Forgotten Valley

Tales of the Two Moons

By

Vince Barrale

To: Mike
My friend
Dungeon MASTer
+ EdiTor
Vince Barrale

This book is a work of fiction. Places, events, and situations in this story are purely fictional. Any resemblance to actual persons, living or dead, is coincidental.

ISBN: 1-4107-3504-4 (e-book)
ISBN: 1-4107-3503-6 (Paperback)

Library of Congress Control Number: 2003094198

This book is printed on acid free paper.

Printed in the United States of America
Bloomington, IN

Cover art by: John Glenn (Crowolf Designs).
Editing by: Mike Muenter (DM)

1stBooks - rev. 06/04/03

Dedication

I had never thought of myself as a writer since as an Engineer, I spend most of my work day reviewing technical specifications and complicated electrical drawings. I guess everyone needs a release, something to take their minds off of the stress of the real world. When I graduated college twenty plus years ago, my release was in the fantasy world of gaming. I really enjoyed getting together with friends and role playing; real role playing involving getting into a mental character. These experiences as directed by an excellent DM, later proved useful. Years later, I became a Dungeon Master myself and began to design a variety of role playing experiences for groups of people as my Engineering career moved me around the country. To create a fantasy world and a story around which it revolves, required making some notes in a short story version. My older brother convinced me to expand on the story and write the complete novel. I hope you enjoy reading it as much as I did living it.

This story is dedicated to all of those real role players and DMs who still play the game with the enthusiasm of a broadway stage actor, and for those in the real world who fight for what is right in their lives.

Prologue

The chamber deep beneath the surface of a land that was once a part of the 'Elven Forest' seemed alive with gaseous motion. It appeared as though the ethereal plane had merged with the cavernous enclosure. In the midst of the swirling energy stood a lone oppressive figure reveling in the atmosphere of evil. Indeed the chamber itself, empty of all except the luminous glow of the gasses was the very core of the evil that had completely ravaged the land above by the vial necromancies of the dark mage it surrounded. For this was the dread summoning chamber of the ancient wizard-priest, Moracles.

For three generations, Moracles had conducted the evil spells that transformed the summoning chamber into a bridge between this unnatural dwelling deep within the highest mound of the now desolate land and the ethereal plane that, even now grew closer with the quickening swirl of the vapors.

The incantations that enabled this transformation acted like a blind snare to a world on the other side, all in preparation for the mage of the valley, to bring forth another unfortunate creature to be his unworldly servant. Another to add to his army from the darkest fringes of the ethereal lands.

Once summoned in this manner, these beings were enslaved to Moracles, a servitude that could only be broken by its death or that of the wizard. Of course of the later there appeared to be no hope; for the mage of the Forgotten Valley was a formidable master whose powerful incantations had transformed the once beautiful Elven Forest into a dark barren wasteland now known as 'Feradune', which translates from the old Elven tongue 'Land of Horrors'.

Now with the preparations completed, the mage opened the graying book of spells that he kept in a large pocket in his hooded robe. The book was light for its size, constructed and bound by the flayed skin of the council of Elves. The pages were written with the blood of virgins captured during the upheaval of Moracles' coming a century past.

With long practiced strokes he carefully turned each page, his blackened nails extending a full inch from each finger. As he spoke, the incantation's voice commands became louder and more powerful. He accompanied the commands with a swirling of his arms in continuous motion. The underground chamber and the fortress that held it, shook to the foundation as it had so many times in years past. As he spoke the words, the gasses swirled like a tornadic funnel centered upon the black marbled circular floor before him.

"Elo et quintarot etherium construit ad moem," Moracles intoned each enchanted word with a precision born of terror, for one slip, one mispronunciation, and the being brought forth would be free of the spell and free to expend its wrath upon the mage.

At the instant of the last word spoken, the funnel exploded into a pillar of such piercing bright light that the brilliant rays extended above the chamber and the surface of the scorched earth above. Then the mage extended his arms, book in hand, in welcoming expectation as he had been taught by the master's of the underworld a hundred years before. The beam of light retracted to its origin and with it a winged crimson red dragon gently landed on the floor of the chamber.

"Excellent," he mused aloud. "A fire serpent, a fine addition to my army of Torgs." Since the spell acted only as a blind snare, Moracles would not know in advance what manner of creature would appear. He only knew that whatever the spell brought forth from the ethereal plane would be his to control.

The dragon was nearly fifty feet in length from nose to tail, with thick leathery wings that spanned fifty feet as well. Smoke billowed from its huge flaring nostrils, and spines protruded in rows down the length of its red back. It's eyes were open and stared blankly, as most of the creatures the mage summoned, waiting for instructions from it's new master.

The 'Torgs', as Moracles had named all the creatures that he had snatched from the ethereal plane, were members of different species, mostly unknown to this world of mortals. Some were fearsome half live humanoid creatures, and some were multi legged monsters, twice the size of men and at least twice the strength. Some were biped, some walked on all fours or sixes like scaly rhinos, and some were even invisible. Others were walking reptiles with frog-like heads and then, on those fortunate occasions, Moracles would summon a powerful creature such as this fire serpent, a crimson Red Dragon that now stood before him.

These past hundred years he assembled this array of unworldly beasts to serve him and to prepare for the mage's grand scheme. With his army of men, sub humans and monsters, he could extend his domain beyond Feradune to the very ends of the continent. No force of earthly beings could stop the disease, that he had unleashed upon the land. No force, that is, except that that he believed to be lost forever upon his arrival so many years ago. As long as the mage lived, his curse would spread throughout the lands extending far beyond the valley's edge.

The evil wizard cringed at the thought that somehow, they might still exist. But only their combined power could stop his necromancies. The legends of these forces had eluded his certainty. Did they ever really exist. Perhaps he would never know, for if indeed they did, his domain could be reverted into the bountiful land it once was.

Moracles' army of creatures took decades to assemble because the dark energies required for each summoning would be drained from him for many days leaving him vulnerable. For this reason he must remain in seclusion to regain his strength after each attempt. Even a failed summoning would drain him of his dark powers, though those failures rarely occurred.

He could only attempt the spell once when each moon was full without high risk of a dangerous costly error. But on the hour of each fullest moon, he would be found deep in concentration, as was tonight.

While looking at the dragon, pondering ways for its best use, one of the smallest Torgs named Quibit, approached him through the thick mist. Though small and gruesomely ugly with horns, a tail and sharp claws, Quibit was endowed with telepathic abilities when summoned by his master. This was not the reason for his interruption; however, for he now had a very important message to deliver. This fact alone kept him from suffering the fate of such an intrusion upon Moracles' summoning chamber. As only Quibit was at all allowed such an entrance to care for his master in his time of recovery, Moracles was not surprised by the approach. Quibit broke the silence with a series of whines and chirps that Moracles immediately understood to be important.

Telepathically, he spoke to his master, "Master, the seekers of the forest tell of riders approaching from far beyond the mountain peaks." The creature gazed upon the mage for a response.

Broken from his train of thought, he replied in an irritated voice. "Riders you say, umm. That would put them at least a weeks journey from here. We must intercept them before they cross the mountain range but of course that is too far to travel in time," he said in disgust. A crooked grin slowly came to the evil one's face, enhancing the long twisted scar on one side. He turned from Quibit back to his new beast. "Methinks my newest pet can traverse the distance before then." His grin turned into a smile as he commanded his dragon with the wave of his arms, still clutching his book of horrors. He already began to feel the drain on his life force, but gave one last command to the Dragon before his time of hibernation began. "Fly my pet. Fly west toward the setting moons and breathe the fire of my wrath on the intruders who would so foolishly enter my realm." The wizard pointed up, toward the opening in the cavern.

The dragon slowly nodded its head, indicating his understanding the orders. It stretched its powerful wings and ascended through the crevice that reached high above the chamber. His leathery flapping wings once again stirred the rancid air of the chamber with a force that nearly off balanced the mage and his tiny servant, clutching the robes of his master. As the silhouette of the dragon rose toward the high moon, the evil laughter of Moracles echoed through the canyon.

Chapter 1
Saviors

The crimson glow of the morning sun crept over the rigid edge of a distant mountain range. Yet there was still darkness along the dense forest path, too thick with foliage to allow even the pre morning light to penetrate. Amidst the mighty oaks and bushes the sounds of the awakening woodland creatures could be heard chirping and chattering their signals to one another, that another day was about to dawn.

A rustling of blueberry bushes and a low growl startled a family of quail, that fluttered away into the safety of the trees. A large black bear picked casually at the berry bush for his chosen breakfast, too lazy to hunt for fish in the nearby stream. A gentle breeze passed a new scent by the nose of the contented bear. As he raised his snout into the air, he determined that a more tasty meal was not far off.

As the brightness of the sun began to peel its way through the cover of living greens, the overgrown path through the forest became more visible. A large gray tailed squirrel hopped through the brush and scurried up a tree with an acorn in its mouth. He deposited the find in his nest and perched himself to overlook a small campfire. Over the fire set several pots and skillets, steaming and sizzling fresh fixings within. Two men tended the fire and stirred the food in the kettles. The aroma of ham and eggs seeped through the blackened lids of the cookware.

"This is the last of our carried rations," the first man said as he carefully lifted a scalding lid with his gauntlet. "We will have to hunt for our food from now on."

"I prefer to live off the vegetation rather than slaughter a helpless animal," said the second man attending the fire. "We do not need to kill our fellow creatures to eat."

In a nearby clearing, another man fed grain to a line of horses tethered to the trees. As he patted them down, he talked to each one softly in a series of snorts and whinnies acting as if each understood him. And in turn several of them shook their heads and returned the noises as if in response.

Nearer the camp, a man packed his bedroll into a neat tight bundle. He tied it down with leather straps behind the saddle of his horse, that was tied to the tree. He brushed off the dirt from his padded leather armor and began to pull the vestment over his head.

"My stomach beckons me to breakfast," said another man, as he pulled on his proective garb of chain mail over his cloth weave garments.

"I too hunger for food," came the higher pitched words of another who was checking the straps of the saddle on her horse. "Gor, fetch the others to eat before we starve," she said impatiently as she secured her crossbow to the saddle."

" I'll not be the one to disturb the lord's morning prayers my friend. I am doing the cooking," the first man said from the campfire. "Grefden, why don't you find the Lords?"

"Not for all the fires of hell," replied Grefden. The man rose to his feet, a full height of 6' 4" strapping on full plate mail armor over his rippling physique. However, his stature and self-assurance led them to believe that he may be able to endure hell's fires; he was not born a fool.

Grefden took a quick glance at the young woman near the horse who was now strapping on her plate mail breastplate and sword. She was muscular for a woman, self assured and attractive in rugged sort of way. Her hair was pulled over the back of her armor vestment and loosely flowed half way down her back. She looked up to meet the other warrior's glance and gave a quick smile; a mutual attraction.

"I shall find the others," came the soft, melodic, feminine voice from the shadow of a giant maple tree. The slender cloaked figure approached the campfire. As she tossed back her hood, the radiance of her beauty and long golden hair brought a different tone to the next words uttered by the soldiers.

In unison they spoke, “Good morning, Lady A’mora”.

Two more warriors emerged from the forest, sniffing the air, that led them to their morning meal. They were carrying several water pouches, that they had been refilling in the cool spring just north of their camp. They tied them to the tethered horses in the line and checked that the saddles were securely fastened.

* * *

A lone figure wearing a black hooded cape knelt beneath a great pine tree. Before him set a large stone with a small lump of smoldering incense upon it. The man’s head was bowed in reverence as a low mumbling chant emerged from his lips. He inhaled the aroma of the incense as he prayed. Beside him laid a sheathed sword, its pummel glistening from a single sunbeam coming through the trees. The golden handle shimmered from the reflections of the intricately sculptured winged beast with inset ruby eyes.

His hands are clasped in devout prayer as his concentration was broken by the gentle touch of a hand on his shoulder.

“My Lord,” she spoke softly, “The others await your presence for breakfast.”

Gently he touched her hand with his own upon his shoulder as he spoke, still with his head bowed.

“I can feel your anxiety A’mora. What is it that troubles you? Have you not prayed this morning?” He slowly arose and turned to face her, still holding her hand in his.

“Yes, I did pray and it was a vision I had that causes me fear.”

He looked deep into her eyes and took her other hand in his. “Tell me of your vision,” he said intently, knowing of the critical nature of their mission.

*   *   *

An anguished cry came from the camp accompanied by a ferocious growl. A large black bear wrestled one of the soldiers near the fire. The man fought to get free of the bear’s powerful paws tearing into his studded leather armor as he defended the food, which was being served.

Grefden yanked his sword out of its sheath with a fierce yell and ran to attack the bear. Several of the other soldiers cried out to him and held him back.

“Do not harm the creature,” they shouted. “It is an act against our Goddess, Mirana.” Since they could not stand to see their companion torn to shreds they rushed the bear, surrounding it. The soldiers stood around with swords drawn poking at the beast in an attempt to draw it off. Their reluctance to attack the creature was due to their strong belief in care for all good life. The deity they prayed to forsake the taking of animal life, as she was a protector of the forests and those creatures living within.

The brave soldier continued his struggle with the bear as it licked the spilled servings of food from Gor’s vestments.

“Enough of this!” Exclaimed a new angry voice. His strong sureness drew the attention of all the soldiers away from the bear. As he drew a dangerously sharp arrow into his bow he said to the tattered and bloody soldier “Gor; hold the beast still so I can pierce its hollow skull.”

“I shall try my lord.” Came the muffled reply from the weary soldier under the weight of the bear. He desperately grabbed the throat of the bear in an attempt to keep it steady.

"No! Shi'roc. Wait," Came a shriek from Lady A'mora. She slowly approached standing opposite the camp fire from the bear and with a swirling motion of her arms and a few mystical words: "In explicore advocatum renius benefissimo duras nato."

The bear released its opponent and stood back from him. It pawed at the knocked over kettles and pots licking at the food it had spilled on the ground.

Shi'roc let out a sigh of relief and lowered his bow, slowly releasing the tension on the string. " Don't just stand there, help him," Shi'roc shouted at the other men.

"Yes M'Lord," came the hesitant reply from the soldiers, still fearful of getting that close to the bear that was now far more interested in the ham and eggs than in the soldiers.

A'mora slowly circled the fire keeping eyes locked with the bear's as he sat lazily down and licked his lips. She approached the animal with out-stretched arms as the others slowly reached for Gor.

A'mora placed her hands on the head of the bear, now cowling at her feet."Linguatorum beastilan vocalori transit," Came the strange words from her lips as she petted the beast. The bear let out a few subdued growls and moans. "He is just hungry," she said. "He meant no harm to anyone."

"That may be difficult to explain to Gor, mistress," came the reply from Grefden, now carrying his limp unconscious companion.

"Well done my dear," Lord Lorentz praised his apprentice, as he too approached the bear. He sat next to her

and tossed back his hood to reveal his strong handsome features. His hair was dark and full with curls as was his beard. The points of his ears poked through the curls to show that he was not entirely human. His eyes had a deep magical brown glow that seemed to enthrall those with whom he had made eye contact.

Shi'roc approached them shaking his head in amazement and disbelief. "I will never understand how you do what you do," he said. "But I'm glad that the two of you are with us, not against us." He motioned back to where Gor now lay as the soldiers attended his wounds. "I believe he will live."

Shi'roc was not an impressively strong looking man. Distinctly pointed ears penetrated his long straight black hair. He too was part Elf. His sharp hairless chin and high cheekbones accentuated his generally jovial character. Though he appeared light hearted to those who knew him, any man or intelligent beast would fear him at a glance; not because of his polished chain mail armor, but for the assorted weaponry dangling from it.

"As long as we have known each other, the best I've learned from Lorentz is a few words to empower this ring that he gave me." Shi'roc reached out his left hand to display a beautifully carved golden ring, that he wore on the fourth finger. He looked at Lorentz. "You said to always wear this and remember the words. I've yet to need it." He scoffed, having little knowledge of the magical powers contained within the ring.

"You can not learn if you don't believe," A'mora said with a twisted smile. Her fondness for the Elf was apparent. "Magic requires extreme concentration and a serious mind devoted to study. Our other powers are granted by our deity for healing and preserving life of a good nature."

"And since you believe in nothing you must remain without," Lorentz sarcastically interjected. Shi'roc was slightly annoyed at the accusation, as this was an on going argument between them.

"I believe," he said. "I believe in my own abilities and strengths. I believe in weapons that I can hold and fight with," he motioned to his sword and bow, "not words with no meaning."

"But the words do have meaning if only you would believe in them, as you do your weapons. Can I not wield a sword as well as hurl a magical ball of fire, or heal your wounds?" retorted Lorentz.

Shi'roc hung his head in disgust, knowing he had lost the argument, once again. For it had been Lorentz who had kept him alive so many times in the past, having been mortally wounded in combat.

"I shall leave the magic to you and A'mora," He said as he stomped back to the campfire to see if there were any remains for breakfast.

"He is a stubborn man," Lorentz mumbled to A'mora as he watched Shi'roc move away.

"But his heart is good." She replied. "You have told me many times yourself." Though they had only been recently introduced, A'mora felt the good nature of the warrior and his complex personality.

"I should tend to Gor's wounds from the bear wrestling." Lorentz went over to where the soldier was being healed and bandaged by his own faithful followers, warriors he had trained himself in the basic arts of healing.

Grefden had gone into the woods earlier to hunt fresh game for the day. He walked up toward A'mora and the bear carrying the carcass of a small freshly killed animal. He stopped in front of them; weary of getting too close to the bear.

Lady A'mora looked up at him in disgust. "Why do you feel the need to kill defenseless animals?" She shook her head. "I suppose that you are going to feed that to the bear?"

The bear looked up at the meat Grefden was holding and growled.

"Just lay it down in front of him. He won't harm you," she said, seeing his confusion on what to do.

"How can you be so sure mistress?" replied Grefden.

"Well if you just stand there with it in your hand, you are sure to irritate him," she said with a chuckle.

He tossed the food in front of the bear and quickly backed away. The bear tore into his meal holding the meat with his powerful paws and ripping it with its teeth.

By now the remainder of the group had returned to the camp, missing the excitement, they sat to consume their morning meal finding that there was none. Gor was setting up on his own power but would not be able to travel well from the loss of blood. The wounds were not too severe; claw gashes and a few broken ribs. The other soldiers had removed his leathers in order to be properly bandaged.

Lorentz motioned the others to step back as he began to chant. With a freshly pulled patch of dew-covered moss, he pressed his hands on the most bloody cuts and ribs. "Manua invocatum coagula noxit fractum et bene sut."

Gor's breathing became more regular and the gashes had stopped bleeding beneath the moss. He quickly appeared to regain some strength. "Thank you M'Lord," he said most gratefully.

The fire was carefully extinguished and the gear stored back on the pack animals. The soldiers seemed agitated not having had a good meal; a necessity prior to a day's ride.

Shi'roc and Lorentz mounted their horses along with the rest of the guard. A'mora was bidding her new friend good-bye with a great bear hug.

"A'mora, we must be getting on with our journey," Lorentz said as he held out the reins of her horse.

The light of the sun had penetrated the dark forest and shown down on the nearby untrodden path. The bear let out a harmonious howl to say good-bye to A'mora as he too began his journey home, now fed for the day.

As they rode, they saw more of the small forest animals. The birds were chirping, the squirrels and rabbits were jumping around as if they had never experienced the sight of people or horses.

Lorentz took note of this and slowed his horse to a stop. He tossed back his cape as he drew out a beautifully carved pendant on a chain around his neck. The ornament was engraved with a great oak tree and a small bird in flight. The roots of the tree formed a large 'M'. This was more than just an ornament of bronze. It was the symbol of a priest, who draws power through it from the Goddess 'Mirana'. Holding out the pendant, he began to chant to the animals that watched in curiosity.

"Avium communicatum rodius explicori sum." He then listened intently to the birds and squirrels chirps and chatters as if he understood their meaning.

The rest of the party had stopped and looked back to watch Lorentz as he began to chirp like a bird and chatter like the squirrels. At first some thought he was just mimicking the sounds, but A'mora and Shi'roc knew better. A moment later Lorentz rode up to the others.

"We are nearing the end of our journey. At the edge of the forest lies the beginning of the wasteland. Just beyond that, hidden in the mountains, live the ones we seek."

"How do you know this M'Lord?" one of the soldiers spoke.

"A little bird told me." Lorentz shot back with a smile and began to trot off ahead of the others.

Shi'roc rode up to him and asked, "have the animals seen these people in the mountain?" he asked seriously knowing from experience that Lorentz had in the past gathered information from animals.

"They had on occasion come to the forest for food in small groups. But it has been many years since they have been here. They don't know their numbers, just that the survivors exist." Lorentz explained.

They continued through the day to ride toward the woods edge. It was later in the afternoon when they reached the abrupt end of the trail.

"Tell the others to be cautious. As we approach the wasteland the possibility of danger will increase," Lorentz warned.

A'mora slowed her horse to pass the word onto the soldiers. Lorentz signaled the others to wait as he rode ahead. At the trail's end the forest just ceased to exist, as if cut off by a knife. Just beyond, he could see the mountain range directly ahead. Between him and the mountains lie a totally decimated area of dead, rotted trees, burnt shrubs and dirt. Not a blade of grass or the color of one flower could be seen.

"What power could cause such destruction in such a finite pattern?" Lorentz said to himself

Shi'roc approached in a slow pace on his horse. He looked at the desolation, that lay between them and their destination.

"What's happened here?" he asked. "Why does the forest end in such a manner?"

"Its of a power far greater than mine," Lorentz said very softly in reply, in a worried tone. He turned to Shi'roc suddenly as if his concentration had been broken. "Do you think we should cross the openness now or wait till darkness falls? It looks like a two hour journey at a fast pace, to the foot of the mountains."

Shi'roc gave Lorentz an inquisitive look. "That depends. How will we find these survivors? How will they greet us if we do? And .." he hesitated, leaned toward Lorentz and added, "and what are you not telling me that you should?" He glared at Lorentz as if trying to invoke the true nature of their mission from him. "You tell us of great danger and now you say we are up against powers superior to your own. Now, tell me what we are getting into."

Lorentz broke off the eye lock that Shi'roc had initiated. "Lets make camp here. We have had a hard ride," was his response to avoid answering the question. He motioned the others to join them just off the path near the edge of the forest. They began to make camp, unsaddle the horses and clear an area to set up a fire. As the soldiers gathered stones for a fire pit, A'mora walked over to where Gor was setting propped up against a tree. He was in much better condition than earlier that morning. She helped him remove his armor and checked his bandages.

"Your bleeding seems to have stopped," she said to him in her soft gentle voice.

"Thanks to Lord Lorentz and you M'Lady. I have not thanked you for removing that bear from my chest. I am grateful." Gor bowed his head in appreciation and respect.

"And I have not thanked you for not injuring the bear as your Lord Shi'roc would have done. Let me complete your healing." She pressed her hands on the bandages and began to chant, repeating the words that Lorentz had spoken that morning. She closed her eyes in concentration for several minutes as she invoked her powers of healing. She removed the bandages and moss from his arm and chest.

"The wounds are completely healed," Gor exclaimed with delight and amazement. The gashes had totally closed leaving barely a scar. His ribs were no longer sore.

"Do you believe?" She asked him, looking into his eyes.

"Believe what?" he replied.

Shi'roc approached them. He carried his long bow in hand and a quiver of arrows. "Gor, you are well I see." Shi'roc said smiling to his loyal guard. "I will be off to hunt our evening meal," he said to A'mora with a slightly perturbed look. "Since your bear decided to eat our breakfast and dinner this morning, we have no meat."

She tried to hold in a grin but found it hard seeing how serious Shi'roc was in his accusation. "Don't be long. It will soon be dark," she reminded him.

"My dear you forget. I hunt best in the darkness." He touched a finger to the point of his ear. "Having mixed heritage has its advantages." Shi'roc began to walk off.

"You should be searching the nearby woods for edible vegetation." A'mora now said to Lorentz. "Some of us will not eat meat," she said, loud enough to be sure Shi'roc would hear.

Shi'roc stopped a moment and spoke to the soldiers. "Stay close to camp and be watchful."

Lorentz turned to the rest of the soldiers and said aloud to them all "Mind your wits. We are near unholy lands, and evil takes many forms. We shall return soon with dinner."

Almost in unison the soldiers replied, "Yes my Lord."

As Lorentz and Shi'roc started from the camp, Grefden approached them and began to follow. Shi'roc turned to him and asked, "Where do you think your going?"

"I must accompany you M'Lord. You should not be in these woods without escort. It is too dangerous." He said with conviction as Shi'roc's personal guard.

Shi'roc chuckled. "Thank you my friend for your concern but we will fare quite well on our own. And you cannot see in the darkness as well as we can. Now return and guard the camp."

"As you wish my Lord." Grefden knew his first duty was to protect Shi'roc and his second duty was to follow his orders. He chose the later and returned to the camp.

A'mora continued her conversation again with Gor. She now sat on a large smooth rock next to him. She had pulled her cloak tightly around her to fend off the evening's cool air. "Do you pray to any Gods?" she asked seriously.

He looked up at her and replied, "My lord does not believe in such things."

She drew a deep breath suppressing some frustration, and said, "I know of Shi'roc's beliefs. What of your own? You must have your own thoughts."

"I don't pray to any Gods but I do believe that there are powers both good and evil that can be controlled. Powers that cannot be stopped by shield or sword." Gor replied with careful thought and conviction.

"You possess an uncommon wisdom. Certainly more than your Lord, Shi'roc." she said with a wink and a smile. "Now that you are as healthy as you are wise, I shall leave you to rest. Tomorrow promises to hold much work," she paused, pondering if she should express her feeling, "..and danger for us all." Her smiles faded into a blank stare at the campfire, which was now burning in anticipation of the dinner it was to cook. The flames burned into her memory of the vision she had that morning.

"How do you know this M'Lady?" Gor asked with a puzzled anxious look. "What kind of danger? Can you see the future?" He rushed the words out before she could answer a single question.

She turned back to him. "Calm yourself," She said with a stern expression. "There is nothing to fear as long as we are careful and alert." She walked away with her robes flowing behind her wondering if she should tell him… tell them all of her morning vision. Would it turn to reality or was it merely her subconscious fears tormenting her. Lorentz had taken it seriously but did not wish to frighten them or make them too cautious, for both would impair their judgment and abilities.

As Lorentz and Shi'roc quietly meandered through the forest searching for a substantial animal and vegetation to feed upon, Shi'roc suddenly remembered that Lorentz still owed him an answer. Somehow Lorentz made him temporarily forget the question earlier at the wasteland with his mesmerizing stare.

He now broke the silence with a whisper. "Well; are you going to tell me what is going on or do I have to guess?"

"Not now." Lorentz whispered back. "Look over there. I think it's a deer." He pointed through the darkness to a shadowy outline of an animal in the distance. You go on while I try to find some fruit bearing trees and bushes." He walked away with a satchel in his hand.

As Shi'roc carefully stepped closer he could see a glowing, red form in the darkness as clearly as any human could see in daylight. Since he was of Elven ancestry, at least on one parent's side, he could see variances of heat radiation in the dark. Warmth of a living creature would seem to him to glow in varying shades of red. The movements of mixing air would help to guide him around inanimate objects such as trees. This ability required some mental focus for him since he was also part human.

Shi'roc maneuvered for a clear shot at the animal. He drew his bow and fired twice, almost simultaneously. The two arrows made a hissing sound as they left the bow on speedy course for the target. A split second later, the glowing form slumped and fell to the ground with a thud. He raced toward the prize to find that their dinner would be the meat of an eight-point buck.

"This will keep us fed for several days," he said to himself feeling quite pleased at his accomplishment. Shi'roc firmly put his foot on the deer's shoulder as he plucked the arrows from it. The two shots were barely an inch apart. "Yes, if we clean it and prepare it well." He continued his one-sided conversation. He was used to hunting with a partner. Though Lorentz' fidelity to his deity was strong, he did occasionally hunt for food. But since they began on this trip, A'mora had put a stop to Lorentz killing any animals. This too weighed on Shi'roc's mind. What was so important that Lorentz felt he must maintain his purity for his Goddess?

He made a stretcher from branches and rope to drag the deer back to camp. The others would be waiting hungrily for their return and it would take some time to prepare the meat.

As he proceeded toward the camp, he ran into Lorentz carrying what looked to be a full satchel.

"I shall tell you all I know of our quest as we eat," Lorentz said suddenly. "The others should hear what I have to say as well." He began to roll over in his mind all of the facts that he had obtained in the past year relating to their mission. How much of it would they all understand? He must sort it out.

Just before they reached the camp, Lorentz told Shi'roc to wait. They set the carcass down. "A'mora would be furious if we paraded in with this." He gestured to the deer. She understands that we hunt only to eat but still is upset by the sight of killed animals. To cut into it in her presence would be more than she could take I'm afraid. Lets do the cleaning out here and bring back only the meat; it will be more tolerable for her."

Shi'roc tossed a worried look at Lorentz as he pulled out a dagger from his belt and began cutting into the hide of the deer. "Why does it upset her and not you?" Shi'roc inquired trying to pry out some deep meaning to it all. "Do you not both pray to the same Gods?"

Lorentz also pulled a dagger and cut into the deer's hide. "Goddess." He corrected. "And yes, we do but A'mora seeks only those powers of good and healing from Mirana. She would only use her aggressive abilities to destroy evil. That is why her healing powers are so intense, and will in time surpass mine."

They continued to fillet the animal removing only the good edible meat. Still they had enough food for days, and proceeded into camp with the meat and various fruits and vegetables stuffed into their pouches.

They sat around the fire exchanging stories of their past to become more familiar with each other. Lorentz had instigated the dialog knowing that they should learn of each other's abilities and strengths to help them through the coming dangers. It may also be the last chance for some of them to pass on their experiences.

It had only been a week since some of them had met. There had been little time to really get to know one another. Though Grefden had made plans to know the young female warrior better. Sha'la was her name, he had learned from Lorentz' other guards. The two sat together during the feast around the fire, laughing and exchanging stories of their past. They seemed to have much in common.

Beyond the loyalties they each had for their masters, Lorentz and Shi'roc, they had no reason to question where they were going. They were soldiers of a cause and did as ordered. Though these men and women were loyal, they were not so because of payment. Of that there was none but the spoils of the enemy. They followed their Lords out of friendship and respect. Lorentz and Shi'roc cared for them in times of need. But until a week ago the two groups had not previously met. They were bound by the kinship of their leaders.

A'mora had no followers of her own since she was young and somewhat inexperienced in the quest. She was loyal to Lorentz, as her mentor, and knew of Shi'roc only by legend and what truths she had been told by Lorentz. It was the stories told of him that infatuated her. As is with all legend, reality is quite different. One could imagine the inflated facts passed on for many decades. She found Shi'roc to be quite self-assured yet humble, shy and out of reach. These real qualities are what attracted her even more.

"Its time that we discuss why I have brought us all together." Lorentz stood up and began to casually pace the campfire as he spoke. "About a year ago, there was a man; an Elf, actually, who straggled into the town of 'Farna', where we all met one week ago to begin this journey."

As he paced he looked into the eyes of each of them. "Life was barely holding him up. He had come from the mountains ahead of us, that he called 'The Three Dwarven Peaks'. He spoke of a great evil that had taken over his land and destroyed the towns and peoples in them. When asked what force could do this, he said but one word; 'Moracles' just before he died."

Everyone was now enchanted with his story. He continued talking while the others listened in silence. Only the crackle of the fire could be heard beneath his voice. He spoke of the people left hiding in the mountains calling themselves 'Survivors' and that for many years no one had been heard from or seen, from beyond the mountains. No one had returned from there either.

"Our quest is to find these people and rid their land of this evil 'Moracles'," he hesitated, and in a muffled voice, "if possible." He continued with even greater strength. "You are the most loyal and bravest of our combined following. Out of all our volunteers, Shi'roc and I have chosen you to carry out this monumental task. Most of you have served us long and know that we would not lead you on an unjust cause. But our foe is very powerful. His magic is strong enough to rival my own." Lorentz was anything but modest. He knew that from what he had seen and heard that his powers alone were out matched but could not let on to the others for fear of their loss of confidence.

He looked down at Shi'roc setting opposite him from the fire. He nodded to him expecting he would want to continue the encouragement of the troops. "Shi'roc, is there anything you would like to say before we retire for the night?" Lorentz encouraged with a nod indicating that he say something.

Shi'roc was not aware that he was expected to do so. He was a warrior, not a speechmaker. His lack of charisma made him uncomfortable doing anything except fighting. The warrior stood up and looked around to all with eyes focused on him, awaiting his great words of wisdom, though Gor and Grefden knew that he was not one who felt comfortable speaking to crowds. To make it worse, Lorentz had caught him unprepared to do so.

He stuttered quickly thinking of something useful to say. He cleared his throat then proceeded. "I've known Lorentz for a long time; since together we fought the giants of 'Thormadore'. I trust in his wisdom and cunning," remembering what Lorentz had said to him about `a power far greater than his own' he said, "and I have faith in his great magical abilities as well to be able to defeat this Moracles." He turned to Lorentz, stern faced, looking into his eyes reflecting the fire. There was a dead silence for a moment. Then suddenly they both broke out into a roaring laugh, followed by the laughter from the others. The bond had been sealed amongst them. They were ready to fight anything to the death if necessary.

A'mora remained silent, staring into the fire once again, pondering her vision of the morning prayer, what should she do? What could she do?

Chapter 2
Survivors

The night air was cold at the mountains second peak. Stars lit up the sky with their multi-colored sparkles of light as if each was sending a signal to the others and responding. Two distant moons cast a chilling blue glow over the rocks and made eerie shadows over the wastelands surrounding the mountains. The air was so clean and clear that one could see for miles from the precipice.

Two figures sat at the ledge looking west over the wastelands between the mountains and the dense forest. They sat alone in the silence of their shadows wondering what tomorrow might bring; probably the same as all the previous days of their short lives. Life for them had been meaningless, without hope for a future other than to grow old and die in the mountain or be ripped apart by one of the evil creatures, that sometimes stalked the lands below their gaze.

For generations, the peoples of the great valley had lived in the hidden caverns tunnels and mines of these 'Three Dwarven Peaks'. Those few who had escaped the initial destruction of Moracles sought refuge in these mountains. It was the furthest safest place outside the edges of his domain at that time.

Their existence was unknown to the evil one, due to the survivors care in not making contact with the creatures of his creation or those of his armies. His evil forces consisted of men know as 'Magdarn' and remnants of other races, too evil and cruel to exist in the civilized lands. They traveled from far away to join up with Moracles and be a part of the most powerful army in the known world. It remained so because no one lived to tell of its existence, not that any would come to challenge it had they known. One would be a fool to knowingly take on the armies of the dreaded Moracles.

The survivors lived in constant fear of being discovered. The Dwarves, who were the original inhabitants of the mountain, accepted the Human towns people and even the refugees of the great 'Elven Forest'. The Dwarves had been a race in solitude, but their social differences were soon forgotten in the face of a common enemy. They lived in their mountain villages high above the valley. On occasion few would travel to the valley towns to trade their goods for needed supplies. They rarely socialized with those outside their race and were thought to be rather elitist by the Elven population who were very open and jovial people to all.

As the first moon cast its light from the western skies, one of the figures pointed toward the edge of the forest. "I think I see a fire in the woods," he whispered as he tried to focus his vision while pointing more precisely. The second figure, shorter and rounder than the first, followed the pointed finger with his eyes and also concentrated his vision.

"I have trouble seeing that far with all of this moonlight," a rather raspy voice replied. "Once the moon sets, I'll try again." Their point of focus was a distance of many miles away.

"I tell you Kura, I can see a flicker like a star, at the edge of the forest near the old hunting path," came the voice of the first figure. His pitch was more energetic and light hearted. "It might be a campfire." He became more excited thinking hard for another explanation. All that came through was desperate hope. "It could be rescuers from another land; maybe an army." He jumped up with the enthusiasm of a boy anticipating a circus.

"Quiet down, Ilo. An army would need more than one campfire. And besides, rescuers would not be stupid enough to light a fire so the whole valley would know they were there." Then all was silent for a while as Ilo pondered Kura's comments.

Moments after the moon set beyond the forest, Ilo asked Kura to look again at the flicker of light. "I still don't see it. It's just your wishful thinking again. You can't go on wishing for miracles all your life."

"It's not wishful thinking. I tell you, I saw something there." He began to jump up and down with frustration. He could not get through his companions stubbornness.

"Come now. What's the commotion? Do you want Moracles to know we are here?" resounded a very authoritative voice from behind them.

"No sir," replied Ilo in a dejected tone recognizing the voice of his father. Two figures approached Kura and Ilo from behind. Their silhouettes were cast in the face of the second moon now cresting the mountains peak. The light of the moon was almost blinding to him after concentrating so hard on the darkness.

"Your watch is relieved. The first moon has set. Go to your homes and get some sleep," the voice commanded.

"But father, I have seen a camp fire at the edge of the forest," he pointed out the area to his elder. "Someone is coming to help us." Ilo was still filled with hope after all the years past when a few brave men attempted to seek help.

Most were greeted to their deaths by a most gruesome display for all to see. In the crossing of the wastelands, the creatures in years far passed, or the Magdarn had come to stop the attempts. They never asked or talked, just tormented and slaughtered anyone not of their kind.

The most recent, Do'bar, left more than a year ago down the old hunting path through the woods. when the path was in fact closer to the mountains. It seemed safer back then to travel. He had made it past the patrols and successfully to the forest unseen. He was never heard from again, just as those prior to him. The few times travelers had come this way, they were met by one of the creatures patrolling the area and killed or mutilated. No one had ever survived to warn the lands beyond not to come, so merchants and transients alike met the same fate as they approached the Dwarven Peaks.

"Show me this fire you see Ilo." Maac-To followed Ilo's pointed finger to where he saw the flicker. "I'm afraid I see nothing." He said with mock disappointment. "Go on home to your wife, son, and dream of a better world," he told him as he patted his son on the shoulder.

Ilo walked off grumbling, "But I saw it." He scurried around the rocky ledges down the mountain, with Kura waddling behind. Ilo often forgot how Kura's short Dwarven legs made him much slower. Though frustrated with Kura from time to time, he was Ilo's best friend, despite their opposing heritage.

The two men now sat in replacement of Ilo and Kura looking out over the wasteland. "I wish I had Ilo's hopefulness of freedom. Do you think he really saw something out there?" Jantez asked. As a Human, born in hiding, he had never known a different existence. His twenty something years of life had been a struggle from the first, having lost his mother at birth and his father from illness years past. The Humans of these mountains were in the minority since their coming, due to susceptibility of disease and shorter life span in general He was of the fourth generation and lucky to be there.

"Long ago, I too had his hopes of being rescued as our towns were being destroyed and our forest homes burned." Maac-To was one of the oldest living Elves among the survivors. He had experienced the ravages of the coming of Moracles. As a young Elf he saw many of his people and family slaughtered or taken by the Magdarn.

"If there is someone out there, they could just as easily be renegades coming to join the Magdarn, as they could be innocent merchants who know no better than to come this way. In either case we cannot let ourselves be known. We can't fight them nor can we help them." He gazed into the sky away from the second moon as if looking for answers in the distant stars. These people had long forsaken any deities they may have once worshipped. No god could have allowed such misery to go on for so long. No prayers had been answered for generations; no miracles, no hope.

Maac-To reached into a shirt pocket as he stared at the sky and pulled out a small object. As it set in the palm of his hand, the blue moon light reflected off of it casting a golden glow.

"What is that?" asked Jantez casually looking into his friend's hand.

"A golden acorn; a gift from the father of the old 'Elven Forest'. When I was a boy, long before you were born, the Elves lived in large communities built into the trees."

Maac-To had begun to drift into memories as he continued telling Jantez his recollection of the past. "The forest extended from the eastern edge of the mountains to far beyond sight from here. We lived with our families safe in the protection of the giant oaks. We were all happy and free to farm, hunt, and play as we wished."

His tone suddenly changed as he began to recall the end of paradise. He looked at Jantez and continued. "One day the earth shook violently. So much that it damaged many of our tree homes. Soon after, we began to hear stories from the merchants in the towns. Stories about evil soldiers who would raid the towns and slaughter people for no reason. They took their food and the young women and would ride off. No one knew where they came from and no one would dare follow. The trees at the eastern end of the forest began to whither and die. In a few years we no longer heard anything from the human merchants. They had stopped coming through the forest to our villages. Some of our village elders began to form scouting parties." Maac-To continued in a sad, depressed voice. "These parties included members of the Elven high council and the best trackers and hunters. They traveled to the nearby towns and to inspect the eastern forest. They never returned or were heard from again."

"What did your people do after that? What happened to the scouts?" Jantez asked, excitedly, reveling in this story of the past.

"Some began to panic. They packed their families and all they could carry and headed off into the woods toward these mountains. The others, as my family, remained in the village."

His tone became even more serious. "Only months after that, the Magdarn came and destroyed our village. This was the first time we had seen them. They rode in on enormously powerful black horses. They wore lightweight chain and plate armor, also in black. Their helmets had spikes or horns and were masked so that we could not see their faces, not that we took the time to try as we ran from them.

"Didn't your people fight them?" Jantez asked now with terror in his voice, as Maac-To went on.

"Some tried with their bows. Our people were experts with a bow and yet the arrows would not penetrate the light armor as the arrows would be deflected. This was not right." He began to talk with anxiety and frustration, reliving those moments of the past.

"My father was a good swordsman and managed to unhorse several of them, but they were very strong. I remember as he was fighting, he yelled to us to run. My mother was slaughtered, as were my elder brothers who tried to fight. My sister was being carried off by one of the soldiers, kicking and screaming. I jumped on the back of one of them and thrust my dagger into the back of his neck as he tried to throw me off. When I fell to the ground, I turned and saw my father fall as a lance was put through him. Two soldiers began to chase me through the woods on their horses. But I was too fast for them and the woods were dense. I saw more of my friends and their families also fleeing into the woods, scattering in all directions as they were chased. Some eventually made it here."

He took a deep breath as if tired by the weight of the memory. He again looked at Jantez who was hanging on his every word.

"The woods were thick with brush. I ran to the west, toward these mountains, until my legs could no longer carry me. I looked around to find that I was indeed lost. I had never been this far into the forest before. It was getting dark and I had to rest. I leaned up against a huge oak tree as I could hear the soldiers in the distance coming on foot. Then, I saw the flicker of torches but I was too tired to move. I hid behind the tree and began to fall asleep between the tree's massive roots."

"How did you escape? Did they not find you just setting there?" Jantez was goading him, anxious for the undoubtedly exciting conclusion to this story.

"Just as I started to fall asleep, the roots that I was resting on began to move. It startled me and I rolled off onto the ground as the tree came to life." His eyes lit up remembering the amazement he felt back then. "Its mighty branches shook as they came down and swooped me up. Each branch passing me higher up, until I was able to see over the rest of the forest. I could see the torches of the soldiers quickly approaching the spot where I had laid below. They stopped for a moment, looked around then moved off into another direction."

"You're saying the tree came to life?" Jantez asked in disbelief. Having been brought up in these mountains he had little knowledge of the powers of life. He had no way of knowing what magic had died in the great Elven forest. "Why did it want to save you from the soldiers? What did you do after the soldiers passed by?"

"From where I was, I could see to the mountains. The moon shone down on the peaks as it does now. Their peaks seemed to glow beneath the blue moonlight. I began to climb down, when I heard a low voice speak to me. It was the great oak tree, the father of the forest."

"What did it say? What language did it speak? Was it Elven? Could you understand it?" Jantez was so excited that he couldn't stop asking questions.

"He spoke in the old Elven tongue; not what my people speak today, but the language of my great grand parents, five hundred years ago. I had learned some from old writings and from my great grandfather. The tree told me that there would be safety in the mountains. He said that the forest would soon die and a great desert would take its place. I didn't understand at the time exactly what he meant. Then he set me down on the ground and told me to pick this acorn from its branch." He held out the golden item again for Jantez to see. "When I did, the acorn turned to solid gold. He told me that some day it would be replanted in that spot to revive the forest once again."

"Did he say who would do it? Did he say when? How would you find that spot in the desert? This is really amazing." Jantez went on with questions.

"I thanked him for saving my life and promised to return the favor when the time came. I am still waiting for that time. I have hoped for so long for some sign." They both sat in silence as the second moon set and the night was once again dark.

"How will you know when its time to plant that acorn, or where to plant it? The Elven forest has long since been destroyed. Hasn't it?" Jantez was now calm and in serious thought.

"I am afraid the time, my young friend, will be beyond my years. I must pass the responsibility of my promise to someone else, someone able to fulfill the obligation. Then again, the time may never come. We may all grow old and die on this mountain from disease or starvation as have your parents." Maac-To was very saddened by his own words and the depression quickly spread to Jantez.

The silence grew between them. Not another word was spoken as the darkest part of the night passed into dawn. Slowly the stars began to fade. Jantez stood up brushing the dust from his britches and walked off. Maac-To continued to stare over the land below, contemplating the fate of all to come as a single tear came to his eye. Were they truly fated to pass into nonexistence? Most had never known anything outside these mountains. None would know of their plight and struggle to survive for as long as they have. What end was in store for them?

"Your watch has ended." Came a distinctly human voice from behind him. Maac-To was shaken out of his trance. The voice spoke in a common language generally understood by all races in the mountains. The mixture of Humans, Dwarves and Elves, living together in hiding caused a mutual understanding of this language.

"Forgive me sir for startling you," he said noticing the sudden movements of Maac-To as he tensed up. "I am here to relieve your duty." The young man spoke quite calmly and respectfully to the elder Elf.

Maac-To peered over his shoulder. "I have long forgotten what it means to be frightened." He rebutted to the lone figure outlined by the orange glow of the morning horizon.

"Its you, Moran, I should have recognized your voice. Have you seen Jantez?" He was forced to speak the same language since Moran would not totally understand Elvish.

"Yes. I just passed him a few moments ago over there." He pointed to the path they all used as lookouts, connecting the vantage points, that overlooked both sides of the mountain range.

"I suppose I should get some rest also." Maac-To slowly got to his feet and walked passed Moran. He stopped for a moment and turned to him with a thought. "Keep an eye out for travelers near the old hunting path at the edge of the woods." He pointed in the general direction, realizing that the path he spoke of had long since vanished. Moran was too young to know of it.

"But sir, that is several miles away." Moran said with a chuckle. "My vision is not as keen as yours."

"Oh yes, that is right. I had forgotten that your heritage is entirely human." He began to walk slowly down the path. "Never mind, never mind. Its probably nothing anyway." He walked on meeting several other of the watchers teams who were returning to the villages underground.

The entire mountain range was honeycombed with tunnels and shafts fashioned by the Dwarves. These passages were originally used for mining the abundant supplies of precious metals and gems. Each of the peaks connecting the range had contained a wealth of different items to be collected.

The first peak to the north was rich with gems ; beautifully colored stones. The Dwarves inhabiting this peak were once fine gemologists. This knowledge was passed through generations..

The second peak was mined for its precious metals. These were used by the fine jewelry craftsmen of that peak to create intricately carved rings, pendants and other beautiful works.

The third peak farthest to the north, was mined for its hard metals used to make armor and weapons, forged in huge underground furnaces. These Dwarves designed and created the best weapons and armor ever constructed.

All of these mined raw materials were traded almost exclusively amongst themselves. The combining of their resources produced the finest jewelry and weapons known in the valley. The craftsmanship of the Dwarven peaks was legendary then throughout the towns. Fortunately for them, they had little contact with the outside world. Only a few had journeyed to towns to trade their finished products with the humans in exchange for essential items that the Dwarves themselves needed. No one knew for sure how to find the Dwarves in their mountains. This fact is what had kept them and all of the survivors safe from Moracles' armies all these years.

As Maac-To traveled slowly through the maze of tunnels he could hear voices whispering in the distance though he could not make out what was being said. He could tell that the voices were approaching. He cautiously stepped into a side tunnel knowing that no one should be coming out this passage so early in the morning. All the watchers were already at their posts. Though old and unarmed, he was still preparing himself to fight. He finally recognized the voices to be those of Ilo and Kura. He was at first relieved but his curiosity made him listen to what mischief the young men must be up to. He remained silent as the two approached.

"We must be careful not to let the watchers see where we are going," Ilo whispered to Kura. "All the watchers have changed so no one will be in this passage this early." He could see Kura's head nodding in agreement in the darkness of the tunnel.

Maac-To listened and watched as he let the two pass his hiding place.

"I've brought some food and water for our trip." Kura pointed to the leather backpack and water pouch on his shoulder sling.

"And what trip might that be?" Came the roaring question from Maac-To. The two let out a frightened yelp as they fell over each other trying to run. They realized who it was as they began to lift themselves from the floor.

"You scared us half to death, father," Ilo scolded as he helped Kura to his feet. They turned around to face the elder Elf who was standing in the center of the passage with his fists planted firmly on his hips. Though there was no light, they could easily see his form.

"Where are you two going?" he said coldly staring at Ilo. "You weren't by chance headed off to the forest in search of your flicker of light, were you?" Knowing full well that it was true, Maac-To didn't expect a reply.

"Sir, I must know if what I saw last night was real. What if there are people out there looking to help us. How will they find us without our help?" Ilo replied exasperated.

Kura was shaking his head vigorously in agreement with Ilo. "He's right," he said to Maac-To.

Maac-To snapped his mouth shut pondering the relevance of the argument. His granite stance had softened and he folded his arms. He began to test the wisdom of the two younger men. "How would you know if they were here to help us without making contact?" The laws of the mountains had expressly forbidden contact with outsiders for the safety of all. He waited for their thoughtful response.

Kura was deep in thought as was Ilo knowing that only the correct answer would convince the wise old Elf. Kura spoke first.

"We will sneak out to meet them half way across the wasteland. If they head off around the mountain we can assume that they are not here to help us but to join Moracles."

Ilo continued the line of reasoning. "If they continue toward the mountain then they must know we are here and looking for us. He looked into Maac-To's eyes for some sign of acceptance.

"What will you do if they spot you? Do you have any weapons to defend yourselves?" the old Elf questioned.

They looked at each other, puzzled. Ilo pulled back his cape to reveal a wooden short sword strapped to his belt, while Kura reached into his backpack and presented his sling and small round pebbles.

Maac-To was pleased at the readiness and courage of the two young friends. It reminded him of when he too was younger. He eyed the home made weapons and smiled. "Can you use them if you have to?"

"We are ready to fight if necessary." Ilo replied bravely as he drew his sword and stood at attention. A gleam of new life emerged from the old Elf, inspired by a courage, that he thought to be forgotten in these mountains years past. It pleased him more so to see it in his son. He turned and quickly moved off into the side tunnel. His voice echoed back. "Wait here," he said, "I shall return in a moment."

Kura looked at Ilo and said, "Do you know where he is going? That tunnel is a dead end." Just then they heard a rumbling noise from the passage, that sounded like scrapping stones.

"What was that?" he said. "Father, Father, are you all right?" Ilo called to the darkness.

Maac-To reappeared moments later wearing a vest of polished chain mail armor. He walked up to them strapping the sheath of a long sword to his belt. He looked entirely different. The Elf had somehow transformed from an old tired man into a warrior ready for battle. Both Ilo and Kura were in shock at the sight of the new Maac-To.

"You are not the only ones with a vision of the future. I have been waiting decades for a hope at saving our people," Maac-To said with a conviction never seen by any of the survivors before. "I am going with you."

Chapter 3
Heroes

A mist hovered over the wasteland, obscuring the mountains peaks as Shi'roc gazed out from the forest path. He had already fastened on his armor and was testing his bowstring, plucking at it like a stringed musical instrument. His years of practice in crafting weapons had provided him with a fine sturdy bow. Satisfied of its tightness, he slung it over his left shoulder.

This was his usual ritual, checking all weapons before an anticipated battle. His exercises trained his muscles and his mind. But this morning was different for he had no opponent to study. There may not be an enemy this time but still he must be ready.

With one swift stroke, he drew his sword from its sheath, that was tied to his belt. He swung it back and forth in front of him, with one hand, as if fighting a nonexistent opponent. He stopped the motion of the sword, now grasping the hilt with both hands; he stood firm, staring at the brightly polished blade. His concentration was broken by the gentle voice of Lady A'mora.

"Praying to your sword?" She inquired whimsically with no response from Shi'roc. "You should eat something before we travel." Slowly she approached him from behind, her golden hair flowing over the shoulders of her cape.

Shi'roc was not alone in his daily preparations for battle. Today, A'mora did not wear the robes of a priestess, but the studded leather armor of a warrior. A soft fur protruded from the neckline of her vestment to keep the chill from her throat. Plate mail padding was neatly tied around her muscular thighs. From her hip was suspended a stone head throwing hammer. Shi'roc turned to look at her. He was at first lost for words having not previously seen her attired for combat. He tried to keep hidden his enthusiasm for her change in appearance. Since they had met, he had respected her as a priestess and student of his friend, Lorentz. It was that fact that helped him to not fall helplessly in love with her. He had tried to dismiss the fact that she was a very beautiful woman. His past experiences had taught him to steer clear of such beauty even though it was painful to pass up such an opportunity. A relationship would just cloud his judgment and his fighting skills, which he knew he would need on a quest as the one they were on. He took a deep breath in awe of her and finally spoke. "I am not hungry; besides I fight best when I have not eaten."

"Or slept?" she interjected. "You were restless last night, pacing around the campfire. Why were you so uneasy? What makes you so sure you will need to fight today?" Though she was trying to be comforting, she knew full well that today her vision could come true. Could Shi'roc also have somehow known? Was it possible for him to have visions of his own?

"I felt as if we were not alone; as if we were being watched." Shi'roc re-sheathed his sword as skillfully as he drew it, without even looking.

"I detected no evil presence near the camp last night," she gestured with a magical sweep of her hands. She had always performed a spell to detect any evil creatures in the area before sleeping. She then smiled and held out her hand to him. "Do you always trust your feelings, your instincts?" she asked. She did not expect an answer, as she had not been able to get close to Shi'roc; few people could. Only Lorentz and Shi'roc's personal guards knew him well.

"Yes." He said firmly as he quickly straightened his back. Then his expression changed, as did his appearance of confidence. "Well no, not always." He graciously took her hand and began to walk back to the camp. He was still fighting the urge to open up to A'mora and expose his fondness for her.

A'mora, for the first time, was able to feel Shi'roc's uncertainty. His touch was gentle but firm. Maybe she was finally getting close. The rest of the party was either eating around the campfire or preparing their horses for the day's journey. Lorentz stood up as A'mora and Shi'roc approached. He had been watching them at a distance, wondering what was being said and puzzled by Shi'roc's reactions.

"Well; are you ready to make history and meet our future this day?" Lorentz asked theatrically with a wide-eyed smile. Shi'roc stopped with his head hanging, staring at his feet. Lorentz gave an inquiring expression to A'mora.

She released Shi'roc's hand, stepped over to Lorentz as he whispered, "What is the matter with him? I've not seen him so depressed since he lost 'Luminex'."

'Luminex' was the one thing that Shi'roc had treasured most in his life. It was a sword of such great power and knowledge. The sword was of a magical persuasion and he happened upon it long ago in a deserted castle buried in a chest of coins and jewels. Since riches were not of great interest to him he allowed his companions his share of the riches in exchange for the sword. No one knew where it had come from or who had created it but the holder must be of good character and pure conscience for the sword to serve. It had saved his life many a time not only in battle but also by warning him of unseen dangers. Luminex was unique in that it possessed an intelligence and could communicate telepathically with its wielder. That is until Shi'roc discovered the swords true nature. It had the power to grant wishes like the proverbial Genie in a lamp. He had discovered this fact quite accidentally while one day polishing its fine blade. Its past was such a mystery to him that he 'wished' the sword could tell him of it's past. There went the first wish. Not only could the sword then speak to him but it also possessed an uncompromising attitude. Unlike Shi'roc, the sword was anything but modest and began to brag of its incredible history of battles in the hands of kings hundreds of years prior.

"I believe that Lord Shi'roc has doubts of our success." She whispered back to Lorentz, being careful not to let anyone hear.

"Did you tell him of your vision?" Lorentz asked softly, hoping that the response would be, no, as she confirmed. He turned to the camp and said allowed for all to hear. "Stow your gear and prepare to ride. We shall soon be on our way."

"Aye, my lord." Came the group response in a half excited tone. Many of them looked forward to the challenge while others, Shi'roc's guard, seemed more apprehensive, but followed their lord out of trust and loyalty.

Gor watched Shi'roc and Lorentz talking as he and Grefden saddled their horses and packed the supplies. "Shi'roc seems disturbed this morning." Gor pointed out while Grefden, once again, made eyes at Sha'la. "Are you paying me attention?" he said.

Grefden recovered from his eye lock with the woman and said, "He was up most of the night during my watch. He would not let on what was troubling him, though I believe he worries about our mission. Do you know what our role is in this rescue?" Grefden looked around and was careful not to let anyone overhear his conversation for fear of passing on doubt.

"I don't fully understand what we are to do, but I do believe that we are not being told everything." Grefden nodded in agreement as they both finished packing.

"Shi'roc let us walk a minute and discuss your concerns." Lorentz put his hand on Shi'roc's shoulder as they walked off back toward the path and looked out over the misty wasteland. The dead, rotted trees seemed haunted. The outline of the mountains was becoming clearer with the backdrop of the suns morning glow. The fog, that hung between them and the mountains, would soon fade revealing once again the barrenness of the land.

"Having second thoughts about our quest? Do you fear the unknown, or do you fear what you do know?" Lorentz was purposely goading Shi'roc into an emotional outburst. He knew full well that Shi'roc feared nothing that he could fight. It was the only way to expose his real fear. He could see Shi'roc tense up as he continued. "Tell me what are you afraid of?"

Suddenly Shi'roc turned and pointing an accusing finger, said. "I fear nothing except what you are not telling me. There is more out there that you have not revealed to us. You are holding back; don't deny it." Shi'roc was almost to the point of anger as Lorentz interjected.

"You are correct my friend." He slowly clasped Shi'roc's pointed finger pulling his clenched fist down from view of the others. "There is much I have held back and for your own protection and the safety of the others. We can only reinforce the necessity to stay alert. Also if we do come into contact with any of Moracles' evil servants, we must destroy them before they can send word of our arrival, if they don't already know we are here."

Shi'roc stared at Lorentz with a serious blank expression and said, "What evil creatures? What do you mean, by `if they don't already know we are here'?"

Lorentz broke Shi'roc's stare. "I never said this was going to be easy." He looked away for a moment. "We just need to be careful. Trust me." Through all the years he had known Shi'roc, Lorentz was unaware of the hatred Shi'roc had for those last two words. `Trust me'.

"The last time I heard those words I had been entranced by a water nymph and almost drowned." Shi'roc put his hands on his hips and was now furious at Lorentz. It was rare that Shi'roc would trust anyone, let alone one who asked to be trusted. It was only through first hand experience that he learned to trust Lorentz implicitly.

"Calm yourself before the others see us arguing," he said quietly. "The last thing we need is for them to loose confidence in their leaders." He held out his arms to Shi'roc in friendship. "I will never use those words again in your presence, I promise."

Shi'roc took Lorentz' arms in his, grasping at the wrist in acceptance. His tension was now released and he cracked a mischievous smile. "She tricked me into taking off my armor. It was quite embarrassing but she was very beautiful."

"She must have been a blond," Lorentz interjected and nodded toward A'mora, knowing of Shi'roc's weakness for ladies of golden hair. He had almost come to the point of encouraging a relationship between the two knowing how well their dispositions would complement each other.

Shi'roc threw his arm around Lorentz' shoulder and they started walking back to the others. Lorentz looked at Shi'roc and broke out in a laugh, that Shi'roc soon added to. The tensions had been relieved through trust and open expression, something that Lorentz had taught Shi'roc long ago.

The party was already mounted and awaiting the command to ride. Grefden handed Shi'roc the reins to his horse as he climbed on. "Is all well my lord?" he asked.

"Yes my friend, all is well." He turned to the others and yelled out with excitement. "Let's ride."

Lorentz mounted his horse as well and reminded, "Keep alert and remember why we are here."

* * *

Maac-To, Ilo, and Kura had only hiked part way to the forest when the sun's glow crested the mountain's peak. The mist was entirely dissipated. The three survivors moved slowly and cautiously from one rotted tree to another so as not to be seen or heard by any potential predators. They also intended to hide from their own watchers on the mountains behind them. So far their journey was uneventful and their stealth had tired them but was also worth the effort. They moved individually and remained separated but in visual contact.

Suddenly Ilo motioned silently to Maac-To and Kura. They focused their attention to the direction indicated by Ilo. In the distance they could see a cloud of dust and could barely make out the forms of many horsemen approaching. Maac-To signaled for Ilo and Kura to join him behind a pile of dead wood away from the main path. Moments later the three of them were joined at the pile of tree remnants safe from view of the approaching riders.

"How many do you think?" Maac-To whispered to Ilo.

"About a dozen I figure maybe more judging from the dust. What should we do? They are heading straight for the peaks. They may be looking to help us," Ilo rushed on.

Kura reminded Ilo of their plan. "If they continue toward the mountain we will follow to determine if they are friend or foe. The watchers will be able to see them and warn the others. If they move off, we can figure that they are unfriendly and we will not make contact."

Ilo peeked through the woodpile to see the riders were slowing. He could now effectively count their number and see more clearly who they were.

Maac-To asked, "How many?"

Ilo responded with a whisper. "Twenty in all."

Kura now also peered through the branches. He concentrated on what appeared to be the two leaders and described them to the elder who was still setting low. "The leader, he is wearing polished chain mail armor and carries many weapons. The other is wearing a robe with a hood. I can't see his face."

Ilo continued with descriptions of the others. "There is a light haired female with them wearing leather armor and a cape. She carries no visible weapons. The others are wearing leather or plate mail armor and have swords and bows. Some have crossbows as well as swords and are wearing helmets. The two younger men had effectively displayed their knowledge of armor and weapons as they had learned in legends of the past. The elder Elf had long ago tried to educate his son and their friend of the various forms of weaponry both for combat and defense. They had not actually ever seen such equipment until today when Maac-To adorned himself. They also had never seen horses up close, only at a distance. From what they had heard, those before them were fine healthy animals.

After rolling over all that information in his mind, Maac-To asked the next question in a very serious tone. “Are they human?”

“Some are for certain, but the leader with the armor could be Elf and so could some of those with helmets. Its hard to say from here.”

“Let them pass until we can be sure who they are or why they are here.” Maac-To said, still in a whisper.

“I can somehow feel that they are good people,” Kura said sheepishly staring in concentration. “I don’t know how but I can feel it deep inside me. I must go to them.” He began to stand up, almost as if in a trance. Ilo pulled him back down just as a thunderous echoing roar came from the sky.

* * *

“There they are my pet. Swoop down on them now and breath your deadly fire. How dare they approach my domain?” Moracles mischievously whined as he hovered over his magical crystal globe. There he stood, alone, in the corner of his misty room circling his hands around the bright glass ball, peering into the wastelands through the eyes of the Dragon beast. Now hovering high over the barren area with wings fully spread to keep his targets directly below him.

He chanted his evil thoughts into the ball, transmitting his commands to the Dragon. "Ubator transit machia sum, fiero brethium uta inferno." He repeated again, entranced with the vision in the large glass ball. Soon he will have incinerated the intruders and could concentrate on more important despicable plans to strengthen his realm and reach out further into the peaceful lands of mankind. Soon the land would be rid of all good creatures and prepared for the coming of the lords of hell.

* * *

Simultaneously, everyone looked up in horror to see hovering over them, with wings fully spread, a great red scaled Dragon with smoke bellowing from its nostrils. Shi'roc and Lorentz yelled out. "Scatter!" This was not a planned maneuver on the part of the soldiers. Never had they fled from a fight in such haste. Chaos struck the novitiates of the quest not all being seasoned enough to have experienced such a sight. Most had never encountered such a creature but only heard of in legends.

They all spurred their horses into a dozen different directions as the fiery beast began his deadly dive from high above. It folded back its wings, tucked its claws under its belly and made an arrow like projection of its body. Lorentz had stopped to turn and see what Shi'roc was doing, remembering what A'mora told him of her premonition. He knew that Shi'roc was not inclined to run from anything.

A'mora had pulled her horses reins, stopping as well and turned toward Shi'roc. She began screaming to him. "No don't do it. You'll be killed." As she reared her horse back to full gallop towards him.

Shi'roc had remained behind and leapt from his horse. He stood staring directly up at the dragon as he carefully reached behind him and drew two silver tipped arrows from his quiver. He nocked one in his bow, drew, and aimed directly at the Dragon's smoking face. He knew from experience that the timing of his shots would be critical.

Grefden and Gor, heard the cries of A'mora and turned back to see. They spurred their horses into a gallop back toward Shi'roc to try and save their leader.

Lorentz began to head back, knowing that he might not make it in time. He quickly recalled from his memory all of the magical spells he had empowered onto his special ring. He pulled the reins of his horse, stopping him, and held out his left hand with outstretched fingers.

As the Dragon opened its mouth to breath his fire, Shi'roc fired his arrow, nocked and fired the other, both directly down the throat of the creature, its only immediate vulnerable spot.

"Fiero protectum." A beam of light shot out of Lorentz' ring toward Shi'roc. It spread out a few feet in front of him as the warrior crouched down drawing his shield over his face to protect him from the fiery blast.

The Dragon choked on the arrows as he spit his fire, causing him to stray from his target and produce only a portion of his capable flame. He reared his head still coughing, trying to dislodge the arrows from its throat. It pulled back from its dive once again extending its powerful wings to climb back into the sky.

The flames had been deflected around Shi'roc by the magical shield, that Lorentz had produced. The ground and brush were all aflame around him as Shi'roc poked his head up around his shield. He could hear groaning behind him. He turned and saw his two guards stumbling off of their horses, singed by the effects of the flame. They had returned, not in time to save their master but just in time to feel the edges of the Dragon's breath.

Moracles' pet had climbed into the sky above, circling for another dive. He had dislodged the arrows from his throat and could produce a full belch of fire at its opponents. It now appeared quite irritated at the group, especially the one who had fired the arrows.

A'mora rushed to aid Shi'roc's injured guards as they lay on the ground. She quickly pulled them to the cover of some boulders and began her healing chant. The other soldiers had taken cover and prepared for another round with the Dragon. The archers had pulled and locked their crossbows while Lorentz and Shi'roc exchanged ideas for a strategy.

"Shi'roc, use the ring." Lorentz shouted as he was almost drowned out by the screech of the creature, diving for another pass. "Slow it down with the web of the spider spell," he suggested as Shi'roc stood with a somewhat dismayed look, staring at the ring on his left hand.

He dropped his bow and aimed his hand at the dragon. Still partially protected by the magical shield spell, he pulled his own shield in front of him as he fumbled the words over in his mind. He knew that only the exact pronunciation and inflections would trigger the power of the spell in the ring.

The Dragon's angry eyes met his own as he began to invoke the spell. "Area..., No! Ahrac.. No! That's not it!" He began to loose the calm he had so carefully mastered. His dubious beliefs in magic was causing him to falter; now almost face to face with his most hated enemy.

Lorentz, himself was worried, hiding behind a small boulder and concentrating on the words of prayer. Though his goddess was one of peace, he was also able to invoke her powers of protection through his prayers. He aimed his left hand at the Dragon wondering how long Shi'roc would wait before giving the command. He looked over to him and finally realized that Shi'roc had forgotten the words.

"A'hrachnia" he yelled out to him. "Now."

Shi'roc repeated the command with renewed confidence "A'hrachnia", he yelled, and a rope-like stream spewed out of the ring at the dragon. It began to spread a large thick web over the Dragon's wings. The warrior moved his hand in a swirling motion, redirecting the web over the long snout of the Dragon, temporarily tying it shut. Not only did he slow down the motion of the dragon but he also kept it from breathing its fire.

The archers fired a volley of arrows into the belly of the now defenseless beast as it slowed its flight. Several of the arrows penetrated the scales of the creature's softer belly area as evidenced by its violent flinch reaction.

Lorentz immediately followed with his own spell. "A'battoir", he carefully pronounced as he aimed at an area directly in front of the entangled red Dragon. A cloud of shimmering blades appeared in the path of the creature.

More than a thousand twirling, razor sharp knives, suspended in air, engulfed the enemy. In a second, the beast passed through with torn wings, and numerous slashes over its entire body.

Shi'roc and others had been sprayed with the mist of blood produced by the red shimmering blades. The Dragon fell limp on the ground with a thunderous thump. His eyes focused still on Shi'roc as he stepped toward the beast to deliver the final blows. The warrior was no longer under the protection of Lorentz' magic fire shield as he walked.

* * *

Moracles was blind with rage as he starred into the crystal globe. His long fingernails trying to grip this insolent warrior through the glass as he could still see through the failing eyes of his precious pet. Once more the wizard in his rage began to swirl his arms in the air. The sleeves flowed with the motion as he began to chant the words into the crystal.

"Equeous nostrum fiero bectus noctua rena voleris." The words flowed and echoed through the crystal into the mind of the dying Dragon. "Rise my pet one last time to obliterate the warrior. He shall never soil my lands with his presence again."

* * *

Lorentz was running up to Shi'roc yelling. "No! Get away."

As the others watched, the Dragon raised its battered head ever so slightly and rolled one last belch from its torn bowels. Shi'roc barely had time to raise his shield as the flying body of A'mora struck him on his left side. The force of her leap had knocked them both clear of the fiery blast. They tumbled to Lorentz' feet.

The mage had drawn his sword and approached the long neck of the creature. He drove his sword fully into it up to the hilt. The Dragon gave one last try to hang on to its life as it lowered its head to die. It laid limp and bleeding as the other soldiers gathered all around. Some stared in wonder, never having seen a live Dragon before, nor dreaming of ever defeating one.

Shi'roc walked up to the beast, standing on its snout, he drove his sword strait down into the skull with all his strength and a mighty groan to accompany it. Now he was sure it was dead. He withdrew his sword as the others watched, and carefully wiped the blade with a rag before returning it to its sheath. He then noticed that all was silent and everyone had their eyes fixed upon him as if waiting for something.

An uneasy moment passed that seemed like an eternity. He could not understand what he had done for them all to be staring at. Lorentz stepped up to him and whispered. "They are waiting for you to lead the cheer of victory."

Shi'roc looked at him, puzzled. He was never one to take part in such rituals. But if it would aid the cause and rouse Lorentz' followers he would do so. He raised his shield arm high, trying to find the right words. "Victory to us all." He yelled out. Everyone followed, repeating it again, "Victory to us all".

Lorentz again whispered to Shi'roc, "We are being watched. They are not the enemy so I believe they are the survivors we seek. Keep an eye out just the same." He walked away and began a quiet chant while bowing his head and waving his arms.

* * *

"Damn them all," Moracles exploded as the vision of the Dragon ceased through the magic sphere. "I will have them. Sooner or later, I will find them and cause them a most unpleasant death." He was slightly weakened from the experience. The emotional strength it drew from him to operate the sphere and transmit his instructions to such a distance was great. He slowly walked away from the orb and into the dark mist, that surrounded him. His long robes followed him, as he went off to some resting chamber. The candles remained glowing casting their light upon the dusty books and scrolls, that lined the shelves behind the heavy oak desk and chair.

* * *

"Did you see? Did you see? They defeated Moracles' monster. They must be our friends." Kura rambled with excitement, still being held down by Ilo behind the brush pile. "They are brave and powerful. They use magic when they fight. They must be here to help us."

"We do not know that for sure." Ilo said looking toward Maac-To for guidance. "They may have simply been defending themselves. We don't know that the creature was sent by Moracles."

Maac-To was deep in thought. "Let us watch them further before we make any moves." Kura and Ilo accepted his wisdom. As they peered through the branches at the newcomers, they saw the robed one approaching.

"You may come out now my friends. We will not harm you. We are here to help." Lorentz was sure of his feelings as he directed his speech toward the brush pile. With dramatic flair he continued his oratory. "We are here to defeat Moracles and his evil armies." He spoke with confidence and clarity. He waited for whoever was behind the bush to show themselves, as Shi'roc and the others remained behind. He spoke in the common tongue of all men.

The survivors froze in place. They were not expecting that their presence had been known. This puzzled Maac-To. They had taken every precaution to remain unseen, yet they were known. What went wrong? Ilo and Kura carefully studied their elder as he pondered the situation.

Kura still had a warm feeling about the strangers, an unexplained feeling of trust. He was the first to move. Before Ilo could stop him again, Kura stood up and walked around to the front of the brush pile. His hands were outstretched in front of him as a show of non-hostility.

Lorentz watched Dwarf carefully. He knew full well from the spell that he had cast, the little survivor was of good nature and frightened.

"Well; my little friend, what is your name?" He tried to lessen the tension as he looked directly into Kura's eyes. He had never attempted his power of calming on a Dwarf before and was unsure of its result.

"I am Kura," was all he said as he studied the robed figure trying to discern any specific features under the hood. "Who are you stranger?" he continued. "You say you are here to help us. How do you know who we are and if we need or want your help? How do you know of Moracles?" Through his feeling of trust and fear came a spark of wisdom.

Maac-To and Ilo remained silent and still as they listened with amazement to Kura's words. They were unaware of his inner wisdom.

Lorentz too was puzzled. Had these words been the result of his calm spell attempt on the Dwarf, or had the spell failed and was the Dwarf actually as cunning as he appeared? He carefully and slowly pulled back the hood from his face to reveal himself to the Dwarf.

"I am Lorentz and I assure you my friend that we have come a long way to help free those who are known as the `survivors' from the torment of Moracles. We know that you have remained hidden from him in these mountains for generations."

Shi'roc, A'mora and the others watched from a distance, unaware of exactly the words being exchanged by Lorentz and the Dwarf. Shi'roc could see that the Dwarf appeared harmless but remembered from his past that Dwarves could be deceitful. He turned to A'mora and said, "I have not yet thanked you for saving my life today," He said as he wiped the dragon's blood from his armor. "How did you know I would be killed? You came close to getting yourself killed too."

A'mora became flustered, not knowing how to answer him. Should she tell him about the premonition or would it anger him, that she kept the knowledge of the danger from them? She looked into his thankful eyes and chose to keep the secret.

"I've seen Dragons before and know of their power. No one could survive a direct blast of fire such as that, which you so foolishly chose to chance." She was putting up a defensive wall so as not to divulge her vision. "I was confident that I could save you without harm to myself," she told him, turning embarrassment into a well-deserved scolding. She smiled, gave him a quick kiss on the cheek and walked away toward Lord Lorentz.

Shi'roc stood staring in shock at the brash response, with his mouth open unable to speak. He watched her walk away as he touched his cheek with his hand. Unaware that anyone had seen the kiss she gave him, he quickly brushed it from his mind.

Grefden walked to Shi'roc's side. He was still a bit singed from the fiery blast, as he continued to watch Lady A'mora walk toward Lorentz. "I believe she likes you my lord."

Shi'roc looked at Grefden with a shot that could kill. He opened his mouth, about to speak but could not come up with the words. Then he stomped off to join Lorentz and A'mora.

Grefden stood and chuckled to himself. "What a beautiful woman can do to a brave man's soul," he mused as he went off to tend the injured horses. Several of Lorentz' guard were chanting over the two downed horses as they massaged the burns with an oily ointment.

Maac-To and Ilo were convinced that it was now safe to show themselves. They stood, and slowly came up behind the brave Dwarf sheathing their swords to show their trust. Kura introduced them to Lorentz. "This is my friend Ilo and one of our village elders Maac-To."

The elder Elf bowed his head slightly in greeting to Lorentz, noticing the point of his ears. Lorentz returned the gesture. Though he noticed the differences between pure Elves and mixed bred, Maac-To suspected that they were of similar age. He had not seen a mixed Elf with a beard before.

"These are my companions, Lady A'mora and Lord Shi'roc." Lorentz gestured to them as they approached and stopped a few paces behind him. "And the others are our personal guards."

Maac-To spoke to Lord Lorentz. "How did you know we were watching you from behind the brush pile? You could not have seen or heard us from your direction."

Out of respect for Maac-To, Lorentz spoke in his native Elven tongue. "I was able to feel your presence, especially the force of the little one's mind," he gestured to Kura. Then in Dwarfish he spoke to Kura. "You possess a power that is yet to be developed. If you would permit me, I will instruct you in the teachings of my Goddess, Mirana."

Ilo spoke up, realizing that they were spending far too much time in the open wasteland. "We must take cover. If that Dragon was indeed sent by Moracles, then he knows you are here." Now looking at his father he said. "We must take them to safety. They can help us gain our freedom."

Maac-To hesitated for a moment, thinking of what the elders of the Dwarven council might say. "Yes we must hide you. Have your people follow us back to the mountain."

A'mora was having trouble keeping up with the conversation since she was not fluent in Elvish or Dwarvish. She quietly asked Shi'roc "What is going on? What are they saying?"

"They fear that the Dragon was sent from Moracles, and that we are now in danger. They want us to follow them back to their hiding place." He hesitated a moment and whispered "I still don't trust Dwarves. Lorentz never said there would be Dwarves here."

Kura tugged on Ilo's sleeve and he bent down to hear Kura whisper, "She is beautiful, even for a human, isn't she?"

Ilo replied, "Yes I suppose she is but what does that matter? There is no time for this. We must get back."

Lorentz said simply "We will follow." Then he turned to the rest of their party and gestured to remount and ride. "It will be faster if you ride with us," he said to Maac-To.

Grefden rode up to them, bringing their three horses. He carefully looked over the strangers as he handed the reins to Shi'roc, A'mora and Lorentz.

"We will have to ride double since we have no spare horses and our pack animals are quite burdened already. You can ride with me," Lorentz said to Maac-To, hoping that this gesture would initiate a friendship, feeling that he held some respect of the survivors.

Kura spoke up. "I will ride with her," he said most assuredly, pointing to Lady A'mora. A wide grin broke out on his scruffy little face.

Shi'roc took the reins from A'mora, stepped up to the little one and handed them to him, and said, "You two will ride together and lead," he gestured to Kura and Ilo. "Lady A'mora will ride with me." He looked to A'mora for a reaction.

The smile quickly left Kura's face as Ilo helped push his pudgy little friend onto the horse. Neither had ever been this close to one let alone ride one. Getting on seemed to be half the battle being as short and awkward as he was. Ilo had less trouble getting mounted since the horses were well trained. The others began to ride off toward the mountains.

"Why did you not let the Dwarf ride with me? I didn't mind," A'mora said to Shi'roc as she put her arms around him. She had no idea of why Shi'roc had ill feelings toward Dwarves though he had made reference to his mistrust.

"I told you, I don't trust Dwarves." He said adamantly. "And I certainly would not want one at your back," he hesitated then added, "or mine. I want them up front, where I can see them."

She laughed and said, "He seemed harmless enough. I think you are just jealous." She did not realize how true that statement was. They all rode off in a gallop, leaving a raising trail of dust, that could be seen even by the human watchers on the mountain.

Chapter 4
Meetings

The sun was high overhead yet the watchers on the mountains ridge could feel a cool breeze. Moran was still on watch over the forest side of the mountain and as Maac-To had requested, he was keeping a watchful eye over the desolate area between the peaks and the forest. They had already sounded their silent alarm as the beast from the sky had attacked the group of riders in the wastelands. The watchers took cover to hide from the creature as it flew overhead. Although still miles away, they had seen the winged creature soaring from the skies above and dive to the ground while breathing its flame.

"Look, the riders are heading straight for the hidden cave entrance." Moran silently signaled to the next watcher. "Send word to Maac-To. He was right about travelers crossing the wastelands." Moran had no way of knowing that Maac-To was with the riders he had spotted.

As the riders drew nearer, the watchers took cover so as not to be seen. They could not know if these riders were friend or foe so they remained hidden. One of the watchers on a ledge overlooking the cave entrance spotted Maac-To with them. He was yet unsure as to why the elder Elf was with them or how he had not been seen leaving the mountain.

Ilo and Kura dismounted their horse at the cave entrance. "That was a new experience," Ilo suggested, helping Kura as he stumbled from the saddle to the ground. Their hearts were still pumping from the excitement of the fast ride. They looked up, wondering if the watchers had seen the battle with the Dragon.

The watchers had indeed, and looked on as the rest of the party made haste in dismounting; all except one. He was noticeably nervous.

"We are being watched; I can feel it," Shi'roc said with caution in his voice. He trotted his horse back and forth along the mountain, trying to get a look at those who he felt were watching.

A'mora quickly chanted a few words and with her hands made a wide arcing motion towards the mountain face. "Yes there are several beings nearby but I feel no evil intentions. Just confusion."

"Of course we are being watched. Our people are very careful to look for strangers or any of Moracles' creatures," Maac-To was quick to point out. "Come, we must get inside before we are seen by more than our own people. Moracles is sure to send something to investigate the death of the Dragon." He too was fearful that the arrival of the creature was not a coincidence.

Shi'roc dismounted at the reassurance of A'mora's spell. His trust in her abilities had grown since they had first met. He was still looking up as he walked his horse toward the rest of the group. "Where is this passage? I see only rock," he questioned the others as he better examined the rough stone surface. A close inspection revealed an optical illusion. From looking straight on, the stone appeared to be flat, yet it was offset and hiding a narrow path, just wide enough for a single horse to pass.

Maac-To led them all through the unseen, narrow crevice in the mountain wall, connected to the tunnels. Ilo and Kura helped the humans find their way in the darkness. The horses were somewhat skittish not being able to see in the narrow passages. A'mora clung to Shi'roc's arm as he was first to follow Maac-To into the dark passage.

They were soon met by the two humans, Moran and Jantez, who blocked their path in the inner tunnel. The two stood motionless and silent in the darkness of the cave.

"Maac-To, what are you doing? Where are you taking these people?" Moran spoke in common tongue, with proud authority standing guard with a ready club in his hand. He feared that the strangers may be a threat to the community and Maac-To was being forced to lead them.

"Stay alert." Shi'roc whispered to his men while A'mora grasped his tensed arm. "There is the voice of one, but bodies of many Dwarves up ahead high on the walls." He said to A'mora concentrating his night vision to determine the many heat forms he saw. "This could still be a trap." He began to distinguish and count the bodies. "I don't like this. There are too many Dwarves back there."

"All is well Moran," the elder Elf called out. "These are the people from the camp that Ilo saw last night Jantez," recognizing the form of the other in the darkness. "They are, as he had hoped, here to help us become free once again to reclaim our land."

They stopped walking as Moran and Jantez lit two torches revealing to all, that the strangers were indeed surrounded. Dozens of Elves, Humans and yes, Dwarves, showed themselves as the walls seemed to come alive. Many were armed with only clubs and stones.

"As you can see, Lorentz, we do all we can to protect what little we have." Maac-To motioned to the strangers and said, "These are our new friends. Welcome them and make a place for them in our community."

On the word of Maac-To, the survivors lowered their weapons and approached the strangers to greet them. It appeared that his words were enough to satisfy the community of the strangers' intentions. It was abundantly clear to Lorentz that Maac-To was indeed a leader of sorts among the survivors as he had suspected.

Ilo and Kura pushed their way through the crowd of strangers and kinsmen toward Maac-To. There was a feeling of joy in the air that had not been shared in a hundred years as they led the newcomers through the tunnels.

"Take the horses to the cavern of water and care for them." He told Ilo and Kura in a soft but stern voice. "I will present our friends to the village elders."

"Yes sir." Came the begrudging reply as they tethered the reigns of horses so as to lead them single file through the narrow passages. The soldiers removed their equipment and gear from the animals and carried what they could over their shoulders. There was much to carry with bedrolls, weapons, cooking utensils and so on. The two walked off down a separate path with the horses in tow.

"I have not been this way for many years." Kura noted as the rocky path slowly descended into the bowels of the southern mountain range.

It was mid afternoon though it was not noticeable in the community except to the watchers who were to begin their ascent of the mountain path.

The rest of the elders and the council of Dwarfs had assembled and were seated in what was their council room; a small underground cavern that was located at the intersection of several tunnels. Lorentz' and Shi'roc's keen senses determined that they were near the center of the mountain range. In the center floor was a long stone table where the elders and Dwarfs had gathered to meet with the newcomers. The walls glimmered with the flickering of the many torches, surrounding the main area. Maac-To was standing in front of the council between them and the stone fashioned benches where the new found army settled in. Around them were the eldest representatives of each of the mountain clans of Humans and Elves as well as the mixed breeds.

"..There he stood alone, facing the fire-breathing beast, that was all but dead. As he raised his sword for the final blow to the Dragon, it raised its head one last time in defiance. Just before the fireball emerged from its mouth, Shi'roc was saved by the beautiful Lady A'mora, tackling him out of the fire's path." Maac-To spoke to the council in common tongue, about the newcomers' cunning and bravery. His manner and flair was second only to Lord Lorentz'.

Shi'roc smiled at the way the story had been told. He sat up straight and took a deep breath, now filled with pride. He would not have thought of the day's events as heroic, as he was not one to think himself a hero. Once again, the stories make the legend and the teller makes it grand.

Having carefully listened to Maac-To's version of battle, the Dwarves began to quietly converse. They spoke in an old Dwarfish dialect, trying to be secretive of their discussion. "Their deeds are indeed impressive," they chattered. "Why else would they come this way if not to help us?" one said. "What good are only twenty of them against Moracles' armies?" retorted another. The murmurs seemed to go on endlessly.

A'mora carefully leaned over to Shi'roc. "What are they whispering about?" not being able to understand much Dwarvish. She would occasionally pick up a word or two but not enough to grasp the meaning.

"I'm not sure. They appear to be discussing us." Though Shi'roc could understand and speak some common Dwarvish learned in his travels, this dialect was foreign to him. It was most probably indigenous to the region. "I don't like it whatever it is. We shouldn't be here." Shi'roc became uneasy at the thought their fate may be left to the old Dwarves. He began to feel as a trapped animal, mentally preparing himself to fight his way out, though he would not know exactly which way to go. They had traversed so many tunnel passages. Though he was attentive of the journey, he would probably not find his way out quickly.

Lorentz had been listening intently to the Dwarv's conversations from across the room. Though he understood standard Dwarvish tongue, he too was unfamiliar with this dialect. He mumbled a few words. "Manua linguatorum cogito sum." He concentrated his thoughts on their words.

A few moments later, he stood up and approached the Dwarves still huddled in their discussion. "May I have your permission to speak?" He then addressed the council in their own tongue and dialect, much to everyone's surprise. They all looked at him and gasped at the thought of an outsider knowing their secret dialect.

"This council is truly wise in questioning our intent and abilities." All the Dwarvs looked at him in shock and amazement. Maac-To was also amazed but smiled with delight at Lord Lorentz who had begun his own oratory. This would surely convince them, he thought.

"Now what is he doing?" Shi'roc said to A'mora. "I can't understand him either?" He rolled his eyes and leaned back stretched on the stone bench. "I hope he knows what he is doing."

"As Maac-To has so graciously been trying to tell you, we possess the knowledge and experience to defeat the armies of Moracles." He looked at each of them. "However, we do not intend to do it alone." He paused with a dramatic flair. All eyes were fixed on him awaiting his next words.

"We are here to teach you the powers of magic, prayer, and the techniques and skills of fighting." He saw doubt and disbelief in the eyes of some who did not think it possible. He reacted to their expressions by saying. "You did not think anyone could know your Dwarven dialect?" he put the question to them though it was a rhetorical question. "I did not know your secret tongue until a few moments ago. Through the powers of magic, I am able to speak to you now. Those of your people who can believe, and possess the wisdom, can learn these powers and together we can destroy the evil forces that have taken your homes and lands and forced you into hiding." Lorentz spoke with a zeal known to his friends and followers as

"The voice of power", where all who could understand him, would be enthralled. It was the power of great charisma, the voice of a true leader. He continued explaining his plan for several minutes.

"...In time you will be ready for the final battle. The war to end this curse that has been placed upon your land has yet to begin." He awaited a response from the council who remained in shock at the words and the way in that they were spoken.

All the others were oblivious, except for Maac-To, since they could not make out a single word of Lorentz' speech. All they knew was that he used the voice for what they expected was to their favor.

Lorentz began to think his power did not work on the Dwarves since a few moments passed in silence. He turned back to Shi'roc who, as expected, wore a puzzled look. The two friends both shrugged their shoulders.

The Dwarf chief cleared his throat, breaking the silence and causing Lorentz to turn back to the council. "Your offer to help us is a bold one indeed." He spoke in the common tongue for all to hear. He did not seem too convinced. "We will make arrangements for you and your party to stay with us in the community while we discuss your plans with the populous. If the people feel that we can sustain such training as you propose, then we will proceed." His words were slow and monotone.

"Surely, you must see the need for the revival of spirits, the renovation of hopes." Maac-To broke in, with the same enthusiasm as Lorentz had demonstrated. "We must learn to fight while some of us can still remember how it was, what we had in years past. The younger generations do not know what life can be like. All they've known is this darkness and fear in which we live from day to day." His words were passionate with disgust and resentment for being forced to live underground for this eternity.

A'mora felt she had remained silent long enough. "I propose that we have a feast for all the communities in a common place, so that they can meet with us face to face." A'mora spoke in a strong yet, sensitive manner, to the council as she stood up and approach the table.

Lorentz turned to look at her. He understood what she was planning and turned back to the council. "Do you have an area large enough to hold all your people?" he smiled.

A'mora stood at Lorentz side and whispered her plan into his ear. He nodded knowing exactly where to go from there.

The Dwarven chief hesitated, and then nodded his head. "Yes, we do have a common auditorium cavern that can hold most of the clans." He paused in thought. "But how do you propose to serve a feast when we survive on roots and rodents?" he questioned holding up his hands in an emptying fashion.

"How many of you are there?" Lorentz asked, thinking that only a few remain. He knew that his powers combined with A'mora's, would suffuce in preparing food for all.

Maac-To approached Lorentz. Even he showed a disbelieving concern in his eyes. "Including wives and children, there are over seven hundred of us."

Their eyes widened, a little shocked by the numbers. Lorentz and A'mora turned to Maac-To, then to each other and said simultaneously, "It will be a small feast."

The Dwarven council paraded out of the room past the others. Each one gave a scornful look at Maac-To as they left. The last to pass was the chief. He too scowled at the Elf leader as he looked at the armor and sword he had adorned himself with.

"Maac-To, show them to the great hall while we summon the clans for this feast; huh!" came the grunt from the skeptical Dwarven chief, Kyman. The Dwarves and elders dispersed down the various passages leading from the meeting room.

Maac-To brushed his hand over the armor breastplate and looked down at his sheathed sword, knowing exactly why Kyman was angry. For a moment he felt a rush of panic and betrayal.

There was a moment of silence as the newcomers all looked at each other wondering what Lorentz and A'mora had gotten themselves into. The others arose from their stone benches and followed as Maac-To led the group down a wide tunnel passage toward the great hall.

"Well; can you do it?" Shi'roc broke the quiet as they traveled in the darkness. Though he was worried it could not be done he was more worried of their host's response to their presence if they did fail.

"Yes we can, but it will take some time and considerable concentration." A'mora responded, a little more abrasive than Shi'roc expected. She and Lorentz had already begun their prayer chants as they walked, and Shi'roc's question had already disturbed the meditation.

By the time they had reached the entrance to the great hall, the chanting had become more noticeable to them all as they made every effort to travel silently. It was not easy for most of them, not being able to see in the total darkness. Shi'roc often took his natural abilities for granted leaving his companions to fumble their way through.

"We have arrived," Maac-To announced standing at the mouth of the cavern. "I will light some torches for your party. The way down is quite treacherous in the darkness."

Lorentz could feel the vastness of the cavern before him in addition to the flowing air currents sensed by his visual abilities. "Not to bother," he replied as he knelt down to scoop up a handful of dust from the floor. "Lumina dochit faux fiero, " he chanted as the dust in his hand began to sparkle like the embers of a dying fire.

As if in synchronous thought, A'mora began to chant as well waving her arms toward the cavern. "Renium zephyra meandrus" a slowly growing wind coming from the passage in which they stood, swept the now glowing dust from Lorentz' hands and spewed it throughout the cavern ahead. In a moment, the walls and high ceilings began to illuminate casting an even light over the great hall.

Maac-To led them down the steep rocky path to the floor of the auditorium. The light seemed to grow and began to spread down the connecting tunnels with the movement of the air. "This is a miracle," he exclaimed, referring to the magical light, as they all looked in awe over the size of this space deep inside the central mountain.

"Yes, it is a miracle," replied Lorentz, "and I will perform as many miracles as it takes to convince your people to fight Moracles," he said with conviction.

* * *

A'mora was deep in concentration kneeling on the hard stone floor. She chanted while slowly waving her hands over the small scraps of dried fruits, vegetables and stale bread, that she had removed from her satchel.

"Maac-To, please leave us to our prayers. We must enlist the help of 'Mirana' if we are to be successful in creating enough food for your people."

"Is there anything at all I can do to help?" The enthusiastic, elder Elf replied sincerely, wanting to become a part of Lorentz' plans.

"Any scraps of food that you could provide for us will help," Lorentz replied. He motioned for the rest of their party to disperse. He turned to Shi'roc as Maac-To headed off towards an outgoing passage. "Gather what's left of the food from our guard. We will need all we can get if we are to feed over seven hundred people."

Shi'roc nodded and went to each of the soldiers collecting their food, that was left from their journey, knowing just what to do, having seen this miracle of the goddess before. He carefully sorted the food into small piles on the ground around A'mora and Lorentz, being careful to leave enough room between piles for the abundant multiplication.

The soldiers found less than comfortable rocks to rest themselves against as they began to remove the more uncomfortable items of gear and armor. As instructed, they remained as quiet as possible and far away from their praying leaders.

Gor leaned over and carefully whispered to Grefden. "How long do you think this light will last?" Looking around at the glittering walls and ceiling. The roof of the cave was full of glowing stalagmites. "I've never seen anything like this before." He gazed up and all around.

Grefden answered just as quietly. "I imagine for as long as Lord Lorentz wants it to." He stared at Gor seeing a quizzical expression on his face. Then he looked over his shoulder to see Sha'la watching him as she was removing her heavy armor. Her skin glistened, reflecting the light from her perspiration. He too was becoming warm staring at her muscular form pressed tightly against her cloth undergarments.

The remaining warriors were sprawled out among the various ledges and carved stone benches. Some were just resting while others were fast asleep. Many wondered if their journey was for naught or their mission failed. All awaited the feast.

Maac-To returned a while later, with a small basket of dried roots and vegetables. A few small pieces of dried rodent meat topped off the meal. This is what they had become accustomed to eating for generations. He did not wish to disturb the prayers so he brought the offerings to Shi'roc, who was watching the two clerics at their form of work. "This is all I was able to collect from the nearby villages." He whispered to the warrior.

Shi'roc carefully looked over the pitiful scraps, sniffed at them and looked at Maac-To. "You actually eat these roots and rat tails?" He asked in amazement almost choking at the thought.

Maac-To was quite flustered and at a loss for words. The proud smile quickly disappeared.

It finally occurred to the warrior that he had insulted his host, seeing the scowl forming on the Elf's face. "Forgive me my friend. I meant no insult to you or your people," came the abrupt and sincere apology. "It must take great strength and courage to survive as you have for so long. How can I apologize for my ill spoken words?" Shi'roc was now the one embarrassed by his own words.

Maac-To looked Shi'roc sternly in the eyes. "You can teach me your skills with a long bow." He put his hand on Shi'roc's shoulder to show friendship and smiled. "Whatever the outcome of this feast, followers or not, I will hide here in the mountains no longer. I wish to fight for what I have lost and avenge my family," he spoke proudly, and then continued. "and so will my son." They shook hands as warriors, grasping each other's wrists.

"Will we meet your son tonight?" Shi'roc asked.

"You already have." Maac-To replied. "It was Ilo who first spotted your campfire last night in the forest. At first we did not believe it possible, but his feelings were so strong that he convinced Kura and myself to venture out to meet you today."

"Spotted our campfire you say?" Shi'roc was amazed. "From the wasteland?" he prodded, not believing it possible from such a distance.

"No. He spotted you from the mountains peak on the first moon's watch." Maac-To motioned up then realized how boastful that must have sounded. "His vision is quite good."

Shi'roc nodded at a loss for words. Was it Ilo's eyes he felt watching him the night before? he wondered, and then proceeded to bring the basket of food to Lorentz. He motioned for the Elf to wait until he had delivered the basket.

"It appears as though we have a new partner." Grefden whispered to Gor, watching the exchange between Shi'roc and Maac-To. He again peered over his shoulder to see Sha'la stretched out on the rocks, playfully urging him on. He became aroused watching her hard body slowly sit up. He resisted for a moment but it was her wink that did him in.

Sha'la gracefully stood up and walked to the shadows of a large stalagmite in the highest corner of the cave. She leaned against it and waited for Grefden's reaction. He quietly stood up, not wishing to disturb the other's rest, then climbed the steep path toward her. As he approached she slipped behind the stalagmite into the shadow. Grefden quickly glanced around to be sure his movement had gone unnoticed as he also slipped into the shadows.

The night was fast approaching with no resulting food, and then suddenly, the quiet chants of the priests were broken by the sounds of an echoing voice, melodic and gentle. Those that were awake looked up and around in the cavern for the source while the others slept peacefully. Lorentz and A'mora, still on their knees, bowed their heads in reverence to the presence of their Goddess, Mirana. The followers of Lorentz, also worshipers, upon realizing the significance of the event, fell to their knees and began to pray.

Sha'la, stunned by the presence, froze in the entanglement of Grefden's arms. The passionate embrace ceased as their pounding hearts stilled.

"What is it?" He inquired. "What is the matter?" As she broke free of his embrace and dropped to her knees, pulling her cloths on around her. He peered over the top of the stalagmite to see the blurred hovering form of the Goddess Mirana.

"Lorentz and A'mora," the voice began, "Your deeds are truly a tribute to me. Your efforts in creating an army to destroy the ones who have decimated my lands and slaughtered my seed will be rewarded. Let your new army of life feast on the foods of your creation." The voice trailed off as the apparition dissipated. "Seek out those least likely to serve my domain."

When the echo died, the small scraps of food began to multiply. The piles grew higher and higher. Fruits and vegetables sprung from the rocks. The pieces of bread turned to multiple loaves. The meat turned into racks of lamb, pork, venison, and even the basket of roots overflowed with fresh leafy cabbage.

Maac-To fell to his knees with tears of joy at the unbelievable sight. "Who is this 'Mirana?" he gasped, "For I wish to worship her too. Please tell me how I can be worthy to witness such a miracle."

Shi'roc stood, being the only one awake and not on his knees, as he watched the vision fade. Though he had not the wisdom to grasp the concept of the powers of any God or Goddess, he had many times been benefactor of her powers through Lorentz.

Shi'roc had heroically fallen in battle many times before, though on one occaision he had not risen on his own power. Near death experiences were not uncommon to such a headstrong warrior such as he. When all hope was lost; when others had given up, Lorentz was able to breath life once again into Shi'roc's battle torn body. Lorentz had attributed this to the powers granted to him by Mirana.

"She grants special powers to those who worship her," he said to Maac-To. "I have no need to worship." He turned to walk away, but stopped as Maac-To replied.

"What is the harm in worshipping one who can grant such miracles?" He asked still on his knees.

"Dependence," was all that Shi'roc said.

Chapter 5
Miracles

Still deep in the southern caverns of the Dwarven Peaks, Ilo and Kura, having tended to the horses, returned to their families. The long walk back through the winding tunnels had made them quite weary and irritable.

"Why do we always have to do everything around here?" Ilo whined as the two strode the uneven cave passage. Kura's short Dwarven legs were trying to keep pace with his Elven friend.

"We all have to do our share for the good of the community," came the thoughtful reply from Kura, "but now we will have help from the newcomers," he said. "Somehow I could feel the strength of their leader, Lord Lorentz. He is a good man," he said confidently. "They all are good people. I could feel it." They continued their walk back slowly ascending into the center section of the mountain range.

When they reached the major intersection of cave paths from the various communities of survivors, they noticed a congested movement of people headed toward the great hall. They saw entire families traveling together. They were all in such a hurry to get somewhere, but Ilo and Kura had no idea of the feast that awaited them.

Ilo inquired as the two were swept up in the flow of bodies. "What's the commotion all about?" he asked one of the elder Humans carrying a torch to light his way. The bearded man was easy to keep up with.

He turned to Ilo and said, "Haven't you heard? The strangers have prepared a huge dinner for all of us. They have invited all the communities to eat and meet with them." Ilo paused in amazement and was quickly shoved forward by the crowds.

Kura had somehow been lost in the shuffle as Ilo said to him, "I guess you were right about them after all. Anyone who could convince these people that they will all be fed on what little they carried with them must indeed have powerful magic." He stopped and looked around. "Kura; where did you get off to now?" It was apparent that he had been swept down one of the other paths by the flow of people.

As the masses of people merged into the great hall from various cavern paths, they could see piles of food amidst the newcomers. The crowds became frantic trying to push toward the food; food of which most had never seen the likes. There was almost a panic until Lord Lorentz stood up on a large boulder in the center of the base of the hall and spoke. His words came forth loud and clear amongst the clamoring crowds; his arms outstretched as a sign of peace and friendship. He motioned to them to quiet down.

"Brave peoples of the Dwarven Peaks; rest thy selves and be silent!" Suddenly the rush ceased and the great hall was still. All eyes were upon him as he turned slowly around to meet the gaze of each and every one of the several hundred participants. Most were crammed into the hall while others still crowded the passages.

"He's doing it again," Shi'roc whispered to A'mora.

She did all she could do to keep from smiling though she was weary from the hours of deep penitence. She knew that he was referring to Lorentz' ability to charm crowds or individuals into listening. She too possessed this power though not with as dramatic effect as her mentor. She had used the power on Shi'roc that morning though it was not as obvious to him. By this time Ilo was finally able to see down into the hall. All were gathered around the center stone as Lord Lorentz continued his speech.

"My friends and I have come to you from far away lands to teach you our ways and help you regain your strength and you freedom. I realize that many of you are too young to know what freedom is, what a town or a city looks like, or even what real food is. Tonight we have prepared a sample of that freedom for you." There was a murmur of sighs from the crowd. "It was not an easy task, but you all are worthy of its efforts having remained safe and whole during these troubled decades. Please eat well and feel free to talk with any of us."

The soldiers had cut up the portions of prepared meats and began handing it out to the crowds. There seemed enough to go around. The mass of survivors calmly began to take food from the various piles. A piece of fruit, a chunk of bread, celery stalks, and so on. They ate, drank and talked with the newcomers. No one had thought to question the mysterious light, that illuminated the many levels of this great open cavern, or how the food came to be. They only knew that there was now hope for their future generations to leave this mountain prison and spread forth through the land once more.

As the crowds mingled in good spirits the newcomers learned more of the heritages of the various peoples. They were told of the cities and communities that once flourished in the valley beyond. Of course much of the stories were passed down through a generation or two by the humans, yet many of the Dwarves remembered first hand of the old days.

Though many stories were told of the valley towns, none were mentioned about the Dwarven communities here in the mountains. There was an understanding amongst the elders not to reveal too much to the strangers too soon. This discrete omission of information was not noticed by anyone except for Lord Lorentz. He noted that conversations with the elders were brief and uninformative. They were careful not to mingle with the newcomers but were there to observe. His efforts in ingratiating himself upon the council were dismissed. He knew there was something to be hidden, possibly something worth hiding. Though he was able to determine no hostilities by them, he felt they were difficult to read. All except Kura, whom he already knew was quite endearing.

Though puzzled by the Dwarves aloofness, he managed to accept it as their way of being and hoped they would in time open their minds to him. For the overall plan to succeed, there must be total trust and understanding amongst them all.

Many of these Dwarves were several hundred years old. Since the evils of Moracles brought them all together in one community, many of the humans mated with the Elves and Half Elves due to the similarities of physical features. This had caused a genetic deficiency in the general long life span known to Elves of pure heritage. It was not uncommon for a pure Elf to live to be over two hundred years old, yet when mixed with Human blood, the life span was greatly reduced though still twice that of a Human.

The Dwarves however had mostly kept their own bloodlines in tact. There was little social contact between them and their refugee guests, descendant from the old cities and forest communities. They did manage to learn toleration for Humans and those of Elven descent. This was due to the natural wisdom acquired from having lived so long.

Now they had a new concept to contend with after all these years. Could they learn to accept the outlanders or would they just be interfering in their copasetic underground world.

As the evening progressed, and all were contented with the food and camaraderie, each one of the newcomers gained a new sense of purpose to help these deprived peoples. They began paying attention to the traits and strengths of the individual survivors. They would learn soon enough which ones could be trained and would be best suited for what type of training. Some would be taught the ways of the gods while others would learn to harness the energies of the elements. Those with the greatest strength and agility would learn to fight with a weapon best suited or with whatever might be available.

"Where are we going to get weapons and armor enough to outfit this small army?" Shi'roc asked the rhetorical question of Gor.

"Perhaps they can learn to make weapons from the elements found in these mountains," Gor replied after a moment of serious thought. Shi'roc glanced back at him with a quizzical eye, not having expected an answer at all let alone a serious one. He had begun to point out to Grefden those of the survivors, that he expected to be good fighters. Most of them were of Human descent or a mixture of Elven like himself. He had also selected several younger, stronger Dwarves. He knew that they had a much greater stamina and strength than would a Human or even an Elf.

"My lord, how can one expect to make a warrior out of one so small?" Gor asked noting Shi'roc's selection.

"Physical size matters not, my friend, only the strength and will to survive. Look around you." He waved his arm out, over the crowd. "Do you see any sickly Dwarves here? No, they have the constitution of a Dragon. They have lived in these mountains for a thousand years." Shi'roc responded, almost as if he admired them. The others knew of his distrust of Dwarves in general, though they had never been told why, and did not understand this sudden change of attitude. Both Grefden and Gor stared at him as though he had been touched by a demon.

Shi'roc scowled at them both, understanding the meaning of their expressions. "I didn't say that I liked them," He snapped then hesitated, still trying to break his friends' stare. "Just that they would make good soldiers."

* * *

Lorentz had gone off with Maac-To for the first night watch. The two figures sat in the mountain shadows of the first blue moon as it rose high above them. The night air chill indicated the coming of another season. Both were wrapped in their cloaks peering over the barren wasteland where they first met.

"Over there; that is the place where Ilo first spotted your campfire." Maac-To pointed to the distant forest edge as the moon cast the mountains shadow over the land. Lorentz appeared to have the same disbelieving expression as did Shi'roc earlier having heard the story. Though the night vision of an Elf was impeccable, the ability was only useful for a short distance. The several miles between the mountains and the forest were totally unbelievable.

"Is this visual ability common among your people?" Lorentz questioned in astonishment, already realizing the advantage of such a talent. This power of night vision far exceeded any that Lorentz had ever heard of. He envisioned the new army to be able to fight best at night with the opportunity to reconnoiter the enemy far in advance of confrontation.

"I don't believe so." Maac-To said disappointedly "At least not to my knowledge." He thought long and hard of other instances involving uncommon sight. "Most of the watchers have been chosen for their visual acuity but Ilo is the best by far."

"Then all of your watchers are composed of Elves and Dwarves?" Lorentz supposed trying to get a feel for the common work ethic among the survivors. He knew that Humans would be useless for night watching unless a full moon was present.

"No, actually those with the 'night vision' as you call it generally take the night watches while the others take guard during the daytime." He thought nothing unusual about the schedules until Lorentz remembered.

"Didn't you say earlier that Jantez sat with you on watch last evening?" He pried, knowing Jantez was human and not prone to have such abilities. He thought that maybe he was there in replacement of another.

"Yes, Jantez teams with me quite often. Are you surprised that a human and Elf would work well together?" Maac-To questioned. "Being confined to these mountains has made us all more tolerable of each other. The Dwarves especially." He continued.

"No, that's not it," Lorentz interrupted. "Your saying that Jantez has the night vision as you and I have?" He was shocked at the prospect of a Human having this ability. As much so as the claim that Ilo had been able to see their campfire from miles away.

"Well; yes. Several of the humans have developed some limited ability having been born for generations in the darkness of the caves. I thought it a natural progression of adaptation for them." Maac-To professed now realizing Lorentz' interest never encountering humans with the vision.

"How many Humans can see in the dark, even those with limited vision?" He pressed on. "This is a remarkable discovery. How many generations did it take in the darkness to develop?"

"Let me think. There are four that I know of with any ability, Jantez being the best. Moran whom you remember greeted us has limited ability." He thought some more and said. "And yes two others." As far as for the time it took to develop; Jantez is the fourth generation I believe and the others are third."

"I wonder if those traits will progress after leaving their homes in the darkness and if it can be passed on to their offspring as well?" Lorentz mused to himself. He was already planning for the best use of those with special talents.

"Having seen what remains of us, what do you think of our chances in defeating Moracles? Can you teach us your ways of combat?" Maac-To was anxious to learn how the

Elves of the outside world evolved after leaving the Elven Forest. He truly believed that Lorentz was a descendent of that heritage. "Where do your people come from?" Referring to Lorentz' part Elven background.

"I am from the land known to most as Thormadore. Have you heard of it?" He asked.

Maac-To thought for a moment and shook his head, "No, I have not."

Lorentz continued, "The area is surrounded by treacherous mountains where terrible Giants once lived. They would come down at night sometimes, raid the villages, take the women, some food and disappear up into the mountains again."

Maac-To listened intently with a look of terror in his eyes as Lorentz spoke. He had never heard of such creatures as he described them. "How could you live with such a feeling of uncertainty, not knowing when they might strike next?"

"We fought back with all we had. Many men died trying to follow the giants back to their mountain caves. They lived much like you do in your communities, safe from outsiders, until, that is, when Shi'roc and his friends arrived."

"You mean he brought an army?" Maac-To corrected.

"No. It was he and a handful of his followers who were sent by a distant wizard," Lorentz began to reminisce.

"I was a young man then. Many times I fought with the elders on the nights the village was attacked. That is when I first learned to use a sword. These giants stood more than twice our height and were at least five times the strength. With much practice and experience I became proficient with the sword."

Maac-To watched Lorentz as the story continued.

"Later, as I grew older I was taught by the village elders. They realized that there was an unseen force in me that needed to be brought out. They taught me to read and understand languages."

Maac-To was enthralled with the story. Lorentz spoke as the Elf had done the night before to Jantez. He told the tale with great feeling so the listener became involved.

"I read many books and apprenticed with both the high priests and the valley mage. All were amazed at the speed with which I learned and the diligence of my studies." It was so natural for him to be able to talk endlessly of himself.

Lorentz suddenly stopped talking. He felt from Maac-To that he was more interested in his people than in himself. "But I think you have been living under a false pretense." He turned to his new friend. "You and I are not from the same ancestry. My parents did not originate from this area. Nor did my grandparents."

Maac-To was in shock. His mouth hung open as if to speak but did not. He had believed for all his life that here in this valley was the origin of all Elves. He was brought up with the understanding that the Elven Forest was the root of all Elven heritages. He finally spoke. "What do you mean? Your grand parents of your Elven half must be from here, or descended from here?" He questioned Lorentz, having shattered his own beliefs.

"No, my friend. There are many lands, on the outside world as you call it, that have bred Elven cultures. There are many types of Elves as well." There was delight as well as disbelief in Maac-To's eyes.

"You would be considered a Wood Elf, having come from a forest community. I have seen Elven villages near and in large bodies of water. My Elven grand parents came from a mountain community called Norgothrond."

Maac-To wanted even more so to be free of this prison and travel to these other Elven communities. He asked Lord Lorentz, "Would you take me with you when we have defeated Moracles?" He paused and a saddened look appeared on his face. "If we defeat Moracles?"

"Indeed, *when* we defeat Moracles I will bring you to lands you had not dreamed imaginable far away from this valley if you wish. But that may not be for years. It is clear that your people are very weak and would require much training in order to effectively assault such great evil."

Maac-To did not understand the length of time involved in preparing for battle. "But why so long. If you have the power to create such miracles as the food we ate tonight and the magical weapons we saw this morning, why must we wait?" He became very serious "I wish to fight now."

Lorentz looked into his eyes and could feel the desperation to be free. He inhaled the crisp night air deeply as he began to explain the apparent powers that he possessed. "You must understand that my magical abilities have been accumulated for over a hundred years. These are not easily shared." He shook his head at Maac-To. "One must study the sciences and the elements to invoke such results. I will seek out those with the highest probability of success and teach them what I can. Lady A'mora will assist those of your people who possess the wisdom to receive the gifts of our goddess. Shi'roc will train the strong of body and courage to fight with the cunning of a wolf. The rest of your people will make clothing, weapons, and armor from whatever materials are available." These had been his true plans from the start. Though he had not envisioned that there would be so many survivors.

Lorentz looked hard at Maac-To with a question on his lips. Should he press him for the answers? "This morning you were wearing a vest of chain armor and sporting a long sword. Where did these items come from?"

Maac-To was no longer wearing them and shied away from the question. He began to try to lie to his new friend but could not. "I… Cannot say where they came from." He turned away from Lorentz in embarrassment. He could not betray the secrets that the Dwarves had entrusted him with all these years as a village elder. He knew that he should not have been wearing the vestments at all.

"Maac-To, you can trust me if there is a secret to be kept. Were they a gift of some sort? Are there more of such items? I need to know what is available to work with if we are to be of help to you." He still received no response from the weary Elf.

"There are several hundred people below that are now depending on us for guidance." Lorentz tried to appeal. "Please, if there are such weapons available, we must be told."

Maac-To continued his shameful silence as he starred into the blue glow of the setting moon. "Please ask me no more, for I can not tell." He turned to Lorentz with an expression of fear and agony at not being able to share what he knew.

* * *

Lady A'mora, still exhausted from the prayers, was now setting on the stone bench. She gently held in her arms a small Dwarven baby. Kura was sitting beside her while most of the others had wandered off or slept from the meal and the wine. Even the newcomers had feasted well after making sure the others had enough to eat.

"What is your son's name?" She asked. Looking at the child with adoring eyes, slowly rocking him to sleep. She had never held a Dwarven infant before.

"We call him Tyme. Named after the great father of all Dwarves." He said proudly then explained. "Of course we were granted permission to do so by the high council. Muga, my wife, is grand daughter to the chief." He boasted with a grand smile. Then suddenly he changed his tone. He looked at A'mora solemnly and asked, "Would you teach me to pray?"

"It is not as much a matter of teaching as it is a gift of the gods. Some have abilities hidden deep inside them that can be brought out and put to use serving their people as a healer or a leader." She began to explain to Kura. She quickly changed the subject back to the child, not wanting to encourage him to peruse that which he could not grasp. For she knew that Dwarves were highly uncommon as priests.

"How old is your son?" She asked looking back at the little one in her arms. Suddenly she felt that someone nearby was staring at her, other than Kura who found her to be very attractive, even for a human. She looked up to see a handsome young human walking toward her.

"Dwarven children grow up slowly that is why they live to be old and wise." Came the voice of the man approaching. "The child is more than three years yet still appears as an infant."

She handed the baby back to Kura and began to stand up. She stumbled from her weakness and was helped back to stability by the young Human. She looked up into his eyes and felt the rush of warmth shooting through her head. He was holding her gently by the arm as she began to sway again. Her eyes were still locked onto his.

"Perhaps you should sit back down before you fall down M'Lady." He gestured to the bench with his free hand. "I don't expect that your dizziness has anything to do with the fine wine we were served at the feast?" He spoke in a pleasant and unassuming tone.

Kura stood up suddenly in her defense as Jantez assisted her to be seated. "Jantez," he blurted. "Lady A'mora has not been drinking. She is weakened by the efforts she put into creating this feast for all of us. You should be thanking her."

A'mora could not break the gaze between herself and Jantez, nor was she able to speak. Kura noticed that she was entranced by his stare. She had not experienced such a phenomenon since she had met her mentor, Lorentz, two years ago. Could this man possess the same potential gifts as he? She thought.

Jantez stood tall and strong. Handsome he was even for Human. How could one grow so fine a body without the proper nourishment? She wondered. He would certainly make a fine warrior she thought, but what of this charismatic appeal he has? Could she be imagining it weakened as she was?

"I am called Jantez." He introduced himself while bowing to kiss her hand. "And I am enchanted to meet such a courageous and beautiful woman." He looked her over with a glance. She was still wearing the tightly fitted leather armor that she had put on that morning. "Even more so knowing now that you possess the powers of legendary wizards."

A'mora finally was able to speak as she broke the stare with great effort. "It is I who seem to be enchanted sir." Almost feeling embarrassed, "And it was not wizardry that created this food. It was a gift to you from the Goddess Mirana." She turned to Kura, still standing there with his sleeping son in his arms. "It is rather late. Shouldn't you be getting yourself and your son back to your wife." She urged, and then created a fake yawn in an effort to be contagious.

"Yes, I suppose I should. Will I see you tomorrow to teach me how to pray?" He said with a broken yawn. She nodded to him. "I will talk with you more in the mor…" He broke into another yawn and turned away toward the passage to his underground village.

Most of the mountains inhabitants had gone off either to bed or to take their turn at night watch. Many of Lorentz' soldiers had also curled up in the rocks and gone to sleep. The magical light that had been created in the room finally began to fade.

Shi'roc sat up on the ledge where he had slumbered off, still holding a flask of wine. It had taken him most of the evening to feel safe enough that he would partake in the wine. He realized that it was not these people who were going to hurt him. The intoxicated warrior noticed that A'mora was still talking with the mountain human. He looked and hesitated. Should he interrupt? He wondered. He knew how tired she was. Why were they setting so close? He thought, and then shook his head. No, it matters not, or does it? He was unsure of his feelings toward her and hers toward him. He didn't have time for women nor did he have the patience, yet emotions were getting the better of him in his inebriated state and he didn't yet know why. He began to climb down the sloped path to the bottom level of the cavern where A'mora and this other person were sitting. He approached apparently unnoticed though as he stumbled, his chain male armor was far from quiet.

"I must go for now. It will soon be my turn on watch and you need your rest." Jantez said softly as he stood up. Just as he turned to walk away he saw the warrior standing in front of him.

"Yes she does indeed need her rest." Shi'roc broke in with a sharp voice. "And how would you know what rest she requires?" Spoken more accusingly though he did not know why he said it. He looked directly at the young human as he turned toward him. Jantez smiled and was about to speak when A'mora stopped him and made the introduction.

"This is Jantez." She said as he nodded to Shi'roc. "He was inquiring about being instructed in the ways of magic." She said quite as a matter of fact, feeling some jealousy emanating from Shi'roc's tone. She also knew he had too much wine as evidenced by his inability to stand still. Shi'roc shifted his gaze from A'mora directly to Jantez. Their eyes locked as Jantez spoke.

"I came to express my thanks to Lady A'mora as well, for the feast that she helped prepare. All of you must be very brave to have journeyed so far to help us." He spoke in a mild but convincing fashion. "We will be in your debt if you can truly defeat Moracles and his armies of demons."

Shi'roc was at a loss for a response at such a gracious compliment. The build up of emotion had passed. "Demons? What Demons? Lorentz didn't say anything about Demons," he mumbled with a confused look on his face.

Jantez nodded to Shi'roc and to A'mora, bidding them good night, and walked off toward the passage leading to the surface of the mountain.

Shi'roc stood staring in a trance as Jantez disappeared into the shadows of the cavern. He regained his thoughts and shook his head. "I don't understand what just happened," He said to A'mora.

She gracefully stood up, and looking into his eyes said, "I believe I finally understand." She gave him a soft kiss and walked over to lie down on a smoother looking space on the floor of the cavern. She opened her bedroll and lay down. She was now convinced that she was getting closer to Shi'roc. She indeed felt emotional warmth that he was emanating towards her, even if he was drunk. Perhaps that was what was needed to lower his guard and allow his emotions to break forth.

Shi'roc slowly climbed back to his ledge and collapsed loudly as he tried to unfasten his armor. With the dim glow of the magical light finally extinguished, they all slept.

* * *

Far from the Dwarven peaks, deep in the forgotten valley, lay the exhausted Demon maker himself, Moracles. His strength depleted from the loss of his Dragon pet having been slain. The demonic, empathic connection was so firm between them that when the creature perished so did a portion of the evil wizard. Thus was the price to pay for summoning creatures from the dark ethereal abyss. Many days would pass before he could fully recover his potency from the loss.

He lay limp in his large soft bed somewhere in his vast secret chamber. Quibit, his summoned servant from the dark forces, set carefully wiping his master's brow with a cloth. All of the energies expelled by the mage would be felt throughout his realm of evil. The other sentient soldiers, of whom Moracles had recruited from the dregs of various races, would continue their day-to-day activities unaware of the absence of their leader. It was not unusual for the great sorcerer to be unseen or unheard. Most of his armies had never even been honored by his visit. Only the terror that he created kept them loyal knowing that any disobedience or failure by them would be dealt with in ways unimaginable.

Days passed as the mage regained his strength. Now pacing the great black marble floor of his study as his dark robes flowed with his movement, he sought deep in his soulless spirit, an evil plan so contemptible as to cause a grin to come through.

"He was called by the name Shi'roc as I recall." He gently stroked the hairs of his wild beard with his wrinkled fingertips. He had learned this through the senses of the Dragon before it was slain. "I have heard that name before, long ago in the castle of Lord Magdalene. Yes it must be the same warrior." He continued to mumble alone in the flickering candlelight. "Why are they here? What is their purpose?" He turned to the large desk upon which stood the candelabra. In its light could be seen the master's volume of mystical spells as it lay open upon the desk. He rounded the intricately carved piece of furniture and sat himself in the chair behind it. Once again he began to flick his long blackened fingernails through the book's wrinkled Elf skin pages while caressing the head of the demon carved in the arm of the great oaken chair. He stared hard into the pages of cryptic writings.

As the candles shortened by inches he studied his evil incantations to uncover a long forgotten and seldom used spell. His eyes widened as a child peering at a piece of well-deserved candy. He read through its several pages over and over again until he had finally memorized each and every sinister syllable. He carefully closed the book and relaxed into the leather padding of the chair back.

"It matters not why they are here," he uttered to no one but himself, staring off into the darkness beyond the light of the candles reach, "because I know how to stop them when they reappear. I will stop him. The one they call Shi'roc." He began to laugh, louder and louder until it began to echo through the canyon crevice into the night sky as the second moon began to rise. The watchers in the canyons shuddered at their master's echoing laughter, knowing that another plan to strengthen his grasp of the valley had been unfurled. More evil would be spread, more destruction, and more death.

Chapter 6
Beginnings

As the days went by, the newcomers became well accepted by all the surviving inhabitants of the Dwarven peaks. Each one of the newcomers adapted specific responsibilities in the caring for, and training of those who were able to learn. The excitement level had grown considerably since the introduction banquet and most of the survivors had vowed their loyalty to follow Lord Shi'roc and Lord Lorentz in a battle against Moracles.

This was not unlike previous crusades in that the brave masters of sword and sorcery turned simple folk into a fighting force. On other occasions they had fought side by side with only a few to help them vanquish the forces of evil and oppressors. From 'Norgothrond' to 'Cerratt', the stories were told of the few who bravely faced the unknown, the Dragons, the Giants, the evil wizards and death itself. For it was their charge in life to fight for freedom and the privilege to teach the unlearned and cure the diseased. Their reward was the gratitude of the peoples and the experience and knowledge gained from each battle. The upcoming battle however would be like none in the past and may never be in the future. Those who had not yet heard of the legends of Shi'roc and Lorentz would indeed learn after this battle, that is, if there would be anyone left to tell the story.

"Shi'roc, Ilo is going to lead me back to where they have been tending our horses. It is time that they be told we have not abandoned them." Lorentz said as he passed Shi'roc, distracting him at the moment when a student had swung his wooden training sword, unbalancing Shi'roc as the blow struck his shield.

Shi'roc quickly recovered from his stumble noticing the smiling trainee glowing from a victorious bout. "What do you mean, 'told we have not abandoned them?" He shot a look back at Lorentz, again taking his attention from his eager student who once again bashed his shield with surprising force. "That was a well placed hit. Strong and steady." He said. "Come at me again Jantez." Shi'roc steadied himself for another strike, holding his shield where he could just see over it. The Human student learned well. He was a natural warrior, taller and a bit stronger than Shi'roc. They continued the melee training.

Grefden and Gor were also involved with students themselves. Each was training one of the Dwarves that Shi'roc had selected previously. As with Jantez, the Dwarves each wielded a wooden sword as Gor and Grefden repelled their blows with a shield. This was quite amusing to Grefden who held his shield low, as it appeared he was protecting his family jewels since his opponent barely came up to his waist.

"Remember, if your opponent is larger than you, as I am, move to higher ground or you may be trampled like this." Grefden yelled as he pushed back the flustered Dwarf with his feet. The Dwarf's agility was profound as he dropped and rolled under Grefden's feet and attacked from the rear stabbing Grefden in his exposed rump. "Aaaahhh" Grefden howled as he swung around to be struck again across the shins. Fortunately, Grefden was wearing his armor though he did sustain quite a bruise to his ankles and ego. Enough he called in truce to prevent the Dwarf from further attacks as he limped over to a bench to sit down.

"You see, my friend what I meant. They are both strong and cunning." Shi'roc bragged as he and Jantez witnessed the bout. Gor was too busy laughing to continue the training. The victorious Dwarf raised his sword in victory and took a bow as well. The other students present stood up and applauded. The Dwarves were all quite enthused and impressed with the quickness and cunning of their friend. Grefden removed his leggings and inspected his battered shins. Though his pride was jostled, the incident had greatly improved the morale of the students.

The great hall, as it was known, was a natural training area for those in combat due to its varying ledges and slopes. Shi'roc and his guards could teach all of the techniques, that needed to be learned for hand-to-hand combat, here. The make shift swords and shields of course would be no substitute for training with real weapons and armor. But for now it was the tactics and endurance, that were being tested. Muscles had to be built, coordination had to be practiced. But most importantly, stamina for enduring long hours of combat had to be learned.

At the base of the cave, others practiced the skills of archery instructed by Lorentz' guard. With this being the principal long-range weapon of their armies, many of the survivors would need to learn this skill. They had made enough bows quickly for use in practice, though they were not suitable for actual combat. Although simple long bows and short bows could be constructed from tempered wood and twisted vines, they could not match up to the force of a well crafted cross bow. There were only a few of these brought by Lorentz' followers. The use of a crossbow did not require the amount of strength that a long bow did and was well suited for the few females among the survivors that wished to learn.

"The first thing you need to learn is to reload the weapon as swiftly as possible." Sha'la instructed as she stood before a dozen of the female survivors holding her prized crossbow. It was a complicated weapon in that it had moving mechanisms for that to operate. "In order to cock the bow you must first place the stirrup on the ground and insert your foot to hold it firm. Then pull back the string until it locks into the catch like this." She demonstrated the technique with relative ease having been considered an expert for a number of years and still alive to teach.

She slowly released the string from the catch and asked each of the women in turn to practice the movement. The human women had little difficulty in cocking the bow. The Elves and mixed breeds were straining to pull the string but in time would build the muscles needed. The last in the row was Kura's wife, Muga, the only Dwarven female to participate. This was not acceptable to the Dwarven council being the grand daughter of the chief, but Kura supported his wife's decision. She took the crossbow, held it with her left arm, and pulled the string quickly into the locked position with her right hand. This demonstration of agility and strength impressed Sha'la.

"Thank you Muga for demonstrating the optimum technique for those with the strength to do so. This will allow you to keep your eye on the enemy while reloading. It is definitely faster then having to lower the weapon and bend over." She demonstrated the same move as Muga but with more precision and speed.

Sha'la continued the lesson by demonstrating loading the bolt into the ready crossbow. Although she was an excellent instructor, much of what she taught required experience to absorb. The days ahead would involve much practice in not only developing muscles and speed but also in aiming and firing the weapon under the pressure and distractions of actual battle.

The crossbow would not be an easy weapon to duplicate. And certainly not enough could be made as was needed. One of the other crossbows had been carefully disassembled so the Dwarven craftsmen could study it and attempt its intricate construction with the available materials. As with the simpler bows and arrows, the children would go out on the mountains surface and collect the branches from the dead trees. These were cleaned and crafted into the arrow shafts and bows. The thin bark was formed and used for the arrow fletchings. Vines and strands of rope were combined to form the bowstrings.

Other easily crafted weapons such as slings and staffs were also in the making by the village women and children. All that were able, helped to further the cause. Rock chips were sharpened for arrowheads and tied to the wedged tips of the shafts.

The swords and daggers were carved of wood as well. They did not have the weight or the sharpness of steel. They would be fairly useless against an armored opponent.

Stone war hammers were created in much the same way. The stronger branches were fashioned into handles while stone heads were tied with vines to the end of them. Spiked clubs were also carved from branches while sharpened rock chips were imbedded into the weapons end.

Shields and armor were far less easy to create from straw and branches. The women gathered old bedding to weave with rope to create these defensive necessities. It was clear that there was much work to be done. The making of the weapons was first priority set by Shi'roc.

The village elders observed the training exercises and the manufacture of the weapons and armor. They were impressed with the enthusiasm and diligence of the newcomers in teaching their people. "They work so hard. But to what end?" Kyman told the Dwarven council members. "They can not wage war with these instruments." He shook his head sadly gesturing to the wooden and string weapons the village women were manufacturing. "They would be led to slaughter if we allowed it."

"If they had real weapons and armor they might stand a chance. Don't you think?" one of the others spoke. "Yes, if they are trained well and long there might be hope." Said another to the chief as he waved off their words with his hand and he walked away. "We shall see how they progress before I make a decision." Kyman wanted no part of sending people to their certain deaths. Especially those the Dwarves have kept in protection for so long. He had seen what weapons of war had done to their ancestors long ago and wanted no more guilt on his hands.

* * *

"What did you mean, Lord Lorentz, about talking to the horses?" Ilo inquired as they headed away from the training area. "Can you really talk to them, and have them understand you I mean?"

"Most people don't realize that animals aren't much different from ourselves Ilo." Lorentz began to explain the powers, that allowed him to communicate with most animals. The grace of that was bestowed upon him by 'Mirana'.

Lorentz' task was to find a way to create a continuous food supply. Though both he and A'mora could create large amounts of food, the time and energy spent could be better used elsewhere. Such draining of their priestly powers was quite exhaustive and if done continuously could cause a lapse of ability. Though as seen fit by the gods who provide the power through devout worship, the overuse of such power was indeed frowned upon.

"You say that the horses have been fed and watered every day. How is this possible? I thought that water was scarce?" Lorentz asked, puzzled as he followed Ilo through the winding tunnels leading in a downward slope.

"The water we do have is rationed since it comes so rarely. We felt it was necessary to apportion some to the horses and to feed them the remaining grain that you had brought," Ilo replied. "What we can grow will not be enough for us as well as the horses and we are out of the grain. We do not have any place for them to graze." As they continued the hurried journey, Ilo became tired and breathless. While his elder, Lorentz, was not at all phased by the trip. Though Ilo was young for a full Elf, only fifty eight years, he had not been conditioned for such vigorous day-to-day activity. As the others who were born and raised in the confines of the mountain, there was little physical work involved except for the watcher duty at night.

"I must rest." Ilo said as he sat on a rock in the passage. "Lord Shi'roc really pounded me today in the training exercise. But he says I could someday be as skilled as he with a sword." Ilo smiled though Lorentz could not see in the unlighted tunnel, he could feel the young Elf's pride.

"Your agility will assist you to this aspiration but for now you all need to learn stamina," Lorentz inspired. "The ability to wield a sword is worthless if one can not do so for long periods of time. Your endurance must also consist of warding off attack by your opponent." Lorentz stood over the young Elf. "No more rest. We must move along."

A short while later they had arrived at the mouth of an enormous under ground cavern at what Lorentz believed was the far south edge of the mountain range. There was a crevice high up on the westward wall allowing a narrow sliver of light to penetrate.

In the distance he could hear the echoing drip of water as it condensed on the cave ceiling and fell. The area was cool and moisture could be felt in the air. Lorentz could see a glimmering pool of water where the light was reflecting. He felt that the ground was soft and moist beneath his feet. Not rock as he had expected. He knelt down and reached into the black earth with his hand and raised it up to his nose.

"I can smell the richness of this soil. Where are the foods you grow here?" He asked Ilo. There was an actual earthy floor in that plants could grow.

"Over there." He pointed off to the left. "The horses are near to it. Can you see?" In the shadows created by the afternoon sun, they could both see the outlined body heat of the horses, standing at the far reaches of their enhanced vision. Lorentz reached into a small belt pouch, began to chant and with the wave of his arms tossed the sulfur dust into the moving air. In a moment, the air began to sparkle and the walls near the horses became aglow with a magical light.

"I wish I could do that," Ilo gasped in amazement, his eyes wide open. They walked over and inspected the animals. As they approached, the horses could feel the priest's presence and began to whinny.

Lord Lorentz carefully looked them over and was satisfied that they were in good health and had been well cared for. The saddles and bridle gear had been neatly stacked and laid out on some large boulders. "You and Kura have done well. I wish for the two of you to always take care of the animals," Lorentz praised.

"Thank you sir. I shall tell Kura when we return that you were pleased. The crops are over there." He pointed at the space where the meager crops were tended. The sun light shown on a small patch of ground.

Lorentz was now standing in front of the horses and chanting quietly while moving his arms in a wandering motion. Ilo stood silently and watched as the horses made a circle around the elder Elf, blocking Ilo's view of the priest. When the chanting ceased, he heard the snorts and whinnying of horses. It appeared to be coming from Lorentz. Then the horses started stomping and stepping while returning the sounds as if they had somehow understood and were pleased that their master had returned.

Lorentz looked over at the small root garden and went to inspect it. He knelt in the soil and ran his hand into it. Puzzled by the few assorted vegetables growing in the small area he asked. "With such rich soil and nearby water, why do you only grow such unflurishing plants? There is so much more that can be grown here. Most of the soil has not yet been tilled or planted." He looked around at the rest of the earthy area, that had not been disturbed.

"I've been told that when Moracles destroyed the farmlands the seeds of all flowering plants had been contaminated." Ilo pointed to the dirt. "This area of land was protected by the mountain from the spreading plague that ruined all soil that it touched. There were no living plants to bring here. This is all that the Dwarves were able to grow for themselves. They used to trade with the farmers in the valley for food since they were not growers themselves. That is why there has been so little for us all to eat," Ilo explained.

"That shall soon change, I promise," Lorentz said with a saddened tone. Quickly, he stood up brushing the soil from his chain leggings. His mind went into a patterned frenzy. "We have soil!" He said pointing to the earth. "We have water!" Pointed to the small pool. "We have light!" As he pointed up to the crevice on the mountain wall. "Ilo, go back and tell the others I am not to be disturbed here for six days." He began to pace around the edge of the pool of water as he talked. "At that time send A'mora and some others of the various villages here with as many bushel baskets and water skins as they can carry."

"Yes sir!" Ilo snappily responded. "But what are you going to do here all alone for six days?" He got no answer from Lorentz who was staring over the riches of the cavern, a plan churning in his head. Ilo turned and headed back to the tunnel.

"I am going to build a shrine." Was the only response that Ilo received from Lorentz as he continued to survey the cavern. Ilo hurried back through the cave entrance to relay Lorentz' message.

* * *

"A shrine?" Shi'roc yelled as Ilo leapt back after delivering the message. Shi'roc was not aware of the phrase, *'don't whip the messenger'* "Why would he waste the time. There are more important matters to tend to." Shi'roc was becoming irritated at the thought. "I will fetch him and knock some sense into his head." He began to storm off to the cave passage out of the great hall. Realizing that he did not know the way, he stopped and turned to Ilo. "Come, show me." As he motioned for the young Elf to follow.

"No, wait!" A'mora rushed to Shi'roc grabbing his arm. "You mustn't disturb him. He is doing what's most important for all of us." A'mora looked into Shi'roc's eyes as he turned to face her.

"What good will a shrine do us in training these people to fight." He exploded with his built up frustration. "Its bad enough that they will be fighting with rocks and clubs." He shook loose A'mora's grip of his arm in a jerky motion

"Don't you see? He wants us to bring the baskets for the food. The shrine is for Mirana. She will help him to grow new crops in the cave. He must feel that there is enough of what he needs to create a source of food." Her firm convincing tone, as well as her powers, eased Shi'roc's tension. He felt her wisdom in the gentle touch of her hand again on his arm. She spoke again, now in a much softer voice. "Go back to training your new troops, 'Vandar'." She walked back toward her students to whom she was bestowing the powers of prayer.

Shi'roc stood there for a moment contemplating the word she used 'Vandar', was an old Elven word for 'a great leader'. She had just paid him a great compliment, but where did she learn such an uncommon Elven word? He then returned to his next round of students.

"Grow crops in six days?" Shi'roc spoke quietly to himself as he walked back to his new Dwarven warriors. "I suppose if anyone can do it, Lorentz would be the one."

A'mora sat back down amongst the handful of people that had come to her to be healers. A few were witness to her and Lorentz' healing powers in the past few days. Several of the survivors had been stricken with disease or malnourished. Their health had improved by the abilities and potions of the two devout priests. Some were so moved as to want to heal others themselves knowing that the future held a grave battle where healing powers would be needed.

The students were still entranced in prayer. Kura broke his meditation to ask A'mora if there was anything wrong with Lord Shi'roc. She reassured him that all was well, with a simple nod, and to continue his prayers. She looked over each one of them, the Dwarf, Humans and part Elf, all deep in concentration. She murmured a few words of prayer and with a motion of her arms spreading out over the lot, she was able to foresee those with the greatest potential.

Quite surprisingly, Kura emitted the strongest aura. She did not believe that a Dwarf could have such devotion to a Goddess. She had witnessed great strength of that race, and heard of profound wisdom, but it never occurred to her that a priest could emerge from one.

She looked over to the Dwarven warriors training with Shi'roc. She could see his diligence in the way of his instruction, making sure that each one would be the best. He was strict as well as encouraging. He would not give up on those willing to keep trying to get it right. Although he was a brutal and cunning warrior when he needed to be, he was also gentle and intelligent in his own stubborn and naive way. This was perhaps due to his optimistic view of life, she thought. "He will make a fine king someday." She mumbled to herself. She kept staring at him as if in a trance. He would also make the right woman a good husband. She thought.

* * *

In the glow of the magical light, Lorentz had begun the creation of a new irrigation system. He climbed the rock up to where the crevice reached through to the outside of the mountain. The priest crawled through the narrow opening to see in that direction the mountainside faced. It was apparent that it sloped west as he watched the sun set into the distant forest from that which came. Pulling himself up to brush off the earth from his clothing, he realized why the rains did not provide more water to the cave through the opening. The rock face of the mountain sloped away from it and the slight overhang of rock prevented the waters from flowing inward. “I can fix this so that the water will flow properly.” He said to no one.

Standing alone on the side of the mountain, he began to pray. “Manua lithos corectum in extra deorum.” The chanting engulfed his mind into such meditation that he could not even feel the cool wind rushing past him. As he stood at the edge of the crevice he swept his arms in an arc downward to the rock. The stone at his feet began to soften and take on new shapes. The crevice widened creating a natural trough for catching the rains as they fell and trickled down into the cavern.

Everywhere Lorentz touched with his hands, the stone yielded to his will. He crawled back through the crevice and formed new paths for the water to flow. In a few hours he had created an entire trough system throughout the cave leading into the pool and garden areas. With the remaining strength left to him he formed a grotto at the base of the troughs. With his artistic fingers, he gently sculpted a statue of the goddess who made this all possible. He reached deep into his memory, having visited the goddess in her world several times before. A perfect likeness of Mirana appeared before him in the stone as he fell to sleep at the foot of his new creation.

The light had finally dimmed and wore away into complete darkness. All that could be heard was the stirring of the horses as they moved about also preparing to sleep.

* * *

It had been ten days since their arrival and the feast, that had been created. The food that they made was almost gone. With Lorentz elsewhere, she was faced with the task alone to feed all of these people. As before she asked that all remaining scraps of food be collected throughout the mountain villages and brought to the great hall. There was very little food to work with. Much less than before since the new soldiers had been training hard and all were becoming well fed. The hall was cleared so that she could meditate in silence. In the flickering torch light, A'mora remained on her knees, swept up in the prayers to the Goddess Mirana in hopes of receiving yet another favor to perform a miracle.

As the hours passed, she became very weak with exhaustion from the energies put forth in her devout prayer. The task of creating so much food was too great for her to bear without assistance. She begged in her meditation to Mirana, sacrificing all her powers to be able to provide for these worthy people, that she had chosen to serve. Finally as she was bent over the small piles of food on the cavern floor, she heard a melodic soft voice whispering in echoes from within her head.

"A'mora" the voice whispered her name. And again. "A'mora, awaken from your trance. Your prayers have been heard." Then it was gone.

She lay asleep on the growing piles of food. Beneath her arose once again fresh vegetables, fruits, and breads. The scraps of meat had grown into a fully prepared feast. She stirred and raised her head from the bounty to see that she had been successful. There was clearly enough food to last them a full week if rationed sparingly.

A'mora straightened her body to stand up but realized too late that her sore, tightened muscles of concentration, would not bear the strain. She swiftly fell backward, loosing her balance and struck her head on a stone. She winced upon the impact but was too tired to struggle against the pain. She closed her eyes and fell into unconsciousness. Her wound was not severe but blood had been spilled and quickly began to cake in her soft golden hair.

*   *   *

The mountain dwellers began to gather in the great hall as word spread of more food having been prepared for the coming days. As they entered the hall from the various passages they were surprised that it was dark. They had become used to the artificial light that Lorentz and A'mora had created while they were being trained in the great hall.

Maac-To carefully made his way down to the base of the dark cavern where he had seen Lady A'mora earlier gathering the food scraps. With his ability to see in the dark he noticed the form of someone lying on the ground. He called to her in hopes that she had fallen asleep. There was neither movement nor response from her. He rushed to her side, tripping over the piles of food, that she created. He cried out to the others.

"Someone bring torches. Hurry; she may be ill." Immediately two torches were lit at the top of the cavern and were passed on down to the base lighting other torches along the way. In moments there was a flickering glow throughout the great hall. Maac-To knelt beside her now with a torch in his hand. Ilo and Kura appeared also carrying torches.

"Look. She is injured." Maac-To gently raised A'mora's head to see the coagulated blood caked in her hair. The stone upon which her head laid was also blood stained.

There was soon a circle of torches as the crowds gathered around Lady A'mora and the food.

"Someone go after Lord Lorentz and tell him what has happened. Where is Lord Shi'roc?" Maac-To ordered.

"I am here." Shi'roc and his men pushed their way through the crowd to where A'mora lay in Maac-To's arms. "What has happened?" He demanded, looking at her blood soaked hair. He quickly checked her for other wounds as Maac-To spoke.

"It appears that she stumbled and hit her head on this rock." He pointed to bloodied stone on the ground. "I found her unconscious. What should we do?" He said almost in a panic.

Kura pushed passed the others and looked seriously into Lady A'mora's passive face and said calmly. "I will heal her." He did not even look at the others as Shi'roc began to scoff.

"What can you do for her injuries? You are not a priest." Shi'roc mocked the Dwarf.

"She has taught me her healing powers." He said fervently, not taking his eyes from his patient. He motioned for Maac-To to move aside and let him kneel beside her. Kura turned her head to the side and parted her hair to reveal the origin of the blood. A small gash was still oozing.

He pressed his stubby fingers onto the wound and began to chant. "Manua invocatum coagula noxit." He kept repeating the chant with his eyes closed tight in concentration. In a few moments, the oozing ceased and the gash began to close. He strained to keep his concentration as the crowd murmured.

"Look. He is healing her." They whispered. "The wound is closing."

Shi'roc stood in amazement with his jaw hanging. He knelt beside her and took her hand in his as Kura continued the chant. Finally the Dwarf broke the meditation and wavered wearily. He was quite weakened from the healing prayers.

A'mora stirred and let out a quiet moan. She slowly turned her head and took a deep breath as if coming out of a long sleep. Her eyes flickered open slightly to reveal Shi'roc bending over her still holding her hand. She opened her eyes wide to see the others standing around with torches, wondering what had happened. She then realized she was lying on her back and suddenly remembered the pain.

"She is all right!" He exclaimed. "Kura, you did it." Shi'roc smiled at him.

A'mora tried to sit up but still felt weak and instead remained in Shi'roc's arms as he gently kissed her hand.

"Thank you my friend." Shi'roc said to Kura. "I shall doubt your wisdom no more, for today you have truly earned the title of healer."

Kura blushed at the praise. "I owe my knowledge to Lady A'mora. It was she who taught me to heal."

"And I shall teach you much more." She said slowly, still dazed. "But now you must ration out the food. Be sure to save enough for several days. I fear that I will not have the strength to create more food for a long .... time...." She began to dose and yawned a wide yawn as Shi'roc sat and cradled her, gently brushing the hair from her face with his fingers. He carefully lifted her in his arms and carried her away from the piles of food to a corner of the cave where he stayed with her as she slept.

The others sorted and rationed out the food to the clans of the various villages as the Dwarven council looked on, again at another miracle. Day by day, the chief felt his control over his people and the survivors yielding to the newcomers. They were indeed strong and powerful with abilities and gifts far beyond what he could offer as a Dwarven chief.

Chapter 7
Garden

The night sky was cloudy. Neither of the moons would be seen and no light would be shed on the Dwarven peaks. The crisp wind blew through the rocky mountain passages as the watchers changed shifts. A crack of lightning followed by the thunderous roar broke the howl of the night air.

"I wonder what Moracles has in mind with this show. It has not stormed like this in many months." Jantez exclaimed to Ilo, crouched down behind the rocks braced against the wind. It was believed that such storms were called forth by Moracles. Each held their wooden swords while they stood watch. It was part of their training to always have the sword in hand. They were to make it a part of them, "an extension of their arm." Shi'roc had said.

"It matters not as long as he brings rain with the storm," Ilo replied. For you see it was seldom that rain would fall during one of these storms just as sure as it was believed to be by the design of the evil one; a storm with no rain. Where his magical powers so great as to control the weather? They could only imagine that it was. But rain or not, the waste land between the mountains and the forest was sure to widen inch by inch as all plant life to be touched by the growing evil would wither and die. The forest would grow further and further away as it had for many decades extending the insurmountable forces of Moracles grasp. To their surprise, it began to rain.

"At last. Water for our people. Lord Lorentz will be pleased. It will help him to grow the food for us." Ilo now beamed with warmth at the thoughts he imagined of Lord Lorentz in the cavern. He could feel the strength and commitment as he spoke to him several days past.

"How do you know what his plans are for food? What makes you think that he can grow plants and trees in that water cave?" Jantez questioned.

"He told me he could. I just know he can," He said seriously as he peered through the rain at the distant lightning.

* * *

The rain was now falling at full force as Lorentz stood in the darkness just outside of the newly patterned crevice with his arms outstretched, still chanting the words, that called the downpour. "Aqua nouri in octo sum." The words came forth as the falling rain channeled itself into the reservoir, that he had created. He broke from the trance with rain spattering off of his face. First he reveled in the soaking rain, and then crawled back through the crevice into the cavern. He had prepared a glowing fire in the rocks away from the fertile rows of crops he had planted the day before. He warmed himself for a moment over the flames and looked out as the flowing water rose over the reservoir and spilled into the garden area.

Once again he stood in the grotto at the head of the reservoir and called forth the powers of his prayer. He began waving his arms in the rolling motion and chanted. "Enzi vegorum et manua sit arbori fructum." Echoed through the cavern repeatedly. His majestic voice slowly faded and all was silent. The storm no longer roared. The rain ceased to fall and the wind faded to a cold gentle breeze outside the mountain. After hours of strenuous prayer, the priest lay rested on the rocks shrouded in his cloak. The deep sleep was well deserved as his prayers were being answered.

* * *

"Kura, where are you off to?" Came Shi'roc's words as he successfully fended off several attacks made by three of his warriors in training. He stood alone, unarmed with only his shield for protection. He was demonstrating the ability to defend against several attackers. The make shift swords and shields were working well in the training maneuvers. He was also pleased that his students were learning quickly. Some had grasped the concept of strategic combat in only a week. He ceased the lesson momentarily.

"I must take Lady A'mora and the others to collect food from the garden as Lord Lorentz requested. It is a long journey and I don't want anything should happen to her." His affection for the beautiful Human was becoming more obvious as was Shi'roc's liking for the little Dwarf. He raised his training sword in salute and waddled off proudly to protect his mentor.

Shi'roc picked up one of the wooden swords and waved it at his students. "Again, all of you, now." Shi'roc shouted to his students as all three of them rushed him on the rocks of the great hall. Each one would swing and parry with sword and then shield simultaneously attacking and defending as the master swordsman had taught. The attacks on Shi'roc continued, as he would back up encouraging the poorly equipped warriors to full contact melee combat as if it were for real. Shi'roc knew that the only way to practice was with a real opponent. No holding back. If one would practice by holding back, this would lead to his defeat in real battle. He had to purge their emotions and turn them into stone. Hard and unyielding.

Two onlookers rested nearby. "Do you remember your first encounters as Shi'roc's student?"

"I do believe that I still have the bruises and scars to show for it, Gor," Came Grefden's reply. "He is the best by far. His teaching is what has kept us alive so long." He referred to the several years of which they had traveled with the Elf. Both Grefden and Gor were in awe of their master as they rested on a stone bench. Both short of breath having been fiercely training their own students.

"And he does seem to enjoy it as well. I understand how he feels in having an ability that can be shared with others." He said to Gor, and then turning to their own students with new inspiration, they continued.

"Lets get back to it men." Gor yelled to the group, that was setting off to the side, examining their own minor wounds and bruises.

"Come on before we give you something to really bleed about." Grefden's serious commands brought them to a defensive posture immediately, swinging a battle-ax at Maac-To. The elder Elf dodged the blow and parried with his shield. His agility made him a superb warrior.

"Keep that shield up." Gor exclaimed as he bashed the Dwarven warrior driving him to his knees hiding behind his shield. "Get up. Fight back. Your opponents will not be likely to stop just because you drop to your knees." Gor backed off to allow the Dwarf to rise. He picked up his wooden sword and with renewed vigor in his heart began bashing back at the Human, as he never did before, forcing him back against a rocky wall. Sometimes all it takes is breaking the will to unleash the warrior. Never again would he yield to an attacker.

The others cheered him on as witness to another graduate of Shi'roc's philosophy in training fighters, stone hard and unyielding.

* * *

With a torch in his stubby little hand, Kura led the way for Lady A'mora and several of the tribe's women. A'mora had chosen representatives of each of the six tribes. She felt they should be witness to whatever lied ahead in the cavern where Lord Lorentz had spent the last week. Although she knew of his powers and what might be expected, she also knew that several of the council of Dwarven elders were still leery of her and Lorentz' abilities. She specifically selected the wife of the Dwarven chief to accompany her. They all carried sacks, baskets and skins to bear the food and water back to their respective communities for distribution.

Several rest stops were made along the way, as the women were not accustomed to long travel. Kura was frustrated, having found in himself the stamina to continue without rest. "If you keep stopping to rest you will not build stamina." He said with encouragement as Lorentz had taught.

"They have not been trained as you and I have been." A'mora reminded him. She turned to the others. "Come, there is much work to do and a long journey back as well," She said. "Then your baskets will be full." She hoped that this would inspire them to continue. She received a disbelieving glance from the chief's wife.

They traveled at an accelerated rate led by Kura and A'mora. Suddenly they saw the glow of a natural light emanating from the passage ahead and hurried toward it. It was different from the effect, that Lorentz had cast on the great hall through his magic.

"We are there," exclaimed Kura, puffing in exhaustion having not rested through the whole journey. He stood with the torch at the entrance to the cavern. The women gathered in the passage behind him as he stepped in. All was silent. He could hear the echo of large drops of water as he slowly stepped onto the soft earth floor. A'mora was close behind leading in the others. A beam of sunlight slowly penetrated the crevice on the wall indicating that it was afternoon. Kura extinguished the torch by pushing it into the soft ground.

The priestess took a few steps in ahead of the others. "Lord Lorentz! Are you here?" echoed A'mora's call out into the openness. She listened for a reply but only heard the rustling of the horses in the distance. She could now see the horses in the sunlight. Suddenly the air began to swirl about them. The room began to glow with the radiance of the luminescent dust, that Lorentz had cast into the cavern. In moments the walls and ceiling of the cave were bright with the magical light.

A'mora realized that this show was obviously for dramatic effect since the sunlight coming through the mountain wall was sufficient. The years had taught her to expect this from Lorentz. She smiled as the other women stood in amazement at the entrance. Their eyes widened and their mouths hung open. Not a word was spoken.

Kura and the tribe's women were in awe of the sight before them. They could not believe what had actually happened. The cavern, now well lighted had flourished into a seemingly endless garden. To the right there were neatly tailored rows of fruit trees. To the left was an acre of flourishing vegetable plants. And in the center of it all was the new reservoir with tributaries feeding to each row of plant life. The colors of the fruits of the yield were brilliant and ready for harvesting. It was truly magnificent.

Lorentz stepped down from the grotto at the cave's far wall. It was apparent that he was quite pleased with himself. "Do you like it ladies?" He called out to them.

Unable to answer from the grasp of emotions they could only nod their heads in confirmation. They began to spread out into the cave from behind Lady A'mora. "Harvest as much as you can carry and return to your families. Tomorrow you will begin learning how to tend the crops for a continual food supply so that the inhabitants of this mountain will never go hungry again." Lorentz started toward them between the rows of trees. He approached Lady A'mora and said. "I've missed you these past days. How are you holding up?"

She looked into his eyes not wanting to yield to his powers of truth. She did her best to not tell him of her accident. "The training is going well. Shi'roc and the others are truly fine instructors. They have already gained the confidence of over fifty of these people." She looked away toward Kura who was scurrying up the nearest apple tree.

"You didn't answer my question." Lorentz insisted. "How are you holding up?" Almost as if he already knew. His concern was genuine as this was the first major quest where she had accompanied him. She was unaccustomed to such a harsh environment. He reached out to hold her hand and she flinched. "What has happened?" He said sternly now grasping both of her arms.

"It is not cause for alarm." She said shaken. She looked into his eyes and continued. "We could not wait for food so I needed to pray for another bounty." She was now uncertain of Lorentz' response.

The priest looked at her quite concerned knowing that it was beyond her abilities to perform that particular ritual alone "You should have waited. These people could cope with a few days of waiting. You should have sent for me if there was a problem. What happened to you?" He let loose her arms.

"You were not to be disturbed. She said defensively. "I was successful and we have enough food for a few more days; but," she hesitated. "I was exhausted by the power and..." With a tear forming in her eye she looked down at her feet. "I passed out and was knocked unconscious, hitting my head on a rock."

Lorentz put his arms around her in a bear hug and began to chuckle. "You need not to be ashamed. I am very proud of you." He whispered into her ear. "Your sacrifice will be well appreciated by Mirana." He broke the embrace and looked into her tear filled blue eyes once again. Gently he wiped a tear from her cheek with a finger.

"Kura brought me back and healed my contusion." She saw a wide grin growing on her mentor's face. "He has been a very devout student of prayer." His grin grew even wider.

"It is as Mirana had said, seek out those least likely to serve," Lorentz reminded her with a smile. She suddenly remembered with a jolt and smiled back. "I knew there was something special about him," he beamed. "Why were you so afraid to tell me?" he exclaimed in a jovial voice shaking her excitedly. He turned to the orchard where Kura was outstretched to pick an apple awkwardly grasping on to a branch with his left arm. "Kura!" He startled the little man to the point of loosing his grip on the branch. Lorentz raced over to the tree just in time for The Dwarf to drop into his arms still grasping the apple in his right hand.

"Would you care for an apple sir?" Kura held the apple up to Lorentz' face who proceeded to take a bite. "How is it?"

"It is excellent of course but not quite as excellent as you." He lowered the hefty Dwarf to the ground still smiling at him. "Lady A'mora told me of your first power." He now knelt down to the Dwarf's level. "Tell me, how did you feel during your experience?"

Kura was silent while he remembered the occurrence three days passed. "When I saw that she had been injured something in my mind took control of me and told me what to do. I felt like it was a dream where I was watching myself do it." Kura was very pensive and articulate with his reply. Still looking at Lord Lorentz he took a bite of the apple and said. "This is excellent." They both began to laugh out loud as the women continued to fill their baskets with fresh greens, oats, carrots, tomatoes, pea pods, apples, pears, oranges and assorted other fruits and vegetables.

A'mora proceeded over to the horses that were grazing on a patch of tall grass. She began to brush her animal with her hand. She quietly spoke a few obscure words "Invocatum equas cogito et renium." She repeated several times. Each re-utterance grew in volume. Anxiety could soon be heard in her voice as her continued attempts at the spell failed. Now with both hands on the horse's forehead she re-iterated once more. "Invocatum equas cogito et renium."

This time was so loud that even Lorentz was able to hear. He turned his attention from Kura toward the horses. He heard a shriek from A'mora. And again, so loud that even the women stopped their harvesting. He and Kura went running over to her to see what was wrong.

They found her on her knees sobbing in front of her horse. The horse was shaking its head up and down and whinnying as they approached. Lord Lorentz quickly dropped to his knees and looked her over for injuries but found none.

"A'mora, what is it? What is the matter?" Lorentz asked as he calmed the horse with a stroke of his hand on its head.

"That is the matter," she sobbed pointing to the horse. "I was unable to communicate with him. I have been unable to perform even the simplest of tasks since the incident three nights ago. I'm afraid that Mirana has taken my powers from me." A'mora burst into tears again. "What have I done to displease her?" she sobbed.

Many of the horses had now gathered around her in sympathy of her grief. Kura attempted to push them away but his size prevented his success in doing so.

Lorentz also feeling crowded by the animals spoke a few simple words and passed his hands over the small herd. "Linguatorum beastilan vocalori transit." He then craned his neck letting out a series of grunts and whinnies. The horses responded by shaking their heads and moved away to another grassing spot.

Kura watched and listened to Lord Lorentz. "Could I learn to do that?" He asked with eyes wide open.

"Yes you can but not today." Came the brief reply as Lorentz again knelt beside the despondent A'mora. Kura walked off toward the garden to check the progress of the harvest.

He put his arm around her as he spoke knowing exactly the feeling she was having. "Don't despair my child." Although in appearance Lorentz was certainly older but the one hundred year difference between this human female and he was not uncommon. "Your powers of prayer have not been taken away. Mirana is not at all angry with you." He consoled her. "How could she be, with all that you have done to help these people? You have fed them, healed them and taught them the ways of our goddess," he continued. "Is that not so?"

She looked up at him with swollen tear filled eyes, sniffed and said, "I have done my best." She wiped the tears from her face with the back of her hand.

"When you took it upon yourself to prepare food three days ago, your devotion to the prayer along with the strain of your teaching the others was just too much for you to handle at this time. You need time to rest. Mirana does not expect that each of us continually pray. We are only living creatures with limited abilities. Your concentration and powers will return soon. I promise."

A'mora was now drying her eyes with her cloak and feeling a little more assured. "How do you know this to be so?"

"Because it once happened to me when I was young like yourself." Lorentz began recounting the story to A'mora. "Many decades ago I was still in apprenticeship at the temple in my town of 'Thormadore'. The mountain giants had again raided the town but this time we were ready for them." He had often told her stories of the giants. "The town watchmen were able to fight them off before too much damage was done. As before, the bodies of the dead and injured were taken to the temple. My master and I tended their wounds and prayed over the dead. For days we did nothing but pray and heal. I was amazed when my mentor brought life into some of those we thought lost. My powers at one time failed all together when I attempted to secure an almost detached arm for one of the soldiers. One giant had ripped it from him before perishing to his sword. My previous healing was on less severe wounds. This one was just to much a strain for me." He looked back at A'mora who was enthralled with the story.

"Were you able to save his arm?" She was so eager to learn once again that she forgot about her own loss of powers.

"I was able to eventually heal the severed arm but just as you, I collapsed at the completion of the prayers. My abilities were lost for several days." Lorentz smiled and told her "It was a turning point for me, a test of my stamina and faith. From that point on my learning increased and my abilities were enhanced."

"I will rest my powers of prayer, except to thank 'Mirana' for her gifts to us this day." A'mora smiled and leaned over to kiss Lorentz on the cheek.

He rose and helped the young woman to her feet. Together they walked through the thriving orchard hand in hand. The surroundings were so pleasant that she only wished that she could be walking with Shi'roc, holding his hand. But then, she realized that he might not appreciate the beauty of what surrounded them. They began to help the others gather the bountiful fruits.

Within the hour, they had harvested enough food for all the tribes and their guests for weeks to come. As Lorentz' magical light faded, the women led by Kura, left the cavern on their journey back to their people. A'mora remained behind with her mentor to pray at the shrine of his creation.

Together they knelt down before the hand carved likeness of their goddess. That which Lorentz had created from the stone surrounding the grotto. They held hands and bowed their heads as if being wed by the spirit before them. Though not being joined in wedlock, the goddess, the keeper of all forests and the creatures within, would more readily receive their prayer combined.

"Oh Mirana; we thank you for this place of shelter to enclose the fruits of nature. As the protector of all plants and animals we ask thee to bless these trees of life to bear yet continuing fruit and that the earth that you have provided should pour forth the nourishing plants from that we derive our strength to vanquish thy enemies." Lorentz spoke with fervor so intense that A'mora could feel his strength of soul.

She continued in the same tone and transcendental state that Lorentz had created. "Help us to deliver these poor souls, that we have sought out, from the great evil that surrounds these lands now."

Chapter 8
Bone

Back in the cavernous depths of the hidden fortress known only to the dark forces of the evil master, Moracles prepared for his journey. This would be the first time that he had left the protection of his wretched domain since he first recruited his armies of Magdarn soldiers nearly a century ago. Though now the majority of his forces consist mostly of creatures called from other species and darker worlds he now would seek out a leader, an enemy of the one known as Shi'roc.

This one he sought would travel far to confront Shi'roc once again. Far away he rested near the land of Lord Magdelan. He has been still since the time before Moracles had come to power.

Known only as an apprentice to the great sorcerer, Lord Magdelan, he had a vague remembrance of the party of warriors and thieves who braved the haunts and legends of the castle hidden deep in the mountain. Moracles never confronted the group directly but watched from a distance as his summoned beasts did the biding of their master.

Yes even at his young age of apprenticeship Moracles embraced the powers of evil. He thrived on the torture and mutilation of all living things, especially those who would intrude upon his master's castle. It was he who unleashed the powerful ape creatures upon the adventurers and watched as they mutilated the brave protector known as Ach'med. He perished to save the lives of others in his party. Others less brave than he chose to run rather than fight.

He lay in a state of unrest entombed in the town a few days journey from the great deserted castle. Now Moracles would return to that land of his former master and seek out the uneasy soul of Ach'med.

"Quibit, soon shall I be away in my travels." Moracles directed his thoughts to his tiny servant. "I bid you to watch and assist the great white Bone in matters of urgency." His words unspoken yet understood by his tiny servant who looked up and flickered his eyes in response. "Yes, little one, I understand your concerns." Neither of them trusting the loyalty of the bony leader of dark forces, a general of sorts for Moracles. "I shall now call him from the plane of mists to guard over my domain in my absence." The two moved from the master's bedchambers to the open area beyond. The cavern mists rolled as the mage and his tiny servant walked to the edge of the candles light.

The little one moved to climb upon the desk knowing of the volatile action, that would soon take place in the center of the room. He did not wish to be inadvertently trodden upon, knowing that the Bone had no fondness for him. Quibit reached into a small drawer to remove two small stones and a swatch of cloth. While listening to his master's invocations, he laid the piece of cloth over the wick of one candle and quickly jabbed the stones together causing sparks that ignited the rag. Having lit the candles, he could now see his master in the final throws of his spell.

"Noxit invocatum spiritus et renium vox," the mage recited as his arms flowed with the swirling motion of the mist emanating from his hands. He now called to his darkest creature that commands his forces from the ethereal plane. Although the creatures' origins reach into the depths of hell itself, he now reluctantly obeys Moracles as a leader of torture and destruction.

As if a shadow coming to life before the mage, a powerful black horse appeared with fiery hoofs and mane. Its red eyes glared as it spit searing flames from its mouth. As it reared up, Quibit could see the great white skeletal creature riding the beast. The figures took solid form as the swirling mist dissipated. Having settled the horse of his transition from the other dimension, the great one spoke to Moracles.

"What is thy bidding my master?" came the rattling voice in the commonly used language of the mortals, his head and that of the horse's bowed in respect though his tone was shaded with sarcasm and deceit.

"I shall soon be on a journey to a far away land," the commanding voice replied. "There is a new enemy among my lands." The Bone raised his head in anticipation. "He and his friends must be found before I return." Moracles' careful words were slow and dramatic.

Still seated bareback on the giant stallion, the Bone inquired. "When I find these people, may I kill them my master?" He grinned. The words were heavy with the pleasures of torture in mind.

"No!" Moracles' thunderous voice raged. "I expect to return in the passing of two full moon cycles." He calmed himself in thought. "All of my forces will be at your disposal. You are to find them only," he continued. "But do not let it be know they have been found. For I wish to do the killing myself. I will have a surprise for them upon my return."

"What is this surprise, my master?" he inquired as he slowly dismounted his steed and stood before Moracles. Even dismounted he towered over the robed wizard. His form was quite intimidating even to the mage. The tightly wrapped white skin was all that seemed to hold the bony frame together. His eyes were aglow with a red fire that could cause fear in the lesser mortals who dared to gaze into them.

Moracles looked up at him, stroking his beard. "That is none of your concern." he retorted. "Mind your place and obey my instructions." He now appeared to be frustrated at having no better choice to serve as his overseer while he was away.

Though the Bone was quite powerful in the planes of hell, Moracles knew he could not be trusted. Not even under the control of the spell, that had enslaved the creature to him many years ago. Its very nature was to twist circumstances and deceive even his master.

"As you wish my master." it responded, once again bowing its head. This time being sure that his was lower than that of Moracles. This was difficult considering that the "Bone", as it was called, was a full seven feet in height. He once again stood erect still poised near his mount. He still held firm a bony hooked spear, that he used to grapple his victims in confrontation while thrashing them with his whip-like tail.

The horse seemed to be a better servant to the Bone than the Bone was to Moracles. The horse, having been a bonus at the time of the spell entrapment, was named "Black Fire" for its majestic power and fiery appearance. It had been in servitude to the Bone when the spell was cast, snaring both into the real world as they traveled between the planes of hell.

Moracles stepped behind his magnificently hand carved desk upon which Quibit sat watching the mage's every move. He waved his hand over the drawers with the careful pronunciation of a few obscure words. He then opened several of the drawers, selectively taking the contents.

Upon the middle finger of his left hand, he placed a plain gold ring. On the same finger of his right hand, he slid another more intricately carved ring. He then carefully tucked into the pockets of his robes several small vials of liquid and a rather thick metallic tube.

The Bone watched his every move, as did Quibit. While the small creature sat on the desk with full confidence of his master, the Bone kept his distance at the edge of the candles reach. There he would remain awaiting his master's departure.

When Moracles was finished, he closed each of the drawers. Then he made small inscriptions on the drawers with one of his long fingernails as he spoke some muffled words.

Quibit noticed that the Bone seemed intent on hearing those words but was unable to grasp them from the distance. He turned his attention back to the mage who was finishing the last inscription.

The sorcerer finally rounded the desk walking back toward the center of the area lighted by the candelabra, that was still flickering upon the desk. He began to chant the words, that would bring him to a state where he could travel the ethereal plane of existence. The extended sleeves of his robe swirled as the mist began to form around him.

The Bone and his mount stepped back into the darkness, away from the area, that had been engulfed by the mist. Through the haze Quibit could see the flames of the horses hooves and mane as well as the Bone's glowing red eyes. They stood in the darkness observing the theatrical exit of their master.

As the mage slowly faded into the brume, that would bring him to the plane of ethereal passage, his sight of the candle lit chamber vanished. He no longer could see into the realm of living beings. Both Quibit and the skeletal creature were obscured from sight. Only the fog of the plane between time and space, reality and the heavens, or hells, surrounded him.

It had been some time since he ventured into this null space where only those creatures of special powers and beings of great intelligence could roam freely. This was the connection between all that is real and the other lands of the gods and demons. This was the place from which all that exist can be snatched and enslaved by those such as him. For it is this place that had yielded his armies of Torgs over the many decades of time. He too was now susceptible to the summoning of those who might be more powerful in the practice of magic than he, though this was unlikely. He too at one time had a master, he thought, as did others before him. What were the chances that he would be enslaved? Minimal.

It was now time for him to invoke his powers of directional finding since the real world was no longer visible or tangible. "In oculi plenum vexit renum volari." He began to chant as he slowly turned in space. His powerful mind focused on the direction he would need to travel if doing so by land. The power of direction would create a straight line of travel between his dimensional location and the place of his origins near the castle of Lord Magdelan. He focused on the chamber of his old master, knowing it now would be empty since the demise of the most powerful dark Lord.

In his minds eye he could now clearly see the mountain range in which was hidden his old master's domain. It was as clear to him now as if he could reach out and touch it. The spell, that he wove, would guide his floatation through the plane eventually taking him to the vision, that he possessed. Though the destination was half way around his world, and by horse the journey would entail a years travel, in this fashion would take but a few weeks. As he passed through time and space he knew the possibilities of encountering other beings. People perhaps, but more likely beings from other worlds above and below the boundaries of good and evil. The journey had officially begun.

* * *

In the dim dreary chamber sat Quibit upon the desk of his master near the candelabra. Behind him were the large oaken cabinets and shelves that contained the library from which Moracles had studied his evil sorceries. He sat staring at the skeletal creature as it paced back and forth over the black marble floor. Each step he took caused his anatomy, or lack of, to rattle his enormous bony frame.

In the darkness beyond, stood the shiny coal black stallion, that was only to be seen by the flames, that flared, from its powerful body, and an occasional snort of flames from its mouth. It too watched the pacing of the pensive, hallowed figure.

The Bone approached the desk. "What are you staring at?" he screeched at the loathsome little creature perched on the desk.

Quibit's fear of the entity sent him tumbling back off the desk onto the floor. He scurried between the legs of the chair and hid in its shadow.

"I do not need you around me to spy on my every move," the Bone continued with disdain. "I will find these intruders in my own way, in my own time. So be off with you," He yelled. He rattled his way across the cold floor back to his fiery beast and mounted it as Quibit peaked his head from around the base of the desk.

The horse reared up with the great Bone creature on its back holding onto the illuminated mane with a bony hand. He held his spear high over his head. "Off to inspect the troops." He said with sarcasm as the pair slowly faded into the surrounding mist. He let out a shrill echoing laugh, not unlike that of Moracles himself, and then vanished back to the ethereal plane.

Quibit, under instruction from his master to watch the Bone, scurried out from behind the desk to the center of the candle lit area and he too slowly vanished into darkness.

* * *

Now floating high above the real world in the ethereal mist, Moracles wished to gloat over his vast domain of evil. Though he could only sense his location, he wanted to see his legendary destruction as he passed over it. He began to chant and swirl his arms. With his eyes open wide the mist dissipated from his vision and he was now able to see beyond the barrier of the plane into the real world. As if peeking his head through a closed curtain, the world around him appeared.

Below him was the great canyon in that his fortress of evil was hidden. The canyon he created with a powerful earthquake to announce his arrival from the hells. He had moved the earth so violently that the surface splintered into dozens of separate passages all nestled in an area sunken below the normal lay of the land. The forests had fallen and the rivers merged into a torrential cascade, that eroded even further the surrounding crusts of earth leaving the rest of the valley dry.

Beyond the crater lies the great waste land of Feradune. As far as could be seen was the reach of his destruction and it grew day-by-day, inch-by-inch. For the past hundred years his spells of deterioration had been eroding all living flora and fauna in all directions emanating from what was the great Elven Forest now known as Feradune.

He floated west and began to pass over the desert, hundreds of feet above it, yet unaffected by the dry heat reflected by the scorching sun upon the sand. This still was not the extent of his evil reach. For beyond even the great mountain range did his destruction spread. Even as he floated in the plane of mists, his deterioration of life inched its way through the forests past the mountains.

Even now he could see the peaks over that he would pass, never once expecting that within lie those who escaped his destruction and those who would be his enemies. And the three forces, that combined, would be the undoing of his years of sorcerers work.

His vision began to fade into mist once again as the powers of his spell lapsed. "Just as well," he mused, "I have seen what pleases me most. The bountiful extent of my talents." As he began to laugh to himself, the mist had engulfed him entirely and as before he could only see that which would accompany him in the ethereal plane. That which he could not see. That which may be friend or foe sharing the same space and time.

He continued his journey unseen by the real world with only his memory of the past to guide him to his destination. Though his former master no longer existed, he would find refuge in the now deserted castle of Lord Magdelan and practice his sorcerer's ways to resurrect the one known as Ach'med from his sleep of over a hundred years.

* * *

The word was spread throughout the underground fortress and to the decimated lands of Moracles' evil realm that the Bone was now in charge while Moracles was away. Most of the dregs of the humanoid races were in fear of the Bone, even more so than of Moracles himself. Other mindless creatures had no perception of the differences. For many years they came to know what the wizard priest expected of them. The Bone on the other hand was unpredictable, being from another world himself. It was known by many that the ominous creature, being a captive servant to Moracles would do whatever possible to break the spell that held him in the servitude of his master. But only the death of the mage would break such a spell as he well knew and that was a fact of which he could not change. The spell, that had taken him from the planes of hell, also made it impossible to bring harm to his master or to directly disobey him. Though his orders, if not precisely spoken, may be interpreted as he saw fit.

He had commanded that all forces of both the real and ethereal lands should assemble in the great cave near the stables. This vast open underground cavern enclosed the horses and other mounts, supplies and shelter for those races of Moracles' armies capable of riding. Many of these soldiers resided in the main parts of the castle.

For an entire week those from outside the fortress came and set up camps awaiting the greeting of the Bone. There was no word or rumor as to why the meeting was called. They arrived through the hidden crevice at the south end of the cavern, that led from the main road through the valley canyon. The others descended from the nearby fortress through a hidden access tunnel leading into the castle. Only the castles inhabitants knew the way to pass through the sliding stone wall and down the rocky stair passage to the cave.

All were present. Both men and creatures of darkness alike were in attendance. They had segregated themselves among their own kind. Many of the races did not mingle. Some were natural enemies held together only by the commonality of their devotion and fear of the master, Moracles. Those mindless beings, that had previously wandered the ethereal planes, were now summoned to serve the Bone.

The area was aglow with campfire and torchlight. Only now did those beings of the ethereal plane arrive. Some were full-embodied figures summoned from the depths of hell while others were only shadows, that could be seen, only by a few, hovering within and above the crowds. They were now all encircled about the stable area. The anticipation was mounting as was apparent by the tension it created among the different species all assembled here for the first time together.

Quibit worked his way through the crowds to take a hasty attendance of the more than five hundred beings at the gathering. Having satisfied himself that all were there and then some, he proceeded to the center of the open area in between the stables where the Bone would soon make his appearance. All eyes were fixed on the tiny creature, that was entrusted with all of the great sorcerers secrets. He opened his mouth revealing his rows of tiny razor-like teeth and emitted a high-pitched squeal almost intolerable to most of those present. The crowds silenced as Quibit quickly moved off toward the wooden stable wall. Indeed it was the wise thing to do since the open area began to twirl with a multi colored ethereal mist. It quickly formed into the form of the Bone once again mounted on the back of his fiery steed, Blackfire.

The theatrical entrance appeared to be the eccentric style of the creature from hell. The crowds were motionless and still silent. They stood in awe of the performance. A moment passed as the Bone gazed into the eyes of his armies. Slowly he turned his head catching the attention of each of them with his red glowing eye sockets. He had refrained from using his ability to invoke fear upon sight. Though there was still enough fear in the minds of those present to go around.

His horse, Blackfire snorted a burst of flame from its mouth, breaking the silence. The polished white surface of the Bone's skeletal body reflected the glistening of the nearby torches. Slowly and sure, he climbed down from the massive black stallion, that was suited to the Bone's impressively large frame.

He began to pace in front of the troops. Even his walk showed a certain arrogance. In the stillness, his bones rattled with each heavy step. It was he who had been put in charge while Moracles was away. They were there to listen to him, obey him, and serve him. It would be a time they would not soon forget because their mission had purpose. This was not going to be a rampage of death and destruction as had occurred in the past. No, this would be an orderly search, a plan, his plan.

"It is said we have a new enemy." He began in his tyrannical tone. "You shall seek them out. You will find them and tell no one but me." He continued his sermon in explanation of his methodical plan to sweep the entire realm. From the edges of the canyon as far as the mountain peaks, they would search. He paced around the circle watching the reaction of each as he passed. The excitement grew amidst the crowds. They were once again a powerful force with the driving ambitions of the Bone behind them. By the end of his speech the segregated races had begun to mingle and drew closer forming a tighter circle in the center of the cavern. An occasional war cry from the various clans would pierce the silence. They were one army, his army. The Bone was pleased. He smiled with an evil hiss.

Quibit still lurking near the feed shed at the edge of the tightening circle became uneasy. He knew what the demon had done and the dangers it would cause for him and possibly for his master upon his return. No longer would the various races look upon him as the master's confidant. The Bone had just taken control.

The crowds had begun to chant. The mumbles grew into a steady unison. The white figure stood tall with his arms raised, a shiny-jeweled dagger in one hand and his bony hooked spear in the other. They were all chanting his name. "Bone, Bone, Bone" was all that could be heard.

He looked down at Quibit who was now hiding around the corner of the stable wall. "You would do well to stay out of our way," he fired at him in a most irritating grumble. "Go away," he said as Quibit peaked around the corner of the structure, meeting the face of the bent over creature. The Bone snarled at him.

Startled at the closeness of his new opponent, red eyes gleaming face to face, Quibit shrieked, jumped into the air and vanished in a puff of mist. This was a natural instinct for his race. When seemingly trapped or startled, he could with some effort, instantly transpose himself into the ethereal plane of existence. What could he do? What should he do? He no longer felt safe in the fortress in the service of his master for he now had no master to serve, none that wanted him, that is until Moracles returned.

Perhaps this was best, for as long as he could remember he had served Moracles. Quibit, as the other Torgs, was snatched from the ethereal plane by an entanglement spell cast by a younger Moracles very long ago. He was the first to be summoned by the self appointed guardian of evil in this realm, back in the time when the land still flourished, before the onslaught of destruction. Yes, Quibit had seen it all. He had been by the side of his master, his captor, since the first earthquake, that created the valley canyons in which the fortress was now embedded.

Now in the center of the circle the Bone stood drawing a map of the region in the dirt with his spear. Around him each of the clan chiefs watched patiently as their new leader outlined the scheme of the search. The campfire flames reflected from the varieties of armor and weaponry they wore. One by one he explained the individual assignments in the native language of each of his new commanders. Though most understood the common tongue, he hoped to avoid confusion by giving instructions in the language each knew best.

"You will take your people and travel back through the canyons to the north." He said, in a gnarly animal growl, pointing to the tallest of the group. The creature was still a bit shorter and quite a bit uglier than the sleek Bone. Its scale male armor covered most of its fur torso.

"Grawlic echk rasul muhaska schlac" The other stood tall and proud in his response, showing his mis-aligned fangs as he spoke. He carried a large shield in one hand and a long lance in the other with its shaft placed firmly in the ground. He bowed his head slightly, turned and walked back to share the orders with his clansmen.

The evil one then spoke to the shortest of the generals. An almost human looking creature except for the fur and dogged face. "Your people will patrol this area." With his spear he gestured to the path drawn in the ground. The area was once a lake and river bed that lay to the north of what was once the Elven Forest, now dried to dust by the spell / curse that Moracles had put on the land.

The dogged faced creature acknowledged the assignment. He drew his short sword from its sheath and held it in front of his face in salute to the Bone. In another swift motion he returned it to its sheath, turned and marched back to the distant campfire where his men anxiously awaited instruction.

This proceeding continued until he had covered most of the known territories of the realm except for the distant mountains near which the intruders were first spotted. He only had one remaining general to assign. The creature was a muscular bulky being seemingly held together by a tight combination of leather and scale male. His face was that of a stuffed pig or better yet a boar with its upward curving tusks protruding from the lower jaw. His intelligence seemed to be low or possibly worse.

The Bone chose his words carefully and spoke slowly so as not to confuse the creature. "You shall patrol the mountain region to the far west." His bone spear trailed all the way off the drawn map indicating its great distance from the fortress. For a moment there was no response from the soldier still staring at the ground and to where the Bone was pointing.

He jerked up his head, "Icht reimer slovat grunsh swiv relig compata," he finally blurted out in disgust of the assignment. Realizing that he spoke before he thought, he suddenly looked up to the Bone with a worried almost frightened expression on his face.

The Bone glared back. His mouth wide with surprise at the insubordination. He snapped his jaws and hissed at the soldier. "Icht ta poo," he spat out. That meant, "You will obey".

The general shook his head in nervous affirmation then turned and hurriedly returned to his camp. "Icht ta poo" he repeated under his breath as he stomped off.

The Bone waited for the others to disperse. They packed up their camps and proceeded toward their assigned destinations, mostly on foot. Those who lived in the fortress returned to their quarters to prepare for their long journeys.

All that was left were the shadows around the fire. Now in the silence of the empty cave, the Bone gave his final instructions. The shadows floated closely around the great white Bone as he spoke. "As for you my friends," the Bone said quietly. "I have a special task."

Chapter 9
Doubts

The small room was lit only by the flickering of the fire, that was set in a crevice in center of the floor. Around it were mounds of stones, that supported a steel rod. Above it suspended from the rod were the iron pots, that contained the evenings meal, vegetable stew. Kura's wife lifted the lid with a forked branch and stirred the meal releasing even more of the welcomed aroma.

Lorentz sniffed the air and released a pleased sigh. "I can only imagine that it will taste as good as it smells," he said to Kura who passed him a bowl and spoon. "Let us pray together in thanks for this meal."

"And those to come," Kura interjected. "You know it is all thanks to you. If you and your friends had not come, we may have not lived much longer out here alone."

Muga spooned out the stew into the bowl and handed it to Lord Lorentz then did the same for her husband and herself. "We are pleased you accepted our invitation to eat with us this evening before your meeting with the high council." She said as she sat down on the matted branches next to Kura. "With all that you have done in this past month you have had little time to visit."

"Now that we are together and the meal is served, let us pray." Lorentz bowed his head but before he could speak was interrupted by Kura.

"Let me say the prayer Lord Lorentz," he requested with a tone of almost insistence. "After all you are a guest in our home tonight. This meal is also in honor of you," he continued nodding his head to the other.

Lorentz nodded his confirmation and Kura began. "Thank you, Mirana, for allowing us this time to share a meal with our good friend." He reached out to hold hands with his wife and Lorentz seated to his right and left respectively. Closing his eyes and going into a deep concentration he continued. "He has come to us from a long way and this was also due to your guidance. He and his companions have taught us many things to help us through these troubled times. But most of all, thank you for opening my eyes to your wisdom and kindness." His voice trailed off into silence.

Kura opened his eyes. No longer was he in his underground home nor was he still holding Muga's hand. He found himself setting on what looked to be an elaborately carved wooden throne. It was cushioned with soft leather wrappings. In his right hand he held a staff carved from oak with a headpiece of gold detailed in the shape of an oak leaf.

He was wearing finely hand woven robes. Around him was a light morning fog. He stood up, looked around as a forest began to appear through the fog. He could hear sounds of animals rustling through the fallen leaves and birds chirping songs, as he had never heard. The sun was now creating shadows through the mist. "Where am I?" he said to himself.

"You are in my forest," echoed a soft voice from in front of him as shadows approached. He could see a female form in a flowing green linen gown accompanied by a beautiful gray wolf. On her shoulder sat an owl and in her hand, a white dove.

Kura's jaw dropped open. "Mirana?" He muttered as he dropped to his knees recognizing her from descriptions by Lady A'mora. He closed his eyes afraid to look up. "How did I get here?" he asked with a trembling voice not knowing whether to question or just accept the fact that he was where he was. "Am I dead? Am I dreaming?"

"There is no need to fear. You are far from being dead." She said with a whimsical laugh. "Your faith and kind words have brought you to me." She said as she reached down to touch his head. As she did so he looked up to see just how beautiful she looked in the reflecting sunlight. The wolf was lying on the ground just behind her. Kura stood up brushing the leaves and grass from his robes.

"I don't understand." He looked up at her in puzzlement. "I was with my wife and Lord Lorentz eating dinner and now I'm here? Why am I dressed like this and what is this?" He held out the staff to her.

"She smiled down. "Lord Lorentz has visited me here many times. That is why I have sent him to you and your people." She knelt down touching his hand, that was still holding the staff. "You are destined to lead your people out of darkness. This staff will be your guide.

Kura was puzzled by her words, almost frightened by their implications. "What should I do? What does the staff…"

"You will know what to do and when to use it when the time comes." Mirana cut off his potential flood of questions. "But now you must return." She stood up and let out a slight laugh. "Your dinner is getting cold." She turned to walk back into the forest.

He felt something squeeze his right hand. "Kura, are you all right?" Muga asked.

He opened his eyes and was startled to see the fire in front of him and Lord Lorentz, still holding his hand. He snapped his hands back and gasped.

Muga was a little disturbed. "What is the matter with you? You seemed to dose off during your prayer," she mused.

"Where is my staff?" he said, still a little disoriented. "And my robes?" He began to quickly look around the room and touching his old tattered clothing.

"That was a fine prayer," Lorentz praised. "That is the sort of meditation that will bring you closer to Mirana." The priest had some idea of what had just happened to Kura though he did not want to pry further.

Kura, recovering from his brief panic said, "I'll say it will." Should he tell Lorentz about his vision, he wondered or was this something he should keep to himself? He continued to look around the room candidly, trying not to be too obvious.

Lorentz knew full well that Kura had just experienced his first spiritual encounter. Still studying Kura's face he raised the spoon to his mouth and sampled the stew. "This is very tasty Muga." She smiled back at him. He directed his attention back to Kura who was now eating his stew still very fidgety.

"You seem to be looking for something. Are you sure you are all right?" Lorentz pressed as he too looked around the small fire lit room trying to discover what the Dwarf was seeking. "You appear to be distracted." With a mischievous smile growing on his face he turned back to Kura. "Tell me about your vision."

Kura stopped fidgeting and froze. With a cold look on his face he stared into Lord Lorentz' face and asked, "How did you know?" He took another spoonful of the broth to his mouth and then quickly put it down. He glanced down into the fire to avoid Lorentz' eyes and was entranced by the flames.

"It is normal to be uncertain of your first experience of your faith." Lorentz continued. But the words were only heard by Muga since Kura's attention was lost in the flames.

Suddenly his eyes opened wide and he reached into the fire yelling, "There it is." Kura thrust his hand past the suspended kettle and deep into the flames before Lorentz was able to stop him.

Muga cried out "What are you doing?" As he pulled from the fire a long thick carved branch. Both the stick and his arm apparently untouched by the flames. The wood was capped in gold just as in his vision. He sat mesmerized with the staff in his hands as Muga examined his unscorched arm. "What on earth prompted you to do that?" she questioned.

"Now, Kura, tell me of your vision." Lorentz knelt beside him in awe of the feat this novice apprentice to the faith had just performed.

Kura continued to stare at the staff, that to him meant more than anything now. It was a gift from Mirana.

* * *

The pathway floors were rocky and uneven as the two traveled. Though it was dark, they seemed to have no problem moving their way toward the Dwarven high council chambers. Kura walked proudly with his staff in hand. His short legs trying hard to keep up with Lord Lorentz' pace.

"Do you have any idea why the council has chosen to meet with us tonight?" Lorentz asked over his shoulder.

"They did not say. Only that you, Shi'roc and A'mora were to be together. I'm sure they will be there." He said, still caressing with his fingers, the golden cap of his new gift. Still examining the staff he noticed that it was slightly taller than he. "Do you think this is magical?" He mused, certain that the priest would know what he was referring to.

"You mean the staff?" Lorentz slowed up his pace a little for the Dwarf to catch up. "I'm sure there is good reason for Mirana to want you to have it. As for its magical properties I have no doubt that it is." He clarified, "Just by the way of its appearance to you would indicate thus."

They were now approaching the chamber entrance. They could see the flickering of torch light just up ahead. Their night vision being enhanced allowed them to see far better at distances.

"Do you think Lord Shi'roc would be able to teach me how to use a staff for battle?" The Dwarf wondered out loud.

Lorentz stopped and turned to Kura. "Shi'roc is only the master of weapons with an edge." He said, "The staff is a weapon of priests and mages. Lady A'mora would be best in teaching you the ways of defense using your staff." Now in a more serious mood he said. "It is not to be used for attack. That would not be Mirana's purpose in giving it to you. We will discuss this further at another time." At times it seemed the priest was frustrated with Kura. Though he was indeed of pure heart and intent, Lorentz could not foresee Mirana's special interest in the apprentice at such an early stage of his training. The Dwarf had only been studying under Lady A'mora for a month, yet during that time had performed admirably in healing. Otherwise, he seemed a bumbling youngster, though his age was past that of most Humans.

They entered the opening to the chamber to find the council of Dwarves already seated around their stone table. The room was aglow with torchlight though the only one who needed light to see was the priestess. She was seated next to Shi'roc directly across from the council elders. Both were silent. They too were puzzled at the request of their presence at this meeting. It had been a month since they last stood in this room to be introduced to the council by Maac-To when they had arrived.

Lorentz walked over to the council, gave a slight nod and sat beside A'mora. She gently took his hand and squeezed it as her face lit up with a smile. "I've missed you." She said softly."

Kura stood proudly at the room entrance with staff in hand. He pretended to be guarding the door of the chamber. The eldest Dwarf looked up at the doorway and cleared his throat to get his attention. Kura looked at the elder and smiled.

"You may go home Kura." He said in a stern Dwarven tongue. Kura quickly lost his smile nodded and turned to go home. He was disappointed at not being able to hear the reasons for the meeting.

He knew he had not been invited but thought he could at least stand at the door. The Dwarf wondered why no one was allowed except the council, not even Maac-To. This was not a democratic society in which the Dwarves lived. A council member was chosen by other council members and this was done only when another member had died. Membership to the council was for life and included only the oldest and therefore thought, the wisest of them. Or so was the philosophy involved.

How could he lead his people out of darkness as Mirana had said if he was not chosen for the council? He thought long and hard on this as he made his way through the tunnels. He was not returning by the same path as he and Lorentz had come. He was headed toward the section of the mountain where Ilo and his wife lived.

Though Ilo was Elven, he had chosen a mate from among the human population. His wife's parents had been children when the survivors of the towns were accepted in the mountain community. Back in the times of the Elven forest where his tribes once lived, it would have been forbidden by the parents of the Elf to wed a human. But since the merging of the survivors of all humans and Elves, this had become a more common practice to mate outside ones own race.

Those Elves with true heritage knew very little of the worlds outside the Elven forest. There were those that had left the villages long before the coming of Moracles, who lived among the humans in their towns. This mixed breeding among Elves and humans tended to shorten the life span of the Elves.

The Elves who remained pure in the forest could see as many as two hundred years. One born only half Elven, could expect no more than one hundred and fifty years of life or approximately three times that of most Humans. The benefits however were that some humans bred with Elven blood could be born with the enhanced night vision of an

Elf or Dwarf if properly trained. It seemed that the slightest percentage of Elven breeding could produce this effect in humans.

Ilo, being one of the few pure Elves born in hiding, was not raised with the same prejudices as his ancestors in the forest. Here in the mountains, all survivors were treated as equals, more or less. The Dwarves, being the indigenous race of the mountain, still held ultimate control over all of their guests.

Kura approached the cave of his friend, and softly tapped the stone outside the entrance with his staff. He heard movement inside beyond the curtain.

"Who knocks?" Came the reply from within.

"It is I, Kura, my friend." He stated in a somber tone. "May I enter?" The cloth curtain covering the entrance was quickly pushed aside from within.

"Of course you may enter. What brings you here on the night we do not have watcher duty?" Ilo inquired as he motioned his friend to enter. "You should be spending this time with your wife and son."

Ilo's home was much like Kura's, except that it contained fewer separate chambers. Seating and bedding was much the same from woven straw through branches. Since Ilo's wife was human the cave was always lit with cooking fire or torch light.

"Where is Caellen?" Kura inquired, giving a quick look around the small rooms before he spoke further. He was now carrying with him a secret to share with the Elf that the wives may not understand. He hoped that Caellen was asleep. Although they got along well, she was Human and he didn't entirely understand her, nor she, him.

"It is late and you know how the Human women need to sleep more than others." Ilo replied with cynical intentions. "And now that she is going to have our first child, she sleeps even more." He then noticed Kura's nervousness and the staff he was carrying tightly gripped in his hand. His stubby fingers fitting neatly around the smoothly twisted wood. "Now tell me what brings you all the way over here tonight?" He motioned for the Dwarf to sit on the nested mats. "What's that you've got?" he pointed to the staff.

"Lord Lorentz was at our place for dinner before the council meeting," he began. "I said the prayer and had a dream about Mirana, but it wasn't a dream," he went on nervously, "It was a vision, or at least that's what Lord Lorentz called it." He looked at Ilo for a reaction, but the other stared back waiting for more of the story before deciding whether to believe it.

Ilo listened in silence as the priest apprentice recounted every detail he could remember of the vision and the events, that took place shortly after it. ".....that's when I reached into the fire and pulled out this staff, just like the one in the dream." He thrust the staff in front of Ilo's face. Breaking his silence he gasped and looked closely at the polished curves of the stick and the bright golden cap in the shape of an oak leaf.

"But I don't know what to do with it." Kura was exasperated and lay back on the mat, taking the staff from Ilo's close inspection. A moment of silence passed as Ilo tried to think of what to say. Then finally the simple words came to him.

"Maybe you need to pray more to know what to do. Ask Lady A'mora, she might know." The silence grew again and both became restless sitting in the torch light.

"I'm going home." Kura said softly getting to his feet and heading for the doorway.

Ilo sat quietly unmoving as his friend left the room. "Was he really destined to lead us?" the young Elf thought.

* * *

"We have asked you here this evening to thank you for all that you have done for our people here in the mountain."

The elderly Dwarf praised them in the common tongue. "You have healed our injured, cured our sickness and provided us a means to grow food to survive." His focus was on Lady A'mora and Lord Lorentz. He then turned his gaze at Shi'roc and said "But we are in fear that you may bring disaster upon us. Our people are growing ever more eager to fight this Moracles' army."

Lorentz could feel Shi'roc's uneasiness growing.

One of the other Dwarfs continued. "They have made crude weapons with which to fight. Bows and swords from sticks and rock. This is no way to fight." He spoke as if knowing the taste of battle himself.

"That is the whole point of our being here." Shi'roc jumped to his feet. Before Lorentz could stop him. He continued to vent his frustration at the little elder Dwarf. "Ever since we have been here we have heard stories of how Moracles and his armies have destroyed your towns and lands, driven you all to these mountains into hiding. Its time to stop hiding and take back what is yours."

The chief spoke up now. "This is our home. Our ancestors have lived and worked in these mountains for thousands of years. It is the Elves and Humans that have been forced here under our protection." He spoke with patience and pride. "After a hundred years we will not now allow these people to be slaughtered in some useless gesture of strength or ego."

Shi'roc cocked his head back. "How do you know it is useless?" We have not heard of, or seen any threat since we have been here. Your watchers have not reported any creatures in the night or the day for that matter. Maybe there is no longer any threat." Shi'roc began to ramble on. His emotions getting the best of him. Now not speaking to any one in particular he paced. "What if they've all gone? What if they got what they wanted and moved on." He became increasingly angered. "Maybe all these stories are just folklore." He mused and let out a fake laugh. "Maybe we should go and have a look for ourselves." He looked to Lorentz for some reaction.

Lorentz stood up. "Enough of this." He blurted out, staring at the council and Shi'roc. A silence fell for a moment. He approached the elders. He spoke now to the council in their own tongue so the others would not understand him. "Is it possible that the threat has passed?" He looked at each of the twelve in turn for a reaction or response. "Would you object to sending out scouting parties of volunteers?" The council members looked at each other, grunted and mumbled amongst themselves as Lorentz took a few steps back from the table.

"Maybe it is time to test their skills as you have taught them." The chief spoke in old Dwarvish to Lorentz. You shall select from the volunteers the most capable to defend themselves." His words were calm and expressed wisdom rather than emotion.

Shi'roc now sat again with A'mora on the stone benches, still frustrated at not knowing what has been said between them. The warrior and priestess listened intently now able to pick up a few words that they have learned in the ancient Dwarvish dialect.

Lorentz then turned to them and smiled. "We will find out." He said in common tongue.

* * *

As the three walked back to their sleeping area near the great hall Lorentz began spouting instructions to Shi'roc. "In the morning you should check on the progress of the weapons being made. Select the best crafted. I know they are only wood and stone but they will have to do." They walked at such a brisk pace through the darkness as to have left A'mora stumbling behind.

"Slow down, would you? I can't keep up with you in the dark." A'mora yelled far from behind them in the passage. "I don't have my lantern." Once again the two had forgotten about Lady A'mora's inability to move swiftly in the dark as they could.

"I am truly sorry my dear." Lorentz called back. He bent over and picked up a fist size rock from the ground. He chanted a few words and passed his other hand slowly around the stone. Instantaneously, it began to glow. It was emanating enough light to see the three of them and the walls and floor of the passage around them. A'mora had now caught up to the two. Lorentz turned and handed her the stone. "Here you are." He said and continued onward with Shi'roc.

She looked at the lighted stone in her hand illuminating the passage. "I could have done that." She said softly to herself as she proceeded forward trying to keep up with the others.

The priestess began to realize that she was not using her magical abilities instinctively as Lorentz had been able. Still young and inexperienced, she had to devote thought to a situation before selecting the magic spell ability to resolve a problem. For her mentor, the many years of wisdom had made that thought process unnecessary and his powers had become a part of his being.

"That reminds me." The warrior spoke over his shoulder to A'mora. "Have either of you found suitable candidates for training in your magic?" Though he did not use or understand the practices, he was aware and appreciative of their usefulness in battle.

"There are very few capable of such abilities." Lorentz pointed out. "I have been training them but with only minimal results so far. But A'mora does have one student of magic. Don't you my dear?" He turned back to her seeing her face glowing to a blush in the light from the stone, that she was holding in front of her.

"Yes. I have been spending as much time as possible in developing his talents." She said evenly hoping to avoid further discussion of the subject.

"Is he good enough to send out with the warriors?" Shi'roc asked. "Can he do anything useful as yet in battle?"

"Why don't you judge for yourself? Tomorrow he will show you." She replied almost bragging. What would Shi'roc think of his abilities after seeing who her student was? "I'm sure he would volunteer."

"Remember, we need volunteers, and only the best of them should be chosen." Lorentz reminded as they approached their temporary home in the rocks.

"Halt, who comes?" Resounded a familiar gruff voice from near the cave entrance. As was usual for him, he hid well in the darkness with extreme silence.

"It's us, Grefden." Shi'roc replied to his bodyguard who had stationed himself on watch over their camp.

Having recognized his Lord's voice he lowered his sword. They entered without hesitation. A'mora, still with the glowing rock in her hand, found her nest on which her bedroll was laid. She would curl up and sleep as she had each night of their stay. They watched her tuck the glowing stone under her cape as she prepared for sleep.

"I will stand watch this night." Shi'roc said to Grefden. "As I have much thinking to do." He told his loyal friend. "Get some sleep with the others. There will be much work for you to do tomorrow."

"Aye my lord, as you wish." Came the reply. Grefden was well aware that Shi'roc and Lorentz required much less sleep than their human followers. There would be times, especially in preparing for battle that Shi'roc would be up for two sometimes three days without sleep. Something about the Elven constitution in them even mixed with human blood gave them more stamina. What was going on? He wondered.

Grefden quietly walked to where Sha'la had been bedded away from the others, and he carefully removed his armor, trying to be as quiet as possible. He lay down beside her on his bed mat. The weight of his body pressed hard on the rock floor beneath.

Shi'roc and Lorentz remained awake, thinking over the prowess of their students. Their strengths and faults. Which ones had leadership skills as well as fighting ability and cunning in battle?

Their concerns were for more than good men but also for the lack of suitable weaponry and armor for their protection should they need it. Perhaps the old Dwarf was right. It would be a joke if they were to have a confrontation with the mere equipment they had constructed. The warriors themselves did their best to teach the others how to craft the swords from wood and stone as well as create bows and arrows from the sticks they could find on the mountainside. They crafted arrowheads as their ancestors had before the art of metalworking. They made clubs with sharp spiked projections, nets and ropes from vines and war hammers from the rocks and dead tree branches. Since there were no raw materials for forging or a forge with which to create the steel, they had to rely on their ingenuity and other learned skills.

* * *

The word had spread by mid morning throughout the mountain range that volunteers were being sought for scouting parties outside the protection of the mountain. All those interested were to meet in the great hall. As was expected by both Lorentz and Shi'roc, the amphitheater like, meeting place was packed with all those capable of fighting. In the past month, Shi'roc and the other warriors had personally trained over one hundred of the survivors in one skill or another. Each one varied in ability level and some more promising students were becoming proficient with more than one weapon. But would there be enough suitable arms to go around.Lorentz began his well-rehearsed speech at the base of the great hall as all listened intently, including the Dwarven council. His words were chosen carefully to not mislead the anxious population and satisfy the Elders request.

As Lorentz gave his oratory, Shi'roc, Grefden, Gor and Lorentz' guards reviewed the assorted weapons that had been used for practice in the past month. Each of them carefully examined that weapon on which he or she specialized. Shi'roc had instructed each of them to select only those of reliable status and put them aside for his final inspection. For he was a master in all known bladed weaponry and his eye could detect the most critical of detail and flaws that would ultimately come to disaster.

Although they had used their own weapons as the models for their skills, the materials available were less than adequate but resourcefulness was their advantage. Many of the weapons had suffered stresses during training. Some would be unsuitable for actual combat and some were repairable.

All factors were checked, the tightness of the vines used for the longbow strings, to the flexibility of the bow. A few of the more skilled guards were able to construct crude crossbows. Few of these were made due to the time and complexities. The arrows were checked for balance and true shafts. The swords and clubs were the crudest of all but the easiest to construct so that the most could be made.

"We have completed our inspection my lord." Gor reported to Shi'roc awaiting patiently as he listened to part of Lorentz' speech. Shi'roc had propped himself at one of the entryways into the base of the Great Hall.

He watched as Lorentz paced while speaking up to the crowds. Of course he could see Ilo and Kura seated on the first bench in front of Lorentz. He looked at the rest of the crowd and could see his prize student, Maac-To, the senior Elf among them. Further up and off to the side he saw Lady A'mora seated closely with her student of magic. Her hand was holding his. The warrior began to have that odd feeling again. He peered closer to see that it was also one of his students, Jantez. "The human that was with A'mora on that first night here in the mountain" he thought to himself. He looked away as the feeling grew stronger. He began to listen again to Lorentz' voice.

"As you know, we are limited in weapons to be used by the scouting parties." Lorentz expressed glumly to the crowd. "But this will be the first test for those more experienced warriors. If what we believe is out there truly is, then this will show if you are ready to take on the armies of Moracles."

"If there are such armies." Shi'roc mumbled to himself.

"What my Lord?" inquired Gor at his master's mumbling. Not quite able to understand the combined Elven and Human dialect that Shi'roc was known to mix.

"Nothing my friend." Shi'roc turned to face him. "Now lets see what you all have chosen for us." They walked off together toward the next chamber where the weapons were kept.

They all stood at attention as he walked into the room. "Well; lets see what we have." They moved aside from the pile of assorted weapons. Shi'roc's eyes grew wide at the anticipation of so many available weapons. He gasped and turned to look at the soldiers. He smiled with gratitude.

"These are what we have discarded my lord." One of them spoke up.

Shi'roc's smile quickly faded.

"This is what we have selected for your inspection." Grefden pointed out a table with the weapons and arrows carefully placed in a row; a short row. "This is all that was acceptable to us my lord. I am sorry we could not find more." He lowered his voice in disappointment.

Chapter 10
Mischief

Although time and space were irrelevant during his spell of ethereal passage, Moracles felt it necessary to check on his progress. He once again invoked the spell, that allowed him to see into the real world as he passed it over. With the swirling of his arms and concentration on the incantation, the mist slowly dissipated from in front of him. As before a window below him emerged allowing him to see the earth. He was now traveling over a great body of water, an ocean perhaps, that he knew nothing about, for his travels prior had taken him directly into the planes of hell where he learned to increase his powers under the study of the gods of evil.

Ahead of him was a great three masted wooden ship with full sails of wind headed in the direction of his travel. A mischievous thought came to him as would be expected during his long boring journey. He began to chant and motion came to his arms as he watched the seas below. The words he used in his magic were unintelligible if anyone had been listening. But thus far his journey had been uneventful as he imagined it had been for the crew of the merchant ship below. That is until now when the calm waters just ahead of the ship began to churn. He could see the crew scrambling to alter course but it was too late as a giant scaled tentacle emerged from the water. It began to wrap itself around the seemingly fragile wooden hull of the ship. Moracles watched with pleasure as he passed, seeing several other tentacles enveloping the water vessel and eventually breaking its wooden craftsmanship into splinters.

So passed his entertainment for the day. Too bad for the crew, as he could see the harbor just ahead with a thriving metropolis surrounding it. This looks much like a town he might have visited in his youth though a lot had changed in a hundred years as one might imagine. He could now see much progress with flourishing businesses and farms bearing the fruits of the labor worked by the peaceful, naive inhabitants of those lands. If they only knew how close they were to being destroyed just by the mere hatred that Moracles had for all mankind. With a minor spell cast over the land beneath him he could plant the seeds of ruin that would spread for miles, as he had done in his own realm, to rot all plants and grasses. But no, not today, he thought. The time would come in the future that his power would reach here and there. All would die that would not serve him. The others would be made sacrifice for his evil purposes to further spread the evil that he had brought from the lords of hell. Only they could appreciate his efforts. Only they could reward him for sending them the once mortal souls of the slaughtered peasants to be enslaved in the lower worlds.

"Soon I feel I will arrive at my destination. The castle of Lord Magdelan will once again be my temporary home." He spoke to himself for no one; no living creature could hear his words. "All of my knowledge, all of my years of study will soon grant me the ultimate pleasure. To bring back from the long dead, a soul once so pure and innocent, so powerful in his brief life, and turn him to darkness as none have done before." His evil twisted mind drifted from its concentration and Moracles fell back into the mists of his travel.

The gods, he thought owed him this greatest of triumphs. He would call upon their powers and gratitude in allowing for him, the dead to rise. For it was not such a challenge to grasp the life soon to be lost from a warrior fallen in battle, as it was to restore life in one that had been dead for so many decades, a body turned to dust rotting in a tomb.

This warrior whom he sought to revive had been entombed for longer than most would live. Left behind by his companions, who he had served so proudly and bravely.

"Ach'med" they would call when they were in trouble. Again they would call when all was lost. But once dead, the Elf would be left and forgotten and succeeded by another. It should have been he that rose to power and glory. He was not the one who would achieve greatness, the one whose name would become legend in his place. Shi'roc was his successor. If Ach'med had not perished in defense of his friends, he would now be the one for that songs and stories were written.

The warrior whom all warriors feared and admired. Feared by those who fought on the side of evil instead of against it, and admired by those whom he served and taught. He was loved by those close to him, as it should have been for Ach'med.

As the days passed in the real world and the two moons would continue to rise and set unseen by the travelers in the ethereal plane, Moracles would continue to ponder his plan. Each day he would recite to himself the many long spells required to bring back the dead and more importantly the prayers necessary to the gods whom he did service. To 'Hartes' and 'Lolith' he would pray and share his plans to spread their bidding in the far reaches of the real world. The world to that Moracles was sent, to prepare for they're coming and rule as King and Queen. By then the world would be dark and barren, as they would have it no other way. Moracles was the messenger of their word and the servant of their evil.

* * *

The first group of survivors chosen to form a scouting party were led by their instructor, Shi'roc. If anything were to happen, he wanted to be there to handle it himself. Not that he lacked confidence in those that were chosen, but he felt responsible for their safety and the completion of their training. Though competent with the weapons at hand, they lacked the experience that he hoped to provide. If these few were worthy of the challenge, they would eventually lead their own scouting parties. It would give Shi'roc the opportunity to test their abilities even if they did not happen into any of Moracles' army. Of this he still had some doubts.

His troop was lined up before him at attention as he spoke. "I must remind you once again before we set out, that it is vital we not be seen or heard. Our existence must not be known or we endanger everyone in the mountain." Shi'roc spoke with concern and sincerity. "If we are spotted or are forced into battle, none shall be allowed to escape. Is that clear?" He looked at each one of them in turn with stern eyes. Each nodded affirmation realizing Shi'roc's confidence that they would be the victors in such a battle.

They proceeded from another hidden passage and headed single file toward the east slope of the mountain. "Where will this take us?" Shi'roc asked Kura as he led the handful of warriors. He had not been in this passage before. The newcomers had been too busy in their chores and training to go spelunking through unfamiliar tunnels though it was in their nature to be curious and investigate all that was unknown to them.

"This will bring us under the old town that my family was from." Kura hurried throughout the passage that was inclining, followed by Shi'roc and the others. He was eager to begin this exercise out in the open.

"I thought all of you Dwarves lived underground in these tunnels?" Shi'roc was puzzled, having not previously been told of Dwarven towns on the mountains surface. He attributed this lack of information to the Dwarven council's stubbornness in trusting he and Lorentz.

"No. We used to live above ground before Moracles came along and all the others fled here." The others continued to follow in silence. "We are almost there. The sun will be at our backs." He pointed out as they would be emerging on the eastern slope of the mountain and it was well past the noon hour.

The tunnel narrowed to a dead end. "We are here." Kura spoke with excitement. "The town is directly above us." He pointed toward the roof of the cave.

Shi'roc and the others looked up. Even with his enhanced vision, he was unable to see any air movements to indicate an opening. "How do we get there?" Shi'roc asked. "There is no way up," he said impatiently.

"Yes there is." Kura countered as he pushed on a lose stone in the wall. The others quickly moved back as they heard the sounds of scraping stone. They began to choke on the cloud of dust that erupted around them. When the noise ceased and the dust cleared, they could see the movement of air coming from a carved rock staircase that had appeared in front of them. A faint light could be seen at the top of the stairs.

"Wait here." Shi'roc pushed past Kura and hurried up the stairs with sword in hand to see what might be at the top. With that much noise, it may have attracted some attention from the outside. He wanted to be ready for any conflict. He stopped near the top to observe any sounds or movement. He found himself peering around the corner of a half opened doorway behind a bookshelf. He was inside the remains of a what looked like a home that was partially built into the mountain side. Kura and the others remained at the bottom of the stairs awaiting the all clear from Shi'roc.

He stepped out from behind the shelf, sword at the ready, as he glanced around the room. Portions of a wood and straw ceiling had collapsed allowing the suns light to penetrate. He moved around the rotted furniture to a set of closed shutters. With one finger he quietly pushed one of the shutters open enough to see the outside. Through the window he could see the remains of many buildings set at various plateaus in the mountains ridge. It appeared to be a once affluent community. Shi'roc returned to the entrance and motioned to Kura for the others to come up. He returned to the open shutters to keep watch on the outside. There was no sound or motion. The town seemed to be deserted.

"You say your people once lived here?" he whispered to Kura. "It looks so peaceful out there." He pushed the shutters open all the way. "This is quite a view." He could now see down over the east ridge of the mountain into the realm of evil.

"Yes. This was my family's home just before I was born." Kura said. "My mother had told me much about it when she was still alive." His voice trailed off at the thought of her voice. "There is a path that leads down the rest of the way to the base of the mountain. It was the old road that was used for trading goods with the towns people long ago."

"How do you know of all this? No one has lived here since before you were born." Shi'roc asked as he looked around the domicile and out the other windows near the front of the structure.

"My mother used to tell me of such things, the way it was in the old days." Kura began to walk toward the doorway. "That was before she died." His voice trailed off. He had not ever talked of his mothers death before. Not even to Ilo.

"What happened to your father?" asked Jantez quite innocently, standing at the center of the dusty room. They were all now in the home, awaiting Shi'roc's next instructions.

"I have heard that my father was killed by the Magdarn when he was trading with the towns people." He said with a sigh trying not to sound grieved at an event that had happened more than seventy years ago.

The others were stunned by this news, not knowing whether to ask how or why his father was killed. A brief silence loomed over the group. They began to search the remains of the home for items that could be used by the villages below. Shi'roc looked at Kura and then broke the silence.

"The wood from the furniture and roof can be used for more weapons." The warrior pointed out breaking the somber mood that had suddenly hit the group. "We will take what we can carry when we return, for now we must move on." He looked around at the others. "For now, close the passage Kura." All were ready to proceed through the town and down the mountain side as Shi'roc had instructed.

The Elf quietly opened the door and motioned for each of them to leave one at a time, practicing what they had learned. The first one out was Maac-To, then Ilo followed by Kura. They had moved very quietly from one shadow to the next just as Shi'roc had taught them using the cover of the natural rock and the buildings to conceal them.

Shi'roc watched each one with great pride at their training. He heard a muffled mumble of Jantez' voice and then waved back for the young Human to proceed out from the room. There was no response. "Jantez, where did you go." He whispered as he looked around the room with his back now to the door. "Jantez!" He repeated.

"I'm right here." The whispered response came from the doorway behind him. It was Jantez' voice all right.

Shi'roc quickly turned around to see no one. He knew it was Jantez' voice. He began to poke his sword at the open doorway. Where was he.

"Ouch." Jantez cried out. "Careful with that sword. I'm right here." He pushed the sword away as he grabbed at his flesh wound. "Being invisible is more dangerous than good." He exclaimed as he suddenly reappeared to Shi'roc's amazement.

"Next time tell me you are going to do that." Shi'roc said aloud, quite irritated. "You need to be more careful with your magic." He began to tie a cloth around Jantez' injured left arm. "Hasn't A'mora taught you that you must use your magic in conjunction with your group?" Shi'roc had well experienced the dangers when a student of magic practiced the art in a group where his talents were unknown. Disaster strikes the unaware.

"No, A'mora had never mentioned informing others when I used a spell. I thought the trade was to be kept a secret?" He spoke of her as a companion rather than an instructor.

"Only to those outside of your working group. Although I don't participate in such practices, magic can be very useful in battle if your allies know of your potential. It is your enemy that you wish to keep off balance." Shi'roc instructed as he completed the field repairs to the wound. He also noted the Human's apparent lack of formality when it came to himself and their party. Although Shi'roc and Lorentz were not typically eccentric about their rightful titles as 'Lords' they did expect that they and their followers be treated with respect for their trades. Jantez seemed to be treating him as an equal as did the Dwarven council.

The two left the doorway together, as the others, taking advantage of every possible cover more as for practice than for necessity. Jantez remained close to Shi'roc. He was intrigued by the others devotion to his task.

"A'mora said you were not fond of magic." The human whispered. "Is it because you can not understand, or don't want to know?" He pried at Shi'roc, not intending to be offensive, but truly curious.

"Lady A'mora and I do not always agree. But you should know that I have no dependence on the beliefs of others." Shi'roc replied, attempting to be tolerant. We should all know each others abilities to be a more effective fighting force."

The reconnaissance group was now spread throughout the small town. Each remained in sight of the next forming a visual net as they proceeded toward the downward path. All of the abandoned home and shops were quickly looked over as they passed, noting anything that might be of use. It was quite clear that the town was deserted long ago and in a hurry. Shi'roc made note of certain oddities as they stealthily left the area. He also noted the many hand signals being used between members of the group. It seemed to be a silent form of communication. He was impressed with this potential advantage they could have over an enemy and wanted to know more about it.

The group gathered again at the end of the town near the old trail that Kura spoke of. The sun had passed well beyond the mountain and cast the peak's long shadows to cover their position. So far the excursion had been uneventful but good practice.

"I have observed these hand signals that you have been using." Shi'roc spoke with admiration of this invention. "Could you teach this to myself and the others?" he inquired.

Ilo was the first to speak up after they had all eyed one another. "Yes sir, we can. It is a code that we had developed, that is among the watchers," Ilo explained. "We needed to communicate across the mountains without being heard."

"Yes, that's right. That is how we were able to gather in the caves ahead of you and your party as you were spotted from the mountain top," Jantez continued, referring to their first meeting. "I would be honored to instruct you while we walk." He smiled proudly at Shi'roc.

"Excellent." Shi'roc returned the smile, and they proceeded down the shadowed path through the rocks. "I don't imagine this can be used in darkness since the movements involved are minute." He continued his discussion with Jantez while the others went on ahead.

Ilo led the way down followed by his father and Kura. Not a pebble had been displaced nor dust stirred as they made their way to level ground. Shi'roc knew that these men had been well trained. These past weeks of intensive training had prepared them far better than those trained sporadically through years of experience. He was confident that they would be able to lead on their own someday soon. The next test was their skill in fighting.

The experience would be new to all except Maac-To who had escaped the murderous Magdarn when he was younger. The rest had been born, and lived in the relative safety here in the mountain. Though they had to fight for survival, the need for killing was not a part of their lives. Would they be strong enough both mentally and physically to withstand an attack and defeat the enemy, to the death, if necessary? Although under these extreme circumstances, no mercy was to be shown. They could not allow anyone or thing to know of their existence. At all costs and for the lives of the rest of the survivors, no opponent could be allowed to live.

Now at the base of the center peak they rested in the cool breeze as the mountain shadowed the land. Maac-To slung his bow over his shoulder and began to stretch out his arms. Shi'roc watched over the vast region of withered woodlands. Not one shred of color could be seen. Only the gray of dead trees extended for miles.

Jantez was leaning against a smooth boulder as Kura tugged at his torn sleeve. "Let me examine your wound." He told the younger Human. Together they carefully untied the field bandage that Shi'roc had applied earlier. The gash had not entirely stopped bleeding and appeared to be getting infected. "This may hurt at first." Kura warned. He placed his nubby fingers across the wound as he began to chant quietly.

Ilo walked over to where Shi'roc was setting on a rotted tree across the path from the mountain base. "What could have caused all this to happen?" The young Elf asked as his instructor gazed off into the distance.

"Magic." He said angrily. "I have seen such as this before but not over so great a region." He went on in a thoughtful, quiet rage. "This is what can happen to those who seek power over all. The magic intended for good is turned to evil." His mind was fixed on the corruption he had seen in his life time. He knew that it was unavoidable for those of weak minds. The taste of power can turn even the strongest beings to the dark forces. "Little by little, greed can do this. Combine it with magic and the world could end if it was not stopped by those like us." He felt his heart pumping and adrenaline flowing.

"Do you really think we can kill Moracles and stop his armies?" the inexperienced young Elf inquired. "I mean,...we are skilled enough aren't we? With what you have all taught us that is." He began to sound unsure of himself watching the angered look upon Shi'roc's face. He knew it was not himself that angered the great warrior.

"We have slain lords of the dark forces with fewer and less skilled than what we have here." Shi'roc motioned toward the mountain. He remembered long ago when he and Lorentz along with a small army, had taken on the great evil twins. One was a wizard and the other a priest in service to the dark world. Their army had perished, all but a few. He did not want to let Ilo know this for fear of discouraging him and the others.

"How did you defeat them?" Ilo urged on.

"Magic, if used wisely, as Lorentz does, can confuse the enemy. But it must be in conjunction with a well trained team. Each must become familiar with his party's skills. To be able to communicate without voice but with action, like you and your watchers did." He smiled now at Ilo. "They must trust each other with their lives." He spoke somberly now remembering the stories that he had been told of his half brother's heroics. He barely knew him, long ago, his death saved others is all that he remembered. "Yes, that is the most important thing. They must trust each other."

Jantez came running up to them with Kura waddling behind. "Look, look at what Kura did." They all looked at the now healed injury. Barely a scar was left. "I can't believe it." Jantez was grinning from ear to ear at Kura.

"Yes, you have done well, Kura." Shi'roc praised. I hope that it will not be necessary again." He threw a glance at Jantez, referring to the mischievous stunt that caused the injury in the first place. "Kura, which way from here would take us to the next set of tunnels back into the mountain?" Shi'roc pointed both north and south along the rock path.

"There is an entrance at each of the three peaks from within the town." Kura answered. "But I do not know where the mine entrances are." He shook his head at Shi'roc. The Dwarf had only been told of the entrance from his family's home into the secret mine tunnels. Those in the other towns would take some time to find not knowing exactly where to look.

"Do you mean that all these tunnels are from mining operations?" He looked accusingly at the Dwarf. "What was being mined through this whole mountain range?" Shi'roc asked the startled Dwarf, who replied by shrugging his shoulders. Then the warrior looked to the others for a possible answer. None could or would reply with anything but by shaking their heads. "Maac-To" he called to the elder Elf who was still resting on the hill side. "What do you know of these towns and the mines below?" Again as the others, no reply. He knew that Maac-To was of an age where he should have been able to shed some light on the mystery. He was not born in these mountains but had fled to the Dwarven peaks as a youngster when his people had been scattered by the Magdarn.

Although as a warrior, Shi'roc did not possess great wisdom, he was exceptionally good at piecing together puzzles. These towns and mines in the mountain began to bother him. Why had they not been mentioned before? He was now convinced that the elders were hiding something.

"That is enough practice for today. Let us return the way we came." He said somewhat distracted as his mind began to work the pieces of the puzzle into place. "Maac-To, you lead us back."

The Elf acknowledged as he retrieved his bow and nocked an arrow at the ready. As before, ever so quietly, the Elf disappeared into the rock's shadows.

Shi'roc gave one last glance toward the withered trees before following the others up the mountain side. Just as he turned to leave, he heard movements, the rustling of the trees in the breeze, perhaps? No, he definitely saw movement through the dead fallen branches. With his sword drawn, he backed away from the dead wood, toward the mountain passage. His eyes were focused on the area of movement.

A shrill screech pierced his ears as the branches bristled with skeletons before him. Creatures or beings brought to life by the powers of Moracles. Their decayed bodies moved quickly toward him as their war cry continued. They waved their rusted swords and shields. There was nothing but bones held together by rotted straps of leather and an occasional bit of metal armor. Torn cloth hung around the arms and waist, yet they were alive and had quickly cut off his sluggish retreat.

Shi'roc found himself encircled as he pivoted with sword and shield ready for melee. His only hope was that they had not seen the others leave up the passage. For these soulless creatures were certainly the creation of an evil priest. He must survive long enough to take them all down. He swore to himself that these skeletons were out numbered. Only eight of them, he thought to himself.

This was not the first time he had encountered undead beings such as these. They were often called upon to serve those evil beings with clerical abilities. Their having been raised from the dead could only be for purposes of evil. There was no reasoning with them. He must destroy them or die trying. They were too close to the path not to wander up it and possibly find the town.

Shi'roc thought hard as they each in turn struck at him from the circle that they had made around him. What would best suit his goal? An all out assault, or to scatter them to take one at a time? The later would be best he decided.

He lunged fully at one of them, fending off its blows with his shield. He knew the only way to defeat a skeleton was to bash it. Since it had no flesh to cut nor blood to spill, the only thing left was to break its bones. The force of his shield and the flat side of his sword were his best weapons. A sharp blade would only pit if hitting these specially reinforced bones of death. He continued his assault flailing his shield and sword, breaking free of the circle as he stomped the first skeletons bones into the dirt.

The other bony forms watched. They became enraged by this and charged at Shi'roc along the rock mountain base. As they passed in front of the mountain path, a large boulder crashed through them as they gave chase, crushing three more to splinters. Another was bashed to pieces mysteriously, as Shi'roc caught a faint glimpse of Jantez as the Human struck from behind it. Another was standing with its back to the rocks as a golden capped staff came crashing down on its head, spitting its skull in two with a thunderous clap. The remainder of the skeleton collapsing from the blow. Kura's new weapon had proven to be much more than just a stick.

Shi'roc had no trouble dissecting the other two as he smashed one with his shield while jamming his sword into the ribs of the other and with an upward jerk, shattered the rib cage. Ilo and Maac-To were busy smashing and scattering the remaining bony fragments.

"Did you think we had left you behind? We heard the screams and returned to see why you did not follow" Maac-

To said evenly. "Do you approve?" He asked timidly as he smiled like a child waiting for a reward.

"Yes, I do approve. Of all of you. And you too Jantez, wherever you are." Shi'roc said looking around for his apparently invisible student. "I shall also tell A'mora of your success." He smiled at the open air. "You have done well my friends. Now you know what proper team work can accomplish."

"Thank you my lord." Came a reply from somewhere up the rock path. "It is getting late and we must return now to the caves." He directed as he proceeded to lead them back.

"No. First we must clean up this area of any evidence that we were here. We must scatter all of these bones and brush these tracks with the dried bushes." Shi'roc ordered, now realizing the true dangers of being discovered so close to their hide out. If they were found so easily, they may be found again.

* * *

After the troop had returned to the relative safety of the mountain tunnels, Shiroc headedback to the small room where they had stored some supplies. He needed to be alone and think about what had taken place that day. As he reviewed the food remnants that were saved from the last feast, he found a water pouch. He was not only hungry but thirsty as well. The water pouch, constructed of animal skin, was designed by Lorentz to keep water suitable for drinking and storage for long periods of time. He sat on the rock floor and chewed on some bread as he reviewed the day's events. He opened the water pouch and sucked out the liquid to quench his thirst.

To his surprise, he found that the sack contained wine, not water. Someone had been hiding this from him, he thought. It wasn't often that his guards would allow him to drink, knowing that good wine would quickly inebriate him, but there were times after battles that he needed to be in that state. He was intelligent enough to know not to drink unless his surroundings were familiar and safe and that his skills as a warrior would not be required for a time. As after the battle with the dragon when they arrived, Shi'roc imbibed after feeling somewhat comfortable in the new surroundings.

Tonight he needed to think, and the wine would help calm his mind, at least for a while. Shi'roc was focused on finding answers. He was determined to learn why they had been kept from the knowledge of the Dwarves' past. If there had indeed been some sort of mining operation here, there was no evidence of it. There should be tools, equipment of some kind, maybe even a forge. These items could certainly be helpful in creating better weapons for their army. He was now drinking more than eating and the wine was invigorating his apprehension.

Lorentz must be told of this. Shi'roc began to stand up, faltering on the scattered rocks. He thought to himself as he stormed his way back to the cave section where they slept. We have to extract some truths from the council. Why are they keeping such secrets? His anxiety increased with every stagard step through the cavern as he approached the opening. There was a lantern lit as he could see from a distance. The curtain was drawn but the distinctive light of the lamp seeped through the edges. He could see the outline of one of his men near the opening.

"M' lord, you should not enter." Grefden warned as Shi'roc pushed his way past. He was in no mood for games. "But my Lord." Too late. He pulled back the curtain as he entered the chamber.

"Aahhh!" A'mora gasped with embarrassment as she pulled her cloak over her beautifully naked body. She had been setting on a smooth cup shaped stone that Lorentz had carved out for bathing purposes.

Shi'roc looked up. Stunned by her bare beauty, his jaw dropped open and he was speechless. Embarrassed himself, he turned away and apologized. "I'm sorry." he began. "I, uh, was expecting Lorentz." He stuttered. "I will go now." He began to walk back out of the room.

This was the first opportunity A'mora had in seeing Shi'roc's guard down and she wasn't about to let it pass. The Priestess could tell that he had found the hidden wine. She took full advantage of his embarrassment. "You don't have to go." She said softly as her face glowed, not only from the lantern light but from her genuine warmth for Shi'roc. She stood up with only her cloak wrapped around her, and stepped out of the shallow bath.

Shi'roc stopped dead in his pace just before reaching the curtain that Grefden had already pulled shut behind him. "Are you covered?" He asked as he peeked over his shoulder, now a little more in control of his thoughts.

"It is all right. You can turn around now." She replied, drying herself with the cloth around her. Her garment did not cover her body entirely as she leaned against the stone. Her well formed legs were still visible up to her thighs. "What is wrong? You seemed upset when you entered. Didn't your students do well today?" She asked calmly as Shi'roc began to turn.

As he turned around, his eyes locked onto her long curved legs. Again he was speechless. With all his strength of will he managed to break his stare and gather his thoughts of the days events, still groggy from the drink. "Yes they did very well under the circumstances." He answered her last question first. "There is indeed a danger out there. A matter that I should discuss with Lorentz. I was attacked."

A'mora was a bit surprised. She did not think that they were going to journey too far from the mountain. "Was anyone hurt." Were her first words. She was genuinely concerned as she quickly looked him over for visible damage.

"No, no one was injured during the battle, except of course for the enemy." His thoughts were still effected by the wine, but no longer clouded by arousal as he spoke of the skirmish. "I was also impressed by your student, Jantez" He said jovially as he began to step closer to her. "Does he do any more tricks than just disappear?" He gestured whimsically with his arms. "Surely you have taught him more than that?" He smiled at her with an expression intended to make her blush.

"Yes I have." She responded evenly. "But that was the easiest for him to learn, and maybe the most useful." She thought of all the mischief she had caused in the past when she learned that spell from Lord Lorentz.

"Jantez will be more careful next time he uses it." Shi'roc pointed a scolding finger at A'mora. "You should have warned him of the dangers that accompany the benefits. I nearly ran him through with my sword."

"What? Why?" She shuddered at the thought. "Is he harmed? What happened?" She demanded, almost not letting him answer.

"He is all right." The warrior cut her off. "It was barely a scratch. Kura took care of it very nicely." He nodded to her acknowledging that once again her tutoring came in useful. "He will let us know the next time he intends to use that trick, or stay out of the way." He laughed.

A'mora felt at ease talking to Shi'roc like this. It was the first time they had talked alone, that is just in general conversation. She could feel his openness now like never before. Was it that they were alone, the wine, or that she was standing there half naked? What made this time so different?

"It sure was useful when he was able to attack those Skeletons from the rear." He laughed again. "It was a strange sight to see the bones fly as Jantez slammed it from behind." He still was smiling from the warm feeling the fermented grape juice provided.

"Skeletons?" She spoke with a sudden panic about her voice. She looked up at him then spoke with urgency. "We must find Lorentz at once." She dropped her cloak and began to dress, totally ignoring the fact the Shi'roc could not help but watch her. She knew all too well that the presence of beings raised from the dead could only mean one thing. That Moracles was not only a powerful wizard, but also a priest serving the lower worlds.

Shi'roc was once again distracted as she pulled on her cloth undergarments. "What is so important........ About the skeletons? There were ....only eight of them and...... They are no longer of concern." He spoke brokenly as his eyes covered her every curve and bounce as she pulled on her tight woven casual attire that she had been wearing since they arrived in the mountain.

"But they are of concern." She said pointedly as she turned around and broke Shi'roc's stare at her backside. "Only a priest serving the lower planes of hell would summon such beings to serve him." She tried to explain knowing that Shi'roc had little understanding of the various realms of existence. He only believed in the here and now, what he could see and touch. Matters of other times and obscure places did not interest him.

His wide eyed smile vanished as she spoke of priests and demons. "I know that the undead are made to serve evil priests. I have been around a while you know." He said with a bit of sarcasm. "And what of it, if he is a priest? Lorentz possesses the knowledge and wisdom to command both magic and use the power of the gods." He pointed out still not realizing the implications. "So do you." He pointed to her, still not entirely stable on his feet.

"Yes. That is true. But we know that Lorentz has those powers." She was evasive in her response trying to evoke some logic from Shi'roc. She pulled the tie strings of her tunic as she stared into Shi'roc's eyes hoping to see the inspired reasoning.

He snapped his fingers and said. "Lorentz does not know that Moracles is a priest." It suddenly came to him. "He thought that there was only magic to contend with." The sparks flew in his mind as the fires of wisdom arose. He smiled feeling quite proud of this deduction as he watched A'mora pick up her lantern and walk off.

"Wait! That also means that we are in for more trouble than Lorentz had expected." He now stood in the darkness as reality set in. He ran to catch up with her as she headed down the tunnel.

"Brilliant!" She called back, still walking as fast as possible that was much easier for her when she carried her own light.

"My lord. What is wrong?" Grefden sounded panicked as Shi'roc moved through the open curtain. He had heard bits of the rather heated discussion.

Shi'roc stopped and turned back to the other. "Do you remember when we first met at 'Cerratt'?" He prodded a long ago memory from him when the castle Cerratt was greatly outnumbered by its enemy. Shi'roc and party vowed to help fight against a wizard and his army. Though the castle was well protected and its soldiers strong and well armed, the overwhelming forces would have succeeded in the battle had it not been for Shi'roc and his friends.

"Aye, M'Lord." Grefden responded, puzzled. He remembered that as the massive army began its assault on the castle walls, he saw several soldiers beating a path through. It was Shi'roc and his friends, hacking and slashing their way through while others followed, each with their special talents. There were bolts of lightning crashing down on the enemy and mystical clouds of poisonous gases that choked the attackers.

"Our situation just became far worse." He said as he turned to continue his chase of A'mora. He had not yet even told her of why he had been looking for Lorentz. If she knew where he was, it was best to just follow and explain later.

* * *

The council chambers of the Dwarven elders were well lit this evening as many of those attending were of human decent. Though it was not normally allowed for the non members of the council to attend, this meeting was not under the direction of the council. Lord Lorentz had insisted upon meeting with the Dwarves and asked that certain representatives of the village clans be in attendance. The room was full with those standing as well as seated. There was, as you could imagine, quite a clamber of languages that filled the chamber. Other than Shi'roc and A'mora, no one knew just what Lorentz had called the meeting for.

Lorentz looked over the crowd to be certain that all were in attendance that were necessary. He saw the Dwarven chief and his ministers, Maac-To, Ilo, Kura, Jantez, and a few others from the various communities. Each had their purpose for being in here though they did not know why.

He stood and gained their attention at the center of the room through his powerful voice. "Tonight is a time for thought." He spoke out firmly with a serious expression. "We are here to communicate to you. There will be no room for doubt or apprehension." He paced around to look at all of them, starting with the now silent council. "For the benefit of everyone, I speak the common language so that there will be no misunderstanding." The rest of the crowds looked at each other waiting for the purpose of all of the dramatics.

"I don't understand." Kura said to Ilo. "Are we here to discuss what happened yesterday?" A brief shoulder shrug was all he got in response.

The rest of the ears were focused on Lord Lorentz' words.

"I speak to you tonight to again define our goals, our purpose for being here." He spun around and gestured to Shi'roc and A'mora. "We have journeyed far to help a people whom we believed required and were worthy of our assistance." He pointed to the remainder of the Dwarves, Elves and Humans. "You were the people we sought to help. You were the ones whom we expected to train to fight for their freedom and to crush the evil wizard, Moracles and his armies." Now even more dramatically he continued in an unusual arrogant tone, signifying to Shi'roc and A'mora, his true frustration with the situation. "We came in friendship. We came in truth. We brought you food and healed your sick. Who among you has been healed by myself or Lady A'mora?" He posed the question to the crowd.

"I thought I would not have lived until you came to me." Spoke one of the elderly Humans who was dying of malnutrition. He now was healthy and had been training to fight.

Another spoke up "I also would have died." And with this came a murmur from the others who had been helped by the newcomers. Even one of the council spoke out.

"I was dead, at least that was what my wife had said as Lorentz reached into the darkness to retrieve my soul. I am very grateful for that." He said with honesty as he was nudged by the chief, Kyman, to keep silent. Still he had not used Lorentz' proper title.

"Is there any one among you who can speak out against us. Any of us who might have done you wrong?" He said with anger. Without waiting for a response, he started to continue but was cut off by Kyman.

"I have been wronged by you. We all have." Came the angered words of the Dwarf as he stood up behind Lorentz pointing his ancient nubby finger. "You have come here to turn our peaceful community into your own personal army."

Lorentz smiled at Shi'roc and A'mora before turning to face his accuser. He appeared as though this whole show was to draw out the truth from the Dwarven chief and was successful. He was so sure that there now was something to hide. Something worth risking the respect of his own council who gasped in shock at their leaders accusation.

"Is it not you who are afraid? You who have lied and misled us to believe that you had lived in this hollowed mountain for generations when in fact you too were in hiding, leaving your towns above on the surface." He looked at the council as they anguished over their deceit. All but Kyman who was afraid of losing his authority to Lorentz.

The remainder of the room stood in silence as Lorentz waited for some response from the council or even the chief himself. What answer was he expecting? What was his next move? It was almost as if the Dwarf's fears had become reality. That Lorentz would indeed turn his people against him.

Now in a more calm voice without the dramatics Lorentz asked simply. "Why did you not tell us that these tunnels were actually ancient mines?" He let the question hang heavy in the air without response. Only the puzzled looks of the council toward Kyman triggered his next question. "You must have tools and equipment, a forge possibly, that we can use to craft better weapons." He watched their faces as they pondered an answer.

"The answer to your first question is simple." Came the commanding voice of Maac-To, as he rose from the bench in the rear of the crowd. "Kyman was not sure as to the outcome of your intentions. He felt that the less you knew, the better control he had of your actions." He walked forward toward the council stepping past the others who eyed him cautiously.

"Mind your place, Maac-To. You do not speak for me." Came the desperately angered voice of the ancient Dwarf. "You are not a member of this council."

"Because he is an Elf and not a Dwarf?" Questioned Kura, also standing to approach the elders, his staff in hand. "This is a new time for all of us." He began to address the audience, not sure why, as if driven by another power. "We must work together as equals, true equals. Not that for Dwarves and then for others. There should be no secrets among us."

"My young friend speaks with the wisdom of the gods." Lorentz said nodding thoughtfully. "Do you still have doubts about our reason for being here?" He asked. "The threat of Moracles is a real one as your people can attest." He gestured to Maac-To and Kura.

Shi'roc now spoke for the first time here. "I have, " he paused and looked at the others. "We have seen the enemy ourselves. As you had requested, I have led a reconnaissance team of your best trained people to test their readiness." He spoke evenly. "I am convinced that they are ready just as I am convinced of the reality of the threat. We ventured to the base of the eastern slope and were attacked by several of Moracles' things." He stood also and spoke directly to the old ones. "Your people fought with courage and creativity," he praised, that was a real honor coming from Shi'roc. "I believe we are ready to send out more of such teams. But first we need better weapons." He now spoke in a demanding tone. "We need your tools to craft better swords and arrows."

"We can use much of the materials left in the towns above." Kura said pointing upward with his staff. "There is wood from furniture and cloth. There may be more items but we did not have the time to look."

"Back to the question of what was mined in these passages." Lorentz was now leaning on the table supported by his two fists. He stared directly into Kyman's eyes, as he leaned over the Dwarf. Just then he felt a hand on his shoulder, gently pulling him back from his intimidating position.

"Jewels, precious metals and hard metals." Maac-To whispered, not to let the others hear. "They do have what we need." He told Lorentz. "Tools and forges to make armor and blades." He said almost in shame.

The truth was starting to come out. Kyman then conceded. "We at one time made swords and armor for the valley people."

Shi'roc's pointed ears twitched. "Swords? Armor?" He said, shocked. "That's exactly what we need." Now in a more serious tone. "Is there anything else you would like to tell us?"

Kyman eyed Maac-To before responding. "No. That is what we manufactured here, jewelry and weapons." He said with disgust. "Most of these fell into the hands of the Magdarn as they raided the villages. They took all the weapons and armament they could find and Moracles used the jewelry to buy the loyalty of more soldiers." The old Dwarf sat back down almost in tears as he recounted the past. "That is why we kept these things from you. We didn't want any more bloodshed on our account." He looked at the others in the room. The Elves and Humans were all willing to fight for their freedom. A freedom that the Dwarves unintentionally helped take away. "You can see now why we fled our villages and took in as many of the towns people as we could find. We were a part of the cause that drove them here."

"We left all of our belongings above for two reasons actually. The first, because of our guilt that the others had no belongings. The second, if the towns were eventually discovered, it would appear as if we had fled in a hurry."

One of the other council members explained. “We hoped that they would search no further and be satisfied with what belongings we left behind for them.”

“Where are these tools and forges?” Lorentz asked evenly. “Are they in working order?”

Kyman nodded soulfully. “We will take you to them in the morning. They should be serviceable.” The old Dwarf seemed rather tired and worn out by the tensions released this night. “We should all retire. It is getting late.” He slowly stood up and made his way to the doorway, ignoring the mumbling of the others as he left.

Lorentz watched the old man, feeling a bit of sorrow over the stories thus told. “Yes. We should all get some rest.” He turned and spoke to the crowd. Tell all that we shall meet in the morning at the great hall. We must make new plans in light of the recent events. Have all craftsmen and women there too.” His voice was without emotion, monotone and lacking his usual spirit.

The rest of the crowd broke up and headed to their varied paths toward home. Not a word was spoken between them. The sorrow of the Dwarven tale had bewildered them. Most were not sure that news to take the hardest. The fact that the Dwarves had taken them or their ancestors into their care from guilt or that there were some comforts that could have made their lives easier that had been kept from them in the towns up above.

* * *

The next morning, the word spread once again that Lord Lorentz had called for a gathering of all the survivors. All the inhabitants of the mountain were there. From the children to the old humans and yes, even the Dwarven council was there to hear the words of their potential new leader. The great hall was full, and bright with torch light, as Lorentz talked with Shi’roc at the base of the cavern.

The chattering of the hundreds of voices began to echo into a massive hum that resonated down the passage ways.

Lorentz began to speak as Shi'roc stepped a few paces back and off to the side. All attention was focused on Lorentz as he began to speak. "This is a day of new beginnings." He spoke loud as he raised his hands. "I wish to start this morning off with a prayer to Mirana for bringing us all together. I would ask those of you who have been taught to commune, to join me down here." He referred not only to his own personal guard but also the new clerical students of Lady A'mora.

Several of the students began to climb down and over the rocks to the base where Lorentz stood. They formed a semi circle facing their audience. A'mora, Kura, two other Humans and two mixed elves from the mountain as well as five of Lorentz personal guard. They all joined hands with Lorentz in the center, bowed their heads and began a chant. The meaning sent forth from the utterances was an acknowledgment to the goddess of the gifts she had brought to them through her messengers, A'mora and Lorentz. Kura was especially grateful, yet still awaiting final understanding of the powers that he believed had yet to be revealed in the staff. He could feel its strength as he used it in battle against the Skeletons.

The silent audience listened to the growing murmur. Some bowed their heads out of respect, while others looked off, uninterested in the event that was taking place before them. Sha'la and Grefden were looking up toward the center of the cavern, in anticipation of another appearance by the goddess in the misty form in that she had shown herself before.

Shi'roc was leaning against the back wall of the cavern with his arms folded staring off into the crowd. He had propped his right boot against the stone behind him. As he eyed the now familiar faces of the council and the chief, he realized that they were all paying close attention to the proceedings. Perhaps the last nights meeting had finally stirred their cooperation.

At last the chanting was over. The circle of priests raised their heads and returned to their previous locations among the crowd. A'mora walked back to where Shi'roc was standing as Lorentz began his verbalization of the events to come. "Is anything wrong?" She asked as the two stepped toward the lower entrance to the caves.

Shi'roc shook his head, no, while his inner feelings said yes. "I still do not entirely trust the Dwarven elders." He whispered. "I feel there is still more they are not telling us; especially Kyman. Do you remember when we first met them out in the wasteland? Maac-To was wearing metal armor and a long sword. Those items have since vanished. Lorentz said that when he asked Maac-To about that he would not respond."

"Perhaps they were very personal belongings. Maybe a gift from a relative, or something that he did not wish to share," A'mora suggested to ease his obvious tension. "They seem quite willing to help us now." She referred to the council as they sat together about half way up the hall seating area. It was easy to see now that the various levels of carved stone were from mining. "Can you imagine that all these rooms and tunnels were cut from active mining?" She looked into his stern face and received no reply except a blank stare. His mind was obviously on other matters. She took his hand and said. "Everything will turn out well. You will have the tools and materials to make better weapons and armor."

"That may be true, but I want to know what happened to the weapons and armor that they stopped making so long ago." He took his hand back, not interested in being soothed by A'mora's gentle ways. He was now thinking of the plans he had developed for a swift and safe extraction of all the useful materials left above in the deserted towns. As

Lorentz completed his explanation of the tasks at hand, Shi'roc approached the center of the speaking area.

"... And now, Lord Shi'roc will assign the tasks for those who will be involved in this operation." Lorentz nodded his head to the other as he moved off toward the lower entrance where A'mora was standing. As he approached, the uneasiness in her stance became apparent. He had a way of knowing peoples feelings by their actions and words, both spoken and not.

"I am pleased to see that all of you have taken an interest in the needs of your community. I especially am grateful to the council for their support in these matters." These words of diplomacy did not come easy to him, but with Lorentz' coaching the night before, the effect would be as was needed. He felt that he would now actually have the elders support even though he felt they were holding back.

"Those of you who are capable of operating the kilns and mining tools please stand and be seen." He counted a dozen of the older Dwarves who let themselves be known, including one of the elders who had previously headed up one of the mining operations. He acknowledged them and said. "Thank you. 'Utar', you will be in charge of renovating the equipment and the mining operations." He knew it was important to give responsibilities to the council members to keep them involved. "We will need additional volunteers to mine the ore for smelting. The younger, the better." Another twenty of the younger Dwarves and some of the Humans and mixed Elves agreed to take on this task.

"Which among you possess the talent that I am in awe of? That talent that was known throughout the land for its fine craftsmanship in the making of armor and edged weapons. He spoke with a real enthusiasm though he already knew who he was looking for. And as he suspected, the remaining members of the council reluctantly raised their hands. "Excellent!" He cried out with a smile on his face. We can now be assured of the best quality in the land with the council in charge." He tried hard not to sound facetious since he still had little trust in the council. "I can be sure that the ladies present will be quite helpful in preparing clothing and equipment from the materials that we will scavenge." He mused whimsically as he heard a loud noise of someone clearing their throat. He pinpointed the direction to see Muga, Kura's wife, standing with her hands on her hips. "Ah, yes." He corrected himself. "That is those ladies who are not involved in combat training." He heard a cheer from the dozen or so sturdy female warriors who had become quite proficient at close combat.

Lorentz had been leaning against the stone wall with A'mora at his side, both listening to Shi'roc address the crowd. "This is unlike him to be speaking for so long." He observed. "He also appears to be enjoying it."

"It must be your influence upon him." She whispered. "I have always said that you were a great influence on me and a fine tutor." Her face lit up with a grand smile.

He turned to her quickly. "Perhaps." Then spoke thoughtfully. "But I believe that it is you who have been the influence. You have touched him emotionally. You bring out what is best in him." He commended her. "Since our group has formed I have noticed his ways have changed. He is no longer just the cold tactical warrior as I had known him. He now shares his feelings and his angers passionately."

Shi'roc looked at the council and spoke with authority. "The mining operation should begin immediately. Utar, please proceed." Utar and the rest of the council stood. He nodded to them again acknowledging their efforts at cooperation. They in turn bowed and headed out of the chamber followed by the volunteer miners and the non warrior females. All that now remained in the hall were the warriors and students of Lorentz and A'mora.

"He is quite good actually." Lorentz commented to A'mora as the council left the hall. "I think I'll let him lead from now on." He spoke jovial and added a chuckle.

"Many of you have learned the skills of a warrior as well as the secrets of magic and prayer." He began to pace the floor of the cavern no longer speaking directly to his audience. He spoke dramatically as Lorentz would. "You have worked hard and long, endured the soreness and injury of the training. "I suggest that now it is time to make a concerted effort to learn as much from Lord Lorentz and Lady A'mora in the ways of prayer and magic as possible in the next few weeks." He had stopped his meandering and stood directly in the center of the floor looking up at the crowd.

"He is ill. He must be, for him to suggest that our ways take precedence over fighting skills." Lorentz pushed himself from the wall and stood erect looking directly at A'mora in shock. "What have you done to him?" He said seriously and then turned back to look at Shi'roc in a new light. "I have not spelled him." He insisted and turned back to her.

A'mora shook her head and responded aghast. "I have done nothing to him," She denied. "I know no such spell." She shook her head. "I don't understand what has gotten into him."

Gor and Grefden looked at each other with puzzled expressions and could only shrug their shoulders. What did their lord have in mind? They could not guess. They could only think that a plan was in the making, and indeed they were correct.

Lorentz and A'mora swiftly walked toward Shi'roc both chanting in a spell casting form. They stopped just behind him and moved their arms in various swirling motions. The crowds saw this action before Shi'roc himself realized what was happening. He turned abruptly, to see them both hovering over him like vultures inspecting their prey.

"I sense no change in his manner." A'mora spoke as she concentrated her thoughts on the swaying of her arms about the warrior.

"I too sense no evil as if demon struck," Lorentz replied as he stared into his friends eyes.

"What form of madness is this?" He shouted at his two companions. "I am trying to put our plan into motion here. What are you two doing?"

Both of Shi'roc's guard jumped to their feet and pushed their way past the others as they climbed down the rocky paths toward their master.

"No, it is definitely him. He is not an illusion nor a morphite." Lorentz was now satisfied that the words were indeed those of the one and only Shi'roc. "Well my friend, it is really you."

"Who else were you expecting me to be?" He retorted as Gor and Grefden flanked him on both sides looking puzzled by the situation. The rest of the audience began to laugh or giggle at the apparent comedy of the scene.

"We had thought from your words that perhaps you had been in some way influenced by the dark forces." A'mora explained as she lowered her arms to her side. "We were concerned for your safety." She said soothingly as the crowd looked on at the incident.

"When you spoke in favor of our powers over that of sword and bow we were certain that something had taken you over." Lorentz explained as he put his hand on Shi'roc's shoulder. He smiled at him and looked at A'mora, pleased that there was no danger here.

"If you will let me continue." Shi'roc began to turn back to his waiting audience when he finally noticed his two loyal guards with swords drawn at his sides. "What are you doing? There is no danger here. You heard Lord Lorentz," he exclaimed. " I am me." He continued as a chuckle arose from the students seated nearest the base of the cavern.

The two frustrated guards sheathed their swords and proceeded to climb back up the rocky path to be seated. Grefden moved off to where he had spotted Sha'la sitting.

"What was that all about?" She inquired with a whisper as Grefden maneuvered himself to set beside her.

"Don't ask me. I just work here." He said with a grunt. He was more accustomed to his master's sometimes eccentric ways.

"Now that is settled..." Shi'roc began as A'mora and Lorentz stepped back a few paces. "Your assignments are as follows: those of you learning prayer will spend all of your waking hours with Lady A'mora." He said with a toss of his head in her direction. "We will need good healers. That includes you Kura." He pointed to the Dwarf setting with his wife and child.

The Dwarf held his staff up high and said. "I would be honored my lord to serve as a healer."

"Jantez and Gol. The two of you will follow on Lord Lorentz' heels for the next several weeks." He pointed to the two young Humans up in the rocks. "Lord Lorentz knows where to concentrate your studies." He nodded to his friend. "The rest for you will remain here for further training and assignments as the others go to their studies." He turned to Lorentz and A'mora, nodded and motioned them toward the lower entrance.

"Well done my friend." Lorentz whispered as he passed. The students followed closely behind as he and A'mora left the great hall. "He must have worked on this plan all night." He said to A'mora. "I am not totally aware of its details but it seems to be well organized." He concluded as they proceeded down the tunnels.

"For the remainder of the day the rest of you will train, train, train. There will be no resting and no holding back."

He looked them over very seriously. Even the experienced soldiers were shocked by these words.

"What does he mean by not holding back?" Sha'la inquired to Grefden.

"I am afraid he means that we push our students until blood is drawn. I expect that is why he sent the others to pray." Grefden replied as he pulled on his beard. He knew that intentions were well placed in Shi'roc's mind but now as before hated to draw blood from one who is not the enemy. Yet he knew it was the only way to learn, the best way to teach, and ultimately the only way to stay alive.

"Those of you who can survive today's combat will be assigned to scavenger duty in the towns above." He continued to pace again as the plan unfolded. "Maac-To and Ilo will also teach their instructors in the art of speechless communication. When we are above, we must be silent and cautious not to be seen or heard." He stopped pacing and asked. "Are there any questions?"

"Yes, my lord." Came a voice in the distance. "What did you mean about those who survive?"

"Today's training will be hard. Some of you may wish to volunteer for other duties tomorrow once you see what real combat training is about." He turned and marched out of the cavern as the crowd remained motionless and silent. They could only think of how hard their training had been thus far. To be pushed harder was almost unthinkable.

*   *   *

His footsteps echoed down the empty hallways. The darkness was no barrier for the sound of his bony feet meeting the smooth stone floors. Alone in his new domain, a castle in the rocks, the fortress Moracles had built, the halls seemed to go on forever. A virtual maze of rooms and corridors, most of which the Bone had never seen. But now he will take the time to learn the secrets of the walls and doors. Time he has plenty of, now that all of the dwellers were out in a search for the strangers who dared invade his territory. They would be found and dealt with most cruelly.

As he walked down the main corridor toward the massive wooden doors that led to the outside canyons, he hesitated near the corner. He felt a slight movement of air that was unexpected. Could the winds of the canyon be so forceful as to penetrate the main doors? He thought, unless… "I believe there is a passage here to be found." He muttered as he let the tips of his fingers scrape across the wall in search of the stones outline. He turned and cursed the darkness as he reached for a convenient torch on a wall mounting. With the snap of his fingers the matted splinters ignited and an orange fiery glow illuminated the hallway's corner.

He slowly moved the torch back and forth along the wall until the flames flickered. "Indeed there is an opening here." He proceeded to follow the stones edges as he outlined the doorway with his finger. Then looking for an opening mechanism, he moved his hand along the outside edges of the doorway. There was no unusual markings or handles. Not even a loose stone as an opener.

He replaced the torch in its holder, as he continued to move both hands across the face of the stone door. "I will find the answer to this puzzle," he insisted. Then suddenly his finger stopped at a small hole in the center of the secret door. A small gap between two of the stones was just large enough for the tip of his dagger, that he pulled from the sheath on his belt. He wiggled and pried the blade, being careful not to damage its fine sharp edge. "The key, there must be a key." The echo screeched down the halls.

He slammed his fist against the wall and walked off leaving the torch to shed its light for as long as it could. The sound of the flickering flame crackled and spit as the splintered wood eventually burned down to a stump of ash in its appropriate place. The corner was again dark where there was a passage; the key to which was held by few and unknown to the Bone. He would continue his survey of the fortress as the armies searched in vein in the distant lands for the handful of soldiers that would invade the evil solitude of the valley.

Chapter 11
Friends

The path was wide nearest the end of the woods heading north. Just as he had each year at the same time, a lone traveler made his pilgrimage into town. From this point the traveler could see the few buildings at the edge of the town called 'Tireth-Tec'. It was a quiet sort of town where most people minded their own business. The horse drawn wagons carried the merchants wares to the gallery of shops in the center square of town. Here there was no need for high walls and wooden gates as crime was at a minimum except for the occasional young pick pocket being chased through the alley by one of the town constables.

Yes, the scenes of today were a far cry from those of the past that the traveler had remembered. Each year of his passage, he saw the continual improvement in the general atmosphere and growth of the town. Now no longer a town, one would consider it a city, complete with a government and democratically elected council. None of these improvements mattered much to this Elf who, as the towns people, minded much of his own business. His purpose was not to inspect the progress of others. He came here each winter, as the trees became bare.

Wishing not to draw attention to himself as he approached, he lowered the hood of his cloak around his neck, people would tend more to fear a stranger if he appeared to be secretive than they would a simple traveler who did not try to hide himself. Elves were not uncommon in these parts, though his wavy blond hair did indicate his being from other lands. His attire would blend in well with the more aristocratic peoples of the community. His fine soft leather boots and blue velvet cloak made him out to be a person of some means.

As he neared the shop buildings at a casual pace, the merchants would nod a cheery good day to him. Of course the gesture was returned by the Elf though he felt no joy in his pilgrimage. He made his way up the main street through town that went directly north. He passed several shops at which he and his companions had done business many years past. The leather shop, the dry goods store, the hotel, all of which had passed through generations of owners since he had taken the time to shop or stay at the hotel. No one here would remember his assorted and sorted companions, or the intrigue that they had brought in those times.

Even the tavern was in the same corner spot across from the hotel. It brought back memories of theft and deception. "I wonder what has become of Grog these days?" he said to himself with a smile, having fond memories of the scraggly Dwarf. He peeked into the swinging bar room door. It looked much the same, but at this early hour before the sun reached its peak, there were few patrons. He might stop in for an ale on his way out today for old times sake. He thought to himself.

Here at the middle of the cross road he stood looking west. Just over the tree line he could see the peak of a distant mountain range more than a day's ride. Back then they could not afford horses or riding equipment, as he remembered the journeys they made back and forth by foot. Food and weapons were all they carried back then. Together on their first adventure to seek out the secrets of legends told in the bar he had just passed.

With his mind lost in the reminisce, he had not realized the fast approaching wagon, as he was in the middle of the street. The whinnies of the speeding horses, rearing up behind him broke his thought. Reactively he turned to see the wagon master had pulled the reins of the horses too hard and the Elf was about to be trodden by the two animals. He swung up his left arm and reached out with his mind to the horses calling, "Slow" and in mid stride, the animals almost froze in place allowing the traveler to step aside. The reared horses slowly descended and were back in step as the driver stared toward the Elf, on whom his horses almost trod. The Elf gave a quick glance to the horses and said "Resume" as he walked off, leaving the horses back to an uncontrolled frenzy as they sped past with a mystified driver and wagon in tow. He had no concern with the safety of other pedestrians that might fall in the wayword wagon's path. Though his gifts were many, compassion was not one of them.

He continued his walk through town toward the temple at the far north end. The structure stood alone, away from any other buildings or houses. Its gleaming white form seemed to glow in the suns light. The Elf opened the gate and walked not toward the main doors to the building, but around to the gardens in the rear. He nodded to the care taker as he was careful to stay on the intended path through the colorful trimmed flowering shrubs.

The path he took led him directly to the quiet hill side where a large stone marker had been pushed away from the opening. The tomb that he came to visit was empty. Shock and surprise ran through him as never before. He quickly looked around to see if anyone was near. Only the care taker was in sight. "Why would the grave be robbed?" He said to himself. "There were no items of value left with 'Ach'med' and the remains of the body itself had been taken." Not that there would be much left but bone fragments and dust, if that much, after ten decades.

He remembered when they first brought the torn remains of their friend back to this temple in hopes of restoring his life. Back then they knew little of such possibilities. Even the priest among them was wary of the prospect, yet they carried the odorous carcass back from deep inside the castle in anticipation of a miracle. There was unfortunately nothing the temple high priests could do for him since he was a full Elf and claimed no deity to reckon with. All they could do was pray for his soul to be accepted at the gates of the heavens . Only the fact that his actions in life as a warrior for the side of good might allow him entrance. For this they beseeched the gods and Goddess' of the seven heavens.

* * *

Now, in the deepest part of the castle where none had been since years past, the ancient one began his recitations and incantations. He circled the candle lit room as he invoked both his magical and priestly powers of the dark forces. His incantations flowed from his lips for hours as he wore a path in the dusty floor around the center alter. The candles had grown shorter by inches when the first sign of acceptance came from the gods, whom Moracles had served for all of his evil life.

"Who doth summon me?" Came a roaring low pitched voice that echoed through the temple. The voice came not from a physical being, but from the god 'Hartes' who had been the inspiration to Moracles' evil ways as an apprentice.

"It is I, my master, Moracles," came the response as he bowed. Spreading himself, and his flowing robes across the floor. For it was only in the presence of his masters that he would subjugate himself in this way, on his knees with his raged white beard pressed against the stone floor. Indeed, he truly admired and respected the gods he served.

"Where do you summon from that my presence may be known?" Inquired the voice of the mighty Hartes.

"From the temple of Lord Magdelan," he answered. "We are truly alone, you and I. There are no other souls in this part of the castle," he assured the god of their privacy. There were few living beings for which Hartes would do the honor of communicating in this way. Only his closest servants were permitted such a conversation.

"What is the purpose of your summons, Moracles?" The voice asked, now in a less commanding tone. Though he was the most powerful god of the dark realms, he also respected those loyal to him and granted favor to the deserved few.

For weeks, Moracles had prepared a speech to gain favor with Hartes in order for him to grant his wish. Moracles slowly arose from the floor and gathered his robes around him once again. He recalled the oratory from memory as if it were a prepared spell incantation. Patiently the god listened as if contemplating ones prayers, or deciding the fate of a lost soul. The evil wizard went into great detail of his plan to expand the territory in preparation for the arrival of the worlds new king and queen.

Hartes was pleased at what he heard of the devotion of his prized pupil. “I will assist you in stealing the soul, of the one called Ach’med, from the gods of the heavens,” the god finally spoke after a long minute of thought. “It will be up to you to enlist the services of my queen, Lolith, to turn his spirit in our service.” His voice was followed by a clap of thunder that shook the entire mountain, signaling the conclusion of the discussion.

“Thank you my lord.” Moracles nodded his head in a general downward direction. His voice was sullen and mischievous as he once again circled the alter, inspecting the bony remains of the once great warrior, ‘Ach’med’, as he began the incantations.

* * *

The daylight shown through the open shutter in the otherwise dismal bar. The lonely Elf downed his third mug of ale. It was early afternoon and there were only a few towns people in the place. He carefully looked them over, though he did not realize his sudden interest in the common folk. What or who was he looking for? Perhaps he should speak to the town magistrate or the chief constable? No, he thought, that would do no good. If there was a reason for the tomb robbery it would be not likely that any one here would know or care and he did not wish to bring attention to their past or having to explain.

He then tried to get the bar wench's attention to order another ale. He was not accustomed to waiting. Normally a person of his station would have wenches at his side continuously on hand to serve him. He began to get frustrated at having to wave his empty mug over his head for attention. He was about to slam the pewter down on the table in exasperation when a voice whispered from the shadows.

"They do not know you here, old friend." The voice was gruff and in some small way, familiar to the Elf.

Surprised, he turned to the figure outlined only, in the shadow at a table in the corner of the bar. Whoever it was did not wish to be seen, yet the Elf cursed himself in his mind for not being aware or observant enough to notice this person sooner. In times past, that could have been a fatal error. More than once, he or members of his party had been the target of assassins sent by evil wizards or the gods themselves. Only through careful avoidance and disguise had he survived all of these years. It was not like him to let anyone or thing sneak up on him like that. His mind was on more important matters. "Who are you, sir, that you would call me friend?" He directed his speech to the shadowy plump figure. The light through the window was obstructing his view of the dark corner

"You do not remember me 'Fendal'?" the voice answered with a wounded grunt. He remained motionless in the darkness studying Fendal awaiting a response.

"You must mistake me for someone else." He was even more shocked at being addressed by name. His mind began to plan a hasty retreat and recall some useful defensive spells if this was some sort of trap. The Elf concentrated his night vision on the features of the stranger. To his surprise, he did in fact look familiar. But the voice was much to gruff to match the person he believed it to be. He could have moved closer, but being a stranger made him more cautious. "Your manner is familiar sir, yet your voice throws me some confusion. You know me by name, yet you hide like a giant arachnid in its web, waiting to strike its prey. "

"Those are bold words for someone who at one time required a body guard when he traveled." The figure leaned forward across the small table, just enough for his face to be visible in the light. "It is I, Koloda," he whispered. The sun light from the opened shutter of the window revealed a mangy looking, stout Elf with long wild black hair. He was obviously well fed from his hefty features. A patch over his left eye yielded to a scar rising up from his cheek to his brow. A gold ring through his ear lobe sparkled in the glimpse of sunlight.

Fendal leaned forward as well, across his table for a better look at the vaguely familiar character. "Koloda?" He repeated in surprise but more in shock. That would explain how he was able to sneak up on me, he thought to himself. Then he suddenly remembered the tale he had heard of Koloda long ago. "What happened to you? I had heard you were dead."

"Good." The portly Elf chuckled. "That was the intent, and it wasn't far from the truth." Although Koloda wasn't know for being an honest person anyway. "I have kept it that way for fifty years now."

"I remember now the story I heard. You were caught and hung for the robbery and murder of some town official far from here." Fendal said in a whisper. He recalled the story slowly as he continued to size up the battered Elf. He looked quite different from when he had know him before

"What you heard was not all true." Though from his old ways may very well have been truth that Fendal would have believed. He corrected with a pointed finger. "I killed the magistrate in self defense, then I robbed him." He leaned back into the chair and into the cover of the shadows. "I knew I would get blamed for his death so I figured, what the hell, why not take what I could." He swung his mug up to his lips and drained the last of the ale down his throat. Then with a healthy belch, slammed the mug on the table gaining the attention of the bar maiden.

"What do you mean 'in self defense'? Why would the magistrate try to kill you?" Fendal questioned, trying to extract the whole story, or determine how much might be the truth as compared to what he had heard.

Koloda grunted a warning of silence as a curvaceous, young maiden came to their tables with an empty tray. Standing in the light, she nodded to the shadow in the corner. Koloda grunted, waving his empty mug. She correctly interpreted this as a request for a refill. She then turned to Fendal as she placed the wooden tray on her hip.

"I'll have another as well," he said quietly, as he eyed the young Elf maiden. "What is your name, my dear?" he said with a raised eye brow. It had been a long lonely journey and the ale was overwhelming his self restraints. The only saving grace of the ale was that its effect prevented Fendal from using magic to win the maidens favor. His natural charm would have to be enough if he intended to have a companion for the night.

Her white tunic top was tightly drawn with laces and low cut revealing her soft healthy upper body. The gray skirt was ankle length yet was slit up the side all the way to her white creamy thigh. With a warm smile, she answered, "Cha'ni" as she leaned over to pick up the empty mugs. Having set them on her tray, she turned and walked back to the bar. Her tight hips swayed with a motion that neither of the two Elves could ignore.

They both noticed the other patrons lustfully watching as well. Not a sound was heard as Cha'ni sauntered away. "I think she is far too young for you." Came the voice from the shadow, breaking the silence of the seemingly long stares at young girl's form. "Forget her. She is all but forty years of age. Much too young for you," Koloda scolded. As Elves go, she was barely more than a child yet physically and mentally fully developed. "Where were we before we were so graciously interrupted."

Fendal turned back to Koloda. "You were telling me why the magistrate wanted to…."

"Yes ,yes." Koloda interrupted. "He learned about his daughter and me. He did not want anyone to know that she and I were, …" he paused, his voice trailed off as he chose the right words. "..intimate. We had been meeting away from town to keep the relationship a secret. We knew that her father would not take kindly to me."

He thought about those days before his face had been disfigured. He was not entirely unattractive back then. There was a time when women could not resist his charms and his story telling. But now he was in hiding and better off since he was self conscious about his appearance. "I had obviously worn out my welcome in that town anyway." He said bitterly.

"That sounds like the Koloda I used to know. What surprises me is that you allowed yourself to be caught." Fendal nodded toward the returning waitress as a sign to discontinue the conversation for the moment.

Cha'ni put the tray on Fendal's table and set a clean mug up for each of them. She smiled again at Fendal as she poured the ale. His focus was not on the ale that she poured, but her cleavage. "Will your business in Tireth-Tec keep you in town tonight?" She inquired innocently, as she bent over toward him while she filled his mug. Fendal did appear to be as a traveling merchant so her question was well placed.

His mind was not on her words as she spoke, but on the alluring manner of her speech, as well as her endowment. He broke from his lustful trance to answer. "I believe I may need to stay a day….. or two." His eyes flashed to Koloda for a nod of agreement. "Yes, I will require lodging. Do you have any suggestions?" He knew quite well where this would be leading but pretended that he was unaware of the hotel just across the street. The same hotel at which he, Koloda and the rest of their party used to stay when visiting this town generations ago.

She leaned over and whispered to him. "Come back later and I will take you someplace where you can stay as long as you like." She turned back and nodded to the shadowy figure once again before returning to the bar.

Fendal leaned over the ale as a grin creased his face. His mind was briefly anticipating the evenings pleasures to come. He quickly reverted to the business at hand. He turned back to Koloda. "So tell me, how did you get caught?" His mind went back to the previous conversation.

"The magistrate's daughter found me robbing the home with her father dead on the floor." He picked up the new mug and took a swig of the frothy liquid. "I was too well known in that town to find a hiding place or to escape from the area."

"Then how did you escape the hanging?" He said just before lifting his drink.

"That was my greatest accomplishment ever. I didn't escape the hanging." Koloda noticed a puzzled look grew on Fendal's face. He slowly unwrapped a scarf from around his neck to reveal a nasty looking scar that went from ear to ear. "I played dead at the end of the rope for several hours and paid off the undertaker to substitute a body in my place in the casket." He re-wrapped the scarf to hide the obvious indication that he was a fugitive. "I barely escaped with my life. I have been hiding in this town ever since. I thought no one here would remember me from the old days." He remembered back when their adventuring team used to frequent the town of Tireth-Tec. It had grown in size and wealth since its tyranny under the evil Lord Magdelan had ceased. "Now, you tell me. What brings you to this town after so many years?" Koloda felt he was owed an explanation of the visit, since it was clear that Fendal was not here for reminiscing.

"I come here each year at this time. The time at which we committed our friend, Ach'med, to the catacombs of the temple." He pointed an accusing finger at Koloda. "If you remember , it was you who caused his death." The ale had gotten further into his logic than he had reckoned.

Koloda winced at the accusation. "Don't put the blame on me." Koloda snapped back. "I don't recall the rest of you rushing to our rescue. I barely escaped with my own life." The plump Elf could remember all too well the attack in the castle that cost Ach'med his life. His response came a bit louder than anticipated and attracted the attention of others now in the bar. Several of the patrons became aware of the two Elves' discussion in the corner. They had, until now, been generally unnoticed

"If you hadn't gone sneaking off on your own and gotten into trouble, Ach'med would not have had to save your worthless hide." Fendal stopped. They both were leaning so far over their tables that they had practically become face to face. They noticed that everyone was watching them. So for a while they became silent and regained their composure. They sat back down until the interest in them had passed.

"So what of your journey? What made you stop in here?" Koloda asked in a quieter voice. "I have not seen you when you say you have come to town."

Fendal took another drink of ale. "Today when I went to the tomb, the stone had been moved and the body was gone." He spoke with a quiet fury. Although he normally cared for no one but himself, he did have feelings of friendship toward Ach'med and would not let the theft of his remains go uninvestigated.

"Of course the body was gone." Koloda interjected. "What did you expect to see after three generations." He leaned back in his chair again.

"No. You don't understand. There was nothing, not even the blankets that we had carried him in. Nothing was there." He continued to get himself worked up again over who, what and why this was done. "Not bones, not even dust was left behind."

"Could there have been a time allotment to the tomb? Perhaps it had been cleaned out to be re-used?" Koloda offered as a possible explanation.

"Well; that is why I am staying around for a while. To find out what has actually happened. But between you and me, I think there is more going on." Fendal finished his ale and stared at the shadow unmoving. "Are you going to help me find out what happened or not?" He said after a moments silence.

Koloda grunted an apparent affirmation of his assistance. "I will be listening." He said after some thought. "I will find you when I have word." He noted that the room had been gradually darkening. The suns light no longer shown through the open window shutter. Could they have lost track of the time?

"For now I will go back to the temple and talk with the priests to see if they know anything of the tomb." Fendal began to stand, or try to. Using the table to steady himself, he stood up and pointed himself to the door of the establishment. After a few steps, he turned to Koloda and found that the shadowy figure had vanished. He chuckled to himself and smiled openly as he crossed the floor. "I shall return this evening as promised." He threw a kiss to Cha'ni before opening the bar room door.

He sobered up immediately as the brisk afternoon breeze came rushing to him from the street. It had become noticeably darker, more so than normal for a winter afternoon. He looked up at the sky to locate the sun's position. He thought he had lost track of the time. To his surprise he could not locate even a hint of passing light. Only the swirling black clouds could be seen overhead. As the wind kicked up, he heard the people around him gasp as the sky filled with lightning. This was not a rainy season in this part of the world, yet it appeared that a storm was brewing. He pulled the hood of his cape up over his head and tied the braided fastener.

More wind and lightning erupted as he proceeded back to the temple. He noticed as he approached the main cross road looking west, in the direction of the mountain range, that the blackness of the sky was concentrated over it. It was almost as if forces of nature were at war with one another. The clouds were swirling and pulling in opposite directions. They would slam together and blasts of lightning would surge. Suddenly, an enormous tornadic funnel seemed to be reaching from the dark sky into the mountain.

Some towns people ceased their activity to observe the phenomena, while others hurried for shelter in the buildings and homes. Several elderly elves pointed and said in the old Elvish dialect, “Its happening again.” They gathered others to look off into the distance and see the blasts of lightning that seemed to be absorbed by the mountain’s peak. “I can still remember what happened the last time such a storm occurred.” The old men were reminded of the oppressive evil that had swept their land over two hundred years past. The lands were obliterated, crops died, famine and disease struck. All due to the wizardry of Lord Magdelan.

It had been a while since Fendal had heard the old Elvish tongue but was still able to understand its meaning. He was not old enough to remember the coming of the evil Lord Magdelan but he remembered the peoples rejoice at the word of his demise. What could possibly be brewing at the evil castle that had long since been abandoned.

Chapter 12
Deceptions

The room deep inside the mountain shook with the force of thunder. There were puddles of wax where candles had melted themselves together all around the sacrificial alter. In the center of the stone, laid the still remains of the once loved warrior. Bolts of lightning struck repeatedly around the bones as the air filled with the electricity of the beginnings of life.

The smell of ozone was exhilarating to the mage. Over the crackling sounds of static could be heard the chanting of the evil one. "Unificatum ex renier sanguitori et deremitatu. Exault Hartes." The chant was continued by Moracles throughout the event.

The reunification of the soul and flesh of one so long dead was a once in a lifetime accomplishment for any priest. But with the assistance of his god, Hartes, who had literally stolen the soul of this warrior from the protectors of good, he had managed to reform the being once known as Ach'med.

At first, the dust had moved to compact itself into bones. Then the bones began to grow flesh around them, and muscles and organs filled the interior cavities. Moracles continued his exhaustive chanting and even to his amazement, the body slowly reformed. Even the severed limbs from the battle that caused his death were miraculously re-attached. The procedure continued for several hours until the unnatural act was complete.

The lightning had ceased to spark as Moracles paced around the alter, inspecting his new creation. Though it had at one time been a man, it was properly called a creation now. He too was baffled by the experience, never having heard of such a feat being successful before. This was to be expected, for nowhere in history had there ever been such a tale told as this one would be in the future. The entire world would know of this phenomenal resurrection, reuniting a lost soul with the dusty remains of its rotted corpus.

He bent over the now smoldering candles to touch the completed body. He was astonished at its almost perfect form, still in its youth as he had remembered it so long ago. The skin was soft to the touch. When he squeezed the flesh he felt strong muscles beneath, though the general fitness was not of a bulky man. He put his face close to that of the Elf and lifted its eye lids, searching deep, for a sign of life.

The body flinched as it inhaled a deep breath, startling both the mage and the warrior. Moracles was not a pretty sight from any distance, let alone waking up to be staring up his hairy nostrils. He lurched his body back releasing his fingers from the Elf's eye lids. He took a few steps back from the alter as the warrior began to sit up.

"Where am I?" he insisted. "Who are you?" His voice quivered as he realized that he lay there naked. He pulled the ragged remains of the blanket around his waist and tied them.

Prior to his entombment, his friends had wrapped his body in blankets, and carried his corpse for a week in search of a priest powerful enough to breath life back into his body, or what was left of it. The group's cleric was able to tend minor wounds and set broken bones but had little hope of restoring the torn remains of his body after his encounter with the ape creatures. Even if she could, she was not practiced in resurrections as her youth had not afforded her the wisdom or experience to do so.

Ach'med's services to the group as a protector, were dearly needed deep inside the fortress of the evil Lord Magdelan, and they had become fond of him and his naiveté as was his good nature to trust everyone and to help any who asked or were in need. None had expected his trust in others would one day cause his death.

As the worrior checked his body, he noticed many long thin lines across his torso, some intersecting as if cut many times with a sharp blade. He looked up at the incredibly ugly Human in the dim, remaining candle light and asked, "What has happened to me?"

"You do not remember?" the priest asked with a calm innocence. He watched as the Elf shook his head. "Exhault Hartes." Moracles proclaimed his profound thanks to his god for this turn of fortune. "Your friends had left you to die alone in battle as they ran." He looked on for a reaction from the Elf, but only received a puzzled look. "Do you know your name? Do you remember the friends that had abandoned you?" He asked mischievously.

The young Elf strained to remember what had happened to bring him here, who he was, who were his friends? "My name is Ach'med, son of Ta'lon." He spoke with some hesitation. He thought a moment longer. "I remember that I was with several others in the abandoned castle of Lord Magdelan." His memory slowly returned, yet not entirely intact.

"Well; Ach'med son of Ta'lon. You are still in Lord Magdelan's castle but it is far from abandoned." The priest was a profound liar as one would expect. "Fortunately for you I was able to save you from my pets." He spoke slowly and cautiously, trying to determine the extent of the Elf's memory and loyalties. "Do you remember killing one of my pets." He said in a more irritated tone, remembering the loss he sustained upon the death of his creation. He also realized that the Elf had no concept of the amount of time that had lapsed since his death. To Ach'med this would seem like only a few days passed if any.

"Your pets." He said somewhat dismayed. He thought for a moment in silence as Moracles observed. "I remember now. Koloda was in danger and yelled for help." He began to swing his legs off the altar and attempt to stand, bracing himself on the side of the altar. "When I found him, he was far off from the rest of us. He was battling with three large ape like creatures. I did kill one of them." The spark came back in his voice. "Those were your pets?"

"Yes they were." The sharp irritated voice said. "I see that you are regaining your memory." He continued. "Do you remember how your friends ran and left you alone to fight with my pets?" He was probing to see what memories he could influence in the Elf and which would be to strong to sway. With a fragmented memory he had the opportunity to implant thoughts and feelings in the Elf's mind. "They left you for dead and then I came along and saved you." He began to implant some feeling of indebtedness. "You were in fact dead and I have raised you from the darkness."

"I don't believe you. They would not have left me as you say." He began to feel uneasy again and took another step back from the old man, pressing himself against the waxy altar. "Who are you? You have not said." He looked around for his cloths and armor, or for a weapon to use, if necessary.

The mage felt the sudden change of attitude and attempted to diffuse the situation. He put on a smile, that was crooked at best from the scar on his cheek. "I am Moracles, and I am the cleric of this castle. The healer, if you will." He bowed his head slightly to the Elf. "You should not fear someone who has brought life back to you? Let us be friends. I mean you no harm." To that there was some truth for he indeed wanted to make the Elf his friend and control his being.

Ach'med still had no idea of the time that had passed since he did battle with those creatures of Moracles' creation. "Where are my cloths, my sword?" He eased back yet another step.

"I am afraid that there was not much left of your belongings. By the time I arrived, my pets had mangled you so badly that your cloths had been torn literally to shreds." Moracles continued his charade in hopes of gaining his trust. "It was difficult enough to retrieve your remains. I did my best to collect your scattered limbs."

Ach'med again checked his body to notice that, indeed, there were more scars about his arms and legs. "My body was in pieces?" he asked in shock.

"You had been quite dismembered," Moracles responded. "you were indeed fortunate that I kept them from feeding on you. If I had not arrived when I did, well, there may have been nothing left to save." He now could see that Ach'med had begun to believe the tale since most of what was discussed was in fact true. "I am afraid that your friends are long gone." He began to play on the confusion of the warrior as he said, "If you wish, I can send for them to be brought back here." This was of course a lie and a gamble. The castle was at this time very deserted and most of Ach'med's party, dead or missing.

The Elf just shook his head having an abandoned feeling, thinking that those for whom he had risked his life would leave him there as the priest had said. How else could he explain his presence here and now. "That isn't necessary. I owe you an apology and my thanks, in fact I owe you my life." The Elf finally admitted. "How can I repay such a debt?" He now felt the debt must be paid, as Moracles had hoped. He had been an honorable man in his previous life. This much he still felt inside though his memories had become obscured.

Moracles immediately jumped at this chance for a commitment. "You can repay me with your company. It is quite lonely here in this part of the castle as you can see." He motioned grandly to the castle in general, though the private temple was small. It had after all been in the chambers of the late Lord Magdelan. The past master of this mountain performed many a sacrificial ritual on this alter. Tributes to the dark gods, such as Hartes, from which Moracles received his initial rites as a mage priest of the dark realm.

"Let me get you some clothing. You must also be quite hungry?" His performance was every bit believable and he began to get caught up in his own version of the story.

The Elf followed as the mage proceeded out of the temple. Just outside the opening in a short hallway was a life size statue. It appeared to be a dark skin bearded man. Strong and muscular yet with a kind face. Ach'med studied it briefly in passing. He then caught up with the mage and proceeded into an adjoining chamber. "Who was that statue?" he asked politely.

"That is my god, Hartes, whom assisted me in reviving you," replied the priest. He knew there was no harm in the truth of this answer since Ach'med had little or no knowledge of any gods, fair or foul. Before reviving the Elf, Moracles had done extensive research on his family heritage. He was not brought up under the guidance of any clerical power. He spent his youth in total oblivion to the powers of those not presently of this world. Those gods who would give pleasure or punish as they saw fit. Some were as mischievous as children while others were as lawful as sacred scrolls of the heavens and hells. This fact, Moracles would use to his advantage.

They had now entered the master chambers of the deceased Lord Magdelan, that now, Moracles had restored to full use during his stay. He had spent several weeks in renovating this part of the castle to make it look as if he had been living here alone for a while. The Elf would never be able to know that these were once the private suites of the Late Lord Magdelan whom his companions had finally slain as was their mission in being in the castle long ago. "Hartes has assisted me in healing others many times." He said as an undetected lie to the Elf who was now becoming more at ease with the mage. He opened a wooden closet containing many drawers of clothing. He selected several garments and held them out in offering to the Elf who was in awe of the grandeur in this room. The ceilings were high and the floor spacious with many lavish furnishings. He was inspecting the four poster canopy bed with intricately carved figures on the walnut posts.

"I have never slept in such a comfortable looking bed before." He turned to Moracles. "Everything here is so grand." He said as he stepped to the mage to collect the clothing.

"I believe these should fit you. I must apologize for the styling and drab colors, but there is little available to choose from." Again, Moracles was subconsciously influencing the Elf by the use of dark colors. "There is a similarly furnished guest room down the hall if you would do me the honor of a visit."

Little by little, the Elf would allow the unnoticed control over him. He carefully pulled on the black britches and hooded tunic top. "Yes, they do fit rather well." He said as he stepped to the mirror and straightened out the clothing. The cloth was smooth as silk and reflected the flickering candle light of the room. "I look good in this. Thank you." He turned to the cleric and nodded his acceptance. "Yes, again. I believe I will stay with you for a time while I decide what to do from here." The Elf was seriously believing that he was safe here, having remembrances of some evil creatures that lurked deep in the castle. Some they had fought and defeated. Others had caused them to flee and seek refuge in hidden chambers or barricade themselves in rooms until the dangers had passed.

Moracles smiled with a gleam in his eyes that even he had not felt since his arriving earth quake in the valley from which his evil had spread. "Excellent. I shall have a feast prepared to mark this day of your resurrection. A celebration of life, a rebirth day." He continued on, actually enthused by the prospects of the willing, naive candidate for the powers of darkness. "I shall show you to the guest quarters so you can rest, if you wish, while I have dinner prepared."

The revived Elf followed the mage to the end of the short hallway. The old man turned the knob of the wooden door leading to the bed chambers. The room was dark. "Wait here a moment while I light some candles for you." Moracles proceeded in not realizing that the Elf would follow, guided in the darkness by his night vision. Ach'med could see the heated form of the mage as well as the movement of the air around him. The swirling patterns allowed him to avoid inanimate objects such as furniture.

With the snap of his finger, he was able to light the first candle and from there lit the others on the candelabra. The room brightened with the flickering light and Ach'med was again in awe of the beautiful rich furnishings of the room. Though only half the size of the master's bed chambers, this room was every bit as well dressed. As well it should be, since this was Moracles' own room while he apprenticed with the Lord Magdelan long before.

Ach'med looked over all of the furnishings, ending with the poster bed covered with soft dark linens. He climbed on the feather mattress and sunk several inches into the soft bed. "I really like this." He said with a genuine smile. Such decadent comforts were foreign to him. It was rare that he even slept in a bed at all.

"Then it shall be yours for as long as you wish." The old priest said with a nod, as he stepped out into the hallway. "I shall come for you later, after you have rested." He closed the door and proceeded to chant in a low tone passing his hands near the closed door, reaching beyond to the Elf. "Dormo bene." He repeated several times, then walked off.

Ach'med was still setting on the bed as the drowsiness hit him. He let out a big yawn and stretched out on the large bed and quickly fell into a deep sleep. This sleep would be full of new ideas for the young Elf as Moracles had begun to fill his mind with erroneous memories.

"Help! Help!" He heard the voice yell from far off, echoing down the corridors. Ach'med followed the continuing cries, running with sword in hand to defend his companion, Koloda. His movement seemed slowed as he approached the opening from where yells emanated. He could hear the growls in the darkness as he saw the forms of three large creatures surrounding his friend. They fought fiercely with razor like claws and large sharp fangs. Koloda swung frantically with his short sword and dagger, keeping them at bay as he attempted to withdraw from the hallway.

He was struck from behind by one of the animals and then again from the side. He began to collapse from pain and exhaustion as Ach'med let out his war cry and began to fend off the furry beasts from his fallen comrade.

"I will hold them off while you get the others." Ach'med insisted, as he cut deep into the arm of his attacker with his sword. Koloda crawled out of the way as Ach'med engaged all three of the apes with his single weapon. The distraction allowed Koloda to escape with his life, as Ach'med struggled for his own. "Hurry! I can't hold out much longer by myself." He yelled as another of the creatures slashed his back with its claws.

Koloda had shuffled off down the hall toward the rest of the party . He eventually found them as they were coming toward him. "No! Go back! Get out of here," Koloda yelled, as he waved his bloody arms in panic. "There are several monsters back there, we don't stand a chance." He tried to convince them that the effort was useless.

"What about Ach'med?" One of the members asked. "Where is he?" The concern was apparent in his voice.

"Ach'med is history. He was killed by the creatures. I barely got out alive myself." He explained as he started pushing them all back away from where the battle was going on. "There is nothing you can do. I tried to save him but it was too late." He confessed as they moved on in

their original direction. He was very practiced at lying since it accentuated his thieving skills.

Without even a single cry for help, Ach'med had managed to kill one of the apes before being overpowered by the intense pain and blood loss from the continued attacks made on him. His leather armor had been ripped to pieces as it hung in shambles from his body. His chest had been slashed several times by the sharp claws of his opponents. He had fallen and his vision was blurred. He beckoned death to take him from the pain as one of the creatures tore his arm from his body. He could make out the vague features of someone holding a torch over him as he finally lost his struggle for consciousness.

"Ach'med, wake up. It is time for dinner." The voice of Moracles penetrated the Elf's dream induced sleep. He stood over him with a lantern in hand ready to lead him to the dining hall.

The Elf snapped out of his dream struggle, panting and afraid. He sat bolt upright in the bed. "It was you who saved me." He said to the mage. "I remember now, all of it. Koloda, the apes the battle and the pain." He lowered his head in sorrow. "And my friends leaving me behind."

* * *

The late night moon shown brightly, casting its bluish shadows over the empty city streets. The clearness of the sky was quite a surprise and relief after the day's deviant storms. There was a chill to the air with a slight breeze from the north. All of the legitimate businesses had closed for the night as Fendal and Cha'ni left the bar. He walked down the street with his new companion clinging to his arm. They proceeded to the east edge of the city where most of the homes were located.

"Yes, I have some fond memories of this town; well it was just a town back then," he reminisced. "Most of these buildings weren't even here when my friends and I would come to rest and obtain supplies for our journeys," pointing to the newest structures on the end of the street. He turned to smile at Cha'ni, realizing that those days were far before her birth. "Back then the people here were still in fear of the Lord Magdelan back in the mountain castle." He gestured over his shoulder with his thumb, as Cha'ni listened to his tales without speaking a word. "Most of the people who lived here then are dead. Humans only live so long you know."

Cha'ni chuckled at his reference to Humans. "Being an Elf has its advantages." She said as she put her arm around his waist, underneath his cloak. He looked at her questioningly. "I'm just trying to get warmed." She said with a smile as she snuggled up to him.

"Permit me to warm you." He said mischievously. He stopped and freed his hands as he mumbled a few words that she didn't quite hear. "Regula manus thurmum." He wrapped his cape around her and allowed her to regain her snuggle hold. His body began to produce an uncommon warmth that began to create a light fog, similar to seeing ones breath in the depths of winter.

They walked into the residential part of town where Cha'ni lived. She had after all promised to show Fendal a place where he could stay for as long as he wished. He was determined to stay as long as it took to discover the reason of Ach'med's missing remains. She pointed to a house up the street that had a short white fence around it. Fendal noticed that the house was small but well kept. They walked up to the door and stopped as Cha'ni searched into her purse for the key.

"Here it is." She held it up and placed it into the lock. She turned it with a click and opened the door into the darkened room. She led Fendal by the hand into the house and closed the door behind him.

"Would you like some light?" He asked, not intending to ignite an actual flame. The light he had in mind was more of the unnatural sort. He barely had time to get out the question before Cha'ni thrust her body against his, pressing him onto the closed door.

Her lips had found their target as Fendal too reacted in kind, holding her body firmly against his. Her sweet embrace was welcomed and anticipated since early in the afternoon. She began to move her hands up and down his back in a passionate expression, breathing deeply into his ear. Their tongues were fighting for space in each others mouth.

Suddenly Cha'ni felt a sharp blade held against her neck. She froze her movement and retracted her tongue in order to speak. "What are you doing?" She gasped as she felt a slight trickle meander slowly down her throat. She wasn't sure if blood had been drawn by Fendal's knife or if it was the sweat of passion.

"I knew you were too good to be for real." He said disappointedly, as he grabbed her by the hair and forced her slowly backward, being aware now of every move she made in the darkness. "I wish for you to return the pouch that you have just removed from my belt." He still held the small knife to her neck.

"Stop!" A grumbly voice emanated from the corner as the sound of scrapping flint could be heard.

Fendal turned toward the sound, now with even a tighter grip on Cha'ni held in front of him with the knife to her throat. His vision picked up a heavy figured outline in a chair just prior to the candle being lit. "Koloda?" He was surprised to see the now familiar Elf.

"You can let her go now." He nodded to Fendal. "I will handle this." His face was stern and filled with anger. The anger was not directed at Fendal but at Cha'ni. Koloda followed her with his eyes as she stepped away from his old friend. He spoke to her in a language that Fendal could not follow, consisting of grunts and hand signals. Cha'ni responded in like fashion.

It was apparent that she was being scolded severely for something that she had done. Her face was strewn with worry and begging forgiveness for her actions. In the light, now could be seen the trickle of blood that was now drying on her neck. Fendal realized that he still held the knife in his hand. He quickly put it back into its scabbard under his cloak.

"Hold it." Fendal interrupted the obscure conversation. "Will someone tell me what is going on here." He realized that although the language was foreign, it was a form of communication used among thieves. He never took the time to understand it though he had observed it on many occasions. "Koloda, what are you doing in Cha'ni's house?"

The heavy Elf grunted in disgust at Cha'ni and ended the secret conversation. "Give it back to him," he insisted. "I will not tolerate this kind of behavior in my house."

Cha'ni reached into her tunic top to remove the pouch that was Fendal's currency. "I was going to give it back to him anyway. I was just practicing what you taught me." She responded as she begrudgingly handed the pouch to Fendal. She shook it once first just to confirm to him that it was still full. And full it was, as he untied the strings to reveal the numerous coins and colored stones. "You shouldn't travel with that much money on you. You never know who might pick your pocket," she added as he re-tied the pouch to the back of his belt under his cloak.

"Now then, tell me why you led me back to his house anyway." Fendal still wanted some answers. "And why does she have a key?" He pointed to Koloda. "Why did you tell me that she was too young for me if you two were…?"

"Because she is my daughter." Koloda chuckled in response to his friends questions as Fendal's jaw dropped almost to the floor. " She is also my student, and as you can see, she is still in need of some practice."

Cha'ni finally thought to check the earlier feeling on her throat. She wiped her fingers gently across her neck to find that she did indeed have smeared blood on them. "You really did stick me you..." She said as she slapped Fendal hard enough for him to take a stumbling step back. She had really caught him off guard.

Koloda just laughed. "Like father, like daughter eh?" he said, then began to laugh again.

Fendal began to chuckle as he held his throbbing cheek. He looked at Koloda. Then Cha'ni joined in on the laughter as she wiped the remainder of the coagulating trickle of blood from her skin.

* * *

The fire was warm as they sat beside it. The glow of the flickering flames reflected off of the white walls in the house. The three acquaintances sat calmly enjoying some pleasant conversation. Cha'ni refilled her fathers cup with wine and also poured for Fendal.

"So when did you find the time to have a family? And where did you find such a beautiful woman to produce this fine young lady?" Fendal said with a note of sarcasm. He nodded to Cha'ni as she smiled and shrugged her shoulders innocently.

"It was back when I fled to this town to hide. I had always done my best to be unnoticed. I seldom went out in public." He drank from his cup. "After a while I began to wonder what the people of the town were all about. It had been so long since I had visited Tireth-Tec, I had almost forgotten my way around." He looked at the fire. Then picked up an iron poker and stabbed at it, releasing a flurry of sparks as the log rolled over. "I went to the bar to quietly observe the habits of the residents and other visitors."

"You mean that you were board and wanted to pinpoint some victims to relieve of their coins." Fendal broke into the flowered story with his own translation. Koloda just grunted at him. He looked at Cha'ni who just smiled.

"As I was saying, I went to the bar and sat in the far corner, the same place I was today. Just as I was getting seated, I looked up and there she was. The most beautiful when..." Koloda stuttered, refraining from using the word 'wench' in reference to Cha'ni's mother. "..waitress I had ever seen. She looked much like Cha'ni does now." He looked at his daughter with the loving memory of his wife.

"Well; what happened?" Fendal prodded. "I have never known a woman to get to you before no matter how beautiful she was. I remember a time when you were almost mesmerized by that water nymph. Do you remember back at the Galladorn castle? After we broke you away, you realized what almost happened and...."

"I ended up almost getting killed trying to save someone else's sorry ass. Where is that bumbling warrior anyway? Have you heard anything of him? Is he still enthralled with every beautiful blond he meets?" Koloda took another drink of wine and looked at Cha'ni. She had just been listening to the tales of her father and his old friend. She hadn't taken her eyes off of Fendal since he started the fire by rubbing his finger on the logs.

"The last I heard was just folklore. He had just saved the town of Thormadore from an attacking army of giants. He gathered some of the towns warriors and led a counter attack up in the near mountains and defeated the giants that were being led by a Dark Elf. He is probably still out there somewhere building armies and saving towns." He thought a moment about how long ago that was. "He is no longer the young fumbling fighter that you and I once knew, at least not from the stories I have heard. He has become something of a legend in various lands." He paused and took a drink from his wine glass. "Anyway, you have not yet finished as to how you were enthralled by a beautiful woman."

"Ah, yes. Well; Cha'ni's mother did to me much the same as Cha'ni did to you." He let out an unexpected laugh. "And was just as unsuccessful. I was impressed with her attempt and took her as my apprentice. Somewhere during that time Cha'ni came along."

"Well then, how could you let such a lovely woman get away from you?" Fendal's eyes again found themselves wandering over to Cha'ni, once again finding Cha'ni's eyes were already fixed on him.

"I think I should be getting some sleep. Its been a long couple of days and I have to work again tonight." It was well into the early morning as the light of the second moon shown through the window shutters. Cha'ni got up and walked behind her fathers chair. She bent over to give him a peck on the cheek as she passed. "Good night, Fendal." She said as she disappeared into her room, closing the door behind her.

Fendal was disappointed that Cha'ni did not remain to hear more of their earlier adventures. Koloda noted his change of expression. "It is best that she left when she did." He explained "Her mother is dead and she doesn't like to be reminded of how it happened. She was very young at the time and did not understand."

"What do you mean? How did it happen?" Fendal was not being nosy, but compassionate, feeling that Koloda needed to talk to someone about it. He had probably never spoken to anyone concerning his wife's passing. It was not his way to involve others in his own pain and misery. Fendal knew him well enough to understand that. Koloda would have kept this sorrow in his gut for eternity rather than wear it on his sleeve for some stranger to take pity.

"It was my fault. I never should have let her continue the practice. She was bound to get caught sooner or later." He poured another cup of wine from the flask. Splashing just a little in his hurry. He took a large gulp of the fermented grape juice and continued. "She was still working as a bar maid at that place. She didn't often try to take jewelry but she must have been attracted to this particular piece. I was there setting in my usual corner. I would always observe the crowds and select someone for her to relieve of their heavy pouch."

"So you had grown more careful since your previous disasters." Fendal said to break the building tension. "I remember when you could just casually walk into that tavern and take the purse from some poor drunk without even thinking."

"I was more careful with her," He corrected. "I didn't want her making the same mistakes that I had in my past. I watched over her carefully, selecting just the right people at just the right time. I told her to leave the soldiers alone that night. They were not from around here. There was something very evil about them. Even their armor was black. I warned her to steer clear of that table. But there was a ring that each of the soldiers wore, a signet of some kind. She wanted one of them." He emptied the cup of wine once more in a single gulp. "They were drunk and unruly. A little rougher than humans normally were with her. She began her playful act with them, setting on their laps and drinking their ale as she kept pouring. She did everything right. She made sure they were falling down drunk before she tried to slip off one of their rings."

"Then what happened?" Fendal had become very involved in his friends story. His anticipation grew, yet he knew the overall tragic outcome.

"The lead soldier was furious when she had finally managed to take the ring from his finger. He knew almost immediately that she had grabbed it. I tried to intervene as he threw her off of his lap and pulled his dagger from his belt. He kept insisting that she took his ring although I kept insisting that he was mistaken. I stood between him and my wife who was laying on the floor. He shoved me aside and kicked her as she was trying to get up. The other soldiers stood up and drew their swords as others tried to help her. I drew my dagger and leapt onto the leaders back driving my blade into him. He swung around and threw me off as if I were nothing." Fendal could tell that Koloda was getting emotionally worked up over the tale and tried to once again break the tension. "I can't believe that the master of the rear attack missed with his dagger. More than once you saved our group with your skill."

"No, I did not miss. It was a good hit. My dagger remained in his back as I was thrown free of it. He turned back to my wife and kicked her again as he tore off her apron. The ring fell out of a pocket and rolled on the floor. He went berserk. He picked up the ring and put it back on his finger. He picked her up off the floor with one hand and began to throw her around the bar. I lunged at him with my other dagger in an attempt to draw his anger from her." He just shook his head. "You know that I am not good in face to face combat." Koloda lifted his shirt to reveal a large scar on his lower abdomen. "He impaled me with his dagger, up to the hilt, and lifted me as he did so. I got a good look at the gold, lions head ring that my wife had taken.

"How did you do that?" Fendal asked as Koloda lowered his shirt and tucked it into his breeches.

"I saw it several times as he mashed his fist into my face." He pointed to his patched eye. I was powerless to do anything to prevent it, being skewered and raised off of the floor. I thought for sure I would not escape death this time. I will never forget that ring, an intricately carved lions head with its mouth wide open. There was a gem set in the mouth." His mind wandered for a moment, picturing the finely crafted jewelry in his mind. "When I awoke several days later at the temple, I had been told that my wife was killed, and being an Elf, there was nothing that could be done to bring her back." His voice had grown weak by this time from the wine and the memories. He fell off to a deep sleep.

Fendal thought at that moment of the same words the priest at the temple used when they had brought Ach'med's body to them when he had been killed. They had also said that he could not be revived as he was Elf. The silence loomed between he and Koloda. There was nothing more that could be said. At least he had let the grieved Elf relinquish some of the burden and guilt by telling someone the story of his wife's demise. He watched the heavy one sleep and poked at the fire to restore some flame.

He had just put another log onto the fire, trying not to disturb his friend when he heard a muffled noise. Fendal looked up from the fire to see Cha'ni standing next to her fathers chair. She was staring directly at him. He was a bit surprised and astonished as he could not help but to smile. She stood in the doorway of her bedroom waving a beckoning finger towards him. The newly restored flames reflected off of her white, bare breasts. He looked closely at his passed out host, asleep and now beginning to snore.

Cha'ni took a step back into her bedroom, still motioning for him to follow. He shrugged his shoulders "What else can I do for now?" He said to himself. He hadn't even told Koloda about the lead he had on what might have happened to Ach'med's remains. That would have to wait until morning, he thought to himself and walked around the large table and chairs toward the open doorway. He took one last look at the back of his sleeping friend's head and closed the door behind him.

Chapter 13
Magic

"Have you seen Shi'roc?" Lorentz' voice called to Grefden in the training arena. The entire force of survivors were intensely battling each other and their instructors. Today would be the day when the real warriors would stand out. The true leaders would emerge from the continuous practice battles. Some would undoubtedly be injured, though not severely enough to be crippling. As Shi'roc had said, "Those who survive today's combat would be assigned to scavenger duty in the old Dwarven towns." And he indeed meant, those who survive. Several of the instructors had already drawn blood, eliminating the combatants from the realistic competition. Though this was friendly fighting, each participant knew that it could just as easily be a fight to the death.

"I have not seen my lord since this morning's meeting." Grefden replied as he ducked a swing of the students sword and parried for the counter swing. "Is there a problem?" He took a breath as he blocked another attack from a second trainee.

"No, not that I am aware of. Continue on." Lorentz turned back into the tunnel out of the great hall with Jantez and Gol close behind. Shi'roc had instructed the two humans to follow and learn from Lord Lorentz' books of magic. Although Lady A'mora had been their initial guide to the secrets of cryptical writings and chants that would enhance the powers of natural and unnatural elements, it was up to Lorentz to complete their mage training. Shi'roc knew that Lorentz would provide them with more offensive types of power than would A'mora. The three proceeded to the study chamber where they would today be exposed to new realms of mystical forces.

Lorentz motioned for the three to set in a circle around a small fire that was burning in the center of the sleeping area.

He pulled two small rolls of parchment from an inside pocket of his cloak. He handed one to Jantez and to Gol. The parchment was neatly wrapped and tied with a golden thread. "These scrolls contain the writings of very useful spell incantations." Lorentz began his lecture. His students sat motionless with the scroll in their hands. "The secret is to not utter a sound while studying them. The words are written with a special ink that reacts to the specific tones of the chant. The ink is created from the various elements required to cast the spells."

The two students were totally focused on Lorentz' words. They were very intent on learning all that he would share, all that they were capable of understanding. These two had been chosen well by Lady A'mora to begin the training. She had taught them much is a short period of time. They had learned to read the basic symbols of the mage chants and to understand their meaning. She had also showed them the countless motions that were performed with the arms while intoning the spells. Each movement was to be timed precisely with the spoken symbols. For certain spells, material components would be required. Usually these items would be natural elements such as coal, sulfur, diamond dust and more. The components would be sprinkled or crushed during the chant to release the energies held within. The secret of magic was in the understanding of science and its natural unleashed powers.

"The gold thread is a barrier that keeps the special inks protected from ambient vibrations. Once the thread is removed, the scroll is susceptible to all the tones of your voice." He paused dramatically. Even in his teachings, Lorentz had a flair for theatrical performance. These were remnants of his youthful performances at the school in his home town of Thormadore. Perhaps it was those theatrics that enabled him to enthrall audiences naturally. His abilities to lead armies also must stem from his past. "Once spoken correctly, the symbols will vanish from the page and the power of the elements released. Therefore, a scroll can only be used once, and it must be used correctly. If you fail in the perfection of its reading by the mispronunciation of the symbols or their order of use, the results may be unpredictable. The forces of the components may be released in an untimely order possibly causing more harm than good to those around you and yourself."

Jantez and Gol were allowed to absorb Lorentz' words of wisdom in a few moments of silence that followed. They each held the scrolls gingerly in their hands almost in fear of their potential powers. Lorentz watched as they carefully untied the golden wrappers and unrolled the thick roughened parchment revealing the symbols of power. They studied the inked markings by the fires flickering glow as Lorentz removed a large book of parchment writings from another pocket in his cloak.

The book was thick with pages and bound with a leather cover and lacing. Though it appeared bulky and heavy in his hands, it had not been noticeable in Lorentz' cloak. He opened the leather straps and carefully paged through it. He motioned his hand over each page as his eyes followed the symbols. His many years of mastery in the sciences allowed him to memorize many pages of the script within minutes. The symbols had become common place for him and this brief review of the spells each morning would allow him to perform almost any one of them on command. He had used most of these powers many times and carried an assortment of the material fragments and powders in the many hidden deep pockets of his cloak.

The two students, after what seemed likes hours of study, carefully rolled up the unread scrolls and retied the golden wrapping string. Lorentz closed and sealed his book of spells and returned it to its appropriate pocket. He reached out to the humans and retrieved the scrolls and pocketed them as he did the book. Jantez and Gol both looked a bit worn from the intensity of their study.

"Is there anything else that you will share with us today?" Asked Jantez, almost too exhausted to speak.

"No. We must take this one day at a time. Too much, too quickly would only increase the risk of error in your learning of the spells." He looked them over carefully. "You two should get some rest." He encouraged.

"Oh, no my lord. We must return to the great hall for our turn at combat training. We do not wish to be left out." Gol said as he slowly got to his feet.

"We thank you for your instruction this day. We shall return tomorrow for our next lesson." Jantez spoke as he also got to his feet to leave.

The two began to bow in respect to Lorentz before departing the chambers but were interrupted. "Who would be your instructor for this training?" Lorentz asked.

"Well; Grefden would be our combatant." Gol spoke as he raised from mid bow. A bit puzzled by the question. Lorentz had not seemed too interested in the training of the warriors since his arrival. He had left such details of the training schedules to Lord Shi'roc.

"The two of you would not survive long in your present depleted condition." Lorentz interjected, as he too stood up brushing the dust from his cloak. As he did, he pulled a small glass vial from another inside pocket. The container held a lightly colored blue liquid. He removed the cork stopper from the top of the vial making a small popping noise. As he waved the open tube under his nose, curiosity struck the two students.

"What is that my Lord, if we may ask?" Jantez pointed to the colored liquid that the mage was still inspecting. There seemed to be less than half an ounce in the container remaining.

"I have been carrying this for quite some years. If I remember correctly, it will return to you the energy you have expended on your studies. It should allow you to compete in the combat with your usual skill." Lorentz was not all together confident that he had the correct potion for the description he gave of its effect. He touched the tip of the vial to his finger and tilted it, just enough to moisten his finger. He then touched his finger to his tongue. The liquid had a sweet taste to it. "Yes, this should be the one. He handed the vial to Jantez.

Gol was not so convinced of Lord Lorentz' assurance. "If it is not? What then?" He asked of his tutor, a little skeptical of the unknown liquid. He and Jantez looked at it and waved it under their noses. It had an aroma of fruit freshly picked from the trees in the water cave. They then looked at Lorentz awaiting a reply.

He shrugged his shoulders and said. "We will have to find out, I guess. Remember, just enough for the both of you." He watched as first Gol put it to his lips.

It did indeed taste like a citrus fruit. The young Human smiled. "This has a pleasant taste. It must be good." He handed the remainder to Jantez who also downed the appealing mixture. He handed the receptacle back to Lord Lorentz and awaited a reaction. The two did indeed feel more refreshed and awake.

"Hurry now, before the potion wears off." Lorentz spoke as the humans passed through the curtain, exiting the chamber. "My regards to Grefden." He shouted after them. "..and my regrets." he added quietly to himself. "..if that wasn't the potion I thought it was."

He stepped back to put some more wood on the fire and returned to studying his book of spells. His concentration started to wander. He became concerned as to where Shi'roc had gone. He could be inspecting the forge and mining equipment. Lorentz thought to himself. No, that would be of no specific interest to him. He is not one to be concerned of how the weapons were forged, but that they were well crafted. Could he have escorted Lady A'mora and her students to the water cave shrine? Yes that must be it. He is inspecting the horses.

* * *

The cold breeze blew through his long black hair in the wastelands to the mountain's west. He had successfully evaded being spotted by the watchers as was his plan. The practice would do him good. The dead remnants of the trees and brush had been his cover as the warrior made his way toward the forest from which he had come more than two months ago. Shi'roc wore only his leathers, leaving his heavy plate mail armor hidden in the mountain caverns. It had been too long since he had some room to think, to be free, having been huddled in the mountain. The practice fighting with his students, had only teased at his keen abilities. There was no challenge for him, so he tasked himself to useful purpose. He followed the same path from which they had come. The tracks of their horses were long since covered over from the blowing dust. Soon he should be seeing the Dragon's remains. That was his first goal. He trotted silently meandering through the fallen woods. He knew that there was a possibility of being spotted by another of Moracles' creatures or worse. At least, being alone, he could not betray the secrets of the mountain if he were to be spotted or captured.

There it was up ahead. The hulking corpse of the red Dragon that they had slain earlier. He recalled that day clearly in his mind. He looked briefly at the ring of magic that his friend Lorentz, had given to him for protection. He also remembered the several words that released the powers enchanted within the ring. He had hesitated when he faced the Dragon, having forgotten those important words. Just last night, Lorentz had refreshed his memory as to the correct pronunciations of the mystical release words. Each word would enable him to unleash a different force at an enemy.

The beast's leathery skin was now tightly wrapped around its bones. Its huge armored scales were beginning to flake off of the now rotting skin. Its crimson color had turned to a pale gray. He walked around the beast as if inspecting a column of soldiers. He bent over to look into the rotted eye sockets. Then Shi'roc laid down his bow to rest on the beasts long neck and reached out to pull open its massive jaws. As he had hoped, the rows of sharp teeth were still primarily untouched. "These should do very well." He said to himself eyeing the rows of smaller teeth surrounded by the larger saber like projecting ones.

"Yes they would do nicely," answered a voice from nowhere and everywhere, startling Shi'roc.

Although the voice was pleasant and female, the shock was enough for him to drop the giant snout of the dragon and draw his sword. He had run into females before that were not as pleasant as their voice. Sorcerers trickery had bitten him more than once. He looked carefully over the other side of the beast, then quickly all around the area. He could not determine from whom or where the voice came. All was now silent except for the wind. That must have been it. The wind was playing tricks on his ears. He thought to himself.

"The smaller teeth make excellent arrow heads." The voice came again almost as an echo just as pleasant and non threatening as before.

Shi'roc was sure now that it wasn't the wind in his ears, so he answered just to play along with whomever was taunting him. "Yes, I know. And the larger ones will provide for excellent daggers. Strong enough to pierce even plate armor with enough strength behind the thrust." He spoke to no direction in particular as he continued to hold his sword and search the area. He began to feel foolish wandering around the dragon searching for the source of the voice, and answering it as well. Was he getting too old for all of this? Was he that exhausted? He did not feel worn and he was only one hundred and thirty years of age.

"You have learned much," the voice continued as Shi'roc continued his search still not able to pinpoint even a direction for the voice. "You have become quite resourceful in the time that I have been watching you."

"Oh? And how long has that been if I may ask?" He continued the game trying to keep some control over the situation. He continued to step backward toward his bow.

"Ever since you and your friends had slain the evil Lord Magdelan." The voice was now focused directly behind him.

Shi'roc spun with sword raised, ready to strike if necessary. He turned to see a beautiful woman wearing a light plate mail breast plate and a golden helmet. Her armor was so polished that it reflected the sunlight like a mirror. She stood straight and tall with the butt of her spear placed on the ground next to his bow. She was a safe distance from the potential swing of his sword. He froze, still posed to strike out. He did not look into her face, for he knew of demons that could control even the strongest of warriors with their stare. "Who are you?" he demanded "How do you know that I had slain Magdelan?" He continued, keeping focused on her mid section for any sign of movement, totally avoiding any eye contact.

"I am Alena," she said simply as a fact. "You need not fear me. I am sympathetic to your cause." She said in her attempt to convince Shi'roc to lower his sword. She was indeed the Goddess Alena and could strike him dead if she so desired. Though Shi'roc had no beliefs in such gods, he was aware of their legend.

"Oh? And which cause is that?" he teased her on. Even if he did believe in the gods of that Lorentz had told him, why would the Goddess Alena come to see him?. She must be a demon sent by Moracles to kill him or worse.

"The cause to defeat Moracles of course." She stood very still having anticipated Shi'roc's reluctance to believe. "I only wish to talk with you. You may look at me."

"No!" Shi'roc snapped. "I will not be overcome by your powers." He said still looking down at her armored body. Her form fitted protection was as overpowering to him as if he had looked into the eyes of a demon. "Go. Leave here or I shall be forced to kill you." He was still trying to get a sense of evil from the encounter but did not feel it. Though alert and ready, he did not feel the rush of adrenaline as when fighting a known evil foe.

Alena became impatient with him. "How can I prove to you that I am who I say?" she said sternly knowing of his disbeliefs. "If I were here to harm you, would I have not attacked you when you were not looking?" She tried to reason with him.

Shi'roc thought for a moment of something that only a god or goddess might know. "If you know that I was involved with the death of Lord Magdelan, then who was with me?" Shi'roc knew that his partners in the triumph had sworn to secrecy not to reveal their involvement. Fame is not something that they relished. Back then, they wished to travel freely, to continue their lives in peace. Shi'roc alone wished to find and destroy evil wherever he could. Unfortunately, those of great power would often be avenged by their underlings or their masters as the case may be. It was best not to brag of such a victory as slaying such a dark Lord.

"Your companions were Koloda, Fendal, Ariel and Grog." She gave him the shocking truthful answer without even a thought. She stood with confidence that this information would convince him of her identity.

Shi'roc slowly lowered his sword as he raised his head to face her. She was stunningly beautiful. Her auburn flowing hair rushed from beneath her golden helmet. Her brown eyes were warm and passionate, unlike any he had ever encountered. Her form was strong yet sensuous. Only a goddess of good could possess such grace and beauty, he thought. He realized that was why he did not feel the fire of combat. Though satisfied with her answer, he was still mystified as to why she should appear to a non believer such as himself.

"You are wondering why I am here." she said as she took a casual step forward. "That, I have already told you. I have been watching you since your youth. It is time that the circle be completed." She spoke with a mystical amused charm.

"I do not understand." Shi'roc replied as he sheathed his sword, still in awe of her beauty. "Complete what circle?" He had caught on to her words of mystery.

"It has been know that you would be the one to defeat Moracles since your encounter with the Golden Dragon." She watched as the pieces began to fall in place in Shi'roc's mind.

"The Dragon that we freed from Magdelan's powers?" He wondered. "What did the Dragon have to do with this Moracles?" He leaned on the carcass of the beast that he had defeated, as an irony came to mind.

Alena moved over to a boulder directly in front of him and sat down. "Though the Dragon was kept by Magdelan's magic, it was Moracles who had entrapped him being Magdelan's apprentice."

Shi'roc bolted upright. "Moracles was Magdelan's apprentice?" He shouted as he turned and took a step away from her. "He must have become quite powerful since then to be able to destroy all of this." He motioned with a wide arc of his arm. He was feeling the rush of battle once again as they spoke of the new dark lord. "How do you know that I will defeat him?" He turned back to her. Then a sudden realization struck him. "In your eyes, my life must consist only of a few days. Less perhaps." He had remembered some of what Lorentz had told him of the gods and their timelessness. The past, present and future were almost the same to them.

"That was a wise deduction." She said with a bit of surprise. "You are correct. In my eyes you have already defeated him. But you must continue on your own path or that future for you may change." She warned.

"Then why are you telling me all of this?" Shi'roc threw up his hands in frustration. "If the future is set, how can I change what is going to happen?" He asked.

"I am here to tell you to be careful. Do not take chances as you have in the past." She said more seriously. "This is not some adventure for you and your friends to play out." She became quite stern as if scolding a child. "The future of the world is at stake here." She stood and moved to be face to face with him. "There are evil gods who wish to move from the lower planes of hell and control this world as its rulers." She said more softly as she reached out a hand to touch his wind worn cheek. "In time, Moracles can make this happen." She reached over to touch his bow. She picked it up and handed it to him. "May your arrows always hit their target." She said.

Shi'roc was still a little confused by this whole encounter. "Thank you." He replied as he slung the bow over his shoulder with his quiver. "But for now I have much work to do." He began to turn back toward the woods where he was going to hunt.

"Why are you headed for the distant forest?" She asked. "Aren't you going to remove the Dragons teeth and scales?" She added as Shi'roc stopped in mid step.

He turned to her to explain. "The smaller of the Dragons teeth will make fine tips for the arrows. We will need strong feathers for the fletchings. I must hunt some large birds for those."

"Wait a moment. I can help you." She then pursed her lips and let out a gentle high pitched whistle. The sounds were those that a hawk or falcon might make. Shi'roc heard the flapping of large strong wings as Alena held out her arm. A large brown spotted falcon appeared from nowhere, just as Alena had to Shi'roc. The bird landed on her outstretched arm fluttering its wings. "This is Dobo, my pet," she said as an introduction. She then spoke softly to the bird. "Shi'roc will need some of your feathers."

"No, please. I would not harm your bird or take its feathers. Besides, I would need much more than he has to give." His words were sincere. He would not harm her pet whether or not she was a goddess.

"Dobo may surprise you." She smiled and turned to the bird. "Go ahead Dobo, shed some feathers for Shi'roc." As she spoke the bird spread its wings and began a flutter that released a stream of feathers. The motion continued until a small pile had accumulated on the ground.

Shi'roc looked on in amazement since the fallen feathers seemed to have no effect on the bird. The falcon showed no signs of distress nor loss of feathers from its wings, yet it had shed enough feathers to create three birds of its size. Dobo stopped the fluttering and squawked as it looked down on its gift to Shi'roc. Alena stepped aside from the pile of feathers so that Shi'roc could gather them up.

"Thank you, Dobo. That was quite a trick." Shi'roc bent down and opened a small sack that he had strapped to his belt. He gingerly fingered through the pile and loaded the feathers into the sack. He could feel that these would make very strong and sturdy fletchings. He stood up again to thank them but found that both Alena and the falcon had vanished. He looked around in all directions as he heard the flutter of the birds wings. He spoke to himself almost in a whisper. "Thank you Alena. I will be careful." He thought for a moment about what had just taken place. There must have been more to her reason for visiting him.

"Your welcome." Came the reply in the breeze as Shi'roc went back to his business with the Dragon's remains.

* * *

Lorentz' concentration began to fail as he mixed his powders and elements by the fire. All day, no one had seen Shi'roc. There was no word of his whereabouts. He carefully set his book aside and reached into the back part of the inside of his cape. From a pocket, he removed a small glass globe that fit nicely into the palm of his hand. The flames of the fire reflected through it providing an orange glow. He then removed from another pocket a small brass supporting stand for the globe. He carefully set the stand on a large stone near the fire and placed the smooth sphere into it. He then paged through his book once again to find a particular spell.

Staring closely into the sphere he concentrated on the intricately carved ring that he had given to Shi'roc. Though powerful with protective enchantments, Lorentz had another reason for endowing the treasure to his friend. He quietly recited the magical words from the book as he stroked the glass sphere with his finger tips in a circular motion.

"Regula videum transit nostra." He repeated as he peered into the purity of the clear glass. A moment later, he could now see the image of the ring that had transformed from his memory into the sphere. Its first cloudy appearance cleared to a sharp vision of the jewelry. As the mage continued to concentrate the picture expanded to show Shi'roc's hand, then more, to Shi'roc himself. Yes, he was alive and unharmed. Panning the vision further, it appeared that he was standing in the wasteland. "What could he be doing out there alone?" He asked of himself and continued the expansion. He saw the corps of the Dragon and it appeared that Shi'roc was not alone. He was indeed talking to someone, yet Lorentz could not locate anyone else with him. As long as he was in no danger, Lorentz was satisfied, yet he just realized that Shi'roc was not wearing his armor.

He sported his bow and sword only. What was he doing out there?

"Your friend is in no danger, actually quite safe." A feminine voice emanated from the sphere, snapping Lorentz' concentration. The image of his friend wavered and faded being replaced by the beautiful image of Alena. Lorentz recognized her image immediately. "Shi'roc will now be under my protection. His safety is vital to your quest." The image faded before he had the time to question the goddess.

"What did she mean by that?" He whispered to himself as Ilo burst through the privacy curtain into the chamber.

"M'lord. You are needed quickly in the great hall. There has been an injury." He puffed, almost out of breath. He must have run the entire way. "Lady A'mora and the others are too far in the water cave to reach in time. Gor has run looking for Lord Shi'roc. Please hurry."

Ilo departed as swiftly as he had arrived. Lorentz didn't even have the time to ask what had happened or to whom. He hastily returned the ball and stand into the appropriate pockets of his cloak. He then grabbed his book, tied it shut and secured it into another pocket before rushing out to the tunnels.

* * *

The time seemed as hours since Ilo had rushed out for help. The crowds of warriors stood in a circle around a single man laying on the stone floor. Sha'la was frantically trying to stop the bleeding from the near mortal wound. They had removed his armor and tied cloth bandages around the torso over the gash. Grefden was barely conscious, fighting hard against the pain in example to his students. If he was to die, he would leave this earth as a warrior without crying out or in shame of his past.

"I can not stop the flow of blood. The wound is too deep for my healing." Sha'la muttered to her wounded companion. As one of Lorentz' followers and a believer in the powers of Mirana, she did possess some limited healing abilities. She held Grefden's limp hand and squeezed hard as she prayed. "Forgive me, my love, for I can not heal you." She whispered into his ear.

"Forgive me sir. I had not intended to defeat you so severely." Jantez apologized as he held a cup of water to the dying man's lips. He had admired him as an instructor and a warrior in the finest meaning of the word. "I owe you for all that I have learned."

Grefden sipped the water as it flowed past his lips. His strength was failing and he would soon drift into the unconscious state prior to death. With his last breath he spoke to Jantez. "Mourn me not, for it is you who will have to lead the rest of these warriors. It was your strength and cunning that overpowered me." His voice faded to a whisper as Ilo called from the mouth of the cavern.

"Lorentz is on his way." He cried over the vast cavern as several of the others looked at him and shook their heads. His enthusiasm dropped realizing that it was too late. He walked over to Grefden as the crowd silently began to disperse leaving only Jantez and Sha'la at the dead man's side. Ilo heard the woman warrior weep for her lover while praying for the Goddess, Mirana, to keep his soul to defend her forest in the heavens.

Lorentz bolted through the cave entrance, pushing his way past the somber warriors. He could feel the anguish in the air as he made his way to the three of them kneeling over the body. He recognized Shi'roc's body guard, Grefden, sprawled out on the rocky ground amongst blood soaked rags.

"It is too late my Lord." Sha'la looked up at him, with tears flowing down her cheek. She still held Grefden's warm bloodied hand.

"Nonsense." Lorentz blurted out as he unwrapped the red bandages and performed a quick survey of the injury. Grefden's abdomen had been cleanly split apart as if an animal being gutted and skinned. His intestines were oozing out among the torn muscles. Lorentz then pulled out his amulet with the symbol of his goddess, Mirana, from under his cloak. He then began to chant the healing words as he pushed the exposed innards back into the body. Sha'la assisted by putting pressure on the muscles to hold the split together. As Lorentz' words began to echo, the cavern became alive with hope.

"I think he is healing." Ilo whispered to Jantez as the others began to reform around the group.

Lorentz now placed both hands around the wound, still oozing but slowly forming back into its original state. His hands and Sha'la's were now covering the wound as they both continued chanting their prayers to bring life back to the warriors body. A slight groan wheezed through the man's lips as his closed eyes began to flutter.

"He is alive!" Exclaimed Jantez, relieved of his grief from slaughtering his teacher. Grefden would soon be back in action, wielding his sword and shield. He thought to himself. The others began to cheer.

Grefden wheezed and opened his eyes to see Lord Lorentz looking closely down on him. "I live?" he asked in a whisper, not entirely sure. He felt weakness and he was still in pain.

"Yes, but barely. I was almost too late." Lorentz said with a smile. "But you were not dead as the others had thought. Only in the state where unconsciousness ruled." He shook his head. "Ilo, get some water for us to clean him up." Lorentz grasped the blood soaked clothing and tried to wipe his own hands of Grefden's blood. "Oh, by the way, I have located Shi'roc." Grefden's eyes widened in query, too weak to actually ask. "He is well and will be back with us soon." Is all the Elf would say.

The crowd began to cheer again as Lorentz got to his feet. He washed his hands in the bowl of water that Ilo brought and then handed it to Sha'la to do the same. She carefully wiped the blood from the wound area and washed her own hands. The gash had still been visible and not entirely healed so with some fresh cloth, she tied bandages around him.

"Leave him still for now and let him rest. I shall return for him later." Lorentz announced to the crowd as he began to leave. "He will be well enough in a few days." He then turned to Ilo. "Tell me, Ilo, what happened here to Grefden."

Jantez approached. "It was my fault." He admitted with his head held low in sorrow. "I was too eager to defeat him and be chosen as a leader. I should not have fought him so. I took advantage of his tired condition having been fighting the others all day."

"No. It was my fault." Lorentz insisted nodding to Jantez. "You were exhausted after your training with me this morning. Do you remember?" Jantez nodded in reply. "I had not realized the mixture that I had given you had become so potent after all of these years in my possession."

"What mixture?" Inquired Ilo. Looking back and forth between the two. Lorentz smiled at the two survivors, turned and walked off without a reply

Chapter 14
Waiting

The dining hall was dimly lit by the flickering light of two lonely candles that were suspended in the chandelier. The rest of the castle was dark and chilled, with no one to light the fires in the kitchens or the sleeping quarters. So much the better for the Bone. It was still to warm as far as he was concerned. He preferred it cold since his native home was icy as the great northern plains. Yes, he was from a level of hell where the warmth of the fires did not reach. Though his kingdom was small and not well known, he had still been its ruler, at least until Moracles had plucked him from the ethereal plane of timeless travel.

The smooth stone walls were richly decorated with paintings and tapestries. Moracles apparently spared no expense when it came to the luxuries he desired. Whether or not the artisans were paid or forced into the efforts of the works, one could only surmise, as did the Bone, who sat at the head of one of the two long tables. Each table was surrounded by heavy wooden chairs and were placed parallel to the length of the room.

All was silent except for the repeated tapping sound of his fingers on the wooden table top. He had slumped his giant skeletal frame into the heavy padded leather chair. Though it was exquisitely carved, it was far beneath the stature of the Bone, let alone too small for him to set comfortably. His legs were extended beneath the table and his hooked tail swayed behind him with the rhythm of his tapping finger.

He was bored. So bored with no one to torture or screech at since all the soldiers and creatures were still on patrol in search of the intruders. He had been through the entire castle. Even through the impassable areas by normal means. Yes, the castle was full of secret passages and unmarked doorways. All of which could be penetrated by way of his flaming stallion, Blackfire, who was able to travel through the ethereal plane and bring the Bone to those locations that he was not meant to see. He had thought about another tour through the fortress.

He reached down into a small black velvet pouch that dangled from his belt. From it he removed a small statue, about six inches tall. The item resembled his powerful flaming horse. It was coal black with a fiery mane and hooves. The skeletal creature set the statue on the table and studied it carefully for a moment then thought better of releasing the animal from its present form. He returned it to the pouch.

The statue was indeed the stallion, Blackfire, in its dormant state or rather, its imprisoned form. It was the Bone's way of keeping his pet handy without fear of it being overpowered by Moracles and taken away. Though they were both trapped within the bounds of the castle while Moracles was away, he could at least travel ethereal within the castle. He continued to eye the wall decorations and tapping his bony fingers until the quiet irritated him so.

"They have been gone for a week with no report from anyone." He mused to himself. "What could be taking so long? The incompetent fools." Even the sound of his own voice became irritating. He ceased his rolling fingers and stood up, pushing the chair back from the table. The screech of the wooden chair against the smooth stone floor broke the silence of the castle. As the echo died he slowly but deliberately paced the floor along the walls and studied each work of art.

Though his twisted morals afforded him evil strengths, he could also appreciate fine craftsmanship and would collect such works for himself. The jeweled dagger, for one, that hung from his belt was such a treasure. It was taken from the dismembered hand of a human warrior during the slaughter. The Bone himself had pried it from his clenched fist. The man had bravely defended his town near the far edge of the once flourishing Elven Forest.

He studied the finely woven threads of the tapestry that had erroneously depicted the so called battle. It was indeed a slaughter as he remembered it. Moracles must have wanted it remembered as a great victory to have the artist sew such a scene. The fabric depicted the army of Magdarn soldiers up against hundreds of armored human soldiers. One section meticulously showed violent hand to hand combat at the foot of the great stone walls surrounding the town.

There were no such walls, or soldiers for that matter. Only a few of the inhabitants had even worn armor. Most of the townspeople were simple farmers fighting to protect their crops with rakes and hoes. The town itself consisted of some stone and wooden frame buildings. Most of the homes were constructed of straw covered wooden frames. Many of the decimated towns of those days were much the same. Each one in turn was destroyed with its inhabitants slaughtered or captured for the purposes of torture or worse at the hands of the Bone and Moracles' other henchmen.

The room was indeed a tribute to the cleansing of the land, as Moracles would have it. Another tapestry was devoted to the flight of the Elves who had remained in the woods as the Magdarn took the women and slaughtered the families. The blood of the young virgins was drained and used in the writing of Moracles great spell book that decorated his desk. The council of Elves had been skinned to bear the pages of that same book. There was no glory or honor in any of these battles, but then that was not the purpose that the evil mage sought. Terror and annihilation of all that was good was the goal. All would either follow his ways or die horribly. This was the way that he was taught. This was the way of the God 'Hartes' and Goddess, 'Lolith' who would some day claim this world for their new kingdom.

The Bone was pleased by what he saw. "Yes. This is how it should be again when we find those intruders." He mumbled to himself as he eyed another painting of his armies trampling human soldiers into the ground. Some of the bodies were dismembered or beheaded. Blood soaked torsos were shown dragged through the mud.

He finally stopped at a painting of Moracles as a younger apprentice. He stood on a rock, wearing his magi robes, surrounded by flowing fiery lava. It appeared to be a cave of some sort. Possibly the center of the world. No, wait. The Bone thought. It was in the underworld, in the realm of Hartes. Moracles was performing a summons of a fire beast that was rising out of the flames. Its skin was crimson red and it had horns protruding from its forehead. Its claws appeared razor sharp. The colors of the paint were vibrant and real. The artists eye was sharp with detail as if he had witnessed the act for himself. "Very impressive work for an earther." He said as he looked for the artists mark. He found a small symbol in the lower right corner. The dim candle flicker was barely sufficient to make out details but it appeared to be an 'H' circled with a flame stroke.

"Could it be?" He wondered. "Do the gods have time for such creations?" He mused at the thought of Hartes actually setting down to an artists easel and painting such a work.

* * *

For a week, the various creature armies had been patrolling the known lands of Moracles. Day by day and step by step, they left no stone unturned in their search for the intruders. There had been no sign of anyone passing through the region. All of the rotted forests and even the great desert 'Feradune' had been scoured by the inhuman and human forces of the dark lord.

There were but a few of the original 'Magdarn' soldiers, hired by Moracles as his personal guard. No more than fifty remained to ride once again the trails that brought them glory. As they were of human heritage, most were now far too old for being warriors. They too were sent out into the vast remnants of the land. Their direction as laid out by the Bone was into the old towns that they had destroyed decades ago. It was they who were depicted in the tapestries, powerful, bold soldiers in full armor plate, black as the night. Though their numbers had dwindled and their age had made them slower, their pride was still in tack, and orders were orders. They would sweep each of the building remains for any sign of life.

They followed the old paths that they had taken years past. Back then, there were forests and animals to hunt. Food was plentiful as they made their way from town to town, pillaging and murdering anyone who could not hide themselves. Now all that was left were dried out tree trunks and tumble weeds. The place where the towns had been were barely recognizable. Still they checked each burnt or fallen roof. They knocked over any remaining stone walls. Even the town wells were inspected and found to be dry.

The last area had been inspected and they were on their way to return to the castle deep into the canyons. Their report would be as empty as the lands they rode. Would it please the Bone? Perhaps not, but they would tell it anyway.

* * *

"Icht ta poo," I will obey, the creature said to itself as a reminder that this long journey on foot was at the insistence of their new leader, the Bone. They did not have horses, nor would their bulky bodies be able to ride well if they did. This general and his clan had drawn the worst possible assignment. It was indeed the furthest away from the stronghold. These piggish creatures had been walking for a great distance and were just now near the mountains ahead. They were nearing the edge of Moracles' power. Another day's walk and they would be at the foot of their goal. The sun had set behind the great mountains leaving an orange glow to the clouded sky.

For two weeks they had scoured the land in between the castle and the mountains. Nothing had they found but the endless dead wood that had covered most of the region. No signs of life, not vegetation or even water could be found. They had run out of food and there was no means of acquiring more. The fifty troops were exhausted and in need of a moral boost. Even a good fight would make their trip seem worth while.

"Rogcha dorca." The general called out to his soldiers as they had spread out through the desolate terrain. The order to make camp was given. It was now in the deep winter for the valley. Several fires were lit to keep them from freezing through the night. There was certainly enough fire wood in the area though no food to be cooked. The ground was frozen hard and sleeping was unbearable.

* * *

For weeks the survivors had been systematically scavenging the remains of the old Dwarven towns. They had started cautiously with the town on the southern most peak, where Shi'roc and his trainees, had first emerged onto the eastern slope of the mountain. The work parties had operated in shifts. One shift to gather any usable items while two others would patrol and watch for any outside activity. Ilo and his father, Maac-To, each led one of the patrol parties that surrounded the town while it was being carefully ransacked. Kura organized the scavenger hunt for any items such as wood, cloth, clothing and metals. These were to be brought below and reworked into useful tools and weapons.

Each town took almost a week to completely search. This was due to the caution required in not leaving any trace of their presence. They maintained silence using their hand signals to communicate and never being out of sight of another. The raids were extremely successful, and no one had been injured or had encountered any outsiders. Everything that was of use was now being recycled by the women and craftsmen of the Dwarven peaks.

Grefden had completely recovered from his mortal wound received during the training contest. He was now back at training those who were not successful in the competition. Although many of the combatants were wounded while exhibiting their skills as warriors, almost all of them returned to continue their training.

Shi'roc was pleased that the grueling training had brought out the best in these people. He had originally thought them to be weak and cowardly for hiding through generations. He had expected far more to drop out of the soldiers ranks and help with the mining operation or preparation of the other equipment needed for the inevitable battle.

Shi'roc was inspecting the weapons and equipment that had thus far been forged and assembled by the Dwarven craftsmen. They had been collecting each piece in a chamber near the base of the great hall. This was the same room where the training weapons were first stored. These new pieces were quite an improvement over the training swords and bows.

He picked up one of the short swords to inspect it as Utar and two of the other Dwarven council members entered the chamber carrying more swords and metal plate armor.

"Does this please you, Shi'roc?" The elder spoke, startling the Elf. The council had never called him by his rightful title of 'Lord' as the others had. They did not believe in titles, though they still held their pious attitudes as the Dwarven elders. Shi'roc had come to accept this since the first meeting of the council.

Shi'roc still did not trust the Dwarves as he felt they held back important information. Information such as the abundance of materials in the towns above and the natural recourses of the mountain itself. He felt that after all this time, the Dwarves would be more open about what they knew. He knew that there was more to be told.

"I am quite satisfied with the quality of your work." He said as he twirled the shinny new sword in his hands. He balanced the hilt on the back of his wrist to check its weight. "I can see why Moracles' armies would covet such craftsmanship." He complimented them with a slight nod as they set up the carried swords and armor for his inspection.

The Dwarves were very proud of their work. Though quality took time and time was uncertain, Shi'roc had hoped that more would have been produced since the operation had begun. He was unskilled at the forging and tooling of metal weapons and armor and he had expected more progress. He continued his inspection as the Dwarves left the room. He had been keeping mental notes of what items had been created for the new armies and what other items were still needed.

Of the newly forged weapons, he counted six long swords, three short swords, various pieces and sizes of plate mail armor. All were of the best designs he had ever seen. There was also a collection of carved items such as bows, arrows, shields and war hammers. They had made good use of the wooden furniture from the deserted Dwarven towns.

The long and short bows were strong and tight. Shi'roc checked that the arrow shafts were straight. A variety of sizes had been carved including short bolts for the cross bows of which two more of the mechanized units had been crafted. He tested both for strength and smooth operation.

As he had instructed, the arrow tips were made from the small teeth of the Dragon, as many as he had collected. These would pierce even his own armor. Unfortunately, there were only fifty such tips. The remainder of the arrow heads would be of the forged metal blades. The feathers provided by the Goddess Alena, or rather her falcon, Dobo, were glued onto the wooden shafts with a tree sap mixture from the recently grown trees in the water cave.

The Dragon's skin and hard scales were converted into an assortment of defensive shielding. The smaller scales were made into bucklers. The leathery skin was used as straps, fastened to the scales to be worn around the fore arm or hand. Some of the scales were large enough for full size shields. He claimed one of those for himself, fearing another encounter with a fire beast. The remaining leather had been sewn into body armor. The sun bleached hide of the dragon was very tough and would easily deflect glancing blows from edged weapons.

There was not nearly enough of the weaponry or armor for all of the people there in the mountain. Shi'roc felt as though he should inspect the mining and forging operation even if he knew nothing of the trades himself. Perhaps his visit could further inspire the workers to increase productivity.

*   *   *

Lorentz was instructing Kura in the use of the staff for defensive purposes as he had promised a month ago. Kura, as all Dwarves, had extended patience since he expected to live a long life of over six hundred years. His wife's grand father was himself just beyond that age now. Kyman had been moving slower and his mind was not as sharp as it had been in the past. He would soon have to pass on the burdens of the survivors to the next elder Dwarf as new chief.

"Hold the staff at its center with both hands. Your right palm facing up with you left down." Lorentz instructed as he showed the younger Dwarf the proper grasp and stance of the heavy piece of wood. The stick that the Goddess, Mirana had given to the Dwarf, was slightly taller then he, at about four feet. Its shaft was smooth and straight with the golden oak leaf head piece that the priest believed to have magical powers.

He gave the weapon back to Kura to practice the motion of snapping the wrists to invoke the speed and strength for which the staff was designed. He lectured on its proper use and the philosophy of when a priest should engage in combat and when not to. "You should never use it to attack. A good priest should only fight as a last resort or in defense of others." Kura nodded his understanding of the instructions and continued the wrist movements.

Lorentz picked up one of the practice, wooden long swords and began a thrusting motion toward Kura. Understanding quickly the use of the stick, he was able to block each thrust with the twist of his wrists. "Notice that when the staff has deflected the blade, your opponent is left with a vulnerable opening to his body. Use the end of the staff to jab at the body." He then showed the Dwarf how to adjust the grip as the motion was made smooth from the block to the jab.

Jantez and Gol were watching their mage tutor instruct Kura with the weapon. "I prefer the sword to a staff." The young Human said to his partner loud enough for Lorentz to hear. The two were themselves practicing with their real swords, having graduated to the proficient ranks of warriors. The two went on battling hard and heavy with sword and shield.

"There is a time to fight and a time to refrain from fighting." Lorentz replied. "Kura should not have to fight as his talents as a healer will be more important to the rest of you." He continued the exercise with the Dwarf, who was intent on being capable to defend himself should the need arise. He was performing quite well for his first lesson. The Dwarf's natural strength aided his abilities with the staff.

Lady A'mora entered the great hall with her other students close behind. Jantez was momentarily distracted as he was facing in the direction of that entrance. He had not been able to spend any time with her since the training assignments had changed. His initial attempts at magic had been instructed and inspired by the young lady. His efforts now were spent with Lord Lorentz as his mage instructor and the rest of his time was used in training as a warrior.

His distraction caused him pain as Gol lunged at him with his sword. They both had become very strong at wielding the weapons that now was not to Jantez' favor. He let out a yell as Gol withdrew the bloodied sword from the injured man's side. The cry caught the attention of all in the cavern. He stumbled backward dropping his shield and sword as he grasped at the gash in his side. He was fortunate to have so many healers near by to assist him. Grefden had not been so fortunate a few weeks before.

A'mora ran up the rocky carved path to the fallen man as did the others. Kura, having been closest, began to chant as he clenched the wound in his own hands. Lorentz looked on as the Dwarven priest performed his rightful duties without hesitation. A tribute to himself and his tutor, A'mora. The blood quickly began to coagulate from the opening. By the time A'mora had gotten to Jantez, the bleeding was almost stopped.

Jantez was staring at the beautiful priestess to keep his mind off of the pain that was slowly dissipating. She reached into the folds of her robe for a bundle of linen bandages that she quickly began to shred into strips. She looked again at the wound that Kura had so fervently been tending as he continued his chant. Her eyes widened in amazement as she saw that the gash had been completely sealed and only the scar remained. It too was much smaller than she would have believed. Kura's healing strength had become equal to her own in the time they had spent together.

One of her other students handed A'mora a cup of water that she held to Jantez' lips. He sipped from the cup as Kura broke his trance. "Thank you M'Lady." He spoke formally to her while in the presence of others. Their conversations in private had been much less formal. "Thank you as well my friend." He spoke to Kura, who had just realized the potency of his healing.

A'mora just smiled at Jantez understanding his attempt at deceiving the others, especially while Lorentz looked on. Ignoring the perceived protocol, she leaned over and gave him a kiss that could not be mistaken as that of friendship.

Kura took the remaining water in the cup and a cloth and wiped gently at the wound area to see for himself that the gash was completely healed. He too was surprised at the result although he did feel a bit exhausted. He looked up at Lady A'mora for her approval of his work. She nodded to him in response. He got back on his feet using his staff to support himself in his weakened state. He turned to the mage and said "I think I should go and rest." As Lorentz nodded to him with a smile.

"That is certainly enough training with your staff for today." Lorentz said.

Shi'roc had entered the cavern from the weapons alcove, having heard the scream and then silence. He too rushed up a stairway carved into the stone, to the landing where he saw the others gathered. He had arrived just in time to see A'mora kissing Jantez. He again became uneasy, not understanding these feelings inside of him. Could this be the pains of jealousy? He wondered. Could he actually care that much for her?

The crowd began to disperse as Lady A'mora spoke quietly to Jantez, still unaware of Shi'roc's presence. "You should rest for a few days to be sure that the healing is sufficient." Although the skin had taken hold and the wound was visibly closed, the internal healing would continue for a while longer. He had not lost that much blood due to the quickness of the Dwarf. He would still be weak from the trauma.

"But I have watcher duty tonight on the eastern slope. I have never missed my turn." Jantez insisted. "I should be on my way to the secret passage to the town."

"I will take your watch." Shi'roc interjected. Jantez and A'mora turned to look at him.

"You M'lord?" Questioned the injured Human, still laying on his back.

"Is there an objection to my standing watch?" He said with a raised eyebrow to the younger man. "I am familiar now with your silent signals as you have taught us. I know the passage to the town above." Shi'roc was being a bit candid about wanting to take watch over the eastern side of the mountain.

Ever since they had ransacked the towns and realized there was an unprotected approach to the hidden tunnels, Shi'roc had insisted that watchers be posted near each of the secret town entrances to the tunnels. The eastern side of the mountains would be the first place that Moracles' forces would approach, if they should be looking. This would also give him the opportunity to think in solitude about how to increase the production of weapons and armor.

"No sir. Not at all," came Jantez reply as he tried to prop himself up. A'mora and Lorentz helped him to his feet. He leaned on her with his arm around her shoulder for support.

"A'mora, I would seek your council on an important matter. Would you walk with me a while?" Shi'roc felt the need to separate her from Jantez. "Your apprentices can tend to Jantez." He said as he turned to walk down the rocky stairs with A'mora close behind him. They stopped momentarily at the base of the great hall.

"What is it that troubles you?" She asked as she took his arm in her hands. They began to walk out toward the connecting passages to the old Dwarven town. He began speaking to her in a language other than those spoken in the mountain. She understood that he intended not to be over heard and after some concentration, she was able to respond in that same dialect. She had been practicing her skills in comprehending other languages, at least the more commonly used ones such as Elvish and Dwarvish.

"There is still something missing regarding the Dwarves here in the mountain." He said again expressing his distrust of them. Not just Dwarves in general as had been his past problem, but the council in particular, Kyman.

"Why do you still think the Dwarves are holding something back? Have they not been mining and forging the metals as they said?" She proceeded through the dark tunnels holding on to Shi'roc's hand for guidance. She had not stopped to create any magical light and depended on Shi'roc for sight on the dark the journey through the tunnel.

"You can tell if someone is lying, can't you?" She answered him affirmatively although he knew that both her and Lorentz had this ability. He had not called upon them directly to use it before, but he had an idea that would expose the council if they had been keeping secrets. "Would you join me in inspecting the operations tomorrow? I may need your support."

"Of course I will help if I can." She said with a smile that could be felt more than seen. She held on close to him as they continued quickly to the stairway that led up into the remains of the town. For some reason, she felt a need to be close to him. She was not sure if her feelings for him were increasing or if it was what Lorentz had told her about his vision of 'Alena' and her visit with Shi'roc. She felt somewhat protective since she had saved his life just before their arrival at the mountain. That action was also inspired by a vision. She had been warned that Shi'roc was in danger and that she must save him.

"Are you going to stand the watch alone?" She asked when they arrived at the stairway opening.

"This post only requires one watcher as I have set up the observers network. I will be in sight of others above. There is no need to worry." His own words reminded him of what the goddess Alena had said about not taking chances. "Do you know the way back to our chamber from here?"

"Actually, I believe I would be lost since I had no light on this journey. I might miss a critical turn or fork in the passages. She said a little mischievously. "Perhaps I should stay with you on your watch." She said with a flurtive smile, though the expression would go unseen.

"It will be bitterly cold up there." Shi'roc pointed up the stairs, again forgetting that the motion would go unnoticed. His relaxed mind was allowing him access to his emotions. She had a natural ability, it seemed, to relax him. Until now he had not related that fact to emotions.

"I will be able to keep warm." She said as she began recounting an incantation in her mind for warmth. "In fact, I can keep us both warm." She moved close to him and put her arms around him. He did not resist as they walked up the stairs to the town.

* * *

There was indeed a cold wind blowing down the mountain face where Shi'roc and A'mora were perched above the town. They had climbed above the house that held the hidden passage. The view of the stars was exquisite as was the overlook into the valley. Shi'roc remained alert to every sound that the wind made. He had made visual contact with the next watcher by way of coded signals. 'We have arrived, all is well.' was the message as he had learned it. The first moon had risen from the eastern horizon casting its bluish glow over the desolate wasteland.

A'mora had fallen asleep in his arms. Her cloak was wrapped tightly around her as she rested her head in his lap. Although their feelings for each other were becoming clearer, his first duty was to the watch. He began to scan the dark distance with his night vision. He concentrated on every moving branch or rolling brush.

It was just below them, at the base of the mountain where Shi'roc had been ambushed by the skeletons. He recalled the situation with anxiety and the turn about into victory by his new students. They had progressed even further in the past few weeks of training. He could tell that they were all ready for the fight that would come.

His concern was for the weapons and supplies required for a sustained battle. He did not even know the type or number of his enemy. They had only been told old stories, some of which had been handed down generations. This knowledge was vital in planning for an attack or to just repel one from the mountain. They did have the advantage of higher ground and access to the tunnels.

His eyes scanned what appeared to be four flickers of light in close proximity to each other. They might even be camp fires. Who would be out there but Moracles' armies. But why would only four fires be lit. Surely that couldn't be all of his forces. He watched for a while to be sure of what he was seeing. He wondered if the other observation post above had seen it too.

"A'mora. Awaken." He whispered so as not to startle her. He gently shook her shoulder until she stirred. "There are camp fires in the distance." I must warn the others. She yawned and snapped awake upon the understanding of his statement. She straightened up to look where he was pointing.

Shi'roc stood up to signal the next watcher. 'Ilo had also spotted the fires. It was too far for the others to see.' Was the response from above. 'Send a messenger below to advise Lorentz.' was the signal he sent. He was impressed with the younger Elf's visual acuity.

Chapter 15
Remembrance

The daylight began to vanish as the two Elves proceeded through the abandoned forest trail. They had not encountered any resistance to their travel except for the over grown brush that occasionally blocked their path. Koloda had been using his sword as a bush whacker to clear the way.

It seemed strange to Fendal to be taking the same path where their friendship had first started. At least then, they traveled with several others. What they needed now was a warrior as a body guard. They needed Shi'roc, Fendal thought. Although he had little need of defending himself or being in situations that he couldn't handle, he missed the idea of having Shi'roc as his body guard. When they were all younger and less experienced, Fendal needed to hire a strong courageous warrior that he could trust to protect him while on their earlier adventures. His initial magical prowess was not up to the standards that it was now. He didn't want to bring in an unknown outsider on this journey. Trust and familiarity were essential to a mission such as this. Too bad that Ariel was long since dead. She would have joined them. She was a strong and fearless woman who also gave great massages, as he recalled.

"Are you sure you want to do this. We can still turn back. It's not too late." Koloda muttered as he hacked his way through another brush pile. It was time to look for a place to camp for the night.

"I never thought of you as a coward before." Fendal replied as he pushed his way through the cut branches. "Do you really think that Magdelan's castle is still inhabited after all this time. We did a pretty thorough job of cleaning it out before."

"You are the one that thinks Ach'med's remains were taken here by some evil powers." He turned around and pointed his sword accusingly at Fendal. "I'm just going along because I can still remember my way around in here. Who knows what might have wandered in and taken over this castle in the past years. I'm not going to protect your butt for you, you know." He was eyeing what appeared to be a small clearing in the thicket. "Lets camp there." The hefty Elf pointed with his short sword.

The two weary adventurers began unloading their backpacks and bed rolls. They had soon gathered dead wood for the fire and cleared a place to sleep. With a flick of his fingers, Fendal ignited the wood pile and waved the sparking embers into a steadily growing flame.

Koloda removed from his pack some prepared food that Cha'ni had packed for their trip. This was the first time he had been separated from her since her mothers death. He wanted to take her along for the experience and the company, but Fendal insisted that it would be too dangerous. He didn't want her where she could be injured or killed. He had become very protective of her in the past few days.

"Tell me again what exactly we would be expecting to find in there." Koloda waved a hand in the general direction of the underground castle up ahead.

"Well; after talking with the temple groundskeeper and the priest, we are looking for some old human. He was the only one that had come looking for Ach'med's tomb before it was made empty." He explained as he continued to eat the hot meal that Koloda had cooked.

"How old could he be for a human? They don't live long you know." He remembered that all of the humans in their original party had long since died or had been killed. "What would this human want with Ach'med's dust anyway?" He said while keeping warm by the fire.

"From the priests description, I would say he was as old as you or I. That is, in human years, maybe one hundred and thirty or so." He shrugged being uncertain of his guess.

"How is that possible?" Koloda grunted. "What human have you ever known to be older than sixty years at most?" He began to gather the cooking utensils for storage in the backpack.

Fendal hesitated in his response. "If this human is responsible for the disappearance of Ach'med's remains, it is quite possible that he is in league with the dark lords of hell." He raised his eyes to Koloda to see his reaction to the possibility. Koloda responded with a blank stare and froze his movements. "I am only guessing of course, but the information I have collaborated recently would point to that conclusion."

"You and I alone against an apprentice of the dark lords?" Are you out of your mind?" Koloda barked back at him as he threw the utensils into the sack. "I am not familiar with the ways of the gods, but I know enough not to mess with them, or their minions."

"So you are not going with me tomorrow?" Fendal spoke sheepishly as he stared down into the fire. A long pause of silence followed as Koloda searched his conscience, or lack of one. "I was right in thinking you a coward then." He turned from the fire and unrolled his blankets. "I will go alone to determine Ach'med's fate." No further words were spoken between the two as they laid down on opposite sides of the fire to sleep.

Koloda tossed and turned all night with the thought of confronting a powerful enemy without the protection of a warrior to hide behind. He knew that from all his experience, he was no good in a face to face brawl. His talent lay in deception and stealth. Strike fast and silent from behind an unwary opponent. He realized that this would be impossible against one with magical or priest's abilities and powers. Then again, with the two of them, they might have a chance if they combined their strengths.

The cold night passed uneventfully as the fire died down. Neither had awaken to keep it blazing during the night. The embers were barely glowing as the first orange light of the morning sun penetrated the forest.

The sounds of the woodlands awoke Fendal. The singing of the birds signaled the time to move on. Fendal rolled over to face the all but dead fire. He could see that Koloda was not there. He sat up and looked around, but he was no where in sight. Fendal wasn't too surprised at this. His only regret was that Koloda had the sack with all of the good food in it.

As usual, the first chore of the morning was to review his book of traveling spells. These were the most common for him to commit to memory. Mostly they were for defensive and evasive purposes rather than to attack an enemy which was not something he would normally do. After a quick review he closed the book and replaced it into his front belt pouch.

He rolled up his blankets and stuffed them into the straps of his back pack and pulled out a piece of dried jerky to chew on as he kicked dirt onto the fires remains. "I guess I will go alone." He said to himself, as he pulled up and tightened the straps of his pack around his shoulders. He gave one last look around as he proceeded back toward the overgrown path.

Once he found the trail he continued west along the mountains edge. He was surprised to find that the brush had been mostly cleared from the path and his travel time was improved. He looked to see that the overgrowth had been freshly cut. Very freshly cut.

"Late sleeper, eh?" He heard the gruff voice from up ahead. It was indeed Koloda setting on a log along the path. "I bet you thought I had turned back," he grunted to Fendal.

"You bet well," Fendal said, relieved that he was mistaken about the shady character. "I was beginning to wonder what had cleared this path so recently. I am glad to see it was you." He smiled.

Koloda stood up, still with sword in hand to cut through the shrubbery. "We will be there soon. The cave entrance should be just ahead." He motioned with his sword ahead along the mountains rock slope. Though the brush and forest were thick with life, there was nothing growing on the mountain itself. Just a mass of rock with a steep vertical rise where they were located. The path approached the rocks themselves and the two Elves searched for the cave entrance that had been undoubtedly hidden by an overgrowth of weeds and vines.

At last they found the opening that led deep into the rocks. After cutting away the clutter, they felt their way along the rocky entrance, using their night vision in the dark passage to spot any living creatures that may have taken up residence within. They could both recall the first time they had been looking for the cave that led to the massive wooden doors.

"Fendal, light a torch." The other grunted back. He had stopped just short of the main doors to the castle. The cave had widened at this point allowing for the outward opening of the doors. Koloda was a little ways ahead.

Fendal reached into his supply pack for the store bought torch and his flint rocks. "What is the problem." He inquired as he knelt to the ground to spark the torch. He did not wish to use any of his magical abilities unnecessarily and lighting a torch could be just as easily done with a flint. Now that they were entering dangerous territory, he would need to reserve his spells.

"Do you remember those big wooden doors that we had to open when we were here last?" He called back, as the now ignited torch glowed enough for both to see. "They have been torn off." Fendal crept up behind Koloda casting his shadow well into the opening where the doors once stood. They both could see the shattered wooden planks that had been cast aside in the opening, obviously beaten down by someone or something long ago from the inside.

"Wow. I wonder what did that?" Fendal gasped, as he inspected the wooden fragments, trying to determine a relative time frame of the incident. He could see from the rot of the fractures that it had been done shortly after their last visit to the fortress. He could clearly see claw marks on the broken pieces of wood. "This appears to be too old to be of any concern to us." He turned to Koloda as he got up from his knees. Koloda silently slipped by into the main hallway of their old nemesis.

"Unless what did this is still in here." Koloda's voice came back as he disappeared into the darkness past the torches light. Fendal quickly extinguished the torch and proceeded to follow Koloda.

* * *

The chambers deep within the castle were deceptively quiet and dark. Not a sound emanated except for the repetitive chanting from the temple. The doors to the sanctuary were closed but a faint flicker of light could be seen through the cracks of the door. Within this domain of evil another deception was taking place. That of Moracles over his new apprentice. Ach'med had become fond of the old man and took to his attentive ways. No one in his previous life seemed to pay him any attention and his helpful nature was abused and taken for granted. He now realized, through Moracles, that he was capable of more and that he mattered. He too could possess the knowledge of magic and had learned to do so in the past weeks that were spent studying under the wizard's careful guidance.

Moracles was pleased at the progress his young, impressionable apprentice had made. He was quite intelligent for being a warrior in his previous life. Those trained to fight with weapons of steel were mostly thought of as having low intelligence or wisdom. Brut strength was their only blessing. But Ach'med was apparently different due to his pure Elven heritage. Moracles had brought out in him a child like inquisitiveness and willingness to learn.

"Concentrate on the candle's flame." The master instructed as he pointed to the alter upon which a single wax mound was flickering. The Elf's chants continued as did the motions of his arms, until the tiny flame erupted into a blazing torch from the same wick. "Excellent," the mage praised.

The enhanced flame illuminated the entire temple revealing a stone statue in the corner of the room. The figure was set in the form of a shrine. It appeared to be a beautiful woman draped in a gown that was delicately carved into a web. Upon her shoulder set a large stone spider.

Ach'med was quite pleased with himself and his master's encouragement. "That is the fourth successful spell that I have performed today." He confirmed to his master. He could feel a renewed sense of purpose within. No longer would he be the warrior who would selflessly risk his life for others. He would soon be well known and respected by all as a great wizard.

"Yes, you are becoming more powerful each day under my guidance." The Human replied sternly, without any hint of joy. "But there is still much for you to learn, that is if you wish to lead my awaiting army." The old man turned to look into the Elf's eyes for a reaction.

Ach'med stood up, surprised by the mage's comment. "You wish for me to lead an army? Where is your army? I have seen no one here but you?" He gave a puzzled look to the wizard.

"Do not question me!" Moracles snapped back. "You must make a decision now. What will it be?" He demanded. Do you want to lead my army and learn the secrets of the great powers of the Goddess, Lolith, or remain in ignorance as those who left you behind?" He was now very serious with the Elf. He turned dramatically away from the Elf's stare to hide the evil grin that was creeping onto his wrinkled face. The bait had been laid, the challenge offered. Would the young apprentice rise or fall.

Ach'med looked briefly at the statue in the corner and thought about how good he felt with the knowledge and power he had gained. Nowhere else could he have learned what he now knew. His lust for power was growing as was his dependence on Moracles. "What must I learn?" He asked. "What must I do?"

With his back still turned he said. "That was not an answer to my question." In an irritated voice. "Will you lead my army?" He asked again almost in desperation. The thought whisked through his mind about having left everything in the hands of the Bone. He needed someone he could trust with his castle and soldiers. What mischief had the Bone gotten into while he was away? Had he found the intruders who had spawned this journey to revive the Elven warrior.

A moments hesitation by Ach'med was ended when he spoke. "Yes, I will lead your army," he said firmly and in control. "Teach me what I must know." He had taken the step into the world of evil and hatred with that reply. He had not dreamed of commanding an army at his young age, nor of having magical abilities.

The mage spun around to face him. His robes flowed around him causing a ripple in the flame that was still emanating from the alter. He looked sternly into the Elf's eyes and took a step towards him. "Even though the knowledge would be burned deep into your soul?" he questioned as the Elf stood proud.

"I am not afraid." He spoke, drawing a breath to stand at attention. "Teach me all that I am capable of learning." He said with excitement. The rush of his adrenaline over powered his senses and his logic. His loyalties had faded from those who were once friends, to this powerful stranger who had just stolen his soul.

"Then pray. Pray to the goddess from which I have drawn my powers. She will have the final say as to your destiny as my 'Vandar', leader of armies." 'Vandar' was a term of the old Elvish tongue that meant, as Moracles had said, a leader of armies, a general in the more literal sense. Ach'med understood this title and would do anything now to have it bestowed upon him. The mage pointed toward the statue of Lolith in the corner of the temple. The spider queen. The evil consort of the God, Hartes, who at his side ruled the greater planes of hell.

Ach'med stepped toward the likeness of the goddess and knelt down in worship. He could see the intricately carved stone that depicted the queen as a very beautiful temptress. Her gown was indeed drapes of a spiders web. He studied her features for a moment, then, lowered his head to pray. From behind him he heard the words of his master, attempting to call forth the powers of Lolith.

"See before me, a new apprentice of your powers. He wishes to join in the splendor of your wisdom as I have for so long." Moracles stood, arms spread wide, while addressing the statue of the goddess. "Please allow him to know the strength of our magic and to follow in our cause." He bowed his head and repeated his plea.

The statue began to glow with a mystical blue sheen, similar to that which the clear moon would give in the deepest night. Though the statue did not move, it appeared to breath and come to life. The sensual voice of Lolith flowed from her mouth as it seemed to move on the statue's face.

"Who summons me?" the voice demanded "and where might my presence be known?" Her words were similar to those that Hartes spoke when Moracles had called upon him to restore the Elf's body and spirit. The dark lords would rarely respond to those of their minions. Having served in her name, Moracles' prayer was able to touch the mind of the goddess and bring her visage to the real world. The sense of the lords would not know to where they had been summoned or by whom. They did not wish their existence to be known by anyone but their most faithful followers. There were but few public temples in their name and each was strongly guarded so that they could not be defiled by the non believers.

Moracles, upon seeing the avatar, knelt down, and bowed his head in devoted service. "It is I, Moracles, your humble servant, that calls, your worship. You are deep in the castle of Lord Magdelan." He answered with a voice of reverence. "The request I have to make is of great importance in serving our cause." Once again he used the 'cause' to gain favor with her as he did when asking Hartes to steal the Elf's soul from the heavens. Moracles was the only one of their servants who was capable of bringing eventual control of the real world to the evil king and queen.

Moracles raised his head to speak directly to the glowing statue. He glimpsed the Elf in front of him, head tucked down, and trembling in the presence of the goddess. It was obvious that the young Elf had never experienced such an occurrence. The mage would use this also to his advantage.

"With the help of our Lord, Hartes, I have revived this young warrior from an untimely death. In the past few weeks I have related to him the powers of which would serve you." Moracles could outsell the best of merchants, if his talents were used more appropriately. For now his skill of verbalization was more powerfully used to coerce the dark powers of Lolith. "He trembles with the anticipation of your blessing, to make him one of your flock, a servant of the spider queen." He continued his sale.

Still in silence, Ach'med listened to the words of the wizard and goddess. He realized that he was indeed shaking, not as much from fear as in anticipation. He did not know what to expect or how to react. Should he speak or wait to be asked a question? Should he raise his head or would that seem disrespectful?

"He is to become 'Vandar' over my army." The mage slowly arose from his knees as he continued to face the statue. He stood directly behind the Elf and said. "He will help me to purge the infectious renegades from our lands." He was of course referring to the reason for the Elf's resurrection, the annihilation of the intruders.

"Will you obey Moracles and learn our ways?" The voice addressed Ach'med, still uncertain as to what to say. The Elf hesitated. "Speak." Commanded the goddess. "Or are you too cowardly to command the forces of Moracles?" She prodded. It was enough to rile the young Elf. No one, not even a goddess would call him coward.

He raised his head to speak. "I will lead his armies and crush his enemies." He said with a scowl. "I am Ach'med. A warrior." He continued with renewed confidence spawned by anger. "No one calls me coward." He concluded as he rose to his feet in front of Moracles. The old man put a hand on the Elf's shoulder in an attempt to calm him.

"You must prove your loyalty to me before you can learn of my power." The voice of the statue was raised slightly in response to the Elf's hostility. "You say you will crush the enemies of Moracles. You may start by proving that." Both the Human and Elf were puzzled by that comment. "There are intruders in the house of Lord Magdelan. You must defeat them. Once this is done, you may contact me again." The voice faded as did the visualization of the statue.

Moracles was not sure of his success in the encounter. Was it favorable? He thought about her last words regarding intruders in the deserted castle. Wanderers or adventurers perhaps? They could only be creatures that had wandered in from the forest, but either way, this would be a good test of the Elf's abilities and loyalty.

"What should I do." Ach'med asked as he turned to his master. "Where should I find these intruders?" He was indeed anxious to prove himself to both Moracles and the goddess.

Moracles just smiled his crooked smile and said "I shall show you the way." The old man pulled his robe around himself and reached deep into a hidden pocket. From it, he had plucked what looked like a small piece of gray fur. He placed it carefully into the palm of his left hand and showed it to the Elf.

"What is it?" he inquired, as he looked closely into the open palm. "It looks like some kind of animal fur."

"Very perceptive," replied the old man. "It is the belly fur of a bat to be precise. Now watch and listen as it performs this task." Moracles began to recall the spell. The words flowed from his lips as the fur began to dance lightly in his hand. "Transium oculi veritas sum." Came the incantation as Ach'med mouthed the words to commit to memory. The fur rose steadily above the hand of the mage and faded away.

"Where did it go? What did you do?" Asked the curious apprentice as he looked up to face his master. But Moracles did not answer, for his thoughts were concentrated on the effects of the spell. His eyes were closed as his mind slowly moved through the rooms and hallways of the castle.

* * *

The two Elves proceeded cautiously through the maze of rooms and hallways in search of clues as to where they might find Ach'med's remains. It was late in the afternoon for them but they persisted in their quest without rest. They proceeded as they had done on their first journey into the castle of the Lord Magdelan, except for now they were aware of the dangers that might await them. They were more expedient in their movement through the dark hallways since Koloda had remarkably remembered the layout of the fortress. They were fairly certain that their earlier travels had taken them to all corners of the underground stronghold. Fendal was amazed that after one hundred and some years, Koloda could remember which way to go. There were over a dozen separate levels to the castle, each with hidden passages and secret stairways. To have remembered so much constituted a miracle.

"I will scout ahead a ways." Koloda grunted to his partner as they stood in the intersection of many passages. "This area is a little hazy in my memory. Wait here and I shall return shortly." The master of thieves swiftly, but silently hustled down one of the corridors as the other casually began to mark the corners of the walls with a piece of special white chalk. Fendal had been marking their path in case anything would happen to Koloda and he would find himself without a guide. Even in the darkness, the fluorescence of the chalk could be seen with his night vision.

Koloda stepped around the corner of the next connecting passage and quickly reached into his satchel for his flint rocks and a candle. He bent to the floor and began scratching the stones and lit the candle's wick. He reached into a pocket and pulled out some folded papers. He held them near the candles light to reveal the dried ink markings of a well detailed map. He followed the path with his finger to the last intersection where he had left Fendal and determined that of the other passages would lead to the hidden stairs. He checked the subsequent pages to verify that they were headed for the main temple that was several levels below them. Previously they had decided that the temple would be the most likely place for anyone to have taken Ach'med's remains. He re-folded the papers and blew out the candle, as he rushed back to his awaiting partner.

Fendal watched the approaching heat form. After careful evaluation of the relative size and walk, he determined it to be Koloda. He had prepared a spell in memory just in case it was not. The two were rejoined at the crossways when the larger Elf spoke.

"We should be going this way." Koloda pointed down one of the other corridors. "I needed to check that path to be sure." He continued his ruse confidently. Fendal would not know that Koloda had kept the original maps that were drawn when the group had first learned of the castles secrets. They continued their uneventful meandering through the fortress passages well into the unseen night time. The only time a candle or torch was lit was for specific searching of rooms where they thought clues might be left.

* * *

The apprentice Elf sat patiently on one of the stone benches, as his master's trance continued. He did not yet know the purpose of the spell or its effects on the intruders. Moracles had only said that he would show him the way. As yet, the Elf had seen little of the castle since his rebirth. He did not remember much of the journeys that had been previously taken by he and his former companions. All of that past seemed like a vague memory due mostly to Moracles' influencing spells. The young Elf's dreams were frequently haunted by unflattering scenes of mistreatment by his associates. Gradually his disdain for them would peak as his new master turned him further toward his dark teachings. Soon his memories would be twisted to make him feel the resentment toward them all.

Moracles was still following his minds eye, floating through the passages that led to the main floor. He could see as clearly as if he himself were walking through the halls with a candle in his hand. Although he was human, the spell allowed the magical detached eye to view all in its path with the same night vision abilities as the common Elf. He was guiding the direction of the entity and its speed as if walking. Finally the mage managed to speak through a concentrated and strained effort.

"I have found the intruders two floors above us." The spell broke and the mage seemed frighteningly awake. "There are only two of them. You should have no trouble in exterminating the pests." He said to Ach'med with his twisted smile. "They were preparing to settle for the night in one of the old guards rooms." He sat down next to his apprentice, like a friend about to reveal a mischievous secret. "Listen carefully as I explain the path to you." The mage described the stairways and halls that would bring him to the location of those who trespassed.

Moracles had indeed convinced the Elf in the past weeks that this was his home as well and all creatures within were invading their domain. This would be his final test before fully turning the Elf over to the goddess, Lolith, for her guidance and the ultimate test. If Ach'med was successful, he would become a loyal follower or, be a mutated half being living the rest of his life spinning webs and preying off of passers by.

The old man had thought this legend to be a manifestation of someone's imagination until he himself had subjected two captured Elves prior to training them properly. He thought that their skills alone would be enough to satisfy the goddess. The male was an adequate wizard with skills superior to Ach'med's. The female was a priestess in the community from where she was taken. Moracles had not taken the time, himself to turn their good nature as he had with Ach'med. The goodness in their hearts was not entirely destroyed by the goddess and her fury at their resistance caused them this fate. They have continued to live quite a long life as the rejected, half breeds, that Lolith had turned them into. They now served as guardians of the temple back in Feradune.

"You should rest now." The mage said to the eager Elf. "They will not continue their journey until morning." He stood up and motioned toward the temple door. "When you awake, study your writings and prepare your spells. They should be your only weapon." The wizard nodded toward Ach'med as he proceeded to his sleeping chamber. The mage remained behind in the temple to offer one last prayer to the goddess.

* * *

The room was dark and quiet except for the snorts of the overweight thief, rolling in his sleep. The beds on which they were sleeping were far better than the hard ground on which they had slept the past three nights, out in the woods. The air was damp and musty but still warmer than that outside the mountain. The straw mattress remains allowed for a more comfortable, deeper sleep for them both.

Fendal's keener senses of time and motion awoke him abruptly from his sleep. His internal clock had determined it to be morning. He quickly reached for his flint pouch and lit the wick of an oil lamp that was left behind on the table. There was sufficient light to show the small room, lined with the remains of six beds. He looked over to see the motionless bedroll of Koloda on the far bunk. He quickly read through his book of magical writings from which his powers were regenerated each day. After securing the leather wrappings into his backpack, he stepped over to his friend who was stuffed tightly into his bed roll. As he carefully attempted to prod his friend to consciousness, he was met with the flash of a daggers blade held to his throat. He gasped to call out but was muffled by a hand over his mouth.

"shhhhh." Whispered Koloda who was standing behind him with his hand over Fendal's mouth. "There is someone, or something out in the hall." He slowly removed his hand from around his startled partner. Fendal turned in time to see the stealthful thief return to the dark shadows near the door. Koloda had quickly reverted to his expert practices of deception when they began this journey. The bedroll was stuffed with straw from another mattress. The thief knew better than to sleep without guard in this castle, no matter how safe it seemed.

Koloda's hand appeared from the shadows, waving a signal to Fendal to extinguish the lamp and follow. The door slowly opened as he silently slipped out into the hall. The stillness of the air made it difficult to see any variations in heat traces. Koloda kept his left hand to the wall for guidance along the hallway. In his right hand he held his dagger in stabbing readiness. He heard the slight creek of the door behind him as Fendal made his way into the corridor. Neither could see any heat traces but each others, yet the paranoia of being stalked was now felt by both.

Fendal whispered to Koloda. "Let me pass and stay behind me." He brushed past his friend and began an incantation, waving his arms as he walked. Upon the completion of the spell, his eyes detected a difference in the air around him. The vision now was far superior to his vision in the darkness. Indeed there was someone there, standing in the center of the hall ahead of them. Fendal could now see this person as if in daylight. He wore dark clothing with a cape draped about him. The form of the figure seemed vaguely familiar. How could it be? "Ach'med?" Fendal called forth questioningly.

"Where?" He heard Koloda call from behind. "I can't see anyone but you." He rushed up to Fendal's side, unable to see what clarity the spell had provided.

"Finally decided to come back did you?" Came the angered voice of the figure. He had recognized Fendal's voice as that of the one who left him to die. "Where are the others?" He asked, still not aware of the vast time difference. "Have you abandoned them too." He called, as he raised the palm of his left hand toward them. "Sur fiero." He yelled. A searing ball of fire emerged with a blast down the hall. It disintegrated the dust and scorched the stone as it moved.

Fendal and Koloda both dove to the hard floor in an attempt to avoid the main blast of the engulfing flame. The heat was too intense for them to remain untouched. The fire moved swiftly over them, burning all that was combustible. They both rolled across the floor to extinguish their smoldering cloths. The fire was put out, but the pain was unbearable, causing them both to lay motionless, barely alive.

"Now I shall leave you as you left me, to die alone." The Elf called to the remains of his former companions. "I will now serve the gods who have shown me the powers beyond your abilities." The vengeful Elf walked off in silence down the corridor, leaving them for dead.

Chapter 16
Combat

The temple was dark when Ach'med returned. The smell of the snuffed out candles was still fresh in the air. His inherited vision was able to detect the warmth of the candles location. They had burned themselves out so that only puddles of soft wax remained setting on the alter.

He could still feel the burning in his blood from the powers that had rushed through him less than an hour ago. He realized that he had not experienced this feeling since he fought for his life against the ape creatures. His courage and strength provided less than favorable results then. Death now seemed like a dream. The passage of time that he had been dead, still was not apparent to him. The once familiar figures in the darkness did not reveal to him that they had aged considerably.

Ach'med carefully listened up the hall for any sign that his master was near. Should he wait, or should he pray on his own to the Goddess, Lolith, telling her of his success. He was anxious to begin training under her tutelage as Moracles had promised. Ach'med could only imagine the increased power he would have after he had learned the ways of the spider queen.

He decided to wait no longer, nor would he seek out his master. He knelt before the statue in the darkness and began to clear his mind, as Moracles had instructed, to allow the goddess to enter through his thoughts. All was silent as it was dark. Ach'med closed his eyes and bowed his head toward the statue awaiting a sign from Lolith. Just as he had completely opened his mind, he heard the voice of Moracles from behind.

"Oh powerful queen of the dark lands, we beckon you to receive our humble thoughts and make your presence known." The voice was grating and deep with reverence. "We wish to serve you with our meager talents." Moracles looked down upon the back of the kneeling Elf. “Your new pupil awaits your commands.” The evil mage ignited the wick of a new candle with the snap of his fingers. He then proceeded around the room to light several other candles from the first. The flickering light cast the same familiar shadows that could deceive one’s eyes.

A moment later, the goddess seemed to breath life into the statue as before. Though the statue was carved of stone, faint movements could be seen by the mage. He knew the difference between her enchantment and the reflective light. Ach’med saw nothing as his eyes were still closed with his head bowed. Moracles knelt as well after seeing the life sign in the statue.

She looked at the two of them, bowed in sufficient reverence and finally the queen spoke with a deep alluring voice. “Has the fortress been secured from the strangers?” She asked of no one in particular. There was a long silence as Ach’med thought his master would answer the goddess directly.

“Yes my goddess.” Came Ach’med’s voice, as he looked up with pride, to the carved stone. “But they were not strangers.” He replied to her description of the intruders. His comment caused Moracles to look up in surprise.

“Then who were they if not strangers?” The mage cautiously broke into the conversation with a whisper to his apprentice.

Ach’med turned his head to address his master. “They were my old friends, Fendal and Koloda.” The mage flinched with a bit of uncertainty. This was not the time to be embarrassed in front of Lolith. The Elf noticed the strain in the old mans face. “Not to worry, they will not be a bother to us again, ever.” He turned back to the goddess. His adrenaline was again pumping with the thoughts of his powers soon to be. “I am ready to learn all that you can teach me." The Elf rose to his feet and stood at soldiers attention awaiting whatever orders would come next.

At that moment, Moracles rose to his feet. He knew that nothing more need be said. From his past experience with turning over candidates to the goddess, he knew it was now out of his hands. The last two had failed because they were captive and unwilling to serve. Ach'med on the other hand was not only willing, but eager for the unknown challenge. He turned to leave the temple when the goddess addressed him.

"You know when to return to see the results of your student." He knew that in the two days of real time, months would pass for the realm of the goddess and her teachings to Ach'med. Much could be learned in that time provided the Elf could endure the pains as well as the pleasures of the dark powers.

Moracles thought back to his training under the instruction of Lolith and Hartes. When he was sent by Lord Magdelan, he had apprenticed for several years in the timeline of the gods. There was still some doubt in his mind that Ach'med was ready, but there was no time to waste. They would have to begin the journey back to Feradune when the goddess released him. Would he remain a man or become another web spinning arachnid? "He will learn well my queen." He nodded to her and closed the temple doors behind him.

* * *

The sun was well into the sky when the reluctant soldiers approached the southern mountain peak. The past cold night had yielded to an even more bitter cold clear day. Having run out of food, they were eager to perform their search of the mountain range and begin their journey directly home to the rocky fortress deep inside the canyon of Feradune. Perhaps they might find some small animals or rodents as they searched the mountain. They were no longer concerned about their new leader's reaction to a report empty of a successful result. Perhaps one of the other parties had flushed out the strangers. Maybe they had been spotted near the desert or in one of the other town remnants. The only driving encouragement in the mind of the general was the last words the Bone had said to him. "Ich ta poo" you will obey, knowing full well what might happen to them if they had shirked their duty.

In order to make a swift pass over the entire mountain he had decided to split his troops into several squads. He directed them to search both sides of the mountain simultaneously and meet at the base of the north end. Each of those groups would split again into small parties that would go up into any pathways they may find. He reminded them that they were not there to engage in battle if it could be avoided. Under normal circumstances, battle would be the first thing on their minds. It was hard for them to stay out of a fight since they saw everyone as an enemy. They were in no condition to be fighting anyway being malnourished and half frozen so there wasn't any resistance to the order. It was agreed that they would meet at the north end of the range in two days then proceed directly back across the northern edge of the desert and into the canyons. The General led his party along the eastern base of the mountain.

* * *

"Orcs!" They are splitting up, Shi'roc thought to himself as he was perched on the southern edge of the Dwarven Peaks. He had selected a vantage point that allowed him to see down the entire southern slope. He could see one of them giving the orders. "That one must be the leader." After carefully counting the number of each of the enemy parties, he signaled back to the watchers.

He was well familiar with fighting their kind. These creatures were strong and normally too stupid to be afraid of battle that made them fierce warriors. What were they looking for? he wondered. It seemed that they were not there for combat or they would not be splitting their forces. It was unlike Orcs to not attack as one unit. They can't be allowed to find the passage ways into the tunnels. This was Shi'roc's only concern.

* * *

"Groika con volu." the General said as he pointed up to what seemed like a possible passage through the sloping rocks. They stood at the base of the mountain, looking around the area for some sign that the path had been used. There were no foot prints or tousled rocks along the path. The withered, dried trees to their right showed no sign of a pathway, yet there were some broken branches. His troops were ordered to search along the rotted trees for any signs of activity.

"Kuch ta manu." one of the soldiers grunted as he raised up the hand of a skeletons remains. He snorted out a laugh that was joined by several others. The search continued as they turned up many more skeletal parts scattered along the tree line. Some of the remains still had remnants of metal or leather armor. They determined that there must have been a battle there long ago. Maybe some of the villagers that had been slaughtered by the Magdarn as they saw in the paintings back at the castle. There was nothing here to be concerned about.

"Chenko sa volu." their leader motioned up the path with his sword. Ten of his troops began to climb the narrow, jagged route. "Ich ta ruanta." He indicated that he would follow them up. "Chenko volu semtar." he waved the others to continue along the mountain in search of other pathways. "Cho ni actu." he pointed to one of them as they passed and appointed him as being in charge of the group. The General stood and waited until the last of his men disappeared up the mountain pass. He looked around to see the others continue north along the mountains base.

It was time for something that he would never have allowed his regiment to see. Unlike the rest of his race, that could hold in bodily waste for weeks at a time, he had the need to expel his fluids and solids more regularly. He climbed up between two of the rock edges and unfastened the straps that held up his lower body armor. Although it was cold, the crevice in which he stood deflected the icy winds while he leaned back against the boulder and relieved himself. Perhaps this regularity was what allowed him to lead. The relief always seemed to clear his mind. The lack of these functions might be what caused his race to be such fierce, raging warriors.

A few minutes later he re-dressed himself, fastening back the buckles while still standing amongst the putrid steam. Then he began the ascent up the rocky passage in pursuit of his men. Their tracks were quite easy to follow as they were not even attempting to hide their movement. There was no real reason to do so. He moved much faster now from not being encumbered by twisted bowels. Soon after, he saw the last of his men disappear beyond what seemed like a ridge up ahead. As he approached the precipice, from around the bend in the rock, he heard what sounded like muffled cries, or warnings. He carefully peeked around the edge of the stone and saw what looked like several stone and straw buildings. Amongst them he could see the sprawled out bodies of two of his men. Several arrows appeared to be protruding from each of the corpses. With sword in hand, he was about to run to their side to determine their fate when he saw several smaller creatures begin to drag the bodies around the buildings, beyond his field of view. Another of these people followed behind, erasing the tracks that the drug bodies had made.

He chose to remain hidden, remembering the instructions of the Bone, not to engage in battle, but only to find these intruders. Found them he had done. Now he must remain unnoticed while rounding up the rest of his hoard and quickly returning to the Bone to report their findings.

* * *

The word had spread thorough the caverns that the mountain was being attacked by Moracles' soldiers. Though the rumor was somewhat exaggerated, all of the warriors had been assigned to either watcher duty, or guard the secret entryways into the tunnels. Shi'roc's instructions were simple. "no survivors." was all he said to each group as they had assembled for their first real battles. The lords knew that there was no real threat based on the numbers that Shi'roc counted. Fifty groveling, Orcs were no match for their newly trained army, especially broken into small groups. Shi'roc and Lorentz alone could match them, yet they decided that this skirmish would provide experience for their new soldiers abilities. From the mountain tops, the two masters observed and directed the almost silent attacks on the raiders. The quick learning of the silent signals was well appreciated in the coordination of the attacks. Messages could be sent, unobserved from either end of the mountain in a matter of minutes, to both Lorentz and Shi'roc.

The first attack in Kura's home town was a great victory. Eight of the viscous creatures were taken down before they even knew they had been attacked. Five dropped with the first round of arrows fired from the roof tops of the town. The remaining were soon after put to death by the Dwarven swords. The Dwarves had vowed that never would Moracles' filthy beings invade their former homes.

Earlier that morning, Lady A'mora had led her student priests to the shrine of Mirana to pray for the warrior's safety. Kura led the way into the water cave where he and Ilo had continued to care for the horses as Lorentz had ordered. On alternate days the horses were fed and walked around the orchard. There was not enough room for them to get in a good run, but the minimal exercise was a must. The large cave had been continually illuminated by the magical radiance of the glowing stalactites over the orchard and gardens. There was always enough light for the plants to flourish and continue to bear the fruits that had been their sole source of nourishment for the past several months.

The apprenticed priests were knelt in a semi circle surrounding the grotto of carved stone that stood at the base of the aqueduct that Lorentz had created. The rain fall over the past months had been nominal, but sufficient to nourish the fruit trees and vegetable gardens that the Goddess Mirana had provided through Lorentz' hands. Throughout the morning they had chanted their words of worship, not only for the safe return of the warriors, but also for the wisdom and healing abilities required should anyone be wounded. They were not yet advanced enough in their training to accompany the soldiers into battle. Though they were becoming capable healers of minor wounds, they had yet developed the necessary defensive and avoidance skills required for battle practices.

Their combined trance was disturbed by an unexplainable evil presence. A'mora looked up from the shrine to pinpoint the source of the aura. The others also experienced the feeling and began to survey the area.

Kura pointed up behind the grotto and shouted, "Look up there." He had spotted two grotesque creatures peering through the rain gully that led to the outside mountain face. Though Lord Lorentz had opened up the trough for the collection of rain water, it was also large enough to allow the curious to crawl through. The two soldiers had spotted the opening from the outside and had crawled through for a look. They had seemed just as startled as A'mora and the others.

"Hold" she shouted as she raised an open hand in their direction. The rest watched as she cautiously climbed the rocks around behind the sanctuary toward the two unmoving figures. They had indeed frozen in place, eyes still fixed on the apprentices with a surprised expression. She carefully examined the lifeless bodies that were mostly still hidden in the crevice. "Help me pull them through." she called to the others who quickly scurried up the ledges to assist her. She then crawled part way through to the outside just to see if any more of them were nearby. Once satisfied that these two were acting alone, she pulled herself back into the cavern and began piling loose stones into the opening, pushing them as far back outward as possible in case others came looking. It would appear as though the rocks had collapsed.

The priests had removed the creatures' weapons and tossed them down onto the cave floor. What should be done with them was the next question. A'mora did not want to kill them, but they needed to be securely restrained so that they could be questioned by Lord Lorentz. Kura had an idea. He ran down to where the horses were tethered and removed several of the leather strapsfrom the saddles and reins that had been stored near the horses.

The others were removing the plate armor from the soldiers as they began to squirm out of the trance. Two of the apprentices concentrated their power through the command word "Hold" they shouted directly at the creatures as A'mora had done, once again immobilizing them. They completed their task of removing their armor. One of the human apprentices began to try on the warriors armor as the others began to tie them up.

"Hey, look. It fits." He said to the others as he completed the buckling of the leg guards. The Orcs were indeed similar in size to a full grown Human. He stood up, holding the sword as he mimicked a fierce warrior. The Orcs were broader but of the same relative build as the human. He walked over to his companions to help them restrain the prisoners. The odor of the creatures finally made him realize that the protective apparel should have been cleaned before he tried it on. "These creatures do smell foul," he unnecessarily pointed out.

"Yes," said one of the others, "And now you do as well. Take that off and go clean yourself."

One of the Elven students volunteered to track down Lorentz for guidance and to interrogate the prisoners. He ran as swiftly as possible out through the connecting tunnels. In the mean time, the beasts had been stripped of all dignity and tightly bound, both feet and hands together and to each other. They were not only neutralized but quite humiliated, when they again broke free of the priests spell. They had not been gagged so when they regained their limited cognitive abilities, they began to rant and rave in frustration. They could only be understood by each other since A'mora and the others had never encountered their species before and did not know the language. This was probably a blessing since their main focus was on cursing A'mora and the goddess that they worshipped. She may have thought again about killing them if she had known. For now all they could do was wait until Lorentz arrived. She then thought it best to silence the creatures by tying the straps around their heads through their mouths.

* * *

Ilo laid still on the straw matted roof. He and the rest of his troop remained in hiding in the town that was nestled among the eastern ridges of the center mountain peak. Some lay waiting on the remaining roof tops while others hid around the corners of the ruins, watching for the nearing enemy. They had been there for at least an hour so as not to miss their opportunity for surprise.

With his back pressed to the rough, aged straw, he gazed up into the gray clouded sky. His thoughts were not about battle, but of his loving wife and the child that she was about to bear. Soon he would be a father. He worried about the risks they were about to take and wondered who would take care of his child and wife if he were to be killed. He hoped his father, Maac-To, would be around for support. Ilo briefly remembered how Lady A'mora was able to touch his wife's bulging belly and determine that it would be a girl. This had given them the time to decide on the name in advance. She would be called, Aliah,

Out of the corner of his eye he could see Lord Lorentz perched upon the mountain peak just as the sun reached through the clouds. The master began to wave his arms in motion of the silent signals. He had spotted ten of the creatures coming up the mountain road. This was to be expected since that passage was the easiest to find from the eastern slope of the mountain. Lorentz had been able to watch the enemy soldiers on their journey from that vantage point. After giving Ilo the signal, he ducked down behind the rocks so as not to be spotted when the Orcs reached the town.

The signal was quickly passed from roof top to roof top and down to those hiding in the shadows of the village structures. They had positioned themselves so that each could be seen by at least two others, creating a net of communication and safety. Those in the higher positions overlooking the towns fringe had nocked their arrows and were ready to draw. The others waited in the town with swords at the ready as the invaders crested the ridge.

Ilo peered over the edge of the roof where he lay. he could see the first few of the enemy as they came up the mountain road. He would wait until all were in the open before giving the signal for attack. They walked single file on the main street toward the center of the town, their weapons drawn and their heads looking in all directions. It was clear that this was not a casual search, but one intended to find the survivors. They slowed as the leader of the ten soldiers waved his sword in the air and grunted what appeared to be orders to the others. Just when they started to separate, Ilo yelled out the attack signal, startling the trespassers. They all looked up in surprise as a volley of carefully aimed arrows found their marks. The survivors on the roof tops and rocky ridges fired several times before the Orcs had a chance to react. Two of them dropped in the street immediately having been punctured with multiple arrows at once. The others scattered toward the shelter of the ruined buildings while their comrades wallowed in their purplish black blood. Some of them had one or two arrows extending from various parts of their body. These creatures were tough and well armored. It would take more than a few arrows to kill them altogether. It was fortunate that the survivors were well prepared and had planned the encounter. The Orcs were certainly better equipped and would have been formidable in a straight up battle even as outnumbered as they were.

One of the creatures with an arrow in his back, ran into the nearest doorway and was met by the short sword of one of the Dwarven warriors. The small but powerful Dwarf thrust his sword completely to the hilt, into the running Orc. It screamed with fright and surprise as the blade penetrated his armor and passed through his abdomen. The Dwarf quickly withdrew the blade with his right hand, as he pushed over the creature with his left hand. The limp body fell backward into the street, pushing the arrow through the creatures chest and piercing its black heart.

Another Orc had managed to duck behind a wall of a dilapidated building. He grabbed at the arrow that had pierced his armor but did not penetrate too deeply into his body. The arrow in his side was awkward to remove but he did so with a quick yank. His blood flowed from the wound and trickled down his side. He picked up his sword again and began to sneak around the another opening in the wall to see what was going on in the street. He was being very cautious to observe any movement or sound from the shadows. He concentrated on a section of roof that had collapsed in the building he was in, creating a visual hazard. The sun shown down through the open ceiling leaving a blind spot beyond it. Just as he was able to make out the outline of two figures hiding in the shadow, he heard the twang of bow strings and felt the sting of two arrows rip through his chest. The short bolts fired from a crossbow at close range, had gone through his body. The tips were protruding from his back. He staggered backward a few steps grabbing at one arrow's fletchings, and then collapsed, dropping his sword with a clang.

Sha'la and Muga, stepped from behind rotted wood and straw toward the dead beast. Both women were dressed for battle in padded leather and metal chest plate. They each set the crossbow stirrup on the ground and put their foot through the loop. Then they pulled back the draw bar, cocking the bow for another bolt. They stepped next to the body to make sure he was truly dead. Sha'la bent down to pick up the sword that was worn but usable. Muga gave a stiff kick to the soldiers side, verifying its lifelessness. They saw that the bolts were set too deep to be removed quickly. The two women looked at each other smiled, and nodded a silent signal to move on.

The battle continued quietly in the streets and inside the ruins. An occasional gasp or grunt could be heard as the invaders were hunted down, one by one and put to death. As Lord Shi'roc had instructed, "no survivors" could be left to report back to Moracles. They continued to silently signal each other as to the locations of the enemy, number killed, and injuries of their own. These messages were relayed to Ilo who was still on the roof, watching over the main street of the town. So far, they had killed eight of the enemy with only two minor wounds to his own people. No casualties. He thought the Goddess must be watching over them. He stood up and signaled to Lord Lorentz that all was well and the battle had been won. The return signal was to gather the bodies and strip them of all usable equipment. That, Ilo and the others already knewn was necessary. They needed all of the weapons and armor that they could find since the Dwarven craftsmen were slow to produce enough for everyone.

Lorentz moved from his location to the next expected encounter site to again observe and direct the fight, if necessary. Ilo watched the master climb up over the crest of the ridge and out of sight. Then, he dropped from the roof to help round up the remaining two Orcs. He had slung his bow over his shoulder and drawn his sword. He cautiously moved from wall to wall, looking into the structures as he passed. As before, he was still in sight of at least two others in his party for visual communication. Across the street, another of his party did the same. They watched out for each other and around the corners for the hidden enemy. They must be found and killed. They were so intent on finding the two remaining soldiers that they didn't notice one of them sneaking behind them and off, down the slope of the ridge toward the valley. It moved with a noticeable limp, but was far enough away from the others not to be heard as it scampered down the main path from which they had come.

The Orc knew that his duty was to report what he had seen. His mission was not to battle the enemy, but to find their hiding place. That had been accomplished, so he ran off to find the rest of his fellow Orcs. This news must be brought swiftly to the Bone. There may even be a reward for the group that found the outsiders, he thought as he limped down the mountain pass. He thought nothing of the loss of his comrades, only his greed for wealth and glory kept him going. His thirst and hunger had left his memory for now. He must find the general.

Ilo gave a signal that he was going into the structure where he heard some noise. He cautiously approached the doorway and with his back to the outside wall, peered around the corner. The wooden door had of course been removed and taken underground for other uses. He saw only darkness as this structure was shadowed by the mountain, since the sun was well to the west of them now. One of his companions began to sneak around the rear of the old house for another perspective of the inside. Just as Ilo entered the doorway he heard a vicious war cry from within. His heart raced as he saw the outline of the figure ready to wield its battle ax. Thoughts of his family flashed through Ilo's mind. In mid swing the creature gasped in anguish as a long sword was thrust through its back. Ilo could see a full six inches of the blade at least, sticking out of the warriors chest. It looked down at the protruding blade and dropped the ax that was poised over its head by two stiff arms. The blade was withdrawn and the body fell forward flat on its face. The purple black blood oozed from the gash onto the rocky ground outside the doorway. From inside the house stepped Ilo's fellow mountain dweller with bloodied sword in hand. The human was quite proud of himself and bore a wild eyed grin as he stepped over the corps toward Ilo.

"We must still find the other." Ilo reminded as they signaled that all was well. No one else had seen the last Orc and all the other structures had been thoroughly searched. After a second pass at searching the town, Ilo instructed that the bodies be dragged into the furthest structure from the main path and recounted and stripped of any useful items. There were indeed only nine bodies of the ten warriors accounted for. A great strain of panic ran through his mind. He had failed the prime order, "No survivors." Lord Lorentz would not be pleased, yet Lord Shi'roc would be even more angered, he thought. This would put them all in danger.

* **

It was inevitable, Jantez thought as he watched the group of warriors approaching the wasteland side entrance. He remained hidden as the eight creatures came close to discovering the crevice that led directly to the main tunnels. The others thought this entrance would be difficult to find, yet there was still this possibility. This was the same entrance where he and the others first confronted the Lords Shi'roc and Lorentz, months ago, when their party arrived. He could hear the Orc in the lead grunt something and point at the dark crevice that they were standing near. Jantez was sure they were going in as he watched quietly from above. He made certain not to move or even breath so as to not disturb any pebbles that may be jostled to give his position notice. One at a time they walked passed him into the narrow passage.

"Glunta rogen" the leader explained to his group. It was indeed narrow. Maybe only three or four feet wide in most areas. The Orcs looked and listened carefully as their vision was not so keen in the darkness. They began to bunch up toward the leader as they tried to find any signs of people having been there recently. They walked deeper into the cave entrance beyond where the daylight could reach.

"Ichna toocha" the leader said. Another soldier knelt down to the floor and removed his equipment pack. He drew out some small stones and a torch. The others stood still in the darkness, looking at the cave walls, as he attempted to grind the stones to spark. Another was holding the torch to be lit so as to see where they were going.

"I thought I saw the walls move up there." One of them pointed up ahead of them in a useless gesture. He began to feel claustrophobic, unable to move freely with a weapon in such a tight area. “Hurry with that torch. My eyes must be deceiving me in the dark.”

“There, look.” The leader pointed directly ahead of them in the passageway. “There is someone there. I am sure of it.” He moved forward, poking the air ahead of him with his sword. The rest followed as he moved.

“Were you looking for me?” a loud Elven voice called directly at the head Orc. Maac-To taunted the leader with a little sword play and kept stepping backward, deeper into the cave. Though he knew the creatures could not understand him, he kept up the mocking and insults in order to keep their attention. Then he stopped retreating and stood toe to toe with the head Orc battling as best he could in the confined space. Suddenly, the ceiling of the cave began raining stones upon the intruders. The high walls came to life as the Dwarves began their assault on their unwanted guests. They had beat most of them onto their knees with the heavy stones that they threw, then the formidable short people jumped onto their prey and battled in the darkness.

The remaining two, finally succeeded in lighting the tinder cloth to be placed on the ready torch. They began to move toward the yells of their companions. As they looked up with torch in hand they saw that the ceiling was truly alive. They were pummeled by large rocks being hurled by six very short persons. The rock throwing continued until the Orc with the torch fell to his knees, unable to defend himself from the pounding stones on his head and upper body. The Dwarves then jumped from the rock ledges and repeatedly jabbed and stabbed the intruders with their daggers. One of them barely managed to ward off the Dwarves as he thrust his sword into the chest of the nearest. He ran as quick as he could, in his damaged condition, toward the cave entrance and out into the light of day. One of the Dwarves began to peruse the Orc but was convinced by another to let it go.

The Orc had managed to bounce his way off the rock walls as he stumbled out of the cave opening. Hurried and gasping for breath, he stopped for a moment to take inventory of his wounds. He had indeed been stabbed several times about the lower body. He found blood running down his armor leggings. He realized that he must catch up with the others of his original party and report his findings. He took a few steps out of the crevice when he heard a voice.

"Where do you think you are going?" Jantez' voice startled the creature. The Orc turned right, then left and finally behind looking for the source of the unfamiliar language. With its sword in hand, it cautiously began to move again.

"Here I am." called the voice once again from directly in front of the Orc. It had little time to react as he saw the human suddenly appear in front of him. Jantez sword was in full swing when his spell was broken by the aggression. He had become familiar with this disadvantage of becoming visible once again during an aggressive move. Something about the shift in concentration from the forces that kept him temporarily invisible, to the adrenaline required for aggressive combat.

The Orc tried to fend off the attack with his sword but wasn't entirely successful, catching part of his opponents blade on his left arm. He swung back as he limped, trying to gain a better posture on his weakened legs. Jantez easily blocked the weary blow with his sword, and began taunting the wounded creature. He would jab then step back, avoiding the Orc's blade each time. They were now several yards away from the mountain base, dangerously in sight of any other Orcs that may be nearby.

Jantez heard the hiss of a speedy arrow that ended with a splat. His opponent jerked as he was pierced through the back by the projectile, and indeed there was the sharp tip of an arrow protruding through his breast plate. Blood oozed from the wound as the creature fell forward, smashing his face to the rocky ground. The human finished the job by driving his sword into the warriors spine, severing it at the head just above the armor collar.

"Good shot, M'Lord." Jantez called out as he looked up to Shi'roc who was standing on a ridge just above the crevice. He bent down and grabbed the body of his opponent by the foot and began to drag it into the cave as Shi'roc climbed down the rocks to assist.

Chapter 17
Loyalties

The halls of the castle were still dark and without sound as Fendal regained consciousness. The smell of burnt clothing and flesh, still hung in the air. He lay face down and could feel the cold stone floor pressed against his left cheek. The memory came flashing back to him as he tried to recall why he was lying on an unfamiliar stone floor in the darkness. It was Ach'med who launched the fiery blast, however unlikely that seemed. It was his voice, he recalled, that had spoken the words of anguish and betrayal. How was he alive once again and what did he mean about abandonment?

Fendal took mental inventory of the various pains in his body as he tried to open his eyes. He did not try to move as he was not entirely certain of his condition. He felt barely alive, and indeed he was just that. If not for the powers of the ring that he wore, he would be dead.. Even at that moment he could feel the pulsing surges of the healing powers moving slowly through his body. The ornately crafted ring had been given to him by the master of his master, many decades ago for services that Fendal had performed. The ring had regenerative powers of healing. It could bring back even those beyond death provided it had been worn at the time of death. The magic was even beyond his comprehension since the healing arts were mostly left to those who followed the gods. In past times he had even offered it to others, who had been critically wounded. But then only on short term loan.

After sensing that the ring was still actively healing him he calculated that he may have actually been dead for several hours before he regained consciousness. To regain his full health he would have to remain resting for several more hours while continuing to wear the ring.

Most of his possessions had been entirely burned away, except for that which was protected under him. Much of the clothing that was on his back was now melded into what was left of his skin. He felt the numbness over the parts of his body that were not in pain. Lying immediately next to him was the body of Koloda. It did appear to have some life force though it could be just the heated residue that his vision was picking up. He gathered all of his strength to take a breath so he could attempt to speak. "Koloda, are you living?" he managed to gurgle out of his disfigured mouth. He had smashed his face into the stone floor when diving to avoid the spherical blast of fire. This too would heal soon.

"Quiet." grunted his fat friend. "Someone approaches." The thief remained motionless as well, also within a thread of his life. Neither had the ability to move, much less fight off another enemy. They remained quiet in hopes of remaining unnoticed, or thought dead, by who or whatever was coming. Koloda was able to feel the light footsteps through the stone floor. As he lay there, he could detect more of the vibration and some minute sounds as the entity moved closer. After a few minutes of deep concentration he could tell that it was definitely bi-pedal and slight of build. He was able to determine this from his vast experience in listening to what lay behind the doors and walls of his past victims. Stealth and acute hearing was one of his learned traits.

The entity stopped just a few yards behind them. They could both hear the sounds of flint rocks being scrapped to ignite a torch or candle, perhaps. They had apparently been discovered. They barely opened their eyes, curious as if they were about to be captured, killed or eaten. Neither of the choices was particularly appealing yet they were powerless to change any outcome. They had been disadvantaged before, but never to this extreme. They could see the reflections of a flickering candle from the walls and heard what sounded like sobbing, or someone crying.

"I'm too late." They heard the voice mumble through the tears, as the light of the candle moved closer.

"Cha'ni?" The gravely voice grunted out. "Is that you?" Koloda did his best to urge some muscle in his body to move and show signs of life. He did manage to flinch an arm muscle, since that was all he could feel.

"Father?" The sobbing voice choked. "You're alive?" she shrieked with joy as she dropped to her knees between the two smoldering bodies. "I thought you were dead." She carefully looked over the scorched backside of her father knowing some about severe burns. She knew better than to touch them.

"Why did you come here? We told you to stay home, it is too dangerous for you here." He scolded, doing his best to sound angry that was hard since he was glad she had found them. "How did you find us?" Before she could answer, Fendal managed to get a word in.

"I have been marking the walls on our path, just in case anything happened to you." He explained as Cha'ni turned to him. She had thought her newest lover dead as well.

"Fendal. Why did you not speak before now? I thought you were dead." She said with joy as she tried to find some way to give him a hug. His back was just as burned as her father's so she could not touch him.

"I thought you might be upset with me for talking your father into this trip." Fendal answered slowly. His mouth was dry and he was having trouble breathing. He just lay there, still unable to move. The pain was creeping back into his mind as he tried to get some feeling into his legs. This was a good sign from the ring's healing reaching out to his extremities.

"Don't try to move." She told them both. "I have something that will help." She carefully set down the candle just ahead of where the two lay, and began to unstrap her back pack. From inside, she removed some linen cloth strips, a jar containing some kind of oil, and two small glass vials. Cha'ni uncorked the first vial and gently held it to her fathers torn lips. He too had met the rough floor, face first. Koloda used his tongue to absorb the bluish liquid. It had a pleasant sweet taste and he knew exactly what it was. Then he closed his eyes and concentrated on the warm feeling that slowly ran through his body. The healing potion would take some time and the powers that it drew from his body had put him into a deep sleep. The effect was proof of how close to death he really had been.

Cha'ni began to sprinkle the oily mixture over the burns on his back and legs. Very carefully, she lifted his legs one at a time and wrapped them loosely with the linen bandages. After tending to her father, she turned to Fendal. Once again with the vial, she prodded him to drink.

"No," he told her, "Take care of your father. I will manage." Already he was able to move some of his muscles and touched his hand to the vial, pushing it away from his lips. "Your father may need that later when you take him out of here." The healing process of the ring was increasing.

"I am taking you both out of here as soon as you are able to walk." She said insistently. "You need this as much as my father does." She pushed the liquid back to his lips. "Now drink."

"No," He protested again more strongly and began to push himself up with his arms. She could see then in the candles light that his burns seemed less severe than when she first arrived. He was also speaking more clearly but she didn't understand how or why. "Do not worry about me. I am already getting better you see."

"How can this be. Your skin is healing itself?" She exclaimed in shock touching his hand. The candle light began to flicker as the flame was being snuffed out by the wax puddle it had created. Once again they were in darkness. "I will light another candle," She said, reaching for her sack of supplies.

"No, wait." Fendall said urgently. "We have been here to long. We must get out of this hallway." He began to push himself up on his knees and slowly stood up with the support of the wall and Cha'ni's help. "Help me carry your father to that room." He pointed to the doorway from which they had come early that morning. Together they lifted the hefty elf, being careful not to touch the bandages around his legs and back. Fendal heard something fall from his friends body as they moved him into the room and laid him on the bed.

"My pack is still in the hallway." Cha'ni reminded as she arranged her father as comfortably as possible faced down on the bed. "I should go and get it." She began to head for the door when Fendal gently took her arm and stopped her.

"I will get it." His renewed strength was showing. He had convinced her to stay with Koloda. Fendal wanted to find out what his friend had dropped in the hall. He also wanted a minute alone to take inventory of his own belongings, especially to determine what damage may have been done to his book of magical spells. He stepped out through the door and proceeded to where Koloda had laid. He reached down and felt around on the floor. He found several sheets of parchment folded tightly together. He picked them up and tucked them into the folds of his remaining garments. As he did, he checked the book. He could feel it still intact. It had been protected under him as he dodged the fire blast.

Fendal thought for a moment, then began a few quiet chants. Still in darkness, he waved his arms in a definitive pattern over the area where he and Koloda had fallen. Even he could not see the results of his spell in the dark but was confident of its success. Anyone passing with light would see the dead remains of he and Koloda still lying on the floor. The illusion was not permanent but would suffice to allow them time to recover and be gone. It was unlikely that Ach'med would return to check the bodies, but there may be others living in the castle that might check. He bent down to pick up Cha'ni's supplies and went back into the room.

She remained holding the thief's hand. Fendal was setting in the corner with a lit lamp that was left in the room. There was sufficient oil left to burn for a few hours. He was devoting serious study to many of the spells in his book. He had already discovered that the folded papers, that Koloda had dropped, were the drawings of the fortress. He had recognized them immediately upon seeing them in the light since they were in Fendal's own writing. Long ago when he and the others had first entered Lord Magdelans castle, he himself was the group's map maker. Once it was determined that the passages were becoming too complex to remember, he began making copies so that if anything had happened to the originals, a copy would suffice in an emergency. These were the originals thought to have been lost so many years ago.

Prior to beginning this journey, Koloda had impressed Fendal by claiming to have remembered the passages so that a map was not needed. Now he had come to find that not only was Koloda an excellent thief and liar, but he was also still not to be entirely trusted. Fendal was somewhat depressed, thinking that Koloda's ways of the past had changed, to find out that wasn't the case at all.

The wizard now felt completely healed from his fiery adventure that morning. It was time to get some rest before he continued on his mission to face Ach'med. It was apparent that the once friendly Elf had risen from the dead and become a servant of evil. Fendal was now determined to know why, and also why the resurrected being was so hateful towards he and Koloda. Well; he could understand why he would hold resentment from the one who had gotten him killed. That is, if he had remembered the gruesome death at the hands of the ape creatures.

Cha'ni had fallen asleep where she had been setting with her father. Fendal quietly walked over to observe the horrid scaring of Koloda's back, realizing that his own body had looked the same several hours ago. He slipped the healing ring onto the fat man's finger tip then walked to the next torn bed and put out the lamp.

He awoke the next morning to see the figure of Koloda setting up in the darkness. "Your health has improved?" He asked as more of a statement. Remembering the ring, he approached his recovering companion and quickly snatched it from his finger before Koloda had realized it was even on his hand. "I think it is time for us to move out of here."

Still groggy from the sleep and the entire day's events, Koloda grunted. "What was that?" He started to stand, almost tripping over his daughter who was lying on the floor next to the bed. Cha'ni then awoke and struggled back to a sitting position as the other two talked.

"You should be fully recovered from your burns now." Fendall replied as he returned the ring to his own finger. "The two of you should return to your home. There is no more you can do here. Ach'med is alive and I alone shall find him." He stated as a matter of fact, not expecting any retort.

"Were going with you." Cha'ni blurted out while striking the sparking stones to light a candle. "What do you think you can do alone?" she asked.

"There is only one way to fight magic, and that is with magic." he responded a little louder. "I hope not to have to fight, but from what we have already experienced, it would be better if the two of you were safely out of here. I must find out what is going on." He began to wrap strips of the torn bedding around himself to tie together what was left of his clothing. Koloda had not yet interjected comment. "Koloda, you should try to find a way to get word to

Shi'roc, wherever he might be, that his brother lives again." he hesitated for a moment. "and that he might harbor ill will towards us all." He completed tying up his belongings and headed for the door.

"How will you find your way without me?" Koloda asked to Fendal's back as he began to check himself out in the candle light.

"With my old map." he turned briefly, holding up the folded papers for Koloda to see. "You can find your way out by following my markings, like I had planned to do if we had been parted." He smiled back at Cha'ni as Koloda patted down his clothing looking for the missing maps. "Don't worry, I have them all," Fendal concluded as he opened the door to the hall.

"Be careful." Cha'ni's voice whispered out to him as he closed the door behind him, leaving the bit of light from the candle behind. She turned back to her father. "Did you want to follow him?" She said softly, offering him her loyalty.

"I am afraid he is right." he replied grimly as he began to tear the old bedding into strips of cloth. "We have nothing to offer against the magic we encountered. If that was Ach'med, he is no longer our friend." Cha'ni helped him to tie together the remaining charred clothing before they began their journey back to Tireth-Tec.

* * *

In the hours of real time, the Goddess, Lolith, tested Ach'med with challenges of loyalty and endurance. The pain he suffered in the conflicts of her teaching was rewarded by the great wealth of knowledge that would have normally taken him years of training in the real world to achieve. Not only was his understanding of magic enhanced, but she also imparted to him the ways of the priests who would serve her. This was a rarity since normally a male Elf would only be allowed the knowledge of magic while undergoing these rituals. Only the females would be given the priestly powers of the dark goddess. Not only was she the keeper of arachnids but also the worshipped queen of the Dark Elves. From her palace in hell, she ruled all of the members of the secret society that she alone created, formed from Elves that she had turned. Those who graduated her academy with honors would bear her resemblance in grace, beauty and her sensuous dark complexion. Even those who failed would bear her resemblance having the torso of a Dark Elf and a lower body of a spider with all of its web spinning capabilities. The arachnoid would also retain the magical or priestly abilities that it had acquired until the point of dismissal from her teachings. Most thought it an honor to share both of her traits as beauty and beast.

There, in the domain of the goddess, weeks had passed and Ach'med had accepted his role in the literal web of evil, for the entity known as the 'Spider Queen' was well named. The palace of the sometimes beautiful woman was indeed alive with various spiders. Some small as to fit in the palm of her hand and some large enough to engulf and crush a full sized man in its mandibles. When in her humanoid form her beautiful white hair would flow over her dark skinned shoulders, and rest on her voluptuous breasts. When she spent time with her pets, she frolicked as a giant furry wolf spider, spinning her webs throughout the palace.

Though he was only experiencing through his mind, the pain and pleasure was quite real to him. He was not aware that his body remained in the real world, still in a trance in the temple. His body had aged yet, only a day while his mind had grown immensely.

He learned to accept and befriend all forms of arachnids. This came about even before he had learned that if he had failed in his tests of loyalty, he would become part web spinner himself as punishment. His gradual liking for

Lolith's pets impressed her to the point of attraction. Even her underworld lover, Hartes, did not seem to enjoy her furry multileged followers. He found no comfort or usefulness to their existence but accepted them as pets of his beautiful queen.

Several times during his training, the young Elf was rewarded with erotic pleasures, as real to him as could be. He had never before known the touch of a woman, the softness of her skin against his. These would not be moments that he would share stories of as if word had ever gotten to Hartes, he would most certainly suffer for eternity. Not even when he awoke from his spell would he realize that it had all been an extracorporeal experience. He would never know that only a day had passed nor would he know that he had never left the temple.

Ach'med was to be the General of the forces of Moracles, holding the title of 'Vandar' back in the real world. Historically, the ancient title was earned by a warrior over a lifetimes service to a lord or king. Rarely was this title bestowed as few would live long enough to earn it. As a loyal protector to a master, the warrior would travel far in the name of his homeland. These things Ach'med had not done nor would ever do to have earned the title of 'Vandar'.

His duties would include serving as the evil wizards apprentice and body guard, though there was little chance that the later would be necessary. He would not only be a capable soldier but also a mage and priest. Having the favor of the goddess as well would someday make him even more powerful than Moracles. As his realm would grow, all of the soldiers who would serve his empire would someday serve Ach'med. What Ach'med did not realize was that Moracles' task was to prepare the world for the eventual rule of Hartes and Lolith. All would be subject to their whims whether it be in servitude or death. The world would just be an extension of their noncorporeal realm of hell.

Moracles slowly opened the doors to the temple at the prescribed time. He looked inside only to see the shadow of Ach'med, frozen in the darkness, still entranced by the goddess. He sighed with relief that his student had not acquired new appendages and had been accepted into Lolith's secret society. He stepped passed the still form of the Elf so as to light some new candles near the altar. Soon would his spirit return to the body and a faithful new companion along with it.

Suddenly, Ach'med's body began to shake while the wizard watched. He could see that the body was being reconnected to the mind and soul once again. This was the first time he had witnessed the event. He recalled that the last two times he had returned to the temple back in the canyon and found that his potential students had been turned into the dreaded arachnoids. The convulsions ceased and the Elf began to change in appearance. The mage's face turned to a frown as the Elf's skin went dark and his hair turned gray. Moracles feared that Ach'med would begin to sprout the spider's legs, but this did not occur. The Elf opened his eyes slowly finding himself once again back in the temple. Not only had his skin and hair changed, but also his physique. He had become stronger along with the wisdom and intelligence of an adult Elf.

"Welcome back." The old man said with a grin returning to his face. He was pleased to have finally succeeded in acquiring a loyal subject. He would not let on how little time had actually passed, or tell Ach'med that he had never really left the temple. "Are you well?" he looked the Elf over as he walked around him. He knew better than to question him about his mind's journey. That would be an offense to Lolith's privacy.

Ach'med looked at his own hands and saw the dark gray skin as that of Lolith. He responded to his master, "I am in perfect health and then some." he smiled back at the human. Grinning at the pleasurable experiences that he dared not reveal. "What are your wishes master Moracles?" he asked.

"First you must rest before making the long journey back to my fortress to meet your new army, Vandar." He addressed him by his new title, knowing that his return as a Dark Elf could only mean that he had passed all of Lolith's tests and was prepared to accept that honor. "Then we will review your new powers and practice some new magic as was taught to you by Lolith. In a few weeks you will be in your new home. Even now, our enemy awaits you."

"Our enemy?" Ach'med grinned. "Tell me more of our enemy, that I may crush them." He was indeed eager for battle in every way. He was anxious to test his new skills and practice the old ways of the warrior, with sword and shield.

"In time." Moracles tried to soothe his lust for battle. "There will be plenty of time to learn of your enemy on our journey back." He motioned his new apprentice toward the temple door with his pointed finger. "We must prepare ourselves to return to my Forgotten Valley far to the east." He put his arm around the young man's shoulder as they passed through the doorway and back to the master's chambers. "Even by ethereal passage the voyage will be a week long," he added as they disappeared past the torch light.

Once the hall was again silent, a shadowy figure emerged from behind the open temple door. It made no sound but was barely visible in the bright torch light. It reached up and withdrew the hood from over its head. Suddenly, Fendal appeared quite clearly, staring down the hall where the two magi had passed. "I know not of this place that they spoke of, but I will find it." He whispered quietly to himself. Fendal knew that the longer he remained in the castle, the greater the danger in being discovered. By now his illusion would have worn off and Ach'med or Moracles might notice the bodies missing.

He thought hard about where he was in the castle. He took advantage of the torch light and pulled out the maps to study. His fingers followed the hallways of ink. Some he remembered but others had long since slipped his mind. It was apparent that he was looking for something in particular. He riffled through the pages to look for the room. It was distinctly marked with a 'P' "The paintings are here," He remarked as his finger found the room and traced its passage back to where he was standing. The room was further into the castle on a lower floor. He determined that it would take all day if traveling carefully through the fortress. "I wonder if 'Zant' might still be there?" he said to himself as he headed off into the direction of the staircase that would bring him close to his goal.

"I'm hungry," He thought to himself as he continued his trek down the dark halls. It had been days since he had eaten last, and then not a real meal. He knew there would be no food or drink to be found here. He should have taken some of the supplies from Cha'ni before he left. A stray thought of her soft body against his crossed his mind but he quickly dismissed it by concentrating on the path. He could not afford such a distraction. There would be time for pleasures after his mission was complete. But first he had to figure what his mission would be. One step at a time. First to find Zant, if he still existed.

He stopped to take a look at the map to be sure of his progress. He bent down to light a small piece of candle that he had scavenged from one of the abandoned rooms. Since being a scavenger was a long ago adventure, Fendal had not done bad this day. He had found several usable candle scraps, flints, a torch, linens and clothing. Most everything he could use except for food. Though his magical abilities could afford him light at any time, he felt better not to waste the energy when other means were available.

Kneeling on the ground with the pages spread out around the small flame, he traced his finger from his target to where he was now. He was on the correct level of the fortress and very near to where the paintings had been found before. He hopped with all his soul that he could once again visit Zant, the Golden Dragon, that had been freed from the powers of Lord Magdelan by himself and his long lost comrades. Perhaps the old Dragon's wisdom could shed some light on the recent events that Fendal had been witness to. Who was this Moracles? and how could he have raised Ach'med from a death so long ago? What powers could have turned him to a Dark Elf and endowed him with instant magical abilities?

So far he had not encountered any person or creature that could threaten him in the castle. An occasional rodent or two was all that crossed his path. He had been careful to listen at every juncture and door that might reveal a potential enemy, or possibly friend. It was indeed possible though unlikely that scavengers or adventurers would be traveling these halls as he once did. He became convinced that the castle was void of all intelligent life except for the mage and his lost friend, Ach'med.

A short while later, he reached the hallway that would lead to the room. Just around the corner and he should see the doorway on his left. Cautiously and silently he proceeded to the corner. He listened, then peaked around in search of living heat. None was to be found. The darkness was not even disturbed by the movement of air, so Fendal used his hands along the walls to find the entrance to the room.

The double doors were closed. The Elf concentrated on a spell that would help him determine the safety of the room. He closed his eyes and mumbled a few mystical words, or rather sounds, and envisioned the contents of the room as if he were actually standing on the other side of the door. He could see everything through his mind's eye like the room was well lighted. There were some tables and chairs. Some were smashed in pieces and others were just knocked over. He let his mind scan the room to the fire place on the left wall. It had not been used for some time. The vision went up the few steps at the far side of the room. The paintings for which he searched were still in place. One was to his left and the other directly ahead. The paintings were faded or dust covered since he was not able to make out any details. He checked the room once more for any signs of life. There was no apparent danger, at least not from any inhabitants, so he decided to end the vision spell and enter the room.

Now he would need to light his torch and look at the paintings for real. He walked up the steps to the end of the room and studied the art work very carefully. He pulled out a piece of cloth and gently stroked the canvas from top to bottom, releasing the dust to fall on the floor. Time had faded some of the coloring but the scene was just as before. The painting showed, up close, some flowering trees and brightly colored bushes. Beyond were the steep canyon walls that seemed to surround the small valley. In one corner he could see a small water fall. He was filled with memories and hope at seeing the painting again.

Fendal quickly moved to the wall on his right and again removed the dusty covering and viewed the scene. This picture showed the same valley from a different perspective. It was closer to one of the rock walls. A cave entrance could be seen through the trees. With the light of the torch held high, he searched the trees for a sign. Fendal almost let out a triumphant yell when he found the tiny yellow canary in one of the fruit trees in the painting.

He stepped back from the wall, and with a grin on his face walked to the center of the room, keeping the two paintings in clear sight. He mentally prepared himself and rolled the words over in his mind. He said aloud the mystical words with his eyes still closed in concentration.

The words had been rarely spoken, only once by himself when he was with his companions so long ago.

Fendal felt a slight breeze and opened his eyes to find himself no longer in the room, deep in the bowels of Lord Magdelans Castle, but in an open wooded area. The air was fresh and filled with pleasant smells of the surrounding flora. It was night and all was dark except for the area lit by the torch that was still in his hand. He did a quick look in all directions to verify his location. Just behind him, he found an old tree stump that had been uprooted from the ground. A deep hole remained in front and beneath it, like it had been purposely dug up. Indeed it had been.

At one time a large chest of coins and jewels had been buried there. This was the Lord Magdelans hiding place, and escape route. Once defeated, Fendal and some of his party, discovered this place by uttering those same words, that meant hiding place. There he realized that the surrounding landscape was almost identical to the paintings in the room. From that point he was able to coordinate exactly where the treasure had been buried by visually aligning himself up with the two picture's scenes. It was just a matter of digging up the stump to find the chest. That was long after their friend Ach'med had been laid to rest in the temple of Tireth-Tec. But tonight, he was not here for treasure. It was answers and wisdom that he sought in this valley.

He was gravely hungry, so he cleared an area of brush and started a small campfire for the night. He had laid down the bundled bed linens and walked to the near fruit trees. Just as he remembered, there was always ripe fruit for the picking, no matter what the season. How he wished he could perform such magic. Filling himself with the delicious variety of fruit, he became tired and laid himself to sleep next to the fire.

As the sun created a crimson glow over the eastern canyon ridge, Fendal awoke to the sounds of a chirping bird. The fire had died and Fendal felt the frost on his coverings. He looked through the dim light at the trees for the source of the chirping. The sounds had stopped. He concentrated on a spell in his mind and spoke the word with a wave of his hand, "Thermium" and a magical warmth flowed through the mage allowing him to think more clearly. He knew that the spell would not last for very long.

He quickly arose from his bedding pallet and began gathering more fallen branches to build another fire. As he walked through the dimly lit trees he heard someone else's foot steps. "Zant. Is that you?" he called as he laid down the pile of sticks on the smoldering ash. He looked up to see the old man standing near a tree at the edge of his clearing.

"Yes Fendal. It is I, Zant. Warm yourself," he said coolly as the fresh pile of tinder burst into flames when the old man pointed his finger "Tell me why you have come to visit?" he asked, still standing at the tree. " Has much happened since I have been gone? I have been out of touch with this world for far to long." Zant often talked in riddles or rhymes.

"I am so glad you remember me after all this time." The Elf replied as he stood by the blazing fire. "Please come join me so we can talk." he motioned for the old man to approach the fire as he himself sat to get warm. "I seek your wisdom and knowledge of other worlds."

"Time has been shorter for me than for you." Zant replied as he stepped into the clearing. "In this form, as a human, it is cold for me too." He came close to the fire and sat upon the upturned stump. He thought about how he met Fendal and the others when they were digging up the lost treasures of Magdelan.

"Ach'med." he started verbalizing his random thoughts. "He was my friend, before he was killed." Fendal said with grief. "But now he has been given life again and turned to a Dark Elf with magical powers. How could this be done to him?" He thought back on how good and righteous Ach'med had been in his former life and how they had carried his body around for weeks after his horrible death trying to revive him. "He accused us of abandoning him."

"So you have seen him. Spoken to him?" Zant was a bit surprised at this fact. He did not know much of recent events that for him, a hundred years was recent, but day to day details would slip his knowledge. "What do you wish to know?" The old man became serious.

"How and why, to start." Fendal blurted, quite comfortably, forgetting to whom he was speaking. He stared and poked at the fire with a stick as he talked. Certainly more respect was due to the guardian of the Dragons' Gate. "and who is this Moracles, that raised him from the dead?"

"Moracles?" Zant roared with an inhuman, thunderous voice of rage. Fendal looked up from the fire and saw a shinning gold dragon floating over him. Just the mention of Moracles' name infuriated Zant to the point that he could not hold the transmutation spell that made him appear as a human. Even the Dragon's magical abilities required concentration. Now, in his true form he was quite intimidating. His golden scales now glittered in the sunlight that had crept over the canyon walls. His long snake like body was thick and curled. He had thick curled whiskers about his nostrils and ears. Though he had no wings, his natural abilities allowed him to fly or suspend himself in the air.

Fendal stood up to face Zant and still had to crane his neck back to speak to him. Though he had only seen the form of the old man previously, he knew what he was and what he was capable of. Still, the powerful image that floated before him put him in awe. "What do you know of Moracles?" he pressed Zant for an answer.

"He was the apprentice to Lord Magdelan. It was he who entrapped me as a gift to his master." The Dragon now spoke in a calmer, more thoughtful tone. "I had expected that he would be dead by now since he is a human."

"He would have to be over a hundred years old at least." Fendal interjected, surprised at the the realization. "Was he here when we defeated Magdelan?" Fendal began to piece the puzzle together.

"Yes. He must have eluded you and your friends when you killed his master. I do not know what his purpose would be with your resurrected friend." The massive creature paused to think. "Remain here. I will seek council from Alena. She may shed some light on this matter." Then the mighty Zant floated up above the tree line. Suddenly, the sky opened up with a swirl of clouds just above the center of the canyon and Zant was gone. He had indeed passed into the heavenly planes to speak directly to the Goddess whom he served.

Fendal stood staring at the sky where Zant was sucked through the air. "That must have been the Dragons' Gate." he mumbled to himself. He of course had heard of the Goddess, Alena, but knew little about her. He did know that she was the Goddess of righteous combat, and protected those who fought for good. He could understand that Zant would have some contact with her since he too was a protector of good.

Chapter 18
Orcs

It had been a long and grueling day for the mountain residents. The sun had set and the night watchers were at their posts. The battles were over and the results tallied. The wounded inhabitants were gathered in the Great Hall as they were tended to by their fellow warriors. Shi'roc had personally congratulated each one of the student soldiers as they entered the chamber. Most carried their wounded or dead. Unfortunately, there were casualties, but fewer than there would have been if they had not been forewarned of the pending attacks. All in all, Shi'roc was pleased at the performance of his new army. The intruders had been stopped from finding their secret passages into the underground villages. They would be safe a while longer while they continued to train for the inevitable war against Moracles' armies.

Lorentz had already gotten word that two of the creatures had been captured by the clerics during meditation. This thought amused him as he made way through the tunnels for the water cave where Lady A'mora had taken the student priests to pray. He knew that his healing services were greatly needed by the others but he must get to the prisoners to learn of their instructions and their leaders. Perhaps he could find out more about Moracles and whatever other dangers may lie ahead.

"Is everyone accounted for?" Shi'roc asked Ilo and Maac-To as they made the wounded as comfortable as possible. They had removed whatever protective gear they were wearing in order to more easily bandage the wounds. The more experienced soldiers of Lorentz' guard helped to field dress the injured Elves and Dwarves. They had many times needed to bandage brave men after their battles against evil Lords under the leadership of Lord Lorentz. They felt privileged tonight to be tending to those who only months ago had never held a weapon in their hands. These people had come a long way from hiding in shadows when they had first arrived, to fighting the powerful Orcs.

"Yes, M'lord. All of our people are accounted for." Ilo replied. "Including the three dead. But…?" He hesitated to tell him of the enemy body count. He knew for sure that one had managed to get away.

"But what?" Shi'roc asked. "Is there a problem? You should be proud of yourselves. You fought well." he turned to address the entire hall. "You all fought bravely today. You have proven yourselves in battle." He turned back to Maac-To.

"Yes my Lord, but what Ilo was trying to tell you was that the enemy body count does not concur with your original estimation." the older Elf tried to ease the pain of reality. "We believe that a few have gotten away from us." He looked seriously into Shi'roc's eyes. "We will be in danger if those two return and warn the others of our whereabouts. If Moracles…"

"You are mistaken, not to worry, the two you have not accounted for are in the custody of Lady A'mora. ." Shi'roc interrupted. "You have the other forty eight bodies collected." he turned unconcerned to walk off.

"No, my Lord. We have not erred. We have collected only forty six of the disgusting creatures," Maac-To responded, irritated and frustrated. All of what they had kept hidden for these decades would now be known by Moracles when the two return. "I am sorry. We have failed you." he lowered his head as Shi'roc wheeled back around, not so much in anger as in urgency.

"Are you absolutely sure there are only forty six?" he asked seriously with a raise of his eye brows. The two nodded, sorrowfully in response. He thought for a brief moment, biting his lip as experience ran through his mind. His strategic analytical process kicked in. "Quickly, instruct the eastern watchers to look for any signs of campfires. If the two have escaped they will be heading back to the valley." He looked around at the wounded men and women. "The healers will be here soon. I must inform Lorentz." He walked off toward the tunnels still rolling all the possible outcomes of the day's tragic events over in his mind.

* * *

A'mora paced in front of the cave entrance awaiting word from Lorentz. She had sent her students to help the wounded worriers. The Goddess, Mirana, had envisioned her that there were many wounded to be tended to. She would have gone herself but did not wish to leave the prisoners alone. Though tied and gagged, it was not prudent to leave them unwatched. If they were to escape or become loose in the tunnels, more harm may come to the villagers. She waited patiently while keeping an eye on the bound creatures at the far side of the water cave, still situated on the rock ledge. The position was perilous enough that too much struggling against the leather straps would off balance them and cause them to fall.

A'mora heard some quickened foot steps in the dark passage way approaching her position. Seconds later, Lorentz appeared in the opening. He was breathing a bit heavy, indicating that he had run most of the way. At his age, that sort of exercise was uncommon, even for a warrior.

"I understand you are to be congratulated." He smiled and looked into her soft eyes. "With courage like that, you should have led the warriors and left me behind with the students." He opened his arms to give her a big hug. He was quite proud of his finest student, having captured two gruesome warriors without even lifting a weapon. "Come, show me your prize." He released his hug.

"I am so glad that you were not hurt in the battles." she said with concern. "I had felt there were a great many casualties and did not know the details." She squeezed his hand affectionately as they walked through the fruit tree groves. "I have sent my healers to the Great Hall. Is that where everyone is?" she asked to be sure that her intuitions were correct.

"Yes, indeed. I passed them along the way. I was just an observer of some of the battles and was in no danger. There were more wounded than I had hoped for, mostly minor." He said grimly. "We had the advantage in every case. Surprise, position, numbers, all except equipment. There was just not enough protective armor and weapons to go around." He said frustrated. "Did you know that some of the Dwarves fought with stones and bare hands in the caves? These are the bravest bunch that I have come across."

"Perhaps it has to do with Shi'roc's training and encouragement," She said questioningly. "He has worked wonders with their skills and abilities," she praised.

"As have you, my dear, with your clerics. They seem to have learned quite a bit from you as well." Lorentz reminded her that they all had part in training and supporting the survivors of the mountain villages. "I hear that your friend, Jantez, is quite a mischievous character." he interjected.

"Is he all right?" She stopped and turned to Lorentz, showing a bit more concern than he would have expected. Realizing that she still had feelings for him even though they had not spent much time together, she tried to cover up her mistake. "Did he perform well? I did teach him a few tricks before you continued with his science training."

"Yes. He did fine according to Shi'roc. Jantez does take chances however, that Shi'roc was concerned about." He continued to walk toward the shrine, above which were the two bound Orcs. "Let's see what your two friends have to say, shall we?" He proceeded to climb the rock ledges up and around the water trough.

A'mora followed slowly behind him. It had been a long day for her, being only human. She was becoming tired having endured the strain of deep meditation and the stress of watching the prisoners. She felt she had done the right thing by sparing their lives so that Lorentz could learn from them what they were all up against. Being familiar with Lorentz' abilities and habits, she began to meditate once again on a spell that would enhance her abilities to detect when the creatures were telling the truth, even though she would not be able to understand the language. Lorentz also began to chant as he knelt before the two grotesque figures. He was praying for the ability to understand their language and in turn communicate coherently with them.

The warriors still were tied back to back, bound from their feet to their wrists and to each other. Each had been gagged with a tight strap by A'mora. They were both wearing an expression of total horror as the two priests chanted in harmony, each with a different melody and tone. They had never witnessed such a recital but had heard of those instances where Moracles had performed rituals. Rituals of death and destruction. Their minds were filled with ideas of how these two strangers might be torturing them with these incantations. The sweat began to pour down their brows and backs. They squirmed to loosen the bindings, even more now than before. What manner of creature would they be turned into? they thought.

The meditation had relaxed the two so that the powers of the goddess would pass through them. At the conclusion of the chanting, Lorentz began to untie the gag straps. They both gasped for air and to exercise their jaws. The priest stepped back and sat to listen to the yet incomprehensible babble. The two creatures cut loose with a deluge of curses and threats, now that they realized they were not being tortured, at least not yet. Lorentz had been exposed to the language before but had never been a master since each group of Orcs he had encountered seemed to have its own variation and dialect. A'mora also sat back to listen to the tones and to feel the passions and anger in their voices. Their tones and inflections would alert her to their honesty or denial. Though she could not understand the language her part was to indicate these feelings to Lorentz as he began to ask questions. After a few moments of concentration, as with the Dwarven council, he began to speak to them in their own tongue. He had remembered that the language was not complicated and consisted of simple short sentences. He had to make the questions simple as well.

"How many in your scouting party?" He started with a question for which he knew the answer already so that A'mora could get a proper feel of the conversation. The creatures gasped at the shock of being spoken to in their language by a human. On occasion they had heard Moracles do so, but not even the Magdarn soldiers would speak to them totally in their own language.

"Hundreds." one of them blurted out almost instinctively. An obvious lie since Shi'roc had counted only fifty. A'mora indicated a negative response that validated its claim as a lie. Lorentz was satisfied since he knew she did not even know the question that was asked. He continued the questioning.

"Did Moracles send you to find us?" He pressed, again knowing the answer in advance.

Their reply in unison was a resounding "NO!" The priestess indicated that as a truthful answer.

Lorentz looked at her puzzled, expecting a lie detected. "Are you sure of that?" He asked her. She nodded in silence so as not to indicate to the beasts that the two were working in unison. He turned back to the Orcs. "How far is your castle?"

The one answered indignantly. "I will not tell you." Lorentz drew a sharp dagger from under his cloak and held it in his right hand to the prisoners throat. His speed and silence was so proficient that none of them, not even A'mora, had seen the movement. She jilted back, startled at the unexpected action. With an enraged stare, Lorentz put his face, nose to nose with the revolting creature and asked again, slowly sliding the blade under his throat. "How far is the castle?"

The Orcs were powerful warriors but not so brave when it came to being tortured. The one to his back yelled out insistently. "Do not tell him." That was easy for him since he could not feel the blade to his comrades neck. "Bone will kill us." He added quickly as a reminder.

"Bone? Who is Bone?" Lorentz insisted as the edge of the blade pressed harder against the prisoners neck, not yet drawing blood from the thick hided creature. It panted as sweat again trickled from his forehead and down his neck along the tip of the dagger. "Tell me or I will cut." Lorentz' apparent rage concerned A'mora. She did not understand the words, but the actions were clearly unlike him.

"No," she shrieked. "Don't do it." She began to get up to keep Lorentz from these dark proceedings. Was his anger that great? What had come over him?

He quickly held up his left hand to silence her. while still staring down the Orc. It rolled back its eyes away from Lorentz to get a glimpse of what was going on behind him. It had regained its nerve, possibly sensing that Lorentz had no intention of harming it. It appeared to the creature that the man in front of him was paying heed to this mere female, a sign of deceit.

"No. I will not," it said emphatically, then spit in Lorentz face. As the green slime dribbled down, the Orc began to chuckle and laugh at him.

Lorentz withdrew the blade from its neck and stood up. He wiped the spittle from his face with the end of his robe, then looked at A'mora. She wore a sorrowful look not having realized that Lorentz rage was an act to terrorize the prisoners. She realized that she may have been the cause for the disruption.

"Forgive me." She pleaded. "I should have known you were only pretending." She lowered her head in shame as she reached for the leather gags. "Should I tie them back up?" She asked gesturing to the straps in her hands. Lorentz tried hard not to be angered and just nodded. The Orcs began to spout more obscenities as she began to tie their mouths with the bindings.

"I wish I had not been pretending." Lorentz protested as he dramatically stuffed his dagger into its hidden sheath. His actions were smooth and effortless, as if a bird in flight. He was disturbed, not by A'mora's actions, but by the words of the prisoners.

"What did you learn from them?" A'mora asked as she completed the binding.

"It appears that our enemy is no longer Moracles. They seem to be more frightened of what they called 'Bone' who must be their leader now." Lorentz began to climb down to the grotto to think. A'mora followed. "We really don't know much more than we did before. We knew little about Moracles to start with." He spoke as he paced in front of his stone carving of the Goddess to which he prayed for guidance.

"But we did know that he was a wizard and a priest." She interrupted. "Who do you suppose this Bone might be?" She thought for a moment and answered her own question with a question. "A powerful servant of Moracles perhaps?"

"Lorentz? A'mora?" Shi'roc's voice echoed from the mouth of the cave entrance. He looked around near the horses and then sprinted toward the water troughs. When he emerged from the fruit tree grove, he saw Lorentz and A'mora awaiting his announced arrival.

"Well; what have you learned from the prisoners?" He asked, catching his breath. He too had run all the way from the Great Hall. "Something good, I hope, because we have a problem." He looked to Lorentz for encouragement. There was a silence for a moment as each wondered what to say next.

Lorentz thought for a moment how to find the good side of each situation. "Yes, there is good news. Moracles did not send these creatures to find us." He put on his mischievous grin. Shi'roc's eyes brightened at the news thinking that all along he had been right about the paranoia. There was no Moracles to worry about. "These soldiers were sent by something or someone called Bone." Lorentz continued to explain as he began to pace again. "Someone that we know nothing about," he added. "And these last two here, aren't about to tell us anything because they are terrified of this Bone." He gestured up the ledge to the squirming beasts that were about to tumble down the rock ledge until Shi'roc looked up at them.

"I will give them something to fear." He said in a growling lower tone as he eyed the gruesome lumps. They looked back into the fearsome warriors eyes and saw only their deaths. They had enough intelligence to know that this one meant business. "We must know our enemy before we are attacked." Shi'roc insisted. "We may not have much time to prepare." He stepped over to climb the ledge, when he was interrupted by Lorentz.

"What do you mean by that? These are the last two who could reveal our hiding place." Lorentz said firmly. "We are in no immediate danger." He turned to A'mora and gave an encouraging smile thinking that they were safe from being discovered.

Shi'roc turned around to speak casually as he climbed the ledge. "There were two others that got away. We had counted these two twice as we tallied up the bodies." He continued as he completed the ascension to the Orcs.

Lorentz and A'mora did not take the news as calmly as Shi'roc had delivered it. They were almost panicked.

"Are you sure there weren't bodies missed on the mountain side?" Lorentz asked hurriedly, in frustration. He had thought everything so well planned that it was impossible to miss any of the enemy. "You must find them, track them down." A'mora called up to the warrior as he eyed his captive opponents. He was apparently not as concerned as they were about retrieving the necessary information. "What can you learn from them?" She asked.

Shi'roc untied the gag straps to hear their rabble. Lorentz' spell had since worn off so that he could no longer understand all of what was being said by the prisoners. "Longa tucha?." Shi'roc spoke directly to the Orcs. He bent over one of them as he slid his dagger under its throat. Both Lorentz and A'mora were surprised that Shi'roc could speak their language, but did not interrupt his interrogation. "Oota longa?" Shi'roc spoke to them as their master rather than the more casual tongue that Lorentz had used.

They recognized these as words of authority and hesitated in responding. It had appeared to the Orcs at this point that the others wearing robes were the servants of this warrior. They could see power and death in his eyes as he spoke. "Tucha dua longa." The one answered as he swallowed hard against the pressing knife blade. "Este longa." He continued after taking a breath. The blade was slowly removed from his throat. The Orc let out a heavy sigh of relief.

Shi'roc looked down to his friends at the shrine. "They traveled from the east for two weeks." He told them very calmly. "That will give us approximately four weeks to prepare if the two that escaped make it back to report." He took into account that they were moving slowly on foot. The two may be wounded and that it would take time to gather and prepare the forces to send back for another attack. He put his dagger back into one of the four sheaths draped across his chest. Then proceeded to climb back down, satisfied with the information.

"How did you know their language?" Lorentz asked. "And why would they answer you and not me?" He seemed surprised and disappointed in his own failure to extract the information. "How do you know they were telling the truth?" He shook his head in disbelief as Shi'roc approached.

"I learned the language at the battle of Cerrat shortly before you and I met. There were hundreds of these creatures attacking that castle. I learned some from interrogating their wounded." He shrugged his shoulders. "As far as why they would not respond to you, you wear robes, not armor." He lightly tugged on Lorentz flowing sleeve. "They are warriors and only have respect for superior warriors. Therefore this "Bone" must be some sort of powerful warrior himself." Though this line of reasoning was a natural result of his experience, the logic of his analysis, amazed Lorentz and A'mora. "They could not lie to me once they were convinced that I was their superior." He nodded to them both as he walked past toward the cave entrance. "We should discuss plans for the attack tomorrow in the great hall. I have already alerted the watchers on the eastern slope to look for campfires. Perhaps we can spot the two who got away."

A'mora and Lorentz looked at each other puzzled. They both looked up at the two creatures tied on the ledge, still spouting off obscenities, wondering what to do with them now. Suddenly a voice echoed from the cavern entrance. "Lady A'mora. The voice called. "Where are you? We need your help." She had recognized the human voice of one of her students. "Ilo's wife is having her baby."

"I will be there soon." She replied casually and thought about re-tying the mouths of the prisoners. Their unintelligible vulgarities began to disturb her. She was a healer not a warrior. Though trained to be able to defend herself in combat, she abhorred the idea of keeping these two tied up.

"She is having trouble with the delivery." Her student called anxiously.

Lorentz took her arm as he looked into her eyes. "Go with him. I will tend to these two." He jabbed his thumb in the general direction of the ledge. "You are better at delivering babies than I." He said jokingly, remembering how they first met. He had been asked to help with a difficult birth while visiting a local temple. Though his healing powers were great, he had no concept of what was involved with a birth or the problems that may occur. His healing strength had been accumulated over the years by healing wounded soldiers in battle and relieving plagues. Gashes and diseases he could deal with quite easily, but a birth was very different. A'mora had been an attendant at the temple. As Lorentz began fumbling through the painful birthing, she had stepped in to help. As the temple attendant, she had delivered several of that towns children and had become aware of the potential problems. Thanks to her, both the mother and child survived the procedure. From that time on, Lorentz had felt the strength of her healing potential and offered her his teaching. She began to travel with him from town to town, healing the injured and curing the sick. He had taught her the ways of the healing plants and how to mix mosses and plant juices as poultices. As his affections for her grew, he knew there would be a time that she would move on and need to be able to protect herself. Following the teachings of the goddess, Mirana, she learned to use a whip and hammer to fend for herself.

A'mora hurried to catch up with Shi'roc and follow the student priest back to Ilo's home in the caves. As she expected, the mixture of Ilo's Elven heritage and that of his human wife had complicated the delivery. First she had to relax the mother and ease the pain. She accomplished this by chanting while pressing her fingers on the woman's forehead. Once the breathing had become more controlled, A'mora concentrated her magical abilities, with her hands on the woman's large belly and communicated with the baby girl. The child cooperated by turning itself around in the womb and untangling the umbilical cord. The child 'Aliah' was born soon after and was blessed at the shrine of Mirana. Ilo held his daughter with pride.

* * *

The floor of the Great Hall had been turned into a large map of the region with as much known detail as possible. Maac-To and the some of the elder Dwarves had directed the layout consisting of small rocks arranged on the far edge as the Dwarven Peaks. Their combined memories provided locations and relative distances of the once flourishing towns and villages. The layout continued east showing the locations of the previously inhabited towns and the now withered forests. The canyons to the far east, caused by Moracles' earth quake, were represented by trenches engraved in the rough dirt floor. This information was provided to Shi'roc by the two Orc prisoners. It seemed there was nothing they would not tell him now.

He had seen to it that they were well treated as warriors deserved. They had been provided with food and some shreds of clothing that had been taken from the combined forty six dead Orcs. No trace of the two that eluded them was ever found. These two remained tied up in the water cave to keep them from knowing too much of their captors. Shi'roc had also learned from them that Moracles had vanished many weeks earlier.

The Orcs did not know why, only that the Bone had taken charge. He had been one of Moracles' henchmen as A'mora suggested, but they did not know where he had originally come from. Lorentz had heard of such creatures that lived in the frozen corners of the lower planes of existence, but had never in his journeys encountered one. He could not determine why it would be here on the plane of the material world.

Shi'roc, Lorentz and Grefden studied the completed map showing the general location of the subterranean fortress of Moracles. They measured the main roads, known by the Orcs, with their swords, estimating their relative distances. Maac-To watched as the masters of battle planned their defense.

The Dwarven council wanted no part in planning such a battle so they went back to their work in the mines, creating and smithing the metals used in the weapons and armor. A task that they were proficient at, yet had previously vowed never to do again after the coming of Moracles. The others were assigned duties in preparation for the impending attacks on the mountain. Some assisted in the mining and crafting of the weapons, while others continued to hone their fighting skills.

Once reasonably certain of its accuracy, Lorentz began to draw a map. From one of the many pockets in his robe, emerged a roll of parchment, quill and a small bottle of black ink. Resting with his back against a rock, he began his artistry. Not only was the map functional, it also would serve as a record of history, provided that anyone was left to tell the tales of the upcoming great battle between the forces of the Bone and the valley survivors. The intricate art work of the quill in Lorentz' hands would enhance the tales told in decades to come.

"I expect that the forces would follow this path, as the Orcs had made." Shi'roc pointed out to Grefden, with the tip of his sword. "Perhaps two weeks as an army at a steady pace on foot. We can not be certain of the number or type of our enemy. That is what troubles me," the warrior said. Though the Orcs had been cooperative, there was much they really did not know. All that Shi'roc could determine was that many races served the Bone.

Maac-To watched as to learn the strategies of these experienced men. He stood back from the miniature landscape and listened to them speak. With his head full of questions, he did not dare interrupt their thoughts. He remembered the old days as he looked at the sand that represented the extinct Elven Forest where he had lived. The memories haunted him of the tall oak trees that surrounded the villages and provided shelter. He reached into his pocket and revealed in his hand the golden acorn, given to him by the greatest of the living trees, the father of the forest. Someday soon perhaps he could keep his promise to replant the seemingly magical item where the tree had stood, and somehow regenerate the mighty oak. He never questioned the instructions he was given, only the memory of his words to replant the acorn remained.

Lorentz studied the map as he drew with the ink and delicate feather quill. He also listened as Shi'roc and Grefden planned the defenses of their new mountain home. They of course had the advantage of the high ground and its familiarity, provided that they were fighting against conventional soldiers such as the Orcs. They could possibly fend off wave after wave of assaults if all of the attacking soldiers were as slow and dim as their prisoners. On the other hand, the Bone may have other, more intelligent, creatures at his command if indeed he was from the lower worlds as suspected. He may be joined by other demons or creatures with magical abilities. Such powers that could not be defended against by arrows or swords.

"If we position our archers here, here and there," Shi'roc pointed to the abandoned village passes. "We could surprise the first wave of attackers, forcing them to move off to less favorable terrain to advance. The longer we control the high ground, the more it should cause them to disperse, thinning their ranks." He looked to Grefden, the man who he helped plan the defenses of the Cerrat army a few years past. Shi'roc's strategies were surprisingly successful in saving the falling castle of Cerrat. It was then that Grefden decided to leave his home and follow Shi'roc on his other adventures.

"My Lord, that would eventually cause the enemy to entirely surround the mountains if the tactic continued," A thoughtful pause, and a glance at Maac-To. "Provided that our newly trained forces could withstand." He showed his friend a look of concern. "We too would be thinning our forces to repel attacks from more than these three locations. There are as I have seen, four main entrances into these caverns and numerous crawl ways." He counted in his head the three village paths and the entrance from the western side that led directly to the heart of the mining tunnels where they lived.

Lorentz carefully breathed on the drying ink as he stood to address the strategists. While crafting the historical map, he had also been absorbing all of the strategic conversation. He looked at Shi'roc and asked "On what did our success against the Orcs depend?" He raised an eye brow then turned to Grefden. "Does the enemy know our numbers, or we, theirs?" He posed these questions to ponder. Lorentz set the freshly drawn map on the rock ledge leaving his back to his puzzled friends. There was silence as they looked at each other to resolve the apparent riddle.

Maac-To spoke up after analyzing the questions. "We succeeded in battle because the enemy did not know we were there." He shook his head then continued. "No, that's not entirely correct. They were looking for someone but did not know where or how many."

Grefden continued the analysis. "We were waiting and ready. We held the surprise as advantage." He looked to Shi'roc. "They do not know our numbers, my Lord. We still have that on our side." He waited for the leaders to speak.

"Would it be reasonable to assume, having talked with the Orcs and knowing how they think, that the two would report back to the Bone and tell him that an entire army attacked them?" Lorentz walked around the carefully architectured floor map to stand behind the representation of the mountain range. "Shi'roc, what would you do in response to such a threat if you were the Bone?"

Shi'roc smiled, realizing where Lorentz wisdom was guiding him. He pointed to the canyon area. "I would lead all of my forces along this path and strike where the enemy was first encountered. They will attack these two village remains first." He indicated the places where they first had beaten the Orcs in the deserted Dwarven towns.

"Since they do not know our numbers and will surely outnumber us if we are where they expect us to be then…" Lorentz paused for Shi'roc to complete the analogy after carefully surveying the known paths and defensible locations.

"..Then we should not be where they expect us to be." Shi'roc looked up at Lorentz and Grefden. "The best way to win a battle is to not be there." Shi'roc became enlightened and inspired by Lorentz approach and continued with the altered plans that had been generated in his mind. He reminded himself of an old proverb that he used to share with his half brother. "He who fights and runs away, lives to fight another day." His younger brother was brash for his age and always sought out the fight even when it was to his advantage to retreat.

* * *

The two surviving Orcs, one having been wounded and both starving, struggled to remain alive long enough to report their findings. The general assisted his wounded lieutenant on the sixth day of their journey back along the northern rim of the desert. Their approach to the canyon from the upper plains led them to familiar ground just before their health had failed them. The two staggered to a halt as they crossed the ridge of the canyon. Their weakened bodies could no longer support their efforts to climb the steep rock grade of the path. They tumbled down the embankment almost uncontrollably and laid lifeless at the canyon trail floor.

The Orcs awoke marginally, at the splash of water in their faces. One of the squads of Knolls had found them and carried them back to the enormous stable cave where they had first received their instructions from the Bone. Although their two species varied in appearance and their language, the code of a warrior was that of dignity and the tall, furry Knolls understood that these two were all that was left of their clan. They quickly brought them back to health, enough for them to face the Bone and report their circumstances.

After escorting the Orcs to the main castle entry, they returned to their posts as guardians of the main passage through the canyon. They patrolled the canyon paths and guarded the two bridges that spanned the once raging river that had been diverged into the canyon as a result of the initial earthquake. These were the only known access roads to the underground fortress. As long as the two wooden bridges were kept at the far ends of the maze of canyons, no one could easily approach the castle of Moracles.

Inside the main hallway of the castle, the Bone held conference with his two defeated subjects. Although intimidated by their master's enormous size and poise, they stood tall to report the outcome of their search.

"We divided small groups. Search mountain." The general spoke in his native language. "All attacked by little creatures." He did his best to describe the Dwarves that he saw dragging off the bodies of his dead soldiers at the first encounter.

"Old towns. Many warriors." The lieutenant spoke of his experience in the second village. "Fought arrows, swords." He described the weapons he saw the survivors use against his people. "Not all little. Some men." He and his people were attacked by not only Dwarves but by Elves and Humans that he described as men.

The Bone listened patiently and deciphered the information being given to him. He bent down to stare into the Generals eyes. "Moracles said twenty." He poked the Orc with his long bony finger. "You say more." The Bone spoke the perfect dialect of a leader or master. The Orcs did not dare attempt to deceive him. What they spoke was the truth as they knew it. He backed away slightly and drew his jeweled dagger from his belt sheath. The Orcs gasped, thinking they were to be killed for contradicting Moracles.

The intimidating creature from the lower world looked at it carefully, remembering that he had obtained the finely crafted weapon from a dead villager during the initial slaughter. He remembered other such weapons and armor being scavenged from the dead defenders of the towns. Piecing the old memories with the information now presented, he realized, "Dwarves!" They must have been in hiding all of these years in the mountains, he thought. The weapons that they had collected long ago must have been of the famed Dwarven craftsmen. Perhaps there are more weapons to be found in that mountain? Perhaps the twenty, that Moracles spoke of, had joined with these Dwarves? The Bones mischievous twisted mind was at work once again. "Call everyone to cave." He said to the Orcs in their own language. "Prepare for battle."

Chapter 19
Preparations

A'mora tended the garden to increase the food production while watching the prisoners. Many of the village women assisted in pruning the plants to allow more productive growths of rapidly reproducing trees. Even Ilo's wife worked in the gardens while caring for her new two week old baby. The output of the blessed cave had doubled since Lorentz had first magically planted the trees and plants. All of this was made possible by the Goddess Mirana for whom the nearby shrine was attributed. They were all aware of the plans being made for their defenses by the learned warriors. They also knew that health and strength came from these crops and that soon they would all need both to survive.

That afternoon, the students of A'mora's teachings gathered to pray and worship together at the shrine. The Orcs, of course, had been moved from that area so as not to disturb the prayer session. Thus far, their prayers had been concentrated on the healing powers for which the priests were primarily known, and for which A'mora had excelled under Lorentz' guiding hand. It was now time that they learned how to remain safe during battle and care for the wounded at the same time. It would be necessary to sneak in during the height of battle unnoticed, and shelter the injured and near dead until well enough to move on their own or continue fighting. This technique was know as 'Giving Sanctuary' and was a most powerful spell to be cast on one's self and the injured.

"Remember that the spell can not be cast while the person is engaged in battle." A'mora instructed as she stood before the shrine. "As long as they are still in combat, their adrenaline will repel the protection that you seek to give them. Only when they are calm, inactive or unconscious will their bodies accept your protection. Only then should you invoke your healing abilities." She looked at each of her students for a sign of understanding.

"Question, M'lady" One of her students addressed. "Will we always be protected by this prayer? and how do we know when it is in effect?" His question caused concern among others except for Kura who stood and answered it in place of A'mora.

"The powers you seek to draw from the Goddess, Mirana," The Dwarf gestured to the statue of the lady of the forest, "come from your faith in her. You must concentrate your beliefs in what you are doing. If your opponent senses your uneasiness or doubt, you will be seen as a threat to him once again." Kura answered the second part of his question first. "There are evils so great that even our sanctuary can not repel. You may not know if the creature is powerful enough to see through your cloak of prayer until he strikes." Kura looked to A'mora. "That is why we must also be trained to defend ourselves physically in case we are noticed or caught unprepared for prayer."

A'mora was quite impressed with his wisdom. He did not have experience enough to know what he explained so well. These powers of his faith must truly be emanating from the staff that he was given by Mirana. Each day his knowledge had grown, his powers enhanced, but only, she noticed, when he had possession of the finely polished tree root that was capped with the ornate golden oak leaf. Soon his abilities would surpass hers.

"That is correct." She nodded to Kura as he sat back down on the rocky ground. "I know that some of you have learned to use such defensive weapons as a staff or hammer." A'mora motioned to Kura who held up both items for reference. The hammer was nothing more than a rectangular shaped chunk of stone well secured to a thick piece of wood with leather strapping. It had been fashioned from a table leg scavenged from the above abandoned towns. Kura had chiseled the stone himself. He was quite proud having mastered the use of both items.

"Kura has been proficient with a sling that is also considered a weapon of defense." The Dwarf then held up a leather thong and straps with a hand full of small smooth stones. A'mora continued her lecture as the prisoners watched from beneath an apple tree, to which they were securely tied. Both their arms were extended around the trunk to the others so that the only way to freedom would be to cut the leather restraints or to cut the tree down.

"Though Mirana is a Goddess of peace, there are times when defense is necessary, especially when serving her purpose of defending all good living creatures of the forests and the forests themselves. Weapons of steel are created for war and are an offense to our purpose of healing. Wielding any weapon will cause the protection of your prayers to collapse and make you vulnerable to be attacked." She paused to look at each one of the students for any sign of confusion.

"Today we should concentrate our efforts on the defensive abilities of prayers. As the Lord Shi'roc would say, 'The best way to win a battle is to not be there.' Just as a hammer may be thrown at an opponent, so can the forces of your faith, in similar form. You must concentrate on the shape and weight of the hammer as if it were actually in your grasp. Then in your mind strike at your enemy. Your thoughts will guide your aim to the target." The priestess walked over to the rock wall and scrapped a circular target area with a small stone. "Kura will try first." She was anxious to see the powers of his concentration. Never had she seen any student of the gods perform the feat on their first try. She herself required several attempts before the faint image of the ethereal hammer would appear.

Kura stood up and closed his eyes in concentration to form the non corporeal weapon. Once satisfied of its reality in his mind he opened his eyes and guided it to the stone wall that was thirty or more feet away. The ghost of a hammer seemed to fly from inside his head toward the rock at tremendous speed. It impacted with a very real crash, knocking a chip out of the target area. Kura was amazed himself, but not as much as Lady A'mora or the others.

"Don't let up on your concentration." She instructed, trying to inspire as much confidence as possible. "Keep the form in tact in your mind and continue to control the movement of the hammer." They all watched as the Dwarf maneuvered the mystical weapon back and forth over the rocky area. Once again he smashed it into the etched area near where he had struck before. Again he managed to chip a piece of the rock, then the image faded. Kura sat down, exhausted by the concentration required to produce the effect.

Each of the priests in turn attempted the same performance. Most of them required several attempts as A'mora had expected. Of those who were successful, none had the striking power or control that Kura had demonstrated. Perhaps his proficiency with the real hammer had strengthened his focus, but more likely, she thought, his strength came through the staff of Mirana.

* * *

As A'mora trained her priests in the defensive arts, Lorentz had gathered his students of magic. The spells that they had already learned had become entrained in their minds so they could be performed on command. The few that had been concentrated on were basic and easy to remember. There were others, more powerful that required them to read from the pages of their newly written spell books.

Lorentz had required them to scribe in their own hand, the pages of parchment that would forever carry the powers of their magic. With the finely tipped quills that Lorentz had fashioned from the Falcon feathers, provided by the Goddess, Alena, they inked the various symbols that only a mage could recognize and pronounce. The concentration on the writings were just as important as the performance of the spell itself, since it was their energies that the ink would encapsulate onto the pages. The slightest error in the script would cause the spell to be faulty as it was read and memorized.

Jantez and Gol had been studying the new spell that Lorentz had earlier demonstrated. Each time a new spell was taught by the mage, the students were required to memorize and then scribe the magical words into the books. This would allow them to carry the knowledge with them and to study the spells when time permitted. The more intricate the spell, the more time and pages were necessary. Thus far, each of their books contained more than twenty pages. Not all of the spells were duplicated as one of the students may have had a better aptitude than the other. Each of the students was unsuccessful in grasping certain concepts of different spells. They would in the future attempt again to learn those spells once their experience had helped to open their minds. But for now each of them possessed varying abilities.

Their excitement of the potential of this particular spell drove their accuracy in the writing. Both of them had total understanding as Lorentz had taught it to them. Although they did not have the experience required to achieve a successful delivery of such a complex incantation, Lorentz was convinced that with practice, they could master this important illusion. The whole key to the outcome of the battle plan hinged on the ability for all three of them to perform this particular illusionary spell with the greatest of accuracy. As not to pressure them, Lorentz had kept the battle plans from them until they were complete in their training. The rushed instruction of the past days was burden enough for the two humans, especially since they were also required to continue their combat training.

Lorentz looked up from his chemical components to see the two hard at work, writing and memorizing the pages before them. They sat near the fire pit set in the center of the chamber. He realized that he could not have found more able and dedicated apprentices, next to Lady A'mora of course. But her abilities and service leaned more heavily on the followings of the Goddess, Mirana, than on the ways of magic. He had only wished he could convince her to spend more of her efforts on the magical abilities that she possessed.

Lorentz returned his attention to his makeshift work bench, mixing powders and various chemicals, herbs and minerals. Before him lay many small glass vials. All of which were empty at present and corked shut. In a crucible he ground the various components, adding an occasional drop or two of water. The mixture when in powder form was of no obvious color, but when placed into the vials and water added, a bluish color became apparent. The candle on the table lighted his efforts in preparing for the upcoming battle.

"We are ready M'Lord." Gol spoke up while Jantez sat muttering in concentration. The words were unclear yet Gol heard enough to recognize the verbalization of the spell that they had been studying. He ceased his incantation as Lorentz approached to deliver his final words of wisdom.

"Remember that as you recant the spell you should be concentrating on the image of which you are trying to produce. Although the person or creature you are visualizing will not actually appear, the details must be accurate in your mind in order to deceive your opponent." The two both shook their heads in understanding the instruction. "Your focus for the deceit should be the minds of as many viewers as possible. At first you may only be able to fool a few of the enemy, but the more ignorant they are, the more susceptible they will be to the illusion. It is quite a bit more difficult to deceive an intelligent opponent." Lorentz waved a wary finger at them. "Your first attempt should be of an illusion of someone of whom you are extremely familiar."

Jantez pointed toward the doorway that was behind Lord Lorentz. The mage turned to see what the distraction was. Both Gol and Jantez stood to greet Lady A'mora who appeared at the entrance. Lorentz bowed slightly as she approached. He reached out to take her hand only to find that his hand passed right through, immediately dissolving the illusionary figure that Jantez had produced. His spell had affected both Lorentz and Gol, both believing that A'mora was actually present. The master began to chuckle. Quietly at first but building into a full laugh by the time he turned to his students. Gol was not certain whether or not Lorentz was angry with the trick or pleased.

"Marvelous," was all he could say as he laughed on. Gor began to laugh as well followed by Jantez himself. "That was a most impressive first try." He concluded his laughter to catch his breath. "I believe that would have been effective on at least a dozen of our friends in the water cave." Lorentz was indeed pleased at the performance. He hopped that Gol would produce as well, but now that he would be expecting it, the attempt would be easily thwarted. Once convinced of the fact of the illusion by touching or disbelief, the recipient can convince others of its falseness. The illusion holds no solidity that is why the concentration of the mage producing the effect must be strong enough to hold the image in his own mind and transmit that thought telepathically to the intended receivers.

Lorentz soon returned to his potions as the new mages studied further their practiced spells. Into the afternoon the time passed as they learned yet another of Lorentz spells.

* * *

As the next days passed, the tension of waiting grew. The watchers concentrated their view from the eastern ridge, awaiting a huge army to appear in the distance. None had appeared as yet. From their viewpoint, such an army would be seen from miles away.

Below on the mountain side, Shi'roc was preparing the new warriors for the upcoming battle. In the towns they rehearsed their assigned movements. Timing was crucial and Shi'roc had planned each step down to the minute. Grefden and Gor were directing the exercises at the second Dwarven town that depicted the same scenario. Placement and timing would be the key factors. The new army must rely on surprise and unconventional combat to overcome the lack of superior equipment and experience. They would be going up against a powerful evil force that would not obey the normal laws of compassion or allow for prisoners. The enemy would be coming to annihilate them all. Leave no survivors, women or children. Though more weapons and armor were being produced by the Dwarves each day, courage and cunning were the mountain dwellers only best weapons.

"Choose your locations well." Grefden called out over the town from the ridge above. From his view he could direct the flow of the combat simulation and identify any weakness in strategy. "You must remain hidden as the enemy would surely be awaiting the strike. They will be ready for you, so you must strike from behind. It is your best chance to disable your opponents." He felt uneasy about teaching capable warriors to attack as common thieves, but the need outweighed the ego. Grefden would never himself strike an unaware opponent from behind. That was not the way of a true warrior. Honorable combat was fought face to face as Shi'roc had inspired. But the situation was desperate and their recourses were minimal. Reducing the enemies numbers was the prime concern before the planned escape.

Gor had walked down the main road from the town as the survivors set up for the practice run. He would return up the rocky path, as would the enemy, and encounter each of the traps being set. The fighter waited for the signal from his friend high up the ridge. He sprinted up the passage and gave out a war cry as he approached the town. As was planned, he endured the simulated attacks from each of the secret locations. Each trap and movement was studied by Grefden from above. By the end of the exercise, Gor was worn out having encountered and fallen prey to half a dozen of the skillfully executed entrapments. Though he was not severely injured by his students, he did obtain several new bruises from the unexpected attacks. He was satisfied at their performance.

Grefden and Gor gathered the training participants in the center of town to discuss and refine the tactics. Very little had to be changed. The two experienced warriors were not entirely accustomed to the strike and run approach that they would be engaged in. Now that the attack patterns had been set, the retreat to the hidden cave entrance was choreographed. Once the women were safely into the town, they would surely be pursued by the gruesome army. Each of the attack teams were to strike taking out several of the enemy and slow the others down, then head for the old town commerce building in which the sliding wall had been placed. Grefden and Gor would remain in the rear to guard the others' escape down the hidden stairs.

"Do not look back. There will be no time for a second strike." Gor said. "We will be sure that they eventually find the hidden doorway." He laughed at the thought. Such a clever plan the Lords had created to lure the enemy into the tunnels. Shi'roc had often told them, "He who fights and runs away, lives to fight another day." Until now he had never understood. That phrase was definitely appropriate for this situation. Running was not the act of a coward, but the cunning move of a wise man. "Run as fast as possible to your designated locations. Remember that everything will be set prior to the attack. You must know when to jump and when to roll." They all shook their heads in unanimous agreement.

"And don't forget to leave a torch burning at the bottom of the stairs for us." Grefden said with a laugh. "We don't see in the dark like the rest of you." They all laughed. All of his fighting force was made up of Dwarves and Elves who often forgot about the human deficiency of not having the night vision. Gor and Grefden would surely not see the tunnel markers to avoid Lorentz' little surprises if they did not have the light to guide them.

* * *

At the base of the eastern ridge, Lorentz' followers were setting up the procedures for the archers and bow-women. They would be the first guardians of the mountain trails leading to the towns. From their previous encounters with the Orc army, weeks ago, they knew that the only entrances into their towns that were discovered were the first two roads. None of the enemy lived to report any of the other findings, except for the two prisoners.

Sha'la instructed her group of women warriors at the base of the second town road. They would be the second line of defense against those who might push past the first encounter of Lorentz' archers.

"You must remain hidden and motionless until the signal is given." Sha'la instructed her troops. "Since our arrows may be weak against their armor, you must wait until they are at close range to be effective. There may only be time for one round of fire, especially for the crossbows." She spoke as she walked along the base of the rocky ridge at the foot of the mountain. She held in her hands her own finely crafted mechanical arrow sling. She was the best at crossbow fighting tactics, though there were still not enough of the devices manufactured to go around. Only four of her dozen women had the new crossbows. The rest became proficient with short bows.

The enemy would not be expecting an assault down at the base of the main road. 'Hit them first and when they don't expect it.' were Shi'roc's instructions. The archers would be the most effective in surprise since the opponent would not be expecting to engage until they had reached the towns. Their defenses would be down and vulnerable to the flight of arrows.

"Make your shots true. We do not have the means for an extended battle. We are to strike and run." It was true that they did not have as many arrows ready as they would have liked, nor were they of the exacting quality needed for combat. Many of their arrows would not even pierce the armor that is why the enemy must be close in order to target un armored areas of the opponents body. "Lord Lorentz will provide a suitable distraction to cover your escape back up into the town."

"How will he do that?" One of the archers asked.

"I do not know what exactly he has planned. But have faith that he will protect you as he has done for many others in the past." Sha'la recalled how she first was inspired by Lord Lorentz as he tricked an overwhelming enemy into retreat with only a few soldiers. She did not understand the ways of his magic as he had saved her town from destruction. All she knew was that she wanted to follow and learn from him. In the past year in which she had traveled with him, she had found wisdom and courage through prayer and learned of his fighting skills. Although he attempted to instruct her in the ways of magic, her mind would not allow her to accept the concept.

She looked up to her soldiers who were scattered on the rocks of the mountain base. "Are there any further questions?" She asked. Their heads indicated none. "Then pick your hiding places as I will travel up the road. When I approach I will give the word to strike. At that time you will make yourselves known." Her intent was to see how well they could hide, even from her as she would be watching for any errors in their means of cover.

Sha'la turned her back to the crowd and proceeded along the mountain base in the direction from which the attackers were expected to arrive. She walked for several hundred feet to allow them time to hide. As she looked over the dead forest to the left and the rocky ridge to her right, she felt a queasy, weak feeling in her stomach. At first she brushed it off as hunger, then it worsened, almost causing her to be nauseous. She quickly sat down on a small boulder and hung her head between her hands staring at the ground. Her mind raced as to what the possible cause of the illness might be. Her concentration helped the moment to pass and she was ready to return to her waiting warriors.

Sha'la watched the rocks as she moved slowly up the road, trying to spot her troops. As the road neared the mountain passage not a singe trace of their hiding places was evident. She was impressed with their skills at stealth. They had been in hiding for generations so that must have influenced their abilities. She called out to them. "Now" and looked quickly up the rocks to see their locations. Of course they would not actually fire, but be at the ready to do so. She still neither saw nor heard them. Where did they go? She called again with no visible response.

"We are here." Muga shouted from behind, startling Sha'la. They had all taken up positions at the edge of the dead forest on the other side of the road.

Sha'la turned around quickly. "What are you doing over there?" She asked as she looked them over. They were very well hidden amongst the brush and dead wood.

"As Lord Shi'roc said, hit them when they don't expect it," one of the archers spoke. "We decided that our advantage would increase since they would be looking up at the mountain. They would surely have their backs to us.

We could strike from the most vulnerable position and run past them during the confusion provided by Lord Lorentz." The others nodded their heads in agreement as they emerged from the woods. The logic was sound and their position would allow them fast access to the rocky passage when running. The Dwarven wisdom once again had shone forth.

Sha'la thought for a moment and looked around at their locations in reference to the escape route. She shook her head in agreement. "Well done. Be sure not to become too entangled in the brush as to slow your escape." The woman warrior was proud of her students and she smiled at their intuition and courage. It would not be an easy task and she knew that they may not all make it to safety. From that time on, they rehearsed the strike and escape, taking into account the yet unknown distraction of the enemy.

* * *

In the first Dwarven town, Shi'roc directed the main body of the force. This is where the heaviest combat would take place. Once Lorentz' archers had fled through the town and into the caves, the 'Bone's' army would arise from the mountain passage. Shi'roc realized that they may not all be on foot. He had planned for every contingency including mounted soldiers. They would be the most difficult to fight. Although the greatest contingent of his trainees were human, the heavy riders of the enemy would have to be unhorsed in order to effectively disable them. He had thought of a way to do that as well.

Maac-To and his son Ilo each led one of striking forces in the simulation. Ilo would lead the strikes on the road into town to cover the escape of the archers. Maac-To would coordinate the final assault in the town itself. They had all taken up hidden locations throughout the passage and in the fallen town ruins. The traps were set and ready to be tested by Gol and Jantez as they ran unsuccessfully up the mountain passage. They were so heavily bombarded by the flurry of unexpected attacks that they could not imagine many of the opposition being able to get through. Each assault was a strike and run and by the time the two had made it into the town, they were too exhausted to continue. The others had fled as scheduled so that the town appeared defenseless from the mouth of the road. Though not severely injured by the practice run, they had been battered up.

"My Lord". Gol yelled out, not knowing where Shi'roc was hiding. "Wasn't the purpose of the assault to lead the enemy into the mines?" He puffed and puffed as he sat leaning against the boulder at the edge of the first building. "There will not be anyone left to find us."

"Never underestimate your enemy." Shi'roc said, startling both Jantez and Gol, from behind. They jumped to their feet. "There will be plenty of them to get through. Believe me." Shi'roc was positioned to strike at the mouth of the passage to guard the escape of the passage attackers. Ilo would be the last one out from the path. After that, Shi'roc would be sure to take down a few of the beasts himself while blocking the entrance into the town. He would buy enough escape time for the first assault team. "I hope you two will have more energy when being pursued by the enemy." He slapped them both across the backside with the flat of his sword. "Now, continue the run. I want to see how Maac-To and his men will fair."

The two continued to trot through the town, encountering several mock attacks by sword and ax. Once again, each of the survivors ran to the house of Kura after his attack. The family home of Kura contained the entrance into the mines. These hidden stairs were the first made in the mountain, and soon would be the first to be destroyed.

* * *

The withered trees loomed as ghostly images of a once vital forest as the army passed. They moved slowly and deliberately in order for the footmen to keep up with the mounted soldiers. All were heavily armed and armored, prepared for all out war. For them it was just following orders. The Bone's orders were vastly different than those that Moracles had given. But the army had thought Moracles long gone and feared reprisal of their new leader, the Bone.

It would be five more days at this pace to reach the mountains. The pack mules strained at the wagons laden with food and supplies for the ten score of troops. Each of the various armies traveled separately since it was rare that any of the varied species could get along well enough to work together. Not only were there vast differences in configurations but they mostly lacked a common language. The Hobgoblins pointed faced features and large size contrasted greatly with their smaller cousins, Goblins, who's puffy rounded features looked more human. The dog faced, pointed eared Kobolds, smaller yet than the Goblins, abhorred the large framed, furry Bugbears. Each race more proficient than others in specific weapons due to their relative sizes and physiology's. The Bugbears preferred the spear or hand held spiked weapons such as a morning star, a wooden club with steel spikes embedded in the outer edges. Kobolds typically fought with short swords or axes. The Goblins all toted short spears, while the larger Hobgoblins were more able with long swords.

Then there were the original warriors of Moracles army, the Magdarn, who were of Human decent. Most of those remaining were elderly and still proud to be the most feared fighting force in the land. None of the other races dared to challenge them due to reputation alone, though the Bugbears or Hobgoblins could easily defeat the old human warriors. The paintings and tapestries of the old wars had depicted the original battles for Moracles territory. Though the pictures were greatly exaggerated, the other races of warriors were not around to dispute the stories told.

The only fact that bound these unlikely allies was the Bone's orders to follow the two remaining Orcs back to where they had found the intruders and the survivors of the valley. The forces were being led by those who had been defeated in combat by the Dwarves, Elves and Humans who were hiding in the mountains. What was the Bone thinking when he put those two inept creatures in charge? They had lost the whole of their army to scavengers, being unprepared.

The Orcs rode at the head of the parade of the combined armies. They marched proud and important, the feeling of command inflated their egos. "Why so slow?" The Orc lieutenant asked the general.

"No hurry." The general responded. "Not going anywhere." He referred to the survivors in the mountain. Indeed, where could they go. They would be in a safer position in the mountain rather than in open land. That was why they headed up such a large force to flush out every possible being from their hiding place. They intended to over run the towns and slaughter all in their path.

"Why us?" The Orc questioned the decision of the Bone to lead the army. He knew they were not deserving of the honor to lead the forces.

"Don't complain." The general said as he looked over his shoulder at the column of creatures and wagons. "We have horses and food." They had never had it so good. For the first time they felt respected.

Chapter 20
Surprises

Final preparations were being made inside the mountain for the battle. All of the warriors were secure in their positions for the assault in the towns and the mountain passages. The watchers continued their detailed assessment of the eastern valley, carefully analyzing any disturbances in the distance. On occasion a gust of wind miles off would startle one of them into thinking the army was approaching. Everyone was on edge thinking that at any time they would see a massive force approaching to wipe them out of existence.

Sha'la had continued to feel the illness growing inside her stomach and became concerned that the sudden rushes of nausea would compromise her during the battle. She took it upon herself to consult Lady A'mora. She would have been more at ease talking with her leader, Lord Lorentz, but he was deep in conference with his student magi. Though she had traveled with A'mora for some time, they had never gotten to know each other well. Sha'la was perhaps intimidated by the closeness between A'mora and Lorentz. Although a capable warrior, she felt inferior of the powers that A'mora had learned from her leader. A'mora possessed the magical abilities that the warrior could not grasp.

The priestess had been continuing her teachings to the student priests at the grotto in the water cave. The rest of the village women had been picking the orchards and gardens clean of their fruits. Many baskets and barrels had been filled in preparation for the upcoming journey, that they would soon take. The Orc prisoners had been adjusting to the fair treatment they had been getting. They had been fed and clothed. They had grown accustomed to the Elves, Dwarves and Humans that surrounded them on a daily basis. Though still under guard, the captives had been allowed to help in the orchards by lifting the women into the trees. The relationship was almost as if they were pets on a leash, allowed some freedom of movement and then chained back up at night or when the others would not be around. On occasion, Lord Shi'roc would pass and they would bow their heads in respect and greet him as their master. He continued to speak to them as such to keep them in line.

Sha'la approached the gathering of the healers and watched as they performed their miraculous incantations. She hoped that A'mora would speak with her and rid her of the malady in her stomach. Cautiously she prepared her words of respect. "My Lady," She began. "I have a matter of urgency on which I request your assistance." It seemed difficult for her being more accustomed to receiving such respect rather than giving it.

A'mora looked up from her students and nodded to Sha'la. "Continue your protection chants." She said as she walked over to her. "With what may I have the honor of assisting you?" she inquired.

The two began to walk away from the others as she spoke. "I have for the past several days become uneasy inside. There have been sudden spells of dizziness and nausea." Sha'la spoke softly, uncomfortable with admitting to a weakness. She had rarely been ill in her life time. She was always the strong confident one of her family.

"Have you been eating well?" A'mora asked. "Are you worried about the battle to come." She prodded carefully.

"The food you have provided is plentiful and nourishing. No, I have eaten well I can assure you. The battle does not trouble me. I am very proud of my warrior's ability to adapt to their training." She stopped walking and looked around. They were safely away from prying ears, even those of Elven acuity. "Is there some way that you can determine the cause of my illness?" Sha'la asked as she sat down on a smooth boulder.

A'mora had a feeling that she already knew what was causing her sickness. "Yes. I can help you." She replied confidently. The priestess clasped her hands together and began the chant of knowledge where she would be able to probe the biological aspects of the female warrior. A'mora slowly passed her hands over the head of her patient. She then traced her hands closely all around her body, feeling for the source of the disturbance. As she had suspected all along, "Your illness is not that at all." She knelt down close to Sha'la to explain. "You are with child." She whispered.

Sha'la's eyes widened with surprise. "I'm what?" she said loudly enough to attract attention from the other women in the cave. "That cannot be." She insisted, thinking now about the times that her and Grefden had spent alone together. They had often hidden away from the others off in the un-traveled cave areas. "This is not a good time." She snapped.

A'mora gave her a quizzical look. "There isn't anything you can do about the timing. Are you going to tell Grefden?" She had known as did the others, that the two had a strong liking for each other or suspected as much. It was only a matter of time before it would happen. "There is nothing to worry about. You are only in the very beginning stages." She tried to comfort the wilted warrior.

"No." She whispered in a deeply depressed tone. "Grefden must not know of this." She looked pleadingly into A'mora's eyes. "Please don't tell anyone. I must face this on my own." Spoken like a true warrior, never to share her troubles or show weakness to others.

The priestess took her hand and said "No one will hear it from me. I promise."

* * *

The cold wind blew down over the watchers of the eastern mountain face. The skies were overcast but it had not yet snowed this season. Very seldom did the white flakes fall until this time during the coldest part of the winter. Soon there would be a blanket of endless frost white snow covering the valley and the mountain passes. If this happened, the outcome of the battle could be seriously changed.

"Look to the south." One of the watchers said to his Human partner. "Can you see that far, the dark line that seems to waver beyond the dead forest?" He pointed to the southern passage below the first Dwarven Peak. It was the same path that the first army of Orcs had used a month ago.

"I do believe I can see what you mean." He squinted and cupped his hands around his eyes to shield them from the blowing wind. "It could be Moracles' army." They both continued to watch the distant wavering line to be sure of what they saw. "We should alert the others." He stood and looked toward the next watcher positions to both sides of him. Both were far enough off to require the use of hand signals. The watchers to the south were signaling to them. They had seen it too.

With a fluid sequence of gestures, they described the column of several hundred soldiers at a day's march away. The message quickly continued north, up the mountain range. Within minutes, the entire watcher grid had been alerted and runners had been sent down to inform the mountain dwellers below.

Later that day, all but the southern most two positions had been abandoned. The first to spot the oncoming army remained to observe their movements and continue to estimate their time of attack. They watched until the sky darkened and the movement halted for the day. Distant camp fires were set aglow. Dozens of fires were visible from the mountain ridges. For now it appeared that the attack would take place sometime in the next day or two.

*　　*　　*

"Lorentz, are all your devices in place?" Shi'roc asked of his long time friend. He knew of course that all was ready though he did not understand what elements of the mountain the wise Elf had been mining. He had been seen collecting buckets of black coal from the forges, and crushing it into a powder along with other whitish and yellowish dust. Lorentz had never let him down before.

"Fear not my friend. The mountain itself has provided the necessary components of the, what you call, devices. The show will go on as planned and at its conclusion, the curtain will certainly fall but no one will remain to applaud our performance." His theatrics once again took hold and from the gleam in his eyes, Shi'roc could tell that Lorentz was in his glory, planning and manipulating circumstances and science. "It will be an explosive finale. My students are ready and will surely have some interesting surprises for our guests." The mage twitched his bushy eyebrows. "One last item remains. What to do with our.... pets." Referring to the captured Orcs. They had grown accustomed to having them around and helping in the orchards. They no longer seemed a threat, yet they feared leaving them behind, and Lorentz would not have them killed. Shi'roc would not allow them any dishonor. The two pondered the subject for a moment.

"I have an idea." Shi'roc spoke up. "Perhaps they would be willing to help us?" Lorentz was a bit surprised at the suggestion. "I will speak with them." The warrior walked off down the passage past the scurrying Dwarves.

Each member of the underground community was hurriedly attending to their assigned tasks. They had been awaiting this day for several weeks and the time had come for the plan to come together. Before the late night had arrived, all was in place for the next day's events. Food was prepared, weapons gathered and wagons at the northern most end of the mountain were loaded. The order was for all to get a good nights sleep as all would be taxed to their extent the following morning.

In their sleeping chamber as the others slept, Lorentz and A'mora held a silent vigil to pray for courage and wisdom in the battles ahead. Although the Goddess, Mirana, abhorred violence, this war was to avenge the slaughter of thousands and to stop the further destruction of the forests and its creatures, beyond the valley. Day by day, the sickness imposed by Moracles spread further out into the world. Even the forest from which the heroes had emerged months ago, had been further deteriorated. Only the death of Moracles could revoke the creeping spell that he had cast on the land decades ago upon his arrival in the valley.

Through the powers of prayer, and the wisdom of the Goddess, Lorentz began to scribe a scroll. Almost in a trance, the words flowed through his hand and the quill to the rolled parchment. Having no foreknowledge of the valley or its tales, the words that he wrote were for the restoration of the great Elven forest from which many of the survivors ancestors had come. Although in storybook form, the scroll that he continued to scribe, told of two powerful magical items that were required to perform the ceremony of forest regeneration.

When finished, the words formed instructions and ended in an incantation that was required along with the two golden items. The acorn and the oak leaf. The instructions told that a young, golden haired female would collect the golden acorn and oak leaf. The priestess would be pure of heart and untouched by the temptations of her womanhood. She was to journey deep into the center of the dead forest, now known as 'Feradune' and plant the acorn into the sand covered by the oak leaf. The blessed waters of Mirana would be sprinkled over them as the incantation was spoken. Once again the father of the forest would arise and flourish. Only after the curse of Moracles had been broken could the ceremony take place.

A'mora was herself amazed at the trance that her mentor had fallen into. She did not disturb his writing, but watched as his quill floated over the page effortlessly with great precision and speed. She quietly crept up behind him to read the words over his shoulder, unaware of what he was writing. Just as she began to read the tale, the curtain over the chamber entrance was pushed aside by Maac-To, who came rushing into the room. A'mora could see by the flickering fire light that he was earnestly seeking someone. Lorentz at that moment had completed the scroll and broke from the trance, startling himself and A'mora.

"Lord Lorentz." The senior Elf began. "Thank the heavens I have found you. The chief has fallen ill." He referred to the very old leader of the Dwarven council. "He has been asking for you and refuses to rest until you come." He noticed that all but Lorentz and A'mora had gone to sleep. Shi'roc was not among them, though he did not wonder why. His urgency was to bring Lorentz to Kyman. "Please hurry. He claims he is dying." It was apparent that the elderly Elf still held high respect for the Dwarven chief, though he did not always agree with his profound wisdom. The secrets he was sworn to keep from the outsiders was certainly tearing at his loyalty.

Without thinking, Lorentz rolled up the scroll in his hands, not even aware of what he had written. He tucked it into the folds of his robe and started out of the room following Maac-To. A'mora also began to leave the room with them until Lorentz turned and said, "No my dear, this is something I must do alone. Remain here, you will need your sleep."

After the two leaders had left, A'mora tried hard to sleep but her curiosity about the scroll caused her to be restless. Why was Lorentz chosen by the Goddess to trance rather than she? What was in the writing and what powers might it possess? Though the priestess did not read it entirely, she did believe that the writing held the key to her quest. Finally, she dosed off, lying on the straw like mat cradled in the chamber floor. As her mind wandered, a soft voice entered her thoughts. "Think not of the scroll, for it is no longer of your destiny". A peaceful deep sleep engulfed her, the kind of sleep that had spawned visions of the future before.

* * *

Lorentz followed Maac-To into Kyman's chambers. His bed was surrounded by the rest of the council. At his side holding his hand was his grand daughter, Muga. Kura stood next to her holding his wooden staff with the golden oak leaf shimmering in the light. The room was bright with torches though none of the inhabitants required the light to see.

The Dwarves knew that Kyman was old and had reached his time to pass on to another world. They did not gather to grieve but to celebrate the life long achievements of their elder. He had ruled over them wisely for two hundred years and was respected by all. Although tomorrow would bring a new way of life for the tribes, tonight was the time for Kyman to depart in his own way. As tradition had been handed down for thousands of years, the departing chief would name his successor. This had always been a member of the council who was wise of age and could command the respect of all as Kyman had done.

Lorentz knew he had been summoned to pay his respects as a leader of the outsiders. He knew he would not be asked to try to heal him as it was age, not illness that was about to take the life of the old Dwarf. He did not offer an attempt to extend his life since the decisions had already been made. Maac-To represented the non Dwarven citizens of the underground community.

Kyman acknowledged their arrival and began to speak. "Tomorrow will bring a new day for all of our peoples." His voice was weak. "I will not be there to see the courage and skill brought out by our new friends and Lord Lorentz." He nodded to the Elven outsider. This had been the first time that Kyman had referred to Lorentz by his rightful title. "Before I go I must name a new leader to continue in my place." Each of the Dwarven council stiffened, anticipating who the new chief might be. Kyman's decision would not be questioned. "In my years as your leader, my knowledge and experience had guided my decisions. But I can see now that there is a great need for us to have a spiritual guidance as well." He coughed. "I believe that both knowledge and wisdom can overcome a lack of experience that is why I name Kura as my successor."

There was a gasp of surprise in the room from everyone including Kura. No one dared to question the old man's wisdom in his dying decision. Kura was far too young even to be elected to the council yet to lead the Dwarven communities. This chief would have to prove himself to gain the respect of the survivors.

After the shock wore off, Kura stood tall and bowed to the other members of the council. He held out his shinny capped staff and said. "I will guide you to victory in battle and to a better life above ground, as foreseen by the Goddess Mirana." Kura could have continued his unrehearsed speech except that Kyman coughed out his last instructions. Probably his most important words.

"Maac-To. You must show Lord Lorentz that which you and I have kept secret for so long." With those last words he passed into a deep coma, and rested easy for all time. Out of respect, no one tried to revive him. They let him pass from this world into another. They did not know how or where though since they had previously not had a spiritual leader. Their beliefs in gods and magic had died generations past. It would now be up to Kura to revive those beliefs.

Maac-To bowed to the retired chief and the council. Even they did not know what Kyman and Maac-To were referring to. He grabbed Lorentz by the shoulder and they left the cave chamber. "Where is Lord Shi'roc?" He asked. "It is important that he see this too." The Elf survivor gave Lorentz a great smile as they left the chamber. They moved quickly toward one of the main mining tunnels that connected most of the tribal communities.

"Shi'roc is at the water cave trying to enlist the help of the captured Orcs." Lorentz said, still puzzled as to where they were going. "What is this secret that you and Kyman kept from us?" He began wondering what could be so important that his last dying breath commanded its unveiling. He became tense and apprehensive, remembering that all along, Shi'roc had said the Dwarves were holding something back, something important.

"I must show you," is all that Maac-To could say. This was a very sour point that he felt had strained his relationship with Dwarven chief all of these years. He had given his word that he would not reveal this secret to anyone. When he had first arrived at the Dwarven Peaks to seek refuge from the slaughtering Magdarn, the Dwarves were still living in the mountain towns. They soon retreated below through the secret passages to avoid being found by Moracles' hoards. They wished to make the towns look abandoned so they would not search further. The younger Maac-To had seen Kyman and several of the now deceased Dwarves, dragging covered sleds full of items to a secret chamber deep within the mines. They were sure that no one had spotted them, but Maac-To watched in amazement as they opened the chamber walls and unloaded the sleds.

"We are almost there." He told Lorentz. They moved into a small passage just off of the main tunnel. Since there was no light, Maac-To felt around on the cave wall for the secret door release. He found and pushed the loose stone into the cave wall with a scraping sound.

Lorentz was startled as the cave wall opened up beside him. He could feel the stale air brush against him as the wall moved. Maac-To reached inside the opening and removed a lantern that he quickly lit with the scrape of the flint. The two Elves eyes lit up with joy as the light spread over the chamber. The room was not large, but its contents glittered with the reflected lantern light.

* * *

Shi'roc paced back and forth in front of the now barren trees. He was hungry and looked for some fruit to eat before speaking to the prisoners. Their fruit had been picked clean and stored for the journey earlier that day. He was intentionally making the Orcs nervous. Even though they were chained, they were never left alone nor were they allowed out of the orchard. They had become more docile as the time passed but still not totally trustworthy. Their Dwarven guards stood nearby as the master swordsman spoke. "Moracles army, here tomorrow, destroy us" Shi'roc spoke the masterful Orc language to their two pets that were shackled to the trees in the Water Cave. "What do with, you captured.?" He knew that they would be disgraced, having allowed themselves to be captured and chained as they had. They would be cast out or worse. They might be beaten and killed anyway. It was unlike the Orcs to think for themselves, but Shi'roc had hoped that they had adjusted well enough to the new way of life not to want to go back. "Help or stay." Was how he put it to them.

The Gruesome duo knew that if they remained to be found, they would be humiliated even more so than usual. Their kind had never been looked upon favorably by the other races that comprised Moracles' soldiers. The assignment of marching to these mountains was proof of the Bone's disdain for them. These people had treated them well over the past weeks, as well or better than even their own people. They had not known if any more of the Orcs had survived the incident on the mountain. They stood as alone as they could and grunted back and forth at each other before giving their new master a final answer. They envisioned the Magdarn finding the two in this position. Their lives would be made miserable. "We help."

* * *

Shi'roc had slept in the Water Cave that night. It was unlike him to sleep before battle but it had been days since he had rested. There had been too many duties and preparations to make for the battle and escape. He performed his usual morning rituals. He would stretch his muscles by arching his body into painful positions. He stood near the grotto as he practiced with the long sword, his preferred weapon. Although he was proficient with many weapons and an expert with a long bow, he had depended on his sword for more than a century.

His skilled performance was watched closely by his two new admirers. The Dwarves had become accustomed to Shi'roc's exercises but this was the first time that the Orcs had been witness to him in action. He truly was a leader and master swordsman in their eyes. They were so inspired that they were not only willing to help, but anxious to serve the Elven warrior. As he completed his sword play and sheathed the weapon, the two prisoners grinned, showing their pointed mis-aligned teeth. They would have gone as far as applauding if their hands had not been tied to the tree.

Shi'roc approached his new servants and instructed the guards to release their chains. "How we serve?" the prisoner asked delightfully.

"Follow warriors." Shi'roc responded and gestured as to what they should do. "Carry supplies." He indicated for them to haul things on their backs. Their pointed teeth disappeared as their smiles quickly left their faces. They had fully expected to be allowed to fight at his side. Payback the others for the years of humiliation and mistreatment. Shi'roc picked up on their desire to serve but could they be fully trusted with a weapon? He thought for a moment as the Orcs grumbled. "You know where is fortress?" Shi'roc asked, leading them on to betray the secrets of the splintered canyons.

"We show." They grunted. "We fight." The one pointed to Shi'roc's sword. Should he let warriors be warriors?

"Then lead." He responded to the two. The smiles returned to their faces. The two Dwarves were still at a loss of the conversation consisting of various grunts and gestures between their mentor and the creatures. "Take these two to the wagons. They will lead us to Moracles' stronghold." He told the Dwarves in their own language. They were a bit leery of his decision to allow them free, and certainly cautious enough to question his desire to let them lead.

"M'lord? Do you trust them enough not to lead us into a trap?" The one guard spoke up. "They may not be as they seem."

"They know that if they disobey or betray me that they will surely die for it. There can be no greater trust." The master explained the relationship between the Orc master and the position of his servants. "In serving us they have betrayed the Bone who was their master. That is why they do not wish to be left behind. They would surely be tortured and killed after being humiliated."

"How do you know this to be true?" The Dwarf spoke as they proceeded out of the empty water cave.

"I speak their language as I do yours. I will honor their word the same." He said nothing further as he ran off ahead to his position in the first town. He too distrusted the Dwarves at first, but learned to accept their word in time. They had become good fighters and many were already fine craftsmen. All of his distrust of the Dwarven council had faded after they began cooperating in creating the weapons and armor for the battles yet to be fought. Soon, Moracles' forces, or the Bone's, would be attacking. Everyone would already be heading to their posts.

Along the way, he passed many of the villagers hustling to their assigned duties. Many of them carrying supplies for the long journey to Moracles' fortress. Others were making final preparations for the intruders to enter the caverns. He traveled mostly in the dark of the unlit caves. At certain points, a torch had been lit to signify the presence of the unseen surprises for the evil army. As he approached the rocky stairwell to the first town, he noticed the dark line of powder that had been neatly tucked along the cave wall. it extended for about thirty paces and disappeared at the base of the opening.

He nodded to the guard posted at the stairs to assist the retreating warriors. He noticed that the Dwarf was well armed. His armor seemed more polished and of better quality. His sword would certainly be put to better use by one of the warriors above. He remembered how short they were of armor and weapons as to have selected the best for those who intended to fight. He, himself had given his secondary weapons, daggers, and ax, to others while keeping his bow and sword for the day's battle. He quickly ascended up into the abandoned town. He saw that the others were settled in place as he trotted through. He was surprised to see that Maac-To had also donned the same mysterious armor that he had worn when they first met. His sword shown unlike the others that the Dwarves had been manufacturing. From a distance, it seemed comparable to his own finely crafted weapon. He nodded to, or signaled the awaiting defenders as he found his place at the foot of the town.

Chapter 21
Courage

"First town passage ahead on left." The Orc general motioned to the Magdarn leader as they slowed their horses to converse. To their right was the remains of the withered forest. The gray limbs seemed almost transparent against the gloomy skies. It was bitter cold as the winds blew the fine flakes of snow that had just begun to form. "Next trail several miles." He added, motioning far ahead.

The Magdarn leader understood the instruction without the over emphasized motions. "We split here." He commanded with a powerful gruff voice. The rest of his mounted troops signaled for others of the foot soldiers to follow. The Hobgoblins and Kobolds joined the force that would attack the second town led by the Orc Lieutenant and a handful of the Magdarn. The Goblins and the Bugbears moved up front with the Magdarn leader and the Orc general to assault the first town.

Once the reorganization of the troops was completed, the Orc general waved the signal to the first strike force to move ahead. The general led with thirty of the Magdarn along the mountain base toward the first town passage.

By the time they arrived at the first passage, the snow had begun to fall more heavily. The Orc general pointed to where the path began its steep climb. The snow was blowing in large feathery flakes as they all looked up to the mountain ridge where the Dwarven town was situated far above at the crest.

"Fire." Came the command in common language from the base line of boulders along the path. A dozen streaking arrows from close range raced toward their marks. Just as the arrows struck the Magdarn soldiers, a second array was in the air. Every shot was accurate and penetrated the least armor protected areas of the warriors. Some were instant lethal blows, piercing through the neck, hitting below the helmet line. Other arrows struck at critical areas such as knee and shoulder joints where the metal armor was flexed with leather strapping. Several of the Magdarn rolled off of their horses to the ground, some dead, some too severely wounded to pursue their attackers.

The remainder of the surprised elderly warriors reared their horses and let out an attack call, as the mountain archers fled up the rocky path. The mounted soldiers drew their weapons and spurred their horses toward the incline when a sudden wall of fire appeared at the base of the path, blocking their pursuit and startling the horses. The animals jumped back throwing the Orc general and several of the Magdarn.

Gol had concentrated his illusionary powers where it was most effective, on the horses. Their minds were the weakest and easiest to control. Once the horses' minds were set that they were not going up the pass, Gol made good his escape. Although the riders did not see the imaginary flames, the result could not have been more effective. The horses continued to wail and rear as the rest of the riders attempted to control them.

Two of Lorentz' archers took the opportunity to leap over the rocks onto two of the downed warriors, stabbing at them repeatedly and grabbing the reins of their horses. Since they were experienced riders, they managed to quickly take control of the animals and flee. They needed as many horses as possible for their escape. Perhaps their stowed equipment would be of some use as well. Amongst the confusion, they had ridden off along the mountain base toward the trail to the next town. Behind them they heard the call of the warriors to pursue, though they didn't take the time to look behind them, nor did they want to, the remainder of the mounted soldiers who had control of their mounts sped along the rocky terrain after them.

The large, furry Bugbears proceeded up the path, not being influenced by the unseen image. Their awkward bodies waddled as they ascended the slope as fast as their thin, furry legs could carry them. The three lead creatures looked up the path ahead and yelled in terror as a boulder was on its way crashing down on them. They looked to see that the walled stone path was too high to scale quickly and the road behind them was their only exit. They gave the call to retreat as they flailed their weapons over their heads while running down the hill.

The next group, close behind them were alarmed by the warning but could not see any danger ahead, only the heavy falling flakes of snow. They stopped the first three from a total retreat and convinced them that the threat was not real. They turned back around to see the boulder had vanished. They realized that there must be a wizard among those they were sent to destroy. They had heard stories of Moracles' powers and became more cautious of their advance. The group resumed their attack up the hill with weapons drawn.

* * *

"That was great." Gol said to Jantez. "What did you do?" The two mage apprentices were hiding halfway up the slope to delay the attacking creatures as much as possible. They had been very successful. The first team of archers were well on their way through the town toward the secret tunnel.

"I just let them think that a large boulder was rolling down the path after them." He chuckled and pointed to the loosened boulder on which they were leaning. The two pushed and strained against the large rock until it began to move onto the uneven path. "Lets see what they think now." He said with a groan of relief as the stone was on its way. "Time to go." The two fled up the path to the town.

Once again, the creatures looked up to see the same boulder bouncing and crashing against the sides of the path as it wandered down the hill. They laughed at it allowed, knowing that this time the illusion would not take hold over their minds. In fact, they ran towards it in defiance of the mage who was trying to control their minds. But this time their pointed ears perked at the sound of the clatter of the crushing rocks. This time they could feel the vibration beneath their bare, furry feet. There was no time to run as two of them pressed themselves against the wall trying to avoid the meandering crusher. The other five fled backward to no avail, being crushed beneath the weight of the stone. It continued down, bouncing and breaking up into smaller chunks that were avoidable by the remainder of the Bugbear force and the smaller Goblins who had joined the attack.

The Magdarn had by now controlled their horses, still not knowing what it was that had spooked them. The spell had worn off from the minds of the animals and they were once again spurred up the hill. The Orc general gave out a yell to clear the path ahead of them as the horses required the momentum to sustain the climb. He was followed closely by the twelve remaining Magdarn. The second force had passed on to the next ridge path as they pursued the two archers who had ambushed them. The Goblins and Bugbears opened a path for the horses as they began their climb up the rocky road.

The two furry warriors were the farthest ahead and raging, after seeing their companions crushed by the stone. They neared the crest of the ridge ready to do battle with anyone who dared stand against them. Their fury had made them abandon their caution and they both tripped on a strong, thin twine, causing them to slide on the loose gravel and snow. As they landed face down, they were greeted by two Dwarves wielding battle axes. With strong steady swings, as if chopping wood, the blades were impaled into the lower backs of the creatures, severing their spines. There was no counter response from the flailing Bugbears as they dropped their weapons. The two attackers quickly grabbed the creatures weapons and fled up the hill as two more Dwarves drug the bodies off of the path and out of sight behind the rocks. The falling snow covered the scuffled tracks.

Several more of the ferocious furry creatures scurried up the now slippery pass followed by the small Goblins. Two of the smaller survivors on wooden shields in a seated position, came sliding down the pass, swinging their swords. The Dwarves managed to maim several of the larger creatures by slashing their exposed legs. The two rolled off of their sleds and engaged the first Goblins face to face in an even battle. Three Goblins to a Dwarf. The remainder of the forces had advanced up the mountain faster than anticipated. The two heroic Dwarves were soon out numbered and were forced to battle to the death, not before reducing the number of the enemy by eight. At the top of the ridge, Ilo and the others had managed to defeat the crippled Bugbears with only minor injuries to themselves. Though the creatures were larger and more powerful than the survivors, their leg wounds were severe enough to slow them down and even up the odds. A'mora's cleric apprentices aided the wounded and helped them into the escape tunnel.

Maac-To and others waited hidden in the shadows of the ruined town for Shi'roc to draw the enemy in. They were anxious to combat their foe, face to face, not sure as to what form of creature would appear. Their lack of battle experience made them leery but the thought of defending their homes, families, and the confidence that their mentor had instilled in them, made up for their apprehensions.

As the lead riders galloped their horses to the top of the ridge, a large vine net was thrown from the boulders on the sides of the pass. The horses were startled and reared, slipping on the slick ice covered rocks. The Orc general and Magdarn leader became entangled and were thrown from their mounts.

"Run, now." Ilo yelled to his companion as they let go of the netting that had slowed the aggressors. They avoided the trampling of the horses unsteady footing and ran past Shi'roc and into the safety of the town.

The master swordsman guided the horses reins as they scrambled and let them run loose into the town. The two unhorsed soldiers had blocked the path of the attacking goblins as they began to hack their way out of the netting. Shi'roc hampered their progress by taking quick jabs at them while they were down. They were forced to defend themselves as well as try to get to their feet, still partially entangled by the weave of string.

The Magdarn leader towered over Shi'roc, peering through his black helmet at the Elf. The Orc general swung his sword wildly while breaking free of the remaining net. Shi'roc took the Human warrior more seriously as they clanged swords. Shi'roc took the defensive posture as he analyzed the old warriors attack. Each blow of the sword told much of his experience and tactics. As the Elf fended off the blows with his blade, grasped with both hands, he could tell that the two were evenly matched. They both parried and blocked continuously, each others blows as the Orc general proceeded to lead the Goblins, and remaining Bugbears into the town.

Shi'roc realized that he didn't have time for this melee. Although he found it exhilarating, he heard the clomping of more horses approaching. He began to take the lead in this dance of swords and guided the warrior back into the path to block the other riders. He swung continuously, never allowing the Magdarn to make a counter strike. He had gashed the Humans armor several times on the arms and legs, weakening his opponent. Their heavy breath fogged the winter air as they continued the struggle. Just as Shi'roc had the warrior pushed into the path of the galloping horses and was ready to deliver the crippling blow, he was struck in the leg with a bolt from a crossbow. One of the approaching riders managed to get off a shot to defend his leader.

Shi'roc stumbled and lost his advantage blows. He began again to defend with his sword while limping back toward the town structures. As he was being backed into the wall of a fallen building, a flash of light exploded in the face of the Magdarn, momentarily blinding him. The flash did not help Shi'roc, but was enough for him to be pulled out of the combat by Lady A'mora, who had awaited for the right time to intervene. Her inoffensive spell allowed her to remain unnoticed and at the same time protect her Elven companion.

While A'mora had grabbed Shi'roc, Jantez suddenly appeared by her side. Taking advantage of the situation, he thrust his sword deep into the belly of the bearded warrior with a smooth outward motion. The Old man stumbled back as Jantez' bloodied sword was withdrawn. In a final act of aggression, the Magdarn swung again at the unsuspecting apprentice. Jantez blocked the swing to the right with his blade and counter slashed across the left thigh leggings, dropping the man to his knees. He fell back in agony, near death while Jantez withdrew.

Shi'roc watched A'mora remove the crossbow bolt from his leg and provide a healing prayer to close the wound. "How did you know to be here at this time?" Shi'roc questioned the perfect intervention of his lady friend as before when they faced the Dragon.

She gave him a mischievous smile as she tied a quick bandage around his leg wound. "You always seem to get yourself into these types of predicaments. Someone has to look over you." She told him as she thought again about the vision she had the night before. It almost seemed to be her hidden purpose in being here, to watch over Shi'roc.

Several of the mounted warriors made it into the town following the other foot soldiers. The survivors were severely out numbered. Maac-To recognized the advancing

Magdarn as those who had slaughtered his people. The anger he had felt from decades passed had resurfaced, causing his rage and giving him strength. Up until now the anticipation of battling against Moracles was but a dream. Now face to face with the Magdarn, his revenge could take form. He slipped from the shadows to wield his sword against one of the riders, slashing him across the thigh. Maac-To, being Elf, could not hope to reach any higher while the Magdarn was on horse back. His only chance, their only chance was to bring them down to ground level.

The Rider, limping from the wound, swung his chained mace at the smaller Elf. Maac-To skillfully bounced the spiked ball from his shield allowing him an open swing to the bearded warrior's mid section. The Humans blood spurted forth looking wet against the black armor. Maac-To swung again and again against the weakened warrior's shield. With a fury to overcome the dark soldier, the Elf had hacked off his arm that allowed the mace to drop. He wanted badly to complete the death blow, but in mid swing, a mellow voice in his head calmed his anger. He hesitated in his final blow and stepped away, still with his sword raised. He realized that the revenge that he sought was not fulfilled by the death of another.

The survivors fought with bravery and courage. Though they had the surprise advantage, they were not experienced enough to be fighting straight up with several attackers at once. Many had been wounded as they attempted the retreat to the mountain tunnel. Jantez ran to assist the others by attacking the evil forces from the rear, crippling them long enough for his companions to break free from combat and head for the secret passage.

Once his wound was partially healed, Shi'roc followed Jantez and relieved the others in combat so they could escape. His main concern was that A'mora may be cut off from her retreat. He battled a path for her to escape and made sure that the others had escaped as well. All were accounted for except for Maac-To. Shi'roc urged A'mora to flea as he would attempt to find his ancestral friend. The creatures had been ransacking the towns remains, looking for hiding occupants. Many of the abandoned buildings had been set ablaze by the Magdarn as they threw lit torches onto what remained of the dried straw and wooden roofs.

Shi'roc slashed several of his opponents as he ran furiously through the town looking for Maac-To. Through the blazing fire, he noticed the lifeless form of Ilo's father laid next to some debris. He ducked the swinging mace of a mounted Magdarn and rushed to his friend's body. He saw that some life still remained as the Elf opened his eyes and reached out a hand for help. Ignoring the attacking hoards, he bent down and grabbed the limp body, carrying it over his shoulder.

He turned to face a wall of fifteen of the Bugbear and Goblin attackers blocking their escape. With his left hand holding Maac-To and a bloody sword in his right, he rushed with all his strength headlong into the mass of creatures. He let out an Elven war cry as he ran.

Most of them suddenly hesitated, turned and ran. They believed they saw not only Shi'roc, but twenty other heavily armed warriors behind him. The result of the illusion left only a few to fight. Burdened with carrying the body, Shi'roc's attacking blows were slowed yet he managed to down two of the small Goblins. While some Bugbears pursued, Jantez reappeared and attacked them from the rear, allowing Shi'roc to flea into the tunnel. A'mora helped Shi'roc carry the injured Elf through the secret passages.

"Why didn't you give him the vile?" She asked Shi'roc as they proceeded down the stone staircase. Each of the leaders were given a small vial of Lord Lorentz healing potion. In case of sever injury, it would hopefully provide enough strength to escape.

"There wasn't time." The two lowered his body to the ground at the base of the stairs. Shi'roc felt around Maac-

To's bloodied body for the vial of healing. Not being able to find it, he reached into his own pocket and pulled the blue liquid container. He pulled the stopper and carefully poured the fluid into the unconscious man's mouth. With a cough, the regained just enough life to feel the intense pain of his injuries. Shi'roc had caught the life of his friend just before it passed, and there wasn't time for A'mora to perform such a concentrated heal. The three proceeded through the tunnels to relative safety.

Having seen Shi'roc and A'mora carry Maac-To into the escape house, Jantez held off the enemy while literally disarming one of the beasts, and stalled for time. He led the others on a chase through the town. Weakened by some minor wounds, he feared that he might not be able to fulfill his crucial mission. The last survivor ducked behind a crumpled wall and stopped long enough to find in his pocket the small vial that Lorentz had given him. He sucked down the clear blue liquid within and proceeded back toward the former home of Kura's family where the stairs to the tunnel were hidden. He weaved through the town, slashing at an enemy he would come across, but not stop to fight toe to toe.

Making sure that he was being pursued by several of the remaining enemy, he ran down the stone carved steps into the depths of the mountain. His adrenaline flowed as the unknown potion took hold of his body. He felt refreshed and he ran barely feeling his feet touch the ground. He grabbed the last remaining torch at the base of the stairs and looked up to be sure his pursuers were still in sight. He fled down the passage allowing the torch to guide his vision. He leaped over the marked area so as not to disturb the welcome mat for their guests. He slowed to look behind him and could see several of the Magdarn warriors and other creatures closing in on him.

He turned to continue his flight as a small projectile struck and penetrated his shoulder with a gripping pain. He dropped the torch on the cave floor as he heard the crowd behind yell in terror as the welcome mat was pulled out from under them. The lead soldiers had tripped on the loose gravel causing them to plummet into a shallow pit, about five feet deep. The two had impaled themselves on several sharp wooden spikes. The followers hesitated and then jumped beyond the pit to continue their pursuit of the Human.

Jantez recovered from the pain through his concentration and picked up the torch again. He took a few more steps as the gruesome clan closed in, and set fire to the darkened powder mixture that Lorentz had laid. As the odd dust, burst into a sparkle of fire, it followed its path backward toward the attackers. Jantez ran with all of his remaining energy to regain his lead in the race. By now there were twenty of the creatures in pursuit, puzzled by the sparkling puffs of dirt that had tracked back behind them.

From a safe distance now, Jantez heard a colossal explosion echo through the tunnels. He could hear falling rock among the screams of surprise and horror as the passage collapsed, sealing off the hidden stairway and burying many of Moracles' proud troops. He continued to run with the aid of the potion allowing him to partially heal so that he could navigate the winding passages and duck several other surprises for any remaining enemy followers. After a long while, he neared the western mountain entrance where he had first met the Lords and their followers.

*   *   *

The two riders had a gained a great lead over the other mounted Magdarn as they reached the path to the second Dwarven town. The snow was becoming heavy enough to cover their tracks. As they neared the passage they slowed to alert their companions not to fire.

From her hiding place in the rocks, Sha'la was the first to see the familiar riders approaching. She waved to the other women waiting in the wooded cover across the road, not to fire at the riders. She stood up and signaled Lord Lorentz who was near the base of the pass. Lorentz stepped out to meet them and she hid once again watching the main road.

"My Lord. There are soldiers not far behind us." Lorentz' guard exclaimed as he eased onto his horse and looked behind them. The heavy breath of the horses rose in the freezing cold air. The enemy was not yet in sight through the heavy snow fall.

"Ride on ahead." Lorentz said. "I have an idea." He waved his men on to continue their ride north as he looked at the fine powerful horses that they had taken. They would meet up with the caravan of the fleeing villagers and join them. The Mage - Priest began a deep concentration as he resumed his hiding place. With a wave of his hand, the riders tracks disappeared completely as they passed. With the spell still in force, he mentally replaced their tracks with new ones that led up the mountain passage.

Moments later, Sha'la heard the thundering clumping of many horses. She could see the dark armored figures approaching, laid against the blanket of white. They slowed to check the snow covered tracks that they had been following. As Lorentz had projected, they hesitated at the base of the ridge to study the tracks leading up. As the Orc lieurenant began to survey the rocks, the woman warrior stood and aimed her cross bow straight into the eye slot of his helmet. With a warriors yell, she pulled the deadly trigger. The creature screeched as he grasped at his face. He fell off of his horse in agony as the remaining soldiers took up arms.

From behind them all, Arrows flew into their less protected areas such as their leggings and necks. As before, several of them dropped to the ground, dead or in agony.

Before the others could recover and turn to face the enemy at their rear, the women had scurried around them in the confusion and headed for the pass.

Some of the Magdarn recovered from the surprise and steadied their horses. With sword and maces swinging, they attacked the fleeing women. While running with her short Dwarven legs to the passage, Muga had managed to reload her crossbow. She turned to the riders just in time to see one of the Magdarn about to crush her friends head with a huge war hammer. the woman ran for her life as the warrior began his circular swing. Muga aimed her weapon and caught the upper shoulder of the warrior with the bolt, causing him to waver his swing and miss the other woman.

Just before the first rider pursued the women up the passage, Lorentz appeared on the road just ahead of the horses and pointed his magical fingers at the riders. He shouted the words, “Fiero Projectum” as sparks flew from his finger tips, lining a path to several of the Magdarn. An explosive burst of flame struck three of them, distracting them from the female warriors as they disappeared into the rocks. The missiles did little damage to the warriors armor yet allowed the safe retreat of the archers.

Sha’la had not retreated with the others. Instead, she chose to remain behind to help her leader, Lorentz. She had reloaded her crossbow and slung in onto her back. With a dagger in her hand, she leaped onto one of the horses from the rocks. A wave of nausea struck her in mid jump. This was not a good time for her physical condition to work against her. Her momentum helped her to knock the soldier off of the mount as she slipped the dagger beneath his helmet, slicing his throat with the fall. She steadied the horse and grabbed the reins. The other warriors swung frantically at her amongst the commotion, some hitting each other with crashing blows. As she sped away toward Lorentz, the sickness increased almost causing her to double over on the horse.

One of the Magdarn steadied his horse and aimed his heavy crossbow at the woman's back, firing once and then again in succession, without having to reload the weapon. Both of the bolts smacked into the back of the pregnant warrior, causing her to slump over the horse. Several other of the warriors regained control of their horses and advanced up the hill.

Lorentz did not understand how the soldier could have fired the crossbow twice without having to recock and bolt the device. He could only watch in amazement as his follower fell limp on the back of the horse. Still again and again the bolts flew at him from the same Magdarn without the weapon being recocked. Acting with the agility of an acrobat, the priest was able to deflect both of the bolts with the bronze bracers that he wore about his arms. He climbed onto the back of the horse to protect Sha'la and rode off in search of the other survivors. Just as they fled, the remaining foot soldiers, Hobgoblins and Kobolds, arrived at the battle site. The Enemy did not pursue but continued their assault on the mountain. With much the same results as in the first Dwarven town, the battle raged on.

* * *

A'mora had been able to restore some strength to Maac-To's depleted body. He had fallen into a deep healing sleep under her spell as she bandaged his severe wounds. There was no more she could do at this time for him. She was becoming tired and still needed to tend to Shi'roc. A'mora had completed the healing process for his leg and had helped him and Maac-To onto his horse so that they could ride ahead and join up with the others on the north point of the mountain. By now the majority of the mountain dwellers had begun their snowbound journey toward the valley's great canyon where the fortress of Moracles had been hidden. She gave him a quick kiss good bye as she insisted on staying behind to wait for Jantez.

She had waited a long time and began to lose hope. Many brave people had died this day and she feared that Jantez may have been one of those lost. The priestess checked the saddle and reins of her horse one last time before looking back to the shadowed secret entrance into the mountain. The battered Human suddenly stumbled out of the crevice, exhausted by the run and his loss of blood. He had made it out alive solely due to the miracle liquid that Lorentz had given him. She rushed to catch him as he began to tumble to the ground, leaning on the rough rock slope for support. She sighed at the sight of blood covering various parts of his armor. She realized that most of it, fortunately, was not his own. A combination of green and purplish blood had been splattered about him. He was too weak to even talk as she rested him on the ground and began to remove his armor. She carefully removed the protruding arrow shaft from his shoulder by first breaking off the arrow's tip. The priestess chanted the healing spell to stop the bleeding from the hole and other assorted gashes on his body. She quickly bandaged him since there was insufficient time to heal him completely and her powers of prayer were becoming exhausted after a long day of healing wounds.

The snow was falling harder and it would be difficult to hide the horses tracks if they waited any longer. She helped Jantez onto her horse and chanted a prayer for the horse to step lightly as they rode. It would take some time for them to catch up to the others and it would soon be dark. It was possible, however unlikely, that some of the remaining Goblins or Bugbears may find their way out this entrance and discover their path. She hoped that the snow would cover any remaining trail of their escape left behind.

* * *

Jantez and A'mora had made it past the northern peak before it became too dark to see where they were going. The snow was blowing so furiously that they could no longer be sure of their direction. She knew that they were still far off from catching up with the rest of the survivors. Without a visible point of reference, they had little chance of finding them, not knowing the exact direction. She had been told generally where the caravan was headed and that the path was not well defined. They should not have been separated by such a distance as the plan was laid, nor were they expecting to encounter such a storm.

The horse reared at the uncertainty of his footing on the heavy slick snow. It was time for them to hide out if possible and to tend to Jantez' wounds. The freezing cold and his weakness from battle caused him to be feverish and ill. She had not been able to pray for guidance or healing abilities since her own powers had been sapped.

The priestess managed to find some large fallen trees that provided a wind break from the storm. She tied the horses reins to the branches and helped the limp warrior to the ground. He was barely conscious and quite heavy, still wearing his protective armor. Her experiences with Lord Lorentz guided her on this battle of survival. The warrior was tucked beneath the fallen tree, sheltered by the snow drift on its other side. She knew that it was too dangerous to try to light a fire. The light may be seen by the enemy that might still be on the mountain. There was no choice but for her to share her bodily warmth with Jantez to keep him from freezing to death. She huddled close to him, wrapping herself and her robes around them both, forming a cocoon in the snow. For now all she could do was to pray.

* * *

"I am going back to look for her." Shi'roc insisted in the Elven language, not wanting the others to hear his disagreement with Lorentz. The words were unimportant as the others could tell from the tone and gestures that there was a problem. It was no secret that A'mora and Jantez were unaccounted for and everyone was concerned.

"No!" Lorentz grabbed the warrior by the arm. "Even with your night vision, you could not find them in this storm. If they made it out of the mountain they are held up in the snow. A'mora knows how to keep them safe. They are probably just hiding for the night and will catch up in the morning."

"And if not?" Shi'roc asked, pulling his arm from the priest's tight grip. "What if they are in trouble? What if they didn't make it out?" His feelings for A'mora were becoming more obvious again as he spoke. He had hoped that Lorentz was right and that they were indeed safe.

"If not, then there is nothing you alone can do for them." Lorentz said quite factually, hiding his fear of losing his student and companion. "Even I could not find them tonight. It would be best to wait until morning." He too cared for A'mora, more than he would ever let on. He looked at Shi'roc's heated form in the darkness then walked off to the make shift shelters where they had hidden themselves in the fallen trees.

They too could not light any fire to keep warm. but they had the abilities and experience of the clerical students and the worldly warriors to help them survive. Wind breaks had been set up with the wagons and carts that had been converted from the old mineral cars in the mine shafts. Several of the priests had used their powers to create warmth from the metal armor. Others had huddled around the heated armor pieces and covered themselves with blankets to contain the warmth. These techniques were useful only for a short time so they prayed for a break in the storm in order to last the night.

Lorentz had begun to heal Sha'la's wounds earlier as they rode toward the caravan. He had crudely and painfully, removed the arrows from her back and plugged the torn flesh to keep her from bleeding. He had bandaged her sufficiently while his prayers sealed the wounds as he chanted the spells of healing. While inspecting her injuries and determining if any residual internal damage had been done, he had discovered accidentally the secret that Sha'la so desperately tried to keep. The child that she was carrying was healthy inside her and unaffected by the damage to its mother. He wondered if she knew. She must know. He thought to himself. It is too far along for her not be affected. Then he realized her dilemma. Not a word would he say to her, he decided.

Grefden stayed with her after the priest had completed her healing. They huddled close together in one of the mining carts. Lorentz had put her into a healing trance so that she would sleep well. After such blood loss, the best medicine after healing the wounds was sleep. Such a warrior could heal herself with complete rest. With Grefden to care for her and protect her from the cold, she would awaken well enough to travel.

Ilo and Kura, also slept with their families in the other mining carts. Together they could contain the heat and protect their children. Kura had offered up a prayer to the Goddess, Mirana before they all went to sleep. As the past Dwarven Chief, Kyman, had decreed, Kura would indeed lead his people to a better more spiritual life. In his prayers, he asked that they be able to return to their homes in the mountain someday. For now he gave thanks for their apparent success in escaping their enemies.

Maac-To had injuries too severe for A'mora to heal so quickly as they escaped from the mountain. She had done her best to heal the gashes in his flesh, but the wounds were deep and she had not been able to effect repairs to his internal organs. Lorentz did the best he could with his prayers for the brave warrior. He mended slowly but for now was sleeping wrapped with a heated metal gauntlet for warmth.

The other student priests tended to the less seriously wounded by binding their cuts and bruises and offering a healing prayer. They had performed admirably under A'mora's tutelage. Though less experienced than he, A'mora was by far the best at healing wounds since she devoted all of her strength to it. Her prayers to Mirana were solely for the betterment of healing powers. Once she grows with experience, she will be able to out perform her mentor, Lorentz realized.

Lorentz chanted for continued warmth through the night as he huddled beneath a fallen tree stump. The horses were cared for as best as possible despite the freezing cold. They were all fortunate enough to have had enough blankets and coverings for everyone so all prayed that the storm would subside.

Chapter 22
Recovery

The frozen white moisture whirled around his head as the Bone stood almost invisible, atop the fortress of rocks. His frost white body blended with the blowing flakes of snow that were large and round in infinite patterns. Although the snow was beautiful and made the Bone feel closer to his former home, he still resented the fact that he was still trapped on this earth and unable to return to his corner of hell from whence he ruled. He could only now be exhilarated by the freezing cold temperatures that were closer to his normal habitat. Ever since he had been captured by Moracles' spell of entanglement, he was uncomfortable in the warmer months of the year. He hibernated in a little known section of the upper fortress where he had created his own frozen environment, a place where he could feel at home away from the mortal beings that resided in the castle of rock.

Now, looking over the frosted Valley of Mazes, he could understand why Moracles had chosen this spot for his underground citadel. This pinnacle stood in the center of the meandering canyons and was the highest plateau from which, on a clear day, could be seen both entrances into the canyons from the lands beyond. The two roads converged at the base of the canyon allowing no surprise to its inhabitants. But the blinding snow fall obscured any visible distances. Along both paths, a bridge was constructed from the fallen woods of the Elven forest, to span the extinct river that had one time flowed through the valley and fed the towns and the Elven Forest. Its path had been altered with the occurrence of the first earthquake that Moracles had created to announce his arrival into the valley.

The river wound through the labyrinth of the canyon, finding its own way from its source to a new destination. Its branches flowed deep into the ground and even into where the stronghold itself now stood, creating many tunnels and pathways. Eventually, the river was dried up by the evil parasite spell that the mad priest had created to suck the life from the lands around him. Each day for as long as the mage should live, the spell would spread in its circular pattern that was centered in this tower of power. Inch by inch, the land would be decimated and the life force of the land would be absorbed by Moracles to extend his life and powers.

Darkness began to fall as the thick blanket continued to cover over the canyons and beyond. Soon Moracles would return from his journey, the Bone thought to himself. He awaited to hear from the army that he had sent out and from the ghostly Wraiths that looked on over the valley. It was a Wraith that reported the intruders who emerged from the distant western forests. Only he knew that the shadowy figures roamed the land and watched the progress of the soldiers as they made their way to the mountain peaks. They had remained hidden in their ethereal form as they spied from the Bone's orders. When Moracles returned he would need some proof of his accomplishments, or have facts in which he could twist out the truth if they had failed.

The Bone returned to the cave entrance that wound from the top of this plateau to the inner castle chambers near to his own chambers. The winds blew through the rough caverns from the opening as he slowly crept down the rough cut stairs. "It has been four moon cycles." He said to himself realizing that his master would return at any day or time, dropping out of his ethereal travel precisely into his study chambers.

Very few knew the way to those chambers as it required a secret magical command to enter from within the castle. The opening above the chambers was a wide crevice at the top of the plateau. It was this orifice from which the crimson dragon had emerged to attack the intruders months ago. The entrance from above was obscured appearing as a bottomless pit though an adventuresome, resourceful being might happen into it and discover the chamber's black marble floors and the master's office.

The Bone had heard Moracles mention the guardians who wandered those chambers though he had never seen any beings in the few times that he had been summoned there. The room was vast and the only light was that of the candles upon the grand desk of the study. These mysterious creatures may very well be hidden in the darkness awaiting an intruder, though he did not always believe his master's boasts. He was more concerned with the valuable magic contained within the desk and on the shelves of the study. Books and scrolls with enchantments and spells lined the cabinets behind the desk and who knows what lay within the desk's locked drawers.

As he neared the end of the rough cave walls, the stone became smooth indicating the corner of the upper level of the castle, his domain. The silence of the darkness was broken by his word. In the language of the Kobolds, he spoke his own name, "Bone". The grinding sound of a stone revealed an opening in the wall had appeared. A low, luminescent light broke the darkness of the cave passage and the towering figure lowered his head and entered the opening.

The hidden doorway was much to small for him, but of the correct size for the Kobolds that normally patrolled this entrance to the caves that meandered just beneath the plateau. It was his own arrogance that caused him to inscribed a riddle on the outer wall above the doorway. The riddle in the Kobold tongue was meant to inspire the Kobold soldiers as well as frighten off any wayward adventurers.

The square shaped room glowed with an unknown and unseen light source. The walls and ceiling were seemingly alive with light. The wall slowly scrapped shut behind him. In the center of the room stood a two tiered fountain that gushed with crystal clear water flowing from level to level. The top spouted the water upward in various patterns. The Bone walked past the living water toward a wooden door on the right wall. He was not surprised to feel a sprinkle of wetness tap him on the arm as he passed. He almost mechanically reached into the pouch on his belt. He turned to the fountain who's water had formed a reaching open hand awaiting payment for passage. From his pouch he withdrew a gold coin and placed it into the watery hand that immediately withdrew into the lower bowl clasping the currency. Through the rippling water, one could see the multitudes of coins, gems and assorted jewelry that had been donated by passers by over the years.

"Greedy creature." He mumbled to himself as he reached for the door's brass handle. "What good is gold if you can't spend it." He opened the door, stooped into its low passage and slammed it behind him. He swore that he heard the water beast giggling behind him.

The water creature was a sentient guardian of the passage created by Moracles long ago. The evil mage had thought it strange that such a being would be traveling amongst the ethereal mists. It had no means of locomotion except as flowing water and no magical abilities other than its inherent shape shifting. He expected that it was cast into infinity by some furious spell caster. It became one of his Torgs and as such was assigned a specific purpose. It was well suited to guard an inconspicuous entry to his domain. Although the being had no means of communication except for watery gestures, it performed its duty well and expected payment for its services. Anyone who tried to pass without payment, or did not belong in the castle would be engulfed and drowned in the waters of the fountain.

The Bone proceeded through the Kobold guard's quarters and into the seemingly endless hallways of the maze. An unsuspecting visitor could be trapped for days wandering the unknown passages. At its center, protected by nothing except its difficulty to find, stood the ice throne of the Bone. His chambers were created to simulate those of his home, his palace of ice. But here he only had the space for two rooms as his small frozen domain. No living creature dared enter knowing of the freezing temperatures, colder than the winter storm outside of the castle. A flesh covered being might only survive a matter of minutes before turning to ice itself.

There he sat upon his frozen crystal throne awaiting word from the watchers he had sent to the mountains. Would he learn of victory or defeat? Either way he needed to know before Moracles returned. After all, he had in his own twisted way, bent the instructions he had received from the mage. He was only to find the intruders and not to attack them. That was for Moracles' pleasure alone. But the circumstances had been different than the old man believed. There were not only the twenty intruders but an entire civilization of Dwarves, Elves and Humans hiding in the peaks. He would use this excuse to his advantage.

* * *

The remnants of Moracles army had searched the mountain passages thoroughly. One way or another they managed to unleash all of the hidden traps left behind by survivors. Several had fallen into mine shafts that had been covered over. The bottoms of some shafts were embedded with sharpened wooden sticks that perforated the bodies of the fallen soldiers.

Other shafts had been used for generations as bottomless waste pits. Some of the creatures had stumbled into these rank pits while searching the passages. Their bodies had bounced off of ledge after ledge as they splattered into the depths of fecal matter, drowning if not already dead from the fall.

The main stairwells had been collapsed by the explosive magical powder that Lorentz had created. Many of the intruders were cut off, above in the mountain towns, finding no other entrances into the mining tunnels.

Those who were trapped inside did find the empty living areas and the tomb of the recently deceased Dwarven chief, Kyman. His chamber had been left as he passed into another world. They found the remains of the torches that surrounded his bed and the lifeless body that remained. A few of the Goblins realized the importance of this person from his surroundings and the placement of his body. Though all of these intruders were of an evil nature, they did not dare desecrate the tomb of the powerful Dwarven chief. They left the room untouched as they found it, fearing reprisal from some powerful spirit if they were to disturb the remains.

The survivors had left nothing else behind but the memories of decades living in these underground villages that they had made. The water cave had purposely been cut off by the explosions so that any of the surviving plunderers would not have access to the plants or water that remained. The trees would soon again be bearing fruit after having been picked clean just days before. Lorentz also wished to protect the sanctity of the shrine that he had built to Mirana. He somehow hoped that she would protect the orchards and gardens left behind for another day.

"We make camps here tonight. Return morning." The Orc general told those who remained in the town. Though the survivors of the battle did not speak Orcish, they understood his intent. They took advantage of the fallen shelters to protect themselves from the cold and snow. By now the fires that had been set earlier had gone out. It was far better than where the previous mountain dwellers were sleeping tonight although he had no knowledge that they had escaped. He believed that they had been trapped below as the tunnels collapsed.

They made fires of the fallen roofs of some of the buildings and stayed quite comfortably as they repaired each others wounds. Though they had no knowledge of medicines or clergy, they did have practical experience with minor gashes and arrow penetrations. There would be no time to bury the many dead from the day's battle. They had not expected such resistance, nor were they expecting to be attacked first.

From what he could count, the Orc general figured there were close to thirty of them left here in the first town. He had no idea of how many others were trapped below or in the next town. Some of the Magdarn who had been wounded in the first attack may also have survived at the base of the mountain. He would report back that they had been ambushed and the enemy had been trapped in their own mountain. He was not sure if this would please the Bone or not. At first light they would make way back to the mountain base and hope that any others would join them there. If they moved at a quick pace through the snow they could make it back to the Bone in eight days.

The Dwarves who had perished in the battle defending their town, made a good meal for the Bugbears. They had no qualms or reservations about eating their enemies. They would have preferred some spices or garnish though. Roasted Dwarf over an open fire needed to be basted or the results would be a dried meal. It was still more satisfying to them than the rations that they had brought and still remained in the wagons below at the base of the mointain.

The Goblins and the Orc General made due with the small amounts of food that they had carried with them. The Orc was not particularly fond of dried Dwarf meat though he had a taste for the softer Elven meat. Especially that of the powerful warrior that had attacked he and the Magdarn leader. Yes, he remembered the way that the roasted Elven flesh had tasted long ago. He was there when the bodies remained after Moracles had drained the blood and skinned the Elven virgins to provide the components for his evil book of spells. That was long ago when the valley was still filled with life. There were towns to plunder and people to slaughter. Here in this Dwarven ruin, he remembered the old campaigns, trampling the humans in the valley's towns and villages. The campfire's scent reminded him of the burning wooden and straw huts. They had sung songs about their victories. Works of art were created by the slaves that had been captured, depicting the battles fought by the Magdarn soldiers. These tapestries and paintings were hung in the dining hall back at the fortress, where he wished he was now.

* * *

In the shadows of the fire light loomed a dark ghostly figure. All seemed well as the army prepared camps for the night. It watched as the Bugbears roasted their enemy's remains on the open fire. Though it had watched during the battle, it seemed to him to have favorable results. The town had been destroyed and the enemy was about to be eaten. It was of no consequence that many of Moracles soldiers had died in the process. The intruders had been captured below in the mountain and would make a grand prize for the return of their master. He himself would want the pleasures of destroying those beings who had invaded his lands. It was time to begin the journey back and report to the Bone what he had seen. He should be pleased of the outcome.

The other Wraith had watched as the same results occurred in the second Dwarven town. There too, the fallen enemy was to be eaten and the remainder entombed in the great mountain awaiting Moracles to crush them. It would be a glorious day to be rid of such offenders of the realm.

* * *

"Soon we will be passing over the great valley out of which you will lead my armies." Moracles said to Ach'med, through the mist of the ethereal roads. There was no visible evidence of which to measure distance, just the fact that Moracles knew that their journey would soon be ended. He had been tutoring his apprentice, Ach'med, in the ways of magic along their journey.

There was nothing but dark mists in their path as it was on Moracles' initial journey back to Tireth-Tec. They had not encountered any other travelers through the timeless void. This he thought was fortuitous since those that had the powers to do so may be unfriendly to them and overpower the mage and his young apprentice. Not only did masters of the dark forces of evil travel by these means, but also the minions of the heavenly Gods and Goddess'. The two would be in great danger if a minor deity were to come upon them.

"I am anxious to see your kingdom, my master." Ach'med, the future Vandar, expressed his loyalty to the old human. "I expect that your fortress is exquisitely appointed as was your previous home in Lord Magdelan's castle." The Elf complimented. The whole journey he had been grasping onto his master's arm. Though he felt safe, he was uncertain as his feet touched no ground and he could see nothing beyond his master's form. Travel through the ethereal realm made him uncomfortable though he dare not show it to Moracles. It would take him some time, perhaps later in his magical life, to get used to this form of travel.

"Once you have defeated the rebel intruders, you will take the army beyond the great mountains and crush all those who oppose me in the west." The mage said with a sinister tone. His greater goal was to prepare the land for the coming of his Gods. The land must be rid of all good where they would set up a home on the earth. By now he thought the Bone would have flushed the intruders from hiding and have them ready for an entertaining slaughter.

But he wanted the one called Shi'roc to die last at the hands of his own brother. He was the reason that Moracles called upon the dark lords to raise Ach'med from the tomb. By preparing his new Dark Elf in the ways of magic and armed with the evil powers of Hartes and Lolith, he felt that his apprentice could defeat the great legendary warrior, Shi'roc.

* * *

Before morning arrived, Shi'roc was already preparing his horse for travel. He was intent on back tracking to find A'mora. The clouds had broken and the wind had died down. There was no more snow falling and it appeared to be the beginning of a clear day. Most of the camp had been completely buried in the snow. It was waist deep for him in some of the drifts, but he was sure that his horse would not fail him.

He stuffed some of the frozen fruit into his saddle bags and rode off before anyone else had stirred. He located the sun's rising position and was able to direct himself back toward the mountains along the path that they came. He knew that Lorentz and Grefden would be furious with him for riding out alone, but he could not wait any longer. He had to find A'mora.

The more he thought about her, the more his feelings of love for her came to be. He realized that soon in his life he should settle down, build a castle and start a family. This would be his last battle, he decided. He was getting too old for all of this world travel, never having a place to call home. He would have A'mora as his queen and rule his kingdom with a firm but wise hand. He would count on her guidance for that.

By the time the sun shone on the blinding white landscape, he was half way back to the mountain. He looked behind him to see that his trail was extremely visible, even at a distance. The snow was churned up as the horse strode through it, leaving a path to follow back to the camp, or maybe be seen by the enemy. Perhaps as viewed from the mountain, the debris from the fallen forest would mask his passage.

* * *

The Orc general had made it clear to the remaining army that they were to head back to the fortress by the same path as that they came. He alone would ride north to search for the others commanded by his lieutenant, that had been sent to the second town. Perhaps they had found another entrance into the mountain where some were seemingly trapped. He would not believe that the assault was an entire failure if he could be sure that the loathsome enemy had been trapped underground in their own mountain. The Bone may be pleased to find that the small ones had been entombed with those who had come to the valley.

He rode north along the base of the ridge as he watched his troops straggle off toward the south road. They had gathered as many of the horses and wounded that they could find still alive after the storm had passed. He could only leave the dead as they were. There was no time for proper burials or rituals of the various races to be performed. They would be remembered as having died in battle and accepted by the great gods of their choosing to continue to fight in another world.

The depth of the snows increased as he traveled. The sun was now rising casting eerie shadows through the dead forest. Although there were no visible tracks, he knew that he should be approaching the second road to the mountain town as was described by his second in command. There must be more of his troops close by he assumed so he began to call out to the mountain in Orcish to whomever could hear him. Up ahead he saw several horses freezing in the high snows. Their saddles and equipment were still in place as if they had been left behind. Finally he heard responses from the upper ridge. He looked up to see several figures waving torches. They had been held up for the night in that town as well.

The various troops began to gather on the road coming down the mountain. Just then the general saw the snow covered bodies of many soldiers, hardened in the freeze. He dismounted to see what had happened. They had all been pierced with several arrows. He found his Orc companion with the crossbow bolt projecting from his eye socket. He was enraged by the merciless slaughter by these ruthless mountain people. He hoped that his men had found another entrance so that he could personally take revenge for these deaths.

He found from talking to the few who remained that once again, many of them were trapped inside the mountain after the tunnel passage had collapsed. They found no other entrance and spent the night in the ruined town as the Orc had done. Again they gathered the wounded and the remaining horses and he sent them back along the south passage. He would continue his ride north and around the mountain to search for others and possibly another entrance.

The leader of the Hobgoblins insisted on riding with the general as he had lost many men inside the mountain and hopped that they would emerge from some other cave entrance. He had convinced the general that the mountain people would surely be dead after so many of their troops had infiltrated the tunnels in pursuit of the enemy. They rode on as the sun glared at them from the eastern sky, turning the blanket of white into a blinding mirror ahead of them.

* * *

The two awoke beneath the fallen tree, entangled in a what might have been a passionate embrace to keep warm.

Their conspicuous position startled them both. Jantez had been too exhausted and delirious from the fever to realize that A'mora had removed his armor the night before. She had done so to keep him warm by wrapping her body with his under her cloak and blanket. The beautiful priestess had broken his fever and his wounds had been healing, yet he was slightly embarrassed by the predicament as was she.

Her horse was hidden behind a snow bank, still entangled in the wild snow covered branches. She sent a few comforting words by thought to check on him and she heard his whinny and snort in reply, letting her know that he too had survived the night. He was hungry as well.

"How do you feel this morning?" She whispered to Jantez.

"Much better than I could expect thanks to you." He whispered back to her, no longer embarrassed and a little aroused at her closeness. He had only dreamed at being in her embrace during the past months, and now his wishes had come true. He had not released her from the warming embrace nor did he want the moment to end.

"I must still check your bandages and complete healing your wounds." She said softly as she moved her hands along his body to unwrap the cloth bindings that had protected his injuries. She chanted the healing words as she pressed her hands on each of his gashes and punctures. When her chanting ended, the wounds no longer needed covering. All had healed completely leaving but small scars as reminders of his battle.

Jantez arousal increased at the touch of her hands on his skin. Her hands were warm and comforting. He could feel the powers flowing through them as she performed her healing talents. Soon he had felt as strong as before the battle the prior day. "You have saved my life." He said. "How can I thank you enough?"

A'mora felt a special warmth inside her, urging her emotionally to hold on to Jantez, even though a part of her said no. She did have strong feelings for him, but also for Shi'roc. At this moment, the Elven warrior was far away and she was about to loose control of her emotions. For a moment, she remembered their overall situation and thought they should hurry and move on to catch up with the others if possible. But Jantez' gentle touch convinced her to stay awhile in his arms. She whispered a few words of prayer to herself.

"I know how you can thank me." She told him as she kissed him gently on the lips. Any thoughts she had of Shi'roc had faded away. Her desire to re-join the other survivors had vanished. All that she could need was here and now.

His muscular arms held her tight as he responded with an even more passionate kiss. They no longer needed any magic to warm them. Their sparks ignited a fire within, that even the Gods could not extinguish. Their limbs became more intertwined as their sighs and gasps became louder. The young Human, now with a renewed vitality, carefully unbound the leather garments of his healer. Her bare skin was soft and unscathed. As their tongues wrapped around each others, he loosened her cloth under garments. Their fervent movements shook the crusted snow that had covered them. Much of it melted as it came in contact with the two lovers. Within moments their desires and passions unraveled as they made love under the blanket of snow.

As their movements slowed and their love was consummated, they realized that they were no longer hidden under the protection of the fallen tree. They had writhed several feet into the open snow. Just then they heard muffled voices nearby. Their first thoughts were that the others were looking for them. But it might also be the enemy soldiers tracking them down. They remained still and unmoving as the priestess chanted a prayer of protection, like she had taught her student clerics, to remain hidden. The blessing was most effective when not being hunted or specifically sought after. They dared not move to arrange their clothing or reach for the buried armor or weapons.

The voices moved closer and A'mora thought to her horse to remain still and silent. She recognized the language as that of the captured Orcs. Though she could not understand what was being said, she did determine that another language was also being spoken. She hoped that their trail of the previous night had been covered by the drifting snow and that her horse was unseen by the soldiers.

After a tense hesitation, the voices moved on back toward the mountain. The two were quite fortunate that they were not closer to the main path and the fallen, uprooted trees were hiding them well. They waited a while before making any motion. Their warm embrace had turned into a chilling fear.

* * *

Through the snowy branches he could see the Orc leader and the single Hobgoblin riding off toward the backside of the mountain. Their horses struggling to walk in the deep snow. Shi'roc quietly stepped back to get his horse that he had left tied to a tree. Upon hearing the voices, he had dismounted and hidden himself in the snow drift. He listened intently to the Orc's commands, knowing that he was in charge from the inflections of the language. They were trying to find the missing soldiers and the easiest way back to the castle of Moracles. He had decided that no one had returned this way. The snow was deepest in this direction and travel would be slower. They were not still looking for the mountain people. They had apparently been separated from the others and were still looking for those who had entered the mountain through the village secret tunnels. Shi'roc wondered why they had given up.

The Elf realized that all of the traps they had set in the tunnels were well worth the effort. The enemy must have also been trapped inside by Lorentz' magic powder. He wondered now if Jantez had made it out in time or if A'mora might have tried to go back in looking for him. If the Orc finds the hidden western entrance, he may realize that they all had escaped, hopefully thinking that they fled to the free western lands through the forest.

The Elven warrior proceeded toward the mountain after remounting his horse. He quietly rode through the deep snow and listened for any sign of Jantez or A'mora. The sun cast a glaring projection through the clear skies. With his keen vision he peered through the blinding white surroundings for her horse. He then heard some rustling to his left, the sound of moving armor. He slowly slid off of his horse and drew his sword. The snow was no place to battle on foot but he may have no choice.

He crept over to the sounds and heard soft voices just beyond a snow bank. He looked around the ridge to find both Jantez and A'mora, laying half dressed on a blanket in the snow. He stood in shock, and then anger, watching her fasten her leather armor around her waist. He remained silent as his anger grew. Though he should have been happy to see them alive, his unknown jealousy took the place of his joy.

Jantez completed his armor straps and reached for his sword and froze as he looked up to see Shi'roc. A'mora saw his sudden halt and looked up, only to gasp. She wondered how long he had been there, watching. She knew when she saw the anger in his eyes. The priestess could not speak as his contemptuous stare seemed to spell her. She looked away in shame, unable to face him any longer as he walked back to his horse and rode off in disgust.

Chapter 23
Discovery

They rode toward the blinding sun. The Orcs drove the two lead wagons that carried the supplies. Although the wagons were quite old, the Dwarves had managed to repair them sufficiently for the journey. Their original use was to carry the superior crafted weapons and armor to the old towns of the humans and trade for goods that were unavailable in the mountains. The Dwarves were not much for farming and food was their greatest need. Though they were good hunters and trappers, the little people could not live on meat alone. The wagons would return with sacks of grains, fresh fruits and vegetables, clothing and more. Now, once again those wagons carried much the same loads but for a different purpose. Not to trade but to survive.

Lorentz rode behind them, still not entirely trusting the Orcs, the seemingly converted enemy. They had been given back their armor for protection but Lorentz would not allow them to carry any weapons. So far they had served well and no longer seemed a threat to the survivors. They may be, as Shi'roc had said, loyal to those who liberated them from their peers. He rode up beside one of the wagons and chanted the spell that allowed communications between them before.

"How far?" He asked in their tongue, using the tones that Shi'roc had instructed. He was at least attempting to be their superior though they still visualized him as a servant of the great warrior, Lord Shi'roc.

"Five days to canyon." The lead Orc replied without hesitation. "Where is Lord?" The creature was inquiring as to why Shi'roc was not with them today. They had seen him the night before as he had caught up to the camp. They had also seen their master arguing with this wizard servant before they slept. The creatures were unable to learn the languages spoken by these people but they could understand names and the meanings of actions and tones.

"Returned, find A'mora." Lorentz said, a little irritated that Shi'roc did not listen to his advise. He only hoped that they would catch up to them soon. He did not relish the idea of planning a battle without Shi'roc. Although he was an excellent strategist, he had found that their best results came from a combined and different point of view. Not yet knowing what would await them in the canyon castle made the planning much more difficult.

"We follow, Protect." The Orcs stopped the horses and intended to go back as well, to see to the safety of Shi'roc, their new leader. They had begun to climb off the wagons as Gor and Grefden rode up to see what was wrong.

"No." Lorentz insisted. "Shi'roc order. You lead." He reminded them of their master's direct instructions. They were needed to guide the survivor caravan into the canyon trails. They hesitated. They were torn between their master's orders and their desire to fight at his side. The two creatures looked at each other, pondering, then nodded to proceed with their orders. They remounted the wagons and urged the horses on.

"What was that about, M' Lord?" Gor inquired to Lord Lorentz. Though Lorentz was not their leader, Gor and Grefden held respect for him as a leader and a friend of their Lord, Shi'roc. "Have you seen Lord Shi'roc?" They too were concerned at his absence and did not at all trust the two pets. They had not understood the words he had spoken to the Orcs.

"Apparently our two friends are entirely devoted to your Lord Shi'roc, As much as the two of you. When I told them he had gone back to look for Jantez and A'mora, they insisted on returning to protect him. I stopped them by reminding them of his order for them to lead." He shook his head as the three watched the rest of the troops trudge by in the snow. "It seems that his orders are just slightly more meaningful than his safety. They are true warriors." He looked at Grefden and Gor with a meaningful nod. Lorentz hoped his words would stir reaction from them.

Shi'roc's guards looked at each other in shock. " Went back? We should go back to find him." Grefden barked. "He may be in danger. Why would he do this without us?" Grefden asked rhetorically. "He should have wakened us." They had been unaware as to their Lord's early departure and were disturbed that Lord Lorentz had kept this information from them.

"Love, my friend, is the only thing that causes such delusions." He looked at the two loyal guards. "Find him if you wish. I will not fault you for your loyalty, but be ware, he may not like what he finds." He watched them ride back along the trail in the snow, past the rest of the caravan. It would indeed lead them straight to their master.

They understood what Lorentz had implied. They were aware of Shi'roc's hidden fondness for Lady A'mora. They also knew that she had spent much time with Jantez, training him in magic amongst other things they only suspected. They pressed their horses hard to catch up, not knowing exactly how long of a lead Shi'roc had.

The others struggled through the snow on foot or horseback. It was indeed toughest on the Dwarves who had been walking waist deep in the white powder. Each of them keeping warm with a piece of heated metal wrapped under their blankets over their armor. They were thankful that the Dwarven crafted metals were lighter weight than other armor. The treasures that had been kept secret for so long proved to be worth the wait. The armor and weapons that the former chief had hidden were of the finest design, both practically and aesthetically. The equipment had proved invaluable during the previous day's battle. They would not have faired well with only the practice weapons and few weapons that the Dwarves had made in the forges over the past months.

The farther away they rode from the mountain the less snow they encountered. The small children rode with their mothers huddled in the horse drawn mining carts. The clear skies allowed the sun to warm them some, breaking from the harsh freezing temperatures of the night before. Maac-To was also laid in a cart, still too weak to travel on his own. Lorentz had done all that he could, but the internal damage to his body was far too severe from the wounds to heal properly. Even the healing potions he had made had little effect other than to keep him alive a little longer in pain. He had lost a great deal of blood and was fortunate to still be alive, though the pain may have convinced him otherwise. His wisdom had told him to release his friend from the pain naturally.

The afternoon sun reflected off of the white sheen, almost blinding Sha'la as she turned to watch her lover ride back toward the mountains. Lorentz had performed her healing with great proficiency and though she was in no condition for combat, she could still ride or defend herself if necessary.

The warrior watched the two as far as she could see. Then they disappeared from sight into the fallen wooded area where they had slept the night before. The mountains looked so majestic, covered in the gleaming snow. She had not imagined how they looked from this distance. The warrior felt sorrow for the Dwarves who were forced to leave their homes. She also understood as a devoted follower, that Grefden must return to his master's side.

* * *

Gor and Grefden stopped their horses as they heard the gallop of another horse and the clanging of armor coming toward them. They drew their swords preparing to do battle if necessary, though they were certain that it was a single horse and rider. Through the snow covered branches they could see that it was their Lord Shi'roc moving with some speed. He did not appear to be in danger as they could see no others followed. The two guards looked at each other fearing the worst. Did their master find Lady A'mora and Jantez dead or worse?

Shi'roc rode past them, paying them no mind as his horse galloped. Not even did he so much as acknowledge their presence. "M'Lord," Grefden called. "Is all well?" The two sheathed their swords again and turned to follow. They were dismayed at the encounter. Did he not hear or see them?

"No, all is not well." Was the response they heard from Shi'roc. He rode on as fast as he could, almost leaving the two behind. His mind was elsewhere. The loyalty of his guards coming to look for him was not of consequence. He barely realized that they were there.

Could he be in some trance? They wondered. Perhaps he had found their two friends so brutally murdered that he could no longer face them. "What has happened M'Lord?" Gor pressed as they rode to catch up. "Where are Jantez and Lady A'mora." He asked more directly after a null response to the first question.

"They will be along." He responded curtly. He spurred his horse to ride even faster, not wanting to be near anyone for a while. The path was becoming well traveled through the snow. It would be clearly visible now to anyone or thing that stumbled upon it.

Now they were certain of what they had suspected. They respected their master's desire to be alone and fell back well behind. Occasionally they had looked over their shoulder to see if Jantez and A'mora had caught up yet. As they had reached the open area with the dead forest behind them, they saw a horse with two riders emerging from the fallen trees. It was indeed A'mora and Jantez.

The warriors slowed their pace so the two could catch up. They were obviously in no hurry to do so. Finally the horse drew near as the guards were now at a walking speed, no longer attempting to keep sight of Shi'roc. Grefden could see that both were in good health. He almost preferred that Shi'roc had not found them at all for the pain that he must be suffering. He only gave them a glaring stare as their horses now walked together.

Lady A'mora was the first to break the uncomfortable silence. "What is the matter with you? Speak your mind." She said in a bit of aristocratic tone to Grefden. What she tried so hard to keep hidden about her past status had just resurfaced. None before had known why Lord Lorentz had introduced her by the title of 'Lady A'mora' when she had not seemed at all like the royalty they had encountered. She glared back at him suddenly in demand of an answer.

Grefden looked back for a moment at Jantez who was holding on to her. He was of no mind to be diplomatic about it. That trait he was learning from Shi'roc. "I fear that you have betrayed my master. He is upset with both of you." He said, trying not to become angered himself.

A'mora could tell from the look on their faces that they knew what had taken place, or at least had a good idea of the reality. She did not attempt to hide the truth but felt a slight rush of guilt. Her gaze moved toward Gor who could only shake his head in disappointment.

Jantez did not dare interrupt the session of deadly stares. He remained silent and unimportant for now. He did feel that he should interject some defense but also felt that none was warranted. Their affair was none of their business as he could see. The only reckoning due was to Lord Shi'roc, not his guards.

The incident went unopened as A'mora spurred her horse to trot on ahead. Gor and Grefden gave them some room before encouraging their horses as well. They should all be reunited with the caravan by dark. They would later see what reaction would take place at the camp. Tonight they should be able to eat a hot meal as they would be safe to light campfires. The night would be clear and cold, but perhaps not as cold as before.

Grefden longed to be at Sha'la's side again, and to hold her through the night for warmth. His feelings for the woman warrior grew each day and more when they were apart. He anguished at the thought of not being with her during battle when she was wounded and needed his help. He had thanked Lord Lorentz for protecting her and bringing her back to him.

Once again she was healthy yet that morning she suffered an attack of nausea. Lorentz had waved off the illness as due to the effects of internal healing. Grefden had not witnessed such side affects before when Gor had been mauled by the bear though. Perhaps it was due to her womanly cycles. A matter of which he did not understand since he had never spent that much time with the same woman. He did not dare ask of such things, nor did he really wish to know.

* * *

"They must have fled west to the forests beyond the wasteland." The wounded Magdarn reported to the Orc general. "We found no other signs that they remained in the mountain and we searched all of the passages through the night. We found only the body of a dead Dwarf that had been enshrined." Although he spoke in the common tongue of men, the Orc was able to understand part of his meaning.

The Magdarn soldier had been one of the few survivors of the traps set by the fleeing mountain dwellers. Their luck continued in finding the western opening to the mountain passages. The crevice in the rocks indicated much traffic in recent days. There were even signs of fresh blood. It was indeed possible that the tracks to the west were covered by the snows, though the brunt of the storm was to the east of the mountains. The western side had little depth to the snow, but it was sufficient to hide any activity beyond the tunnel opening.

The General ordered the Hobgoblin to lead the remaining soldiers to the south and follow the path back to the castle. They would be indeed a day behind the others who had left early that morning. He would head back north and make one more pass at looking for stragglers. The upper road back to the castle would be more heavily laden with snow, but the distance was shorter along that route. Traveling alone on horseback, he expected to reach the fortress just prior to the main force following the south passage. He wanted to make his report to the Bone prior to the return of his diminished forces, unaware that the Wraith spy's would report far ahead of him.

The order was followed as the mounted Hobgoblin trotted off south with the remaining twenty something soldiers close behind. The angered Orc proceeded north, reaching the mountains bend just before the clear sky turned a bright orange with the setting sun. He had been following the tracks that had been his own earlier until he noticed that into the rotted woods began a second set of tracks near where they had stopped that morning. It was too dark to continue by then, but he proceeded to investigate the origin of the tracks that they had not seen previously. His immediate thoughts were that more of his army had survived and spent that night in the woods. He dismounted with sword drawn and followed the paths off the road. There was no evidence of a campfire but there was much disturbed snow and many sets of foot prints that he could distinguish as well as horse prints. He saw that the trail led through the woods to the north passage where he intended to follow as well. More prints were added to the first sets. He wished to continue but it was now too dark to travel. He would make camp and resume his tracking in the morning. For now he was happy to think that more of his troops were on their way back to the castle.

* * *

The Bone curiously inspected the intricately carved statues on both sides of the alter in the dimly lit temple. To the right of the alter sat the stone carved statue of a young Human warrior dressed in battle plate armor wearing a crown of jewels. The carving was very life like. The features were so detailed that it seemed to move as the Bone peered at it. The figure sat prominently on a throne with his sword in an outstretched hand with his palm on the pummel and the point balanced on the foot of the throne.

He knew the features of this carving to be that of the God, Hartes, who ruled the upper planes of hell far above the Bone's origins. He remembered having to ask for passage of the greater god, through his domain so as to travel to the material realms of the universe. It was during that journey when Moracles had snatched him and his flaming steed from the ethereal plane.

Now he wondered if it had been Hartes plan working in conjunction with Moracles, to trap him and keep him here. That thought had never crossed his mind before. Hartes always was greedy and in search of more territories to conquer. It would be like the god himself to find a way to keep the Bone from his domain so that he could rule it as well. "No, it couldn't be," the Bone said as if speaking to the statue. "Hartes despises the cold."

The Bone walked slowly around it, watching it in the shadows. His tall frame was bent over the life sized statue as he caressed the stone crown with his finger. If only it were real he thought. He could buy an army of his own with the value of the gold and gems. The chaos he could cause on this earth might make the imprisonment worth while. But first, he must be set free of the powerful magic that held him in this forgotten valley. Moracles must be killed before that can happen.

On the other side of the alter stood a beautiful woman carved from a black marble stone. The woman's features were well defined. Her curvaceous body was draped in an intricate cloak of webs. The points of her ears protruded through her finely combed hair indicating her Elven nature. Upon her shoulder sat a large furry spider that was also carved form the same stone. It signified her title as 'The Spider Queen' well known to all as the goddess of the fallen Elves.

She was worshipped by all dark Elves known as Drow and would empower them with special magical abilities if they could survive her excruciating tests of loyalty. As evidence of such failure, two such beings resided outside the temple in the caves as guardians. They were half Drow and half spider, known as Dryders. The male possessed magical abilities and was a powerful eight legged warrior while the female possessed only evil priestly powers but too was capable of fighting.

It did not surprise the Bone to see the statue of Lolith in the same temple as that of Hartes since they were known as the lovers who rule the lower lands, far beyond the confines of space or time. They were the two most powerful gods of the lower planes and together they controlled the destiny of all humanoid creatures after death: that is the ones who were not snatched away to the heavens to serve the Gods such as Alena or Adolpho.

He knew that for some reason, Moracles, worshipped both the mighty God and Goddess for his mystical gifts. He drew upon Hartes for his priestly powers and turned to Lolith for the magical spells such as the one with which to trap unsuspecting travelers of the ethereal planes. Unlike the powerful mage / priest, the Bone maintained natural magical abilities. He had no use of the greater gods for his powers, nor did he need to study spells from a book or chant prayers as did Moracles. His abilities were at the ready and only a thought was necessary to evoke them.

Although he was restricted to serve Moracles, he still could call upon his own servants to assist him such as the Wraiths he had sent to spy upon the Orc General and his army. Yes, the shadowy figures had been following the army and its actions in order to report their findings back to the Bone before the army itself had returned. The ghostly dark figures resided between the earthly realm and that of the ethereal plane allowing them to remain hidden in the shadows and travel quickly.

The temple was poorly illuminated by only one torch lit on the side wall near the worshipers stone benches. The flame flickered and sputtered as it cast varying shadows around the altar. As the Bone peered through the darkness with his glowing red eyes, a low whisper called to him from the center of the temple.

"Bone, we have returned with grave news of your army." The first Wraith spoke as the Bone walked toward the voice from the alter with three large steps.

"Tell me what has happened." The large creature could now see the floating outlines of the two shadow beings. "I wish to know exactly what you have seen." He spoke with respect to his cohorts. Although they were his servants, he admired their abilities and did not treat them as he did the humanoid creatures of the earthly realm.

The Wraiths spoke in echoing whispers. "They have fought the small people known as Dwarves who were led by the other intruders you spoke of." The second voice said. "They attacked your army at the base of the mountain." He continued the report without emotion or apprehension as the Bone listened intently.

The two described all events as seen through their eyes with precise detail. They did not hesitate to reveal any event or try to withhold the unfortunate truth. The Wraiths had split up as did the army, so they had both described similar events as seen at the two deserted Dwarven towns. In each case, the little people had been led by Humans and Elves.

Clearly the outsiders had trained these warriors and persuaded them to attack Moracles' forces.

The Bone did not interrupt as he absorbed the slightest details of the defeat of his army. He hung his head low as he sat on the stone benches that to him were quite tiny and uncomfortable. The Voices told of the precision and cunning of the enemy warriors. The accuracy of their archers and the skill of their swordsman did not seem possible to be learned in such a short period of time.

The Bone raised his head when he heard of the use of magic by the intruders. This was a surprise to him, especially the expertise at which it was performed as described by the shadow figures. A new glimmer of hope crept into the Bone's twisted mind. Perhaps these beings could defeat Moracles after all and break the spell that controlled the Bone. Moracles death by the hands of the outsiders would release him to roam free once again, even to return home to his ice palace beneath the fires of hell.

His new hopes were shattered as the Wraiths indicated that the intruders and the Dwarves had fled deep into the mountain and collapsed the tunnel passages behind them apparently sealing themselves off inside. At that point the Wraiths had returned to tell their story to the Bone. At its conclusion, the large creature stood up tall and stretched his long limbs and tail causing a resounding grinding and cracking of his tightly bound bony frame. He tucked into the back of his mind the possibility that somehow the intruders would use their magic to destroy the mage who had entrapped him in this world, more precisely, the one who confined him to the area of this canyon. These intruders now seemed to him to be more friends than foes.

"Very well." The Bone nodded to his faithful servants of the darkness. Their shadows faded as they moved through the walls of the temple. He pondered a while longer as he thought of the trapped intruders in the mountain. What would he tell Moracles when he returned from his mysterious journey?

* * *

"That seems to be a peaceful forest in which we can rest." The great Gold Dragon said to the rider on his back. "We should also be getting close to the lands Alena spoke of where Shi'roc and his friends have gone to." The spell of ethereal passage was dissipated and the Dragon and his rider found themselves hovering over the frost covered forest below them, shimmering in the moonlight.

"We must be careful not to be seen, especially while you are in your present form." Fendal reminded the Dragon. "We do not want to bring attention to ourselves as it may somehow forewarn our adversary." The mage then untied the leather straps of the intricate saddle and leapt from his traveling companions back and gracefully floated down with his arms spread as a bird. He sailed through the tree tops in search for an open area where they could set up a camp.

"There is a good spot." He said to himself, knowing that Zant could hear his thoughts and would follow in his own way. He landed himself in a grassy area amidst the trees. While he waited for the lawful one to arrive, he began to set up a campfire and discovered the remains of one that had been set long before. He quickly established a new flame with the fallen branches and sat to warm himself.

A while later, a yellow canary fluttered above in the trees near the fire. It circled over the mages head, bouncing from tree to tree, then slipped into the darkness of the forest. Fendal knew that it was Zant looking for him. He also knew that the powerful transformation of the Dragon was not to be witnessed by humanoids. Moments later, Fendal heard a rustling of someone walking in the woods. He paid it no mind, thinking that Zant was approaching in his Human form.

"Welcome, set by the fire." The Elf said without looking at the source of the movement. He heard no reply and turned, expecting to see the old man. Fendal jumped to the other side of the fire as he saw, standing upright, a large black bear, at the edge of the trees. He took a breath and noticed that the bear was not attacking or growling. The bear set back down on his four paws and slowly approached the fire, sniffing the air as he stepped.

"Hibernating, he is not. Toward the fire he goes, is hot" A voice from behind Fendal made him jump again. It was indeed the old man Zant, speaking again in rhymes. "Not so ferocious is the bear, as he walks he sniffs the air."

"I wonder what he wants, or is looking for." Fendal whispered to the ancient one, as he kept stepping backward away from the fire and the bear. As a wizard he had no abilities to speak with animals as would a priest. His instincts told him that this was a friendly bear, but the Elf was not inclined to take the chance. He did not wish to injure the creature. He would probably only make it mad anyway, so he began to climb the nearest tree and urged Zant to do the same.

"I am not accustomed to climbing trees." The old man said as he watched Fendal do his best to get into the branches. The Elf appeared odd to the Human trying to get away from the bear. He stood by the tree and watched the bear as he meandered around the campfire as if awaiting for someone or something to happen. The bear made no attempt to follow the two into the trees, it only circled the burning branches a few times then trotted off the same way he came.

"I believe it is safe for you now." The old man looked up at the Elf clinging to a thick branch in a very undignified position.

"I wonder what that was all about?" Fendal said as he began to scurry down, trying not to snag or tear his clothing. "I hope it doesn't come back. I really need to get some sleep tonight."

"Fear not. I will handle the situation should it arise." The exalted Dragon said as the two returned to the warmth of the fire. "You need not be awakened."

Fendal put some more wood on the flames before curling up and going to sleep. He did not argue the point about allowing Zant to keep watch all night. Normally he would share the duty but the Dragon had much more stamina than even the Elf.

So far their journey had been uneventful, even when traveling in the ethereal plane. They had not encountered any other creatures of good or evil persuasion. Though Fendal had the ability to travel for short known distances in that manner, it was Zant who had the knowledge of their general destination. He was quite trusting of the Dragon since it was in service to one of the greater gods. Though he did not have such faiths, he knew enough to trust in a follower of Alena. As a Gold Dragon, the magical creature could do nothing but good deeds as evidenced by allowing Fendal to ride him. Such an action would normally constitute a lowly servitude so Fendal surmised that this journey must mean something important to Zant or to Alena to allow the mage to tag along.

As the old man stood watch and tended the fire, he pondered the Goddess' words to him. They were cryptic as always, not allowing the whole truth to be known. Her meaning was not entirely clear but it felt as though she were saying that this would be his final task for her. It was possible that she meant he would be killed in fulfilling this mission to find and protect Shi'roc. He too felt that there must be something more important to the outcome of this journey.

Chapter 24
Traveling

The first moon had risen, showing only a part of itself in a sharp crescent blade as Shi'roc perceived it. The sky was clear and the stars shown as tiny distant fires. He could feel the skin on his face burning with the cold of the wind as he continued to press on, riding to catch up to the camp. They too had gone far this day, heading for their impending attack on the fortress of Moracles, or the Bone, thatever was really running this valley now. They had hoped that it would be left unprotected, with the majority of their forces dead or left behind on the mountain. The Orcs were leading the survivors on what was thought to be the shortest path from the Dwarven Peaks to the great canyon where the hidden fortress lie. The path was without question shorter, though the snows had caused a less than favorable pace for the column of survivors.

Shi'roc looked ahead in the darkness and could see several camp fires in an open area. He slowed his horse for a moment and sniffed the air to see what might be cooking and in what direction the wind was blowing. It was not sending him the aroma of food that he gravely needed. He had not eaten this day and was quite starved. He rode on, determined to drive the last bit of anger from his mind before reaching the camp. He did not want to show any emotion in front of the others. He had almost forgotten that his guards, Grefden and Gor, were well behind him, and behind them rode A'mora and Jantez.

He slowed his horse as he approached the camp. With his night vision, he could see the outline of several figures near the path with weapons drawn. The watchers were performing their duty even as they traveled. He heard one of them call out, "Its Lord Shi'roc." It was the voice of Ilo that called out. The new young warrior had fought well during the attack on the mountain. Shi'roc thought of the boys father who had been mortally wounded during the battle. A'mora and Lorentz had only been able to keep him alive a while longer as his injuries were too severe to be fully healed. He trotted past the night watch, nodding his head in greeting.

"Where are the others?" Ilo inquired with alarm, as he saw no other riders to the extent of his night vision. Everyone knew that both Gor and Grefden rode after Shi'roc in search of Lady A'mora and Jantez. Ilo had expected them all to ride back together and feared the worst as he saw only his instructor ride back alone.

"They are not far behind." Was Shi'roc's reply. "Keep watch for them." He rode into the center of the encampment and stopped his horse when he saw Lorentz looking after Maac-To. The Elf was lying near the campfire for warmth. Lorentz had been attempting to heal his internal injuries but was too late. His body functions were failing and he was growing weaker. Shi'roc dismounted and handed the reins to an awaiting Dwarven soldier.

Shi'roc approached Lorentz, ignoring the day's events. His thoughts only on Maac-To for the moment. "He is still not recovered and there is little I can do for him." The priest said in a saddened tone. "Only the miracle of Mirana could save him now. It must be her will that allows him to die." The priest looked gravely into Shi'roc's eyes. "He has been asking for you. He knows that its just a matter of time now before he..." Shi'roc looked toward Maac-To near the warmth of the fire. He stepped past Lorentz as he heard softly, "Did you find A'mora?"

Not looking back at his friend, his eyes still fixed on the fire, he replied, "Yes, and Jantez as well." He gave no report as to their condition nor did he let on what he had seen. He walked over to Maac-To and knelt at his side. He took the Elf's hand and the dying man smiled.

"You have returned safe." He whispered. "And the others?" His look of concern for Jantez and A'mora told Shi'roc that he must respond.

"Yes, they are all well." He looked into the Elf's eyes to reassure him he was telling the truth. Though he was incapable of lying or deceit for any reason. Even if he had tried to deceive, it would be so apparent. "You should rest now." We will have a long journey yet before you fight Moracles." Now he was trying to boost the man's spirits, knowing that he would not make it to the canyons. Even if he did, he would be in no condition to fight.

"I fear I will not be with you for the battle." Maac-To said solemnly as he held tight to Shi'roc's hand. "I wish to give you something." He slowly reached into a pocket under his armor within his leather vest. From it, he drew the golden acorn. His shaky hand, held it out to Shi'roc as it reflected the firelight. "You must take this and guard it."

"I cannot accept such a gift from you." Shi'roc responded as he held the glowing acorn in his hand. "It is much to valuable." The warrior could tell that it was solid gold, having some experience in the past with rare items. Through the years he learned appreciation for fine craftsmanship of many sorts. He carefully looked it over. Its carvings were entirely accurate and other than its great weight and color, one would think that it was a real acorn. "You should keep this for your son, Ilo."

"It is not just a gift." Maac-To explained. "It is a debt that I owe for saving my life." Shi'roc looked puzzled. "I was to return this at the right time. Jantez will know what to do." The Elf faded into a deep sleep.

Shi'roc slipped his hand away, laying Maac-To's by his side. Then he lifted the blanket around his shoulders and effectively tucked his friend in for the night, hoping he would see another day. He was grateful that the man felt no pain in his dying condition, thanks to Lorentz for that. He pondered what Maac-To had said, that Jantez knew about the acorn. What did it mean? Where did it come from?

Shi'roc's thoughts were interrupted when he heard the call of the watchers announcing more riders. They had identified Grefden, Gor and A'mora with Jantez. He grasped the acorn firmly in a fist and thrust it into a pouch he kept under his arm pit. A safe place for hiding valuables. He had learned this trick from his earlier years when his traveling companions included less reputable acquirers. The armpit was never accessible to pickpockets in a crowd no matter what the conditions, and when sleeping as well. His thoughts turned again to food.

He could indeed smell cooking though he was uncertain of its origin. He stood up and looked around for the fires that had pots and kettles suspended over them. He walked past his guard as they were dismounting, paying them little attention as he proceeded toward the nearest food. Lorentz hugged A'mora upon her return, again gaining no attention from Shi'roc. He mearley spoke at Lorentz as he passed that Maac-To was sleeping.

Hot food was being passed out at several of the camps. Mostly it consisted of stews with meat and vegetables. Fruit had been thawed as well for the meal. All in all a very healthy dinner. He could tell that the meat had been Lorentz' doing, knowing that they had but scraps when they left the mountain. He asked one of the women where the meat had come from. She replied that Lorentz and his men had stolen it along with the horses, from the enemy at the mountain. He had indeed enhanced the amount as well as the portions of the frozen foods that they had brought. Shi'roc just nodded and thanked the woman for the bowl of stew and apples.

He looked around at the other soldiers who were also being fed. Again it came to mind that the armor and weapons they all wore, he had never seen before. He realized that Maac-To even was wearing the same breast plate as that which he was when they first met. It had mysteriously disappeared the next day. Now thinking back as to where these items might have come from. Did we get them from the first band of Orc's that attacked the mountain? No. They were wearing heavy leather with armored plates. Several of the Human soldiers were still wearing those. Fortunately they had been cleaned from the smell and blood when the beasts bodies were stripped.

His thoughts were again interrupted when Grefden and Gor sat down to eat beside him, quite uninvited. They felt it was time to break this useless silence and get back to the business at hand. There was much to discuss about the battle past and ahead. They needed to compare notes with regard to their attackers. What were they? Were they the same at both mountain villages?

"M'Lord." Grefden was the first to speak. "We have heard that your group fought Bugbears and Hobgoblins along with Moracles' Magdarn soldiers in the first town. Did you know which was in charge?" This was an important question since the species of the leader would indicate the style and strategy of the entire army. It was rare that so many uncommon species could be banded together to create an effective fighting force.

"They appeared to be led by an Orc and Magdarn." Shi'roc spoke straight ahead while staring into the campfire. He still did not feel like conversation. "I killed them both." He spoke without thinking. His statement was not true. His mind was still in turmoil and his thoughts were not yet clear. His anger was clouding his reality. The others could tell that Shi'roc was different somehow. He seemed to be wandering into a different reality. He continued to stare into the fire.

The flames seemed to form an image before him. The face of a man that he did not recognize. It was human, rugged and handsome, with a finely trimmed beard. The vision spoke to him. "That was your first step. Take another, and another. Let your hatred grow. Let go with your emotions." Shi'roc continued to stare into the fire as his companions watched the apparent trance he was in.

He did not move yet the face of the vision faded away and was replaced by another more familiar face. It was that of the Goddess, Alena who had come to him months before and assured him of his importance in this quest to destroy Moracles. He remembered her beauty as he finally had looked her in the eye. He had at first thought her to be a temptress, demon of some kind until she had convinced him otherwise.

The vision spoke from the flames. "Shi'roc, do not listen to Hartes." She said. "Your honesty is your strength. Do not hold on to anger as it will destroy you. It is your pureness as a warrior that Hartes wants to corrupt. Don't let him win. Tell the truth no matter what it is." The face of beauty and truth faded as well and Shi'roc broke from the trance.

"It was not exactly as I had said." He began to correct himself. Shaking his head of the visions and his angers. "I had fought both the Orc and Magdarn leaders but the killing blows came from Jantez. He had surprised the Magdarn with his magical powers and caught him off guard. The Orc went into the town and I did not see him die." He thought more about the last day's events and remembered that he had seen the same Orc looking for the remainder of his army just before he found A'mora and Jantez.

"Yes, the Orc still lives." Shi'roc finally looked at both Grefden and Gor. It was the first time today that he faced them. He had released his anger and his memory returned with his honesty, just as Alena said it would. "I saw him again this morning near the base of the mountain when I returned to search for A'mora and Jantez." The day's events came flooding back to him in a revelation. "I heard him talking to one of the Bugbears about finding the others who were missing." He felt a great burden pass from him as he talked more casually to his men. "They were on horse back and continued around the back of the mountain."

"It would appear that we were successful in our escape." Grefden surmised. The fact that he did not follow in this direction means that he did not see your trail." Those listening to Shi'roc's story let out a sigh of relief.

"We may also have trapped and killed more of them than we first hoped in the caves." Gor added with a smile. They began to think that this raid on Moracles castle may not be so tough as they first thought. With the majority of his armies destroyed or trapped, it might be as simple as walking into the valley and letting the two Orc companions lead them through the door of the castle.

* * *

The journey would end this night in the ethereal plane for Moracles and his new apprentice. The misty path had heightened the Elf's senses and his magical abilities. During the weeks of passage, Moracles had tutored him in both magical and spiritual spells. The training he had received at the palace of Lolith had been enhanced significantly during the travel. Ach'med was eager to try some of the more intricate spells that his master had taught. It was not possible for him to practice during the timeless trip in the mystical area. Most of what he learned was in the ways of offensive spells and of deception.

Moracles had told Ach'med stories of glorious battles with armies at his side. All were fabrications of course to entice his loyalty, as Moracles would never allow himself to be is such a predicament. He encouraged the Elf to recount stories of his own regarding his past, his family, his half brother. The old man was able to gain knowledge of the legendary warrior to be used against him in battle. He had known of Shi'rock and his friends to be the ones who had slain his master Lord Magedlan. He knew that stories were told around the region of the great warrior Shi'roc having led armies himself against evil wizards, hoards of Orcs, etc. He needed to find a way to turn Ach'med against his half brother without allowing the apprentice to realize the length of time that he had been deceaced.

"Before we left the castle on this journey, I received word that your old friends had acquired the services of a half breed Elf warrior who seems to match the description of your older brother. It seems that he was to take your place in their adventures." The old man was beginning to spin a dangerous web of lies that would turn Ach'med. "Since you have eliminated your oppressors, it appears that your brother is seeking you out in revenge. As you have already noted to me he is a quite determined person." The mage allowed his student to ponder the repercussions of slaying some of his former associates. "My sources tell me that he and the others are attempting to track us down even now, so you must be cautious when outside of my valley." Ach'med would have no way of knowing that Shi'roc had been in the valley even before Ach'med has been raised from dust.

The journey had been otherwise uneventful. Moracles felt this to be a fortunate occurrence, since he did not wish to tangle with any spirits or other beings that were not otherwise under his control or command. But now they were within the boundaries of the valley, he felt confident that they would not be disturbed. "Would you like to see the valley over which I rule? It is night, however the moons may cast enough light for a glimpse." Moracles enticed the young, impressionable Elf. With a spell of vision, he could open a window as he did before, from the ethereal plane to the real world below.

"Yes, I would be interested in seeing your realm." The dark Elf exclaimed. He had no concept of where they actually were since time and space had no meaning. Such travel and vision was far in the future of his magical powers.

Just as the great mage was about to begin the chant, his concentration was interrupted by the telepathic message of his obedient servant, Quibit, who had been eluding the Bone after he had been banished. Though the creature had feared for his existence, he had obeyed Moracles and covertly kept an eye on the Bone and his dealings. Moracles had instructed him to watch and assist the Bone while the mage was away. The Bone neither wanted his help, nor did he want him around. The tiny creature had been anxiously awaiting the return of his master and had frequently popped in to the mist to attempt contact. This time he was successful. His master was within his telepathic range and the excitement of the creature was apparent as Moracles felt his mental emission.

Ach'med noticed the concerned expression on his master's face. It was obvious that his concentration had been broken from the spell preparation. "What is the matter, my master?" He inquired. No response was received as Moracles attention remained on the thought transmission of his obedient pet.

Moracles had mentally communicated back to his fearful pet, Quibit, to join them. "We will soon be joined by one of my servants." He said as he recovered from the concentration. He was quite disturbed at what Quibit had told him of the Bone. The psychic transmission was weak due to the distance even in the mists of the ethereal passage. The mage then returned to his chant for creating the window in space to view the lands below.

Ach'med listened carefully to the intonation and watched as his master skillfully moved his arms to evoke the energy of the spell. A moment later, like peering through the clouds, the window opened to the real world. Though physical distance was only imagined, Ach'med felt dizzy at the idea of being hundreds of yards above the snow covered earth. It took him by surprise and he grabbed at the robes of his master to keep from falling through. He saw behind them the great mountain peaks of which his master had spoken. Below he could see several points of flickering light. He believed them to be campfires.

"Do not be alarmed." Moracles slowly pried the Elf's fingers from his death grip on the robes. "You can not fall. It only appears that we are so high." They looked together in wonder as the moon indeed shown its crescent shape upon the white blanketed land. "You see below are a part of the armies of which you will lead." The wizard pointed to the scattered points of light, confirming his young apprentice's suspicions.

"Can we go down... I mean go to see them now?" The anxious Elf inquired. He was eager to meet those who would follow him into glorious battle. He had no idea that Moracles army consisted of outcast hordes of various species.

"It would be unwise to suddenly appear to the soldiers." The old man explained thoughtfully. "They are intimidated by my direct presence." He grossly understated, knowing that his armies would tremble and grovel even at the sight of their lord, Moracles. "No, we will wait for the proper time. They appear to be returning from their search for the intruders. Perhaps they will entertain us with stories of their journeys." He looked beyond the fires toward the canyon. "I expect a report of their findings when they return to the castle. Then you will meet the leaders of the various groups and lead them to slaughter those who dare attempt to invade my lands." He remembered that he told the Bone to only find the intruders. From what little Quibit was able to convey, the demon may have overstepped his bounds of authority.

The campfires were no longer visible as they passed beneath them and the window began to fog as the spell ran it's course and ended their evening's entertainment.

Suddenly, a high pitched squeal followed by several cackling noises broke the silence of the mist. Ach'med reflexively drew his sword for battle and peered ahead in the darkness. The mage had provided him with the weapon since he felt the need to carry it.

"Not to worry young one." The mage soothed. "That was the call of my pet Quibit." And instantaneously, the gruesome little creature materialized on Moracles' shoulder. The excited little beast scurried around like a monkey stalked by a predator. "Calm yourself little one. It is good to see you too." The master soothed. "Everything will be all right here. I have brought help to rid us of the dangers. His name is Ach'med." He motioned to the figure still clinging on to his master's robes.

Quibit leaned over the human's back to get a better look at the dark Elf. He flashed the lids of his big black eyes, never having seen a dark skinned Elf before. All of those brought to the castle for torture or slavery in the past were a pale white skinned type. This Elf had midnight skin with wild white hair. Since his master trusted him, Quibit must too, and his instincts told him that this one was far more controllable than the Bone. He looked nervously at the sword in the man's hand then the creature squeaked a greeting to Ach'med.

Ach'med had not thought of the sword still being drawn but quickly put it away. The Elf spoke greetings as well after seeing that the creature looked rather tame although he did have fangs and razor sharp claws. "Hello, Quibit." He nodded up to the beast but did not make any motions to pet it. He felt it might be an intrusion on the relationship it had with Moracles, and he was right. Ach'med was satisfied that the creature would not harm him and seemed totally loyal to Moracles. The ugly little thing, satisfied with the greeting, crawled down to perch himself on his master's arm.

"Now tell me little one what troubles you so." He stroked the short fur on the creatures mane as he cooed.

They once again went into a concentrated telepathic communication as Quibit explained the events after the mage had left. Ach'med stood quietly by and watched the magical encounter between his master and servant, spy.

He told of the gathering of armies by the Bone at which time he had been banished from the castle. He had watched the various divisions of species go off in different directions in search of the intruders. Moracles became visibly enraged as the little one explained that the army of Orcs had all but been destroyed by the intruders and that the newcomers had joined other survivors in the mountains. The Bone had called them Dwarves. Quibit was unfamiliar with this word. Although a few Dwarves had been captured long ago, they were not called as such.

The mage was even more outraged when Quibit told him that the Bone had re-gathered the armies and sent them to destroy the survivors and intruders. They were to mount a major attack on the mountain and annihilate any living creatures therein. This was directly contrary to what he had instructed the Bone to do. He was not to confront them, only find them. Moracles wanted the pleasure of ruthlessly torturing those who slaughtered his dragon. Especially the one called, Shi'roc. That is why he enlisted the help of his half brother, Ach'med.

Quibit hesitated to continue, feeling his master's anger, not towards him but in general. He coward slightly as he finished the story of how the Wraiths had been spying on the armies and reported their failure to the Bone. The mountain tunnels were apparently sealed with the enemy inside. At least that part was partially pleasing to his master. Yes, Moracles would have the opportunity still to slaughter them himself.

Moracles recovered from his concentration and calmed himself with a few deep breaths before speaking. "It would seem that the one I left in charge while on this journey has betrayed me." He sighed. "This was not entirely unexpected. He has managed to have the armies trap the intruders and some Dwarves in the mountains over which we passed." He went on to explain to Ach'med.

"Name this one who betrays you and I will slay him," the Elf boasted loyally. Quibit gave him a puzzled look over the shoulder of the mage. The little creature slowly shook his head in warning.

"His name is Bone, at least that is what he is called," the mage responded, not taking seriously the promise or threat the Elf had made. "Ah, we have arrived," the mage said with relief.

Ach'med felt a solid floor beneath his feet for the first time since they left the old fortress. Still clinging onto his master's robes he asked. "Do we live in total darkness, master?" He looked around for any signs of life or light. He saw Quibit leap from Moracles' arm and run off, beyond his night vision ability. Then he saw a large heat form slowly crawling toward them from the opposite direction. It was long with many legs and a tail. The Elf warned his master as he drew his sword. "Master look."

"No need for alarm." He said to his apprentice. Then in a louder more masterful tone he announced. "It is I Moracles, I have returned." Then back to the Elf, "Just remember never to look that creature in the eye, for you would surely be turned to stone." Moracles was referring to one of his Torgs, a creature of six legs that was one of the guardians of his secret chambers. Its long scaly body was slow to move but apparently had abilities to compensate.

Ach'med watched as the creature turned with its slow, powerful, six legs and walked off. Just then the glow of candle light appeared from behind him and he could see the scaly tip of the monsters tail dragging into the darkness. The candles glow approached as Quibit returned holding the ornate candelabra. He had gone off to get the light for his master.

They walked toward the light over the polished marble floor. Although the air was chilled, and the mist hovered over them, Moracles did not seem to notice. Ach'med on the other hand was being watchful and noticed everything. This was an entirely new experience for him. As he walked behind the mage, he was looking around to all sides wondering what would appear next through the dark shadows. Off to the left and above him, something large and round with many tentacles floated past, again headed for the cover of darkness.

"Master, what are these creatures doing here in your home?" he asked as he re-sheathed his sword, now confident that he was safe in the presence of his master.

The mage stopped walking and Ach'med walked around to his side. They were standing on the edge of what appeared to be an office. It was very open and tucked into the corner of what he now knew was a massive room. There were book shelves lining the walls and small pigeon holes on some of the shelves. A small statue of what looked like the mage himself was setting on a shelf, overlooking the grand desk and intricately carved chair. Quibit carefully pushed the glowing candles onto the desk to the limit of his reach, then skillfully hopped up on its edge. He looked even uglier in the light, Ach'med thought.

"The creatures you have seen are my guardians. They live here and protect my belongings when I am away. You will soon come to know them and they you." The wizard explained calmly as he proceeded to his throne behind the desk. "Quibit, prepare quarters on the lower level for Ach'med and have the armorer meet him there in the morning to suitably fit my new apprentice." The mage spoke in common as a courtesy to the Elf. The creature instantly disappeared from the desk. Not by leaping or any conventional method of transportation of which Ach'med saw. He simply squeaked his acknowledgment and vanished.

"It has been an exhausting journey for both of us I am sure. Soon you will be in your chambers. Quibit is quite efficient. He will return soon and take you there." The mage rose from his chair, visibly exhausted. An ethereal journey such as that would take days for him to recover the energy drained from him. "Remain here and wait for Quibit. I must retire for now." The mage dismissed himself and wandered directly away from the office along the left wall into the darkness.

The Drow quickly became nervous not knowing what to do if any of the creatures returned to inspect him. He would no longer be under the obvious protection of his master. He sat on the desk looking around behind him at the dusty books and rolls of paper. He knew better than to touch anything but his curiosity was tempting him. He slid back off of the desk toward the shelves and began to look at them more closely. He also could see that the desk had many drawers with key locks that he knew also not to touch. He thought back briefly to the times when he and his friends would have literally died for the chance to ransack this furniture. Grog and Koloda would be frantically trying to pick the locks while Fendal would be carefully browsing through the books and rolls of… He paused in his thoughts and looked more closely at some of the pigeon holes that contained rolled dried skin. He bent over and reached out wanting to see for sure but he stopped himself. Yes it was dried skin.

He suddenly felt a presence behind him and jumped back while turning. There in the darkness just beyond the candles reach he could see several shadows of varying shapes. There was also the floating ball that seemed to be swooping in and out of the candles light. It seemed to have a mottled rough surface with a mouth and one big eye. Tentacles were definitely meandering from the top of the spherical creature. Ach'med froze in place. As he feared he was alone with only his sword. He concentrated on his teachings rather than draw his sword. It was time for him to prove himself worthy as Moracles' apprentice. Knowing that these creatures were his servants he did not wish to harm, just convince them of his loyalties to the mage.

He chanted a few words in meditation then spoke as Moracles did, in the common language. "Do not fear me," he started. "I am not your enemy. We serve the same master." So far they did not move or make any action against him. They simply watched from the shadows. "I have been called by the great Lord Moracles to lead his armies to victory against the intruding forces." He was unable to detect any response.

Suddenly, Quibit appeared perched on the desk as quietly as he left. He found himself between the Elf and the guardians of the mist. Ach'med was surprised but it did not affect his concentration on the matter at hand. He ended his speech as Quibit handed him a small scroll. The Drow unrolled it and saw some writing in the common language. The creature motioned for him to follow. The hideous creature blew out the candles and headed off toward the center of the chamber. Ach'med quickly followed as the guardians parted way and headed back to their unknown lairs.

Quibit led him back to what seemed to be the center of the room from which they had started. He could not understand the squeaks and clacks of the creature's language, but with his night vision, he could see the beast motioning for him to read what was written on the scroll. In the darkness he could not read it but called upon his quick memory as to what it had said.

"Where there is light, Darkness shall rule forever." he spoke in the common language as it was written. He felt no movement but was suddenly somewhere else. There was a bright light that shown from above casting his shadow on the floor. He found himself no longer on the polished marble floor, but in another room. He looked up at the beam of light that emanated from a high ceiling. The room was bare with four smooth walls and a wooden door. There was no furniture or decoration. Just the cold reality of dungeon walls. “Is this to be my chambers.” He mumbled out loud.

The door opened and Quibit lurked around its edge motioning for the Elf to follow. They walked down corridor after corridor. All were but five feet wide. There were no other doors to pass. Only endless hallway laid out in what appeared to be a maze. The walls of wonder ended at a steep stairwell going down only. They proceeded down the rectangular flights of stairs. Ach’med noted several revolutions in the downward direction. Each corner landing grew closer together until the stairs spilled out into a great dining hall.

The room was somewhat triangular with the stairs ending in the bottom corner. There were three large rectangular tables, each surrounded by twenty or more chairs. Double doors were arranged on the right and left walls that seemed to open inward to the room. At the far wall, two single doors led into what he expected to be storage rooms or a kitchen. He had no time to nose around as Quibit had already opened one of the doors to the right that led into another hallway.

By now, Ach’med was as tired as his master and ready to drop into a bed at any moment. Any bed would do. The Elf continued to follow the little creature past several doors and around a few corners until the hallway ended at a single door. The room was lit with the flickering flame of an oil lantern and the door was open. He looked around the room as he entered. The light showed a comfortable bed, some tables, an upright chest cabinet and a desk with chairs on both sides. From the rooms size and layout, he imagined that it had belonged to one of the officers of the army. Fitting enough for him now that he was Vandar, leader of the armies.

He turned around to thank the tiny beast so that he could get to bed. He was even too tired to check out the furnishings, as he would have done as an adventurer in his past life. No drawer would remain un opened. No wall would slip by a search for secret doors. That was the past. This was his new present and he wanted to get some sleep. Quibit was nowhere to be seen as he looked toward the still open door. He stepped back to check the hall and close the door to his room when a monstrous white skeletal creature appeared at its entrance.

Ach'med looked into his eyes and leaped back, startled at the size and features of this being. Was this it's room that he was in? The skeleton's red eyes gleamed as Ach'med tripped over himself and the table trying to bury himself into a corner. He was trapped as the thing entered the room and closed the door behind him. He could not control his fear. This was unlike him to panic even before a more formidable enemy, if he was an enemy. He looked away from it and realized that a spell of some sort had been used on him. He concentrated his efforts on breaking the fear and kept his vision away from the creatures eyes.

"What have we here?" The Bone said with an irritating screech. "An intruder in my castle perhaps? A thief come to steal my property?" He stood fully upright with his hands fisted on his hips. "You Drow should know your place which is away from me." He said tapping one foot rhythmically. The clicking sounds of his bony frame gave Ach'med something to concentrate on. The distraction helped him to break the spell.

He straightened himself up, still looking beyond the creature, focusing on the door so as not to look into his eyes. "I am no intruder, nor a thief." He said firmly. "I am Ach'med. Apprentice to the Lord Moracles, Servant of the Goddess, Lolith." His pride and confidence was regained as the creature's mouth opened wide and his foot stopped tapping.

The Bone had realized that his enslaver must have returned from his journey and brought this Elf with him. What information could he extract from this Drow? How much did he know about the intruders? "Why are you here? I do not believe that Moracles would travel so far just to obtain an apprentice." He said sarcastically, with a hiss at the end of his last word.

"Moracles has raised me from the dead." The creature did not seem to be impressed. Perhaps it was not so uncommon to be reborn. "I am to be Vandar," he said with even more authority. "And who are you?" he demanded now, knowing that this creature must also be a servant of the great mage.

"What is 'Vandar'?" The Bone said mockingly as he began to walk about the room. "This word means nothing to me. Why did Moracles bring you back here?" He sneered, trying again to instill fear into the young Drow Elf.

Ach'med was becoming angered and his thought was not clear. "Vandar is the ancient Elven word for leader." He emphasized the last word, leader. He emerged slowly from behind the table in the corner of the room. "You have not yet told me who you are." He demanded again.

"Leader? Leader of what?" The white creature continued his tormenting of the Elf. "What would so young a boy do as a leader? Hmmm?" He again tried to look into Ach'med's avoiding eyes, but the Elf turned away. "Perhaps you will lead servants in the kitchen?"

That was the last insult that Ach'med was about to take. He began to chant quietly as his anger grew, directing his voice at the creature. The intensity grew as he began to form the spell in his mind.

The Bone made no moves against him or tried to retreat. He simple stood and watched the Elf's actions and listened to his mumblings as he had seen Moracles so many times before. Magic did not impress the ruler of the fifth level of hell, nor was he intimidated by it.

Ach'med waved his hands at the climax of the enchantment and threw an invisible power at the creature, dispelling the force that allowed the creature to cause fear with his eyes. Ach'med could now look directly up into the red gleaming eyes of this thing and not be tormented by its spell. He stood as straight as he could and faced the creature that was twice his height. "I will lead Moracles' armies," he said with a growl. "I shall ask once more. Who are you?"

"They call me Bone." The giant said as he turned to leave the room. The rattle of his feet against the stone floors echoed for a time and his tail drug, scraping the floor.

In a matter of hours from his arrival, the young Elf had already made a most powerful enemy. He knew that he would again be confronted by the one who he was to replace, the one for whom he swore vengeance against for the betrayal of his master, the one called Bone.

*   *   *

The dawn broke to yet another clear morning as the camps prepared to move out toward their deadly destination. Lorentz looked over a ridge that had not been noticed the night before. It was south, but not far from the camp. The cool breeze from the north blew his cloak against his back. He could see that the rocks overlooked what appeared to be a once lively lake bed. The scene was beautiful in his mind. He could imagine that at one time, there were towns around the lake and boats sailing amidst the waters with fishermen casting their nets. He could see the entire circumference of the lake and studied the contours of the now melting snow. The night had not been as severe as before and the previous day's warming had begun to turn the snow into large pools in the lake. He saw just off to his left what appeared to be caves at the base of the rock faced cliff.

Lorentz felt the touch of a hand on his sleeve. He turned from his vision of the past or future, to A'mora who had been tending to the sick and injured. Many of the elders and the women would not be going into battle with the rest of them. They needed to find a safe place for them to take refuge with the small children until the conflicts were over and the valley would be safe again. He wondered about the caves he had just seen. A possible hiding place for the few to be left behind? He had no doubt that they would be returning soon for them.

"My Lord." She interrupted. "I fear that Maac-To should not be traveling any longer. There are a few of the Dwarves too old to be of help and the infants should not be with us." She looked deeply concerned. Part of her concern was that she had failed in her efforts to completely heal the elder Elf. She felt responsible even though her abilities to heal could not always reach such critical injuries. Her strength had been drained and her efforts were rushed due to the circumstances of the flight from the mountain.

"I may have found a refuge for those we must leave behind," he said as he pointed to the caves below. "I will send someone to investigate the possibility before we leave." He motioned to some of the Dwarven soldiers to come. "We may not find a better hiding place along our path." He said as the three warriors arrived at his side. He spoke to them in their native language of the caves he had spotted and they hurried off along the ridge in search for a safe path down to the lake bed.

Not too far to the eastern curve of the lake the three found a suitable path. One that could be traveled by the elders and women without too much trouble. The path was muddy but there was enough rock to it so as not to slide down. At the base of the lake , near the caves, the Dwarves spotted tracks of what appeared to be a large animal. The prints in the snow indicated that the animal traveled on four feet.

They drew their weapons as they followed the tracks into the largest of the cave entrances. The Dwarves walked quietly into the mouth of the cave. Using their inherent visual abilities, the warriors carefully checked the interior of the cave for other heat forms. The foot prints in the snow of the animal were fresh so it could not be far.

From a ledge just above their heads they heard a fierce growl as the beast leapt onto one of the soldiers. Its razor sharp claws and teeth gouged deeply into the Dwarf. The others quickly attacked the furry creature with sword and spear to drive it off of their companion or kill it.

It reared back from the fallen Dwarf having been punctured by the spear. Now on its hind legs it attacked again as would a bear, swiping its claws. It was able to move as well on only two legs as with four. It also seemed to have a visual sense in the darkness or possibly relied on its keen sense of smell. It continued its attack, lunging first at one Dwarf and then the other.

Realizing that the only way to save their friend was to kill the snow creature, they fought hard to drive it back, stabbing and slashing at it. Little by little, the animal became exhausted by the blood loss and finally collapsed. For good measure, they drove their spear and sword deep into the body of the beast to be sure it would not retaliate.

One of them ran outside to call for Lord Lorentz as the other tended to the wounds of his friend. He was severely injured and unconscious. The brave man was loosing a lot of blood so he did his best to bind the wounds until help arrived. Once Lord Lorentz had been summoned the first Dwarf continued his search of the cave to determine if it was safe for the others to remain. The cave was deep and it appeared that they were not the first to have ventured inside the creatures lair. He had found piles of bones scattered about further back from the entrance. He found no other passages in the rear and no other dangers to those who would be staying.

Moments later, Lorentz was at the side of the brave warrior chanting his healing spells. He quickly sealed the wounds and checked for any severe internal damage. As he meditated over the wounded soldier, the others drug out the body of the bloodied beast. Its thick white fur was stained and matted with a light blue colored blood. They carried it up to the departing camp so that it could be prepared as food for that nights dinner.

They also reported to Shi'roc that the cave was secured for leaving the elderly and the children behind. It was time to move on as the sun crested over the eastern horizon. There was no time to waste. Shi'roc instructed his Orc followers to again lead in the wagons. Everyone was mounted up or already headed in the direction of the canyons. Lord Lorentz' and Lady A'mora's horses were left with one of the Dwarven warriors at the lake ridge.

A'mora helped carry Maac-To into the temporary shelter. It was decided that Ilo's wife, Caellen, would remain with their daughter. The Elf kissed his human wife and baby daughter, Aliah, good bye as they descended with the Dwarven elders into the lake bed. He grasped his fathers hand, not really wanting to leave him behind. Maac-To squeezed back knowing they might not see each other again. His father had brought him up well and he respected him for that. Ilo was brave and ambitious. It was difficult for him to see his father wither away without a chance to survive.

Despite much protesting by Muga, Kura convinced his wife to stay with their son, Tyme, as well. Muga, being trained as a warrior could defend the small group and the infants, if any unfortunate circumstances arose. The three eldest Dwarven council members also would remain to protect the children and the wounded as best they could.

Lorentz and A'mora bid them all farewell as the wounded Dwarf rested, now conscious and healing. He saw to it that there was sufficient fire wood and food left with them all for a week. He felt sure that he would return by then to get them.

* * *

The sun appeared as a full flaming ball as it rose over the horizon. The General could feel its warmth as he pressed his horse to gallop through the muddied snow. He intended to catch up with those troops that he had thought to come this way. He saw signs of several horses and hoped that their riders were either Magdarn, or other soldiers of his attacking army.

He believed that he had lost many of his soldiers at the hands of those ruthless mountain people, that had now fled to the west away from the valley. He thought the Bone would be pleased that the enemy had been driven from the mountains. He was unaware of Moracles' original intentions.

As he rode following the trail in the melting snow, he saw signs of an encampment. This must have been where they rested the previous night. But what was this? Many tracks of wagons. He had accounted for the wagons that he sent on the southern path back to the canyons with his army.

He rode on east finding new tracks of even more people and wagons. What could this be? Could the enemy not have fled west as he had believed? Were they on their way to the canyon to raid the fortress? His fear and anger stirred. He not only wanted to obey his master but also sought revenge against those who slaughtered his people.

As the warmth of the afternoon sun, now to his back, melted away the snows, he could clearly see the muddy path was that of an army, not his own. He saw the long shadow of himself on the horse trotting before him. He dug his heels into the horse pressing faster to catch the enemy. "I kill." He said to himself under his breath. "Kill all."

Chapter 25
Slaughter

The sun had just begun to set behind the mountains as the Orc saw yet signs of another camp. Again the wagon tracks and hoof prints indicated a wide spread of an army. He found ashes where several campfires had burned out. It was evident that these survivors had no intention of covering their path. It would be near impossible with the snow and now the muddy trails left behind. He decided himself to camp here, knowing that the others would be a day ahead of him but he would catch them soon. A breeze blew past him as he dismounted his horse near the ridge of the lakeside. Here too he could see footprints of soldiers along the overlook. This had once been a grand lake he thought.

The General piled some dead wood in a careful spire. Now on his knees, he struck the flint rocks to spark some shreds of dried branches. In a few moments he had the beginnings of a fire. Carefully he placed the burning branch into the wood pile and watched it begin to glow. He had saved some dried foods from his personal supplies. The General had not originally intended to be separated from the army's food wagon so he had to eat sparingly.

The night air was warmer than it had been in past nights. He laid back looking into the night stars wondering what to do when he met up with the enemy armies. He was but one and he saw how his own experienced soldiers had been killed at the hands of but a few of them. Perhaps he should find a way past them and warn the castle. Yes, that would be best since he would not survive any attack he made on his own.

He appreciated the solitude of this journey. It allowed him to think more clearly. It also provided the opportunity for him to do freely what he would hide in the past from the other soldiers. Another urge had come over him, just as before the attacks on his Orc troops at the mountain. His stomach was again too full to hold its excrement and it was time again to rid himself of the pressures.

He sat up and looked around self consciously to be sure he was alone. It would be absurd that any living creatures would be nearby. The wind was blowing slightly from the north over the lake bed. Even he was aware of the putrid odors that would emanate from his body, so he walked over to the rocks near the lake and dropped his lower body armor. The general leaned comfortably back on the rough ridge and relieved himself with a deep breath and a sigh.

The night silence was disturbed by a faint noise. It seemed to echo from all around him. It sounded first like a small animal howling in the lake bed. Another breeze brought the distinct echo of an infant crying. He peered into the darkness of the open lake bed in front of him as he completed re-strapping his armor. There was a faint glow of a fire coming from a cave at the base of the ridge just below him off to his left. The Orc stared at the area and could see the reflected flickering of a fire within a cave. The sounds were coming from there.

He began to walk along the ridge toward the direction of the cave. What or who was in there? He wondered. The warrior stepped back to his camp to retrieve his sword and shield. Walking along the ridge, he found a path. It lead down into the lake bed. His night vision was not too clear but the bulky Orc managed to maneuver his way down the muddy slope trying not to create too much noise.

With his sword drawn, the general crept closer to the now clear reflected fire light. He peered around the corner of the cave to see a handful of beings. As his eyes focused beyond the light, he could see that there were Dwarves, an Elf and a Human woman carrying a baby. That was the sound he had heard. A Human child. He was not interested in the woman or the baby. These were some of the people who slaughtered my men, he thought. He was enraged. I will have my revenge. He thought to himself as he charged in.

On his first step into the cave, the Orc let out a war cry. Before he could take another step, his armor was pierced by the bolt of a crossbow. He had not seen the female Dwarf hiding in wait on a ledge above the cave entrance where the snow beast had been the day before. His body jerked back but his rage kept him strong. Not even stopping to pull out the shaft, he swung his sword wildly at the three Dwarf soldiers. They defended as best they could with shields and spears. The female Dwarf ducked down behind the rock where she had been hiding and managed to re-cock her bow while the Human woman just grabbed a second child and screamed, running for the rear of the cave. The Elf just lay on the ground near another of the Dwarves. They were obviously injured or ill. The cave echoed with the sounds of clanging steel as his sword met shields and armor plating. The screams of the woman and children played second to the sounds of battle.

The injured Dwarf attempted to get to his feet. He was not about to die without a fight. The cave creature had caught him off guard that morning, but this enemy he could fight toe to toe. He was still weak from the blood loss from the claws of the snow beast, but Lorentz' healing was thorough and he felt less pain. The issue here was to save the children at all costs. That he was willing to die for.

The elders had held their position between the Orc and the injured and children. They had not experienced the training of Lord Shi'roc, but now wish that they had. Muga climbed onto a rock for a clear aim at the enemy soldier. She fired the second shot from her crossbow into the Orc's chest while the Dwarves stabbed repeatedly with their spears. The fierce warrior flinched and hesitated at the jolt from the arrow. One of the little people thrust a spear into the opponent's leather armor releasing a gush of thick dark blood. His courage was repaid by the Orc that slashed the old Dwarf across the chest with his sword. His short body slumped to the ground with a mighty groan. Even the Dwarven crafted armor was no match for a direct hit from this powerful Orc. Red blood spewed from the gapping wound as the life expired from his body. His last breath carried the name Mirana as he passed on, hopefully into a better world. It seemed the teachings of Lady A'mora and Lord Lorentz had been of some inspiration to even the Dwarves.

Maac-To was too weak to do more than watch the battle from the ground. Still lying on the wrapped blankets, he reached for the spear of the fallen Dwarf, but it was just beyond his grasp.

Beaten and bloodied, the two elders fought the Orc desperately with their last ounce of strength. They had repeatedly taken minor blows from the creatures sword. None more than bruises under the armor plate. The stubborn creature would not die despite its wounds and the two arrows sticking from its chest. With one mighty blow, the Orc felled the two small men, hacking at them again on the ground to finish them off. As it looked up he faced the female Dwarf still standing on the rock ready to release another bolt. As she pulled the trigger, he blocked the bolt with his shield. At point blank range, the arrow had pierced the shield, impaling it onto the creatures arm. He yelled with rage as the bloody tip of the bolt protruded through his forearm.

Caellen still held the two children wrapped in her arms. She felt trapped at the rear of the cave but did not know what to do. Muga yelled to her to run while they tried to hold off the creature. Caellen had learned to understand the Dwarvish language having been born in the mountains herself. She clung to the walls as she tried to creep past the ongoing battle.

The injured Dwarf jabbed frantically with his spear, knowing that his reach would be useless with a sword.

There was no choice but to attack with himself being the only standing warrior beside Muga. He wanted to distract the bloody enemy long enough for the Human woman to get by safely with the babies. He could tell that the Orc was severely wounded by the slowness of its actions and its wild swings with its sword and shield. With a wide swing of its shield arm, impaled with the arrow, it knocked Muga from the boulder on which she was standing. She had lost her balance while trying to reload her crossbow and fell backward striking her head on the cave floor and rendering her unconscious.

The Dwarf took the opportunity at the Orc's unprotected stout body and drove the spear into the creature, gouging another hole into its torso. In retaliation it turned and thrust its sword at the little man. The warrior managed to deflect the sword thrust with the shaft of the spear. The deflection unintentionally aimed the sword at Caellen who had been attempting to squeeze behind the Dwarf in combat. It cut deep into her unprotected body, but did not harm the infants. She eased herself from the swords blade and collapsed onto the ground slowly allowing the children to softly slide from her arms onto the cave floor.

The General was horrified. He had not intended to harm the Human woman or the children. He was a warrior, not a butcher. He gasped in shock as did the Dwarf, causing a moment of silence and inaction. Now both were even more enraged at the loss of an innocent's life.

During the scuffle, the spear that Maac-To had been reaching for had been knocked closer to him and within grasp. He pulled the shaft of the spear closer and tried to use it to prop himself up. He wanted so badly to finish the Orc, that he now recognized from the battle on the mountain. He was indeed one of the leaders of the assault on the first town. He remembered how Shi'roc battled both he and the Magdarn leader at the start of the battle.

The Orc slashed at the Dwarf having recovered first from the unfortunate incident. The warrior did not react quick enough and his red Dwarven blood was spilled from his chest wound. The sword had penetrated the chain mail vestment that had been forged in the Dwarven Peaks long ago.

Maac-To had propped himself up enough to raise the spear. He would die in battle, not from lingering wounds. With a mighty yell, he made a short lunge at the Orc leader who had also lunged with his sword. The two fell at each other, both penetrated by the others weapon. Both satisfied that their revenge had been fulfilled.

The two children laid crying on the cave floor huddled in their blankets. No one in this world could hear their frightened tiny voices. No one was there to care for them. Their protectors had given themselves so the children would be safe. Now they were more exposed than ever to whatever might wander into the cave. Any creature would be a predator.

* * *

Ach'med stood proudly beside his master's grand office desk. His polished black chain mail glimmered in the flickering candle light. The armorer had done well to fit him with such precision in such a short time.

It was but early this morning that the Elf was awakened by the knock at the door of his new chambers. He awoke, felt his way in the dark through his new surroundings and opened the door. He was sourly greeted by a grubby looking Dwarf carrying a lantern and small tool box. Ach'med remembered that he was to be met by the Armorer this morning and surmised this must be him. After last nights encounter with the Bone, he had no trust in anyone of Moracles' servants thus far except for Quibit. It did not help matters that this armorer was a Dwarf. His past relationships with Dwarves had not been so good. Never the less, It was Moracles' wish for him to be fitted with proper protection and he would not turn down the opportunity.

The Dwarf entered and set his lantern on the desk with the box. He opened the box and withdrew a measuring rope, a quill, rolled parchment and an ink bottle. Without a word he wrapped the rope around various parts of the Elf's' body, each time writing down the measured results. Then the Dwarf took a few paces back and spoke. It was clear that the old man did not speak Elvish or even common. He gestured to Ach'med what seemed to be a question about what type of weapon was preferred. He motioned a sword, bow, spear, and hammer.

Now, he watched his master out in front of the desk toward the open area of the misty room. He listened to learn all he could from his master's chanting and motions. Many of these incantation components, sounds and gestures were as yet beyond his grasp but he tried just the same. He was unaware just what Moracles was conjuring. Quibit sat up on the desk, watchful as well.

The mist swirled in front of the mage and an enormous black stallion with fiery hooves and mane appeared. Upon its back was the Bone, that the Elf alienated the night before. Quibit leaped behind the desk in terror at the sight of the Bone and his deadly mount. The tiny creature peered around the corner of the desk to continue his observation.

Ach'med stepped quickly to his master's side and drew his new short sword with a twirl in his wrist. He had never before possessed such a finely balanced weapon and it felt natural in his hand. His action to defend his master drew a vile reaction from the white demon and a smile from Moracles. From the top of his mount the Bone leaned over the stallion's head and hissed at the small Elf. His gritted teeth made a horrid display as the dark Elf stood ready to fight.

"I see the two of you have met." The mage said evenly as he began to step back toward his desk. He showed no concern at the incident, but was amused and was ready to get to business with the Bone's report on the dealings with the intruders. He side stepped around the frightened Quibit, still hiding in fear, and sat down in his exquisite throne chair. "No need to fear little one." The old man soothed. "No one here will harm you."

The Bone stepped off of his horse, the black stallion from hell. He spoke the word 'Blackfire' and the horse transformed immediately into a small statue. The creature bent down, picked it up and placed it into the small pouch that hung from his belt. The horse had the power to travel in the ethereal mists that was the only known way for the Bone to enter his master's chambers when summoned. Although the horse was servant to the Bone, it too had its limitations and could only use its powers for such travels for a limited time each day. As he turned to face the Elf, he once again bent over and sneered at him trying again to instill terror as he had done the night before.

The Drow carefully stepped backward to his master's side, still with sword in hand, never taking his eyes from the giant Bone. He would not fall for the same trick twice and avoided looking into the Bone's red eyes. He had paid close attention to his actions and was fascinated by the command that the Bone had used for the horse. He had no way of knowing the devil horse's power but was willing to find out. 'Blackfire' seemed an appropriate name since its coat was shiny black with a fiery mane and hooves.

Once the Elf was safely beside his master, he put his sword back into its sheath. The Bone stood before them all as Quibit jumped back up onto the desk. Again the Bone hissed at the sight of the creature that he had thought banished months ago. The tiny creature flinched and jumped back into Moracles' arms like a frightened monkey. There was much resemblance between Quibit and a circus monkey, in mannerisms and reactions, though this creature was noticeably uglier.

"So, tell me of your progress in the search for the intruders." Moracles said calmly, expecting full well to hear nothing but lies and deceit from his soon to be former leader of soldiers. He stroked the furry mane of his tiny companion that was content to be in safety of his master's arms.

"The intruders that you spoke of have joined forces with renegade Dwarves who dwell in the far mountain range. The mountaineers attacked and slaughtered my…" he paused to correct himself, "your army of Orcs. Only the general and an aid remained alive to report back to me." The Bone spoke carefully and slowly. There was no sarcasm in his voice and he spoke the truth so far as he knew it.

Moracles detected the truth and was surprised at this. He prodded the Bone further, awaiting the opportunity for him to falter. He looked directly up at his servant. "What actions have been taken to secure the western lands from these renegade Dwarves?" The mere question made the Bone nervous since his instructions were only to find the intruders. "I have seen no soldiers in the castle since my arrival. Where might they be?" He knew full well that they were returning along the north passage as they had seen the night before. What explanation would the Bone have for this.

Moracles must have learned that the army had been committed to the quest. "My lord," He hesitated, choosing his next words carefully. "Your armies were sent to confront the enemy in the mountains and were successful in trapping them all inside the underground caverns." He progressed along a logical path with his truthfulness in tact, knowing that any deviation would be detected. "Even now the remaining forces return along the southern path, as they were sent. The Wraiths have informed me personally that there were many casualties but the warriors were successful in holding the enemy for your return to do with them as you will."

"Very well." The mage replied calmly to the Bone's report. He had not detected any lies in his speech, yet there was one puzzling inconsistency. "You are incorrect about the armies traveling along the south pass," the evil one corrected. "We had seen them camping on the northern route as we returned last night. Ach'med had wished to see the valley as it shown in the moonlight and we briefly passed over the many campfires near the lake bed." He looked up to the Bone for any reaction.

"The Wraiths assured me that the soldiers had returned south due to the impassable snows of the northern route." He smiled ironically "Perhaps they were mistaken." He bowed his head to Moracles as he turned to leave.

"Have My army assemble in the cave so that I may congratulate them on the success of their mission." Moracles added to the shadows. He saw the Bone hesitate for a moment in his stride.

The demon feared that Moracles would realize just how many warriors were lost in the battle if they were all gathered together. Even he was uncertain of how many were dead or missing. "As you wish my Lord." He replied over his shoulder. He could not keep his failure a secret for much longer. As yet, his deceit had not been detected, at least not outright. He knew that the assembly would be for the purpose of turning the armies, or what was left of them, over to the Drow. He felt anger yet he was also relieved that Moracles had not disintegrated him instantly for misusing the power he was given over the armies. He was obviously saved by the fact that the enemy was safely imprisoned in the mountains. The mage found some amusement in that.

Quibit, now feeling safer, jumped onto the desk from his master's lap. He turned and looked at the old man and then at the young dark Elf standing beside him. He squeaked a low sound to his master so that the Bone would not hear, not that he could understand the message anyway.

"Not to fear little one." The mage whispered. "Our friend here will replace him soon enough." He nodded his head from Ach'med to the Bone who was in the distance preparing his exit. The three of them watched, as in the shadows, the fiery creature reappeared. The Bone climbed on the beast's back and muttered some instruction to the horse. Suddenly, the two had vanished and the three were alone in the candle light. "He will torment you no more." He told Quibit. "It is time for your studies," the mage said over his shoulder to the Drow. "You must learn to react with your mind and not with your sword. Personal combat must be your last recourse, not your first."

"Yes, my master." Ach'med replied, consciously removing his hand from the pummel of the sword at his side. It had been natural for him to draw a weapon, a sword, at the first sign of conflict. This was due to his initial training as a warrior in his past life. The schooling he received from the Lord Ranger Goth was still fresh in his mind. He would now learn to control that habit and use his mind first and foremost to defeat his opponents.

"Soon you will meet your armies. You must reach out to them with your mind and let them know that you truly are their leader." The old man said as he unlocked and opened the desk drawer and withdrew the volumous book of spells. This was the compilation of all the magic known to Moracles. It was over a hundred years in the making. From this he would instruct the Drow to be the most formidable member of his domain of evil.

* * *

"Tell me, Lorentz. Where did all of these fine weapons and armor appear from?" Shi'roc inquired as the two walked the perimeter of the camp. They had had little time to converse privately over the past few days. It was taxing on both them and their people to be encouraging to the survivors and keep the caravan moving at a rapid pace through the treacherous mud and snows. The carts and wagons required continuous looking after and repairs. Even the Dwarves had difficulty keeping the rugged terrain from destroying their vehicles.

Tonight, they were checking on each of the watchers as this night brought them dangerously close to the valley canyons. They were there to reassure their new troops as Lorentz had sensed growing hesitation and fear from their camp. Some wondered if after all of the past few days events, that it was all plausible to defeat Moracles or whomever, to regain control and peace in the valley.

"These were a final gift to us from Kyman, the Dwarven chief, just before he died." He reached under his cloak and withdrew two beautifully engraved daggers. Their handles both embedded with jewels. "These are for you." The wizard held them out for his friend's inspection.

Shi'roc halted his step and faced Lorentz. It was too dark to see the weapons clearly, but even in the slivers of moonlight reflected off of the blade, he could tell that these were the finest of craftsmanship. He took one of the daggers and ran a finger down the flat of the blade, feeling the engraving. He held its handle and checked the most precise balance. These would be fine replacements for the daggers that he had given to the survivors.

He had given up many of his extraneous weapons to supplement the few good arms that they had during training. He had also parted with a well crafted battle ax. It was an item he had acquired from the mountain giants of Thormadore, the place where he had first met Lorentz. The weapon was but a small hand tool to the giants, yet a heavy two handed weapon for Shi'roc.

After checking both daggers, he placed them into two of the empty sheaths on his shoulder belt. They fit well and he felt some relief at having two additional combat weapons to rely on. Although he was formidable with a one or two handed sword, he often relied on his daggers during close combat.

"Thank you." Shi'roc smiled at Lorentz. It had been a while since he had actually smiled. "These are indeed fine daggers. But you haven't told me where these and all of the other weapons actually came from."

"Do you remember the armor and sword that Maac-To had been wearing when we first met? They were part of a hidden treasure that only he and Kyman had knowledge of." Lorentz related as they headed quietly back for the campfire. "These items were what had been created long ago by the Dwarven master craftsmen and had been ready for sale or trade in the valley towns. Once Kyman and the others had heard of the destruction of the towns by Moracles' armies, he hid them away in a secret cave for fear that these weapons would fall into the hands of evil if they had been over run." Lorentz continued the tale as Maac-To had told it.

"I have learned that Kura's father was one of the master armorers and the Dwarven trader who would travel into the towns with their creations and return with necessary supplies that he had traded for. Just before word of the valley's destruction came from the towns refugee's, the trader had been seen traveling through the towns. That is how young Kura learned of his fathers death. He never returned from that trip, and soon after, more and more of the towns people had escaped to the mountains and were taken in by the Dwarves.

The night air was cool but not as severe as previous nights. The two Elves grew nearer to the camp fires as Shi'roc listened. All he could think of was leaving Maac-To behind, dying a slow death by the hands of his enemy.

Shi'roc scowled having known all along that the Dwarves had been hiding something from them. "Why? Why would they keep these from us knowing how important the weapons and armor were to defend themselves?" The warrior shook his head. "I don't understand how Maac-To could betray us like that!" He thought of the Elf that they had left behind to die in peace, knowing that he wanted so much to fight for his freedom and that of his people.

"Do not blame Maac-To for this deceit." Lorentz scolded. "He was sworn to secrecy as a young boy who had mistakenly watched Kyman and the other craftsmen hiding these treasures. The other Dwarves had since died of age or illness and only the chief and our friend Maac-To retained the knowledge of the hidden passage." Lorentz looked at the puzzled expression on Shi'roc's face as they reached the camp. "Maac-To wanted to tell us of these needed items when we began to train the survivors, but Kyman forbid him, still not trusting in our intentions or abilities." Lorentz paused in thought for a moment. "He suffered long and hard by keeping this a secret from us. He kept his word of honor as an Elf as misplaced as it may have been."

"He seems to be good at keeping secrets." He reached into his under arm pocket and withdrew the shinny golden acorn. It shimmered in the fire light as they sat near the warmth of the flames. "This too is a mystery that he gave to me to solve." He said showing the item to his friend.

Lorentz suddenly remembered some of what he wrote on the scroll during the trance that Mirana caused him to have. The golden acorn, a golden oak leaf, and the spell of restoration that he himself wrote during the trance. The puzzle was complete. Would it be A'mora's destiny to fulfill this prophecy? Was she the one, pure of body and soul? The scroll described her features perfectly as a young, blond female. She would be the emissary of Mirana sent to restore the Elven Forest, yet she did not know of it.

"Yes, Maac-To told me to seek out the answer to this mystery from Jantez. Apparently he knows of a tale from where this originated and what is to be done with it." The Elf put the acorn back into the same pocket for safe keeping until the riddle unfolded.

Lorentz was about to speak, then realized at the mention of Jantez, that A'mora was no longer a candidate to restore the wastelands to the original Elven forest. He must meditate on this subject now that he knew of all three components, Scroll, Acorn and Oak Leaf. Was there another to be destined or has A'mora somehow broken the path of time by sharing her love with Jantez? What should or shouldn't he do? There were many paths that may be taken in life. To decide to do or not do a thing could change the course of future events. Lorentz understood this well but did not speak of it to others. As priest and mage, he knew of the relation between action and time. This was how the Gods remained timeless and ageless.

Lorentz walked off to the south to meditate. He was somehow subtly pulled in this direction, not knowing that he gazed out over Feradune, the once great Elven Forest. He prayed for guidance from Mirana. Perhaps she would provide some sign as to what actions should be taken. She was forbidden as a Goddess to interfere directly with the passage of time, yet she could provide wisdom and inspiration.

The priest stood in the breeze and removed all thoughts from his head. He closed his eyes and opened his mind to all existence, all eternity, to reach out for an answer. A deep voice whispered in his mind, "It is not yet time." He was startled by the unfamiliar voice, expecting the sweet whispers of Mirana. He opened his eyes and saw a faint shadow in the distance. The outline was that of a mighty oak tree, similar to that which was engraved on his clerical medallion. He reached into his robes and pulled out the bronze piece dangling from its chain around his neck. The medallion acted as his holy symbol of Mirana. He ran his fingers over the engraved great oak tree on the medallion that matched his vision. Now he understood.

* * *

Moracles watched from his throne chair behind the desk as his pupil recited the words. He had been studying that spell for hours from the pages of his master's book. Moracles had allowed Ach'med to select at random any incantation he wished, no matter what difficulty. Despite his warnings of the dangers of this spell to the caster, he admired the young Elf for his tenacity and courage. The old wizard knew full well that the spell chosen was quite beyond the Elf's abilities yet he kept his promise to instruct him in all of its aspects. Such determination was impressive to the old mage. What he did not realize was that Ach'med had always been self motivated in whatever he appointed himself to. He had become quite an accomplished warrior at his previous young age. By now he would have been a Lord or King if he had lived.

Ach'med still had not realized the passage of real time that he had been dead. As far as he knew, what Moracles had told him was the truth. He had been resurrected only days after his encounter with the ape creatures. He had no way of judging time from what he had seen since his rebirth. Moracles had carefully controlled the circumstances of his apprentices perceptions. The wizard's creation of the perfect apprentice was about to unfold.

Though the mage was still weakened from the long journey, together they had pronounced the words one by one, being very careful to get them exactly correct. Moracles had made it abundantly clear that the slightest mispronunciation could mean disaster or at least failure of the attempt. Once the words were committed to memory, they rehearsed each associated movement of the body. The energy generated from within was tremendous for this complexity of spell and each impulse must be timed precisely to the enunciated sounds.

It had taken all night but the Elf had been well rested after their long journey. He was eager to practice the powers that Moracles had been preaching during the long ethereal trip. Now, in the presence of his master and Quibit, he was about to prove his worth. With the most enthusiastic performance of the ritual, he recited each syllable and elaborated the most minute movement. As the dark mage had done before, the light mists of the room began to swirl. The candles on the desk flickered with the movement of air.

Quibit rushed to protect the delicate flames from being blown out by cupping his tiny hands around them. He watched with as much enthusiasm as he did his own master. Very seldom was Quibit present when Moracles had created or snatched life from the mists of the beyond. He once was one of those creations that the mage had taken from another place or time.

Moracles himself stood in amazement as the area above the black marble floor lightened with the illusion of flames, as if hell itself had been transported to the chamber. Within the flames he could see the movement of several creatures. Upon the completion of Ach'med's incantation, the flames died away leaving three beings hovering gently above the floor. Their leathery bat-like wings slowed them to a standing pose in front of the Elf. Their eyes were fixed on the Drow awaiting instructions from their new master.

Ach'med himself was physically drained by the energies required for the spell. He stood as dumfounded as his awaiting servants. The three small devils were slightly shorter than the Elf. Their toughened red hides covered them completely from pointed head to the end of their spiny tails. He let out a sigh of gratified relief over his success as he looked into their shinny black eyes. The devil creatures each carried a spear weapon with a sharpened two pronged point. The forks were as long as their owners were tall.

Ach'med had no idea what the creatures were nor what natural abilities they might possess. It was evident that their origins were from somewhere in the upper levels of hell itself. What would he do now that he had them? He thought. The thrill was in proving his abilities as a mage to his master. That he had succeeded in doing. Moracles could not have been more proud of his student.

"How should I command them?" He called over to his mentor from the misty shadows. He was aware that they would be under his control for as long as he lived or voluntarily disengaged the spell. They would do or perform any task he set them to providing it was not self destructive or beyond their capabilities. He thought about making them his personal body guard but that somehow seemed a bit presumptuous.

Moracles stepped around the desk toward them to inspect the catch of the day. He could see that Ach'med was near exhaustion and not capable of thinking clearly on the matter. "They are yours to command, but be careful of your words. Remember that they are not here of their own will and may misinterpret your instructions unless you are very specific." He instructed the Elf with a pointed finger. The old man stroked his beard as he circled the three beings. He was certain that he had seen such creatures in his own travels while apprenticed to Hartes, the God of the Hells. Perhaps these very creatures were once his servants, now snatched by the Elf to do his bidding. If that were so, The God may be irritated and demand their release. "Perhaps you should rest first before defining any tasks for them. For now, have them follow you to your chambers and act as your guard." Moracles presently feared that the Bone may make some trouble for the young Drow.

"Yes master. I shall retire to rest for a time." He responded to the mage as he proceeded to the center of the darkness. "Follow me." He said to the creatures who immediately and witlessly walked single file behind their new master.

* * *

"The view is breathtaking isn't it?" Lorentz said, sitting on his horse overlooking the ridge of the great valley canyons. This very place was created by the Dark Lord Moracles almost a century ago. The broken ground left a maze of endless canyons with steep walls. Only an earth quake of great magnitude could have transformed the once peaceful vibrant lands into this desolate rocky landscape.

"Yes. We should be able to see quite well where the path lies in the morning when the sun rises." Shi'roc said as he walked his horse past his friend. The sun had already set behind them, leaving just dark shadows ahead in the canyon. "The Orcs have done well to lead us here to the canyon road. Wouldn't you say?" He pressed for Lorentz response knowing that the priest had some doubts as to the trust that should be given to the new followers of the warrior. From the time of their capture, many including Lorentz did not believe that the Orcs could be turned from their evil ways. Shi'roc had proven that with the proper respect for another being and learning of their ways and language, that they could be retrained as they were.

"I do concede that they have led us well to this place. But I will be more certain of their loyalty after I have determined if we are walking into a trap," Lorentz replied. "Let us set up camp and discuss our approach to the canyon over a good meal." It was time for a full meal again and a good nights sleep. For most of them it had been several days since the last real meal. Lorentz knew full well that Shi'roc would not sleep the night before a potential conflict. His keen senses would remain ready to fight at an instant's notice. It was best that they plan well tonight.

The two leaders directed the troops as to how best to defend their position if they were assaulted that night from below the ridge. They should have the advantage with the watchers having an overlook position into the canyon. They stayed well off of the known road into the canyons and the ridge was too steep to be climbed easily by heavily armored warriors. Any attack would have to be made from behind them along the road just traveled or from the canyon passage. Either way, they would be ready.

A'mora and Lorentz both took part in the food preparations by increasing and improving on the remaining food that they had carried this far. It was true that there was little to work from but in the end there was enough from their mystical multiplication to feed them all and have leftovers to carry on.

With the campfires burning, and the watchers at their posts, the most experienced leaders gathered around the Lords Lorentz and Shi'roc for a conference. Grefden and Sha'la sat close together as did A'mora and Jantez. There were no more secrets about their feelings for each other so there was no longer a need to hide it. The only secret that remained was concerning the child that Sha'la was to have in the distant future.

The Orcs had done their best to draw a rough map of the road through the canyons onto the soft ground with a stick. Despite the apparent bickering amongst themselves about that way the road turned, the result was close enough to plan from. They had noted a large wooden bridge that spanned a ravine over a now dried river bed. The main cave entrance into the fortress from the stable area was not far past that. The Orcs indicated through Shi'roc that the actual entrance was hard to find and only wide enough for one horse to pass, as they put it, that meant a very narrow crevice, similar to the secret west entrance into the Dwarven Peaks.

After the conference they all went to their beds, which consisted of blankets on the ground. Lorentz still was apprehensive of the information, so readily given by the two Orcs. Though Shi'roc was dead certain of their new loyalty, Lorentz did not wish to end up dead. He would do his own reconnoitering of the canyons in the morning. But for now he would sleep well.

The Watchers continued to trade shifts through the night as they had on this trip so that each would get sufficient sleep for the next day's travels or battle. Nothing stirred in the night except for Shi'roc who had several times arisen and paced the perimeter of the camp to check on the watchers.

While Shi'roc was performing his ritual exercises with his sword and new daggers, Lorentz approached him. "What are you doing up before dawn? The warrior asked. "You should continue your rest." Shi'roc sheathed his sword and daggers with precise quick movements.

"I must make an observation over the canyon. I wish to inspect the mountain in which the castle lies." He motioned toward the center of the great broken ground to the east. "I will be back before you break camp." He started to walk off toward the main road. He was fully dressed for battle with his armor and sword covered by his flowing cloak.

Shi'roc caught up to him and grabbed him by the arm. He felt the silvered steel gauntlets beneath Lorentz' sleeve. "What is your purpose to travel alone?" He asked puzzled. "We know where we are headed."

"We know the direction. But we don't know what lies in wait at the fortress." He turned and spoke in his soothing voice. "We must know what to expect when we arrive without any surprises. Our best advantage is our planning." He put his hand on Shi'roc's shoulder. "You have trained them well." He indicated to the survivors who were all asleep except for the watchers. "But they may be no match for an experienced army who's back door we are about to enter. This is their home. We are the invaders," he reminded Shi'roc. "As was on the mountain, the defenders have the advantage. I must find a way to even the odds." Shi'roc nodded his head in understanding. "At dawn, have them ready to travel and I shall return with a plan."

Lorentz walked past the horses and toward the main road. He chanted and waved his arms in the distance as Shi'roc stood and watched. Suddenly a mist formed around him and he was gone. As many times as the mage had performed such spells, Shi'roc was amazed each time. They would wait for his friend's return.

Chapter 26
Betrayal

In the dim light of the approaching dawn, Lorentz glided over the canyon plateaus. He had been able to ride the winds and channel the air within his cape, diving and rising with the updrafts. Any bird would be envious of his ability to soar above the desolate peaks and valleys. The spell that he cast upon himself allowed his body and equipment to have almost negligible weight. That, with his knowledge of air movements within a cold environment allowed him to travel silent and unobserved within the dark shadowy mazes of the canyons.

Earlier that morning he had studied several of the spells that he would need for this mission. Around the campfire, Lorentz opened his book of magic and breezed through the pages that he knew so well. The more he would use a spell, the easier it was for him to memorize the incantations. As his experience with the art increased, so did his ability to memorize more and more. At this stage of his ability, his mind could encompass as many as fifteen spells each day of various complexities. He could remember them in detail throughout the day until forced from his memory by sleep or unconsciousness in the event of injury. His spells almost never failed to produce the desired effect. He had on occasion, fumbled a pronunciation of a word or gesture while performing a chant that was new to him or beyond his entire comprehension.

Lorentz knew that he would be alone this day and must rely on his cunning and intuition to penetrate the secrets of the enemy terrain. He had focused his study on spells involving penetration, mobility and stealth. For defense, he carried his sword of many wonders as some knew it. It possessed its own magic and had been blessed by the healing Gods. He would never part with this gift, and relied upon it heavily in battle.

As he flew over the canyon passages, he had been looking for signs of hidden soldiers along the path below that their army was to follow. Other passages meandered through the caverns in a continuous maze. If it had not been for the map the Orcs drew, they might have wandered for days or gotten lost in the seemingly endless crevace passages. The road was just as the Orcs had said and he could see no signs of movement until he saw the bridge. It spanned a great gorge that had apparently restrained a river at one time. He saw several tall creatures at both ends of the wooden bridge. From the distance he was flying, he could not make out any details. They appeared to be patrolling or guarding this portion of the road. He knew he must be close to the hidden fortress. He swooped down beyond the bridge and behind the vision of the guards. The road turned, then proceeded along a straight canyon passage where the Orcs said the hidden entrance would lie on the west side. It was too dark to see for sure but with his night vision, he was able to see a heat transfer pattern in the air along an edge of the wall. That must be the place.

The sun was about to crest the eastern horizon and it was time for him to land as his spell was due to expire. He headed for the tallest plateau that was along the path just ahead of the bridge. He felt that from here he could determine where to start his search. The plateau had many interesting features. He could quickly see that from there, the entire canyon could be surveyed. Most of the deep walled passages terminated at the base of this plateau like the spokes of a wagon wheel meeting at the center hub. This must be it, he thought. The main road was just below him and the apparent opening was also at the base of this plateau. He stood now near the center of the massive area and could see that there was a deep gorge of darkness that nearly split the top of this place. The priest chanted quietly for a moment and raised his arms. Just as the orange beams of sunlight warmed his face, he vanished into a mist.

From the ethereal realm he could travel through the rock and directly into the fortress that he felt was far below him. As he tried to move through the dimension of space, he was halted by an impenetrable force. He reached out to the rock and felt it as solid. This was not supposed to be. The only force able to repel travel by this means was a mixture of iron and lead.

This rare combination was sometimes forged into sheets and used by a mage to protect his private laboratory or library. Sometimes used to build small chests that could protect spells and magical items from outside forces. He himself traveled with such a chest containing a variety of devices and magical clothing that were very special. It was currently in one of the wagons back at the camp.

It didn't seem possible to manufacture such a wall that continued as far as it did. The installation would have been an enormous project at immeasurable expense. For wherever he tried to penetrate, he was met with smooth stone. He could penetrate all of the surrounding rock but the inner walls that had been cut and smoothed were filled with these minerals. This must be why Moracles chose this location. It was naturally protected from travel by ethereal means. No mage would be able to penetrate the fortress unseen.

Still in the plane of mists, Lorentz found what seemed to be a secret opening in the smooth stone wall. This must be an entrance of some kind, yet he found no lever or mechanism to slide or lift the stones. Perhaps some magical incantation would open it. There were other means of penetrating the wall but he would have to materialize and perform some other spells to allow him access. He was not certain where this would lead or what cave passage he would find himself in if he called down his ethereal spell. For now he had wished to remain outside of the material plane and unseen by any passers by.

Suddenly he felt a sharp pain at his ankle as if he had just been bitten with sharp teeth. What could it possibly be here with him in the mists? He looked down and saw nothing. Again, something had jumped on his back and stabbed him in the shoulder. He jerked around in the darkness and drew his jeweled sword. In front of him stood a small ugly creature. Nothing like he had ever encountered before. Almost like a minstrel's monkey, this thing had a long sharp tail and bared awesome pointy teeth. His paws were clawed as well. It stood there shrieking, almost inviting Lorentz to swing his sword.

As the mage whisked his weapon through the air at the creature, a violent urge of weakness came over him. He managed to strike the creature despite the extreme disorientation he was now feeling. Ignoring the gruesome animal, he proceeded to move through the mist back upward and out toward the canyons. It had been a long time since he had encountered a being while traveling the mists. It was rare that he traveled in this way. Perhaps this creature lived near or was a part of Moracles' forces.

Just as he felt he had passed through the rock surroundings, Lorentz encountered another creature. A black horse breathing fire stood before him blocking his path. Flames shimmered around its hooves and mane. Upon its back was a rider, almost twice his own size. The creature was almost skeletal, wearing tightly wrapped white skin and carrying a hooked bone spear. Could this have been the 'Bone' that he had heard of from the Orcs?

"Who are you?" asked the creature. "What business have you at my doorway?" The demon held the fiery manes of the horse, looking at Lorentz. Its eyes glowed the frightening crimson red that instilled fear in all who gazed into them.

The mage was not certain if it was the creature in front of him, or the wounds that were causing his nausea, but he felt about to pass out. He replied almost out of fear. It seemed uncontrollable. "I am Lord Lorentz, of Thormadore." He spoke firmly, trying to regain his self control and authority. He raised his finely crafted sword in preparation for battle with the demon horse and its rider as he swooned back and forth. "I am here to defeat Moracles and his minions." He straightened up, fighting off the dizziness and pain. "You are 'Bone' I presume?"

The Bone realized that this was one of the warriors that Moracles feared. He was supposed to be trapped in the mountain, but with the powers he seemed to possess, it was no trick that he could be here now. Perhaps he could kill Moracles and break the cursed spell that kept the Bone trapped on this earth. "Yes, I am." He said slowly. "Do you have the power to defeat Moracles alone?" The Bone inquired, debating on whether to help this man or not. He was unaware that the Elf had been injured by Quibit, Moracles pet.

Lorentz was puzzled by the conversation, expecting to be attacked and killed, not questioned. Was this some sort of ruse intended to determine the strength of the survivor army? "Yes, I am alone and will end this realm of Moracles." He boasted having decided not to divulge the survivors advantage.

The Bone leaned forward over the head of the horse and spoke softly. "Good, then I shall let you live." He reared the horse back and rode past Lorentz into the mist toward the fortress. He let out a blood curdling screech as he disappeared beyond sight.

Again Lorentz felt another jabbing pain from his back. The tiny creature had followed him and clung to his cape as he continued to claw at the Elf releasing more of its poison into him. Lorentz attempted to swing around for a strike with his sword but could not rid the creature from clinging to his back. He finally unfastened his cape and tossed it to the uncertain ground covering the beast. With his last ounce of strength, he hacked at his lumpy cloak with the sword, chopping up the vile creature inside. Then he slumped into the mist high above the canyons, dropping his sword and entered the unconscious state before death overcame him.

* * *

"Quibit?" The mage called out in question. His mind link with the creature was suddenly broken. He had called to the mage in warning. A wizard was attempting to penetrate the castle walls on the upper levels. The little creature's telepathic abilities went beyond words. Moracles could almost see in his mind the images that his little pet had sent. The man had pointed ears of an Elf and was indeed dressed as a mage would travel.

After Quibit had managed to call out to his master, Moracles felt the pain of his summoned creature as the Elf mage had struck him with the sword. At that point the creature's pain blocked out any further telepathic contact with its master.

Quibit had told him where the Mage was but he could not know if he had managed to penetrate the castle walls within the rock mountain. He did know from the lack of concentrated contact, that Quibit was with him no longer. He would deal with this intruder himself, most horribly, for killing his pet. Moracles was very attached to those creatures that he had captured from the mystical planes of travel. He did not quite understand the reason for his feelings toward them.

Quibit had been with him for a long time and served him well as servant and pet. The feelings were somewhat different with the Bone. That creature had a supreme intelligence and a mischievous malice, yet Moracles had been patient with him just the same. There was something about the spell itself that bound the creatures in its grasp to the mage and an emotional tie from the wizard himself to those who served him.

His thin fingers gingerly swept through the massive book of spells that lay open on his desk. He would fill his memory with various spells designed for combat and defense. Since he had no way of knowing the powers of this single mage, he would have to be prepared for anything if indeed there was a confrontation.

Then he began to think about the mage that his dragon had encountered when attacking the intruders. Yes there was a mage with the warrior, Shi'roc, who had caused the defeat of his pet and drove him to a brutal and bloody death. Although the others may be trapped in the distant mountains, perhaps this one was powerful enough to escape. Of course he was. If he could travel the mists he could easily escape the confines of the collapsed mountain passages.

*   *   *

The campfires had been extinguished. The horses and wagons were packed and ready to travel. They waited patiently near the canyon's road for Lorentz to return. Kura had gathered the clerics to pray for guidance and wisdom during the upcoming battle. Although they were well taught, battle experience was something they had little of. It was one thing to heal an injury when concentration was possible and time was plenty, and entirely different to use the combined efforts to evade the enemy and bring sanctuary to a downed soldier in the middle of a battle. This they had only experienced once during the last attack on the mountain by Moracles' army.

Shi'roc peered into the gleaming sunrise, shading his eyes with one hand while holding the reins of his horse with the other. He needed to know what Lorentz had found awaiting them and if he could find the entrance into the fortress. He looked over at the two Orcs setting on the wagon, awaiting his word to proceed. He knew that they could show them where the cave entrances were.

It had been two hours since Lorentz had left on his reconnaissance, and even A'mora was becoming worried. She was unaware of her mentor's intentions to covertly sneak out into the canyons that morning. If she had, she would have insisted on going with him. She was very familiar with his abilities and had often worked in concert with him to enhance their powers of magic and in prayer. She prodded her horse to walk toward Shi'roc.

"I should go and look for him." She said quite as a matter of fact. "It is unlike him to be detained." She stared at the back of Shi'roc's head as if to force a response. His jet black hair flowed in the breeze.

He continued to survey the skies above the desolate area. "I agree." He said as he turned toward her. "You are most capable of finding him." He continued as he nudged his horse closer to hers. "Don't let on but I believe that he is in trouble and I don't wish to leave until I know what has happened." He leaned over and whispered to her. "Work whatever magic you require, but find him." His concern was quite evident. His words were more an emotional order than a request.

"I will M'Lord" She replied as she turned her horse back to where she had left Jantez. She dismounted and handed him the reins of her horse. The Lady quickly pulled a tattered binding of papers from one of the folds in her robes. Holding the papers to the sun's light she scanned several of the spells she would need, or thought she would need to find her master. These were incantations she had known well, so not much time was required in their memorization.

A few moments later she gave Jantez a kiss, then walked back over to Lord Shi'roc and said, "I am ready." She walked out to the ledge overlooking the canyon beyond where the road slopped down. Gracefully she spread her arms letting the flowing air catch her robes and dropped off of the rocks.

There was a gasp from all those nearby watching as she disappeared from sight. Then a moment later she reappeared floating among the currents of air over the canyon passages, soaring like a bird. Jantez and Gol watched until she was too far to be seen any longer. Shi'roc was both amazed and impressed at her devotion and courage. The two young mage apprentices were inspired. They had been taught such spells but had as yet been given the opportunity to put them into practice.

A'mora had swooped down low and high among the flats of the broken earth. She saw nothing. No movements, no vegetation, no living creatures at all. Below her was the road that Lorentz would have followed to find the castle in the rocks. Then she saw the bridge where there were several Gnolls pacing about. She wanted to drop down for a closer look but was afraid to be seen. There did not seem to be any commotion in the area as she floated by.

The flying priestess turned to soar over the bridge when she noted what appeared to be a body, in a free fall. This was large enough to be a human. She raced towards it almost in a dive, like a Falcon attacking its prey. She could see that it was indeed a body and began to chant as she flew closer. "Avium dochet fidera" She concentrated her thoughts on reaching out to the falling body. She could not be certain of who it was as yet. Still a hundred feet or so above the canyon floor she managed to touch the persons arm and relinquish the spell to them. It was a probability that Lorentz had been in conflict with some creature encountered in the ethereal mists.

A'mora then threw open her cloak to catch the updraft of air before crashing to the road below. Her body slowed with the ballooned effect of her clothing. She watched as the body below her floated gently to the ground. As her feet touched ground, she rolled with the momentum of the fall. Her plan had worked well, for her landing had brought her within a few feet of the limp unknown entity.

The priestess knelt over the body and rolled him over to see who it was. As she feared, it was indeed her master, Lorentz. She checked quickly for any signs of life and tears came to her eyes as she discovered the bleeding gashes in his back. She began to weep for her lost mentor, praying to Mirana for a miracle.

She suddenly realized that they had landed dangerously close to the bridge where she had seen the Gnolls. She looked up the road to find a handful of them headed toward her at a rapid pace from across the bridge. Their long legged bodies had a great movement advantage over humans or Elves. Gathering her wits, she lifted the limp body of Lorentz over her shoulder and instantly knew that she could not outrun the approaching enemy even without the added burden of a dead body to carry.

She looked back up at the ridge where the survivor army awaited. Lorentz would have been able to escape from such a predicament by using a spell that could cause them to traverse the distance instantly. She remembered the words that he had taught her but was uncertain of the inflections and motions.

A thought suddenly came to her in the panic. Was he still wearing his magical ring of spells? She grasped at his dangling hand to find the ornately carved golden ring still there. She slipped it from his limp finger and put it on the fourth finger of her left hand. She spoke the words as she remembered hoping that he had empowered the ring with the energies of that incantation. If so, she would only need the correct words to release the energy. "Distare Transversus Renum," she spoke carefully as she concentrated her vision on the ridge. Although she could not actually see the details of that distance, she still held fresh memories of the area from just an hour before.

She glanced behind her just in time to see the five Gnolls ready to pounce on her. It was too late to attempt another course of action. She repeated the words as she looked at the ridge and re-arranged the emphasis and the pronunciation. "Distare Traverseus Renium." Her memory focused on where she last saw Jantez standing with her horse.

* * *

The first Gnoll jabbed at the beings with his lance while in a full run. Just before the pointed blades reached them, they vanished. The large agile creature was in shock as he ran through the space where they had stood, and tripped on the rocky road. The others behind him also gasped as the humanoids disappeared and they followed suit, tripping on their fallen leader. The five lay in a heap on the ground, grumbling and cursing each other.

"We must report this intrusion." The first Gnoll rushed to his large padded feet as he pushed the others off of him. "I will go back to the cave. The rest of you back to the bridge. Remain guarding this side" He shouted the orders, clearly the head guard posted to defend the bridge. He ran at a full sprint carrying his lance.

The others casually crawled back to their feet and trotted back to take up positions on the western side of the bridge. Those guarding the far side had remained across the ravine. They were then notified by the guard leader as he ran across the bridge toward the cave entrance of what to be looking for.

His barefoot speed was astounding due to the long strides the agile creature could take, even with the heavy armor plating the species wore over their muscular furry bodies. Within minutes he had run from the bridge to the cave entrance. As he entered he noticed that the cave was truly empty except for the stable slaves that normally tended the horses of the armies. He ran from the mouth of the huge cavern to the deepest part. The sheds were all empty except for two horses and some equipment and the slave creatures sat idly by watching as the head guard approached.

"Where are others?" He grunted out in his best humanoid tongue. He rarely had to use his ability with this commoners language. Most of the others he dealt with understood and spoke Gnollish, though there were fewer than twenty of his kind in Moracles' service. They were generally considered the most intelligent and best of the non human warriors. Their size, agility and strength even surpassed the aging Magdarn humans that Moracles had as his original personal guard.

The harry fanged creatures looked strangely up at the Gnoll that towered above them, for they were only waist high to the warrior. "There no others for long time." The shameless creatures noted that they have remained unneeded as stable hands since the armies last rode out weeks ago.

The intelligence of the Gibbers, as they were called, was so low that even as slaves they had no desire to leave even when ignored for weeks at a time. They made the perfect servants to tend to castle needs. They wore no clothing and their furry unwashed aroma was less than pleasing to most of the other races, save the Orcs.

The guard nodded and grunted his understanding as he trotted off toward the hidden passage from the cave to the second level of the fortress. The cave area was quite dark where the passage led into the castle. The Gnoll stopped to light a torch so he could more easily find the hidden door mechanism. He never did see the need for the passage to be such a secret. No one other than Moracles soldiers and servants would be using the passage.

With enough light at hand, he walked along the south western wall. When he found the empty torch bracket, he knew he was in the correct location. He placed the torch in the bracket and took a few steps further to where the wall would move. The warrior felt down for the handle that was embeded in a crevice in the wall. He reached into the shadow and yanked the lever to the left. The wall groaned as it moved inward to a rocky stairwell.

With torch again in hand, he sprinted up the uneven stairs until the passage ended again at a false wall. As before, he grabbed at the rock handle and pulled the lever releasing the latch on the hinged rock. The slice of wall pulled to the right as it slid into the rock. In both cases the stone doors were quite heavy so as to not be moved by smaller creatures.

He entered the dim, torch lit hallway of the castle to look for other soldiers or perhaps the Bone so he could report what had happened in the canyon. He proceeded in the direction of the master's temple, not really knowing who might be there. Up ahead he heard a door open. From around the corner coming towards him he saw a silver haired Elf wearing a black cloak and shimmering black chain mail vestments.

With his lance ready for combat the Gnoll spoke. "Who are you? What is your business here?" The words came out in a very broken common language of men realizing that the Elf probably didn't speak Gnollish.

At first surprised, Ach'med stopped and looked at the large menacing looking creature. Even without the sharp lance, he wouldn't want to tangle with this being's fangs and apparent strength. The Elf mumbled a few inaudible words and waved his hands. "I am Ach'med, Apprentice to the Lord Moracles." The words flowed in a smooth Gnollish tongue. "Who are you?"

The guard was now set off balance. How was this Elf able to speak his language? Was this Elf who he said he was? He was uncertain of trust at the moment but decided to answer anyway, in his native language. "I am Quintar, leader of Gnolls." He was impressed with this small creatures ability to speak his language. He may be a wizard, but he was not told of Moracles' return, or of a Drow apprentice. The Gnoll was aware of the existence of Dark Elves since he attended ceremonies in honor of Lolith and had seen the Elf / spiders guarding the temple. "If you are apprentice, where is Moracles?" Of all the races employed by the dark lord, the Gnolls were the least afraid of their master, yet the most respectful, though a voice from behind him sent a shiver down his spine.

"I have returned to an empty castle." The wizard, priest responded from the shadows down the hall. He also spoke in the Gnolls native tongue. "Are there none here to protect my sanctuary?"

The Gnoll turned and lowered himself to a bent knee. He bowed his head and addressed his respected leader. "My Lord. The Bone has sent out all but my men to attack the enemy in the distant mountains. We guard the bridges into the canyon's main road that lead to the castle." He looked up to his master. "It is of a grave matter that caused me to seek you out."

"Rise, and make your report." The mage said sternly as Ach'med approached the towering warrior from behind. "What has caused you to leave your post?"

"We saw two people drop from the sky over the northwest road. One appeared to be injured and the other was a woman." The Gnoll tried to relate each detail knowing that it may be important to Moracles. "They were both robed as you are. When we attacked, the woman spoke words we do not understand and then vanished."

"So, the Bone believes that these intruders are safe inside the mountain awaiting me to do with as I will?" He spoke to Ach'med who was now standing at his side. They conversed briefly in Elvish. "I believe now that the army we passed was not our own, but that of the enemy." His voice became increasingly irritated. "You will lead the

Gnolls and hold them at the northern bridge until the others return." Ach'med nodded his understanding.

"Ach'med is your new leader now." Moracles again spoke to the Gnoll warrior. "The Bone is no longer to be trusted. You will address the Drow as Vandar." He motioned to the young Elf. "Gather your men and meet him at the north bridge. He will instruct you then."

The Gnoll bowed his head in a hesitant gesture acknowledging the Elf as the new leader. He then bowed even deeper to Moracles and took his leave to return to the cave. There he would take a horse and ride swiftly to the southern bridge and gather the remainder of his men.

Moracles and Vandar proceeded up the hallway where they entered the dining hall. There, a hearty breakfast awaited them, prepared by a few of the castle Gibbers. The two magi sat at one of the long dining tables as Ach'med's personal guards stood by. The two discussed strategy and defense of the valley from the bridge. "I believe you should have your guards accompany you." Moracles motioned to the three demons near the doors to the hallways. "They could be of use if I remember their abilities correctly."

"Yes, I shall," the Elf responded as he pondered their usefulness. "I am looking forward to assessing their abilities myself." He nodded with respect and excused himself from the table. The mornings meditation to Lolith had inspired a confidence and wisdom that he had never felt before. No longer would he be the uncertain warrior, but the ever aggressive mage. His past had been completely erased and he now sought the pleasures of power.

He motioned the spinned demons to follow as he opened the double doors, leaving the dining room. Soon he will have what he sought, what Moracles had promised, an army to command.

* * *

The two appeared at the camp as suddenly as they disappeared from the canyon road, at the spot where she had left Jantez. The entire group had taken up positions along the ridge looking over the canyons for their return. No one had noticed them pop out of the air just a few feet behind them.

When she had recovered from the breathtaking teleportation, Her sorrow had re-emerged. She hefted Lorentz body from her shoulders and gently laid it on the ground before her. Once more, the tears of anger and loss flowed down her cheeks. Her gentle sobbing drew the attention of all Elves keen hearing.

Ilo, Shi'roc and several others with pointed ears, turned to see Lady A'mora weeping over Lorentz who was laying on the ground. Shi'roc leaped from his horse and ran to her side before the others could even move. At that moment, the rest of the survivors realized what was happening. Though they did not understand how, A'mora and Lorentz had returned.

"I was too late." She sobbed, speaking to Shi'roc as he put his arm around her. "I found him falling from the sky near the bridge. All I could do was to keep him from crashing into the ground." She looked at Shi'roc with her sad swollen eyes and gave him a crushing hug.

"No!" He insisted. "He can not be dead. I will not accept that." He gently broke her embrace and held her firmly. He looked deep into her eyes and shook her. "You can still save him as he had done for me before. You can't give up so easily." He brushed the tears from her cheek with his finger. "I believe in you as Lorentz did, or does. He is probably waiting for you now if you would just try to revive him." Her sobs lessened as he spoke. "He once told me that your healing powers were greater than his and in time you would possess a far greater clerical power."

By now, most everyone had gathered around them. Kura had already taken hold of Lorentz hand and started to pray. The other cleric apprentices joined in with the chants. Their words of reverence to Mirana inspired the priestess as did Shi'roc's confidence. Perhaps, together, there was a way to bring him back to this world.

* * *

The cave was dark and cold as the babies cried out in vain. The fires had died with no one there to tend to them. The bodies of the children's guardians lay lifeless around them, all except one. There was a stirring in the cave behind a rock as a lone shadow approached the children.

The baby Dwarf, though small was old enough to crawl on his own. He had managed to wiggle out of his blanket wrappings and crawl toward the deeper section of the cave to seek out warmth, while the newborn woman child could do nothing but cry out for a mother who's lifeless body lay but a few paces away.

The shadowy figure passed by the first child as it maneuvered over the decaying bodies. As the being knelt down over the small Dwarf it was startled to hear the sound of a crossbow being cocked behind it. Muga had managed the strength in a delirious state to protect her child. She had just returned to consciousness after the concussion she received from her fall.

A silent mumble emerged from the figure and the cave began to glow from the walls and ceiling. The being, no longer a shadow to Muga, picked up the infant Dwarf, Tyme, and turned to its mother holding the baby. The Dwarven warrior gazed into the eyes of the robed figure and immediately lowered her crossbow. She felt dizzy as the effects of her injury returned. Again she collapsed onto the floor and fell back to a deep sleep.

The being knelt over her and wrapped the infant in its mothers arms. The figure laid its delicate hands on Muga's head and mumbled a silent prayer. Then it whispered into her mind, "Your son will one day be a great leader." It then returned to the crying woman child, Aliah, near the cave entrance and picked it up. Wrapped warmly in its blanket, the two left the cave as if not ever having been there.

* * *

"We should be nearing the valley as Alena described it to me." Zant said to his Elf companion as they neared the dense forest's edge. Both were in awe of the vast devastated land that stood before them. Zant had remained in his human form as they traveled the woods since the night before. They had traveled so long in the ethereal mists, that Zant was weary from the concentrations of the spell.

Fendal was not yet acquainted with the ability to travel in the ethereal plane for such a long time, in real distance. He had occasionally made short hops in and out of the mists to elude an enemy or to transverse an impassable wall. It was a far different matter to navigate half way around the known world without a keen sense of spatial and temporal abilities. The task was fairly simple to Zant who could live among several different worlds on the real plane or of the heavens.

Fendal had remained upon the Dragons back during the entire trip. Although the creature had no actual wings, he did remain in the floating state the whole time. It was fortunate that Zant had kept the specially crafted saddle that the good wizard, Kalicam, had made for him many years before. Zant had served many kings and wizards in his two hundred year life span after being freed by Shi'roc and his friends. Now he served the heavenly Gods such as Alena. He was considered old for a dragon yet many dragons lived beyond the measure of old and were considered ancient. That was not a prospect that Zant looked forward to. He always anticipated being killed in the service of the Gods, fighting evil sorcerers or demons. This may indeed be his last journey from what he had learned of Moracles.

"There, just ahead." Fendal pointed to a large mountain range as they proceeded through the dead forest. "That must be the Dwarven Peaks." From their direction and distance, the three distinct towers of stone shown almost equidistant from each other on the mountains ridge. They were presently a full day's walk through the desolate wasteland of dead trees and shrubbery devoid of all foliage.

"Perhaps we should hide ourselves and float our way to the mountains above this land." The old man suggested. He walked up ahead of the Elf to find a suitable open area where he could transform himself to the magical golden Dragon that was his natural state. When he was ready, he called to Fendal who resumed his position on the creatures back. They began to hover over the dead trees as Fendal invoked the spell that would render them invisible as not to frighten those they sought to help. The sun reflected from many puddles of muddy water below them that the snows had left behind.

They remained at their floating elevation of only a hundred feet above the ground. They saw no movement as they approached the mountain. They carefully hovered over the treacherous terrain and found the remains of the Dwarven town on the eastern side of the ridge about half way up the rocks. Remaining silent and observing all they could see, Fendal was overcome by the sight of the dead decaying bodies just below them.

"We may be too late," the Elven mage whispered to his golden companion. They floated slowly toward the ground so that Fendal could have a closer look on foot. He made a short jump from the dragons back, appearing in mid jump from the air. He was now visible to anyone who might be watching. He scurried from shadow to shadow, looking into the abandoned dwellings. He looked over some of the bodies. Some Human, some Bugbear and some Goblin.

There were no Elves or Dwarves among them. He breathed a sigh of relief.

"The battle was recent." He called up to Zant hiding somewhere above him. "These must all be enemy soldiers. No Dwarves or Elves." He looked around some more to be sure of his assumptions. "There is no one here."

"Alena had said that the survivors lived within the mountain." Came a voice from behind Fendal. The great dragon had once again taken human form. "We should find a way below the rocks." They split up to search the edge of the town nearest the incline. They went from house to house checking through the debris.

"Here. I have found something." Fendal shouted. "There is a secret tunnel in this building." He was standing at the doorway of a home waving to Zant to follow. He had found the open stairway behind the shelving. He could not see too far down in the darkened rock passage. With a few magical words he cast some light on the problem. Instantly he found that the stairway had been collapsed. An impassable avalanche had blocked the passage about twenty feet downward.

"We must find a way in." He spoke to Zant who was now beside him viewing the wreckage. "They may be trapped inside."

"No. Not necessarily." Zant remembered what Alena had related to him about her encounter with Shi'roc. "There is a passage that leads out from the western side of the mountain, as I am told." He expressed relief to Fendal. "We only need to find that."

What they did find was the remains of the enemy soldiers that had fallen into the traps that had been set by the survivors. There was no trace of the those who had lived there for generations. The one thing they did recognize was the shrine set up for the retired Dwarvan king. They continued their search through the fallen cave passages, passing the sprung snares and spikes. The two magi were careful not to trigger any untouched surprises. They were certain that the inhabitants had escaped after a truly brutal battle for survival.

"What is this place?" Fendal asked as he stepped through what seemed to be a large cavern opening. The ground was soft with dirt rather than rock. The two could see with their enhanced vision that there was a movement of air and the cavern was immense. Water could be heard dripping in the distance as they walked. "Lumen" Fendal called out to the open air as a jet of light sprung from his hand toward the distant stalactite ceiling. Numerous stone shapes began to glow with an eerie yellow light, casting shadows throughout the water cave.

"There." Zant pointed past a grove of trees. This place reminded him of the Dragon's Gate that he had been guarding for so many years. "There is a shrine of some sort." The two approached to get a closer look and maybe find a clue as to the whereabouts of Shi'roc and the others. "This is a statue of Mirana," the old man said. "I do recognize her as she is akin to Alena." He examined the carving more closely. "This is of recent construction." The wise man said as he passed his fingers over the stone. "It does not follow, as she is the Goddess of the forests. Mountain Dwarves would not know of her unless the ancient Elves had brought her wisdom to these caves."

"It would not have been Shi'roc that brought this knowledge to them as he knows no gods." He had thought of his friend from the past, never bowing to any deity, good or evil. Perhaps that was what had kept him so pure of heart for so long. "Except of course for Alena, now that she has made herself known to him." Fendal filled his water skin with the fresh water of the melting snows. It had trickled into the cave from a crevice that led to the surface.

The two left the cave puzzled by the lack of evidence of anything except the battle. They continued their flight towards the east as Fendal had convinced Zant that Shi'roc would never run from a battle. He was more likely to take the battle to Moracles himself. It had become dusk as the two floated above the soggy desolation. Zant had returned to his natural Dragon appearance so as to use his abilities more easily. They had found evidence of a large army with horses and wagons along the southern edge of the mountain peaks headed east. Fendal urged the gold Dragon to follow the path until darkness made it impossible to see the trail.

They made a campfire as best they could with the remains of old trees and shrubs. The Elf was not as accustomed to sleeping outdoors as he was when he was younger and traveling with his cohorts. With Zant laying nearby, he felt relatively safe and went to sleep. He figured that no one would dare disturb a sleeping dragon. Though the dragon's powers were limited, Its ominous form would frighten any half intelligent creature. What the survivors were up against must not be very intelligent, Fendal thought, because if they were, they would have fled at the first sight of Shi'roc. He knew he was out there somewhere.

Zant also was fatigued from the long journey and the use of his magical abilities to transform. He snorted as his deep sleep brought him to the world of dreams. Yes, even the most powerful of dragons could dream.

"Zant? Zant, can you hear me?" A mellow voice drifted into his sleep. His mind raced to incorporate the voice into his dream. He had recognized it as that of his Goddess, Alena.

"Yes my queen, I hear you." His mind voice responded in the dream. Was it a dream he thought? "How may I serve you?" He remained respectful as he felt it was more than a dream, but a vision.

"Do you remember how bravely Shi'roc fought to free you from Lord Magdelan's control? Do you remember how he fought to defend Cerratt against the hoards of Orcs?" She said in a tranquil voice.

"Yes my queen. I do remember those deeds of the Lord Shi'roc. I owe him my life." The gold Dragon replied in his mind. His own words almost involuntarily, reminded him that this may be his last quest, his final mission for the Gods, to return the favor of saving the life of the Elf warrior.

"In two days the two moons will become one and the world as you know it will end if Shi'roc is not successful in defeating Moracles. You must see him through this. Those of good heart are depending on him, and you." The vision told Zant more energetically and emphatically. He then passed into a deep dream or vision. He saw himself in his natural Dragon form hovering over a great canyon. The mage Fendal was riding in the back saddle as they battled with the evil Moracles. "This must be the vision of my fate," he thought as he felt himself plummeting into a deep ravine.

The vision of Alena spoke to him from her throne in the clouds as Zant's mind had envisioned her. He was still uncertain of the dream or vision but either way would not fail her. As he suspected all along, this mission may be his last. The words that Alena spoke were those of finality.

He continued the long deep sleep until the morning dew began to trickle down the golden scales of his spine. The dragon awoke with a snort. He raised his massive head and looked around to see Fendal tending the fire and cooking a small rodent. He was huddled over the warmth wrapped in his cloak and shaking. Before him was an open spell book that he researched feverishly running his hands over each page quickly as he memorized the words written in his own hand.

During his sleep, as with all wizards, the strength and energies required to cast spells dissolve. Each morning all magi must re-read the incantations that they intend to use during that day. Unconsciousness or sleep of any kind would endanger the effects of a memorized spell. Presently he was studying a warmth spell.

Once completed, he was able to stop his shivering and continue his studies as Zant lay patiently by. Once the sun had risen and the dew had dissipated, the two were ready to resume their search for the armies that they knew Shi'roc was leading against Moracles.

Again, Fendal climbed into the hand-crafted leather saddle that was strapped to the gold Dragons back. This would normally be considered an indignity for the creature as only those of the most lawful and good would even be permitted to approach him. As Fendal was of some questionable nature, this would not be happening. But in this one instance, Fendal's mission to assist Zant for the good of all worldly beings was considered a true act of valor as seen by the heavenly gods.

"We must hurry." Zant urged as Fendal strapped himself into the plush seat. "We have only this day to find them." His words were direct but cryptic.

"Why have we only one day?" Fendal asked. "What will happen after that?" He shrugged not knowing how important this journey really was. Nor that he may be killed as well for the good of the world as they knew it.

"I have it on good authority that we are nearing the end of our journey." Was all that Zant said. He would not let on what he knew in whole, for the mage may change his mind about finding Shi'roc and warning him of his brother's resurrection against him in the service of Moracles. Fendal may never know the true nature of the part he was about to play in history. If they were not successful, it would be no matter.

Chapter 27
Resurrection

The night passed quietly for the survivor army. The watchers had kept focused on the canyon road as they had the night before. Several had positioned themselves just below the crest of the ridge so as to get a better view down the canyon walls. Ilo had taken charge of the night watchers as his father had done while living in the Dwarven Peaks. Ilo's extraordinary night vision allowed him to spot campfires down the canyon road near where Lady A'mora had described the bridge. As before, no one else was able to confirm his findings but knew better than to question them.

The nights seem to be longer now that Maac-To was not with them. The apprentice priests prayed for his recovery as they asked their Goddess, Mirana, to protect those who remained in the cave with the children. Lady A'mora had a much more pressing need of the Goddess' powers. She had found a scroll that Lorentz had always kept in the folds of his robe. This scroll contained the chant of life that only a high priest would normally be acquainted with. Due to her profound healing abilities and her studious efforts under Lorentz' tutelage, she was able to comprehend the meaning and inflections of the prayer.

Shortly after she had retrieved Lord Lorentz' body that morning, the student priests had provided the superficial healing rituals for the bites and gashes that they had found on his body. The poisons that actually caused his death were removed from his blood so that, if resurrected, he would once again be healthy. The question was, could A'mora perform such a miracle.

The priestess had studied the scroll the entire day and began the ritual early that night. She was determined not to fail. Shi'roc had given orders for her not to be disturbed while performing the ceremony. He too knew the importance of her concentration. What mattered most was that Lorentz be revived to full health soon so that he could relate to them the cause of his death and what secrets he may have uncovered at the fortress. Any further delay in their attack on the canyon might allow the enemy army time to return from the southern path.

While A'mora studied her chants, Lorentz' two mage apprentices grew restless. Jantez and Gol had approached Lord Shi'roc with a plan. Under the cover of darkness, they suggested flying over the area where Ilo had spotted the campfires. Using the best of their combined abilities, they would remain unseen and be able to see what was awaiting them at the bridge.

Shi'roc, fearful that Lorentz may not recover, allowed them this mission. He ordered them to observe and report their findings. The two students gathered all of their scroll spells and studied vigorously by the campfire light. They discussed all that Lord Lorentz had taught them and devised the specific combinations of spells that should be used. Since each was limited as to their abilities, they had to work in concert to support each other.

Once prepared, they leapt from the ridge into the valley canyons and soared on the rising air currents. Since Jantez had some limited night vision abilities, though Human, Gol had to rely on his sense of direction in the darkness. As they approached the area near the bridge, they could see the campfires below. Jantez concentrated on his abilities to remain unseen and silent as he landed closest to the enemy camp. Gol had perched himself on a low plateau overlooking the path to the bridge. From there he could observe from a distance and assist Jantez if he were to be discovered.

Both silent and invisible to normal vision, Jantez crept up to the campfire to get a good look at the enemy face to face. He observed several of these tall, muscular furry creatures, some sleeping and some keeping watch. They were just off of the road at the foot of the bridge. He had not seen these beings before, but there was something else very unusual at the camp. He saw a young Elf dressed in black armor and cape, talking with the warriors. His features were unusual, he thought, not ever having seen a Dark Elf before.

There was an even more frightening sight. The Elf was flanked by three short, winged creatures. From stories he had heard, fables or myths, these creatures seemed to be demons from the many hells. They seemed to follow the dark Elf wherever he went. Their leathery red skin and wings accentuated his shinny black armor. This couldn't be Moracles he thought, yet he did seem to be in command of these troops and the demons may be his servants.

He could also see a camp at the other end of the bridge though he was unable to tell how many were there. He did his best to count those around him when suddenly the Elf stopped in mid sentence, and began to look around. Jantez froze in place thinking that he had somehow been detected.

Gol watched from above and he too suspected danger. He crawled to a position where he could best watch the man in the black armor. When he heard the call to alert the creatures, he knew it was time for Jantez to make a stealthful retreat. The young apprentice stretched out his hand down toward the warriors and spoke the words to release the energies from his finger tips. "Fiero" he called out as jets of sparks flew from his hands at the camp. He had been particularly aiming at the leader in black.

Jantez heard the call from above and watched a shower of fiery sparks explode upon the Elf with no visible effect. The Elf's cape should have burst into flames as the missile of fire struck, but it seemed to bounce off of an invisible barrier surrounding the Dark Elf. The sparks flew and did manage to singe some of the nearby furry creatures. The demons also seemed unaffected. The Drow shouted to the warriors around him and pointed up the canyon wall. Jantez took this opportunity to run back up the road at full speed not caring if he made noise or not. He heard another launching from Gol as he had cleared from the area.

The winged demons flew up the rock wall with forks in hand ready to skewer the intruder, but Gol dove off of an opposing ridge to begin his soaring climb back into the sky. Jantez soon joined him though Gol could not see him. He made sure that the winged demons had not spotted their escape. They had avoided being seen by the enemy so they were not followed. He shouted to his companion a thanks for the timely distraction. The two returned to their camp sometime later and reported the nights events to Lord Shi'roc.

Shi'roc was not pleased to hear that they had engaged the enemy, but understood the reasoning for the attack. The information that they brought back was valuable in case they would have to fight without Lorentz' insights. That was a prospect that the Elf warrior didn't want to face.

He was concerned at Jantez' description of the Dark Elf. The apprentice indicated a resemblance between he and Shi'roc. Why would a Drow be serving as a leader for Moracles or was he Moracles? This was a matter best understood by Lorentz. Could it have been the Drow who defeated Lorentz? He sent the two off to get some sleep as he stood over the canyon's edge and reminisced a moment. Demons were not a force to be taken lightly. They may possess their own magic as he had discovered in past situations.

Shi'roc remembered the time when he and Lorentz first met. Shi'roc and his party were sent to help a town rid themselves of the mountain giants. There at Thormadore, the two became friends as they fought side by side against the Drow who led the giant Neanderthals. That was when Lorentz learned the true powers of his gifted sword. It had been forged and blessed by the heavenly gods to seek out the minions of an evil goddess. This was how Lorentz explained it. The sword would take control of its wielder and attack any Drow within fighting distance. He realized that A'mora had returned with Lorentz but the sword was not with him.

Shi'roc well knew the powers of enchanted weapons since he himself had experienced similar control by his old sword 'Luminex' that was destroyed long ago. He had not since been fortunate enough to find as fine a weapon as that. He had found it hidden away in the deserted castle Norgothrond. How it got there and who had created it, no one could tell.

If only Lorentz could be resurrected to wield that Drow slayer sword again, Shi'roc would be pleased. He left word not to be awakened before sunrise as he needed to get some sleep after his briefing with Lorentz' apprentices. It had been days since he had gotten some real sleep. He looked over toward A'mora who was still performing the rituals of life over Lorentz' body. Her silhouette shown near a small fire as she waved her arms in healing prayer.

* * *

The morning sun had crept over the edge of the canyon's shadows and its gleaming orange light was cast on the sleeping Shi'roc. It was odd that his instructions were not followed and he was allowed to sleep so long. The others had been up and milling around the camp. They had not packed nor were they preparing to move out.

Shi'roc finally awoke by the gentle nudging of a foot at his ribs. He stirred and opened his eyes at the second such violation to his person. Who dared to wake him in such a manner, he thought as he saw the sunlight, and why were his orders ignored.

"I ordered to be awaken before sunrise." He said firmly, clearly irritated at the person who stood over him.

"Yes, M'lord, but you needed your sleep." The figure spoke, almost sarcastically.

Shi'roc recognized the voice though the face was obscured by the sunlight in his eyes. He leapt to his feet and hugged Lorentz. "You have returned to us. I was so at a loss when A'mora found you dead." He gushed with joy at his friend's appearance. "She is as you said, a great healer. She studied all day and prayed all night." Shi'roc was almost in tears to see his friend breathe once more. "I must thank her. Where is she?"

"Yes, she is, but she had a fine teacher." Lorentz gloated, showing once again his lack of modesty. "She told me what had happened. I sent her to rest. She should sleep most of the day after her exhaustive prayer." He looked around at the camp. "Now I am at fault for holding up the attack, but what I have learned may be worth the delay." Lorentz became serious once again. "I have a plan that we must discuss."

The two leaders sat alone, away from the camp exchanging information from the past day's events. Lorentz confirmed that the main road did indeed lead to a dark crevice in the base of the tallest mountain wall. The bridge had been guarded by soldiers.

"Yes, I know, Gnolls." He said confirming Lorentz' suspicions. "A'mora found your body falling near the bridge and you were both seen by them. She whisked you away just before being run through by a lance, as she said." He winced at the chill of the thought of the beautiful woman being pierced by the Gnoll had her spell of escape failed.

Lorentz continued to explain of the lead lined stones of that the castle walls were made. He described the little creature who attacked him and inflicted him with the poisons from his bite. "I believe that I managed to kill it before succumbing to death, but I also remember a delusion." He thought hard trying to separate the reality from the delirious memory in his mind. I remember, as I fled from Moracles' servant I may have seen the Bone."

Shi'roc gasped. "How do you know it was he?" He asked not understanding what Lorentz was relating.

"I asked him." He stated simply. "He was riding a black stallion from hell, breathing flames. The Bone was a demon himself as described to me long ago." He paused to give thought to a simple description for Shi'roc to understand. Though he had been exposed to many unearthly creatures in the past, Lorentz wanted to be able to draw a comparison. "Do you remember fighting the Lytch and his evil twin brother a year earlier?"

"Yes, how could I forget. It was your healing powers that brought me back from near death to help you defeat the brother." Shi'roc remembered that even then they had led armies against a superior enemy.

"The Bone is taller and his skeletal structure is tightly wrapped with white skin and he has a tail." He thought more about how to warn Shi'roc and the others of its powers. "Also, if you encounter it, do not look directly into his eyes, for he can instill fear in you with his stare."

Shi'roc scoffed at the fear in its stare. "I can look any enemy in the eye, just before I take its head." He laughed. "So it was the Bone who defeated you?" Now Shi'roc wandered if Lorentz had been delirious.

"No. It seemed that he did not wish to cause me harm." He thought some more about the conversation." He said that as long as I was there to defeat Moracles that he would spare my life." They both stared at each other quite puzzled. "I must have been ill with the poison."

"While A'mora was in trance, your two apprentices surveyed the bridge area. They counted ten of these Gnolls and possibly more on the other side of the bridge." He was trying to break the bad news slowly. "They were led by a Drow."

Lorentz was now shocked. At the mention of the word, his hand instinctively reached for his sword. It was not there in the scabbard. He panicked for a moment and then remembered that he had used it last in the mists against the small creature. He must have dropped it there when he died. He may never find it in the ethereal mists.

* * *

Having been eaves dropping at the temple doors, the Bone had learned of Quibit's death. Of that he was not sorry. Moracles had been praying to his Gods, Hartes and Lolith, telling them of the death of the mage that Quibit had encountered in the mists. He was gloating of how no one on this earth could defeat him now. Apparently Quibit had stumbled onto the mage and managed to defeat him somehow as he himself was killed. What a useless creature he was. The Bone thought to himself. His best chance at escaping Moracles' spell was now gone. That Elf Mage might have been able to defeat the old man if he had found him first.

Perhaps there were more of these people wandering around nearby attempting to penetrate the castle. The army would be returning soon so he had best help these intruders find a way in before they arrive. He slowly moved away from the temple doors as quietly as his bony frame would allow. Once out in the clearing of the great ravine he pulled his little horse statue out of the sack on his belt and placed it on the rocky ground. With the word 'Blackfire' the horse sprang to its full size, puffing smoke and ready to stretch.

Off into the Ethereal plane they rode, near where he had found the mage the day before. He knew that they were somewhere above the canyons though he could not see into the real world. They floated aimlessly around the area, looking for anything suspicious, or anyone who might serve his purpose. He would not dare discuss his plans of betrayal with his Wraiths because they too served Moracles. He must find a way alone to help the intruders. They had apparently not been trapped in the mountain as he was led to believe, but were obviously somewhere nearby as he gathered from his master's conversations with the Gods.

The Bone saw something laying in the mist. He could not dismount from Blackfire as he did not alone have the power to travel in the plane between worlds. He leaned over from the back of the horse and looked carefully at the gleaming sword. He recognized it as that which the mage held when they met. It had a gold and jeweled pummel with a shiny silver blade. A fine piece of craftsmanship, something that the Bone could truly appreciate. Somehow the sword must have possessed its own magic that allowed it to remain in the misty plane on its own. He reached out to pick up the weapon and as he got a firm grasp of the handle, it let out a tremendous shock, burning the demon's hand. He dropped it instinctively as he let out a screech. It disappeared from sight as it fell from the mist into the real world.

* * *

"Look at that." One of the Gnolls pointed at the shinny item falling from the sky. The other guards at the bridge stood up to watch where the item had landed. They were all curious as to what it was, but looked to Vandar for permission to investigate.

"You two. Find that item, but be weary as it may be a trap." The young Elf spoke with authority as he pointed to two of the guards. They hurried off down the road away from the bridge. The Drow was still leery of the happenings the night before. He was now suspicious of everything and everyone.

The two Gnoll soldiers stopped near where they thought the shimmering thing might have landed. They were near where the two strangers were the day before. They both drew their swords and looked around for anything or anyone. "There. Up on the ledge." The one pointed to the mirror like reflection on the canyon wall. The sword had landed on a ledge about twenty feet up.

He began to climb up the ragged rock face to the ledge and saw the beautiful sword. He reached up and grasped it with his left hand while balancing with his right for support. Again the sword was dropped after delivering the shocking jolt in its own defense. The Gnoll cried out in pain. It tumbled to the ground in front of the other soldier. "Don't touch it." He called down. "It is trapped somehow."

"How did it fall from the sky?" The other asked as he stood staring down at it laying on the ground. "Perhaps the Gods dropped it." He said scratching his head as the other walked over to him.

From around the corner of the path, Vandar came running with the three demons floating at his side. He was taller than the red skinned creatures but appeared quite small next to the large bodies of his new warriors. He was actually only half the height of the Gnolls. "What has happened?" He demanded as he saw the two standing in the middle of the path looking at the ground.

"It is a cursed sword." The first Gnoll said.

"Nonsense." The Drow blurted out as he approached them. "Pick it up." He stopped and pointed at the item in the road. He put his hands on his hips, testing his command.

"But, sir, it is trapped or cursed." The injured warrior reached out his hand, scorched from the blast of the sword, for Ach'med to see.

The other obeyed the command and was determined to hold on despite any violent reaction to him. He bent over and put a firm grasp around the golden hilt. The moment he raised it from the ground he was jolted by the sword but he kept a firm grip as his body flinched with the shock. Then the sword began to vibrate with a powerful energy.

Ach'med and the demons stood on guard as the reaction of the other was mystifying. He began to loose control of the weapon as he grasped it with both hands trying to break free of it, but it was too late. The magic of the weapon had taken control and the Gnoll and raised the sword to attack the nearby Drow. Realizing that his soldier was no longer in control of his faculties and tried to resist the pull of the weapon, Ach'med stepped back behind the winged demons who had raised their spears for his protection, putting themselves between their master and their ally. They were serving as perfect personal guards.

Still, the Gnoll was on the attack and the others were forced to fight him as he tried to get to the Drow. The sword seemed to have a mind of its own as it flailed at the spears of the Drow's, protectors. The demons danced and fluttered their wings to block the advances of the Gnoll since he had height and strength to his advantage. They had taken several slashes from the weapon as they managed to pierce the furry warrior with their steel forks.

Vandar remained behind his demons and prepared a spell in case they had failed in defeating the Gnoll. It was apparent that the warrior was trying hard to fight the control of the sword and Vandar did not wish to have to kill one of his own troops. He continued to concentrate on the enchantment until the right moment occurred for its effect.

The other Gnoll, not wishing to harm his compatriot, but wanting to stop the battle, jumped and tackled the possessed warrior. He intended to knock the weapon from his hand, but the spell released by the sword was causing a tight grip with both hands and could not be broken. The two wrestled on the ground as they heard Vandar's word.

The Drow had stepped out in front of his body guards and released the energy of his spell with one word. "Hold." he called to the two fierce warriors battling for what might have been their deaths. As if time had stood still, the two entangled bodies froze in place with muscles locked.

The one Gnoll had grabbed the two wrists that were clenched around the handle of the sword, and had been trying to pry them free. Vandar stepped firmly on the clenched fists. He had put on a pair of specially made gauntlets that would enhance his strength and manual dexterity. He reached down, pried the fingers from the sword and kicked it away from the two Gnolls.

The two motionless warriors were well aware of the happenings. The spell itself did not stop the minds of the creatures, only the voluntary muscle control. They were fully capable of breathing and had maintained their senses so they could still see, think and hear. The Mage then released the spell that held the two and their tensed muscles collapsed upon each other. They had let out a sigh of relief with the sword out of reach.

The Elf walked over to the magnificent sword, now helpless without someone to wield it. With the protection of the gauntlet he reached down and picked up the sword. It caused no injury and posed no threat to himself or those around him. "I must put this in a place of safe keeping." He said to himself as he inspected the intricately carved blade and the gold and jeweled handle. "Perhaps, someday I might be able to convert its powers to suit my purpose."

* * *

"We must wait no longer." Shi'roc said as darkness fell over their camp. All was ready for their attack on the canyon bridge. Once across, they would continue on into the castle itself to find Moracles. "Lorentz. Are your people ready?" He asked his magical friend.

"They have been studying all day. Their combined abilities will be of great use provided they stick together and do not get separated." Lorentz replied as the students approached. A'mora and Jantez were holding hands, with Gol walking slightly ahead of them.

The other group leaders joined them for a final review of the plan. There were many doubts about the success of the attack due to the uncertainty of where Moracles' army would be. They may still be far from the castle and they may be there already. Either way it would be a tough fight, not knowing what they were truly up against.

"Remember, I want to take the Drow alive if at all possible." Lorentz pointed his finger to no one in particular to exemplify his point. "He may be forced to tell us what we want to know." He turned to Shi'roc and asked. "Do you remember the words of enchantment for your ring?"

Shi'roc began to speak. "Of course, Ara.."

"No." He was quickly silenced in unison by the shouts from everyone around him, knowing that the utterance of the words would release the power from the ring springing whatever magic was at hand.

He reached into his pocket and pulled out the ring. "Its all right. I'm not wearing it." Knowing full well that the words were safe as long as he who spoke the words was not wearing the ring. He held up the ring with his two fingers and placed it safely back into his pocket. "Arachnia, Fiero, Medicum, and Traversus." he spoke confidently. "I am ready." He smiled.

The road through the canyon to the bridge was narrow and steep from the starting point, so they would leave the wagons and carts behind. It would be hard enough for the horses to negotiate the rock slope without the extra weight behind them. Each group had their plan as before on the mountain, but this time it was they who were the aggressors. If all went according to Shi'roc's calculations, they would be attacking the bridge just before dawn.

The warriors were split into several groups to be dispersed after they had crossed the bridge. Ilo and Kura refused to be split up so their group would be the strongest. Gor and Grefden each had their own forces combined with Lorentz' archers and crossbowmen. Sha'la as before led the women warriors with a special mission plan.

They moved as quickly and quietly down the dark canyon path toward the bottom of the crevices. From A'mora's description, the road would wind through the canyon passages and lead to the bridge over the ravine. That would be their first confrontation. Lorentz had come up with a clever plan to split up the enemy forces at the bridge. Although the survivors would greatly outnumber the Gnolls, there were concerns of the Drow and his demons.

Most of the guards were asleep as was the Drow and his servants when Jantez and Gol looked down over the ridge of the plateau. They could see the campfires with only two of the Gnolls standing watch on the road. Across the bridge on the far side of the ravine they could see other fires as well as torches lit on the bridge itself "How do you know what a female Gnoll looks like? Maybe they are female." Gol whispered, pointing at the creatures below them. The two apprentices were preparing for the first phase of the attack.

"I don't, exactly, but its dark and they probably haven't seen a woman for a long time." Jantez whispered back. "Get ready, there they are." He pointed down in the canyon passage just beyond the light of the fires reach. The young mage closed his eyes and concentrated hard. He tried to visualize the image and its reactions to the events about to unfold.

* * *

The two furry guards stood furthest away from the campfire at the start of the canyon walls of the road. They were alert and cautious, not knowing what to expect if anything from the supposed attacking army. Anyone would have to be a fool to attack on such a narrow pass to the bridge, especially at night.

They heard what sounded like a giggle coming from up the passage. Then just at the edge of the light from the campfire they saw someone or something moving. Whatever it was stood just at the curve of the road. They readied their weapons for a fight when they saw what appeared to be a sleek light furred female Gnoll wearing tight black leather armor. She had leaned back against the far rock wall showing off her sensuous curves and held out her tempting paw. The two guards looked at each other and then back at the female as they heard another giggle from her. They lowered their weapons and decided to investigate a little closer.

The two casually and confidently walked over toward the female, not worrying about waking their companions. With only one woman, why invite the others. Just as they crossed the path within talking distance of the woman, one of them spoke. "Where did you come from," the first said in their native tongue. The only response he heard was another giggle that this time came from off to the left. They looked up the road in the darkness and saw the shadows of a mass of people. Before they could utter a warning or react at all, they were flurried with a volley of arrows from less than twenty feet away. At least six arrows penetrated each of the creatures armor, some above the neck line.

All that they could mutter were gurgling sounds as they grabbed at the protruding arrow shafts in their throats. The next thing they felt was the sting of long swords being thrust into their sides. They fell over dead as the others caught them to keep from making unnecessary noise. The bodies were dragged around the bend and stuffed into an open crevice along the road.

"Looks like it worked, whatever you did." Gol said to Jantez. He was not influenced by the spell since it was directly aimed at the two guards, so he could only imagine what had happened. "Try it again." He urged, really getting into the spirit of the magic.

"Just watch what's going on down there and be ready." Jantez pointed to the small group of soldiers moving slowly and silently toward the campfire led by Lord Lorentz. Not a sound was made from footsteps or armor as they moved in on the sleeping enemy.

Knowing the powers of a Drow, Lorentz had planned a special surprise for the dark skinned Elf as he awakened. He had also wanted to include the demon creatures in his plan. The dawn began to lighten the sky above as the Gnolls awoke to see themselves surrounded by the enemy soldiers. They cried out just before being skewered with swords and their own lances. The disruption was enough to send the demons into a scurried flight around the waking Drow. The leathery creatures were quite the watchdogs.

"Silentium." Lorentz called toward the dark Elf and his servants. Lorentz had taken a sword from a dead Gnoll and advanced on them. "There will be no magic emanating from your lips, Drow." He taunted as he began his attack. The dark Elf moved his lips as if giving commands or casting a spell. No sound could be heard, nor was there any sound from the screeching demons.

The Drow sprang forward to face the sorcerer with his new shiny jeweled sword in hand. He was yet unaware of the powers of the sword and knew that using it would be the only way to determine its strengths. He swung it fiercely at the priest but the blade was blocked by the mage Elf's sword. The devils immediately intervened blocking Lorentz sword blows with their military forks.

In the dimness of the morning glow, Lorentz recognized the weapon that the Drow posessed. "That sword is mine!" He demanded, seeing for the first time that the Drow did indeed have possession of the blessed weapon. He attacked the demons with every effort now enraged that his sword was in the hands of the one it was meant to slay. For his efforts he received several gashes from the sharp claws and forks of the leathery creatures. Lorentz realized quickly that he was outnumbered and backed off from his attack on the Drow.

The silenced Drow knew he had to withdraw until the spell of silence could be broken or its effect had worn off. He fled across the bridge as his guards protected his escape. As he did the creatures began their flight over the survivor army that was now advancing on the bridge.

Since the spell that Lord Lorentz cast had eliminated the ability to use verbal magic for the Drow and the demons, they had resorted to their natural defensive abilities. From their leathery skin protruded a line of bone spines down their backs. From flight above their enemy they released these bone fragments as a defense and the falling projectiles would burst into flame upon impact. This seemed quite effective on the crowd in the narrow passage. Many of the survivors were burned as a result of these attacks.

Shi'roc observed the happenings just ahead of him and notice that the demons were gathered at the narrowest point over the passage. Several of the archers had taken shots at the creatures with little effect. They were quite agile in flight and managed to deflect or avoid being hit by the arrows. The Elf warrior reached into his pocket and quickly put the ring on his left hand. He reached up aiming his arm at the leathery devils and announced, "Arachnia." From his hand sprung a white net of webbing that he had aimed above the area of the flying demons. They quickly became entangled with the sticky substance and together fell into the crowd of warriors below.

The creatures were quickly jabbed, stabbed and rendered incapacitated, then trampled as the group yelled its victory cry. With the Gnolls dead and the Drow now running across the bridge, the army proceeded triumphantly toward their goal. Lorentz resumed his chase of the Drow onto the bridge.

"Fiero" Gol called out, concentrating the aim of his magical spell at the Drow, fleeing across the bridge. The line of sparks flew from the ridge and slammed square into the back of the Dark Elf.

Ach'med lurched forward and his cape exploded into flames as it should have before. He rolled on the log bridge and tore the fiery cape from his back, casting it into the waterless rivine. The Gnolls on the other side of the long bridge saw the encounter and began to run across the bridge to the defense of their new leader.

Lorentz had almost caught up with him to take back what was stolen. The precious sword, blessed by the Heavenly Gods created to eradicate the race of Dark Elves must be retrieved. As the Dark one got back to his feet, Lorentz saw the oncoming group of Gnolls from the other side of the bridge. Knowing he was outnumbered, he signaled for Jantez and Gol to meet him beyond the bridge. His body was racing too hard to concentrate on casting any spells from memory. He knew he must get past the blockade and allow the army to handle the Gnolls. He called upon the powers of his ring to escape. Leaping from the bridge and spreading his cloak, he again allowed the updraft of the ravine to lift him up. He soared as light as a bird around the stone mountains.

The Drow ran past his attacking Gnolls, motioning instructions to them to hold the enemy on the bridge. He continued his flight, running toward the castle, knowing that he must retreat to warn Moracles and find his new army. Without the powers of magic he could not be of much help against the survivor army. He could stand and fight with his sword, but would only be defeated by shear numbers and no one would remain to warn his master.

The Gnolls now had an advantage although greatly outnumbered. They blocked the bridge with two rows of warriors. Anyone who could get through the first line of soldiers would be killed by the next. Those in front used their long lances that kept the shorter enemy at bay. The next four held swords at ready.

The survivor army suffered many casualties from the conflict. Some of the small Dwarves were able to swarm around the Gnolls first line and get past their lances. They hacked at the legs and lower bodies of the tall furry creatures. Several of the Dwarves sacrificed themselves at the pointed end of the lance so the others could get through.

Some of the Human fighters climbed past the bodies of the downed Gnolls and fought the enemy face to face. The swords and shields clashed as the battle continued a little closer to their goal. Screams echoed as the wounded soldiers fell or were throne from the bridge. The tall furry creatures were eventually overpowered by the slashing blows of the Dwarven swords on their legs. They had collected the Gnoll weapons and pushed their dead bodies over the side of the bridge.

* * *

As the morning sun crested the canyon's edge, Zant and Fendal finally reached their goal. They could clearly see the army below ahead of them crossing the long wooden bridge. Someone on the bridge was waving frantically at the warriors encouraging a swift march. The horses pulled the heavy wagons behind at the top of the ridge. Those soldiers mounted on horse back broke into a gallop after crossing the bridge.

"Look. There they are on the attack." Zant said elated that they were in time to join the battle. He felt that his time was at an end and today would be his final chance to die gloriously in the service of the gods. "Is that your friend Shi'roc leading them across?" They floated down for a closer look.

"No!" Fendal gasped. "That is not at all like Shi'roc." He then realized that the army they were seeing was not the mountain people at all but Moracles' wretched outcast army.

* * *

"Hurry." Quintar, the chief of the Gnolls was waving frantically to the approaching army. "The enemy is going to attack from the other end of the canyon. My men will try to hold them off until you arrive." The Gnoll yelled in his best common tongue, then joined in stride as the Bugbears, Goblins and Hobgoblins began to run across the bridge. "Moracles has returned with a new leader to guide us," he said with great enthusiasm. The few remaining mounted Magdarn warriors broke formation and galloped on ahead. Their sole purpose was to protect Moracles at all costs and they were not content to wait for those on foot. Qunitar remained on horseback to lead the others as they ran on foot across the bridge. Within moments, the Magdarn were out of site.

"Look, above. It must be Moracles come to join in on the battle." One of the Bugbears pointed at the Golden Dragon and rider floating past, above the bridge. Since most of them had never seen Moracles in person, the rider wearing robes could seem to match the rumor of his image. "He has captured a powerful dragon to help us defeat our enemies." The airborne mage followed the canyon road just behind the Magdarn warriors. The sight of their returned leader inspired them all for the long run to the other side of the canyon. This battle would be more glorious than the conquering of the valley towns had been.

*   *   *

Once the survivors were safely across the bridge, the priestly apprentices tended to the wounded and prayed for the dead. The loss of life was expected but many were disappointed at their own performance in combat. This was the first time that they did not have a scheme to give them full advantage over an enemy. The first toe to toe fight and although they won, it was at extreme costs. Shi'roc encouraged them to press on.

At this time, the group leaders' special tasks became apparent. The survivor army broke up into its various teams. Ilo and Kura led their men to follow Shi'roc toward the castle, searching for a sign from the others along the canyon walls to mark the entrance. Shi'roc was flanked by his two pet Orcs. Although they had not yet been trusted with weapons, they still insisted on fighting at his side.

Lorentz had previously instructed several of the Dwarven miners in a special task and the five of them were hard at work on the bridge cutting into the binding ropes and notching logs. The Dwarves were quite agile when it came to climbing and scurried about the underside of the bridge supports like ants at a picnic.

The other groups would take up positions hiding in the crevices high and low along the canyon walls. Grefden and Gor would command the foot soldiers, while Sha'la would take the archers to higher positions overlooking the canyon road near the cave entrance once they arrived.

A'mora awaited her mentor and the others at the cave entrance where they were to meet. She was concerned at the wait since she had spotted the enemy army approaching the south valley bridge a little while earlier that morning. She had made a reconnaisance flight toward the south end of the canyons while the others had been setting their trap for the Gnolls at dawn. She must warn them that they were running out of time.

"There you are , my dear." He said as he slowly floated down to the road followed by Jantez and Gol. "The army should be beyond the bridge by now. I will lead Shi'roc here while you find the inner entrance that those creatures spoke of." Lorentz motioned toward the cave. "Go on and be careful. We will be along soon." He was about to begin his run to flight when A'mora broke in.

"You must hurry. The other army has already crossed the bridge." She sounded somewhat desperate. She knew that their quickly trained survivors were not a match for a head to head battle with experienced soldiers. “This might all be for nothing if you don’t hurry.” She said softly in a defeated tone.

“Not to worry, my dear,” Lorentz said with his famous smile. “We have a plan.” With that he made a short run and opened his cloak, lifting his body into a soaring flight like a bird. Moments later he spotted Shi’roc and the others in a quick paced march up the road. He noted that there were distinctly fewer now than before the assault on the bridge. He sighed at the loss of those lives that he convinced to follow on this quest.

A’mora Jantez and Gol hurried into the darkened cavern to find the hidden passage that the Orc had told them of. Once inside the cave, she grasped a handful of dirt from the floor and with a few mystical words, tossed the glowing dust up into the air as her and Lorentz did back in the Dwarven peaks to light the great hall. The cave ceiling and walls began to shed some light as the three passed. They could see the stable areas up ahead and knew that the passage was beyond them.

“Look.” Gol pointed to the awful grimy creatures that had appeared from the wooden structures. “What are they?” He wasn’t worried since they were naked and obviously unarmed.

“They must attend to the horses and equipment of Moracles army,” Lady A’mora replied as they quickly moved passed them. She hesitated then turned toward the small crowd of gauking beasts as the two men continued on. She chanted a quick verse at the stable hands and ran to catch up to her lover and his friend.

“What was that about?” Jantez wondered as she rejoined them. “They looked harmless enough.”

The three had reached the back wall of the cave and began their search for the wall that was to open into a stone stairway. They chanted as they moved their hands over the rock walls to enhance their abilities to find any edges of a doorway or mechanism to operate. Again A'mora urged expediency in their search.

* * *

"Shi'roc." Lorentz called from his lofty position. The warrior halted and looked around for the familiar voice as did the others. They did not see him ahead or on the walls. "Up here." He called again as they all looked up, continuing their march. "We must hurry to the castle. Moracles army is returning." He waved ahead as he swooped past. "The cave isn't far ahead on your right side." He returned to join his apprentices in the cave and assess their findings.

"Here is cave." The gruesome Orc pointed out the hidden cave entrance to his new leader. "Main door ahead." He pointed up the road.

"All right. You all know what to do." He called out, deploying his troops. They immediately began searching for crevices to lie in wait for the enemy. The archers began their climb to protect the entrance from above. He halted two of the climbing archers. "You will not be needing these for now." He said as he took their swords and turned to his two unarmed followers. For his plan of deception to work, his two pets needed to be armed, not only for show, but for self protection should anything go wrong.

Shi'roc then spoke to the Orcs in their own tongue. "Tell army, go bridge." The crafty warrior pointed toward the direction they had come from. "Tell of battle now in canyon, there." He pointed again to the north bridge. He handed them each a sword. One hurried off to the main doors of the castle up the road to divert the impending attack. The other remained at the cave entrance as Shi'roc led Ilo and Kura's troops inside.

All the archers and bowmen were in position on both sides of the canyon road to overlook any attack. They were all thankful for the rest time as they waited for the events to unfold. Just as Sha'la was beginning to calm down and relax a while, She had another sudden attack of nausea and became dizzy. She overcame the urge to vomit but the wooziness and the height caused her to question her footing and began to slip from her hiding place in the rocks. She held on to the stone around her as she tried to slowly slide into a sitting position without falling off the ledge.

Grefden noticed the slide of loose rocks and dirt and looked up to see Sha'la sitting on the ledge. If he could spot her from his position, the enemy would surely see her as they approached.

Chapter 28
Invasion

The torches flickered in the large temple as Moracles chanted to the lifeless stone statues of his evil gods. Both stone carvings of Hartes and Lolith stood motionless as the light created shadows around them. The temple was silent and empty except for the lone figure who himself was laid out before the alter in penitent prayer. Tonight would be the most important and eventful time of Moracles' centuries, for it would be on the first day of the of the new calendar that the two moons would be aligned. This could happen only once in a hundred years. The last time announced the coming of the great mage himself, for on this eve, his powers would be enhanced by the gods of the underworld.

A century ago this night, the evil priest had created the valley canyons with an enormous earthquake that was felt as far as the Dwarven Peaks. The face of the land had changed, altering the paths of the rivers and streams. The springs dried up soon after and the land began to die all around the center of the disturbance. Moracles had unleashed such a deadly spell that all earthly life, plants, trees and water would dry up and wither away. Such was the fate of the great Elven Forest and the Father of the forest himself. For these years since, the plague had been spreading and now extended far beyond the Dwarven peaks creating a wasteland that grew inches each day so that eventually all the world would become as desert.

Fortunately, the heavenly gods through their minions knew of this plan to decimate the goods of the earth and empowered the Goddess of the forests, Mirana, to create three such powerful devices as when used together would combat the lifeless plague. The hope was that one day, the three items would be united by one who was good and pure to renovate the land that had been destroyed and restore the

Father of the Elven Forest. Those items eluded Moracles and were thought to be only myth. He believed that by mercilessly murdering all the inhabitants of the valley that his spell of death would continue to grow. No one would remain to stop him.

His ultimate plan was to bring the lives of Hartes and Lolith to this world by creating an entirely evil realm for them to preside over. Tonight was such a night for the likenesses of the two dominant beings to come to life and reward Moracles for his servitude. With the two moons aligned and his powers enhanced, he would call on the statues to breathe and fulfill his promise to those who had given him such power. All was ready for the night's events. Moracles was certain that the intruders would be, by now, eradicated so that no presence of good would interfere with the coming of Hartes and Lolith.

Though it was only mid morning, the preparations were under way for the nights events. He would call to life the statues in the temple and they would all revel in the safety of this evil realm that Moracles had created. Ach'med, being his apprentice and being favored by Lolith during his initial training, would also be present to participate in the ceremony. Moracles was quite proud of the accelerated learning of his student. Although not experienced in the twisted usage of his powers, he was capable of calling forth demons from the ethereal mists.

* * *

By the time Ach'med had reached the inner hallway, the spell of silence that had been put on him by Lord Lorentz had dissipated. He was now able to hear his own voice and movements as he ran toward the temple shouting for Moracles.

As he passed his own chambers, he stopped and looked at the door. He still held the shimmering jeweled sword in his hand. It might be wise, he thought, to hide this from anyone, especially since the mage who claimed it was so intent on getting it back. If this sword fell into the wrong hands, he himself would be in danger, for he had witnessed what the sword would do if grasped by an unprotected hand. His own guard had been turned against him, unable to control the unstoppable powers that the sword seemed to possess. Yes, possess was the correct word since it enthralled its wielder to attack without end. The Drow would have to study it further before determining its power.

He opened the door to his room and looked around for ideas as to where to hide the weapon. For now, he slipped the sword into the armoire in the corner of the room where it should be safe. He closed the door to his room behind him and continued down the hall and crossed the stone bridge that spanned the ravine which separated the main castle dwellings from the temple to the Gods. He was certain that his master would be praying, preparing for the ceremony.

He went down the dark cave where Loliths special spider creatures resided. Moracles had allowed them to serve as guards of the temple since they had been cast out in disgrace by Lolith herself during the rituals of loyalty and endurance. Neither the Elf mage nor priest could pass the excruciating tests that would have allowed them the powers of a Drow. Their punishment for failure was to live out their existence as half Elf and half spider.

The cave walls were sticky with webs and Ach'med knew he was near the side entrance to the temple. His night vision allowed him to spot the creature clinging to the wall of the cave. He was in no danger, for the eight legged servant knew that Ach'med was a Drow and apprentice to Moracles. If however a stranger would have attempted to pass, the being would have attacked with his magical spells and his bow to ward off any trespassers.

The Elf ran down the narrow hallway from the webbed cave. As he approached the side door to the temple, he slowed down to listen for his master. He could hear the chants from the high priest, Moracles, reverberating through the double doors. He was deep in concentration of his prayers in preparation for the dark arrival of the Gods. He did not wish to, but his master must be disturbed. He opened the door and stepped into the dimly, torchlit temple and saw his master floating over the alter, hovering between the two statues of Hartes and Lolith. His chants continued as the young Elf approached. What should he do? How could he interrupt at such a moment. Moracles was not even aware of his presence. He stood and waited a few moments in silence as the forces of evil enveloped his mentor.

The chants subsided and Moracles slowly lowered himself to a standing position behind the alter facing out toward the rows of stone benches. The mystical forces faded away and the old man opened his eyes. At first he was startled by the presence of his apprentice at the foot of the alter, but then took a deep breath and posed a question. “Has the enemy been defeated? Are they all dead?” His mouth formed and evil twisted grin that allowed his rotted teeth to show.

“No my Master.” Ach’med hesitated. “The Gnolls were holding them back at the bridge, but my army never arrived.” He seemed depressed and frightened at his real failure. “There was a mage who cast a spell of silence over me so that I could not use my powers. I fought with my sword,… his sword, and my demons protected me so that I may return to warn you.” He carefully worded the events so as not to let on that he fled the battle.

Moracles was shocked at the mention of the other mage. He had thought his pet Quibit had killed the magic user. Perhaps this was another? He thought back to the first encounter when his crimson dragon had met with the intruders in the wastelands. There was only one wizard to his recollection. He thought carefully as how to next proceed.

"Come, we shall see what has happened to Quintar." He motioned the Elf to approach the altar. The mage placed his hand on the young man's shoulder and the two vanished from the temple with a magical word from the mage. A moment later they found themselves in the mist of the master's cavernous chambers where those special creatures, the Torgs as he called them, guarded Moracles' secrets. It was dark save for the reflective glow of the sun penetrating the open crevice and illuminating the hovering mist.

Ach'med found himself standing before a large crystal ball supported on a three legged pedestal in what seemed the corner of the chamber. The device stood alone away from any furnishings. Moracles waved his hands and concentrated on the image of Quintar, the Gnoll leader who had been awaiting the arrival of the army from the southern bridge. The Mage was capable of finding almost anyone he chose provided he had a clear image from personal contact of the being in mind. As long as the subject did not have a knowledge of the search or a special magical resistance, Moracles' spell would be able to find them within the valley. Quintar was well known to him and did not know that he was being sought. The ball began to glow with its own mist as the wizard chanted into it and caressed the smooth surface. In a moment, a picture of the Gnoll appeared amongst several others running through the canyon, with weapons in hand.

"Ah, you see there." The mage spoke with some relief. "The army has arrived and is on its way here now. They will meet with the intruders and finish them off." He turned to the Drow. "You should meet them at the main entrance and lead them to victory against the intruders. No one of them should live." He smiled. "The valley must be cleansed of all creatures who do not serve Hartes or Lolith." He motioned for the Elf to go.

Now revitalized, Ach'med ran to the center of the chamber and spoke the words that propelled him through the floor of the chamber into the mazes of the castle. He had well learned his way back to the long winding stairwell that led down to the large dining hall where just yesterday he shared a breakfast with Moracles. He had already been through most of the passages and hidden hallways as his master introduced him to the castles' secrets. The master knew it would be sometime before his apprentice could travel more easily by way of the ethereal mists. So for now he would have to run from place to place within the castle. Once down the stairs and into the dining hall, he would hurry through the castle toward the main double doors of the fortress.

* * *

Shi'roc lead the way into the cavern as both Kura and Ilo led their troops behind, all keeping a watchful eye and weapon in hand. They noticed the slight glow of the cave walls and ceiling and knew it was the work of their companions. The way must be safe they thought so they picked up their pace to a run toward the wooden structures. As they passed, they noticed the five furry creatures huddled together near one of the stable doors. They did not move but stood staring.

"Ilo, Take a few men and check them out, I don't want to leave anyone behind us who might make our presence know." The small army continued on to the back of the cave where Lorentz and his students awaited at an opening in the wall. They had lit a torch in a nearby holder to better illuminate the doorway.

"Jantez found the moving wall and the hidden handle to open it." Lorentz greeted Shi'roc and held out his hand.

"He also disarmed the trap around the wall itself that contained these." He let the handful of spiked needles fall into the warriors hand. "Be careful, they are dipped in a strong poison, clearly meant to keep strangers out." Shi'roc held one up to the torch light to see the tip of the needle had a dark coating on it. "It is now safe to pass."

"Then what are we waiting for? We have an evil mage to find." Kura spoke up from behind Shi'roc. His men were eager to end the hundred years of destruction by Moracles.

"Let us go in first and I will signal you from the other end of the stairwell." Shi'roc nodded in quick agreement, then the four magic users were on their way up the dark hall. The stone stairs were rough cut and uneven, making it difficult for A'mora and Gol to move too quickly. After a long tangled climb, they reached a dead end. Lorentz knew that there must be another lever to be pulled or loose stone to be pushed allowing a wall to open.

Shi'roc and the others stood at the entrance awaiting a signal from Lord Lorentz as Ilo approached. "What were those things at the stable?" He asked Ilo.

"I do not know but something had made them motionless." He said confused. "They were frozen in place but still alive. We found some rope and tied them all together in case they did try to move."

"Good work, Ilo." Shi'roc motioned for the others to gather around. "You two wait here and guard the entrance in case Moracles' men show up behind us." The warrior selected two of the biggest Humans for that task. "The rest of us will have to stick together once Lorentz gives the signal."

"What is the signal we are awaiting?" Kura asked wisely as he looked up the dark stairway.

Shi'roc thought a moment and then replied, "I don't know." He shrugged his shoulders. "He didn't say." They all listened intently from the opening for any kind of noise that might be a signal. After waiting a few minutes longer with no sound he said, “Lets go.” He motioned the survivors to follow him up the passage.

With swords in hand the group made their way as quietly as possible to the opening at the other end of the stairwell. They could see the distant flicker of reflected torch light. It seemed that the stairs ended at a narrow hallway within the castle. Shi’roc carefully peeked around the corner in both directions. To the right he saw some lit torches on the wall illuminating a clear path. He saw several doors along the smooth walls. To the left he saw only darkness, but again, no movement. Still no word or warning from Lorentz or the others.

“Ilo, Kura.” He whispered. Once he got their attention, he motioned with the hand signals for the two to lead the men to the left to check out the dark end of the hallway. Shi’roc would go alone to the right, apparently deeper into the fortress hoping to catch up to the others. Shi’roc went first, quietly moving along the walls with sword in hand. Although he realized that the fight with Moracles would be with magic he also knew that there would be other sources of distraction where a warrior might be needed.

He followed the hallway that cornered to the right without any sign of the castles inhabitants. He remained as silent as possible to allow his Elven ears to listen for distant signs of Lorentz and his apprentices. He cornered to the left and found that the passage opened into a great cavern. He heard distant voices shouting, that from where he stood echoed as whispers. He ran out toward the cavern and across the stone bridge. He relied on his acute vision in the darkness to guide his footsteps. Soon he found himself at the other side of the ravine at a set of carved stairs going down. The voices were distinctively louder and he recognized them as those of his companions. They were apparently battling someone or thing with magical incantations.

He ran down the winding stairs into the cave entrance where he could distinguish the heat signatures of his party as well as a multileged creature some distance ahead of them. He could tell that Gol had been wounded by the weakness of his stance. He had apparently been struck in the leg by an arrow. Jantez was caring for his friend as A'mora and Lorentz worked in concert to defeat the spidery form in the cave. He knew better than to disrupt the concentration of his magical friends, yet he did not wish to sneak up on them either and be turned upon mistakenly as an enemy.

The warrior suddenly noticed that the spider creature had magical abilities as a ball of fire began to shoot towards his friends down the center of the pathway. Despite their need for concentration to protect themselves, they had to dive for the cover of rock outcroppings of the cave wall. Shi'roc found himself with no where to hide as he was at the end of the growing ball of flames' path. All he could do was turn and run back up the stairs around the corner, but it was too late for that. He fell to his knees and pulled his dragon scale shield in front of him to give himself some protection. Just before the flames hit him, he heard some familiar words from Lorentz.

The ball of fire roared past them and impacted on Shi'roc's location. Perhaps he was the intended target to begin with. The spell that Lorentz cast had deflected most of the heat around his friend as it had done before with the crimson dragon's breath. Now they had all noticed that Shi'roc had arrived at a most inopportune moment but they were glad to see him.

"Are you all right." A'mora called out as Lorentz immediately began another chant to combat the Dryder. Shi'roc remained curled up behind his shield motionless and unresponsive. Was he so injured that he could not respond?

The others had been tucked tightly behind the rocks to avoid the majority of the heat as it passed, but the creature had advanced on their position after the fiery spell had been cast. It was determined to finish off any survivors of the flames and had its sword in its Elven hand for that purpose.

It was for that reason alone that Shi'roc remained motionless, to draw the creature nearer. He carefully peaked over his shield and could see that the beast was just up to Lorentz position.

The priest sprang up in front of the Dryder in surprise and cast his spell of silence, removing any possibility of the creature casting any more spells. Simultaneously, Shi'roc had leapt up himself with a war cry to either frighten the creature or alert the others of his approach. With both hands wrapped around the hilt if his sword he swung determinately at the creature head on.

With swords clashing Shi'roc yelled out but could not be heard for he had put himself within the range of the silence spell that had been placed on the spider. He battled the creature back up against a cave wall and it had the ability to fight from a horizontal position. This allowed room for the others to get by safely and on to the hallway that led to the temple. The creature was as skilled with a weapon as he was with magic. Though Shi'roc inflicted several wounds on the creature's spider legs and Elven torso, he himself was injured by the blows of the failed Drow's sword. He was eventually forced to back off the attack and flee after his friends.

His goal had been accomplished in getting them past the abomination of nature. "He who fights and runs away…" He muttered to himself as he ran. "..lives to fight another day." He fought back the pain of his wounds as he leaped down the steps to the narrow hallway, falling and rolling, back to a running position. He was now on smooth floor rather than the uneven rocky cave area. He turned to look back and see if he was being pursued by the Dryder. He had heard its thin armor coated legs clacking behind him. It was standing just at the head of the stairs now with a drawn bow taking aim at the warrior.

"Run, Shi'roc" He heard a yell from behind as he noticed that Gol had been pressed against the wall next to the stairs that he just jumped past. The Elven part of the creature was set back on the spiders body just far enough as not to see Gol waiting. With a powerful swing, he hacked at one of the spiders spiny front legs, causing it to misdirect its aim. It stumbled forward down the stairs just a little. The arrow flew wildly, bouncing off the smooth walls of the straight hallway.

Shi'roc hesitated before continuing down to find A'mora and Lorentz. He wondered what Gol would do, fight or run? He hopped that after the successful attack he would take the initiative to get away from the beast before it recovered from its stumble.

The Human warrior took the opportunity now with the creature's torso in attacking position to do just that. The Dryder only had his bow in hand and had not had time to reach for its sword from the sheath on its back. Gol thrust his long sword at the Elven chest, but the blow was blocked by the bow. The sword had silently broken the Dryders bow as it had used the weapon as a defensive staff. It had sacrificed its long range weapon to defend itself, allowing it time to again stand upright. It wavered, not yet used to only having seven legs and it did feel the pain as well. This left Gol in an awkward position.

The Dryder had pushed his attackers sword away and reached for his own. He used his powerful shelled legs as a shield from further blows by the sword. The Human had managed to cut off the front part of another of his legs causing him even more pain. The creature again stumbled but then thrust the pointed tip of a remaining good leg at the warrior. The spell of silence had just been expired as the Dryder pierced his armor and drove through his chest with a ripping sound through the metal as the spines tore into him. He let out a tremendous scream as life left him.

Shi'roc had not realized that Gol remained behind to fight the creature until he heard the agonized scream. He turned to look up the dark passage but the fight was beyond his night vision. He sighed with grief at the loss but knew that if he returned he would be unable to do anything for him. He peeked through the partially opened door to the temple where he saw a magical battle in progress. The Human that must be Moracles, stood behind an alter between two statues. In front of that stood A'mora and Lorentz, all throwing spells and casting chants at one another. Jantez lay limp on the floor nearest the door where Shi'roc stood. To enter at this time would be suicide. He waited at the doorway for the opportune time to enter.

* * *

Ilo and Kura had led their warriors cautiously down the dark hallway and discovered a recently used dining hall. There were three large tables with many chairs around each. They searched the other doors along the walls only to find a food storage room of sacks of grain , vegetables, and fresh hanging meats. The other adjoining room was a kitchen where two smaller creatures, like the ones found at the stables, were preparing a meal. As was done in the cave by Lady A'mora, Kura quietly chanted a spell to keep these furry creatures from moving about. Then one of the warriors tied up the servants with some twine from the stables.

The Humans in the group had to move carefully as not being able to see in the darkness as the Elves and Dwarves. They had been standing guard near the double doors of the hallway. Still with the dining hall dark save for the light of the kitchen fire, the Elves had found another set of double doors to another hallway opposite the entrance from which they came. Again, two more guards were posted there.

In a far corner there were stairs that had been unnoticed until Ilo spotted them. He and Kura quietly led the remaining Dwarves up the short flight of stairs to the first landing. Even in the darkness, Ilo's keen sight was able to detect that there was a hidden doorway on the wall. Something there should move and open into a passage or another room. He passed the word through the Dwarves down the stairway to light a torch from the wall of the dining hall and bring it up so they could search. When Ilo and Kura were satisfied they could not reveal the secrets of the wall, they turned to go up the next flight of stairs.

With torch in hand, Ilo led the way up the stairs with Kura close behind. There were several other survivor soldiers behind them. The flickering light revealed that there was another landing up ahead. Suddenly from around the corner of that landing appeared a Dark Elf. It was the same Elf that Lord Lorentz had battled at the bridge. Lorentz had called him a Drow, though one of this kind had never been seen in the valley until now.

It was unclear which was more surprised. Ilo or the Drow as they stopped dead in their tracks. It was clear that the Drow was in a hurry to get somewhere or away from someone. Though seemingly uncertain, the Drow was still a threatening sight with his black chain mail and plate armor.

"By the powers of the Goddess Lolith, I shall kill you all." He shouted as he began his chant of protection from the presence of good. They were in too tight of space for the Drow to use any offensive spells without endangering himself, so he drew his sword and charged down toward Ilo.

Immediately, Ilo dropped the torch he was carrying down the stairs back toward the others. He could not effectively use his shield if he was also holding the torch in his left hand. The light faded and their night vision instinctively took over as their swords clashed. The smooth stone stairway did not provide enough room to get a full swing of a long sword, so most of Ilo's attacks were jabs up at the Drow. The Drow's short sword was more adaptable to the narrow surroundings.

Kura picked up the torch and backed the others down the stairway to allow Ilo more room to fight. He watched the sparks fly as the swords would occasionally strike the walls around them. He thought of what he could do to help as his friend fought the Drow single handedly. The Dwarf looked at the staff he was given by the Goddess Mirana, then at the war hammer hanging from his belt. He suddenly remembered what Lady A'mora had taught about fighting with the invisible hammer. He would not need to be close to the enemy, only within sight. He handed the torch to the soldier behind him and began to chant.

Ilo had suffered several wounds from his attacker's sword while inflicting little damage himself on his dark opponent. With no assistance he began to tire when he saw the Drow flinch dramatically. He was uncertain what caused the reaction as the Drow himself was taken by surprise. With his ability to see better in the darkness, he detected that the Drow received some sort of injury to the head. He pressed his attack harder thinking he had some ally attacking the dark Elf from behind, perhaps what the Drow was running from. Their swords continued to clash as Ilo took a few steps up toward his weakened foe. Again he saw the Drow flinch from the mysterious blow to the head. Ilo as yet could see no attacker even with his night vision.

* * *

The clatter of hooves echoed through the canyon walls. He knew the horses were near but stood steady at the secret entrance to the main doors of the castle. The Orc waved his sword at the Magdarn soldiers to direct them to the bridge.

"Battle, cross bridge." The turned warrior exclaimed in his only language. Fortunately the instructions were simple enough for the Magdarn to understand.

They had already been told by Quintar the Gnoll, that there would be a battle at the northern bridge into the valley. The Magdarn existed for the sole purpose of protecting Moracles, and if he had returned, they would not be seeking battle outside of the castle. It was apparent that the intruders had not made it this far into the canyon so the old soldiers rode past the main entrance off toward the stables in the caves.

Again they spotted an Orc soldier guarding the cave entrance. He too waved them past to the bridge. "Go, bridge." He said in the Orcish tongue that some of the Human Magdarn knew. "Help Gnolls. Push enemy." He demanded, almost in a panic.

"You two, Take our horses and see to the master's safety. We will remain here to guard the canyon if the cowardly Dwarves make it past the bridge." The lead Magdarn motioned to his men to dismount and hand the reins to those who would proceed into the stables. With the horses reins tethered together, the two old warriors proceed quickly into the narrow cave entrance. The eight remaining Magdarn drew their weapons and stood in formation across the canyon in two staggered rows awaiting the enemy attack. "We will let them come to us this time, rather than walking into another trap." One of the bearded warriors said.

"Those devious peasants fought like women." Another of them said and laughed. "And ran like them too." A third joined in. They laughed with their gravely voices and the comments were followed by several others derogatory remarks.

The Orc insisted again that they move on to the battle at the bridge. He was noticeably nervous about something as he stood just behind them at the crevice in the wall listening but not understanding their conversation. It was apparent that they were not going to leave and follow his instructions.

One of the Magdarn closest to him turned and took a few steps toward the Orc while pointing his sword at him. "We stay. Protect Moracles." He insisted. The words clear to the Orc as spoken by a master rather than an equal. A thought then struck the Human as being odd. He turned to the others and called out. "Didn't that Orc general claim that all of his men were killed and he was the only surviving Orc in the valley?"

The others turned around while thinking over the situation. "That's right. There were no more Orcs." Another said as he too approached the Orc with sword pointed.

Although Lord Shi'roc's new guard did not understand exactly what they were saying, he did know that the Magdarn were becoming increasingly threatening. He raised the sword Lord Shi'roc had given him and prepared to defend himself, not realizing what he had in his hands.

"Look at that." The Magdarn said with surprise. Then he spoke to the Orc in its own language. "Where you get?" The warrior pointed to the beautifully crafted weapon in the Orc's hands.

Thinking as quickly as the Orc could, he came out with an amazingly good lie. "Kill mountain leader." Though plausible, the Magdarn soldiers were not entirely fooled by the Orc, but they did lower their swords while they thought it over.

The pause was just enough. "Now." The word came from Grefden to attack. First the archers fired arrows at close range from just above road level. Their aim was to perforate as many of the eight old Magdarn as possible and distract them. At that range, many of the arrows were accurately placed to penetrate the gaps in their armor. Some aimed for the legs while others aimed for the upper areas of the arms and chest. Since most of their backs were to one side of the canyon wall, several were critically incapacitated with spinal injuries from directed arrows.

Sha'la had also managed to get to her feet and put a crossbow bolt through the shoulder of a Magdarn between his breast plate and shoulder plates. A finely placed shot. By the time she reloaded, the rest of the survivors had emerged from their shadowed crevices along the road to assault the enemy.

"Traitor." The Magdarn shouted at the Orc as an arrow pierced his back, clearly done to assist the Orc. A single arrow was not going to take a Magdarn out of a battle so the two attacked the Orc. With both hands on their swords they swung fiercely, outmatching the Orc despite their wounds.

Though he knew his death was imminent, the Orc knew he had accomplished his goal in setting the trap for the enemy. He could die a proud warrior. He wished for his new master, the Lord Shi'roc, to know that he died well in battle, so he fought with all his strength against the two Human warriors. Their swords clashed as the Orc battled one, then the other. He had not realized that his actions were enhanced by the graceful balance of the Dwarven sword in his hand. It seemed to flow with his bodies' movements which were far from that of a graceful warrior, hacking at the old Magdarn. Each of them receiving serious wounds as did the Orc.

The brief battle with the six remaining enemy warriors continued in the canyon path. Grefden, Gor and their twenty survivors, each taking their turns at the Magdarn soldiers. Even having been wounded and outnumbered three to one, it was an even match. They still held their own down to the last one. Swords and shields clashed as the injured survivors wore down their enemy. The archers remained in their perches ready to take advantage of any clear shot at the Magdarn soldiers. Another opportunity did not present itself as the combat was close and fierce.

The two Magdarn attacking their former ally had left their backs plainly unprotected and open to more arrow attacks. The archers on the far wall of the canyon carefully placed their shots as not to hit their new Orc friend. Arrows or not, the Magdarn continued their assault hacking at the fallen Orc, trying desperately to defend himself to his last breath. The old Humans turned from their victory, each still with arrows protruding from their backs, their chests and arms covered in their own blood. They had gotten their revenge by killing the traitor. Gor and Grefden made the final death blows to the Magdarn, severing their bearded heads from their bodies in one swift swing as the bearded ones laughed at death.

Two more of the survivors had been killed and eight more severely wounded during the conflict. The cleric apprentices had done what they could for their wounded companions during the combat, removing them from harm as other fighters took their places. They bound the wounds and performed what little healing powers they had to stop the bleeding, but much of the damage was too severe. The other soldiers assisted each other with the more minor wounds. Not one came away unscathed, except the archers who remained perched above the canyon pathway. Even Grefden and Gor, the most experienced warriors, were covered in blood, some of it their own. All of them were staggering from exhaustion, but Grefden managed to look up to Sha'la and give a wave to let her know that he had survived.

* * *

There was barely enough torch light to guide the two Magdarn to the stables, unaware of the battle that took place after their departure. It had been so long that they were gone, there was no point in the Gibbers keeping the whole cave lit. They aimed the string of horses for the single light at the end of the cave. Normally the stable hands would come running out of the wooden structures to assist the warriors with their horses. The riders detected no movement in the shadows as they approached. Could they all have run off while the army was away? That would not be unrealistic.

"Take the horses." The one said. "I will go on ahead up the passage. Meet me in the dining hall." He then dismounted in front of the stables, handing the reins to the other. He then saw the group of Gibbers tied together at the stable doorway, struggling to get loose. Their small hairy bodies wriggling to break free of the ties and the gags in their mouths. He drew his sword and raced for the secret passage. The torch on the wall was lit, showing that the doorway had been left open. This was not allowed by the castle rules. "Hurry, someone is inside the castle already." He called to his companion.

The other Magdarn had just cut the Gibbers loose when he heard his friend call. The smelly creatures hurried to tend the horses brought in by the Magdarn warriors. They had no other thoughts on their minds like trying to explain their circumstance or who had caused them to be bound and gagged. They continued about their work like nothing had ever happened. "I'll be there shortly." He called back.

The first warrior awaited at the stone passage doorway. From the shadows behind the torch came the sword thrust of another Human warrior. The Magdarn, unprepared caught the full thrust of the blade in his back. He cried out, more in rage than in pain. He pulled himself away from the cowardly rear assault, turned and drew his sword to meet his attacker. The young Human was surprised that the elderly warrior could still fight and lost his advantage of surprise. He was slashed on the arm by the first swing of his opponent, causing him enough pain to drop his weapon. The raged Magdarn swung again showing no mercy for the unarmed man. The Old warrior was more than able to keep up a good fight. The survivor tried to fend off the crashing blows of the sword with his shield, but was unsuccessful in the end. The strength of the seasoned warrior was overpowering, knocking him to the ground.

The old warrior drove his sword in a downward thrust as he stood over the young man, tearing through the Dwarven armor. He retracted the bloody sword and staggered back as the other survivor again jabbed his short sword into the lower back of the Magdarn. Blood was gushing from the two deep wounds and the crusty soldier toppled over when the sword was withdrawn.

His companion raced to join the fight with the intruders. He avenged his friends death in a violent berserk reaction, yelling as he thrashed the other young Human with barely a struggle. The Human's short sword was no match for the Magdarn's battle ax. Though wounded by the brash youngster, he remained ready to continue the fight. He quickly looked around for more of the enemy, then rushed up the dark passage.

* * *

Ach'med became annoyed at the unseen attacker behind him, but assumed that it was some result of the chanting he was hearing from down the stairwell. As a Drow, he was aware of such incantations. He became even more furious at his enemy and jabbed repeatedly at the Elf below him, knocking him off balance as he continuously defended with his shield. Although he had called for the blessings of his evil god to protect him from these powers of good beings, somehow the spiritual hammer had broken through his clerical shield of dark magic.

Kura kept focusing the attacks by the invisible hammer, directing it with his own war hammer in hand, as a conductor would direct the minstrels in a king's gallery. There was something special about his concentration through the war hammer. When he had created the hammer back in the mountains, he carefully engraved his name and that of the Goddess Mirana, on the handle. He had meant it as a tribute to her teachings and the spiritual guidance that he had received by her. But now she had somehow enhanced his strength and the hammer had become a blessed artifact. Kura could feel the power pulsing through the carved wooden handle but was uncertain of its effect.

The fighting became more vigorous as the Drow had backed down Ilo's advances. The Dwarven soldiers wanted so badly to advance and help him but there was no room to move past. They could only wait until one of the Elves was victorious. Both seemed to be wounded and exhausted from the continuous melee. They were now fighting halfway between stair landings.

Ilo now realized why Lord Lorentz was so insistant that stamina drawn from the adrenalin within the body was so important in a battle. It was all that kept him from collapsing under the weight of exhaustion. Ilo, frustrated by his lack of progress in the combat became increasingly more aggressive in his swings, opening himself up for dangerous strikes. The Drow saw the opening and took advantage of it, jabbing into Ilo's unprotected chest area. Ilo collapsed with a crash of shield and armor onto the stairs.

Kura shouted his last invocation and with all his strength, threw his war hammer directly at the dark Elf. It flew as straight and hard as if an arrow flung from its bow. The hammer bashed into the tightly woven black chain mail armor, knocking the Drow several steps back up the stairs. To his own surprise and to that of the Dwarves watching, the hammer, after hitting the enemy bounced back directly into the Dwarf's hand as if commanded by some magical source.

Kura, being more concerned for his friends safety, rushed to Ilo. He and another Dwarf carried the limp body down to the first stair landing where he began his healing incantations. The other soldiers assisted by removing the battered armor from his body and binding the bleeding wounds. With the light of the torch he was able to see his progress, pressing on the open gashes and calling forth the healing powers of the goddess.

Whispers were passed up from the dining hall. "Someone is coming." The humans who were guarding the main doorway retreated to the corners as they would be unable to fight in the darkness. The Elves moved across the room to better hide in the shadows and see who it was that would enter the room. The Dwarves were gathered at the stairs hiding around the corner.

The door slowly opened as the Elven warriors used their superior night vision to identify if Lord Shi'roc had returned. As the warrior stepped into the room, it was plain to see that he was much taller and larger than the Lord Shi'roc. The young warrior shouted out in Elvish, "It is not Shi'roc." and the battle began.

* * *

He looked in both directions as he reached the torch lit hallway. Again he found that the secret doorway had been left open in violation of the master's orders. There must indeed be intruders inside the castle. The hallway to the right showed no sign. To the left, the hall was dark. He ran toward the darkened dining hall doors and found that one of them had been left open a crack. With the bloody head of his weapon, he slowly pushed the door inward to the right. The room was also dark. He stood in the doorway ready for battle while he peered into the room looking for shadows.

As his eyes adjusted, he saw flickering torch light from the corner of the room at the stairs. He took a few steps in with a raised shield on his left arm and ax in his right hand. He was startled by a shout in the language of Elves and was suddenly attacked by several small warriors. He swung his ax and shield wildly as he was at a disadvantage in the dark. He could barely see that small shadows raced from the stairway into the room. All the Magdarn knew was that there were several shorter beings attacking him from all directions. His shield clashed with swords and he felt the sting of edged weapons at the back of his legs as well.

He continued to move through the room, slashing and clanging his way, feeling the pain of his wounds. He could only guess that he had wounded or killed several of his attackers as it seemed less movement. He swung his powerful ax again in a downward motion to clear his forward path. It came down with a thunderous crash as its blade was buried in one of the dining tables. Before he could pull the weapon from the solid wood, he felt three more stabs of pain from his legs and lower back.

He fell to his knees and drew a short sword from his sheath as he was continuously hacked by his enemy, eventually driving him to the floor from pain and exhaustion. The last thing he saw was several torches being lit around him as his eyes closed forever.

Chapter 29
Sorcery

Still watching from the double doors at the side of the temple, Shi'roc could see that both A'mora and Lorentz were being worn down by the dark powers. For some time the three had been bantering back and forth their magical spells and calling upon the gods for resistance against the other. He was hesitant to disturb the concentration of his friends but needed to find some way to give them the slightest advantage, a way to distract the old Human enough for Lorentz to take charge of the combat.

Though only minutes had passed, it seemed like hours to the Elven warrior. He wanted to take action and was growing impatient at not being able to help his companions. He regarded Jantez scorched body laying just inside the room. It was apparent that the impetuous young Human had tried to sneak up on the evil priest and was torched by some walloping flame for his attempt. His sword and shield were still in his grasp.

Through the slightly open door he had watched the three conjure up similar spells to use against one another. The alter and walls behind it wore evidence of the flames as did Moracles and Lorentz. How long could they hold out against the powers of the evil gods?

A blast of lightning from Moracles finger tips caught A'mora by surprise throwing her back over the stone benches. The Elf's anger almost exploded, but he held his composure knowing he could do her no good in a rage. He thought about what he had just seen. Shi'roc had been exposed to magic long enough to notice that the spell was not invoked from the mage's memory, but instead released instantaneously from a ring on Moracles' finger triggered by a single word. He suddenly remembered that Lorentz had empowered the ring on his own finger with spells. One of which would throw a blast of flame as he had seen used before.

With A'mora, possibly badly injured and his rage growing, he was certain that now was the best time to intervene, before Lorentz too was overpowered. He saw Jantez move slightly as A'mora had been hurled back by the lightning bolt. He might have also just been waiting for the right moment to attack. The Human warrior had learned something after all about knowing when to fight and not to. He had been feigning death or unconsciousness long enough to be ignored by Moracles. A good plan, Shi'roc thought, but one that would get the boy killed.

Seeing his love tossed about the room caused him to react. But before the raged warrior could get to his feet, he heard a call from behind him. "Fiero" echoed through the room as another intense ball of flame soared over his head toward the alter, behind that the mage was conducting his spells. The blast took the evil priest by surprise and enveloped him in flames briefly. He could see the scorched Human turn in surprise and anger, as he called forth the powers of his ring to take him to another place. He had vanished from sight and the room fell silent.

Jantez reached under his armor for a pocket in which Lord Lorent'z blue potion of healing awaited its use. He was in such pain that he could barely sit up. With his scorched finger tips he delicately held the vial to his mouth and grabbed the cork stopper with his teeth. With one toss he downed the sweet liquid that he believed would begin his healing process. He lay back down as he could feel the warmth of the magical spell rush through his body.

The air was foul with the smell of fire, burnt flesh and the ozone of a lightning strike. Shi'roc and Lorentz both rushed to A'mora who had been rendered unconscious from the fall more than the lightning bolt itself. Her clothing was still smoldering from the strike. Her golden hair was soaked with blood from hitting her head on the stone bench.

She was struggling to regain consciousness on her own when Lorentz placed his hand on her forehead to heal the wounds from within. He chanted the blessings of his goddess and moments later, A'mora opened her eyes.

They all sighed a breath of relief as she looked at each of her friends in turn. In a struggling weak voice she spoke. "Did we win? Is he gone?" She asked as she began to sit up between the stone pews.

"Yes, Moracles is gone." Lorentz answered. "But we have not won." He shook his head in disappointment, now feeling the pains from the wounds he suffered at the hands of magic. It was not the first time that the elements and studies of science had been turned against him, but it was the first time he had been defeated by them. He looked at Shi'roc. "We must find him again. He must have transported himself to a secret place of safety where he could hide and heal." He helped A'mora to sit up on the floor. She was far from being well enough to go chasing after the mage again. The others were also in need of mending and rest. For now they would remain here in the temple.

* * *

"Look." One of the archers shouted. "A Dragon has been sent to destroy us." All of the bowmen drew their sights on the large creature that was descending upon them. Panic struck the others thinking that these were their final moments.

"No, wait!" Grefden shouted as he could see that the creature had no wings. Although he had never seen a Gold Dragon before, he had heard tales from his master Shi'roc about a great wingless Dragon that he had helped sometime in the past. The warrior remembered that the Golden Dragon was a sign of good, not evil. "The dragon will not harm us." As it came floating closer they could all see that it had a rider who appeared to be an old bearded man. Could Moracles have captured such a creature to be used against them? It was possible as he knew of Shi'roc's tale.

"Where is Shi'roc?" The voice called down as the golden scaled wonder hovered just above the passage. "We are here to help." The old man said something to the Dragon then jumped from the saddle and floated to the ground thirty feet or so below him.

The archers had lowered their bows, realizing that even at that close range they would have been dead by now if the dragon had wanted them so. None of them had ever encountered such a creature but the stories of the bards that some of them had heard, told of these creatures destroying a town with one blast of their fire breath. This dragon was not as large or gruesome as those described in legend. Their minds were all filled with these stories that were now to be erased. This dragon had a grace and beauty, floating magically in front of them.

"Fear me not." The dragon spoke to them all without a sound. He looked at the archers on the walls. "I too wish to destroy Moracles." The thought of the words somehow filled their minds as he ascended back up and over the crest of the canyon walls. His words brought them peace and comfort, a new courage to continue the fight.

Fendal could see that the area had evidenced the battle just fought. Although the Magdarn bodies had been drug into the cave entrance, the ground was clearly scarred with scuffled foot prints and drying blood. "Moracles army is just around the bend in the canyon." He told the Human warrior who towered above him. "What is your plan? you will not defeat them with the few you have here." He gestured around to the troops that were all in need of healing except for those high on the wall.

"Our main forces are down the road near the bridge." He pointed with his sword. "Moracles army is to believe that they should continue on to there to fight the battle. We will hide here." His men were already climbing back into their rock crevices to await the passing of Moracles troops.

Fendal looked around disapprovingly at the blood soaked ground. "What did you intend to do about all of this?" He looked at the warrior and received nothing but a shrug. "Go and hide yourselves. I will take care of it." He waved off to those above as well. "Hide! Hide!" he called.

He bent down and scooped up two handfuls of dirt. The mage began to speak to the skies as he held out his arms to his sides and spun as fast as he could, leaving a circular trail of dust. The movement of his robes created a sort of wind that increased in strength as he twirled faster, clearly now not of his own power but from some unseen source. A whirlwind had arisen from his spot that was powerful enough to cover the ground with dust and even to cover the foot prints of the battle and the entire area. The old man disappeared in the funnel of wind.

As the wind died down, Grefden and the others could now hear the shouts of the monsterous army approaching. What they were saying could not be understood, but they were in a hurry. There was a powerful looking Hobgoblin riding a horse leading the pack with the Gnoll riding along side. The rest were marching at a fast pace toward the intended battle sight. They had been instructed by the Orc at the main entrance of the castle to hurry to the bridge. The area was still filled with flying dust that helped obscure their sight and helped to hide the survivor soldiers as the evil army passed. Grefden watched in silence from his hidden crevice as the last of the enemy had moved beyond their position. There were more than he had thought left alive after their battle in the mountains. He hoped that Lord Lorentz' plan worked at the bridge.

*   *   *

The lone Orc waited at the secret main entrance to the castle as he was told. He had succeeded in convincing the enemy, his former allies, that the battle raged on at the bridge. The good Orc stood tall as the two horse drawn wagons slowed to a halt before him. "What you do?" He spoke to the furry creatures who had been driving the wooden carts. They seemed not to be interested in answering him. The Orc was used to being ignored by the more powerful soldiers in Moracles' ranks but not by the castle slaves. He grabbed one of the little beasts by the arm as it carried in a sack of leftover food into the castle. "What you have?"

The Gibber dropped the sack, spilling its contents of breads and dried meats. "Take food to kitchen." The servant replied as he bent down to gather the spilled food. The others passed him by as they too returned the unused food supplies to the castles main kitchen pantry. They had left the horses and wagons unattended since there was no passage wide enough to bring the bulky carriages. They would return later to walk the horses to the stables at the other cave entrance.

As the dirty creatures continued down the dark crevice to the main castle doors, he noticed that a chunk of previously cooked meat had been left behind from the upset sack. The Orc looked around to see that no one was near then reached down and scarfed up the meat. He ate frantically as he had not eaten much for days. The survivor army was very conservative with what food they had and the Orc was accustomed to eating quite well, especially lots of meat. He consumed the unknown shank and tossed the bone back up the road. Satisfied now that he was fed he rejoiced with a loud disgusting belch.

* * *

Ilo slowly opened his eyes, only to see staring down at him the unexpected but familiar sight of Kura's face. It had been several minutes since the Dwarf had begun to heal his friend. He was badly cut and bruised during his long battle fighting the Drow single handedly. "Was I dead?" The Elf managed to whisper out of an exhausted breath. He could see from the torch light that he and Kura were alone. He recognized the stair landing that they were on.

"Not quite, but it was close." The Dwarven priest replied as he helped his friend set up against the wall of the stair landing. The same wall that they believed to be some sort of secret passage, possibly like the one they came through from the cave. They were still unable to find a way to open it

"Where are the others?" Ilo asked seeing no movement up or down the stairs from that point.

Kura began to check his friends bandages again to be sure all of the external wounds were healing. "They have split up and gone searching for the Drow again." He did not wish to upset him by telling the whole truth, how he had stopped the Drow with his war hammer and then did not finish him. He quickly changed the subject. "While you were unconscious there was a Human warrior like the ones we fought in the mountain. We stopped him back in the dining hall." He exhaled an anguished sigh and continued. "Kendra and Grek were killed before it was over. They were already dead before I got to them. There was nothing I could do." The two then sat in silence, awaiting word from the others of the Drow's whereabouts.

* * *

Moracles chanted the words of healing as he lay on the bed of his private chambers. His ancient body torn and scorched by the one he was to destroy. An irony he thought, to be hurt by fire from the one whom he had sent his powerful dragon to roast several months ago. This half Elf that would hopefully die at the hands of his own brother that he himself had turned against the warrior. He expected that even now, Ach'med the Drow, was hunting down the desecrators of his domain.

"Master are you here." The voice echoed in the vast open chamber. "It is I Ach'med." The voice announced to ward off the encroaching Torg's that lurked in the darkness to protect Moracles' private chambers. Though Ach'med knew the creatures would not harm him as an apprentice chosen by their master, he still felt safer in Moracles' presence. He looked all around through the mist for signs of movement and listened for a reply. Just as he was about to speak the secret words that would propel him back to the castle, he heard Moracles' voice.

"Why are you here?" Moracles approached from the far corner of the chasm. His voice was less than pleasant, almost as if he were irritated at the Elf.

"The castle has been invaded by the enemy. I came to see that you were safe here." He then realized what his night vision was telling him about his approaching master. The varied heat patterns indicated that he had been disfigured in some way. "What has happened, my master?" The Drow asked.

"I have met with our enemy face to face." He said, holding out his arms, scarred from the magical flames that had engulfed him. Any average being would have been killed by such a burning but Moracles had been partially protected by his own magic. His robes were scorched but did not propagate the flames due to their magical fire resistance. "I believe it was your older brother who was leading the enemy against us. What happened to our army?" He said through clenched teeth.

"They must have passed them in the canyons, or the enemy entered before my army arrived and moved on to the bridge." Ach'med regarded his master. "Did you say, my brother was with them?"

They walked over to the office area and Moracles lit the candles one by one. He regarded the Elf now apparently angered with his enemy's actions. "I see that you too have met the taste of battle. Why did you not use your magic?" He carefully helped Ach'med remove his armor so they could more effectively heal his wounds. Blood also was caked in his hair from the head bashing he received from the mystical hammer.

The Drow was turning his pain into anger and focusing it towards his brother as Moracles had twisted his mind into doing. The wizard's teachings and manipulation were now having the most desired effect. "I will hunt him down and slay them myself for attacking you, my master. He turned to his master. "Were the others with him?" The bitter warrior referred to his former friends that he was convinced had left him behind. For Ach'med, the incident happened so recently. His anger towards Koloda, Fendal, Ariel, Grog and the rest had grown to such proportions for leaving him there to die, in the castle of Lord Magdelan.

"I did not recognize the other priest or the young woman with him." These were of course not the same companions that Ach'med kew long ago. Moracles did not wish to let on that he too had been surprised by the combined powers of the woman and Elf. He continued to mislead his apprentice into doing his bidding. "The young woman seemed quite attached to your brother." He knew of no such bond but remembered that it was she who tackled the warrior as the crimson Dragon was about to belch its final flames on the Elf. Again Moracles wished to plant an evil seed.

Ach'med smiled an evil grin, a trait that he picked up from his master. "I shall start with her then. It must be Ariel." He chanted quietly to himself various spells of protection from his enemy as Moracles sealed his bloody wounds. His anger grew so deep that even Moracles could feel it while healing him.

"First you must meet our army. Go to the bridge and send them back here to search the castle. Then you can have your way with Shi'roc and his friends." The mage whispered the suggestions, penetrating the thoughts and concentrations of his apprentice. The healing continued as the Drow's powers grew from his anger. "Visualize your camp at the bridge. See it in your mind. Visualize every stone, the fire, the foot of the bridge. Put yourself there now." Moracles instructed.

The apprentice mage emerged from his healing trance with a vigor and power he had not felt before. He was ready to find and crush his enemy once more. "I must go, find my army and bring them back to flush our enemy from the castle." He said commandingly. "Teach me the words of travel from one place to another." He spoke of the powers of teleportation, that were normally far beyond a mage of his experience. "I shall return and take my revenge on those who left me, and their friends." He put on his black chain male armor over his shiny dark Drow skin, as his master regarded him.

"Once you have gone, I shall return to the temple to complete the ceremony. Your friends will have been gone by now." He looked at the anxious warrior. "Repeat the words carefully after me and see in your mind where you wish to go, my friend."

* * *

The canyon walls grew wider as the army approached the long wooden bridge. They were beginning to tire as they had been marching at a hurried pace from the opposite end of the canyon since morning. Still they had seen no sign of the Magdarn who had bolted on ahead of them when they learned that Moracles had returned. Perhaps they returned to the castle to protect their master as was their original duty.

When they reached the bridge, they saw signs of dead campfires but no Gnoll soldiers. Quintar wondered what had happened. They must have driven the enemy back and chased them through the canyons. Still, he thought, someone would have remained to guard the bridge. He pulled his horse to the road side near the bridge. As the others marched on, he stopped and stood aside the path to think as the Hobgoblin on the horse led the column of troops to the bridge.

The Gnoll leader looked over the abandoned camp sites for clues as to where his men were. The fires had burned themselves out. The bed rolls were still in place around the fire pits. Tracks all around the camp led him to believe that more than just his soldiers had been here. He dismounted and looked more closely to the loose areas of dirt. There and there, he saw other footprints. Smaller ones, much smaller ones. Blood stained rocks, drag marks to the edge of the great ravine, these were all signs of a battle. His investigation led him to the edge of the bridge where the last of Moracles' soldiers had just passed. He realized that the enemy must have already been through there.

Two small trails of sparkling dark dirt, hissed and fizzled past him as they made their way along the opposite edges of the bridge. He had not seen such a phenomenon before. He took a few steps onto the bridge to watch the direction of the quickly burning dirt. He looked ahead to see that the dark trails stopped half way across the long log bridge. He was unaware of its reason. The last of the Goblin soldiers, the smallest and slowest of the groups, were now scampering past the bridges mid point.

Quintar called out to the Goblins in their own language. "Return to castle. Enemy has already passed." They stopped and looked back to see the Gnoll waving his spear over his head indicating for them to return. The column of small warriors halted and reversed their direction. The furthest of them ran on to catch the rest of the army up ahead of them that had already passed the far end of the rivine.

* * *

Ach'med suddenly found himself standing in the middle of, what was the night before, his campfire. Fortunately for him it had burned itself down to ashes. His focus for the transportation spell had been on the campfire itself. Having never experienced the effects, he did not realize how accurate the results of the teleportation would be. The last of his army was rushing past him toward the deep canyon trails. "Stop. Go back." He commanded in the common language that he expected that most of them understood.

He saw the bodies of those who stood with him in battle early that morning. Some of the dead Gnolls lay where they awoke, only to be attacked, defenseless in their beds. Others managed to get to their feet barely in time to grab a weapon and fight. He could see that there were no weapons left behind. Those scavengers must have taken them he thought. He did not see the remains of his personal demon guards. He wondered where they had gone.

Some of Moracles' soldiers, his soldiers though he had not been properly introduced, ran over to him as if to attack. Ach'med realized that they did not recognize him or his authority and shouted again. "I am Vandar, apprenticed to the great Lord Moracles." He held up his hand in a commanding gesture. Before him stood several large bug bears and Hobgoblins. "We must return to the Castle. The enemy has already passed here and is in the fortress.

Just then they heard the yells of a small Goblin running to the end of the bridge. He indicated to them, and the Drow, that Quintar ordered them to return to the other side of the bridge. They could see the Gnoll waving his arms frantically over his head and the band of Goblins returning across the bridge.

"Yes, rally the others," The Drow commanded. "We must hurry." All of them hastened back across the bridge with the dark Elf in the lead. He noticed just as they approached the center of the bridge, the sparkling dirt leaving a trail on both sides of the wooden logs. It disappeared between a joint as an enormous eruption exploded the logs into splinters, throwing them into the air. Some of them bounced from the supporting bridge frames as they fell aimlessly downward.

The Gnoll and the goblins watched as the other soldiers fell into the great ravine, their screams of pain and terror at having the bridge ripped from under them, echoed through the canyon. As the smoke cleared they spotted several bugbears dangling onto the shredded wood and ropes. The gap in the bridge was only a jump apart for the agile Gnoll but a bit of a struggle for the bulkier Bugbears and Hobgoblins. The Drow had also disappeared from sight having been in the center of the explosion, he too must have fallen to his death or been blown apart in the blast.

Suddenly, the bridge head was filled with Dwarves, attacking the evenly matched Goblins in one on one combat. Though the evil creatures were more experienced in battle, the Dwarves made up for it with superior strength and cunning. Many of the small Goblins broke free of the skirmish and ran back toward the castle. The others were soon defeated by the Dwarven warriors.

The Gnoll quickly found himself disadvantaged by several of the savage creatures hacking at his furry legs with their swords and axes. He reeled in pain as he responded with low sweeping motions of his spear, temporarily driving them away. He swept in front and was attacked from the rear. He turned and was gouged again. Though he inflicted seriously damaging wounds on several of the small

Dwarves, their moral seemed not to be disrupted. Quintar jabbed in anger as he fought for his life. The stakes were now different. His life was more important than serving the great mage who had not appeared to help his armies during battle.

Overall, the combat went well for the survivor army, though some of the enemy had gotten through. The Dwarves had held up their duty in destroying the bridge thus separating the army from the castle. Still, the bulky Hobgoblins and Bugbears made attempts to jump the dismantled bridge with little success. Their armor was too heavy for them to gain any agility for the long jump. Others were still hanging on to the ropes and fallen logs trying to climb back up.

One of the younger Dwarves who was not quite old enough to fight, remained hidden in one of the rocky crevices away from the battle. His mother and the others who did not learn to fight were also in hiding back further along the road away from the bridge. Borak was carrying supplies for the soldiers and was instructed to stay put until the fighting was over. He watched his father battling the enemy with a strength and courage that inspired him. Some day he too would become a protector as his father. He saw many of his neighbors fall in the combat. Some were killed while others were rescued by the powers of the mysterious cleric apprentices. He watched as the prayers kept them from being noticed by the enemy so they could tend to the wounded and drag them from the battle area.

Nearly all of the enemy on this side of the bridge had been slain but at a great cost to the Dwarves. Borak saw his father fall as he battled the giant furry creature with the long spear. The young Dwarf cried out in anger as one of the priests rushed over to his father. There was nothing to be done for him as his wounds were beyond their abilities. Through his tears he noticed that one of the other larger creatures had crawled up from the foot of the bridge. It looked pretty badly beaten by the explosion but nonetheless was going to attack the unsuspecting Dwarves.

Borak called out, but his warnings went unheard. He dropped the packs of supplies he had been carrying and ran toward the creature who was still climbing up the edge of the ridge. On the way to the enemy, he picked up a sword that had been tossed aside and lifted the heavy weapon over his shoulder. He ran as fast as his stubby legs could carry him and with all of his strength, swung the sword in a sideways motion. Though the creature was much larger than he had thought, it had just gotten to its feet when the sword struck its left leg, cleaving it viciously from the rest of its body. The creature didn't even have time to react before the weight of its body hurled him backward into the rocky ravine, wailing in agony.

The young Dwarf had never thought himself to be especially strong, but never had the chance to test it. He was always given the boring tasks to do in the mountain because he was not considered old enough or smart enough. None of the other soldiers had noticed what had just happened but turned back to see the lad standing near the edge of the ravine with the sword in his hand. They did see that the Hobgoblin leader that was on horseback had cleared the path on the other side of the bridge and was about to jump the hole in the bridge.

The remaining Dwarves gasped at the sight of the powerful warrior with plate armor, successfully leaping the gap to their side of the bridge. He galloped onward swinging his huge war hammer. It was apparent that his first victim was to be Borak who was still looking down into the ravine at the fallen Bugbear. What was that he was so intent on seeing?

"Borak, look out." called one of the Dwarven warriors. The few that were left to fight looked at each other in dismay then cried out an attack, knowing that it would probably be futile. Their deaths would be imminent after attacking this mounted menace.

Just as the mounted enemy soldier reached the end of the bridge, Borak looked up and ducked the massive wooden headed hammer, causing the attacker to be off balanced by the weight of his swing. It seemed that he was intent on massacring the little one, as he recovered and reared his horse back toward him in a run for the bridge. Borak now stood in the center of the road at the first log taunting the angry beast. It charged and swung again at the child who ducked and rolled to the edge of the ravine causing the soldier to over run the mark by running back onto the bridge.

The Dwarven soldiers were still running toward the bridge now behind the creature as they saw the youngster duck and roll to the side of the bridge. Just then, they saw a golden Dragon arise from the canyon alongside the enemy. The dragon carried a saddle with what appeared to be a wizard in flowing robes. The Dwarves stopped dead in their tracks fearing that Moracles had just appeared. They noted that the dragon flew casually without having any wings.

The enemy that had been trapped on the opposite side seemed to rally just before the amazing creature blasted the bridge and it's occupants with its fiery breath. It engulfed the horsemen and several of the other soldiers who had been climbing along the wooden supports. Their screams echoed as their flaming bodies plummeted into the canyon ravine. The remainder of the enemy fled to the safety of rock on the other side of the canyon.

Borak climbed to his feet brushing himself off as the other Dwarves ran to his side. They all looked over at the hovering dragon and its rider who waved a sign of friendship, then floated up above the canyon walls.

* * *

"I wonder what is going on." The Bone spoke to the statue of his magical steed that he held in his hand. The once powerful leader had been hiding, no, waiting in his self made ice chamber in the center of the upper maze of halls. He had hoped that those who he suspected of attacking and possibly defeating his enslaver, Moracles, would soon make it so. "He has not called upon me as of late. He must be preoccupied with his new apprentice or preparing the ceremony of the dual eclipse." He mumbled to himself.

The fact that the dual eclipse of the aligned moons would enhance the powers of a mage was well known among the rulers of the lower planes. It was said that Hartes himself had managed to arrange for such an event once every hundred years. It had started as a joke among the evil Gods until the clever ones learned to use it to train apprentices. This was the case with Moracles. He had once before, on this hundred year anniversary, used such enhanced powers to create this land of canyons, this Valley of Mazes to announce his arrival and completion of his training by Hartes himself.

The room was barren of any furnishings save for the carved throne of ice on which he sat. He had no need of gaudy possessions. His residence in the castle consisted of this room and an adjoining sleeping chamber, also created from the ice that he called forth. His bed consisted of rotted branches and vines, not unlike the nest of a large bird. The freezing temperatures were self imposed and reached out to the nearby meandering halls. No one dared disturb him so there were no doors on the rooms, just sheets of ice and dangling icicles.

Suddenly a disturbing feeling overcame him. Yes, as he had feared, Moracles was summoning him from his secret study chambers. As much as he would like to resist the summons, he could not. This was indeed proof that his tormentor was still alive and well. Once again, the Bone called forth the mighty black horse from his miniature statue condition. "Blackfire" he said, as the tiny creature came to life in the full size, snorting its smoky breath. The former master of the coldest corner of hell mounted the steed and vanished into the plane of mists that was the fastest way to Moracles chambers.

In the blink of an eye, the two materialized on the black marble floor in the center of the massive chamber. Before him stood his master who showed the signs of being in some sort of battle. The refracted sunlight through the top of the open gorge allowed the Bone to see his master's condition. The wizards robes were burned and his arms scarred from a fire. He also noticed that some of his long white beard had been burned away as well. The mage was tired and angered, but the Bone did not know why as yet.

He dismounted the steed and bowed as usual with mock respect for his master by default. There was no point in resisting and he might learn what had been going on by cooperating. "What are your desires, my master."

"Where have you been?" The old man demanded. "Our enemy has penetrated the castle and eluded our armies. Why haven't you stopped them?" His anger out weighed his usual diplomacy and tact, leaving the Bone ample opportunity of a reprisal.

The thin large frame of the creature again stood upright, holding a secret rejoicing at knowing his enslavement may soon be brought to an end. Once the enemy had vanquished Moracles, the spell that held him on this world would be broken. "If you had allowed me to control the army, this would not have happened." He said evenly. "Your new apprentice may not be up to the challenge of commanding such a force as I had." He bowed his head slightly to Moracles.

The evil priest ignored the Bone's insolence. "I was attacked in my own temple by a pair of mages and warriors. You will go there and make sure the room is vacant so that I may continue my preparations for Lolith and Hartes." He insisted.

The Bone fought hard to keep a smile from his gleaming white face. He bowed his head. "Yes my master. I shall go to the temple and rid it of your enemies." He mounted his horse with a new zeal hearing that the Elf wizard, thought dead, was still alive and now inside the castle. He must find him and somehow help him to find Moracles again.

* * *

Shi'roc carefully examined the passage leading out of the opposite side of the temple from which they came in. The hallway had no door making it extremely dangerous. He noted that just beyond the opening was a small door, maybe to a closet or adjoining room. With sword in hand he quietly stepped past the door and checked with his night vision down and around the connecting corridor. It was similar to the hallway from which they came, long and narrow. He remembered how Gol gave his life to stop the spider creature from following them. He knew it would be difficult for his friend, Jantez, to accept, but he had told him what had happened.

The Elf then stepped back to examine the wooden door. The handle seemed to be unlocked indicating that there was little importance to the rooms contents. There was no sound nor light coming from under the door. He moved the handle to the opened position and pushed the door open just a crack. No response led him to push the door open further with sword at the ready. Nothing was revealed as he peaked his head around the corner and looked into the small room. He had been right, just a storage closet of some type.

He glanced back into the dimly lit temple where Lorentz had been concentrating his healing powers on A'mora and Jantez. If they were to continue their pursuit of the old mage priest, they would have to be at their peak performance. Shi'roc was the first to be healed so that he could stand guard over the others while Lorentz prayed. The wounds he received from fighting the spider-Elf were closed but his body was still sore, especially from his acrobatic jump down the stairs. It was far from graceful considering the weight of armor he wore.

So far they had been lucky that Moracles had not returned or called on any of his creatures to attack them in the temple. Perhaps there was some sacred creed as to not fighting in this temple. He wanted so badly to examine the finely carved stone statues on either side of the altar but he needed to stand guard on this open area. He turned back and listened again with his acute Elven hearing for movement around the corner of the hallway. Nothing there, he determined.

Jantez apparently had recovered from his serious burns and walked down the center isle of stone benches to the main double doors that were still closed and had not been checked. Shi'roc noticed that the young Human was not as agile or enthusiastic after hearing of his friends death. Perhaps A'mora could help him through his loss when this was all over.

Just as Jantez had disappeared into the dark area near the double doors, a great black stallion appeared in the center of the temple with a huge white creature on its back. The horse breathed fire and its mane and hooves also glowed with a flame. Shi'roc stood fast against the wall around the corner from the temple. Jantez position was also obscured behind the creatures. This would give them some advantage when they attacked.

Lorentz looked up from his healing of A'mora and recognized the creature who had allowed him passage through the mist before falling from the poison inflicted by Moracles' pet. The blond woman laid back down between the benches to hide as well, leaving Lorentz as the only one to be seen. He stood up straight to gain the Bone's attention. "Why are you here." He asked to determine his intentions. "Has Moracles sent you to destroy me now?" The Elf mage spoke boldly against uncertain odds. He had learned long ago not to show fear but to attempt to take charge of any uncertain situation. He attempted to throw his potential opponent off guard.

"As a matter of fact, he has." The Bone screeched with his intimidating voice and glowing eyes. "But I would prefer that you remain hidden as my master will soon be here. You must destroy him so that I will be free." The Bone steadied his 'Blackfire' which appeared to be nervous in the presence of a being of such good nature. Its first instinct would be to attack all those of such moral standing. What the Bone did not realize was that he and his horse were surrounded by such people.

Jantez stood ready in the darkness with his sword perched over his shoulder and both hands gripping it tightly. Shi'roc had drawn his bow and arrows ready to strike. Neither of them understood what was taking place, only that they had an overpowering urge to attack the pair of creatures. A'mora as well was concentrating on defensive spells and calling upon the powers of Mirana to complete her own healing now that she had regained some strength.

Lorentz realized what the Bone was saying. He was a prisoner of Moracles, entrapped as a creature of servitude. He called out to the others not to attack. "Quickly, do as he says. Remain hidden and await Moracles to return. This may be our last chance." Shi'roc and Jantez were confused at the trust Lorentz had put in the words of this evil being. What if this was some sort of trap to keep them here while reinforcements arrived?

The Bone was confused as well, thinking that he was alone with the Elf mage being the only other in the room. He looked around hurriedly and saw behind him a warrior standing in the shadows, and another lurking near the cloak room of the temple. “Steady, my friend.” He said to his horse. “You must remain calm if we are to convince Moracles.” The Bone was impressed with the Elf and his stealthful companions. “You must all leave the temple before Moracles arrives.” He bowed his head to Lord Lorentz.

A’mora and Jantez moved out of the temple through the double doors from which they had first entered. Lorentz went to the hallway to join Shi’roc who had moved to hide around the corner of the opposite hallway near the closet. A moment later, Moracles appeared at the raised alter. Though they could not see him from their hiding positions, they all listened to his words with the Bone.

“As you can see, my master, the Temple is quite empty.” The Bone and the horse both bowed their heads in a respectful gesture. “Do you have any further need of my services?”

“Yes, I do. You shall remain here to protect me while I complete the ceremony preparations.” The mage said with bitterness in his voice. The flesh on his arms had healed a bit more since the Bone had seen him last. “I must retrieve my fresh robes to continue.” He looked at the burned and tattered garments that he still wore. “These will not due in the presence of Lolith and Hartes.”

Lorentz and A’mora both froze in shock. They realized that they must act now to catch the evil priest by surprise before he called forth his gods. They had no idea of the mage’s intent to open up this world to the lords of evil. He must be stopped before it was too late. A’mora peeked through the space in the double doors to see the old Human walking over to the area where Shi’roc was hiding, away from her general direction. Though she feared for his life, she also knew that if anyone could slay the mage in personal combat, it would be Shi’roc. They now knew that they had inflicted great damage to the evil one before his escape.

The warrior and mage quietly remained around the dark corner of the hallway so as to not alert Moracles. The mage was headed for the closet door that the Elf had found earlier. Shi'roc perched his sword ready for one swift stroke to attack the old man knowing that if he missed or did not incapacitate the mage, he would be killed himself. The mage was almost to the temple opening when he stopped.

The Bone heard the clashing of swords and the banging of armor outside the main double doors of the temple. There was some shouting in the Dwarven language and suddenly one of the doors burst open. At first it startled the evil beings. It also surprised the rest of the group who remained in hiding. The Bone turned to the open door and screeched at the tiny creatures while shooting his glowing red eyes at them.

The Dwarven soldiers halted in terror upon seeing this massive blast of evil from within the room. One of the Dwarves pushed his way through the others and fled from the doorway. The others stood fast and repressed the urge to run in terror. The brave soldiers advanced into the room to attack the Bone on his horse.

Moracles ran back to the alter just as Shi'roc turned the corner to strike. "Kill them." Moracles shouted to his servant "When you are through, I will be waiting atop the plateau." Moracles would never participate in such a battle of swords. The mage recanted a magical phrase and vanished from the temple.

Lord Lorentz ran out from the hallway into the temple to stop the impending battle between the Bone and the Dwarves. "No, don't fight," he called out to his friends. An echo of his warning came also from A'mora entering from the other side of the room. They knew that the loss of life would be senseless.

The Elf priest called in his best command tone to the Bone. "Resist your orders." He knew that the Bone would fight to the death if necessary to carry out the orders of his enslaver. As long as there was any life in the old man, the Bone would have to obey any orders given to him by Moracles. "Fight the powers of the evil one. Leave here if you must but you have to be strong for a while longer."

Shi'roc ran to Lorentz side as he saw what was happening with the Dwarves at the door. It was too bizarre for him to understand. Lorentz was giving commands, using his voice powers of persuasion to turn such an evil creature. He had heard what Moracles had said and realized that the Bone might be helping them after all.

The Dwarves had halted their attack within the temple. The Bone reared his horse who was snorting his fire breath, both trying to resist the command to kill the little warriors. This was direct enough as not to allow any stretching of the command as he had done previously. He fought as Lorentz had commanded and the pain running through them was great, but subsided a bit as the horse let out a great whinnies and the Bone shrieked.

"Follow me through the mist to Moracles." He cried out as he and the stallion vanished. He did not know how long the pain could be controlled, if they could now fool Moracles while holding back on the direct command.

"We must go quickly while I can still track them." Lorentz grabbed Shi'roc by the arm and the two vanished with a simple word. The Bone was just ahead when he passed back through to the real world. They found themselves floating through the mist for a brief minute. Before Shi'roc could even protest the means of travel, being grasped from normal space and time, they had rematerialized. The two had followed a ways behind their suspicious benefactor, not knowing where exactly it would take them. Moracles had mentioned the plateau, possibly above the castle.

They found themselves behind a ridge of rocks that was on top of a plateau. Lorentz surmised that it was the highest point of the canyon where the castle was hidden. Lorentz remembered this spot as he had searched the canyon for the hidden fortress just two days prior. Behind them there seemed to be a cave or tunnel of some sort, perhaps another entrance to the fortress from the top. Yes, that was the entrance to where he had found the impenetrable wall of lead rock. Around the ridge, Lorentz saw the Bone and his horse bowing to the great evil mage. So far the two had convinced him that the temple was once again rid of the enemy.

Lorentz concentrated on the few offensive spells that he had studied for the day's work. There was no time to review any new items from his book of spells and his memory was becoming weary. He had used most of his magical powers in the temple earlier while battling Moracles. In conjunction with an attack by Shi'roc, they might be enough to incapacitate Moracles if caught off guard.

Moracles had just given the Bone instructions to take him back to the temple on the Bone's horse. His magical spells had been overtaxed for the day and he knew that there were only a few surprises left on his ring. The Bone of course resisted the idea though he knew he had to comply and so did 'Blackfire'. Just then, the evil mage saw a large shadow rise up from beneath the edge of the plateau. The magical beast came up from behind where the Bone and his horse stood. It was a shimmering golden scaled, wingless Dragon. Moracles began to panic, realizing that somehow, the great Dragon, Zant, had come for him. The creature he once hunted and trapped, now was hunting him. How did he find the mage after all this time?

Chapter 30
Traps

The Dwarven soldiers guarded both double doors leading into the temple. They had carried or dragged the wounded inside the temple so Kura and A'mora could tend to them. Though she was far from recovered from her encounter with Moracles, A'mora was still able to help heal the wounded soldiers.

The other Human soldiers lit more torches on the temple walls in case they did need to fight their way out. It was also a help to Lady A'mora with her healing abilities. Several of them were lying down on the benches or the floor still trying to recover from their own combat encounters. They had found their way through one of the secret stairways from what appeared to be the second floor of the castle, down to the main entry way. After meandering around they met a handful of smaller creatures with dogged faces, guards of some sort. They battled them without too many injuries to themselves. Although the size of the creatures was equal or larger than the Dwarves, the compact strength of the mountain people proved too much for the castle guards.

They eventually found the large opened double doors that led across the bridge where they met up with Kura, Ilo and the other Dwarves who were fighting the Elf / Spider creature near a cave entrance. It took a great effort by all of them to put down the already wounded beast. It was apparent that it had just been in battle with the likes of Shi'roc. The loss of the use of its spiny front legs slowed the actions and agility of the abomination.

Jantez stood near the open hallway where Shi'roc was previously positioned. Though he was only Human, his vision in the darkness and hearing was far better than most. He was not recovered himself from his burns or the loss of his friend, Gol. He did not see the final battle between Gol and the creature, but Shi'roc had told him that the Human had died bravely.

A'mora had explained to him about the legend of the creation of the Elf / Spider creatures referred to as Dryders, though she had never actually seen one before today and hoped never again. The males were known to have magical spell abilities, while a female would possess some powers of the evil goddess who caused their form to be. Jantez wondered what the Lords, Shi'roc and Lorentz were doing and why they were trusting the Bone. The enemy army could return at any moment and have them all trapped in the temple. They had no way of knowing what had happened outside the castle in the canyon passage. Had the enemy been brought down by their surprise forces or had Grefden and Gor been defeated by Moracles army?

Ilo slowly approached the alter to examine it and the statues around it. He too was still recovering from massive wounds that Kura deemed near fatal. He was certainly in no condition to be fighting and hoped that it would all be over soon so he could get back to his family left in the cave back at the dried lake bed. He wondered what his wife and daughter would think about all of this fighting. He never thought himself to be a warrior at all until a few weeks ago.

"Who do you think they are?" The Elf asked Jantez from the altar. There was enough light now to see the carved stone figures with relative detail. The evil spider queen all in black webbed robes with a spider on her shoulder.

"That must be Lolith, the creator of the spider creatures." Jantez replied after recalling what A'mora had told him. He stepped toward the statue to join Ilo for a closer look. "She looks so beautiful. But Lorentz taught us that evil mostly hides behind such beauty." He was tempted to run his finger along the smoothly polished stonework, then thought better of it. Lorentz also taught he and Gol not to touch anything unfamiliar to them without first checking the item for possible magical properties. These statues would certainly hold the promise of magic.

A'mora was exhausted from her healing rituals and had just finished with her last patient. It was a minor sword slash of one of the Human warriors. She was just tying off the bandage over the wound when she glanced over to see Jantez and Ilo at the statue near the altar. She thought nothing of it for a second and then realized that no one was guarding the corridor opening. The hiss of two flying arrows brought her attention to the spidery legs of another Dryder at the hallway entrance where Jantez had been standing. She called out to him but it was too late as the arrows had found their mark in Jantez' back.

The Human warrior felt the sting of the two arrows piercing his armor from behind, yet he turned with sword in hand to face his enemy. Ilo knew they could not fight and survive having been so seriously wounded earlier in the day so he ducked down behind the alter and yelled for Jantez to do the same.

"You can't win against it." Ilo called as he crawled to the far end of the altar's protection. But Jantez did not heed the warning and ran toward his attacker.

A'mora also tried to convince her lover not to stand up to the creature. She knew that they had all taken a beating and should not be diving into such a battle. The creatures were powerful in many ways. "No, don't do it," she cried as she saw Jantez run toward the spider. She then saw as the creature fully emerged from the opening that the Dryder was of female origin, a priestess with powerful spell abilities.

The rest of the beaten warriors were scrambling to their feet from whatever resting positions they were in on the floor and benches. Kura was urging them all to flee through the main doors as he helped the seriously injured Dwarves in that direction. Wisdom told him that they could not easily win against a healthy Dryder after the injuries incurred by a half beaten one.

The majority of the warriors ran to follow Kura's lead through the main double doors that led out of the temple and back toward the main entrance of the castle. They stood a better chance against the smaller guards that they had previously defeated in the main hallway, provided that there wasn't a horde awaiting them.

The Dryder chanted as she delivered two more arrows accurately into Jantez torso, piercing his armor with a screech of grinding metal to metal. He cried out as he fell onto the temple floor. There was no more he could do, laying on his side is stabbing pain. Then the creature let loose the spell upon the warrior.

It all happened so fast A'mora had barely the time to chant a spell of her own, calling upon her goddess, Mirana, to grant her a power that she had never before desired to use. Her anger had never been stronger, seeing her man struck down in such a merciless way. She prayed for the same gruesome death blades that Lord Lorentz had called forth against the crimson Dragon months ago. "Firestrum sogito abatorium sum" She chanted at her opponent as she stood alone in the center of the temple. From where she stood, she could see Ilo leaning against the far side of the altar to the right, safe from any residual effects the Dryder may retaliate with.

Jantez, immobile as he was, began to cry out in excruciating pain as the spell effect of the Dryder caused all metal on his person to heat to incredible temperatures as if it were once again being forged in a furnace. His sword became too hot to hold onto any longer. He struggled to remove his armor as the growing red hot metal seared his skin. He broke off the arrow shafts to slide off his breast plate, but had no more strength left as he passed into unconsciousness from the pain.

As she saw her lover move no more, the flash of the shimmering blades engulfed the spider creature, cutting into every part of its body. The spinning hundred blades chimed as they cut into the armor plated spiny legs dropping it to the ground. The fallen priestess of Dryders screamed as its upper torso was slashed repeatedly by the sharp magical instruments. Its bulbous spider aft spilled its oozing web liquids over the temple floor as it died horribly. Its blood had been spattered about the corner walls of the hallway and as far as where Jantez lay lifeless on the floor.

When the sounds of the blades ceased, Ilo crawled around the corner of his shelter to see the great creature laying in a pool of its own fluids and his friend Jantez, covered in its blood and his own. He arrived at the body just as A'mora arrived, weeping over a corpse she had not the power to resurrect. The heated metal armor had burned so badly into his flesh that it had become a part of him.

As much as they wanted to remove his remains from that evil place, they did not have the means or the time. They both knew they must flee and follow the rest of their party or be left behind. Neither one in their weakened condition could make it far alone so they clung to each other, the Elf and Human hurrying out of the desecrated temple. As they passed through the door and into the temple antechamber, they heard the sounds of battle once again up ahead.

Lady A'mora chanted once more while still holding on to Ilo. Her prayers were now for her own protection, that she and Ilo may pass unnoticed through the combat. They hurried up the stairs that led to the great cavern opening. Up ahead in the torch light, they could see their own battered army battling with several small but vicious warriors.

The main focus seemed to be getting across the main bridge to a set of open double doors on the other side. The torches on the bridge walls and through the doorway indicated that the enemy had been waiting and had planned this defense to keep the survivor army from escaping to the main castle.

A'mora chanted once more, now weaker than ever. Ilo now held her up as she stood at the foot of the bridge and spread her arms toward the combat. She prayed for her goddess to give her people strength and protection from the evil attackers. Then she and Ilo safely passed amongst the swinging swords and axes as the combat continued. They had made it through to the other side of the bridge weaving in and out of the path of flailing weapons to where the doors were parted.

They found themselves in a main hallway with several smaller passages connecting to it. "Which way to the main entrance?" A'mora asked as the two helped each other along.

The smaller hallways were unlit but the main had enough scattered torches to see by. "I know not." The Elf replied. "I did not come from this way, but I would guess that the widest path would be best."

* * *

As wounded and worn as the Dwarves and Humans were, the battle against the dog faced guards went well. The enemy's sword swings seemed to glance off the superior Dwarven armor. Also for some unknown reason, the wounded warriors themselves felt a rush of adrenaline that improved their accuracy and strength. Within a few moments they had cleared the bridge of the guards, slicing them open or throwing them over the bridge wall into the ravine. The resulting casualties were minor as compared to those they would have sustained if they had remained in the temple to fight the Dryder.

"Look up ahead!" one of the Dwarves exclaimed. "It is Ilo and the Lady A'mora." He pointed to the hallway far ahead with his blood drenched sword. “How did they get past us?” He looked behind to the foot of the bridge with the hallway that led back to the temple. There were no other nearby passages that they could have taken to get there.

“Lets go,” Kura directed as he pointed his staff forward across the great bridge. He held in his right hand the hammer that Mirana had somehow blessed for his defense in combat. It seemed that with only one blow, he could take out an opponent.

As they helped each other scamper across the bridge, the large iron doors began to close. A shadowy figure now floated just ahead of them between the survivors and the main hallway to their escape. One Dwarf jabbed at it with his spear that seemed to pass through the misty dark figure.

The shadow laughed and spoke to them. “You shall all die here and now.” It floated toward them just above the ground. The aberration had general human features though the details were indiscernible. It reached out with its right arm and touched one of the smaller Dwarves. The effect caused the Dwarf to feel weak and faint. No other pain or injury was felt.

Several of the Humans tried to slash at it with swords but to no avail. The edged weapons seemed to slice right through the ghostly creature without any effect. Again it touched one of them causing the already wounded warrior to collapse to his knees in exhaustion. The dark figure meandered through the crowd toward Kura, knowing that their weapons were of no threat.

“Run for the doors.” The Dwarven priest called as he raised his hammer over his head. He whispered to himself as the others ran. “May the powers of Mirana pass through this weapon.” Then with all of his strength he hurled the hand crafted stone and wood at the servant of Moracles.

The blessed weapon struck the Wraith with an unexpected thump that knocked the floating form over the wall of the bridge and into the ravine. Kura did not wait for the return of the hammer as it seemed to impale itself into its target. It vanished with the Wraith into the darkness below.

Kura barely made it in time to squeeze through the closing doors to the castle as the warriors struggled against the forces that were closing it. There was still enough torch light in the hallway for the Humans to see their way back to the main entrance they had found earlier.

* * *

The Elf's supposition proved correct, but as they were approaching what might have been the main entrance, a lone guard stood in their way. Ilo leaned Lady A'mora against a closed door as he bravely drew his sword and staggered forth to confront the creature. The two faced off, one on one. Ilo's weakened state put him at a disadvantage although the dog faced creature was about his size. He must get Lady A'mora out of the castle to relative safety. He hoped that she would try to slip by while Ilo kept the guard occupied.

Just as their swords were about to clash, the creatures eyes widened with fear and it fled down a dark narrow hallway. Ilo felt a rush of pride having stared down his opponent. He dared not pursue it at this time. When he turned back toward Lady A'mora, his pride turned to embarrassment as he saw the remainder of his soldiers led by Kura coming quietly up behind him. It was they who had scared off the guard, apparently feeling outnumbered.

A curdled scream emanated from the narrow passage where the guard had headed. The survivors waited and listened quietly to determine what had happened. They looked at one another to account for all who were with their raiding party. None were missing and they were mystified as to what had happened to the guard or at his hand.

A quiet but steady sound of footsteps emerged from the direction of the scream. The warriors froze as they saw an old Dwarf who they did not recognize, come around the corner wall. He wore finely crafted armor and held a bloodied sword. They saw dragged behind him the dogfaced guard that he had just slain.

"Who are you?" One of the younger Dwarves called out across the wide hallway in the ancient Dwarven tongue. The man's apparent age would indicate his familiarity with the older form of the language.

"Father" Kura cried out. "Could it be?" He pushed his way past the others to get a closer look at the once forgotten head armorer of the Dwarven Peaks.

"Kura?" The old man questioned, as he let fall the corpse of the enemy soldier. He dropped his sword as well and opened his arms to receive a loving embrace from his only son. The younger Dwarf cried, thinking his father had been killed so long ago.

It was indeed Kura's father, Koda, who had been thought slaughtered decades ago when the human towns had been destroyed by Moracles' army. He had been last seen trading goods in the most southern town in the valley, never to be heard from again. Fortunately for him, Moracles recognized the use of such a fine craftsman and spared his life to become the sole armorer for the evil army. His wagon of armor and weapons had been confiscated and dolled out to those creatures who were in need of it. It was as the late chief, Kyman, had said, the weapons and armor from the Dwarven craftsmen had indeed been used against the people of the valley, rather than in their defense as was its original intent.

*   *   *

Shocked at the site of the great Dragon, now grown to its full size after so many decades, the evil mage's first thought was that of protection. He had one more offensive spell remaining on his magical ring. Without warning, he launched the most powerful of fire spells with one command, “Fierum Maxima” and a blast of fire emanated from the ring. The fire was larger than any Lorentz, or Shi’roc had ever seen before, even from the mouth of a Dragon.

Zant was unprepared for such an attack and became fully engulfed in the intense flames causing him serious injury. He instantly endured so much pain that it caused him to loose concentration on his flight and began to plummet into the canyon. Fendal was also singed but mostly protected from the flames by the massive torso of the great one. He held on tight to the straps of his saddle hoping desperately that Zant would pull out of the dive. He knew that the blast alone was not enough to totally incapacitate the power of the Gold Dragon.

Just before reaching the bottom of the canyon, the great one regained his composure and ceased the descent and quickly regained his altitude following along the gorge to approach the evil one from a different direction. He then realized that the vision of the night before was to warn him not to underestimate Moracles, a warning that he had not heeded. It was not his death at all that he anticipated. Now, ready to do battle, he ascended the crest of the plateau much to the surprise of the mage.

The old Human ran as fast as he could, toward the Bone and his horse to escape the wrath of the golden Dragon, Zant. Before the trio could escape into the ethereal mists, the magical creature let go a blast of his fire breath, causing both the Bone and the mage to dive for the cover of rock. The horse, Blackfire, being a creature of Hartes’ fiery hell was unaffected by such magical flames as he too possessed similar powers.

“Command your horse to attack the Dragon.” Moracles insisted. “We must flee.” Moracles for the first time had shown his face of fear and desperation to the Bone. Never in the time since Moracles had arrived in the valley had he been so defenseless, having to defend himself from so many in one day. Although his magical and priestly powers were great, they had been worn down throughout the day. All that was left was his ring and it too had already been used during his battle in the temple.

The Bone yelled out to 'Blackfire' "Go, destroy the Dragon." That he knew was a suicidal act and would not be carried out. The magical powers with which the Bone had enslaved the horse, were the same as those used by Moracles against him. It was meant for creatures without independence or wisdom. It could not drive one to carry out fatal or suicidal commands. The horse was highly intelligent in its own right and would not obey such an order, nor would the Bone. This was an obvious sign that Moracles was becoming panicked since he knew that such an order would not be accepted.

'Blackfire' puffed his flaming breath and stomped his front hoofs in rejection of the command, as the Bone knew he would. He enjoyed seeing his enslaver nervous and vulnerable to thoughtless decisions, even though it may mean his own death as well. At least he would no longer be enslaved.

Although the skies were gray, as yet they had produced no threat of rain, when a sudden swell of clouds raged over the plateau. Lorentz continued to chant from behind the ridge. He stood up, having witnessed the confrontation of Moracles and the unknown Dragon. It was time to take advantage of the Dragon's distraction and it was apparent that Moracles had lost his confidence and most probably his spell abilities, though Lorentz too was lacking sufficient magical energy to continue an extended battle.

Shi'roc also went into action in conjunction with Lorentz magic. He quietly crept around the ridge and up behind the cave entrance. His goal was to get behind

Moracles in some way. He had continued his romp over the rocky terrain and was suddenly halted by a huge crevice in the top of the plateau. He had lost his footing on the loose rock and almost fell into this pit. It was cleverly disguised by a natural visual phenomena. He looked carefully at where he was standing and in the area beyond. To anyone not intently watching, the crevice was invisible to the eye, yet by tilting his head and leaning to ground level, he could see a vast opening that now appeared quite deep and it reached out near to where Moracles and the Bone were laying.

Being careful of his footing, the warrior crept along the edge of the secret crevice to get closer to Moracles from the other side. He could see the gold Dragon now floating and perched in front of the evil ones that were cowering behind a rock ridge. The fiery horse was standing just between them and the edge of the invisible pit. The Dragon seemed to ignore the warrior though he was in plain sight from the Dragon's perspective. Shi'roc could also see that the magical creature had a rider on it's back, hidden from Moracles' view. This was no random occurrence, he decided. Why would a gold Dragon be here to help them defeat Moracles? How could anyone know what had been taking place this day?

* * *

"Is that Shi'roc?" The wizard queried the Dragon, whose vision was keen at such a distance. The two did not wish to be distracted at this time of vengeance. They were still observing the cowering Moracles and his demon servant. They waited patiently as the tension grew. Why had the old man not launched some magical attack upon them? Why was he hiding behind that rock? Fendal had been concentrating on a defensive spell in anticipation of an attack by the evil wizard.

The Dragon took a quick glance at the warrior who was trying to sneak up on the evil ones. “Yes, I believe it is Shi’roc, though I have not seen him since he helped to free me.” It had been several lifetimes for most, but for the life span of a Dragon it seemed fairly recent history. “He carries the courage and confidence of the one I remember.” The Dragon said to his rider. “Who is that one conjuring up the storm?” The Dragon referred to the robbed Elf behind Moracles and his servants.

Fendal replied with surprise. “I thought it was you who conjured the storm.” From the back of the Dragon, his vision was obscured directly ahead by its great neck. “I see no one else.” Zant lowered his head slightly for the wizard to see past him directly beyond where the evil ones had hidden. “I do not know this one. It must be a compatriot of Shi’roc.” The Elf surmised.

“Only a Priest of the elements could create such a storm and call lightning in this fashion. Perhaps it is Moracles himself performing this ritual.” Zant offered as an explanation as to why the old man had hidden himself away to conjure a spell.

The lightning began to flash more violently as Lorentz’ chanting became louder. It was now evident to the Dragon that it was indeed he who brought forth the storm. The priest called out to Moracles. “I call forth the wrath of the heavenly gods to strike you down and banish your soul to hell from whence it came.” The power and intensity of his voice echoed as thunder.

Shi’roc had drawn two arrows, remembering the blessing that the Goddess Alena had placed on his bow. Though he had no actual faith in such things he drew his bowstring taught. “May my aim be true for Alena.” He said to himself awaiting for Moracles to stand.

Moracles looked back toward the Elf wizard whom he had faced in the temple. He then looked at the Bone in disgust of his betrayal. The Bone could only returned a wicked smile. Then the old Human jumped up and ran for the horse that stood unaffected by the goings on around him. He stood dangerously close to the hidden ridge that dropped far below to Moracles' secret chambers. He desperately tried to mount the flaming horse as a means of escape, but Blackfire would not hold still for the mage to mount him. He bolted and bucked to keep the wretched Human off of his back.

A lightning bolt came flashing down from the sky at Lorentz command, striking the old Human down. Moracles, now totally outraged, crawled to his knees facing the Elf with his back to the Dragon. He began to recite an incantation as he rose to his feet. He turned to Zant just as the Dragon released a burst of its fiery breath. The flames seemed to envelope the mage but in reality had passed around him. When the bright yellow fire had ceased, the old man was still standing tall on the edge of his hidden domain. The incantation of the wizard had surrounded him in a globe of fire protection.

The evil one had apparently not exhausted all of his powers. Shi'roc now had a clear shot at the great wizard. He knew from his experiences with Lorentz that a mage must have vocal ability to recite incantations or to trigger commands for a ring with such powers. Moracles swung around again to face Lorentz and extended his hand as if ready to use the powers of the ring against him. Before the mage could utter the command words of his enchanted jewelry, Shi'roc had fired his first arrow.

The metal tipped projectile soared without a sound to its target, cleanly clipping the finger from the mage that held the ring of spells. As the arrow struck, the warrior nocked the second arrow and aimed. He released the bow string with a twang as the finely crafted arrow hit its mark.

Moracles was aghast at the loss of his finger but more importantly his ring. His only escape would be to fake a fall at the next opportunity and call forth the last of his remembered spells allowing him to safely float down to the floor of his chambers far below. He turned to see his enemy to the right with the bow and began to call on the power of the evil God, Hartes, to strike down this insolent being. Just as he began the words of his chant he felt the a force of pain on his throat and could not continue. The arrow had gone clean through his neck preventing him from speaking the words required to summon the evil powers. As he grasped at the hole in his throat, another bolt of lightning struck him. This time the force of the strike and the flash jolted him from his feet, throwing him backward into the crevice.

"May Hartes take you back to the depths where you belong to burn in hell." Lorentz called as the last lightning strike obliterated the mage. The flash was so bright that he could not see himself and had to shade his eyes with his left hand.

The great golden Dragon jolted backward with the blast of the lightning in front of him. Fendal was almost thrown from his saddle on the great one's back but held on to the straps as the Dragon recovered from the turbulence. "It is fortunate that the Elf is apparently our ally." Zant exclaimed as he searched for Moracles body in the cloud of vapors. He saw no remains of the mage, just the horse stomping about, jittery from the blast.

"I am free." He screeched. The Bone stood at the thought of Moracles demise. He ran for his horse just in front of him, ready to leave this plane of existence. With Moracles dead, the spell that entrapped him in the valley was now broken and he would be free to return home and reclaim his throne in the frozen depths of hell. "Go Blackfire, back home through the mists." The mystical horse and its evil rider reared up as the others watched.

"Zant, stop him from escaping." Fendal called to his companion. The wizard began to conjure a spell himself to restrict the evil servants of Moracles from leaving. As the tall bony creature mounted the horse, Zant began to wrench forth another dose of his intestinal flames.

"No, don't." The Elf priest called out to the gold Dragon. "He is not our enemy. He was forced into servitude by Moracles." The Priest was waving his arms to gain the attention of the grand creature, still unaware of the rider on its back. Indeed, his message was received as the Bone reared up on his horse and saluted Lorentz as the two creatures vanished into the mists of the ethereal plane. Lorentz bowed to the great unknown Dragon as it swallowed its fiery belch. "Moracles has been reclaimed by the fires of hell, I am sure." He called out to Shi'roc who had been climbing his way over to Lorentz.

The two Elves embraced, patting each other on the back at having completed their mission. "Our work here is completed." Shi'roc said indicating the destruction of Moracles. "Who is your Dragon friend?" He asked, pointing to the creature who was now approaching them about to land on the plateau. He then saw the rider on its back.

"I do not know." Lorentz replied. He seemed to come from nowhere at just the right time." He addressed the Dragon and the rider who was now visible to Lorentz for the first time. "We are grateful for your assistance and honored by the presence, oh great ones." He bowed with the distinction of diplomacy, though his own appearance was quite tattered from the battles of the day. "We are wondering how you came to be here at such a time?'

Now, low on all four legs, the dragon appeared to be quite massive and intimidating even to those of good nature. The rider slid from his saddle to the ground. The man appeared still as an elderly Elf with long whitened hair and beard. As he approached the two, his form changed to that of a much younger Elf, one that Shi'roc began to recognize. "Hello my old friend." Fendal said in the Elven tongue as he extended a hand in greeting. "It has been a great many years since we have last seen each other."

Shi'roc grasped his arm in friendly recognition. "Fendal, is it really you or some illusion?" He looked deep into his friends eyes for truth as he replied.

"I assure you, this is me. What you saw before was illusion." He motioned back to his former appearance as an old man as he dismounted the Dragon. Then he pointed to the golden beast that was resting on the rocky ground in front of them. "Do you remember Zant, the one you rescued from Lord Magdalan's castle?" The great Dragon nodded his recognition of the warrior.

"This is Zant? He has grown so much since then." It had been a hundred years. Shi'roc sometimes had difficulty in relating time and age with having encountered so many different species in his travels with different life spans. "This is my friend Lord Lorentz." He introduced his battered companion to both Fendal and Zant. "How did you find us at exactly the time we need your assistance of distraction?" Shi'roc was amazed still at the timing of their arrival.

"Why or how we are here is unimportant. What is important is that we are together again and Moracles is dead." Fendal decided not to relate the real beginnings of the story. For now, as long as Shi'roc was in no further danger from Moracles, he would not tell him of the unholy resurrection of his dead brother Ach'med. The evil, turned Elf was dead once again having been blown from the bridge into the ravine. Fendal had seen this as he and Zant waited below, determining their usefulness in the battle.

"What's left of your army is relatively safe now. The bridge is destroyed with the enemy off into the canyon passages now." He looked up to the darkened sky as the clouds dissipated from the storm that Lorentz had created. It was now late in the day and the wind still blew a chill on this plateau top. He addressed Lorentz. "That was quite a storm you conjured." He pointed to the sky. "Not unlike one that ….." Fendal stopped himself as to the story would lead back to Ach'med's resurrection. "Never mind. It is good to make your acquaintance." He nodded a good bye and began to walk back to Zant.

"Where are you going now? Shi'roc was surprised at the sudden departure. "Stay a while longer, won't you?"

"We have other business to attend to, now that Moracles is dead. I shall return someday to visit. I will find you. Your legend lives on and will continue to grow long after your death I believe." The wizard remounted the Dragon's back saddle and the two began to effortlessly float up into the sky. "I will give Alena your regards." The Elf called down to Shi'roc.

The warrior waved back as he pondered what was meant about seeing the Goddess, Alena. How could Fendal know about his vision in the dessert? He was not at all a spiritual man.

*   *   *

With little life left him, from the blood loss and the fall, the old human mustered what remaining strength he had to crawl toward his bed chamber, hoping to rest and recover some self healing vial of liquid. As he heard the motions in the dark mist, he remembered that he had not announced himself to the guardians of his secret domain. He pushed himself up onto his knees, realizing his Torgs that he captured from other domains would not recognize his beaten and charred body. He must stand and declare his presence or be destroyed by his own security forces.

From more than one direction they came towards him, floating, crawling, slithering as their anatomy allowed. He managed to get to his feet though broken bones caused him to waver, and tried to speak. With all of his remaining concentration, he held his torn hand out to the multi legged reptilian creature approaching him and tried to call to it but it was too late. The gurgled cries were unrecognized as was the magi's form. His eyes had met those of the magical being and all consciousness was lost.

The eyes glowed from the spell that it cast upon the Human, instantly turned his flesh to stone. The mage became a statue of himself, a fitting tribute to his life of evil. The creature, having fulfilled its purpose, returned back to the dark corner from which it was hiding. The other Torgs as well went back to their places in the vast chamber, leaving the statue of the unknown intruder standing guard in the center of the floor. Soon, they thought, their master would return and praise them for their expediency in arresting the one who entered the sacred chambers.

* * *

The top of the plateau was now vacant of all signs of the earlier battle. Those who slew Moracles had left the area and rejoined their remaining troops. The sun was setting in the west behind the distant mountain peaks as a shadow appeared near the secret crevice that led to Moracles chambers. Only a trained eye could notice the vast opening in the rock from whence a crimson Dragon had emerged only months ago.

The clouds had dissipated from the earlier storm that sent lightning down upon the canyon peaks. The shadow figure slowly paced the edge of the crevice as if searching for something, being careful not to slip on the loose rocks. He stopped and bent down to pick something up from the rocky surface. The dark hand held it up to the splintered rays of the setting sun to examine. It was a bloody finger with a golden ring still wrapped around it. Though the finger had been severed from its hand just an hour earlier, it still possessed some life of its own. The figure carefully wrapped the gruesome find in a dark cloth and placed it into a pocket for safe keeping. As long as he had kept it alive, there would be still hope for the mage.

* * *

Deep in the ethereal mists, the Bone rode to what he believed was the extent of the valley to escape what once was his prison. As he reached the edge of the realm he rejoiced at the thought of being able to return to his throne deep inside the frozen part of hell. "Free, I am free once again." He exclaimed as he commanded his free spirited mount, Blackfire, to return to their origin past the fires of Hartes.

As they emerged from the mist they found themselves once again atop the highest plateau of the canyon, back in the forgotten valley. "No! This can't be. Moracles is dead and I have the right to return to my domain." The Bone was enraged at the defiance of the spell to cease. Once Moracles was dead, he knew that the spell that enslaved him and his horse there would be broken.

The fact that the ethereal plane could not take him from this place could only mean one thing. Moracles was somehow, still alive. The Bone let out a blood chilling screech into the night air that echoed through the entire canyon. The two stood there motionless at the point from which they had started their journey. The mists had taken them full circle through the folds of space.

* * *

Darkness grew over the canyons as night fell. The remains of the survivor army had gathered in the cave area where the stables and supplies were kept by Moracles' mounted soldiers. Shi'roc expressed some concern for those of Moracles army that were still somewhere in the canyon. After the Dwarves had related their story of the actions at the bridge, Lord Shi'roc realized that they may still be in danger if they remained in the castle.

"We must take what supplies we can gather and leave by the bridge that still stands at the far side of the canyon. If we do not we will be trapped here when the enemy returns." Shi'roc discussed the situation with Gor as they inspected the horses left behind by the Magdarn soldiers. Although the hairy creatures that tended the animals were still lurking about, they did not seem hostile towards the survivor army.

"M'lord, many of our people can barely travel. If we have to fight our way across the bridge, we may not fair well against a fresh enemy. They would be whole and well rested." Gor reminded Shi'roc that the faction of the enemy army that had been cut off by the broken bridge were the larger soldiers and had not yet engaged in battle with the survivors. He nodded over to the campfires where Lorentz and the apprentice priests were tending the critically wounded as A'mora cared for the others.

The day's losses were heavy as expected but Lorentz knew that the sacrifice was well worth it. Some did not yet realize the importance of this day. A new future for the valley and its free people would start. The priest had prayed and given thanks to the Goddess, Mirana, for the victory against Moracles. With all of his magical powers exhausted for the day, he used his powers of healing to save those brave soldiers who were near death from the battles fought.

A'mora however did not seem to feel the same. She still mourned the loss of her lover, Jantez and had separated herself from the others to meditate alone. Although she had only known him a short time, she had somehow become more than just attracted to him. She was uncertain just what caused her feelings to be so strong. As she prayed for his souls' acceptance by the heavenly gods, she thought briefly of how Shi'roc's soul would wander forever, not accepting any gods as his own.

Most of the wounded were sleeping well after Lorentz healing trance. He gazed from campfire to campfire seeing just how few of the soldiers were left, mostly Dwarves. Some of his own followers had been killed over the past few weeks, during the battles on the mountain and here today. He wished he had the power to bring them all back from the dead as had been done for him, but such miracles of the gods were rare. Only a true healer could perform such a feat.

Sha'la lay with her man Grefden. He had slept in the healing trance that Lorentz performed as Grefden's wounds were healed. She regarded him and wondered briefly if she was worthy enough to bear his child that she carried secretly inside her. She knew that the secret would not be possible to keep for long.

"Kura, where will we go when we leave here?" Ilo asked as the two friends stood guard, together once again at the cave entrance.

"We will go to rejoin our families back at the cave." He referred to their wives and children that they had left behind with some of the elders along the journey. It had been only five days yet it seemed to them to be like months since they had seen them.

"No, I mean after that. Where will we live?" Ilo thought about what might be left back in the mountain, but Lorentz had told them before that the magic powder would likely destroy many of the tunnel passages.

Kura contemplated the subject. No one had given any thought about that outcome. They could not see beyond the battle itself. "We will rebuild our towns in the three peaks as when my father had lived there." He spoke solemnly as if in some trance.

Kura thought about how his father had survived all those years of servitude to Moracles and his armies. Fortunately he was allowed to perform the duties he was best suited for, making armor and weapons. It would take some time for the elderly Dwarf to regain his comprehension of various languages. He had been subjected to so many monsterous forms of speech that even the common languages were confusing to him. He couldn't even carry on a complete sentence in Dwarvish.

"We will rebuild the towns in the valley. People will come from far away to live in the prosperous new lands. There will be castles and farms and great forests …." Kura's voice faded off and he seemed to break from the trance.

"Kura, what are you talking about." Ilo shook his head. It would take miracle upon miracle to rebuild the towns and plant new forests." He looked at his friend in the darkness and shook his head. "Lord Lorentz believes that the catastrophic effects of Moracles spell may never be broken."

Chapter 31
Return

With the wagons loaded with the severely wounded warriors, the survivors headed on the road leading out toward the remaining bridge at the southern end of the valley. They had been careful to watch for any of the remaining enemy soldiers who might be lurking in the canyon passages. The mazes of the canyon walls provided every opportunity for a counter attack by the evil creatures that they had tricked several times before. This time, the enemy had the advantage. It was the survivors who were treading through unknown territory in the home of Moracles army. Although they had been traveling all day, they had not encountered any of the remaining scattered enemy creatures along the road. Perhaps they had massed for an attack at the bridge to cut the Dwarves off from the rest of the valley. Lorentz had passed it off that the enemy had fled from the canyons in fear rather than face the slayers of the evil Moracles.

Shi'roc was more realistic about the situation and surmised that they would rather take their chances in the desert than return to the castle and face Moracles in defeat. They had no way of knowing that Moracles had been disintegrated by lightning, his soul sent back to the planes of hell. Most of the survivors thought Lord Shi'roc's, a more plausible story.

"Perhaps A'mora could fly above the canyon road ahead to check for enemy traps or ambushes." Shi'roc spoke to Lorentz as they rode just ahead of the first wagon.

The remaining Orc, last of his breed in the valley, guided the slow moving wagon as he grieved for his friend who had been slaughtered by the Magdarn the day before. He had died valiantly while serving their new master, Shi'roc. It was his choice to die in battle, at least following the orders of his own choosing. These new people were far more pleasant to work for than the likes of the Magdarn or the Bone, or even Moracles himself. He was quite relieved to hear that Moracles was gone forever and that the Bone had returned to his own home. He would not be allowed to live having betrayed his former employers for the better life offered by these strange little beings.

"A'mora is still in shock over the loss of Jantez," Lorentz reminded. "Her thoughts are not at all focused and would not be able to successfully prepare the spell." He nodded to Shi'roc. After the two had returned from the final bout with Moracles, they learned of what had transpired in the temple. The story was the same from each of the warriors who had witnessed the bravery of the young Human. A'mora could not yet bring herself to talk about what had happened or her burst of sudden rage when Jantez was killed. "I shall go, but I still believe that I am correct about the army having fled from the canyons." They both smiled, realizing that their roles had now reversed from that of a few days earlier when it was Lorentz who was being cautious about entering the canyons and Shi'roc was the bold one. The mage dismounted his horse handing the reins to Shi'roc. He lifted the folds of his cape as he chanted and began to run on ahead down the road. His body once again became feather light and the wind lifted his cape as a bird's wings. As he disappeared from sight, he rose with the currents above the passages and above the canyon walls.

In the light of the afternoon sun, Kura spoke carefully to his father trying to reestablish their relationship. Though the two recognized each other, much had passed in the decades they were apart. Kura was most proud to talk about his son, Tyme. He knew that one day he would become as fine a leader as the ancestor for that he was named.

The weather was mild, the most pleasant it had been in months. It seemed almost warm in comparison to the recent freezing temperatures that they endured on their long journey without shelter. Even the canyon was still of winds though Lord Lorentz had found enough air movement to be gliding overhead to scout for enemy traps.

Grefden and Sha'la rode side by side in the rear of the column to protect from any rear assault that might be made on the group. Grefden was still in a healing process having been quite badly injured in his fight with the Magdarns, but was still strong enough to ward off any offending creatures. Sha'la was suffering from quite another malady. The nausea had become too strong to suppress any longer and had caused her to stop along the rocks and heave. Her worry was how much longer could she keep the truth from Grefden of her pregnancy? Soon her body would begin to show the signs of being with child. It was neither the time nor the place to be raising an infant. She was needed more as a protector than a procreator. Warriors should not be tending babies. But in this time, when many of the survivors had been slain in battle, a new generation was needed to carry on and tell the stories of recent events.

Having left the canyons behind them, Kura had decided for the Dwarven people to head back to their mountain and try to rebuild their towns on the eastern slope. Shi'roc and A'mora led the wagons of the wounded off along the southern path that Moracles' armies had followed from the canyons to the Dwarven Peaks.

Grefden had led a small group to travel around the western edge of the canyons and try to gather the horses and wagons left behind on the ridge. They had hoped that the wagons had not been taken by the creatures whom they had driven off. They also hoped that there wasn't a trap awaiting them.

When they finally did arrive at the fateful ridge, they found their belongings intact. The wagons, horses and supplies that they were forced to leave behind days earlier were just as they had left them. All around the lower ridge were scattered bodies of the enemy creatures. The Survivors dismounted to investigate what had happened to the largest of these beings. There were no visible signs of injury as they poked at the soldiers with their spears and swords. The furry creature's armor and equipment were still intact and quite usable, so they stripped what was useful and hauled the bodies to the nearest crevice.

With the horses and wagons they began their journey back to the mountains along the northern road. This journey, made by them in reverse just weeks ago, seemed like a horrible memory, but they had survived the bitter blizzard, the battles, the horrible deaths of their friends and family. Now it was time to face the trials of renewal.

* * *

"I would like to visit that dried lake again where we left the others. Might I join you on your journey to the cave." Lord Lorentz asked of Ilo and Kura whom he knew would be headed off to rejoin their families. "I have ideas about that lake. I am getting to old to be traveling the world." He pulled at the white hairs in his bear and hair, indicating his age, even with Elven blood in him.

Kura smiled. "We would be honored that you would travel with us." Kura replied. Ilo nodded his approval also. "What will you do at the lake bed once we arrive?" He asked of the elder Elf.

"I believe I will try to find the source of the original spring and to revive it. If I can, I would like to build a home overlooking the lake and settle down." He looked behind the small caravan at the shadows of the canyon in the distance. "Somewhere back there a river will emerge again now that Moracles' powers are gone and the land will stop eroding. I will do my best to revive the lands for growing crops again for food."

Ilo looked at Kura and stretched a great smile across his face. "Do you think it is possible to rebuild the towns again as they were before?" He asked Lorentz eagerly, remembering what Kura had been babbling the night before.

"No." Lorentz said firmly. "We can not build the towns as before." Ilo frowned. We must build them better, stronger, with high walls to help defend against others like Moracles in the future."

"It will take some work, but we will bring people from other lands to help rebuild, and live here." Shi'roc joined the prophetic conversation. "I am tired of all this fighting as well, Lorentz. I too wish to settle and even raise a family if I can find a woman who will have an old war horse like me for a husband."

Now that the fighting was over and the mission completed, Shi'roc's aura had begun to change. His softer side was beginning to show that there was more to him than just a warrior. He slowed his horse so that A'mora would catch up to him. They had not spoken since Jantez' death. Perhaps now she would accept some consoling.

* * *

Muga sat on a rock at the edge of the cave with her young son, Tyme, in her arms. They had been alone for at eight days now, though she may have lost count when she was unconscious. She still was unaware of the events that had taken place in the canyons. The woman could not know if the battles were won or lost. Had they been abandoned, left to fend for themselves?

There was sufficient food for several months based on her careful usage. She was used to stretching small amounts of food for long periods of time having endured it continuously back in the mountain. They were left enough food for all nine of them for a week before the attack. They should have been back by now if her husband and the others had lived. Perhaps she would wait another day or two before making other plans. She sat thinking with her child in her arms and crossbow at her side.

She had dug graves for all of those killed defending the children. Seven rock piles were neatly laid out in the dried lake bed away from the cave. The ground had been soft from the melted snow run off. She could not believe that she and her son were the only survivors of the assault by the great Orc warrior. What did he want from them? Why was he so determined to slaughter them?

As Muga sat near the edge of the cave looking out over the empty space, she wondered what had happened to Caellen's daughter. Was it a dream she had about the shadowy figure in the cave who swept up the child and vanished? How would she explain it to Ilo if he returned to find his wife slain and his daughter missing. Combined with the expected death of his father, Maac-To, he would be devastated. All that he lived and fought for was lost.

Muga thought she heard someone calling her name. The wind in the lake bed was playing games with her, she thought. Then again she heard it more clearly this time. It was Kura calling down from the rocky ledge. She stood up and ran out in the open with Tyme in her arms. Muga was elated to see the new Dwarven chief climbing down the ledge. Although Ilo was also in sight, she was less anxious to face him. He was calling out for Caellen as he climbed down.

Lorentz and the others had remained up top, overlooking the situation from horseback. Even before the two survivors approached the cave, the priest recognized the shallow graves. He had seen his share of unplanned stone piles in his life to know that something had taken the lives of his friends and their families. He sighed at the thought of Ilo's pain as he could see his disgust when he approached Muga.

The young Elf yelled out in anger. "No, they can't." He sobbed heavily as he knelt beside the rocks that Muga indicated was Caellen's grave. "What will I do now?" He asked of no one in particular. "What has become of my new daughter? No one could answer what fate had in store for Aliah. If she had indeed been taken, then by whom and for what purpose?

Lord Lorentz remained behind to survey the lake bed and surrounding lands as Grefden and the others met up to continue the long journey back to the mountain. They gathered up the remaining food and other supplies. Muga and Tyme rode in the wagon as Kura drove the horses onward. They debated upon leaving the bodies behind, but as with the battle in the canyons, they were forced to leave their dead buried as remembrance. Perhaps their spirits would remain and protect the lands from any evil doers who would pass.

Epilog

The survivors had all done their best to clear away the rubble and decayed enemy bodies from the old deserted towns of the Dwarven Peaks. They began to plan reconstruction from what materials they could scrounge. They had decided that stone would be their primary foundation material. It was in abundance and they had the tools to shape it. As they began to re-dig the tunnels to the mines, the excavated materials were then used for forming the foundations of their new homes. Shi'roc was not surprised with the resourcefulness of the Dwarves as their new community began to take shape.

Kura began to set up a temple to the goddess Mirana, and prayed for her guidance and wisdom in leading the remaining Dwarves to rebuild their towns and their lives. He had decreed that they would no longer live in isolation as their ancestors had. The Dwarven people would build and prosper. Kura felt this deep inside from his meditations. His people would trade freely with other towns people and welcome outsiders into their towns as well.

A'mora had been continuing to care for those who had been wounded in the recent battles. Several of them were already well enough to be helping with the town reconstruction. There were a few others who did not survive. They had been too seriously injured to endure the journey back to the mountains despite A'mora's best healing efforts.

Sha'la had become uncomfortable keeping her secret from Grefden. She felt she had to leave before her pregnancy was too apparent. The warrior had been able to hide her morning weaknesses from her mate but knew that wouldn't last too long. She confided in A'mora that she did not want to have the child in the mountains and did not wish for Grefden to know about the child.

The two conspired to search out others from distant lands, who would relocate to the newly freed valley. They would journey together as ambassadors of the region to invite craftsmen of all trades to avail their services. They would travel for at least a year before returning to their companions back in the valley. By then, A'mora expected that Lord Lorentz would have restored at least some vegetation and crops for the survivors to live from as they rebuilt their communities. In the mean time, they could easily live from the vegetation remaining in the water cave they had left behind. Though it was not convenient relative to the towns being rebuilt, they would have to make weekly pilgrimages to the shrine to pray and gather food.

In years to come the valley would be thriving with new towns, farms and shops. Craftsmen from around the world would migrate to the new land. Children would be raised knowing this land was safe and kept that way by those who would be known as heroes of the great war against Moracles.

* * *

The Bone returned to his icy throne deep in the maze of the castle halls. Somehow, he was still trapped by the spell that Moracles had cast upon him. This fact indicated to the creature that in some form, Moracles still lived. The same spell also restricted him from directly causing any harm to the evil mage, even if he could find where he was being kept alive. "I will find a way." He said to himself as he stretched his bony frame out on his icy rock

He pondered what to do with the remains of the army who returned to the castle long after the battle. What few had survived the onslaught of the mountain dwellers no longer seemed to have a purpose now that Moracles was gone. Who would they serve? Would there be a time of vengeance?

Vandar, broken and beaten, remained hidden in the cavernous hide out of his master. There he had discovered the stone resemblance of Moracles, now lifeless. He would devote his powers to the reincarnation of the evil wizard by keeping live the mages finger. As long as it remained, there was hope for restoration. He would study all that his master had left behind and eventually uncover the secret that would revive the evil one.

* * *

Zant and Fendal returned to their respective homes after the long journey back. Each wondered what would become of their friend Shi'roc now that Moracles had been defeated and Vandar was dead as well. The wizard never did tell Shi'roc of his half brothers' resurrection, or how he came to be in the canyons at the time of the final battle between good and evil. Was it all coincidence or were all of these events orchestrated by the gods? No one would know for sure. Life would go on.

The next spring, Fendal traveled to Tireth-Tec, no longer to visit the tomb of A'chmed, but instead to see Koloda and Cha'ni. His first stop was at the tavern where he knew Cha'ni would be working. He also expected to find the hefty Elf Koloda lurking at the corner table in the shadows. He hoped that his friend had healed completely from his injuries by now.

"Pardon me, sir. Is Cha'ni working today?" he asked the burly human behind the counter. Fendal noticed that the tavern was quite empty except for the Human and himself. He did not even see Koloda's shadow in the corner.

"She stopped coming to work last season. I don't know why, She just stopped." The man said in an irritated manner. "Business has been slow ever since." The man humphed and turned back to cleaning the bottles behind the bar.

"What about the fat Elf named Koloda,who used to sit in that corner?" He pointed to the small table in the dark area.

The proprietor looked to where he was pointing. "I don't know of any fat Elf named Koloda or otherwise."

It didn't surprise the wizard that the tavern owner had never seen Koloda or knew who he was. It had always been the Elfs greatest desire, not to be noticed. He was the best thief he had ever known and that was due to his ability to never be seen unless he wanted you to see him. He could remember times long ago when Koloda would leave the group of adventurers unnoticed, sometimes for days, while lurking on his own.

Fendal rushed down the street and to the outskirts of town toward his friends' home. As he approached he noted that a board was nailed across the front door. He looked around through a window and determined that the house was now empty. He spoke to a neighbor.

"Madam, can you tell me where they went?" he pointed to the boarded up house. "I have been away for a while and have lost track of my friends."

"I hardly ever knew that anyone lived there. A young girl and her father I think. Is that who you mean?" The elderly Human woman did not seem too sure when they left, let alone where they would have been off to. Perhaps the events in Lord Magdelans' deserted castle convinced them to move on. "If they had wanted me to find them, they would have left some clue." He said to himself walking back to the deserted house. He pulled the plank from the door of the small house and tried the handle. It was unlocked so he pushed it open. It had been apparently vacant for some time. He left it open as he searched so that the daylight would be available. He checked for writing on the walls, floor, anything that would be a clue. He was about to give up, but as he went to close the door behind him, he looked behind it.

On the back of the door he found an old curled piece of parchment fastened to the door with a small dagger. It looked like the one that Koloda used to keep up his sleeve. He pulled the paper from the blade and unrolled it. Holding it up to the light Fendal recognized it as the original map that he himself had made long ago, showing the path from the town to the mouth of the cave; the entrance to Lord Magdalan's castle.

"He wouldn't. Would he?" the Elf whispered. As he examined it further, he saw an additional note, more recently written as it was not faded like the rest of the map. The writing was in the old Elvish tongue. "Unfinished Business" was all it said.

The End?

The tale continues a generation later, as the valley is restored by the grace of Mirana, in the next book, ‘Arena’s Sacrifice’

About the Author

Since 1981, Vince has dedicated his professional career as an engineer, to be the best in his field. He is a graduate of the University of Missouri at Rolla, with a degree in Engineering Management. All along the way he maintained a secret passion for writing and story telling. In truth, he is a Bard, Mage and Warrior all in one as would be attested by those who have endured his meticulously created role-playing games upon which, this book is based. He promises more to come and hopes that you will join him for an adventure into his fantasy world of wizards and heroes, love and deceit.

"Remember not, the names of the characters in this story, as they are not as important as the deeds for which they should be remembered. It is their courage and wisdom that will be engrained in your memories forever."

Prepare yourself for the first of Vince Barrale's 'Tales of the Two Moons' that pour fourth in the following pages

Printed in the United States
1350000009B/3